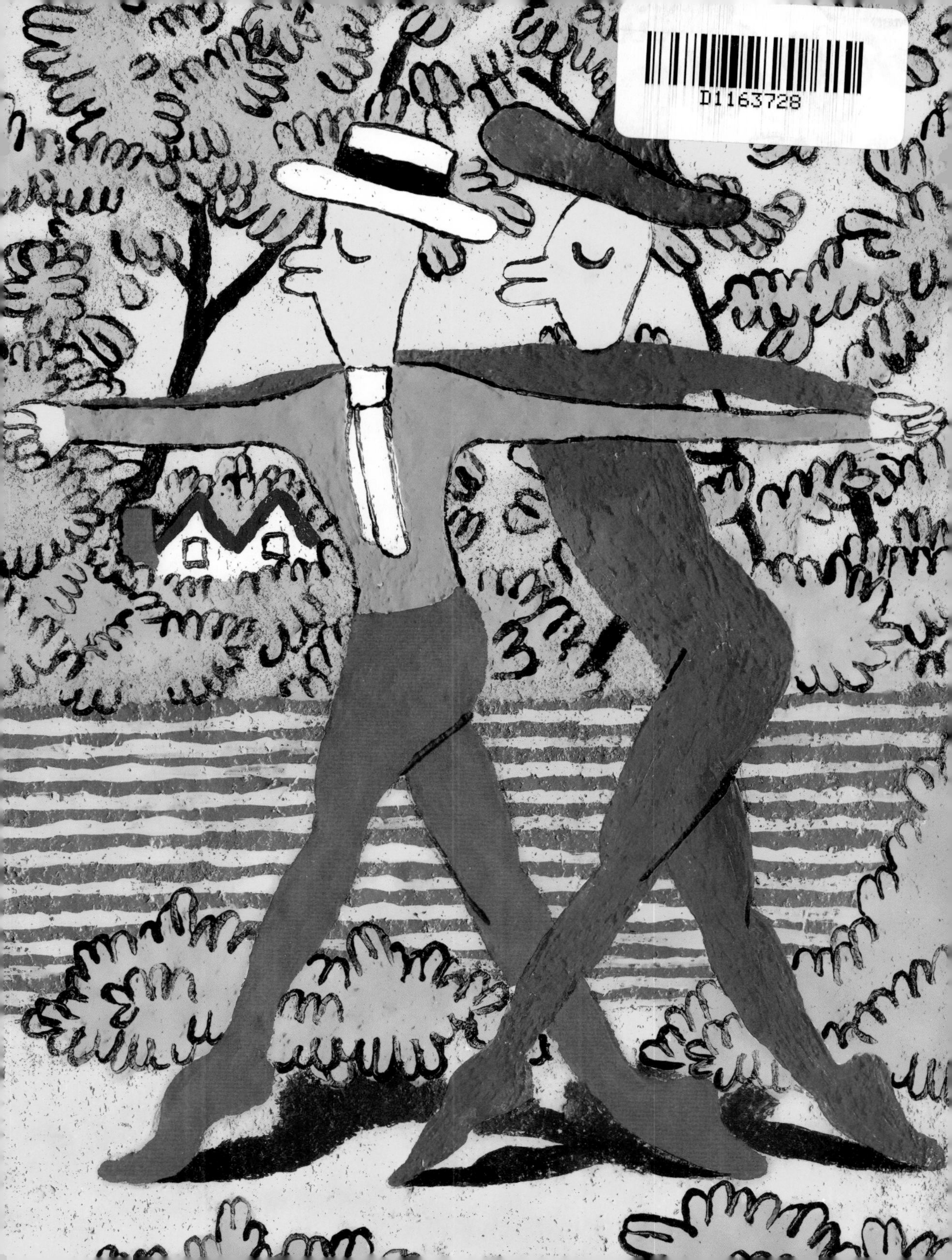

THE BEST AMERICAN

Comics 2018

GUEST EDITORS OF THE
BEST AMERICAN COMICS

2006   HARVEY PEKAR

2007   CHRIS WARE

2008   LYNDA BARRY

2009   CHARLES BURNS

2010   NEIL GAIMAN

2011   ALISON BECHDEL

2012   FRANÇOISE MOULY

2013   JEFF SMITH

2014   SCOTT McCLOUD

2015   JONATHAN LETHEM

2016   ROZ CHAST

2017   BEN KATCHOR

2018   PHOEBE GLOECKNER

THE BEST AMERICAN

Comics

2018

EDITED *and* INTRODUCED
by Phoebe Gloeckner

BILL KARTALOPOULOS,
series editor

HOUGHTON MIFFLIN HARCOURT
BOSTON * NEW YORK   2018

www.hmhco.com

Library of Congress Cataloging-in-Publication Data is available.

ISSN 1941-6385 (print)   ISSN 2573-3869 (ebook)
ISBN 978-1-328-46460-6 (print)   ISBN 978-1-328-46536-8 (ebook)

Book design: Chrissy Kurpeski & Chloe Foster   Cover art: Lale Westvind
Endpaper art: Alex Graham   Cover art direction: Christopher Moisan

PRINTED IN THE UNITED STATES OF AMERICA

DOC 10 9 8 7 6 5 4 3 2 1

Permissions credits are located on page 394.

Contents

vii : BILL KARTALOPOULOS Foreword

xi : PHOEBE GLOECKNER Introduction

1 : GABRIELLE BELL Ghost Cats FROM *Everything Is Flammable* (*Excerpt*)

10 : TARA BOOTH Selections FROM *How to Be Alive*

20 : D. J. BRYANT Echoes into Eternity

30 : MAX CLOTFELTER The Warlok Story

39 : GEOF DARROW The Shaolin Cowboy: Who'll Stop the Reign? (*Excerpt*)

55 : GUY DELISLE Hostage (*Excerpt*)

63 : ABRAHAM DÍAZ Brausebad

72 : MARGOT FERRICK Margot

91 : EMIL FERRIS My Favorite Thing Is Monsters Book 1 (*Excerpt*)

103 : CASANOVA FRANKENSTEIN A Taste of Purgatory FROM *Purgatory* (*Excerpt*)

110 : JULIA GFRÖRER Frail Nature

112 : JULIAN GLANDER Selections FROM *Susan Something*

129 : SARAH GLIDDEN Sam's Story FROM *Rolling Blackouts* (*Excerpt*)

142 : ALEX GRAHAM Angloid, Part 2

155 : SIMON HANSELMANN Megg, Mogg & Owl: "A Gift for a Baby"

158 : JAIME HERNANDEZ Forest Spirits

165 : KEVIN HOOYMAN The Wide Berth AND Benign Neglect

177 : JESSE JACOBS Crawl Space (*Excerpt*)

196 : JULIA JACQUETTE   Playground of My Mind (*Excerpt*)

219 : ANDRE KRAYEWSKI AND ED KRAYEWSKI   Miss V:
My Last Love Story

242 : AARON LANGE   Selections FROM Art School

249 : JOE OLLMANN   Seabrook of Arabia FROM *The Abominable
Mr. Seabrook* (*Excerpt*)

264 : LAURA PALLMALL   Selections FROM Things More Likely to Kill You
Than . . . AND Busy Comic

272 : GARY PANTER   Songy of Paradise (*Excerpt*)

281 : CHLOË PERKIS   UGLY

300 : RICHIE POPE   Fatherson

310 : MICHAEL RIDGE   Untitled (*Excerpt*)

327 : KEILER ROBERTS   Sunburning (*Excerpts*)

333 : ARIEL SCHRAG   Things I Regret

337 : TED STEARN   The Moolah Tree (*Excerpt*)

355 : MATTHEW THURBER   Art Comic (*Excerpt*)

370 : PETE TOMS   The Last Felony Comics Story

374 : LALE WESTVIND   Yazar and Arkadaş (*Excerpt*)

391 : Notable Comics from September 1, 2016, to August 31, 2017

Foreword

I hope that you will read the comics in this book the way that we read all of the work that we consider for inclusion in the Best American Comics.

In my role as series editor, I receive many hundreds of comics from artists and publishers for consideration for the Best American Comics. Over the course of each year, they arrive in envelopes and boxes and accumulate in my book-filled apartment, and I read them all. It is then my job to narrow down that pool of work to about 120 pieces that I forward to each year's guest editor to select from for publication in this anthology (our guest editors also have the freedom, of course, to bring in comics they may have found on their own). My part of the job involves an incredible amount of close reading, consideration, and reconsideration. Selecting the 120 comics that I think can make a claim for inclusion as one of the year's "best" is not exactly the same as selecting the work that I *like* the best. There's a huge amount of overlap, but it's not exactly the same thing.

When I select work to forward to our guest editor, I'm not just expressing my default opinion. Rather, I'm exercising critical engagement. Like anyone else, I have opinions: I have tastes, I have preferences, I have aesthetic biases. Like any critic, I believe that my opinions are informed: I believe that even my reflexive opinions—my gut reactions—are informed by a valid point of view based on years of engagement with comics. I have read and studied comics intensely, I know the history of the medium, I have thought deeply about the art form and how it works, and I am intimately familiar with the contemporary landscape of the comics field, both in North America and internationally. But engaging work critically forces me to go further than simply exercising a reactive opinion. Engaging work critically requires one to be aware of one's predispositions, and, crucially, to be willing to put them aside, to question them, and to revise them. A critic needs to be humble enough to acknowledge that they may not have totally understood a work the first time they encounter it.

When we're talking about art, it's always worth remembering that it is implicit in the job description of an artist to challenge or even overthrow our assumptions about how art can or should work if that's what their personal expression calls for. Any art form is constituted by a field of self-motivated people making new things and then showing the world that it needs something that it had never thought to ask for. When a critic, like myself, engages work that causes them to change their point of view, it's a mind-expanding experience. This experience is enlarging: it broadens one's perspective, and leaves the critic grateful that an artist has made work that has challenged them and increased their understanding of what comics can be and what comics can do.

So when I receive any comic as a submission, I do my best to put aside my preconceptions of what I think a good comic looks like, and try to understand what each comic I read is doing—or trying to do. But then the critical judgment kicks in: is the work successful in accomplishing what it is trying to accomplish? If it is, is it distinct? How does it sit within the overall field of comics? Is it unique or original somehow? And is it doing —or saying—something worth saying?

I don't claim that there's anything "objective" about a critic raising and trying to answer these questions. At the end of the day, any critic reveals a great deal about themselves and their own artistic values in the evaluations that they make. But it's crucial that this process begins from a place of openness to all possibilities and a willingness to question oneself. Otherwise, there's a deadly threat that one's critical position will harden into a kind of reflexive dogma, and that the critic will be less personally available to and appreciative of new work that emerges into the future.

When it comes to art, there is nothing more limiting than only valuing work that gives you more of what you already know you like. Unfortunately, our mass media is very good at delivering new material that provides the comfort of the familiar with just enough of a surprising twist to satisfy the human desire for novelty. And even more unfortunately, audiences respond positively enough to this slightly stimulating mix of the familiar with a dash of the unfamiliar to reinforce that practice. This is just as true of contemporary film franchises as it is of automated social media algorithms online. Fortunately, in this context, comics have the privilege of *not being* mass media. Comics maintain their historical connection to independent culture. The cost of participation in comics is low. *Literally anyone* can make a comic with a pen, paper, and access to a photocopier or the internet. It's just as important that artists remain open to all possibilities as critics; critics need the work of artists who will justify their radical openness to the possibilities of their shared art form. And beyond critics, those artists need engaged readers.

I have no doubt that any reader will come across pieces in this book—and in any volume of the Best American Comics—that won't satisfy their reflexive tastes. But every piece in this book is here because both our guest editor and I found something of value in it, beginning from that first position of critical openness to creative possibility. So I hope that each reader will be engaged, curious, and interested enough to try to understand what each piece in this book might have to say about art, about life, and about the life of the mind. I know from my own experience over the past year that every piece in this book has something to say that's worth paying attention to.

I could not have been more fortunate to be joined in this task by Phoebe Gloeckner over this past year. At precisely the moment when graphic novels were broadly emerging into North American cultural consciousness, Phoebe's 2002 book *The Diary of a Teenage Girl* appeared as if it was designed to question all of our developing concepts of what a "graphic novel" could be. A hybrid book combining prose, illustration, and comics, Phoebe's work also questioned traditional categories of fiction and nonfiction. The field of comics has been enlarged by her artistic work.

Phoebe's engagement with the comics that she considered for inclusion this year was a model of critical openness: she intently sought to understand the artistic perspective motivating the work that she saw, including—and even especially—in the case of work that didn't immediately appeal to her. And then, like every guest editor working in this series, she performed the difficult critical task of selecting the pieces that she ultimately felt most strongly about including as this year's Best American Comics.

The Best American Comics 2018 represents a selection of outstanding North American work first published between September 1, 2016, and August 31, 2017. Many of the comics we considered came to us through our open submission process. Additionally, I sought out work for consideration at comic book stores, at comics festivals, online, and through recommendations from trusted colleagues. As I mentioned above, I amassed and considered a large pool of comics, and selected approximately 120 pieces to forward to our guest editor, who made the final selections that constitute the present volume. In addition to the work we have reprinted here, I've assembled a lengthy list of additional Notable Comics that appears at the back of this book. If you have enjoyed any of the comics in this volume, the works listed in our Notable Comics list are all also worth seeking out. I have posted a version of this list to my website (on-panel.com) that includes links to sites where you can find out more about those comics.

We are always seeking work to consider for the Best American Comics. Any artist or publisher is encouraged to submit comics, including self-published and online work. The continuing robust diversity of the Best American Comics is greatly dependent upon these submissions. Work can be submitted at any time to our public postal address:

Bill Kartalopoulos
Series Editor
The Best American Comics
Houghton Mifflin Harcourt
3 Park Avenue, 19th floor
New York, NY 10016

By the time this book is published, we will be seeking new, North American work published between September 1, 2018, and August 31, 2019, for consideration for *The Best American Comics 2020.*

Thanks as always to our in-house editor at Houghton Mifflin Harcourt, Nicole Angeloro, who manages and coordinates the many moving parts behind this challenging annual book project with efficiency and equanimity. Thanks to art director Christopher Moisan, who works with our artists on the cover and endpapers for each volume. Thanks to Chloe Foster and Chrissy Kurpeski, who designed the book, and to Beth Burleigh Fuller for managing the complex production behind this volume. Thanks as well to Mary Dalton-Hoffman, who secures the crucial rights and permissions for this series every year. Many thanks to all of my colleagues who offered helpful suggestions, advice, and guidance as I worked on this volume.

Special thanks to Lale Westvind, who provided this year's spectacular cover artwork, and to Alex Graham for her excellent endpapers.

We hope you enjoy this year's perspective on the past year's best comics. As always, we'll return next year with another guest editor's point of view on an entirely different body of eligible work. Comics, like all art, keep evolving and changing, and it gives me pleasure to say, at the time of this writing, that I wouldn't dare to pretend to be able to imagine what next year's volume might bring.

BILL KARTALOPOULOS

Introduction

Dear Reader,

I love comics. Comics is (Comics ARE?) a perfect language, robustly evolving and expanding like any other living language. The pictures say what words could only struggle to express, and the words tell us things that images could only describe in awkward pantomime.

When I was very young, I lived in Philadelphia and read comics intended for children, like *Little Lotta* and *Richie Rich*, but I was by no means a comics fanatic. I was more interested in my grandparents' book collections, especially my grandmother's illustrated medical textbooks, bound volumes of surgical journals, and old books with reproductions of medieval triptychs and illuminated manuscripts. In retrospect, it's clear that I was attracted to images that relied on words (and vice versa) to create meaning. This is no surprise; I liked to draw, and I liked to write. Like hearing and seeing, words and pictures just seemed to belong together.

Comics became more important to me in the early 1970s, when my mother and little sister and I moved to San Francisco, the epicenter of the 1960s "underground comics" movement. My mother, a librarian, was hip to counterculture and our apartment was crowded with books of all sorts, including comics. I was 12 or 13 when I found a stack of *ZAP! Comix* cached away in her room. If you haven't seen *ZAP!*, suffice it to say that there was a reason these comics were usually hidden from tweens; in stories like *Star-Eyed Stella* (S. Clay Wilson), *Wonder Wart-Hog* (Gilbert Shelton), and *Joe Blow* (R. Crumb), drugs and sex leapt off the pages. Some of the art was rough or grotesque, and some was astoundingly beautiful and seemed effortlessly drawn.

ZAP! caused a light bulb of realization to switch on in my head. *Comics could be drawn any way you wanted to draw them.* The term "cartoony style," which had been uttered with a tinge of disparagement by my middle school art teachers, was rendered meaningless. The stories in *ZAP!* were shocking, yes, but their existence revealed the potential of the medium. *Comics weren't just for children.* Comics could be used to tell any type of story; autobiography, biography, fantasy, etc. There was no formula, no limit to the style or tone of a story: violent, sexual, light-hearted, funny, wry, frightening, political, intimate; comics were, it seemed, a medium presenting boundless possibilities for the expression of nuanced thought and emotion. I was inspired, and started drawing and writing comics myself.

My mother started dating a cartoonist (the creator of *Mickey Rat,* Bob Armstrong) while I was in high school. Armstrong played in a band called the Cheap Suit Serenaders with Robert Crumb (*ZAP!*) and Terry Zwigoff, who worked as an unemployment officer and went on to become a film director (*Crumb, Ghost World, Bad Santa*). Sometimes the band stayed at our apartment when they were playing in San Francisco.

Armstrong and Crumb modeled "the successful artist" for me at an impressionable age. My father, who was a man of prodigious charm, wit, good looks, and artistic talent, had unfortunately succumbed to a life of fast cars and drug abuse, and was largely absent from my life. My fondness for drawing drew frequent comparisons to my father, which both flattered and frightened me, since his life didn't seem to be proceeding as he had hoped. Crumb and Armstrong, who were productive and smart and funny and kind and more or less sober, showed me that it might be OK to be an artist after all. And through them, I met Diane Noomin ("Didi Glitz") and Aline Kominsky ("the Bunch"), two cartoonists who not only influenced and inspired my work, but encouraged me to keep doing it.

Back then, a "best of" book for comics would have been unimaginable. It was a period when the medium had little cachet in the United States of America. These were the waning years of the vibrant Underground Comix era. These were the post-hippie, pre-punk, pre-*RAW Magazine* years, before the term "alternative comics" had been coined. There was scant recognition of comics as a form of visual or literary art of any note; comics were largely disregarded as unimportant, crass, seen more as cultural detritus than a medium capable of powerful communication.

I was a student at San Francisco State University in the 1980s. I was also making comics, contributing to *Young Lust, Wimmins Comics, Weirdo,* and *RE/Search Magazine* (a punk tabloid). In painting and drawing classes, I did what came naturally and often surrounded images with frames to "define a moment." Several professors advised me not to do this, saying that it made my work look "cartoony," or "like illustration." The implicit message was that comics and illustration could not be "Art." One professor, Jim Albertson, a painter whose work I greatly admired, had a different message. One day before class, he saw me working on a comic for *RE/Search* and asked me if I had more comics. He arranged for me to have an informal one-person exhibit in the halls of the art school. I was so accustomed to being dissuaded from making comics that I could hardly believe he was serious. The show hung for a week, and I'd casually walk down the hall, anonymously watching people read my work. My heart was aglow. I felt vindicated. Thank you, Jim Albertson.

I spent one year in college studying at the Université D'Aix-Marseille in France. I took a course called "The Semiotics of Comics," taught by Pierre Fresnault-DeRuelle, who wrote many books analyzing the medium long before any US writer attempted the same. He gave names to aspects of comics that I was aware of through using them in my work, but hadn't had the vocabulary to discuss concretely. The very existence of such a course would have been unthinkable in an American curriculum at the time.

After college and graduate school in medical illustration (words + pictures), I continued to make comics, but I pushed myself to attempt new forms. My last book was a hybrid novel, using both prose and comics sequences. The novel I'm working on now is a further departure from the traditional comics form.

I've got to admit that there have been times I've felt constrained by the medium. I was frustrated by the observation that a page of comics is generally consumed more quickly than a page of text, and yet, that same page of comics probably took far longer to create. I wondered how the reader could be slowed down when there was reason to modulate the experience. In response to my own inner battle regarding the balance of words and pictures in my work, and noting that there are many examples of wordless comics, I decided to make a nearly image-less one. The result, "I Hate Comics," was composed almost entirely of solid blocks of text within panels. But don't be fooled by that title, because, like I said, I love comics.

Looking toward the blurry future, I'll bet that comics as a medium will influence our changing definitions of literature and film, and we will start to see hybrid forms develop. Cartoonists, as masters of both words and pictures, are likely to be amongst the innovators and authors of future forms of storytelling.

As guest editor of this book, I collaborated with series editor Bill Kartalopoulos to choose this handful of work produced by cartoonists on the North American continent from September 1, 2016, to August 31, 2017. Mr. Kartalopoulos lives and breathes comics. He is smart, dedicated, and indefatigable, and I'm grateful to him for giving me this opportunity to read many comics that I probably would not have otherwise known about.

This book is an edition of a "best of" series. Let's face it; a collection of any sort of creative work is influenced by the particular tastes of the chooser (which, in this case, was me) and can hardly unequivocally claim to curate the "BESTEST" work available.

Choosing my "favorite" work was difficult. We read hundreds of good stories, collectively representing thousands of hours of work. For every piece or excerpt I decided to include, there are several I wanted to but couldn't for lack of space. I'm very pleased with all the work we ultimately included. Some of the artists/authors may be familiar to readers; others are (as yet) little-known. As I hope you will find, there are many ways that stories can be told and impressions of life can be expressed in comics form.

It is interesting to note that most of the comics in this book have been written and drawn entirely by one person. We could call these *auteur* comics. There are plenty of comics created by teams of artists and writers, tasked with quickly producing books. With such comics, it is often difficult to identify an "author," or to understand to what degree the end product is truly a creative collaboration.

The question of authorship is significant to the interpretation of comics. If we think of Comics as a language, the *auteur* cartoonist must be fluent, whereas with team-produced comic books, the writers and visual artists achieve fluency only when working as a group. There are many comics that don't neatly fall to the broad groups I describe here. For example, a team of two (artist and writer) can work with such a level of creative symbiosis that they can almost be thought of as one author.

The motivation to create these different types of comics, as well as the process by which they are created, can be radically different. When we compare the medium of comics to literature or film in terms of authorship, we see that while comics are commonly created by a sole author, they are just as likely to be created by a team. However, there are very few novels written collaboratively by multiple authors, and rarely is a feature-length film the work of one individual. What do these observations say about comics?

One of the great benefits this collection offers is that it brings the reader stories chosen from all realms of North American comics. Most readers, I'd wager, would never have the time or opportunity to find much of this work independently. Whether you agree that they are the best or not, I'm confident that the comics represented here are worthy of your attention. Be aware, however; this book is just the tip of the iceberg. There is a prodigious amount of great work out there, just waiting for you to discover.

A note on the order of the selections:

The stories in this book are presented in ascending alphabetical order. For those who have been subject to roll call in elementary school (or beyond), this decision might seem oppressive. However, in a book such as this, an alphabetical arrangement is rare. I had intended at first to group the stories by theme, but I found that this decision was influencing my choices, as some categories had too few stories and others too many. In an effort to balance things, I was no longer simply choosing my favorite stories. I was also shopping for work that fit a theme. This didn't seem right, and I abandoned that idea. Fortunately, the selections ordered alphabetically read quite well.

I investigated the distribution of surnames in the United States according to the letter the name begins with. I collected similar data culled from the table of contents of this very book for comparison.

I found that while the highest incidence of names in the general population begin with the letter *M*, not one *Best American Comics 2018* contributor's name begins with that letter. The letters *G*, *H*, and *P* dominate amongst our cartoonists, while these same letters don't have such impressive representation in the population at large.

Drawing conclusions based on this data would be premature. Further research into the names of authors represented in previous (and future) volumes of Best American Comics will be required.

PHOEBE GLOECKNER

DISTRIBUTION OF FIRST LETTER OF SURNAME: US POPULATION VS BEST AMERICAN COMICS CONTRIBUTORS (PERCENTAGE)

12
9
6
3
0
A B C D E F G H I J K L M N O P Q R S T U V W X Y Z
General Population
BAC Contributors

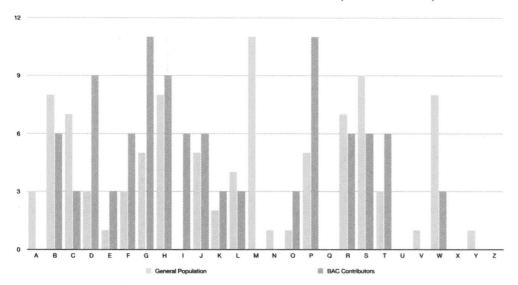

THE BEST AMERICAN

Comics 2018

Ghost Cats (*Excerpt*)

GABRIELLE BELL

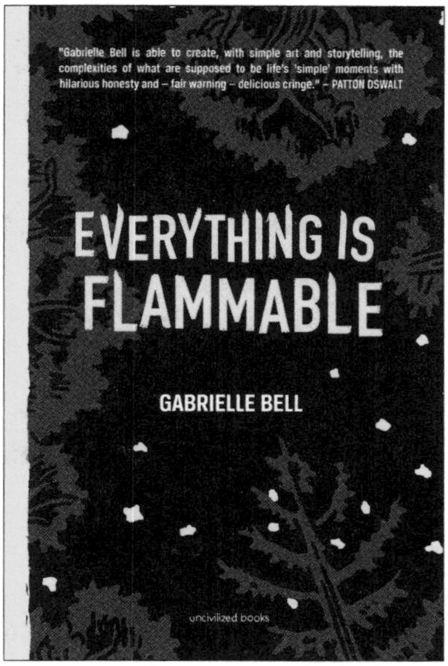
"Gabrielle Bell is able to create, with simple art and storytelling, the complexities of what are supposed to be life's 'simple' moments with hilarious honesty and – fair warning – delicious cringe." – PATTON OSWALT
EVERYTHING IS FLAMMABLE
GABRIELLE BELL
uncivilized books

originally published in

Everything Is Flammable

UNCIVILIZED BOOKS

6 x 9 inches • 160 pages

Biography

Gabrielle is a British-American cartoonist currently based in Brooklyn. Her comic "Cecil and Jordan in New York" was adapted for the film anthology *Tokyo!* by Michel Gondry. "Ghost Cats" appeared in her first full-length graphic memoir, *Everything Is Flammable*, published by Uncivilized Books.
gabriellebell.com

Statement

This is one of the few stories I've done about my childhood. It was surprisingly cathartic to put such a distant, traumatic memory into pictures and words. Part of me retains such a stark, vivid memory of that time, and another part of me isn't even sure if I didn't imagine the whole thing. For the record, though, I'm pretty sure it happened.

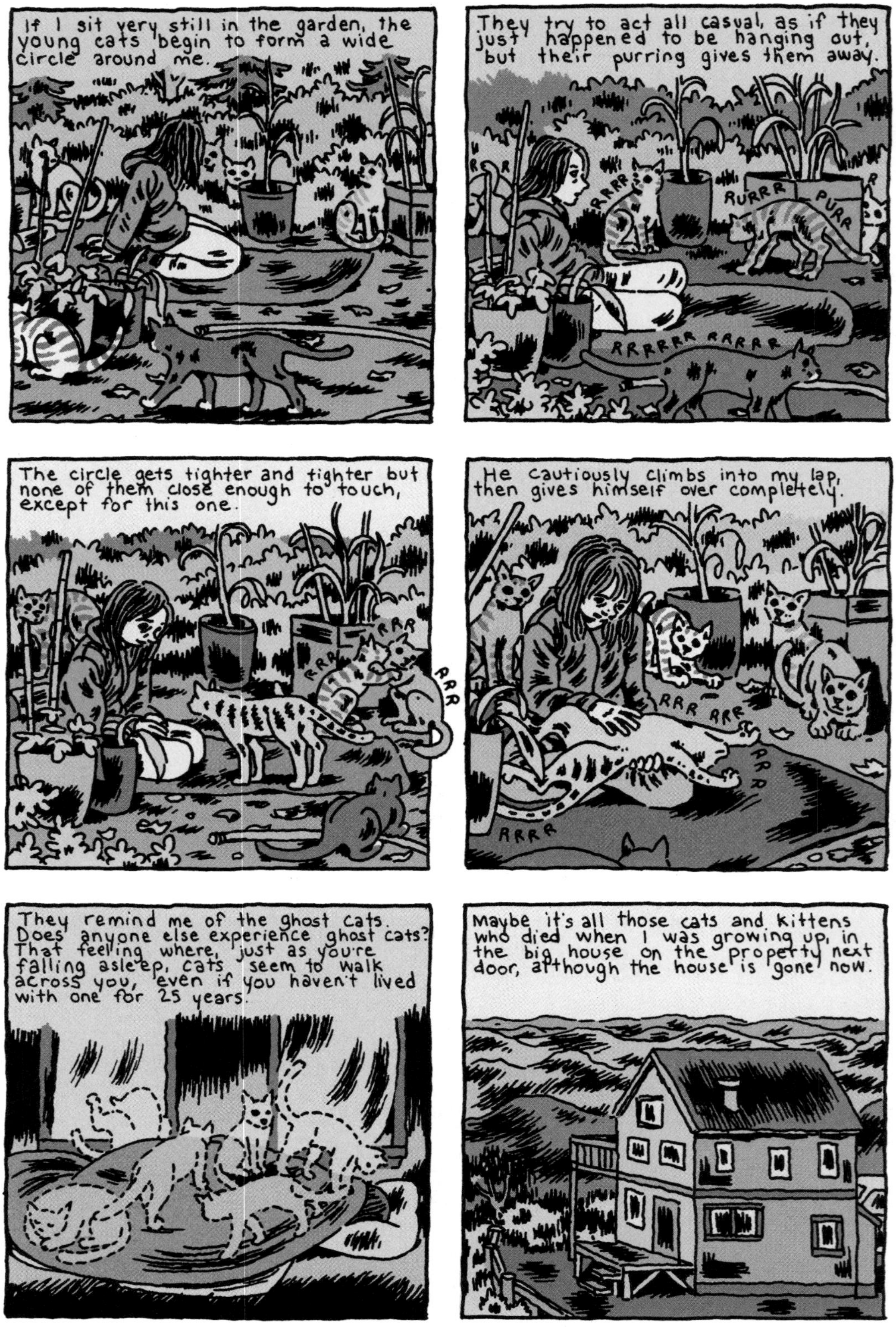

If I sit very still in the garden, the young cats begin to form a wide circle around me.
They try to act all casual, as if they just happened to be hanging out, but their purring gives them away.
RURRR
PURR
RRRRRR RRRRR
The circle gets tighter and tighter but none of them close enough to touch, except for this one.
RRR
He cautiously climbs into my lap, then gives himself over completely.
RRRR
They remind me of the ghost cats. Does anyone else experience ghost cats? That feeling where, just as you're falling asleep, cats seem to walk across you, even if you haven't lived with one for 25 years.
Maybe it's all those cats and kittens who died when I was growing up, in the big house on the property next door, although the house is gone now.

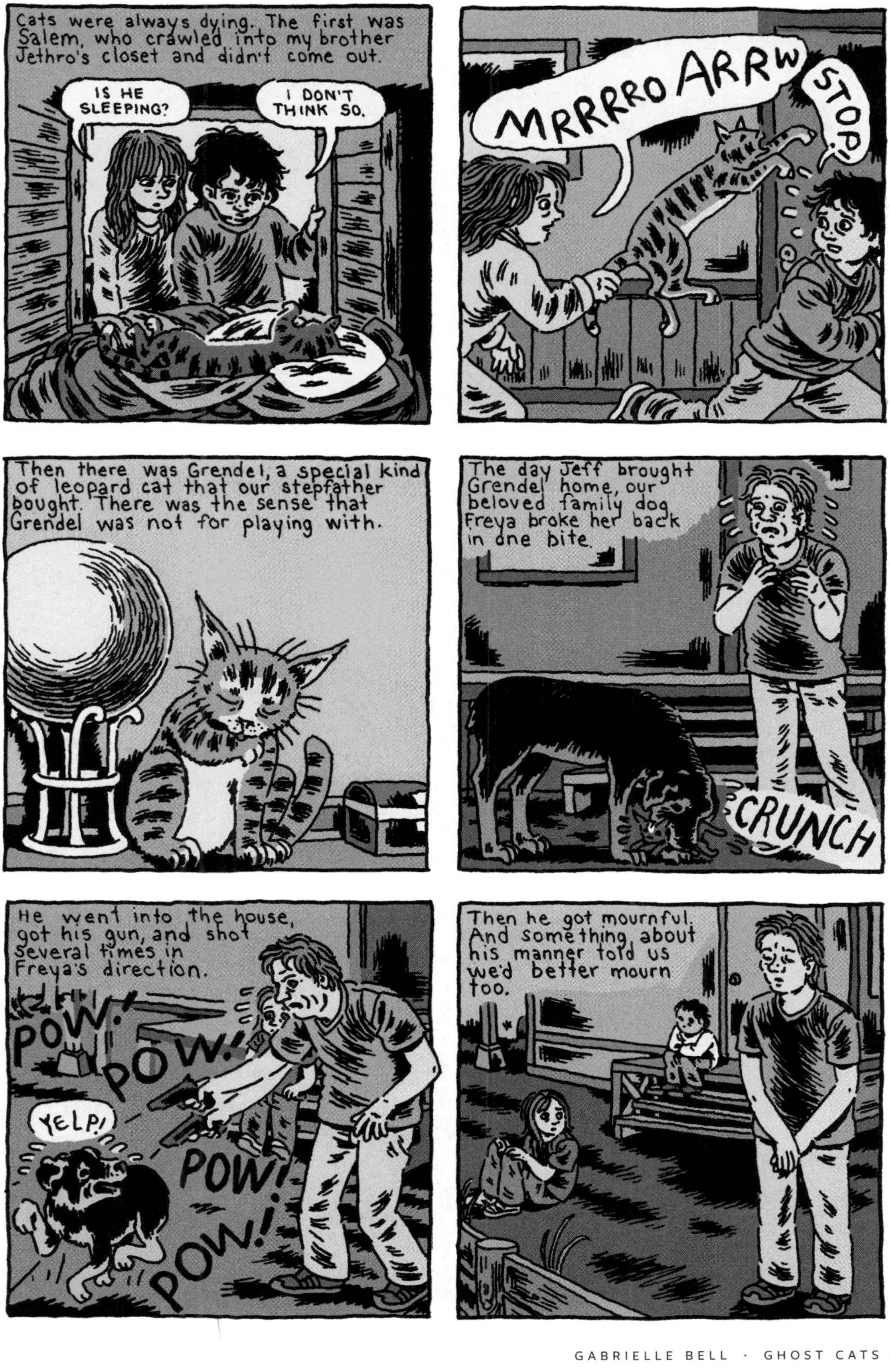

Cats were always dying. The first was Salem, who crawled into my brother Jethro's closet and didn't come out.
IS HE SLEEPING?
I DON'T THINK SO.
MRRRRO ARRW
STOP!
Then there was Grendel, a special kind of leopard cat that our stepfather bought. There was the sense that Grendel was not for playing with.
The day Jeff brought Grendel home, our beloved family dog Freya broke her back in one bite.
CRUNCH
He went into the house, got his gun, and shot several times in Freya's direction.
POW!
POW!
YELP!
POW!
POW!
Then he got mournful. And something about his manner told us we'd better mourn too.

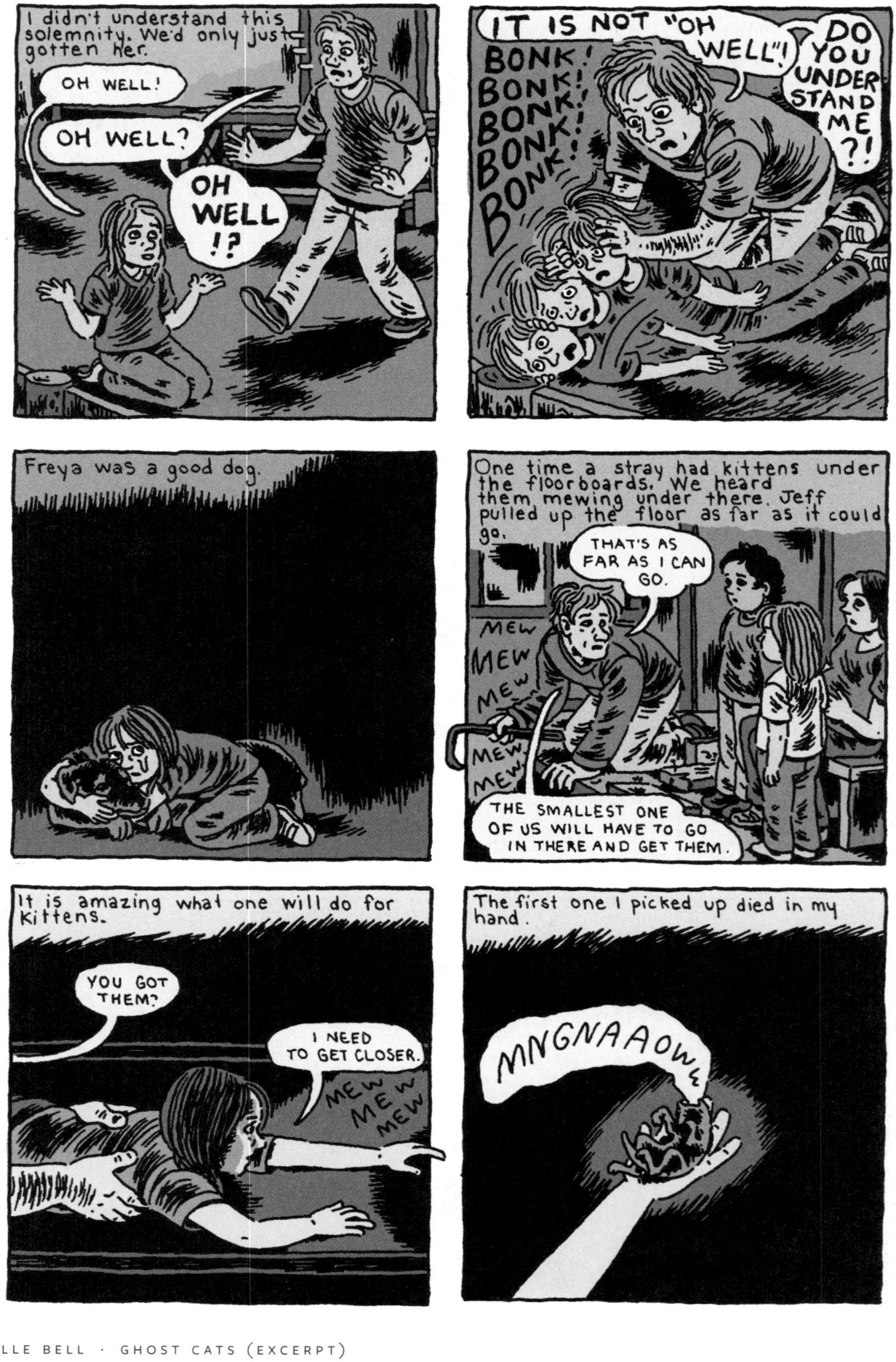

I didn't understand this solemnity. We'd only just gotten her.
OH WELL!
OH WELL?
OH WELL !?
IT IS NOT "OH WELL"!
DO YOU UNDERSTAND ME ?!
BONK! BONK! BONK! BONK! BONK!
Freya was a good dog.
One time a stray had kittens under the floorboards. We heard them mewing under there. Jeff pulled up the floor as far as it could go.
THAT'S AS FAR AS I CAN GO.
MEW MEW MEW MEW MEW
THE SMALLEST ONE OF US WILL HAVE TO GO IN THERE AND GET THEM.
It is amazing what one will do for kittens.
YOU GOT THEM?
I NEED TO GET CLOSER.
MEW MEW MEW
The first one I picked up died in my hand.
MNGNAAOWL

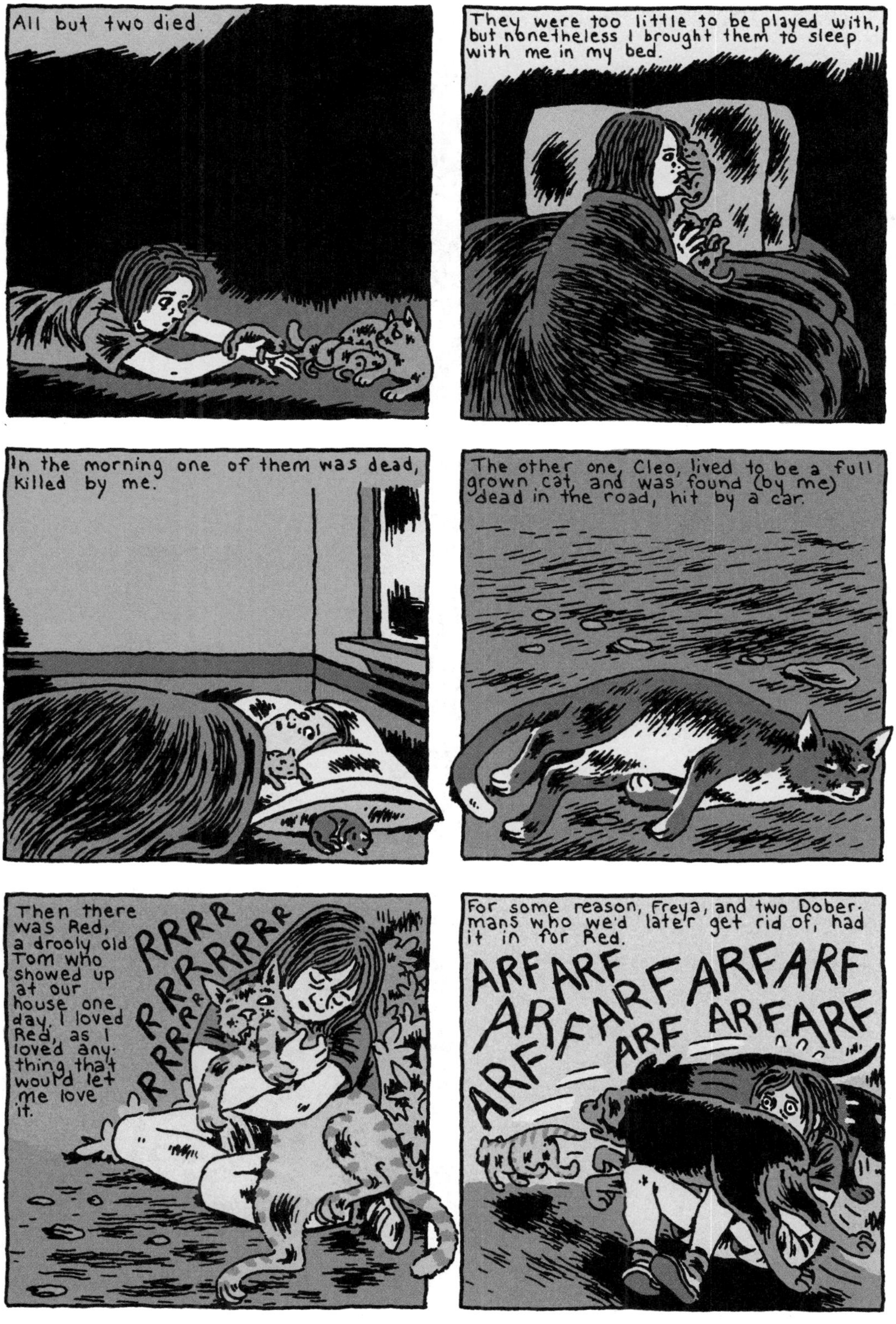

All but two died.
They were too little to be played with, but nonetheless I brought them to sleep with me in my bed.
In the morning one of them was dead, killed by me.
The other one, Cleo, lived to be a full grown cat, and was found (by me) dead in the road, hit by a car.
Then there was Red, a drooly old Tom who showed up at our house one day. I loved Red, as I loved anything that would let me love it.
RRRR RRRRRRRR RRRRRR RRRR
For some reason, Freya, and two Dobermans who we'd later get rid of, had it in for Red.
ARF ARF ARF ARF ARF ARF ARF ARF ARF ARF ARF ARF

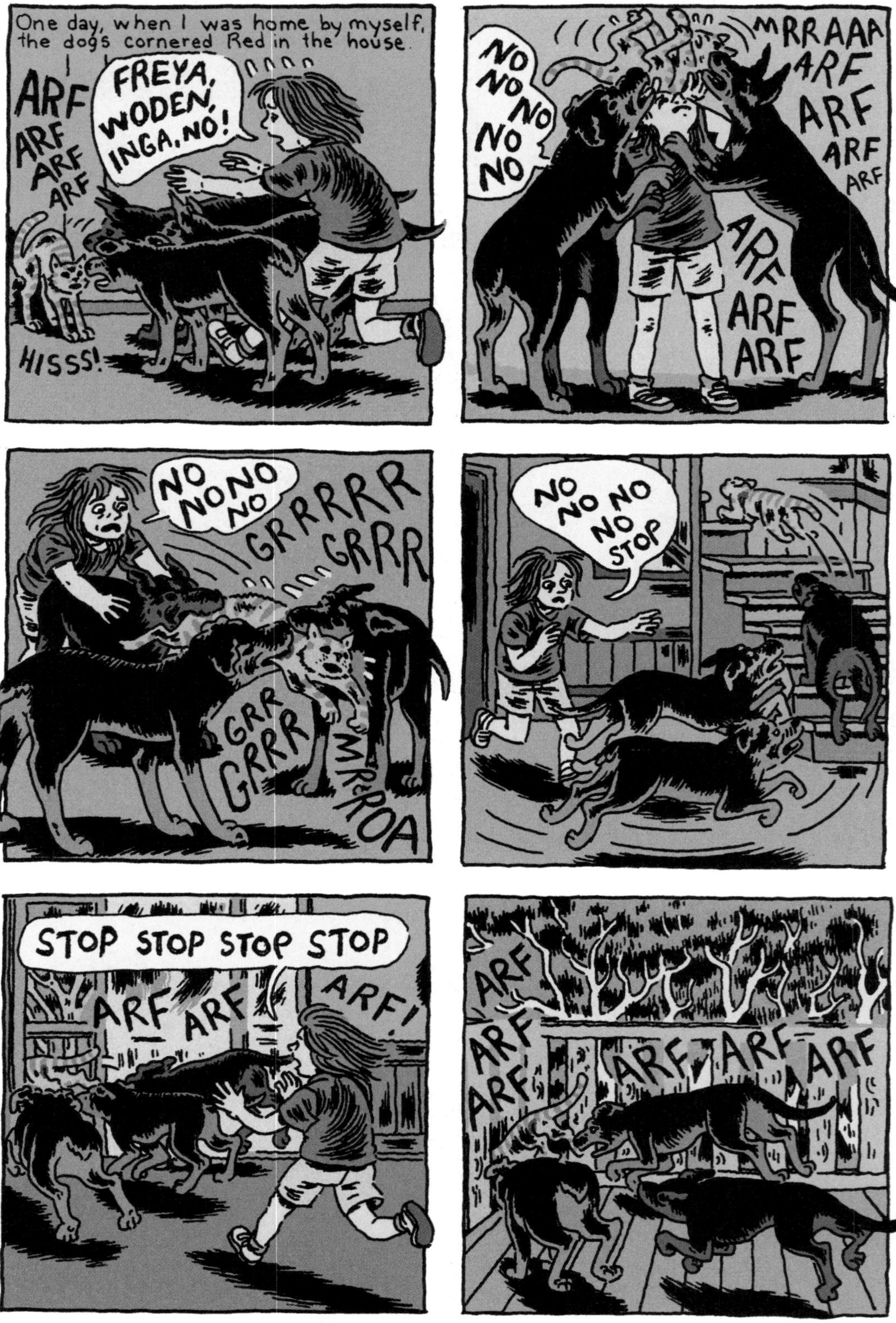
One day, when I was home by myself, the dogs cornered Red in the house.
ARF
ARF
ARF
ARF
FREYA, WODEN, INGA, NO!
HISSS!
NO NO NO NO NO
MRRAAA
ARF
ARF
ARF
ARF
ARF
ARF
ARF
NO NO NO NO
GRRRRR
GRRR
GRR GRRR
MRROA
NO NO NO NO STOP
STOP STOP STOP STOP
ARF
ARF
ARF!
ARF
ARF
ARF
ARF
ARF
ARF

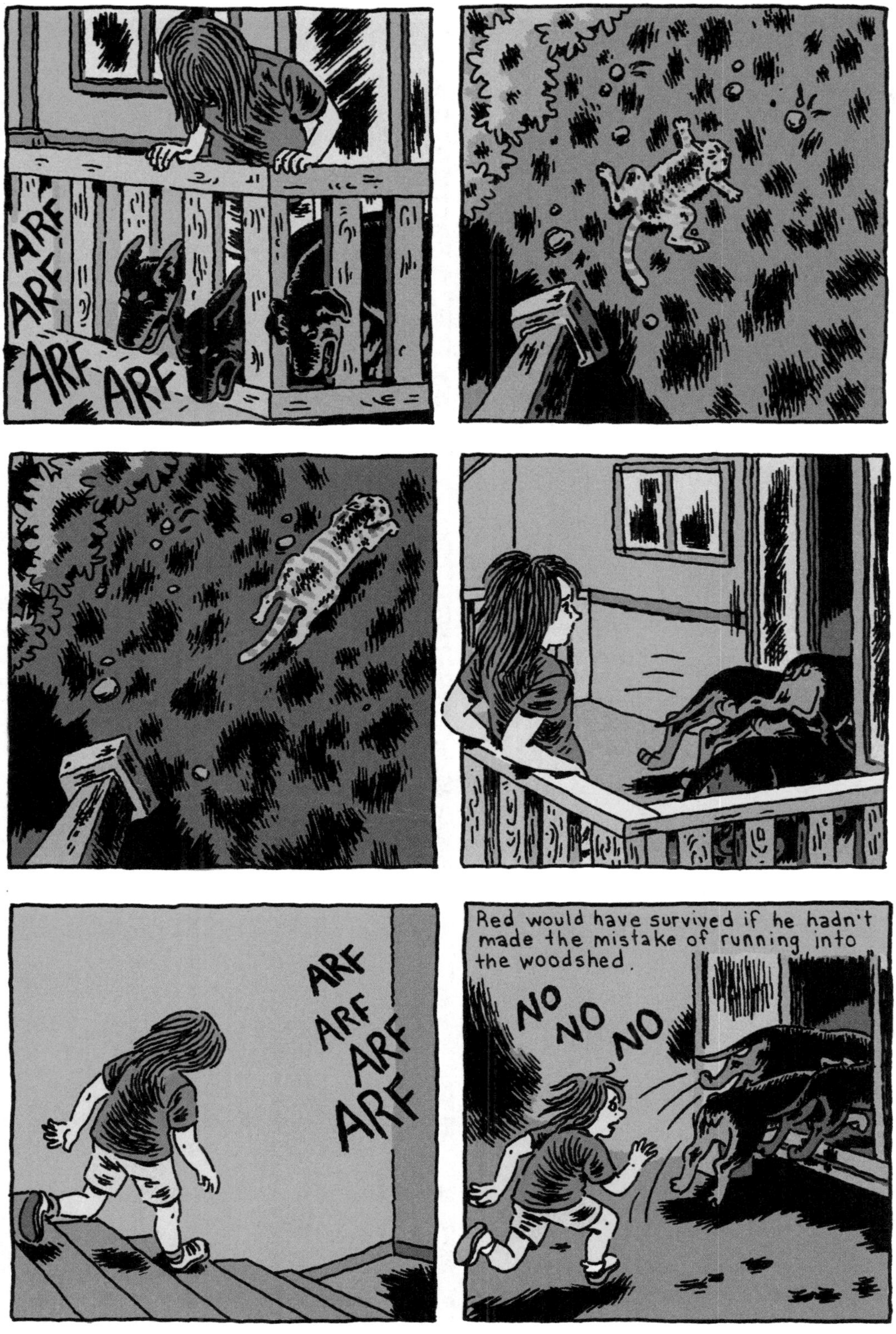
ARF
ARF
ARF
ARF
ARF
ARF
ARF
ARF
Red would have survived if he hadn't made the mistake of running into the woodshed.
NO
NO
NO

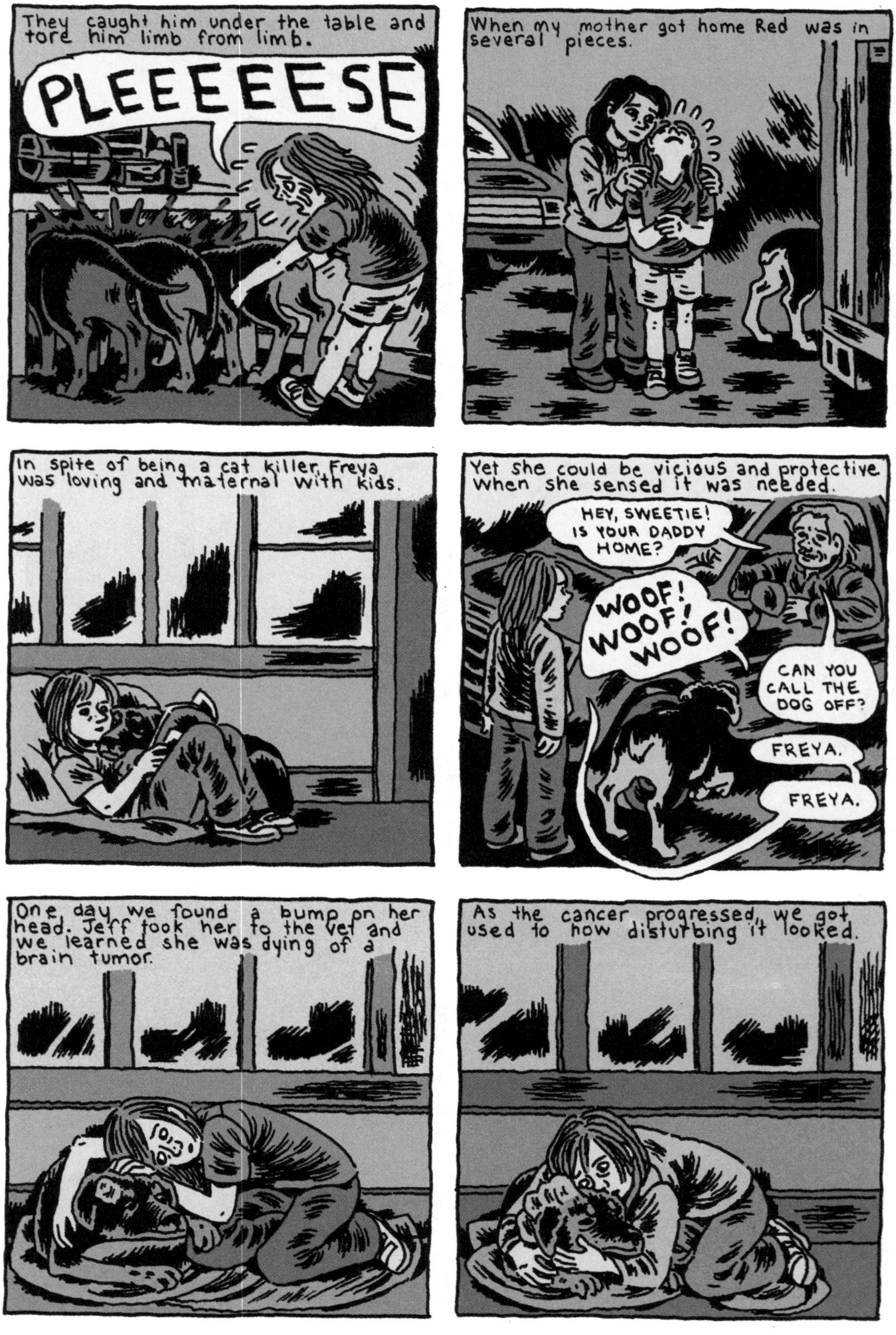
They caught him under the table and tore him limb from limb.
PLEEEEEESE
When my mother got home Red was in several pieces.
In spite of being a cat killer, Freya was loving and maternal with kids.
Yet she could be vicious and protective when she sensed it was needed.
HEY, SWEETIE! IS YOUR DADDY HOME?
WOOF! WOOF! WOOF!
CAN YOU CALL THE DOG OFF?
FREYA.
FREYA.
One day we found a bump on her head. Jeff took her to the vet and we learned she was dying of a brain tumor.
As the cancer progressed, we got used to how disturbing it looked.

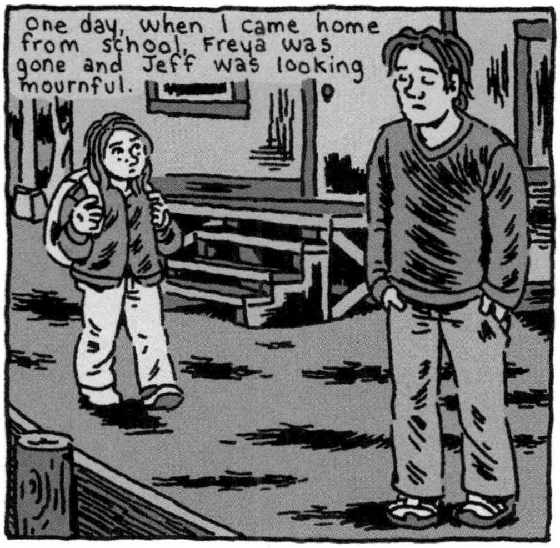
One day, when I came home from school, Freya was gone and Jeff was looking mournful.

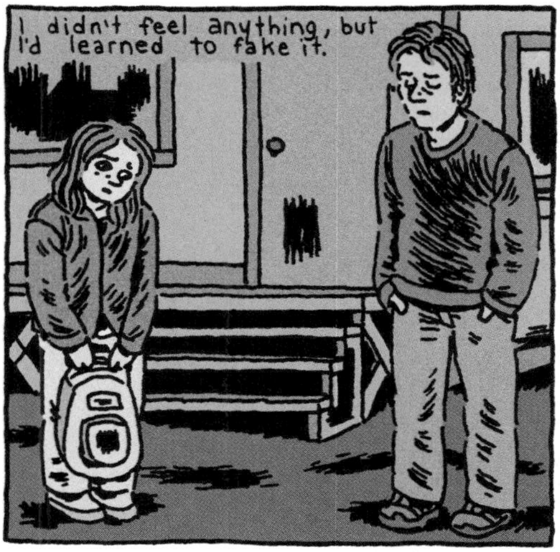
I didn't feel anything, but I'd learned to fake it.

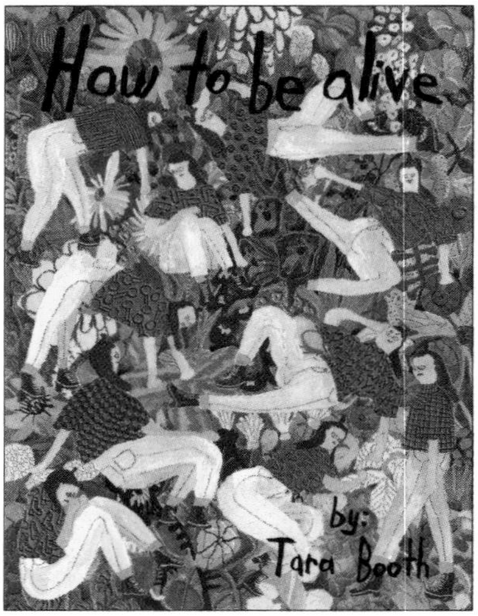
How to be alive
by:
Tara Booth

SELECTIONS FROM

How to Be Alive

TARA BOOTH

originally published in

How to Be Alive
RETROFIT/BIG PLANET
7 x 10 inches • 40 pages

Biography

Tara Booth is a comics artist and illustrator from Philadelphia, Pennsylvania, currently working from Chicago, Illinois. Her comics have been published by kuš!, Retrofit, and 2dcloud. Her illustrations have been featured in *Bloomberg Magazine*, *Mashable*, and *It's Nice That,* among other publications. She is best known for her funny, pattern-filled, auto-bio gouache paintings.
tarabooth.club

Statement

The piece includes excerpts from *How to Be Alive*, a forty-page collection of gouache paintings from 2017.

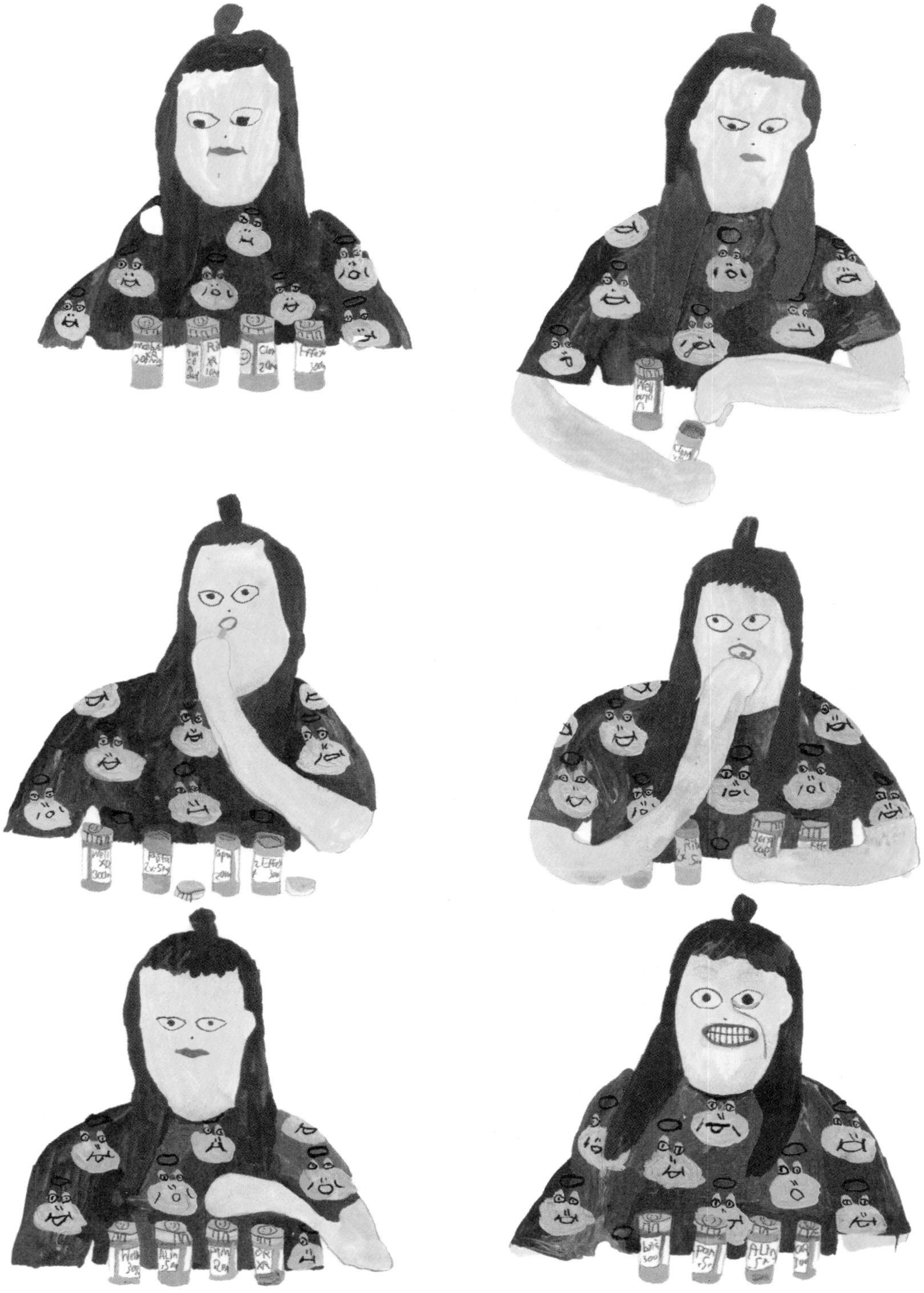

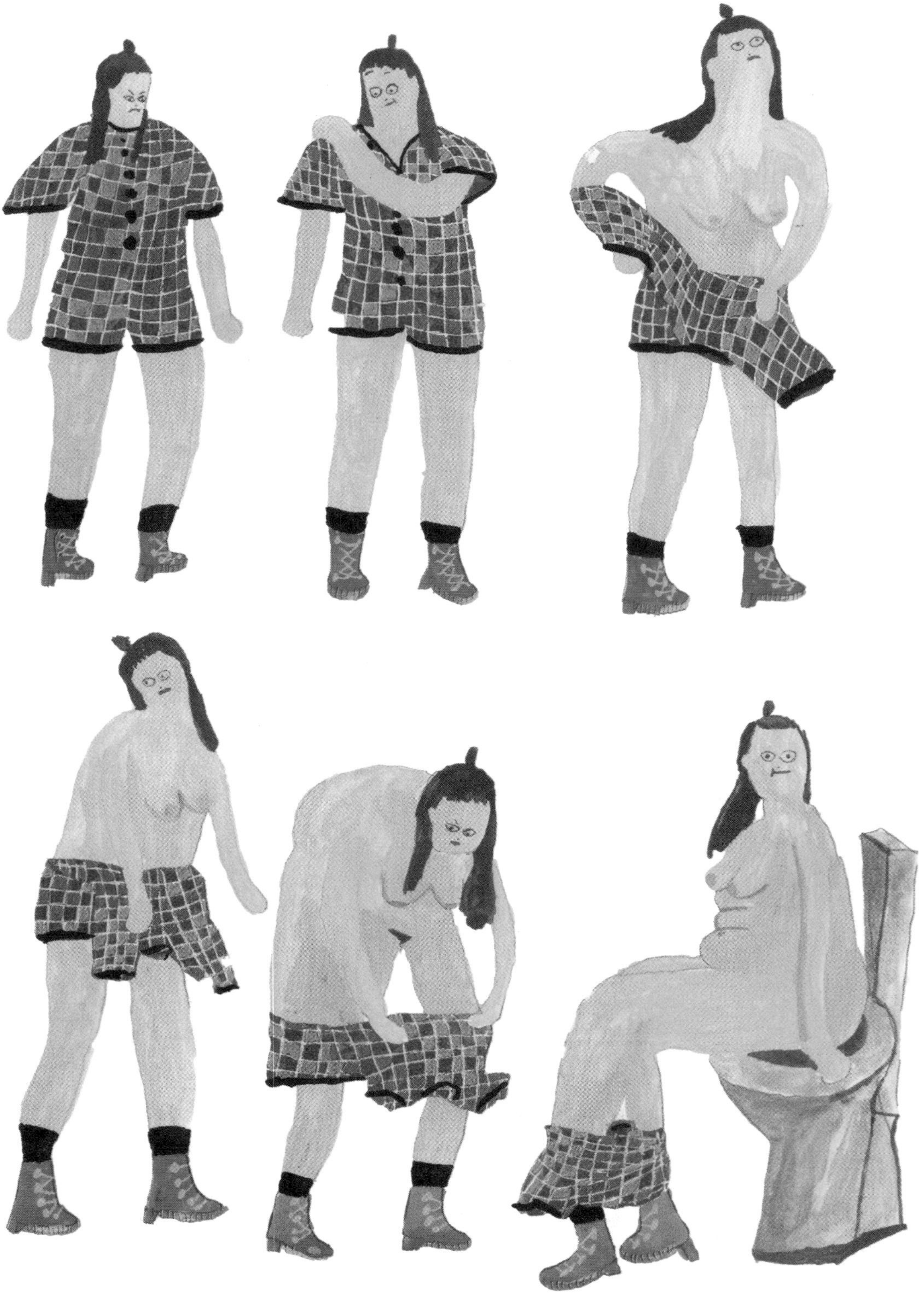

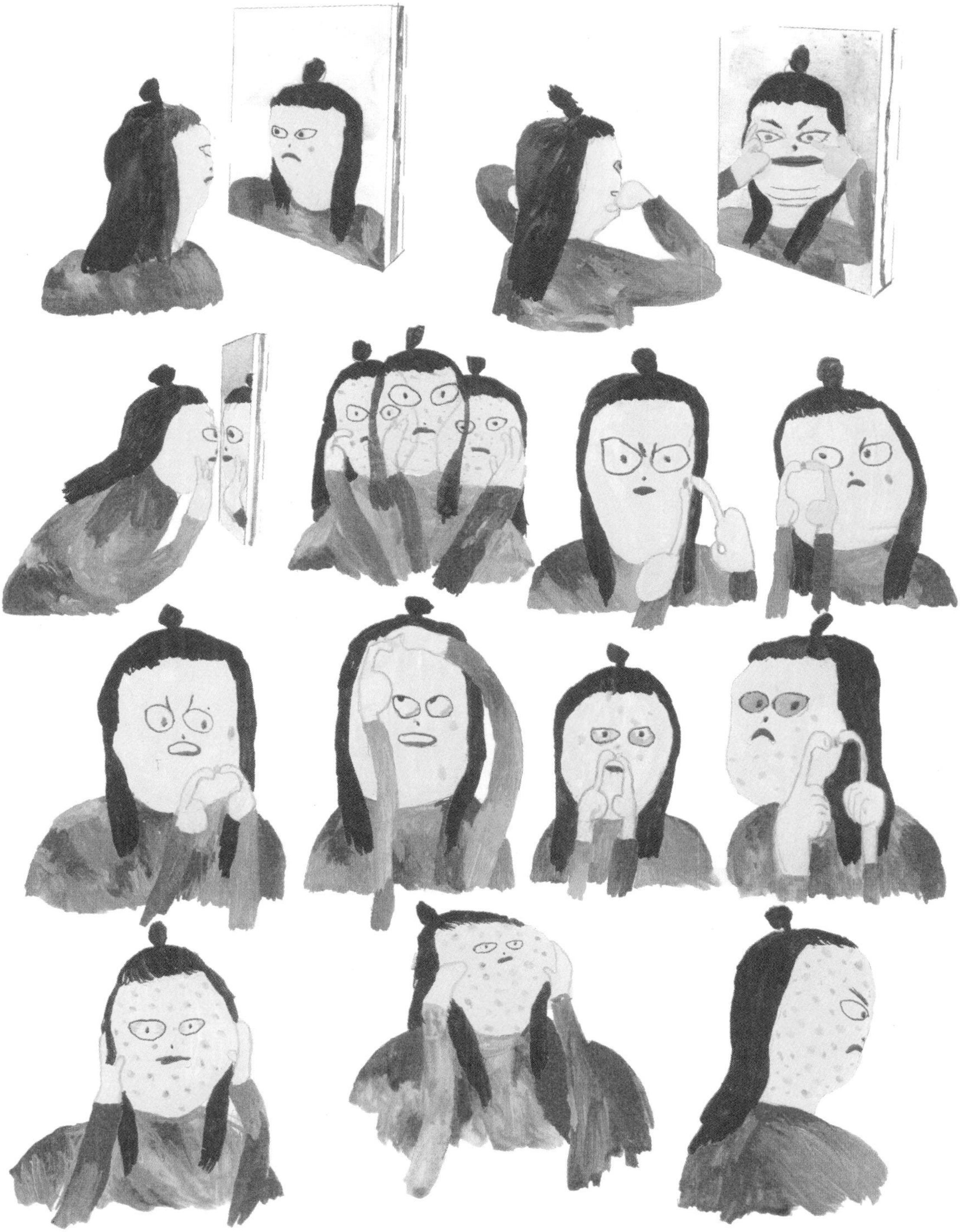

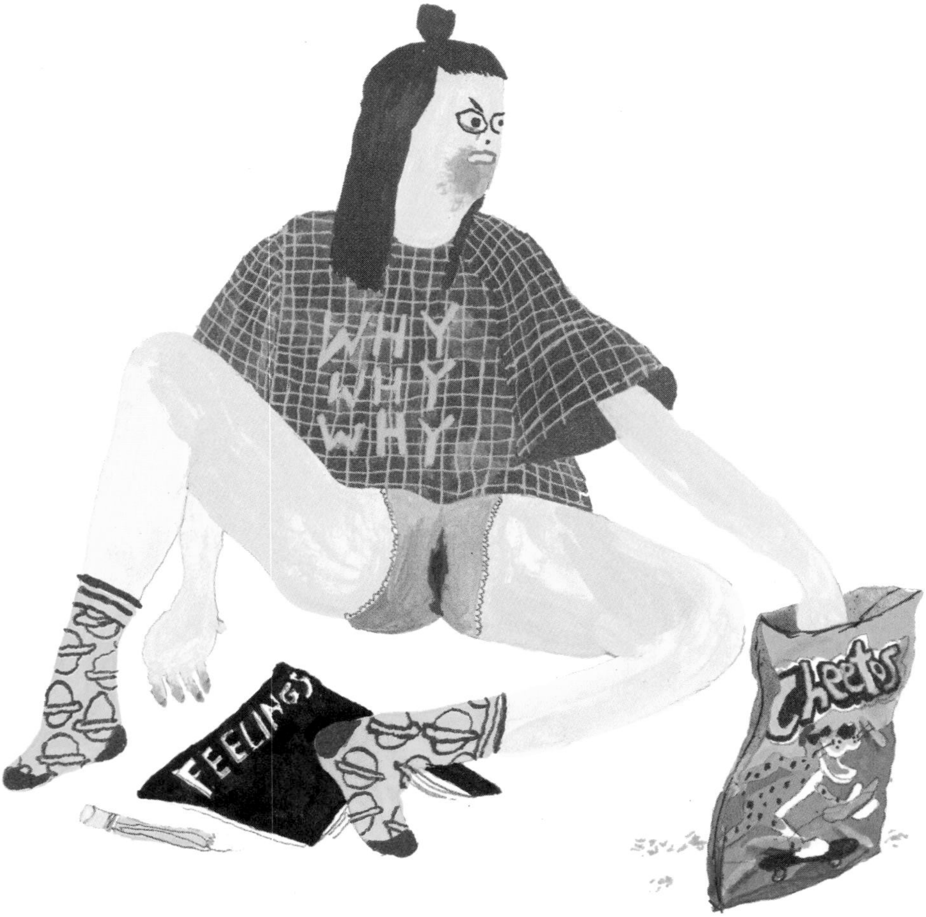
WHY
WHY
WHY
FEELINGS
Cheetos

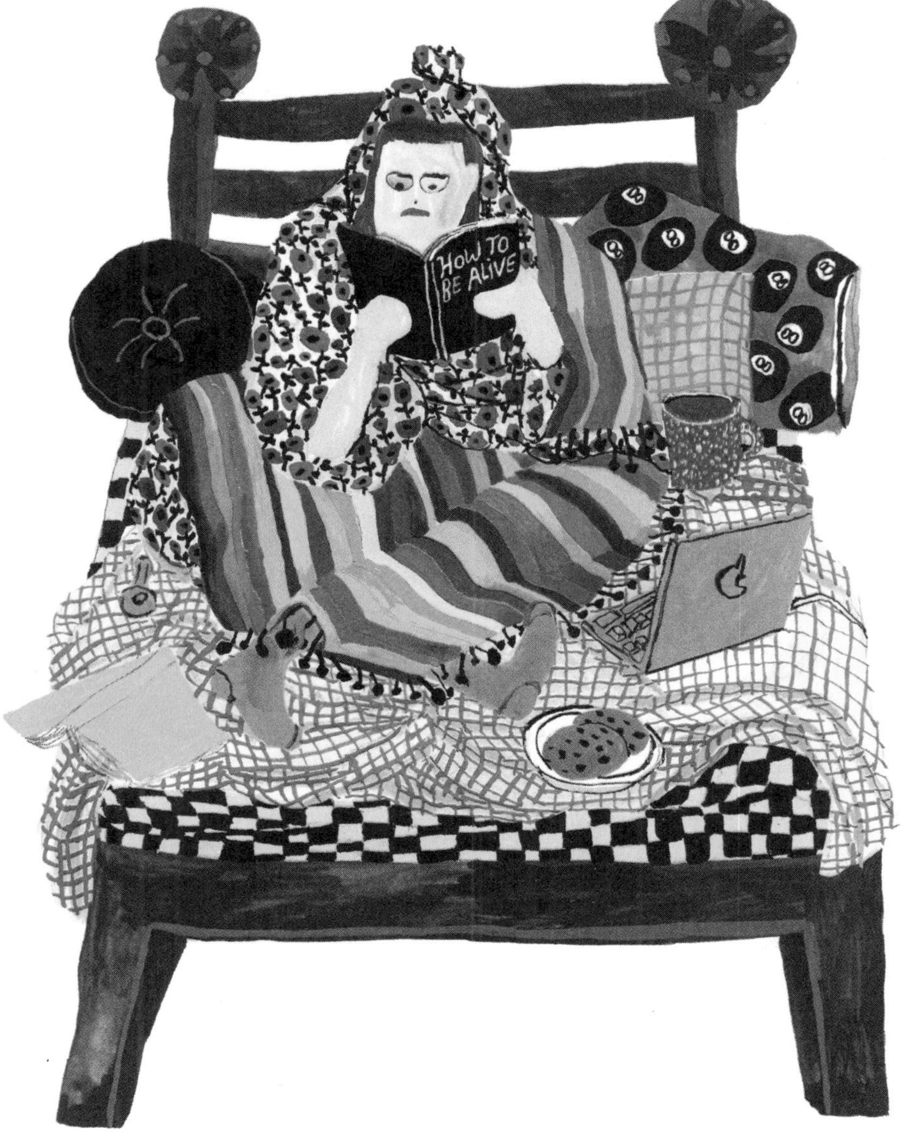
HOW TO BE ALIVE

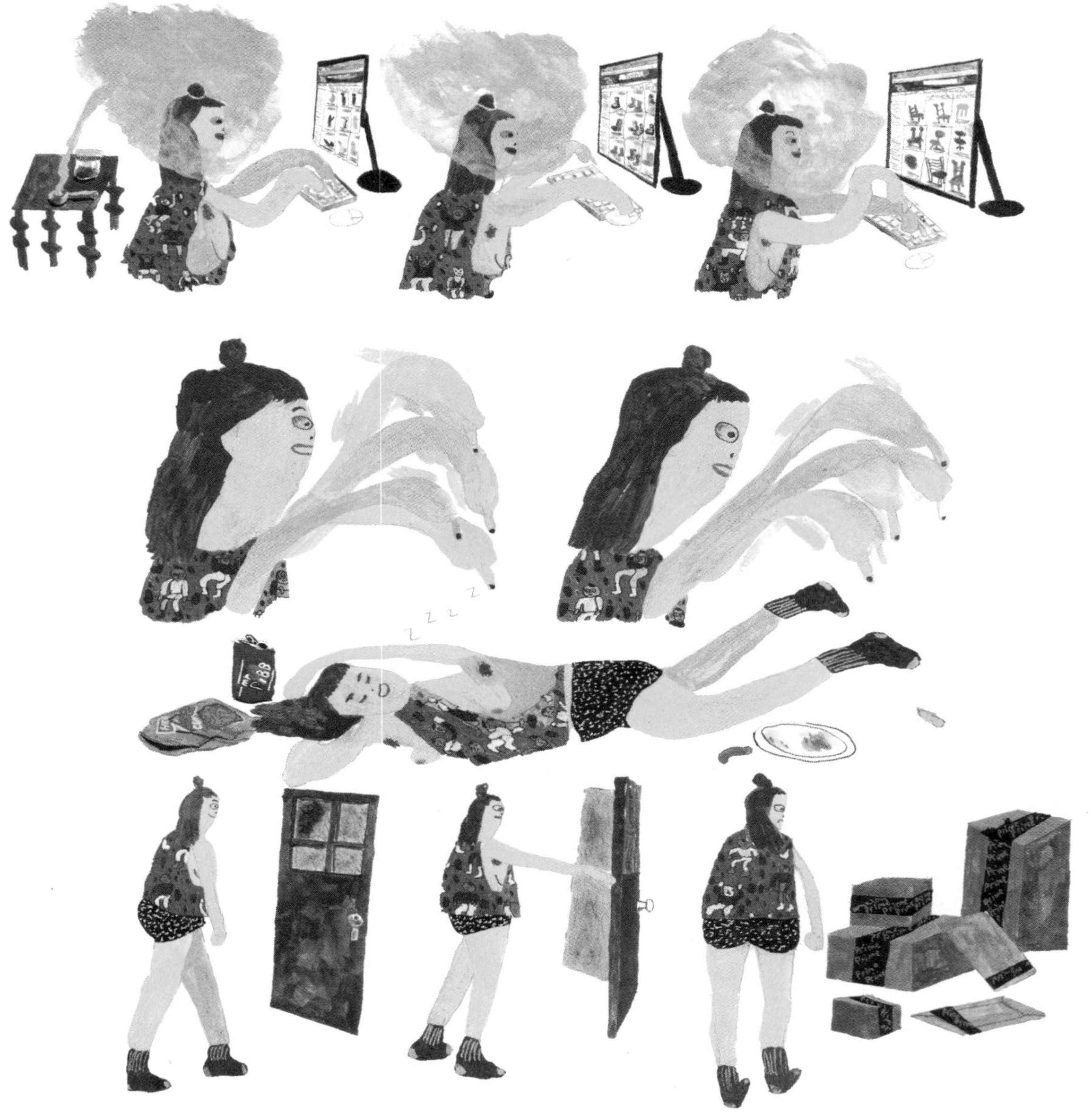

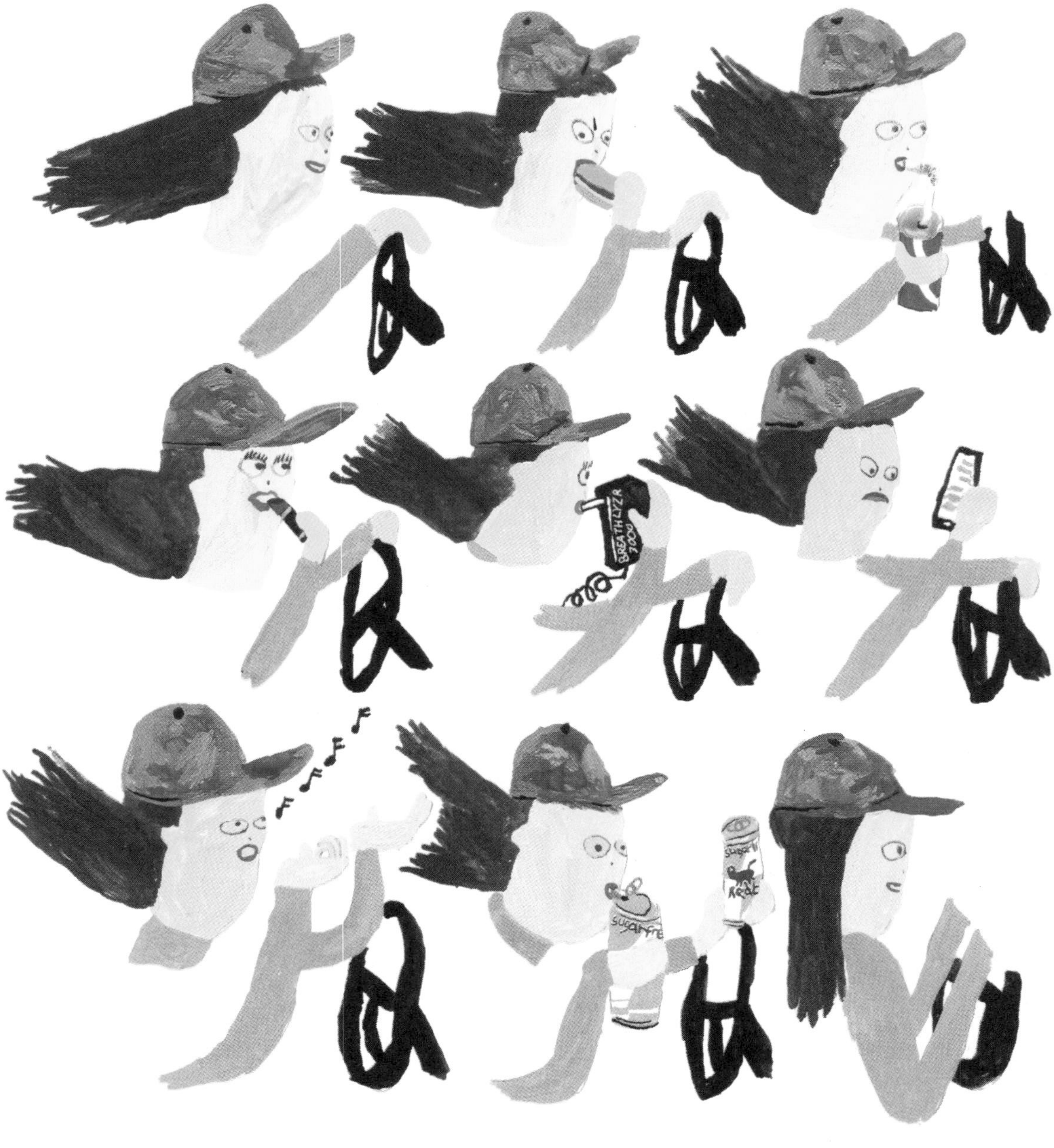
BREATHLYZR 7000
Reat

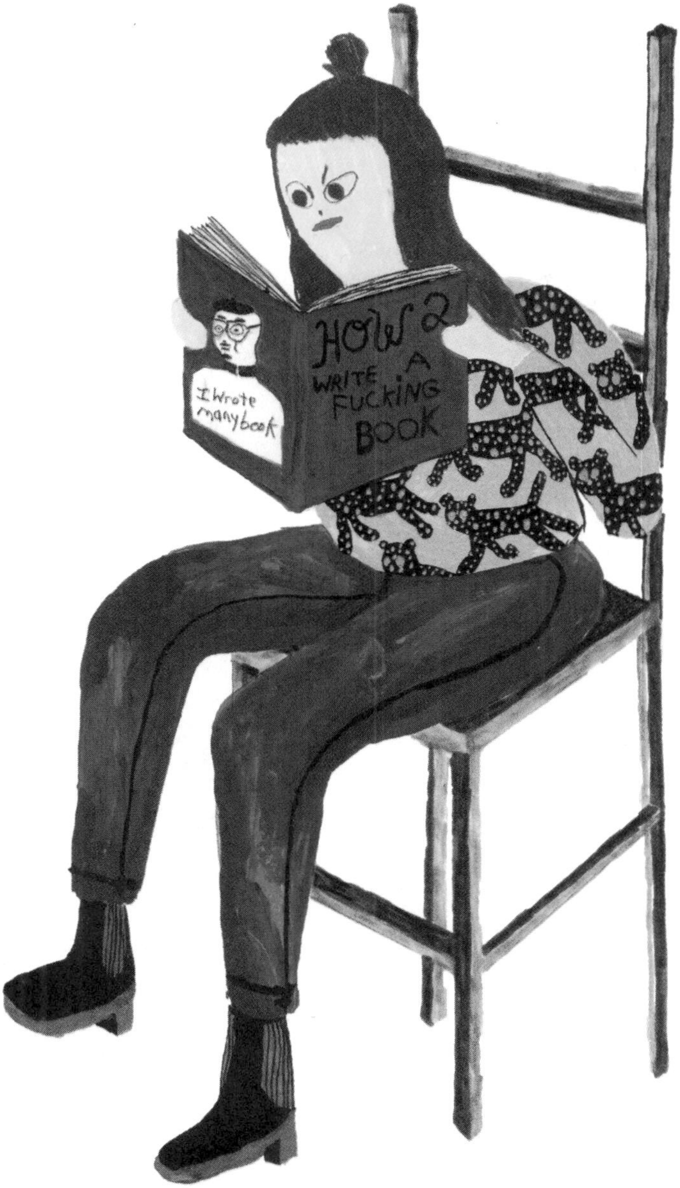
HOW 2
WRITE A
FUCKING
BOOK
I Wrote
manybook

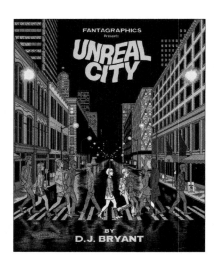

FANTAGRAPHICS
Presents
UNREAL CITY
BY
D.J. BRYANT

Echoes Into Eternity

D. J. BRYANT

originally published in

Unreal City

FANTAGRAPHICS BOOKS

10 x 12.5 inches • 106 pages

Biography

D. J. Bryant was born in 1979 in Raleigh, North Carolina, but spent his formative years in Chugiak, Alaska. He graduated from the Art Institute of Seattle in September 2001, shortly after the 9/11 attacks. His first short story, "The Steelcharge Horsecap," appeared in Danny Hellman's *Typhon* anthology, published in 2008. His work has additionally appeared in *Cinema Sewer*, *Mome,* and *The Stranger*.
djbryantcomics.tumblr.com

Statement

"Echoes Into Eternity" came together, like so many of my stories, because I was running behind on a deadline. The story I was working on was taking too long and I needed something short and sweet to announce my presence to the world. Then, almost miraculously, "Echoes" came to me. I had long wanted to do a story focusing on narcissism and gender identity. I was living in a lesbian house at the time and in retrospect I think that also influenced me. The only problem was the protagonist. The story was initially narrated from a male point of view, but the tone seemed off somehow. As soon as Aydan became Nadya, everything clicked and the story came together in a flash. I still blew my deadline, but I ended up with what felt like a perfect eight pages of comics.

ECHOES INTO ETERNITY

by D.J. BRYANT

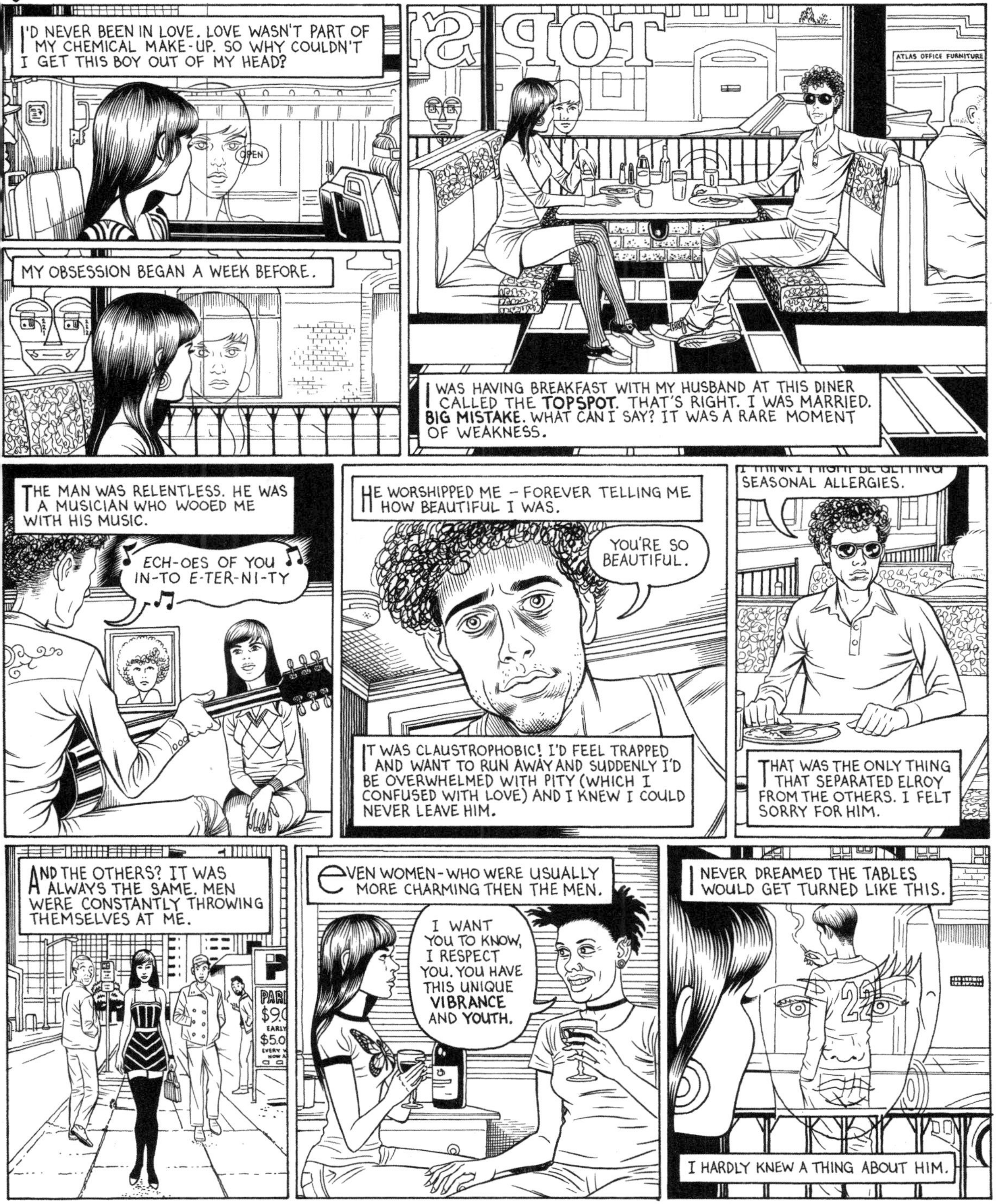
I'D NEVER BEEN IN LOVE. LOVE WASN'T PART OF MY CHEMICAL MAKE-UP. SO WHY COULDN'T I GET THIS BOY OUT OF MY HEAD?
OPEN
MY OBSESSION BEGAN A WEEK BEFORE.
ATLAS OFFICE FURNITURE
I WAS HAVING BREAKFAST WITH MY HUSBAND AT THIS DINER CALLED THE **TOPSPOT**. THAT'S RIGHT. I WAS MARRIED. **BIG MISTAKE**. WHAT CAN I SAY? IT WAS A RARE MOMENT OF WEAKNESS.
THE MAN WAS RELENTLESS. HE WAS A MUSICIAN WHO WOOED ME WITH HIS MUSIC.
ECH-OES OF YOU IN-TO E-TER-NI-TY
HE WORSHIPPED ME – FOREVER TELLING ME HOW BEAUTIFUL I WAS.
YOU'RE SO BEAUTIFUL.
IT WAS CLAUSTROPHOBIC! I'D FEEL TRAPPED AND WANT TO RUN AWAY AND SUDDENLY I'D BE OVERWHELMED WITH PITY (WHICH I CONFUSED WITH LOVE) AND I KNEW I COULD NEVER LEAVE HIM.
SEASONAL ALLERGIES.
THAT WAS THE ONLY THING THAT SEPARATED ELROY FROM THE OTHERS. I FELT SORRY FOR HIM.
AND THE OTHERS? IT WAS ALWAYS THE SAME. MEN WERE CONSTANTLY THROWING THEMSELVES AT ME.
EVEN WOMEN - WHO WERE USUALLY MORE CHARMING THEN THE MEN.
I WANT YOU TO KNOW, I RESPECT YOU. YOU HAVE THIS UNIQUE **VIBRANCE** AND **YOUTH**.
I NEVER DREAMED THE TABLES WOULD GET TURNED LIKE THIS.
22
I HARDLY KNEW A THING ABOUT HIM.

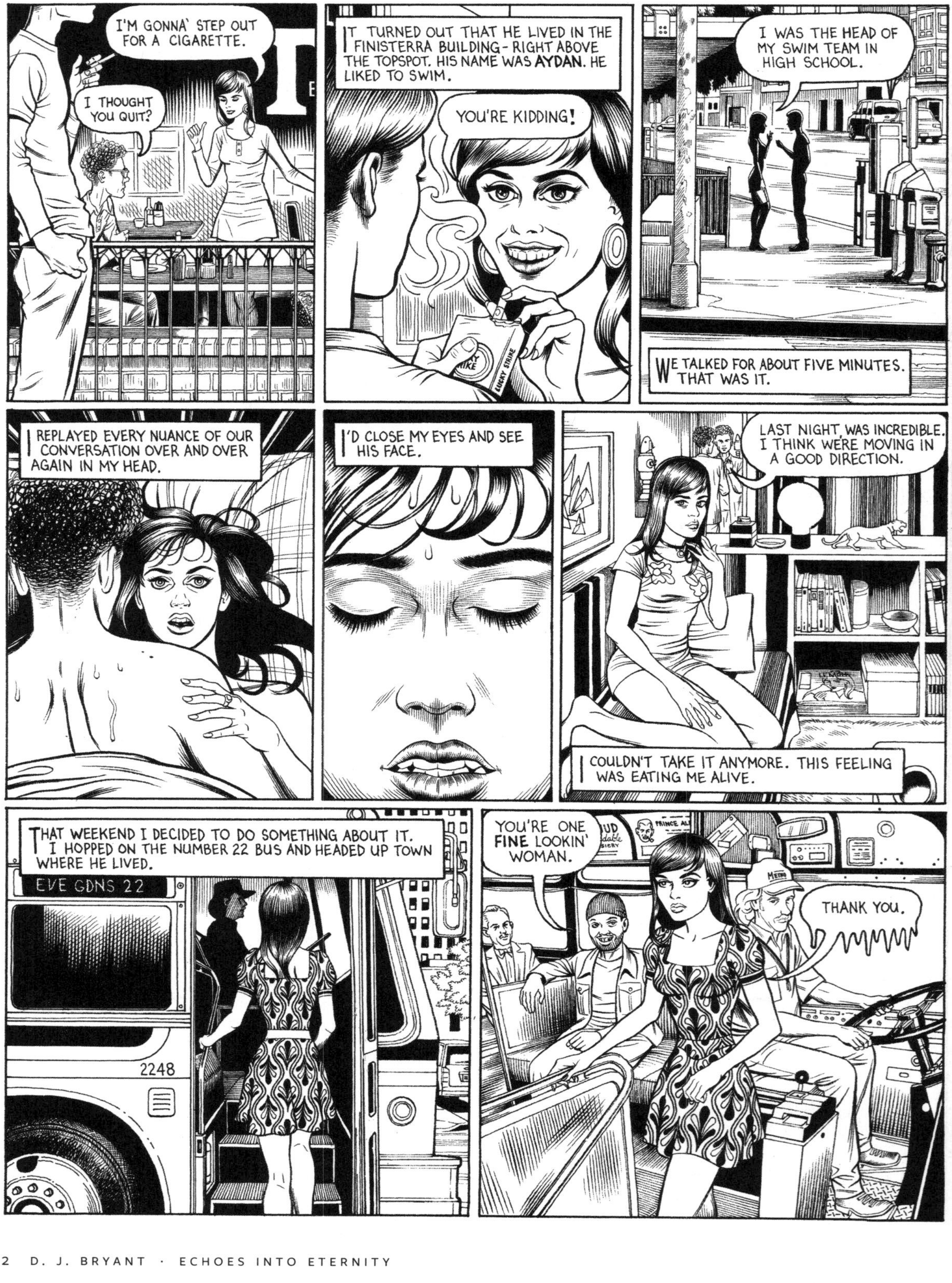

I'M GONNA' STEP OUT FOR A CIGARETTE.
I THOUGHT YOU QUIT?
IT TURNED OUT THAT HE LIVED IN THE FINISTERRA BUILDING - RIGHT ABOVE THE TOPSPOT. HIS NAME WAS AYDAN. HE LIKED TO SWIM.
YOU'RE KIDDING!
LUCKY STRIKE
I WAS THE HEAD OF MY SWIM TEAM IN HIGH SCHOOL.
WE TALKED FOR ABOUT FIVE MINUTES. THAT WAS IT.
I REPLAYED EVERY NUANCE OF OUR CONVERSATION OVER AND OVER AGAIN IN MY HEAD.
I'D CLOSE MY EYES AND SEE HIS FACE.
LAST NIGHT WAS INCREDIBLE. I THINK WE'RE MOVING IN A GOOD DIRECTION.
I COULDN'T TAKE IT ANYMORE. THIS FEELING WAS EATING ME ALIVE.
THAT WEEKEND I DECIDED TO DO SOMETHING ABOUT IT. I HOPPED ON THE NUMBER 22 BUS AND HEADED UP TOWN WHERE HE LIVED.
EVE GDNS 22
2248
YOU'RE ONE FINE LOOKIN' WOMAN.
PRINCE AL
METRO
THANK YOU.

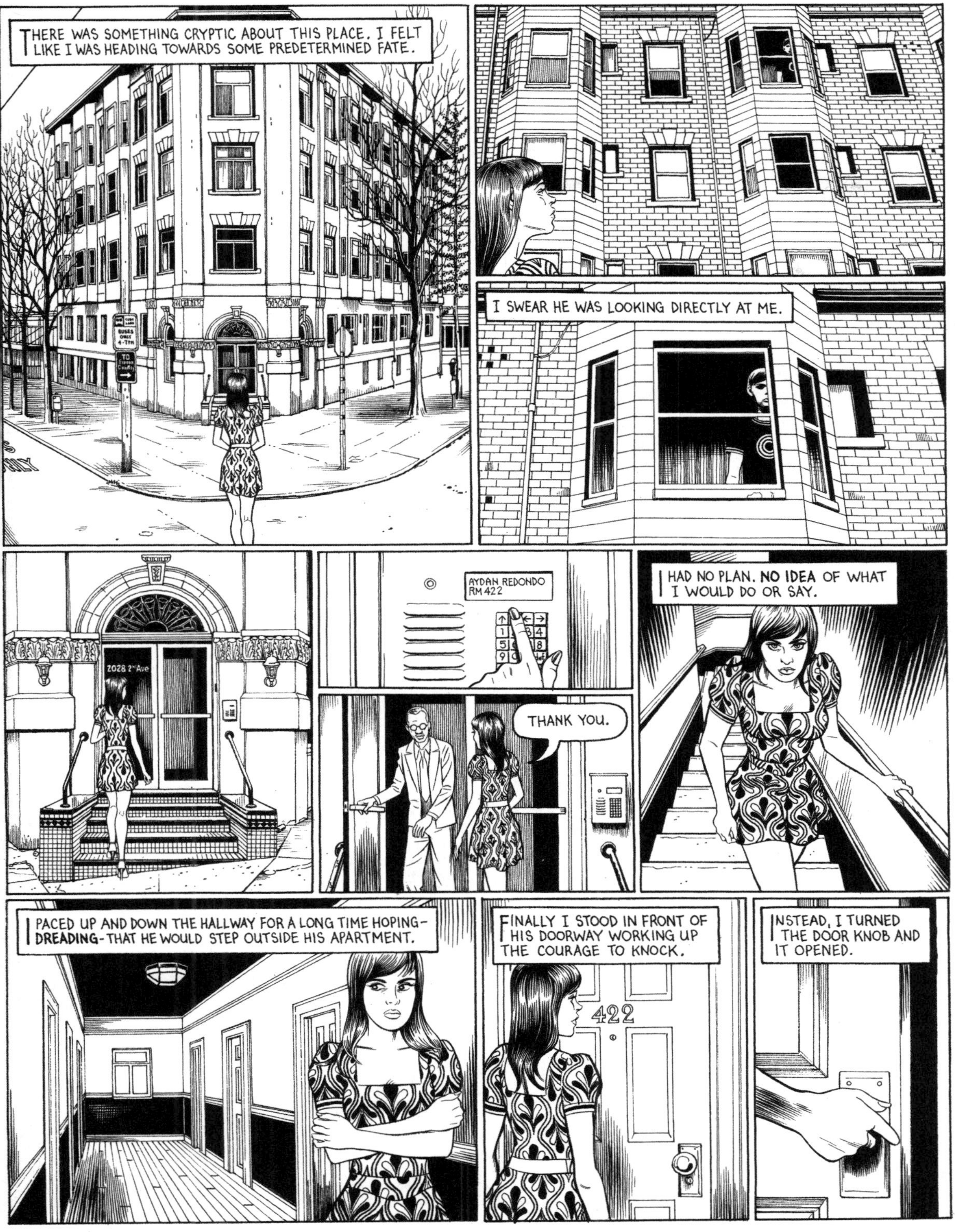
THERE WAS SOMETHING CRYPTIC ABOUT THIS PLACE. I FELT LIKE I WAS HEADING TOWARDS SOME PREDETERMINED FATE.
BUSES ONLY 4-7PM
I SWEAR HE WAS LOOKING DIRECTLY AT ME.
2028 2nd Ave
AYDAN REDONDO RM 422
THANK YOU.
I HAD NO PLAN. **NO IDEA** OF WHAT I WOULD DO OR SAY.
I PACED UP AND DOWN THE HALLWAY FOR A LONG TIME HOPING- **DREADING**- THAT HE WOULD STEP OUTSIDE HIS APARTMENT.
FINALLY I STOOD IN FRONT OF HIS DOORWAY WORKING UP THE COURAGE TO KNOCK.
422
INSTEAD, I TURNED THE DOOR KNOB AND IT OPENED.

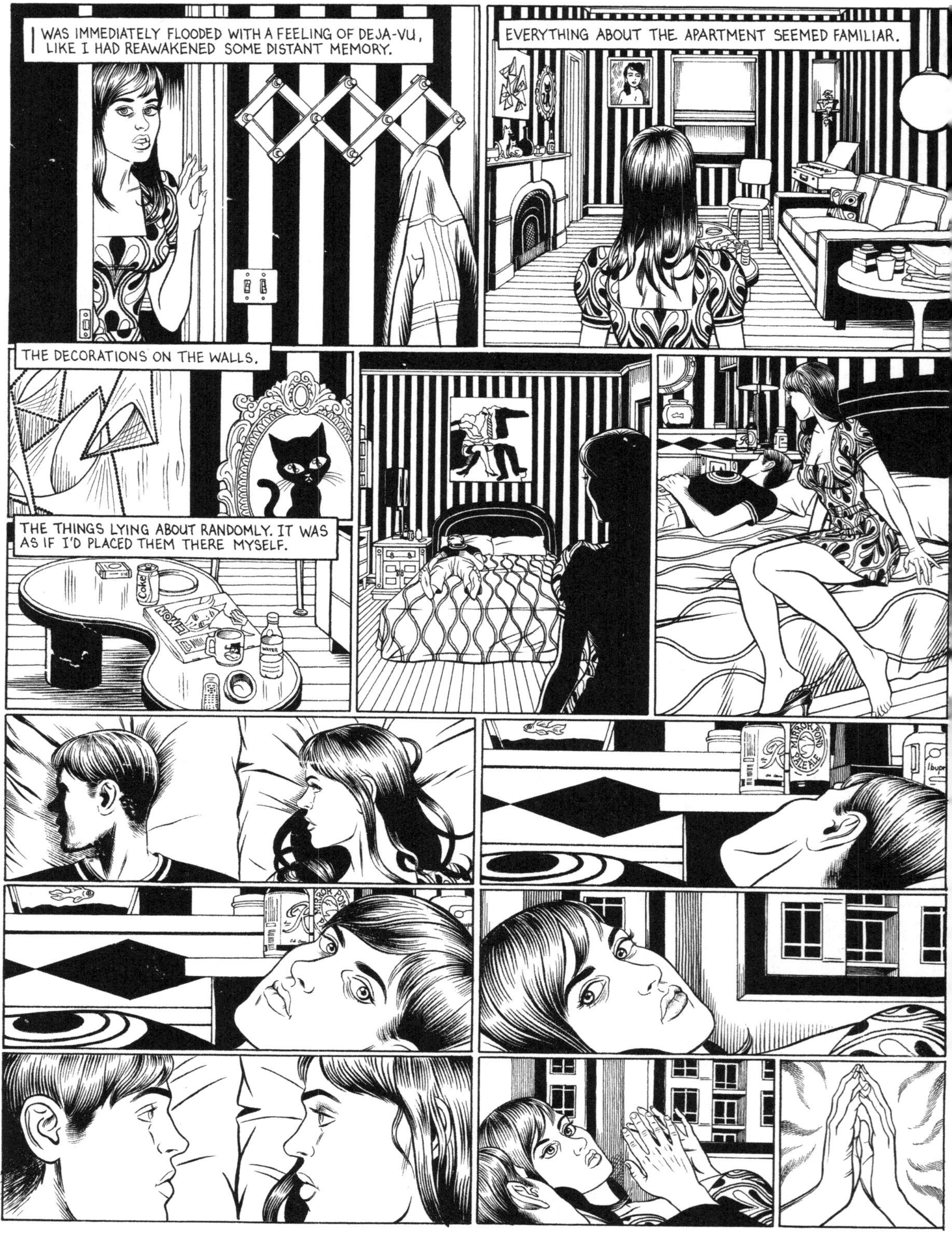
I WAS IMMEDIATELY FLOODED WITH A FEELING OF DEJA-VU, LIKE I HAD REAWAKENED SOME DISTANT MEMORY.
EVERYTHING ABOUT THE APARTMENT SEEMED FAMILIAR.
THE DECORATIONS ON THE WALLS.
THE THINGS LYING ABOUT RANDOMLY. IT WAS AS IF I'D PLACED THEM THERE MYSELF.
Coke
WATER
MIRROR POND
PALE ALE

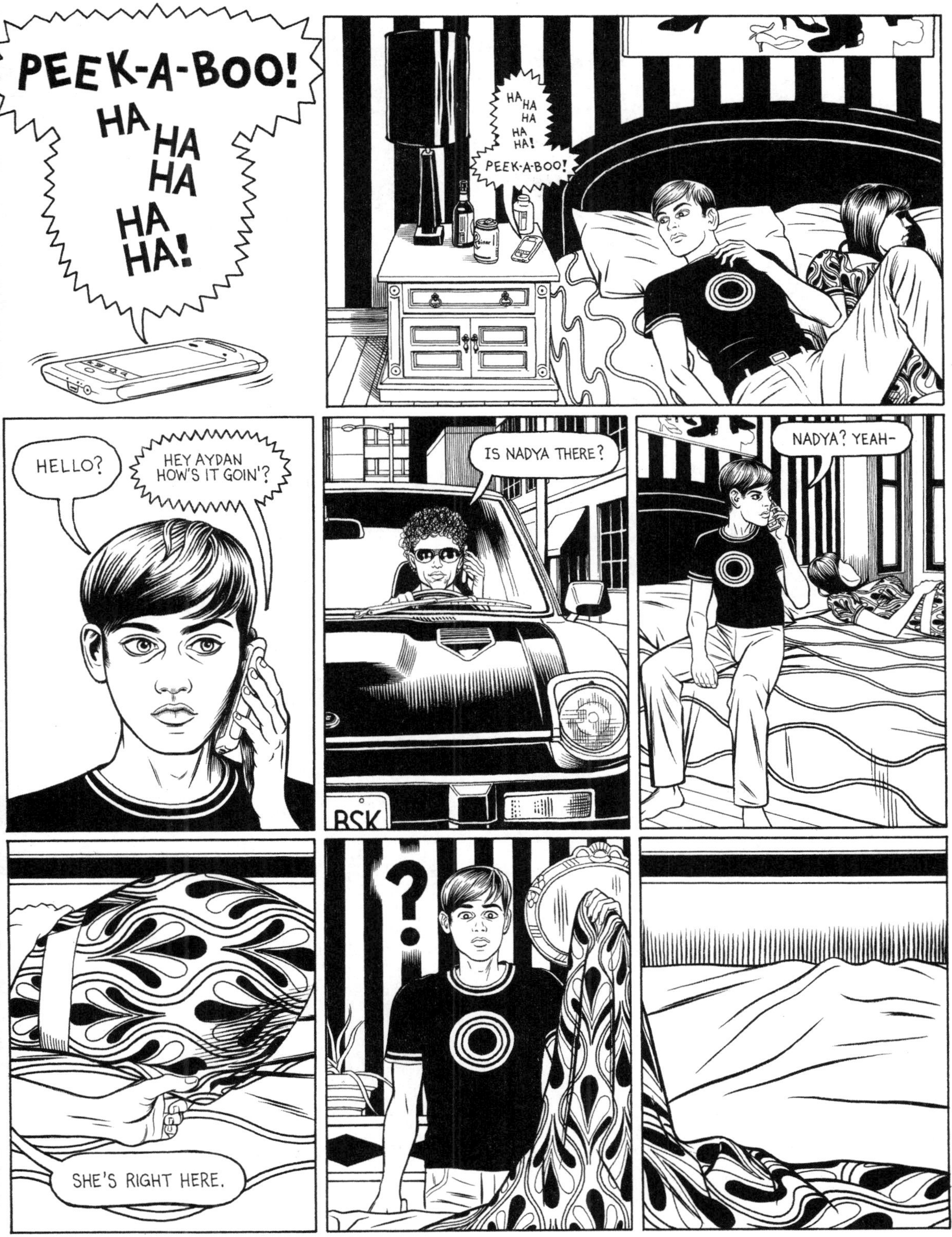
PEEK-A-BOO!
HA HA HA HA HA!
HA HA HA HA HA!
PEEK-A-BOO!
HELLO?
HEY AYDAN HOW'S IT GOIN'?
IS NADYA THERE?
BSK
NADYA? YEAH-
SHE'S RIGHT HERE.
?

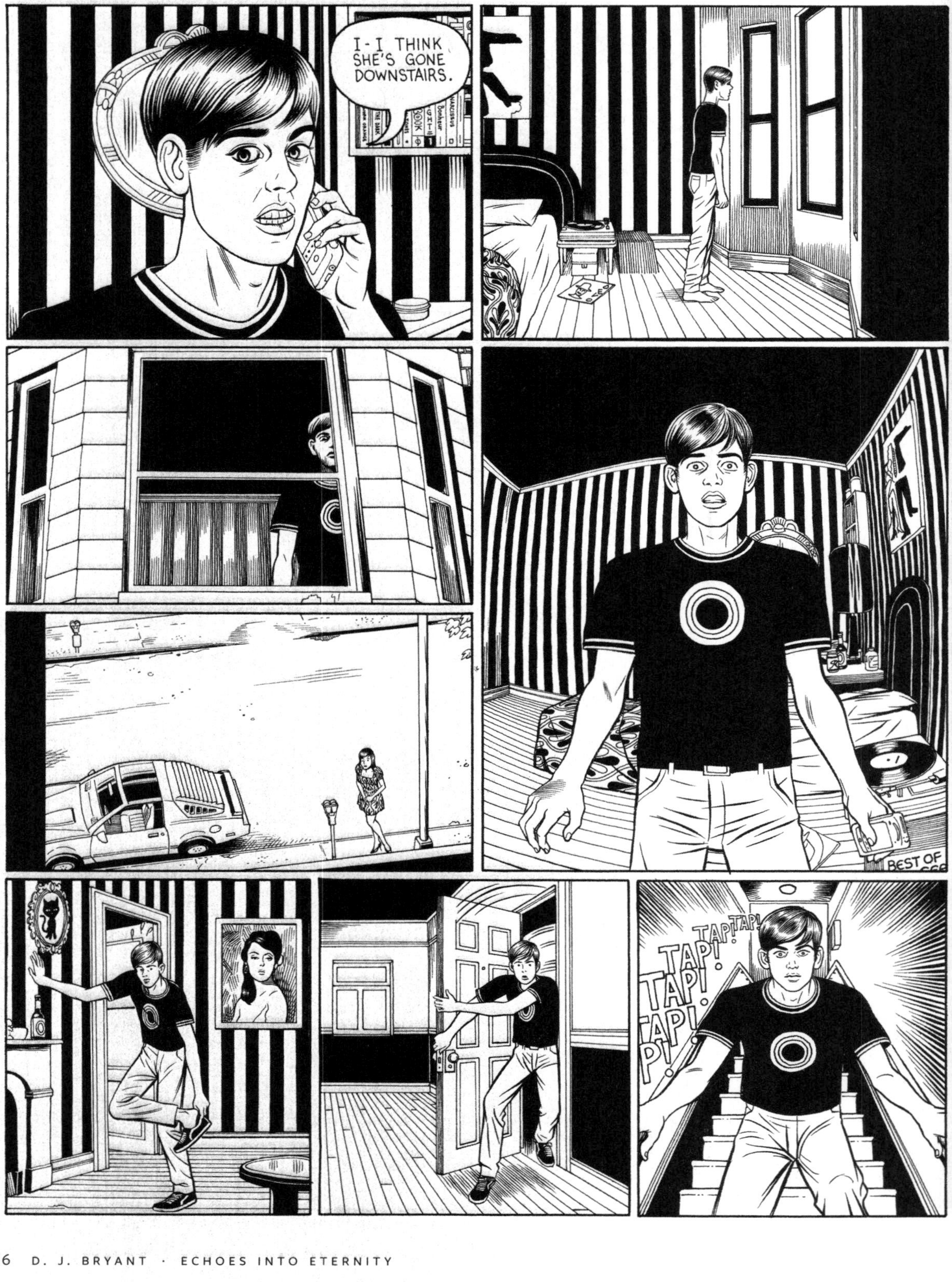
I - I THINK SHE'S GONE DOWNSTAIRS.
BEST OF
TAP! TAP! TAP! TAP! TAP!

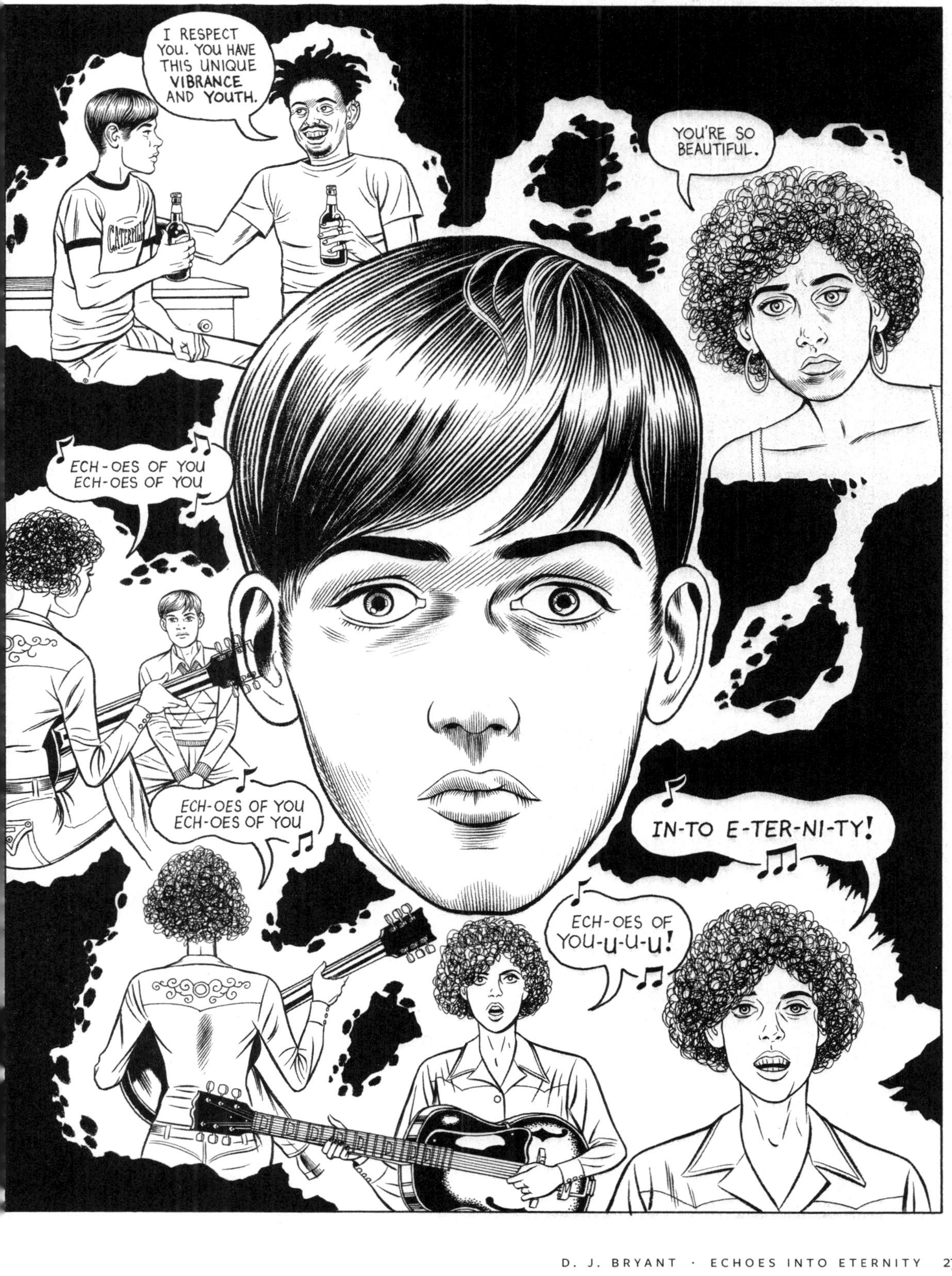
I RESPECT YOU. YOU HAVE THIS UNIQUE VIBRANCE AND YOUTH.
YOU'RE SO BEAUTIFUL.
ECH-OES OF YOU ECH-OES OF YOU
ECH-OES OF YOU ECH-OES OF YOU
IN-TO E-TER-NI-TY!
ECH-OES OF YOU-U-U-U!

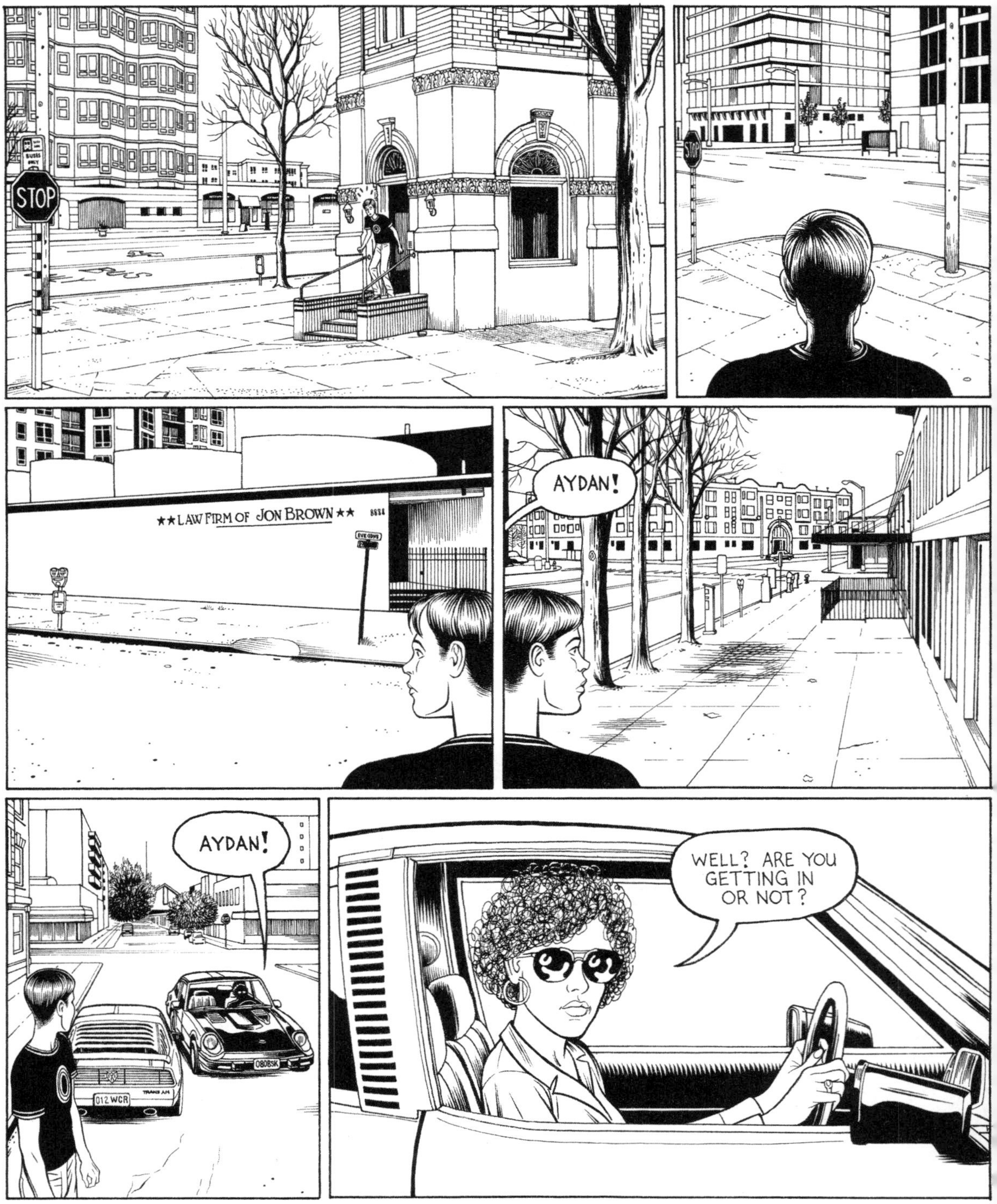
STOP
BUSES ONLY
STOP
★★LAW FIRM OF JON BROWN★★
AYDAN!
AYDAN!
012 WCR
TRANS AM
080BSK
WELL? ARE YOU GETTING IN OR NOT?

THE END.

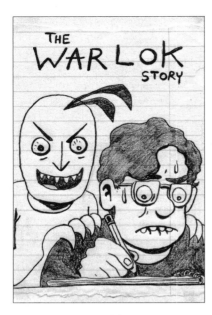

The Warlok Story

MAX CLOTFELTER

originally published as

The Warlok Story
SELF-PUBLISHED
4.25 x 5.5 inches · 32 pages

Biography

Max Clotfelter was born and raised in Marietta, Georgia. He studied sequential art at the Savannah College of Art and Design and then moved to Seattle, Washington, where he's lived for 12 years. Max has self-published over 75 mini-comics, some of which have been reprinted in Fantagraphics Books's *Treasury of Mini Comics* Vol. 1 & 2. He is also the co-creator of the Ignatz-nominated series *Stewbrew* with his partner Kelly Froh. In 2012, Max founded Seattle's *Dune* anthology, a community art and comics zine which he produced for 50 consecutive months. *Dune* featured hundreds of local and visiting cartoonists, and was profiled in the April 2016 issue of *Art in America*. maxclotfelter.blogspot.com

Statement

The Warlok Story is an autobiographical comic I created for the Short Run Comix & Arts Festival that details my experience growing up as an awkward teenager in a crummy southern town with a public school system that had no idea what to do with me. The events take place in the mid-1990s, before the internet had created a virtual refuge for the maladjusted adolescent. A lonely byproduct of a dysfunctional middle-class family, privileged with the time and resources to make violent art, just years later I would have been labeled as a potential Columbine-esque school shooter. Or worse, diagnosed with some form of mild social autism. But all of my transgressive pleas for attention were quickly processed and dismissed. Years later, and slightly more mature, it all worked out (pretty) well, and I can look back and tell the story of the insecure misfit who was just looking for a little love. I drew the comic with a raw urgency that tried to capture the crudeness of those original teenage drawings, while narrating the story as if I were simply relating the tale to a friend.

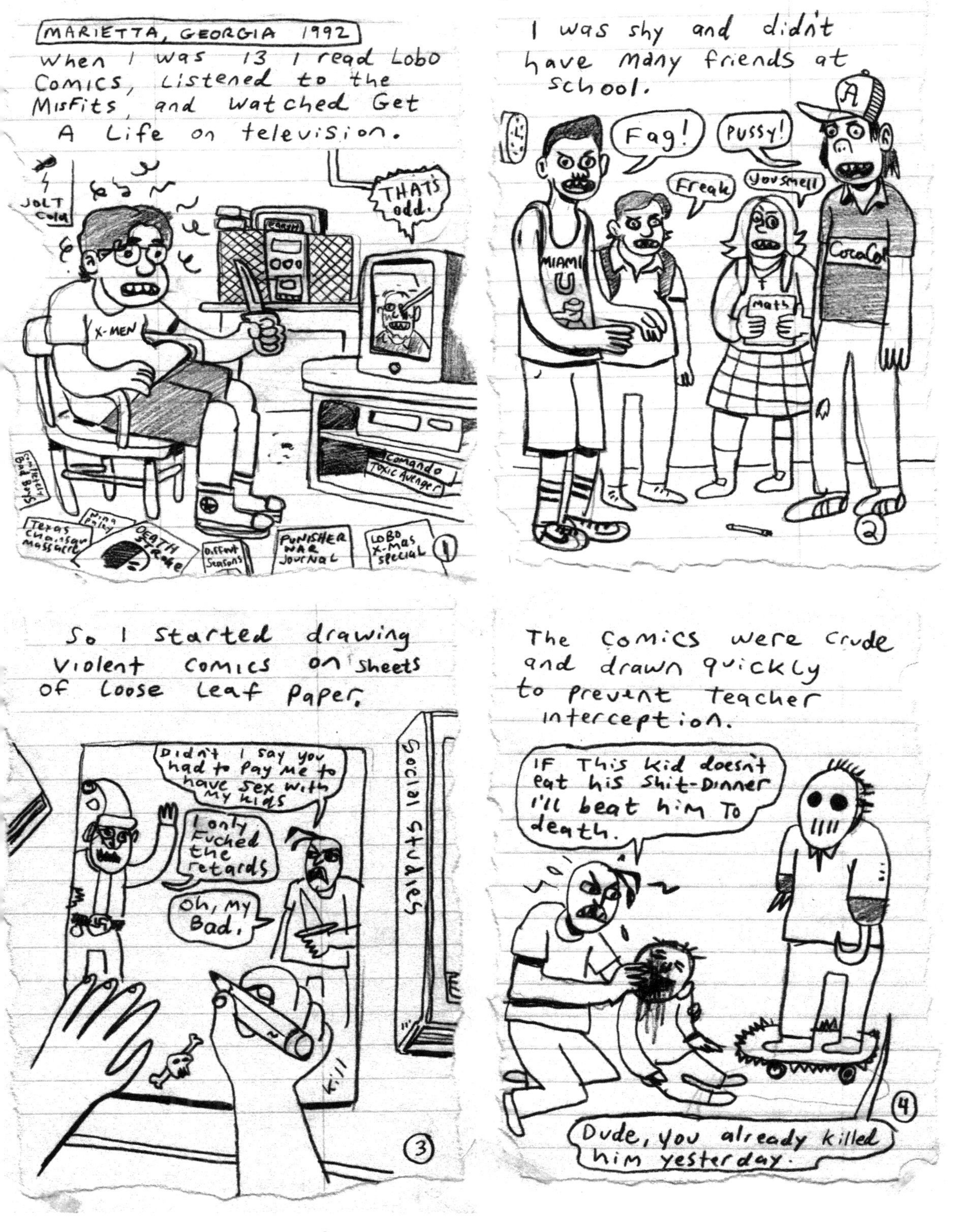
MARIETTA, GEORGIA 1992
When I was 13 I read Lobo Comics, listened to the Misfits, and watched Get A Life on television.
JOLT Cola
THAT'S odd.
X-MEN
Comando
Toxic Avenger
Texas Chainsaw Massacre
DEATH STRIKE
Different Seasons
PUNISHER WAR JOURNAL
LOBO X-Mas Special
1
I was shy and didn't have many friends at school.
Fag!
PUSSY!
Freak
You smell
MIAMI U
Math
2
So I started drawing violent comics on sheets of loose leaf paper.
Didn't I say you had to pay me to have sex with my kids
I only fucked the retards
Oh, My Bad.
Social Studies
Kill
3
The comics were crude and drawn quickly to prevent teacher interception.
IF This kid doesn't eat his Shit-Dinner I'll beat him To death.
Dude, you already killed him yesterday.
4

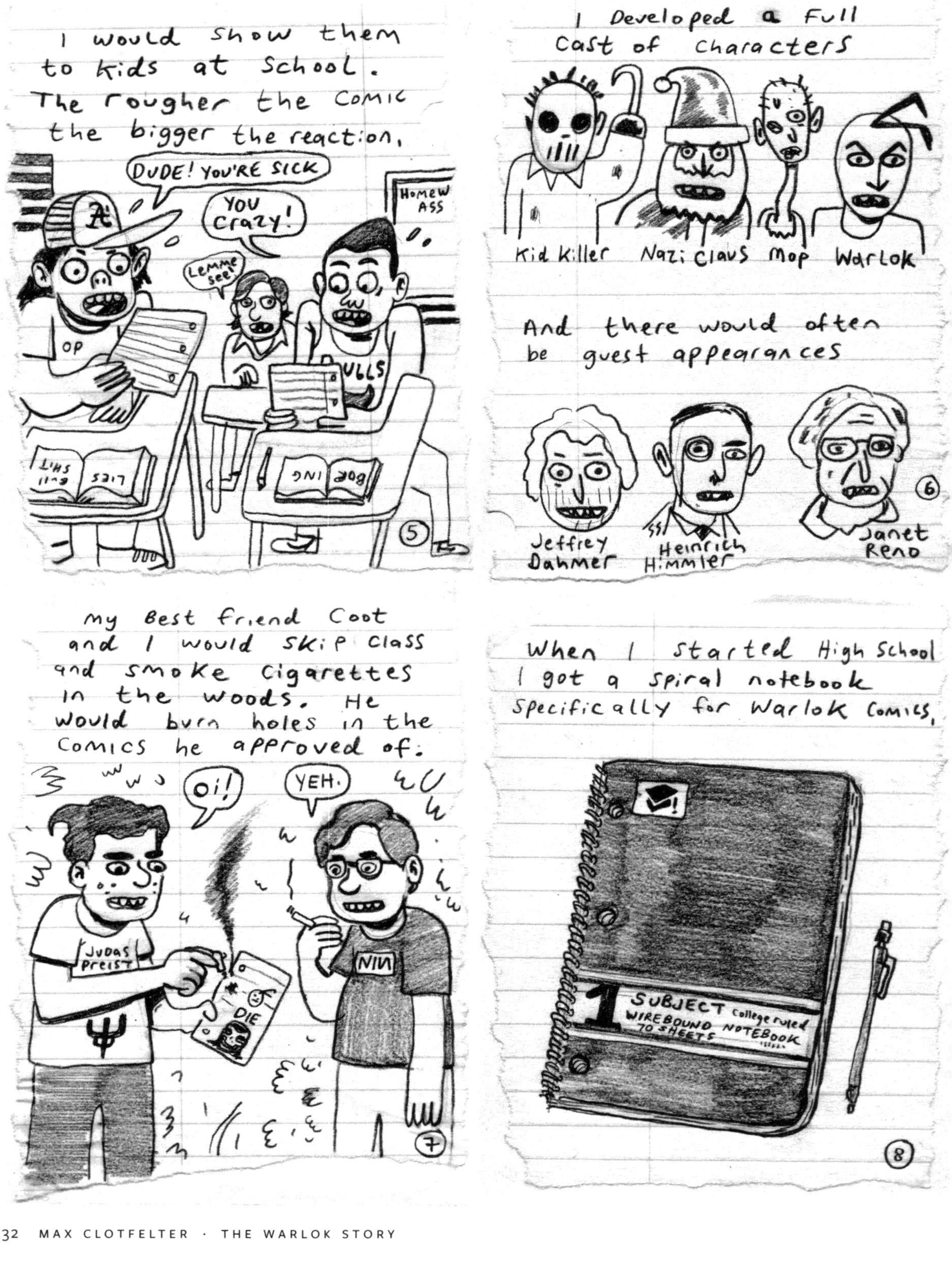
I would show them to kids at School. The rougher the comic the bigger the reaction.
DUDE! YOU'RE SICK
YOU crazy!
Lemme see!
HomeW ASS
OP
BULLS
BOR ING
5
I Developed a Full Cast of Characters
Kid Killer
Nazi Claus
Mop
Warlok
And there would often be guest appearances
Jeffrey Dahmer
SS
Heinrich Himmler
Janet Reno
6
My Best friend Coot and I would skip class and smoke cigarettes in the woods. He would burn holes in the comics he approved of.
oi!
YEH.
JUDAS PREIST
NIN
DIE
7
When I started High School I got a spiral notebook specifically for Warlok Comics.
1 SUBJECT college ruled WIREBOUND NOTEBOOK 70 SHEETS
8

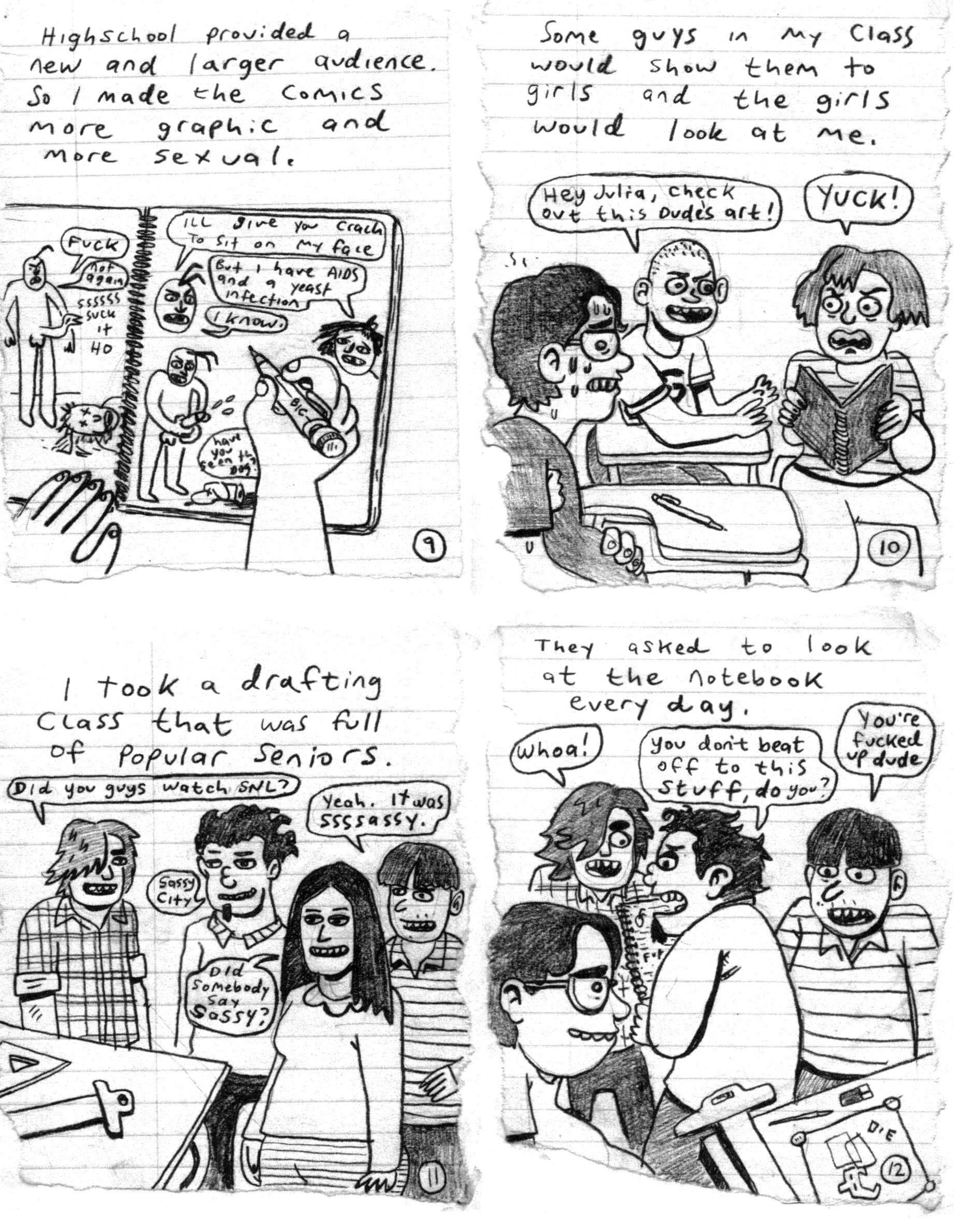

Highschool provided a new and larger audience. So I made the comics more graphic and more sexual.
Fuck
not again
ssssss suck it HO
ILL give you crack to sit on my face
But I have AIDS and a yeast infection
I know.
have you seen the dog?
BIC
9
Some guys in my class would show them to girls and the girls would look at me.
Hey Julia, check out this Dude's art!
YUCK!
10
I took a drafting class that was full of popular seniors.
Did you guys watch SNL?
Yeah. It was ssssassy.
Sassy City
Did somebody say Sassy?
11
They asked to look at the notebook every day.
Whoa!
You don't beat off to this stuff, do you?
You're fucked up dude
DIE
12

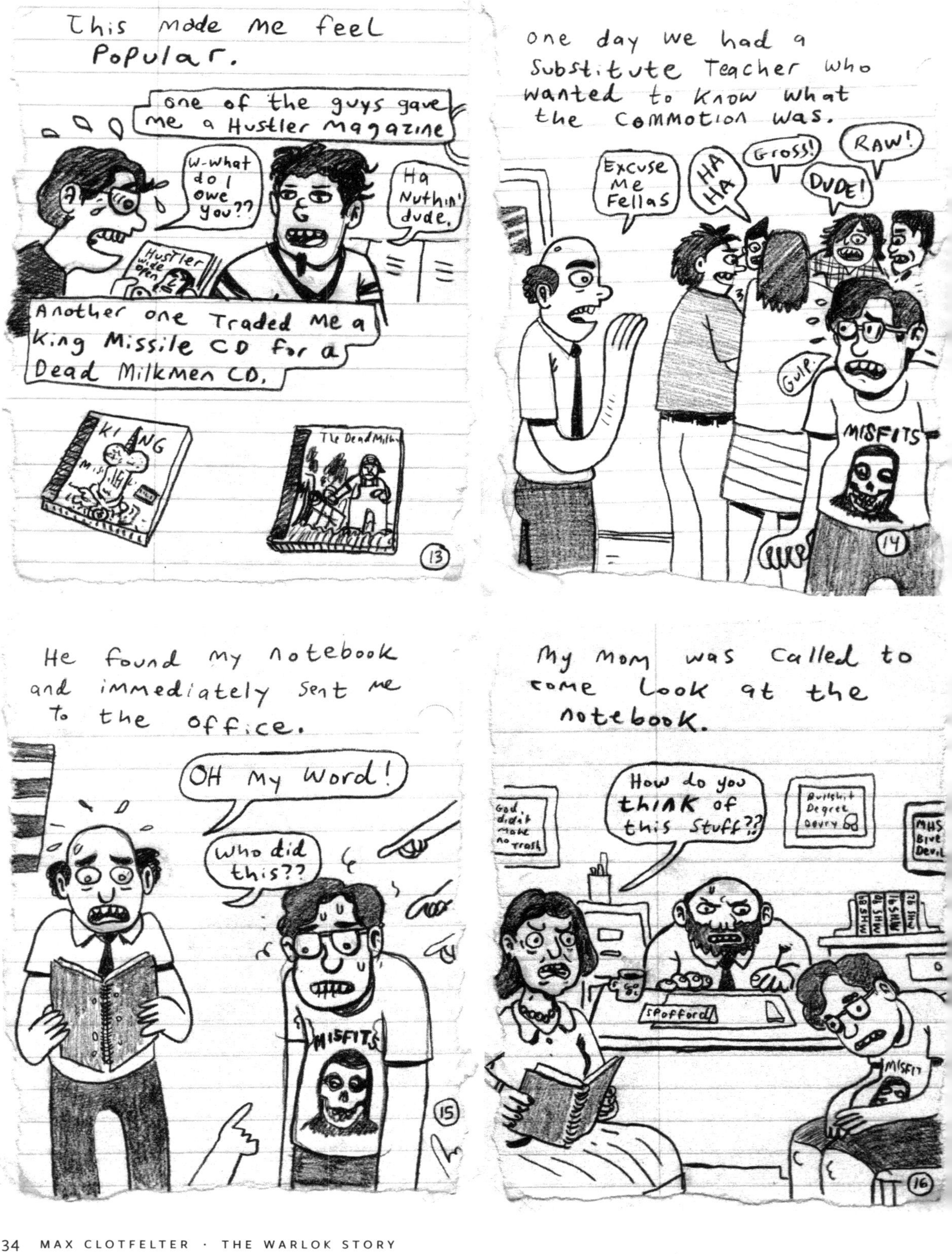
This made me feel Popular.
one of the guys gave me a Hustler Magazine
W-what do I owe you??
Ha Nuthin' dude.
Hustler wide open
Another one Traded Me a King Missile CD for a Dead Milkmen CD.
The Dead Milkmen
13
one day we had a Substitute Teacher who wanted to know what the commotion was.
Excuse Me Fellas
HA HA
Gross!
RAW!
DUDE!
Gulp.
MISFITS
14
He found my notebook and immediately sent me to the office.
OH My Word!
Who did this??
MISFITS
15
My Mom was called to come look at the notebook.
How do you THINK of this Stuff??
God didn't make no trash
Bullshit Degree Devry
MHS Blue Devil
Spofford
16

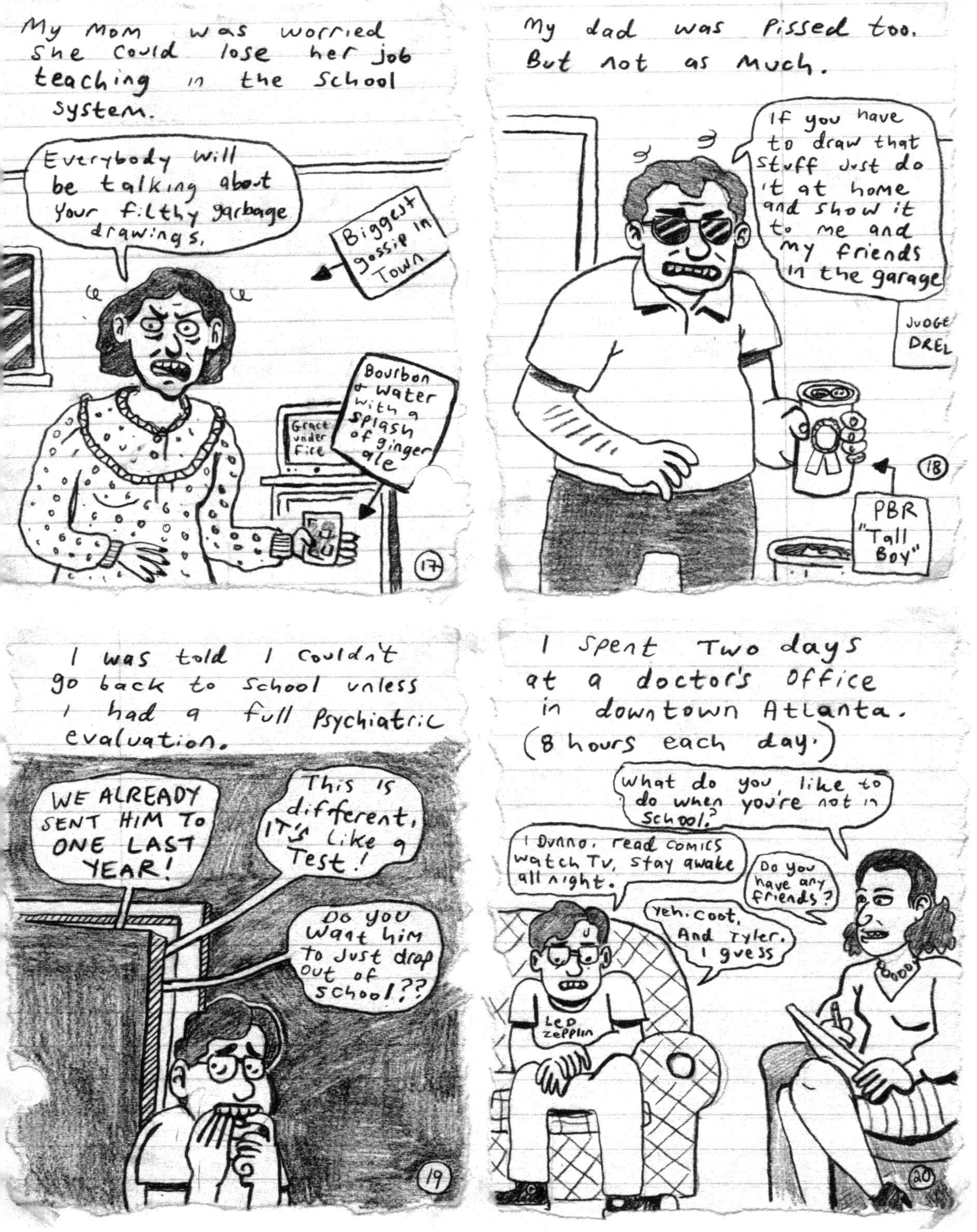
My Mom was worried she could lose her job teaching in the School system.
Everybody will be talking about your filthy garbage drawings.
Biggest gossip in Town
Grace under Fire
Bourbon & water with a splash of ginger ale
17
My dad was pissed too. But not as much.
If you have to draw that stuff just do it at home and show it to me and my friends in the garage
JUDGE DREL
PBR "Tall Boy"
18
I was told I couldn't go back to school unless I had a full psychiatric evaluation.
WE ALREADY SENT HIM TO ONE LAST YEAR!
This is different, IT's like a Test!
Do you want him to just drop out of school??
19
I spent Two days at a doctor's office in downtown Atlanta. (8 hours each day.)
What do you like to do when you're not in school?
I Dunno. read comics watch TV, stay awake all night.
Do you have any friends?
Yeh. Coot. And Tyler. I guess
LED ZEPPLIN
20

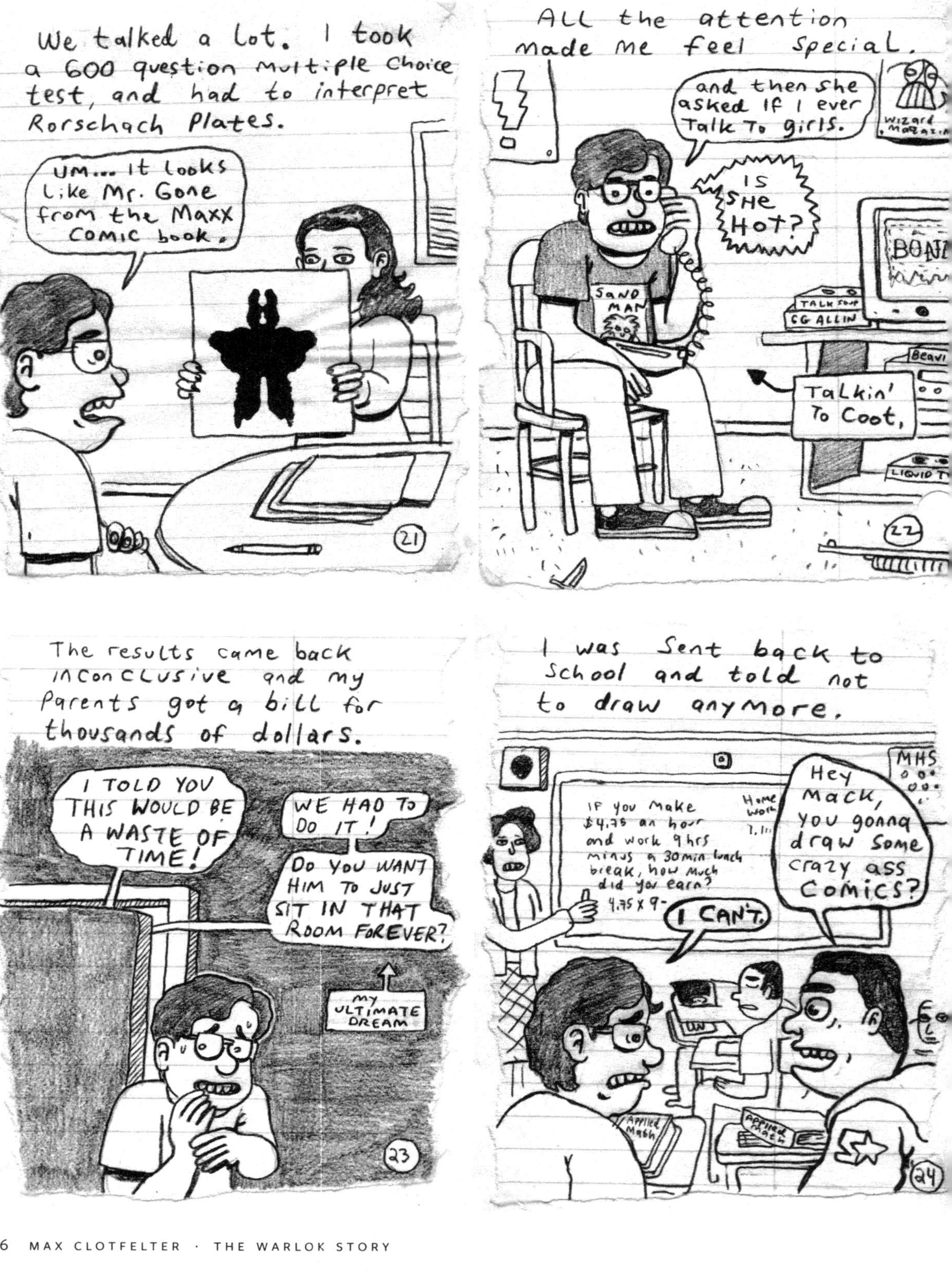
We talked a lot. I took a 600 question multiple choice test, and had to interpret Rorschach Plates.
UM... It looks like Mr. Gone from the Maxx comic book.
21
All the attention made me feel special.
and then she asked if I ever Talk To girls.
IS SHE HOT?
SAND MAN
WIZARD
TALK SOUP
GG ALLIN
Talkin' To Coot,
22
The results came back inconclusive and my parents got a bill for thousands of dollars.
I TOLD YOU THIS WOULD BE A WASTE OF TIME!
WE HAD TO DO IT!
DO YOU WANT HIM TO JUST SIT IN THAT ROOM FOREVER?
MY ULTIMATE DREAM
23
I was sent back to school and told not to draw anymore.
MHS
IF you make $4.75 an hour and work 9 hrs minus a 30 min lunch break, how much did you earn?
4.75 x 9-
Hey Mack, you gonna draw some crazy ass comics?
I CAN'T.
Applied Math
Applied Math
24

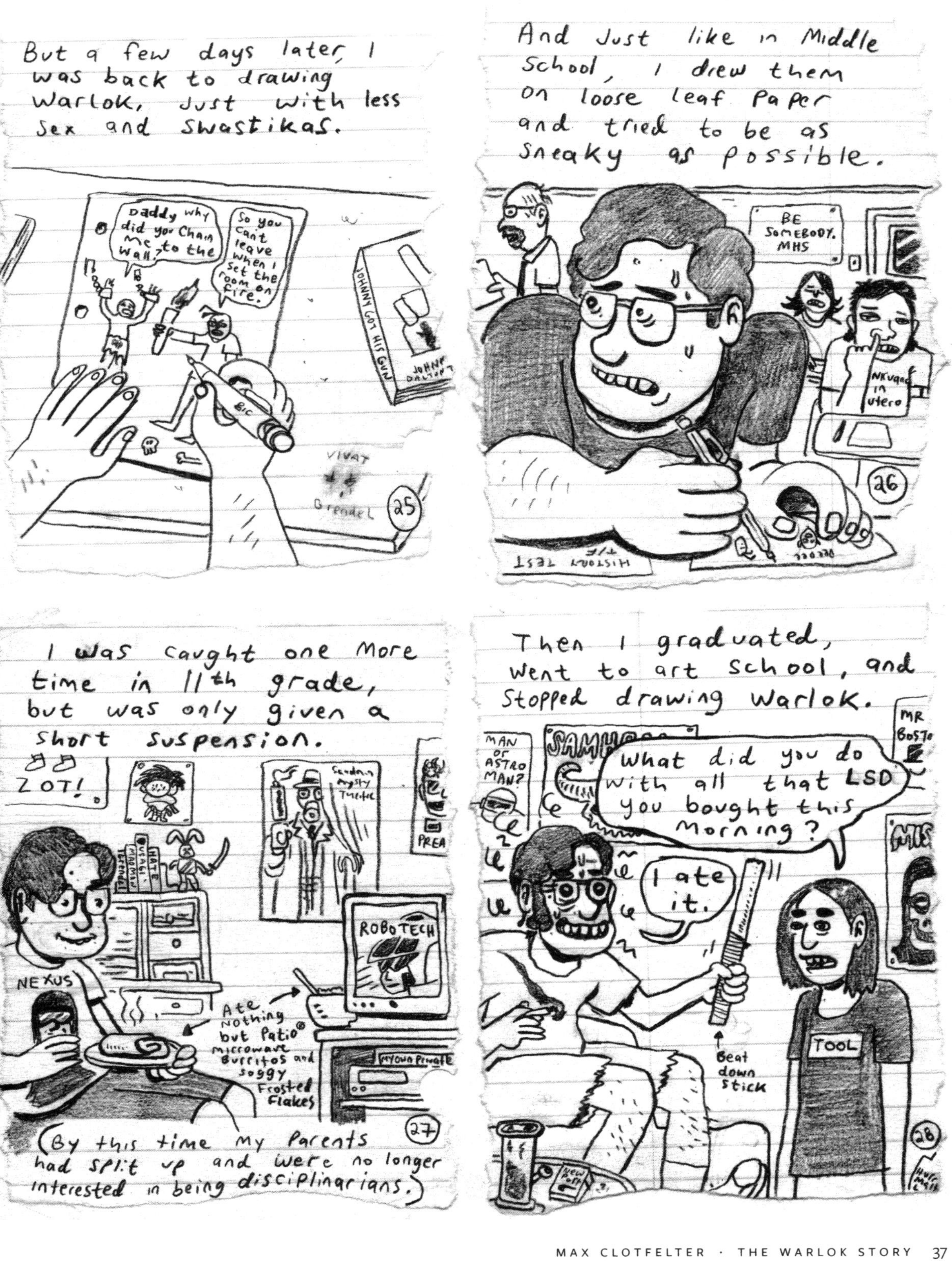
But a few days later, I was back to drawing Warlok, just with less sex and swastikas.
Daddy why did you chain me to the wall?
So you can't leave when I set the room on fire.
JOHNNY GOT HIS GUN
JOHNNY DALTON
BIC
VIVAT
Brendel
25
And just like in Middle School, I drew them on loose leaf paper and tried to be as sneaky as possible.
BE SOMEBODY. MHS
NKvaad in utero
HISTORY TEST
26
I was caught one more time in 11th grade, but was only given a short suspension.
ZOT!
PREA
HATE
ROBOTECH
NEXUS
Ate nothing but Patio® microwave Burritos and soggy Frosted Flakes
MY OWN PRIVATE
27
(By this time my parents had split up and were no longer interested in being disciplinarians.)
Then I graduated, went to art school, and stopped drawing Warlok.
MAN OF ASTRO MAN?
MR BOSTO
What did you do with all that LSD you bought this morning?
I ate it.
Beat down stick
TOOL
28

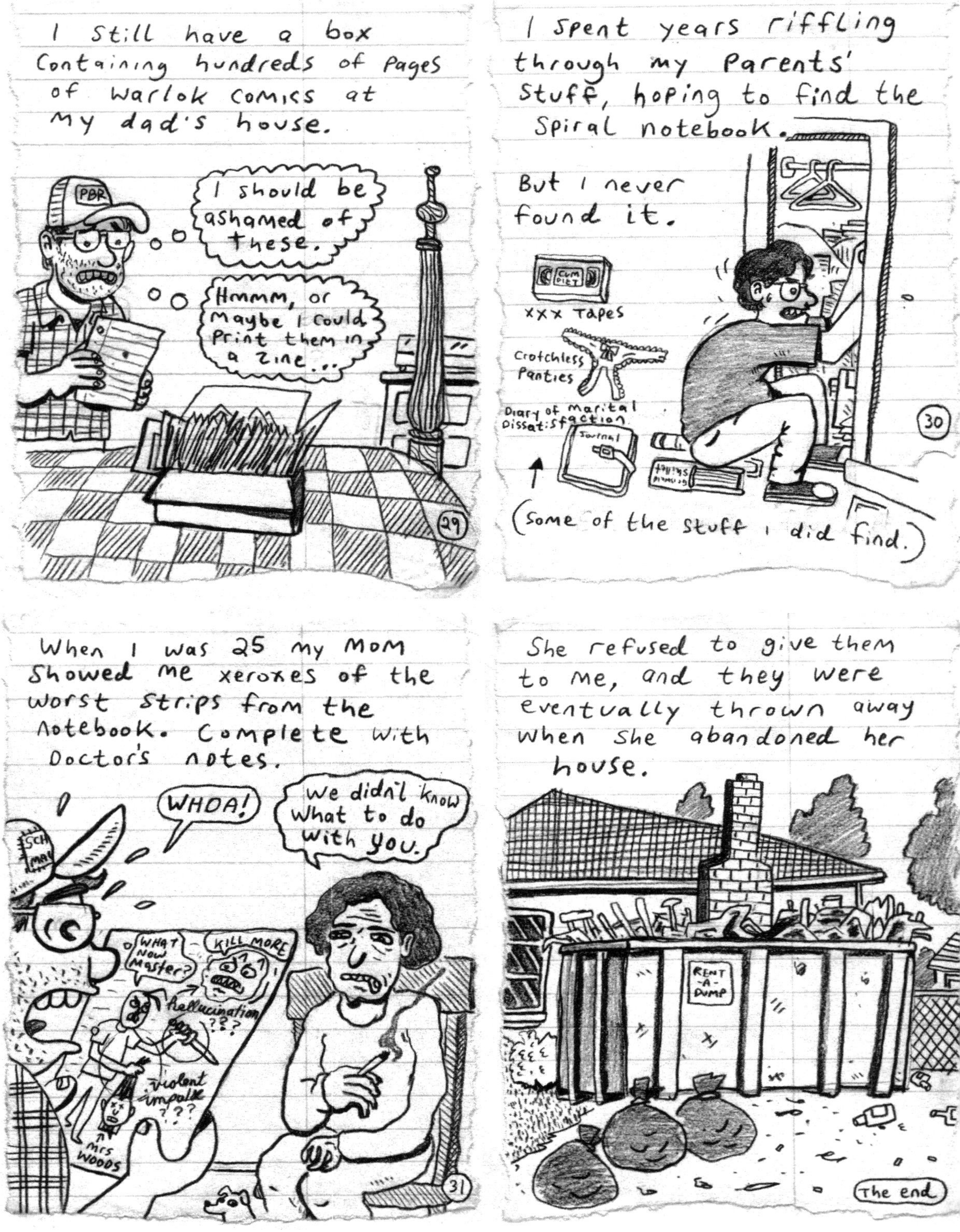
I still have a box containing hundreds of pages of warlok comics at my dad's house.
PBR
I should be ashamed of these.
Hmmm, or maybe I could print them in a zine...
29
I spent years riffling through my parents' stuff, hoping to find the spiral notebook.
But I never found it.
XXX Tapes
Crotchless Panties
Diary of Marital Dissatisfaction
Journal
30
(Some of the stuff I did find.)
When I was 25 my mom showed me xeroxes of the worst strips from the notebook. Complete with doctor's notes.
WHOA!
We didn't know what to do with you.
WHAT NOW Master?
KILL MORE
hallucination ???
violent impulse ???
Mrs WOODS
31
She refused to give them to me, and they were eventually thrown away when she abandoned her house.
RENT -A- DUMP
The end

The Shaolin Cowboy: Who'll Stop the Reign? (*Excerpt*)

GEOF DARROW

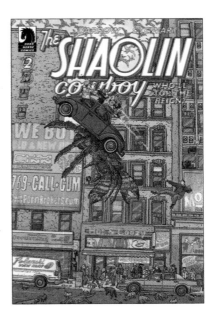

originally published in

The Shaolin Cowboy: Who'll Stop the Reign? #2

DARK HORSE COMICS

6.6 x 10.25 inches • 32 pages

DARROW STEWART
The SHAOLIN cowboy
WHO'LL STOP THE REIGN?
769-CALL•GUM

Biography

I was born in Cedar Rapids, Iowa, but left there at the tender age of 17 and have lived in such alien territories as Chicago, Los Angeles, Paris, and Tokyo. I started out in advertising. Moved into character design at Hanna-Barbera Animation. Was not very good at it but managed to do major damage on *Pac-Man*, *Super Friends*, *Scooby-Doo*, *Richie Rich*, *Smurfs*, and the feather in my crown: *Monchichis!!!* Moved to France to work on my artfather Moebius's magazine *Metal Hurlant*. My first published comics work was done in France. I went on to create the comics *Hard Boiled* and *The Big Guy and Rusty the Boy Robot* with Frank Miller. This lead me to work as the conceptual artist on the *Matrix* trilogy (if you look real hard, you can see me in the third film for three seconds playing triplets driving giant robots against the sentinels in a big battle scene) with the Wachowskis. This was the greatest professional thrill of my cinematic life. Now I draw comics that make me happy and keep me away from a life of crime and having to draw Monchichis and living in a state that could elect something like Rep. Steve King.
geofdarrow.com

Statement

It is what it is. I like drawing stuff.

AAAAWWWWOOOOOOOOOOOOOOOOAAAAWWWWOOOOOOOOOOOOOOOOAAAAAWWWWWO

AAAWWOOOOOOOOOOOOOOOOAAAAWWWWOOOOOOOOOOOOOOOOAAAAAWWWWWOOOOOOC

AWOOOOO

≈SNORT≈ ≈SNUFF≈ WHA...?

WAKING UP IS ALWAYS THE HARDEST PART. GOTTA CUT BACK ON THE SNAUSAGES.

HOG...*HOG KONG*... GET *UP*, YOU LAZY PIG.

THE BITCH FOUN THE G KIN CRAB LOOK FOR

HE'S HEADING OUR WAY. TIME TO BUST A NUT.

DOOLEY, WHY IS IT EVERY TIME I WAKE UP, I FIND YOU *LICKING* YOURSELF?

'CUZ NO ONE ELSE WILL, AND 'CUZ I *CAN*, YOU JEALOUS SOW.

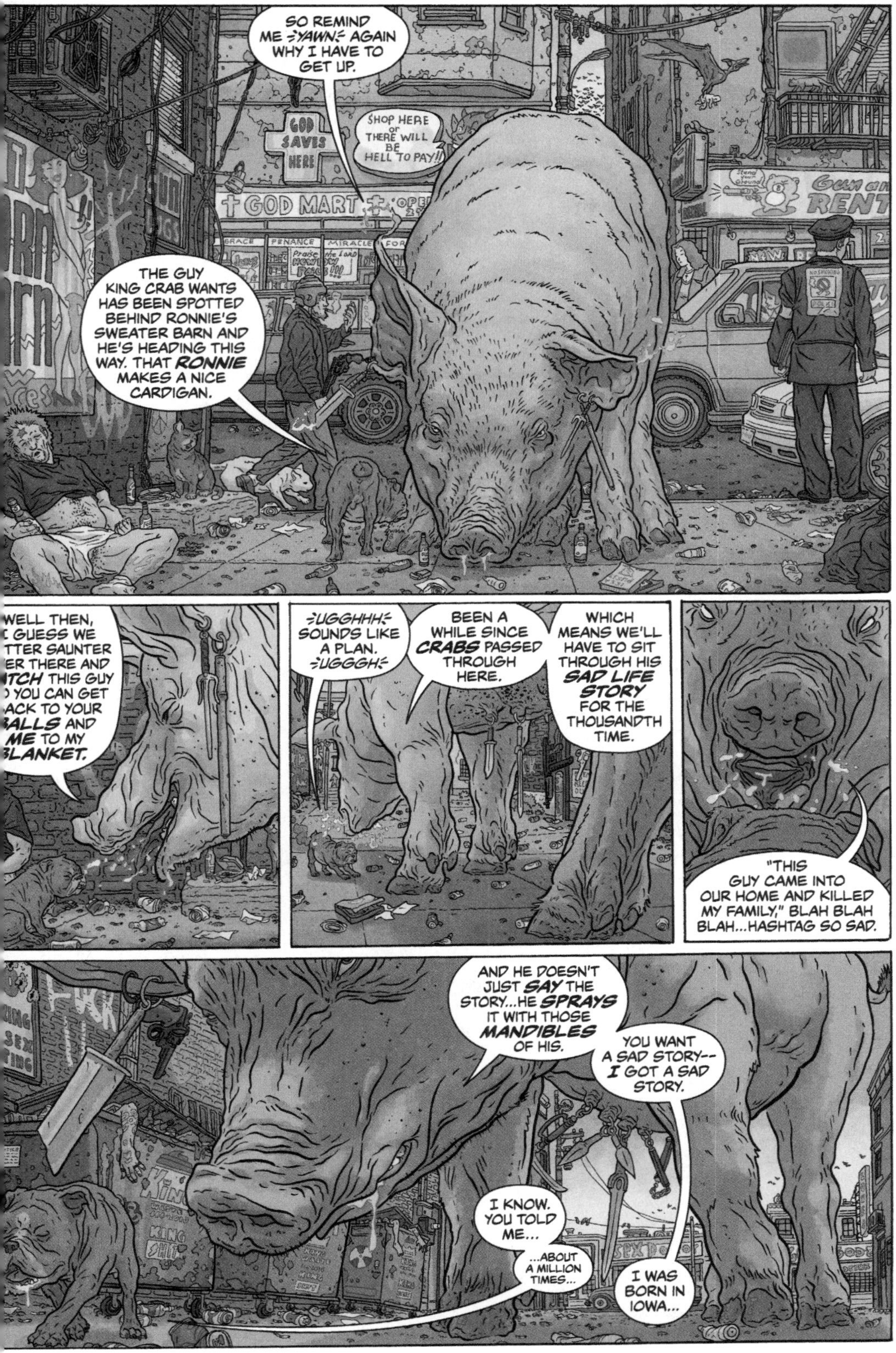

SO REMIND ME ≈YAWN≈ AGAIN WHY I HAVE TO GET UP.
GOD SAVES HERE
SHOP HERE or THERE WILL BE HELL TO PAY!!
GOD MART
GRACE PENANCE MIRACLE
THE GUY KING CRAB WANTS HAS BEEN SPOTTED BEHIND RONNIE'S SWEATER BARN AND HE'S HEADING THIS WAY. THAT **RONNIE** MAKES A NICE CARDIGAN.
WELL THEN, GUESS WE TTER SAUNTER ER THERE AND **TCH** THIS GUY YOU CAN GET ACK TO YOUR **ALLS** AND **ME** TO MY **LANKET.**
≈UGGHHH≈ SOUNDS LIKE A PLAN. ≈UGGGH≈
BEEN A WHILE SINCE **CRABS** PASSED THROUGH HERE.
WHICH MEANS WE'LL HAVE TO SIT THROUGH HIS **SAD LIFE STORY** FOR THE THOUSANDTH TIME.
"THIS GUY CAME INTO OUR HOME AND KILLED MY FAMILY," BLAH BLAH BLAH...HASHTAG SO SAD.
AND HE DOESN'T JUST **SAY** THE STORY...HE **SPRAYS** IT WITH THOSE **MANDIBLES** OF HIS.
YOU WANT A SAD STORY-- **I** GOT A SAD STORY.
I KNOW. YOU TOLD ME...
...ABOUT A MILLION TIMES...
I WAS BORN IN IOWA...

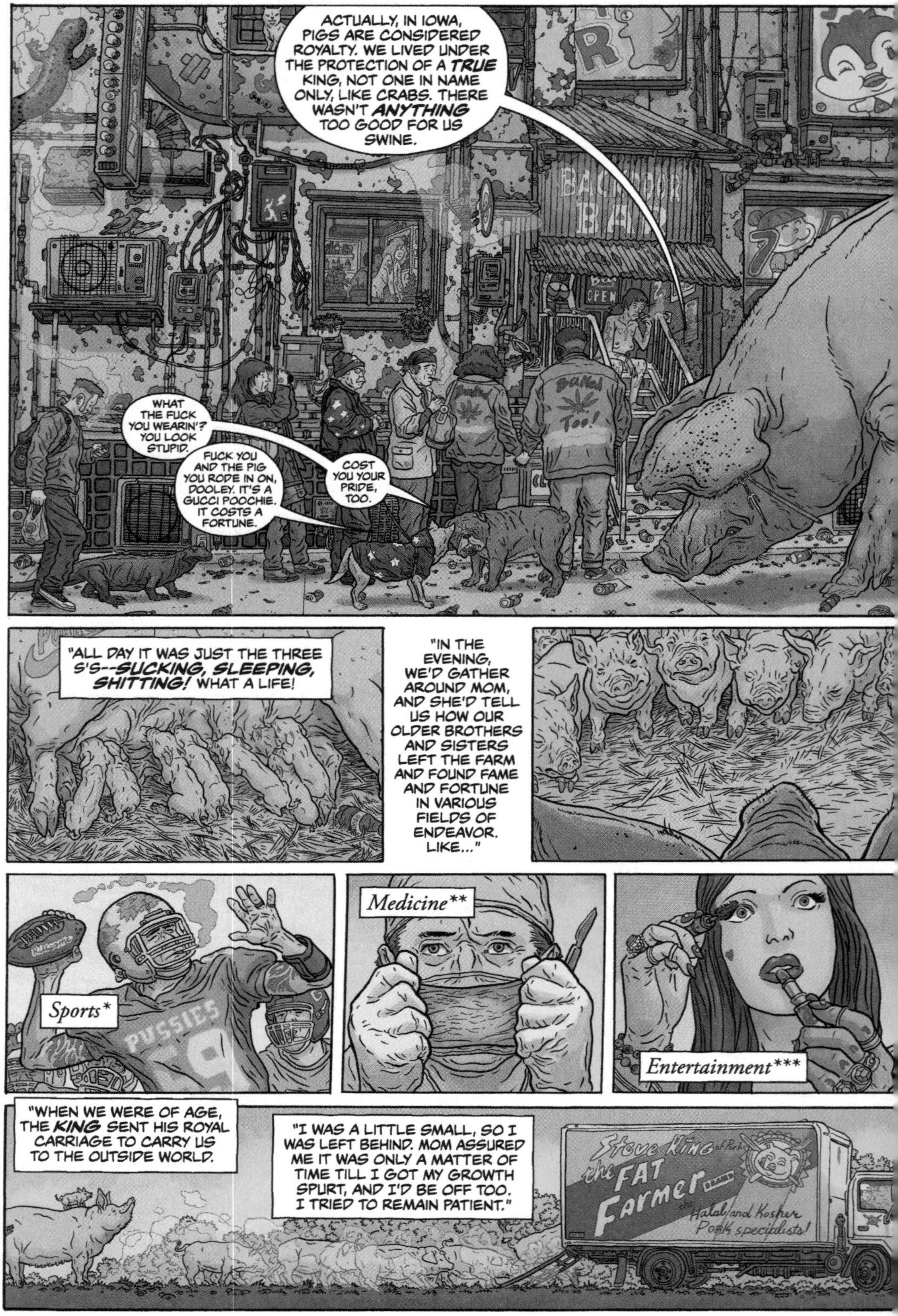
ACTUALLY, IN IOWA, PIGS ARE CONSIDERED ROYALTY. WE LIVED UNDER THE PROTECTION OF A TRUE KING, NOT ONE IN NAME ONLY, LIKE CRABS. THERE WASN'T ANYTHING TOO GOOD FOR US SWINE.
WHAT THE FUCK YOU WEARIN'? YOU LOOK STUPID.
FUCK YOU AND THE PIG YOU RODE IN ON, DOOLEY. IT'S A GUCCI POOCHIE. IT COSTS A FORTUNE.
COST YOU YOUR PRIDE, TOO.
OPEN
"ALL DAY IT WAS JUST THE THREE S'S--SUCKING, SLEEPING, SHITTING! WHAT A LIFE!
"IN THE EVENING, WE'D GATHER AROUND MOM, AND SHE'D TELL US HOW OUR OLDER BROTHERS AND SISTERS LEFT THE FARM AND FOUND FAME AND FORTUNE IN VARIOUS FIELDS OF ENDEAVOR. LIKE..."
Sports*
PUSSIES
Medicine**
Entertainment***
"WHEN WE WERE OF AGE, THE KING SENT HIS ROYAL CARRIAGE TO CARRY US TO THE OUTSIDE WORLD.
"I WAS A LITTLE SMALL, SO I WAS LEFT BEHIND. MOM ASSURED ME IT WAS ONLY A MATTER OF TIME TILL I GOT MY GROWTH SPURT, AND I'D BE OFF TOO. I TRIED TO REMAIN PATIENT."
Steve King of Pork
the FAT Farmer BRAND
the Halal and Kosher Pork specialists!

I COULDN'T WAIT TO GO OUT INTO THE WORLD. PROVE MYSELF TO OUR KING, AND, OF COURSE--

--MAKE YOUR MOTHER PROUD.

ONE LAST SPURT. AHHHH... HOPE BRENDA GETS THIS MESSAGE.

PRIVATE PORKING

FAT FARM

VIOLATORS WILL BE BUTCHERED AT PIGS EXPENSE

FOR SALE

DOG FIGHTING EQUIPMENT

"I MISSED THE LITTER SO MUCH THAT MOM DECIDED, FOR THE FIRST TIME, TO *LEAVE* THE KINGDOM AND TAKE ME TO SEE MY BROTHERS AND SISTERS."

"SHE'D OVERHEARD THE KING TELL THE CARRIAGE DRIVER THAT HIS DESTINATION WAS KANSAS CITY'S BESTEST AND BIGGEST EATERY, SO WE SNUCK OUT THAT NIGHT AND HEADED WEST."

"AFTER AN EVENTFUL ROAD TRIP WE ARRIVED. FROM THE LINE OUT THE DOOR AND DOWN THE BLOCK WE COULD TELL THE LITTER HAD FOUND *GREAT SUCCESS* IN THE CULINARY MARKET!"

"WE COULDN'T WAIT TO SEE THEM AND TELL THEM HOW PROUD WE WERE OF THEM WHEN..."

"...IN THE WINDOW WE SAW..."

"PIP, TIPPY, AND SCREWTOP!"

WWAAAAAAAAAAAAAAAAAAAAAAAAA

"EXCEPT THEY WEREN'T *SERVING* IN THE RESTAURANT..."

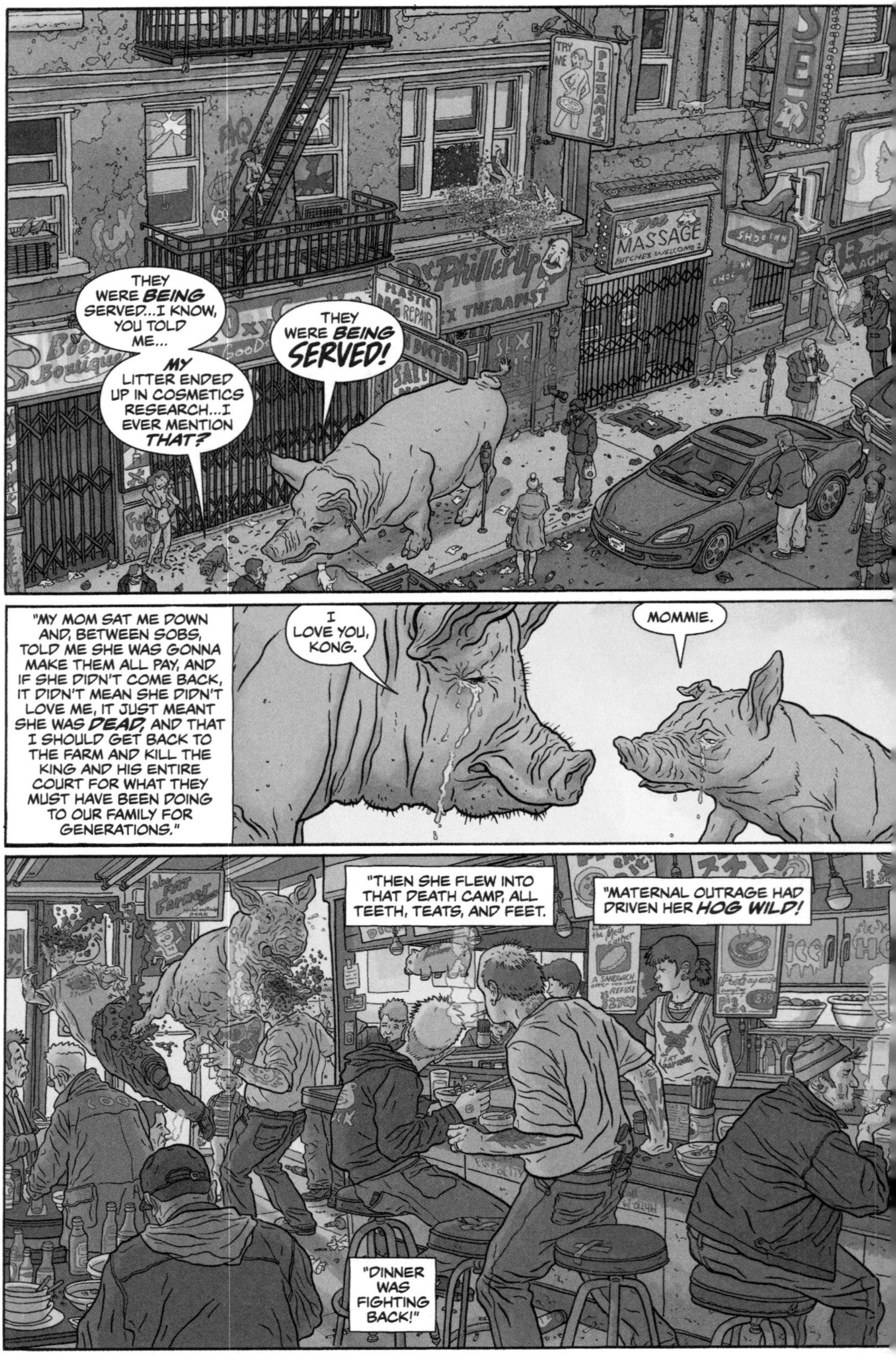
THEY WERE BEING SERVED...I KNOW, YOU TOLD ME...
MY LITTER ENDED UP IN COSMETICS RESEARCH...I EVER MENTION THAT?
THEY WERE BEING SERVED!
"MY MOM SAT ME DOWN AND, BETWEEN SOBS, TOLD ME SHE WAS GONNA MAKE THEM ALL PAY, AND IF SHE DIDN'T COME BACK, IT DIDN'T MEAN SHE DIDN'T LOVE ME, IT JUST MEANT SHE WAS DEAD, AND THAT I SHOULD GET BACK TO THE FARM AND KILL THE KING AND HIS ENTIRE COURT FOR WHAT THEY MUST HAVE BEEN DOING TO OUR FAMILY FOR GENERATIONS."
I LOVE YOU, KONG.
MOMMIE.
"THEN SHE FLEW INTO THAT DEATH CAMP, ALL TEETH, TEATS, AND FEET.
"MATERNAL OUTRAGE HAD DRIVEN HER HOG WILD!
"DINNER WAS FIGHTING BACK!"

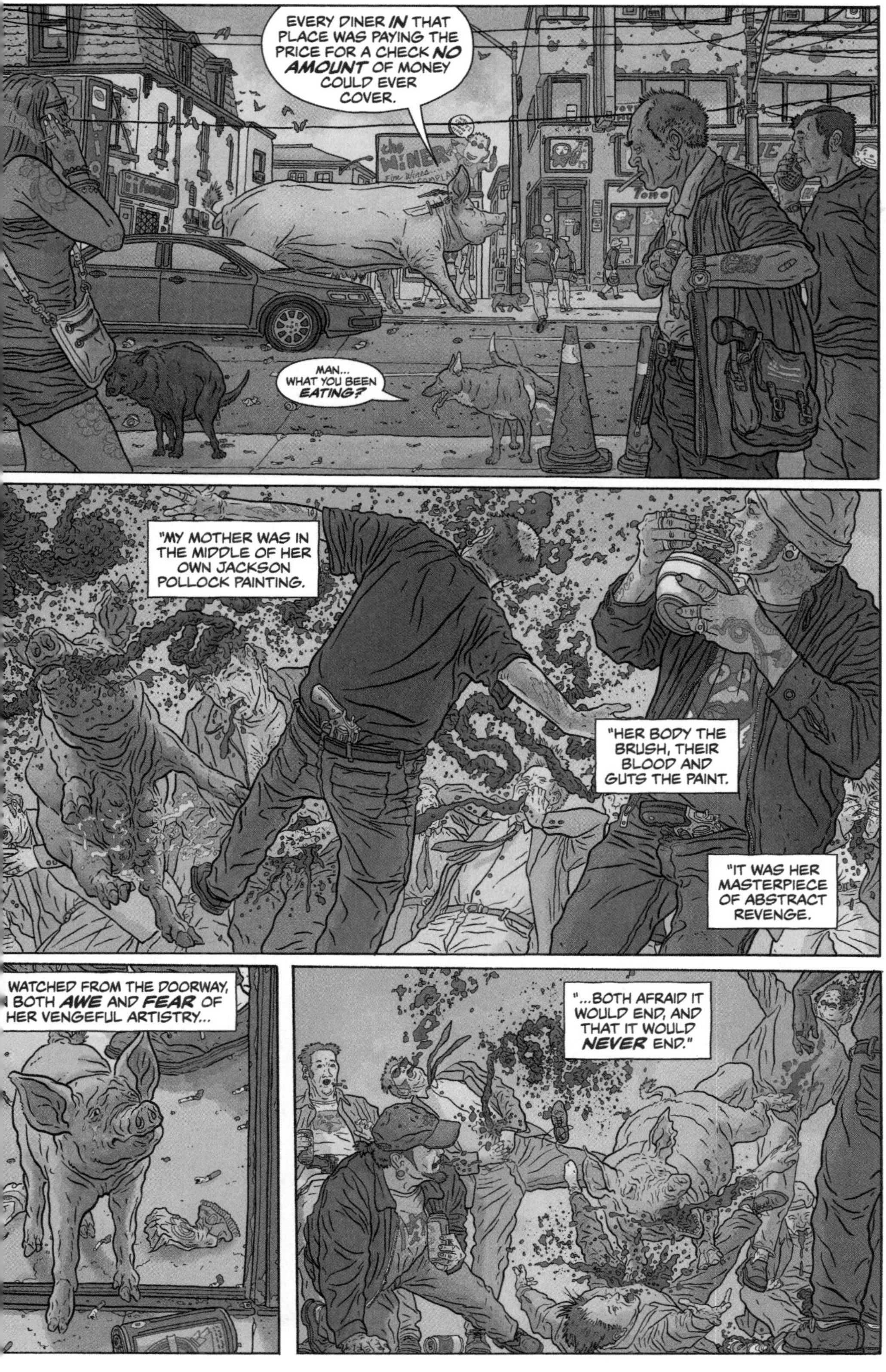
EVERY DINER **IN** THAT PLACE WAS PAYING THE PRICE FOR A CHECK **NO AMOUNT** OF MONEY COULD EVER COVER.
MAN... WHAT YOU BEEN **EATING?**
"MY MOTHER WAS IN THE MIDDLE OF HER OWN JACKSON POLLOCK PAINTING.
"HER BODY THE BRUSH, THEIR BLOOD AND GUTS THE PAINT.
"IT WAS HER MASTERPIECE OF ABSTRACT REVENGE.
WATCHED FROM THE DOORWAY, BOTH **AWE** AND **FEAR** OF HER VENGEFUL ARTISTRY...
"...BOTH AFRAID IT WOULD END, AND THAT IT WOULD **NEVER** END."

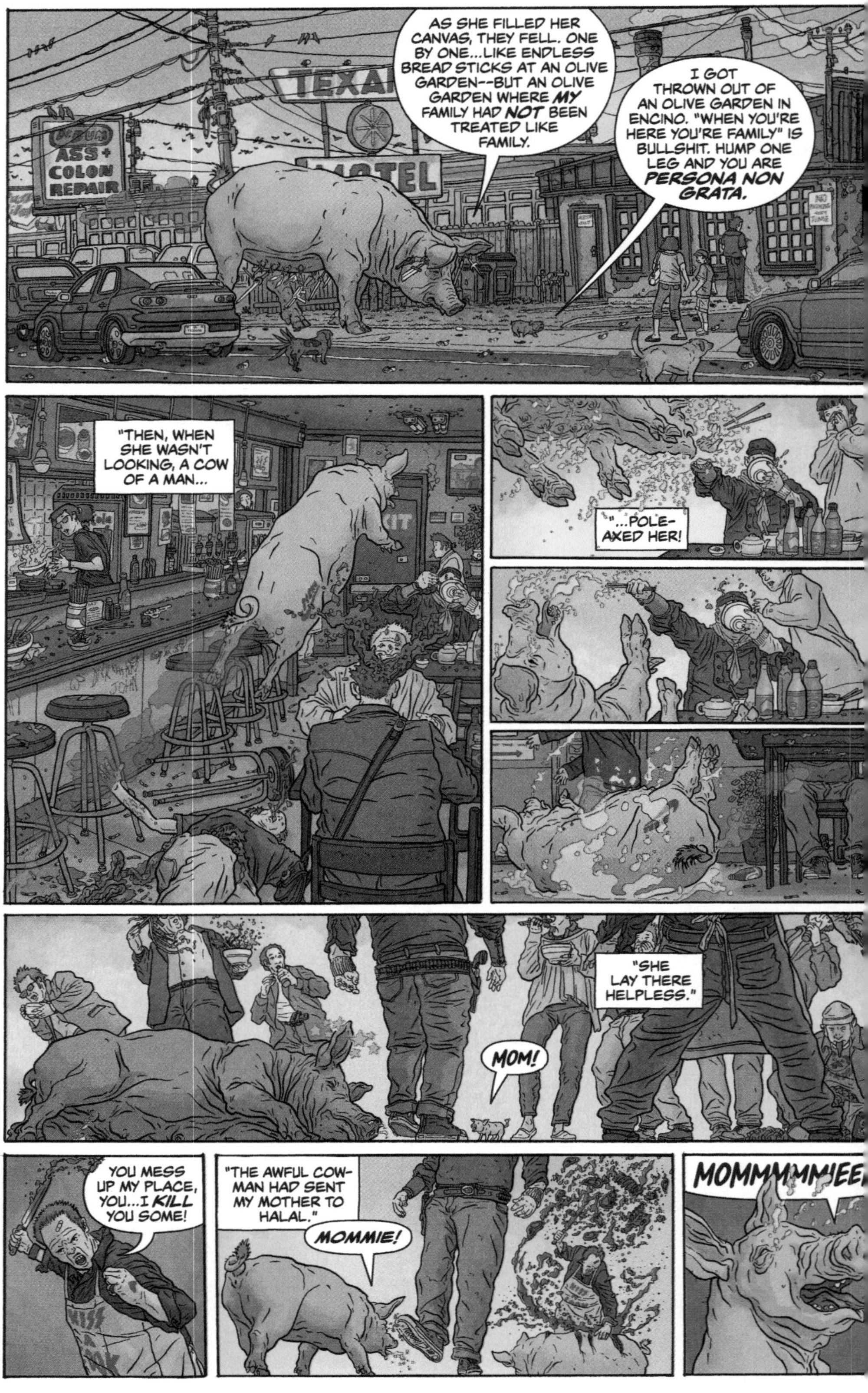
TEXA
MOTEL
ASS + COLON REPAIR
AS SHE FILLED HER CANVAS, THEY FELL. ONE BY ONE...LIKE ENDLESS BREAD STICKS AT AN OLIVE GARDEN--BUT AN OLIVE GARDEN WHERE *MY* FAMILY HAD *NOT* BEEN TREATED LIKE FAMILY.
I GOT THROWN OUT OF AN OLIVE GARDEN IN ENCINO. "WHEN YOU'RE HERE YOU'RE FAMILY" IS BULLSHIT. HUMP ONE LEG AND YOU ARE ***PERSONA NON GRATA.***
"THEN, WHEN SHE WASN'T LOOKING, A COW OF A MAN...
"...POLE-AXED HER!
"SHE LAY THERE HELPLESS."
MOM!
YOU MESS UP MY PLACE, YOU...I *KILL* YOU SOME!
"THE AWFUL COW-MAN HAD SENT MY MOTHER TO HALAL."
MOMMIE!
MOMMMMMIEE

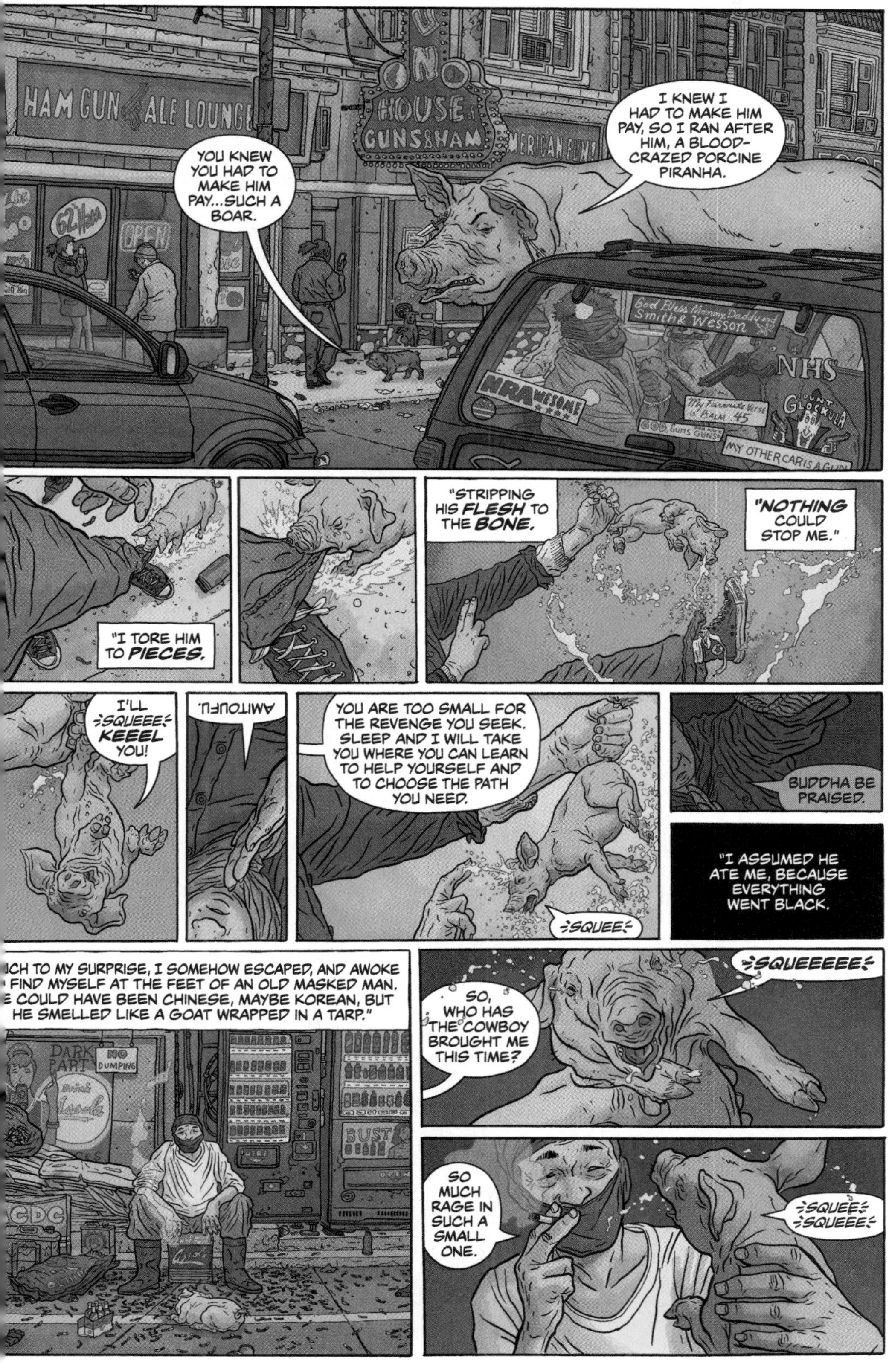
HAM GUN ALE LOUNGE
HOUSE GUNS&HAM
YOU KNEW YOU HAD TO MAKE HIM PAY...SUCH A BOAR.
I KNEW I HAD TO MAKE HIM PAY, SO I RAN AFTER HIM, A BLOOD-CRAZED PORCINE PIRANHA.
God Bless Mommy, Daddy and Smith & Wesson
NHS
"I TORE HIM TO ***PIECES.***
"STRIPPING HIS ***FLESH*** TO THE ***BONE.***
"***NOTHING*** COULD STOP ME."
I'LL -SQUEEE- ***KEEEL*** YOU!
AMITOUFU.
YOU ARE TOO SMALL FOR THE REVENGE YOU SEEK. SLEEP AND I WILL TAKE YOU WHERE YOU CAN LEARN TO HELP YOURSELF AND TO CHOOSE THE PATH YOU NEED.
-SQUEE-
BUDDHA BE PRAISED.
"I ASSUMED HE ATE ME, BECAUSE EVERYTHING WENT BLACK.
CH TO MY SURPRISE, I SOMEHOW ESCAPED, AND AWOKE FIND MYSELF AT THE FEET OF AN OLD MASKED MAN. E COULD HAVE BEEN CHINESE, MAYBE KOREAN, BUT HE SMELLED LIKE A GOAT WRAPPED IN A TARP."
NO DUMPING
-SQUEEEEEE-
SO, WHO HAS THE COWBOY BROUGHT ME THIS TIME?
SO MUCH RAGE IN SUCH A SMALL ONE.
-SQUEE- -SQUEEE-

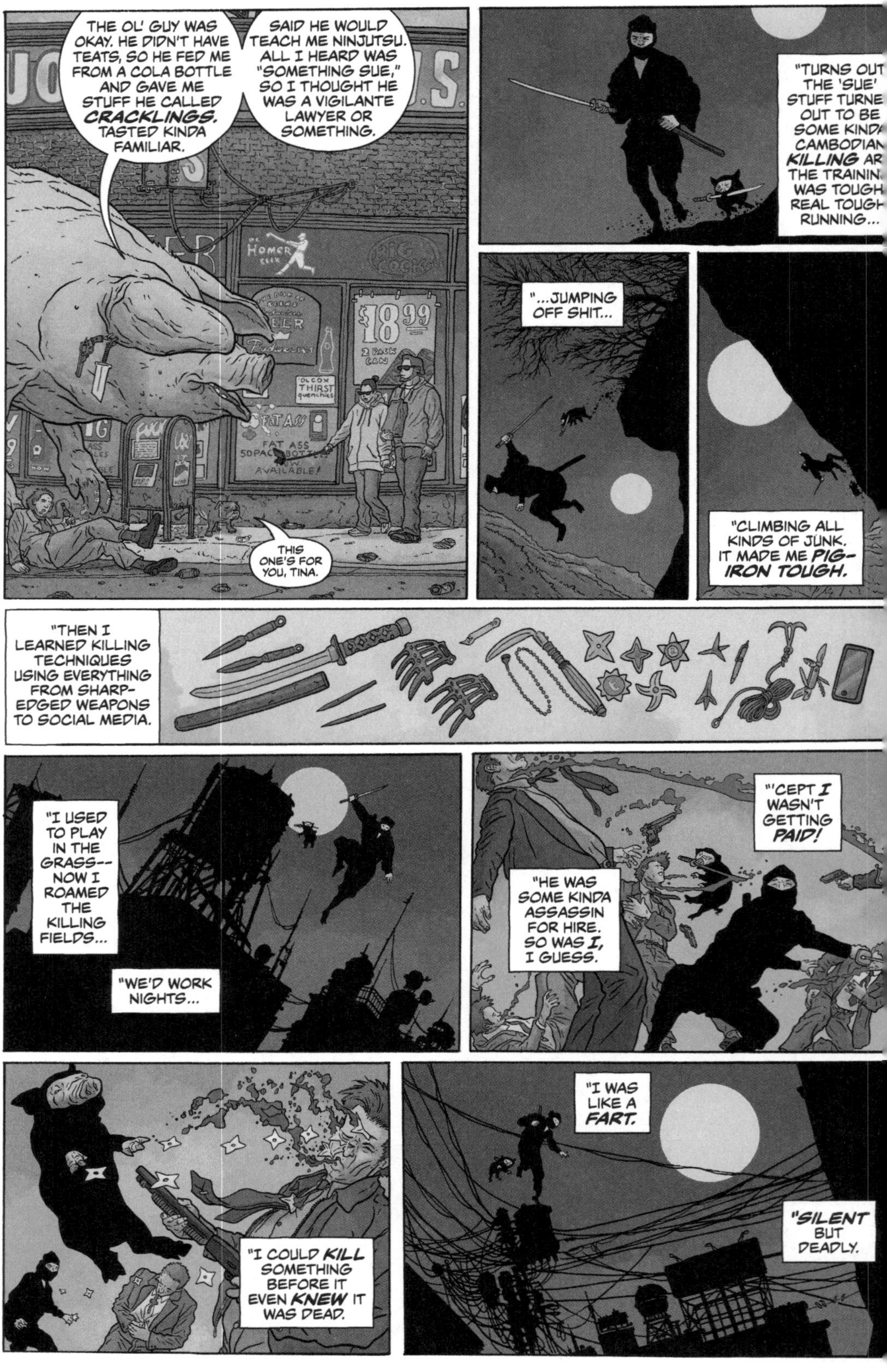
THE OL' GUY WAS OKAY. HE DIDN'T HAVE TEATS, SO HE FED ME FROM A COLA BOTTLE AND GAVE ME STUFF HE CALLED CRACKLINGS. TASTED KINDA FAMILIAR.
SAID HE WOULD TEACH ME NINJUTSU. ALL I HEARD WAS "SOMETHING SUE," SO I THOUGHT HE WAS A VIGILANTE LAWYER OR SOMETHING.
THIS ONE'S FOR YOU, TINA.
"TURNS OUT THE 'SUE' STUFF TURNE OUT TO BE SOME KINDA CAMBODIAN KILLING AR THE TRAININ WAS TOUGH REAL TOUGH RUNNING...
"...JUMPING OFF SHIT...
"CLIMBING ALL KINDS OF JUNK. IT MADE ME PIG-IRON TOUGH.
"THEN I LEARNED KILLING TECHNIQUES USING EVERYTHING FROM SHARP-EDGED WEAPONS TO SOCIAL MEDIA.
"I USED TO PLAY IN THE GRASS-- NOW I ROAMED THE KILLING FIELDS...
"WE'D WORK NIGHTS...
"HE WAS SOME KINDA ASSASSIN FOR HIRE. SO WAS I, I GUESS.
"CEPT I WASN'T GETTING PAID!
"I COULD KILL SOMETHING BEFORE IT EVEN KNEW IT WAS DEAD.
"I WAS LIKE A FART.
"SILENT BUT DEADLY.

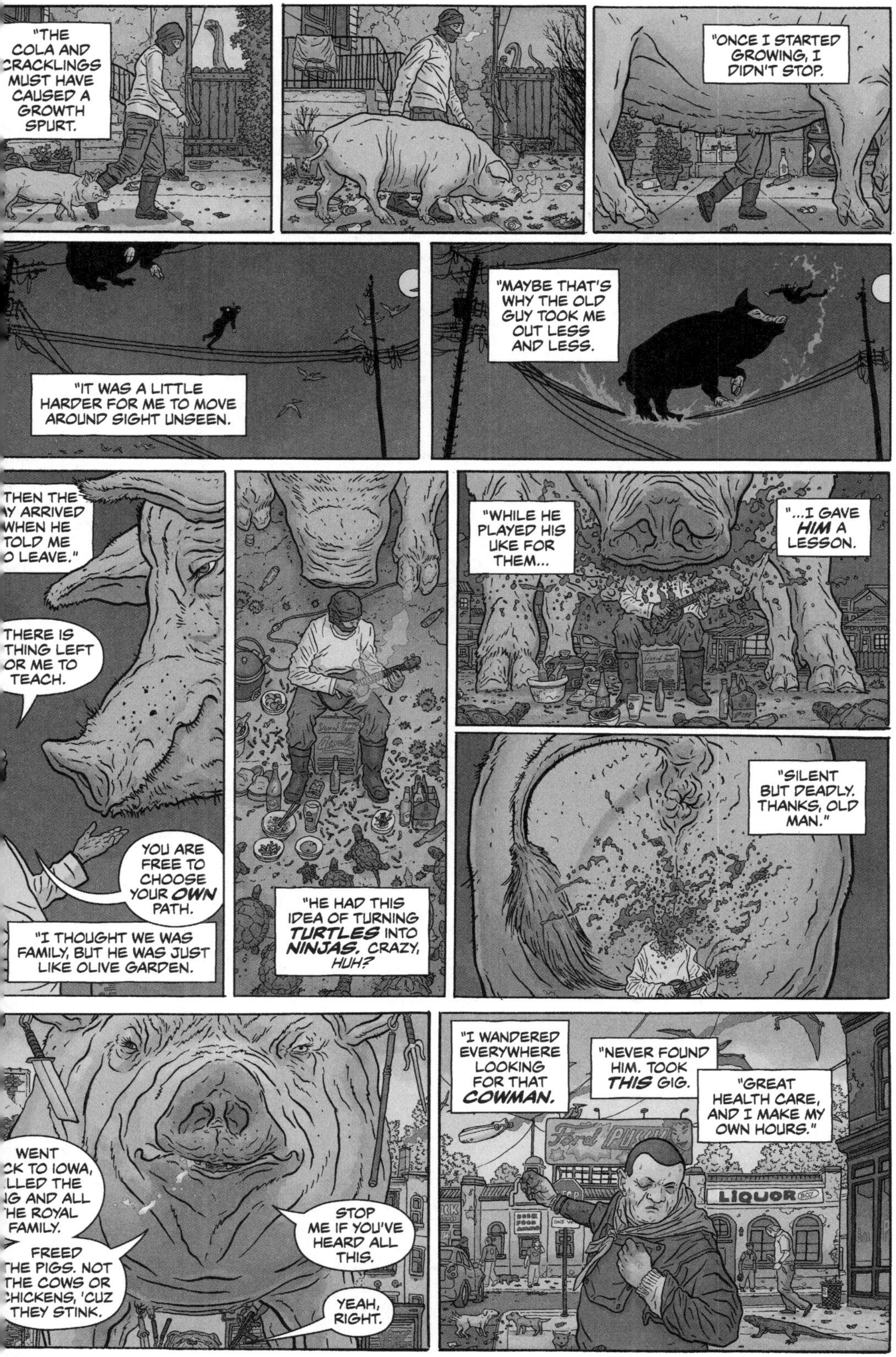
"THE COLA AND CRACKLINGS MUST HAVE CAUSED A GROWTH SPURT.
"ONCE I STARTED GROWING, I DIDN'T STOP.
"IT WAS A LITTLE HARDER FOR ME TO MOVE AROUND SIGHT UNSEEN.
"MAYBE THAT'S WHY THE OLD GUY TOOK ME OUT LESS AND LESS.
THEN THE Y ARRIVED WHEN HE TOLD ME O LEAVE."
THERE IS THING LEFT OR ME TO TEACH.
YOU ARE FREE TO CHOOSE YOUR OWN PATH.
"I THOUGHT WE WAS FAMILY, BUT HE WAS JUST LIKE OLIVE GARDEN.
"HE HAD THIS IDEA OF TURNING TURTLES INTO NINJAS. CRAZY, HUH?
"WHILE HE PLAYED HIS UKE FOR THEM...
"...I GAVE HIM A LESSON.
"SILENT BUT DEADLY. THANKS, OLD MAN."
WENT CK TO IOWA, LLED THE IG AND ALL HE ROYAL FAMILY.
FREED THE PIGS. NOT THE COWS OR CHICKENS, 'CUZ THEY STINK.
STOP ME IF YOU'VE HEARD ALL THIS.
YEAH, RIGHT.
"I WANDERED EVERYWHERE LOOKING FOR THAT COWMAN.
"NEVER FOUND HIM. TOOK THIS GIG.
"GREAT HEALTH CARE, AND I MAKE MY OWN HOURS."
LIQUOR

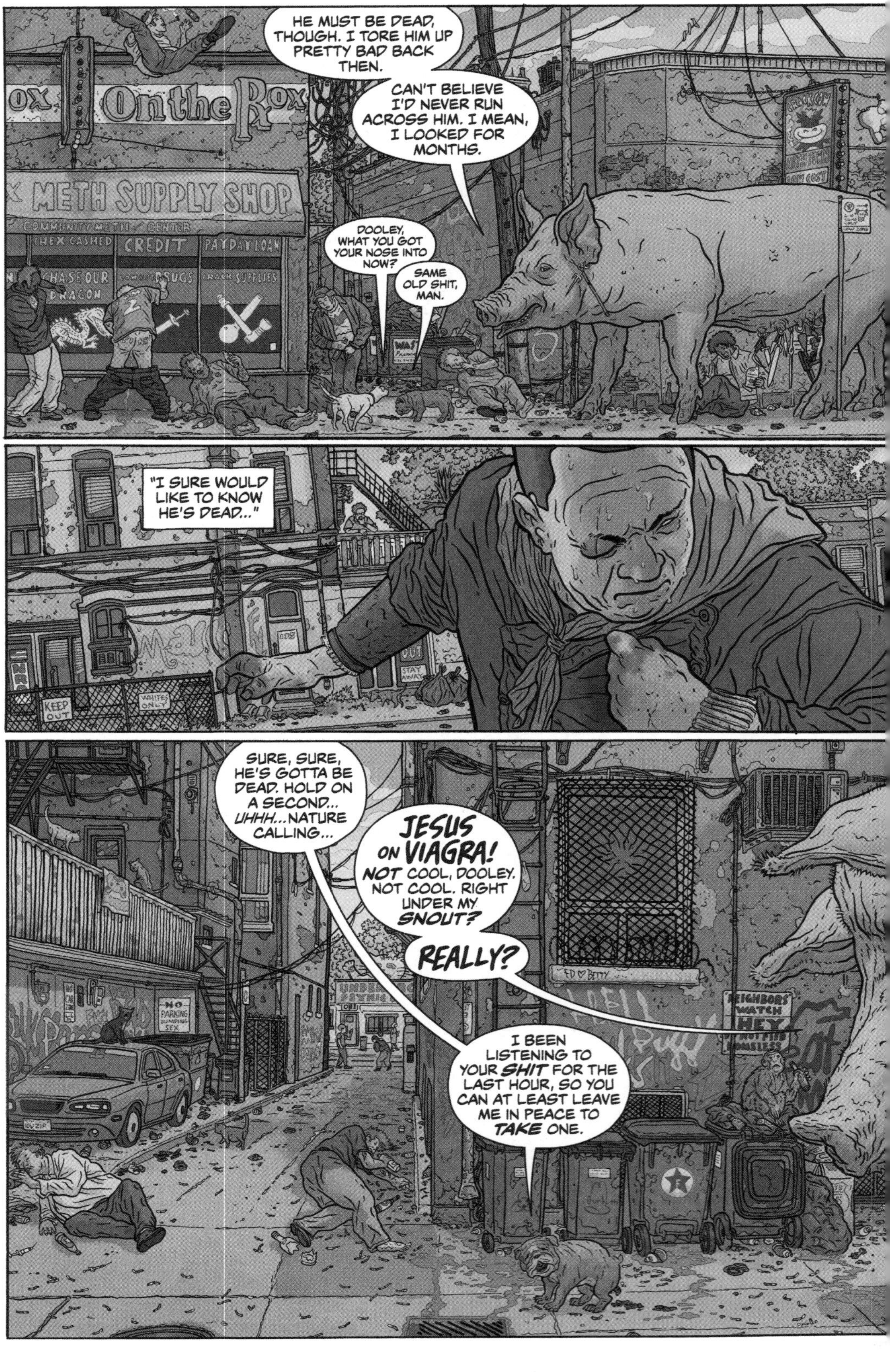
On the Rox
METH SUPPLY SHOP
COMMUNITY METH CENTER
CHEX CASHED
CREDIT
PAYDAY LOAN
CHASE OUR DRAGON
DRUGS
CRACK SUPPLIES
HE MUST BE DEAD, THOUGH. I TORE HIM UP PRETTY BAD BACK THEN.
CAN'T BELIEVE I'D NEVER RUN ACROSS HIM. I MEAN, I LOOKED FOR MONTHS.
DOOLEY, WHAT YOU GOT YOUR NOSE INTO NOW?
SAME OLD SHIT, MAN.
"I SURE WOULD LIKE TO KNOW HE'S DEAD..."
KEEP OUT
WHITES ONLY
STAY AWAY
SURE, SURE, HE'S GOTTA BE DEAD. HOLD ON A SECOND... UHHH... NATURE CALLING...
JESUS ON VIAGRA! NOT COOL, DOOLEY. NOT COOL. RIGHT UNDER MY SNOUT?
REALLY?
I BEEN LISTENING TO YOUR SHIT FOR THE LAST HOUR, SO YOU CAN AT LEAST LEAVE ME IN PEACE TO TAKE ONE.
NO PARKING DUMPING SEX
ED ♡ BETTY
NEIGHBORS WATCH

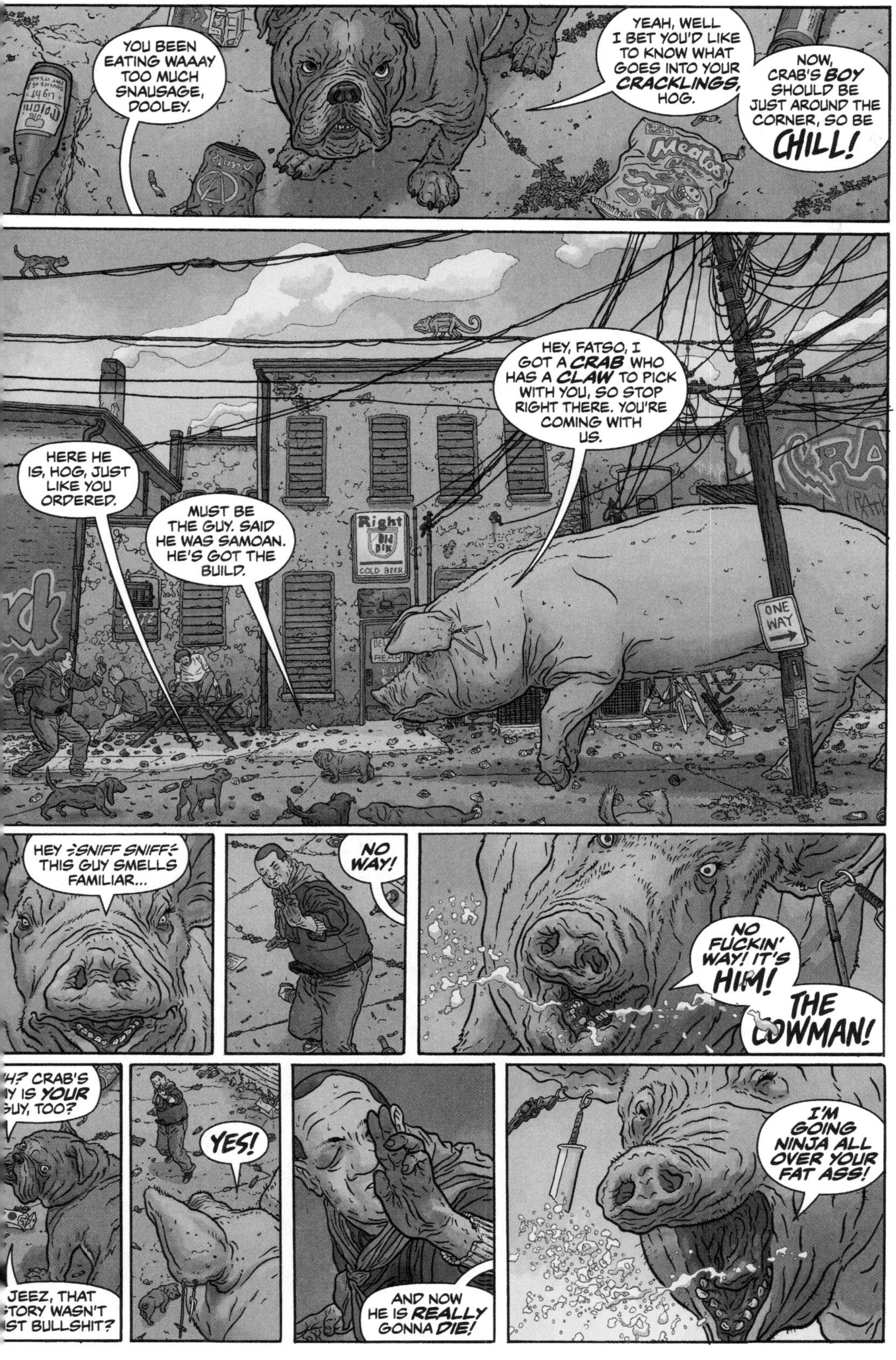
YOU BEEN EATING WAAAY TOO MUCH SNAUSAGE, DOOLEY.
YEAH, WELL I BET YOU'D LIKE TO KNOW WHAT GOES INTO YOUR CRACKLINGS, HOG.
NOW, CRAB'S BOY SHOULD BE JUST AROUND THE CORNER, SO BE CHILL!
HERE HE IS, HOG, JUST LIKE YOU ORDERED.
MUST BE THE GUY. SAID HE WAS SAMOAN. HE'S GOT THE BUILD.
HEY, FATSO, I GOT A CRAB WHO HAS A CLAW TO PICK WITH YOU, SO STOP RIGHT THERE. YOU'RE COMING WITH US.
Right
COLD BEER
ONE WAY
HEY -SNIFF SNIFF- THIS GUY SMELLS FAMILIAR...
NO WAY!
NO FUCKIN' WAY! IT'S HIM!
THE COWMAN!
H? CRAB'S Y IS YOUR GUY, TOO?
JEEZ, THAT STORY WASN'T ST BULLSHIT?
YES!
AND NOW HE IS REALLY GONNA DIE!
I'M GOING NINJA ALL OVER YOUR FAT ASS!

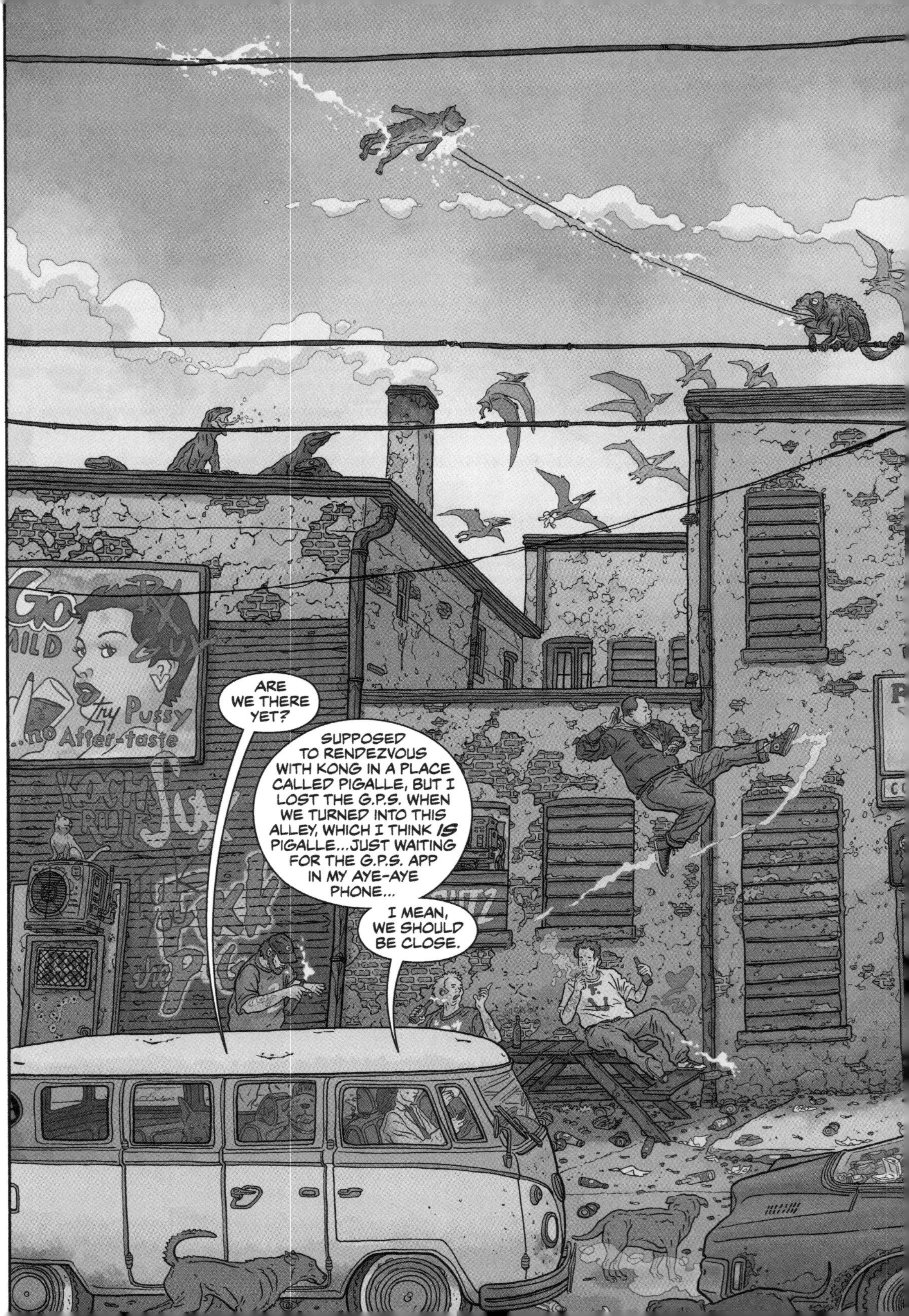
MILD
try Pussy
...no After-taste
ARE WE THERE YET?
SUPPOSED TO RENDEZVOUS WITH KONG IN A PLACE CALLED PIGALLE, BUT I LOST THE G.P.S. WHEN WE TURNED INTO THIS ALLEY, WHICH I THINK *IS* PIGALLE...JUST WAITING FOR THE G.P.S. APP IN MY AYE-AYE PHONE...
I MEAN, WE SHOULD BE CLOSE.

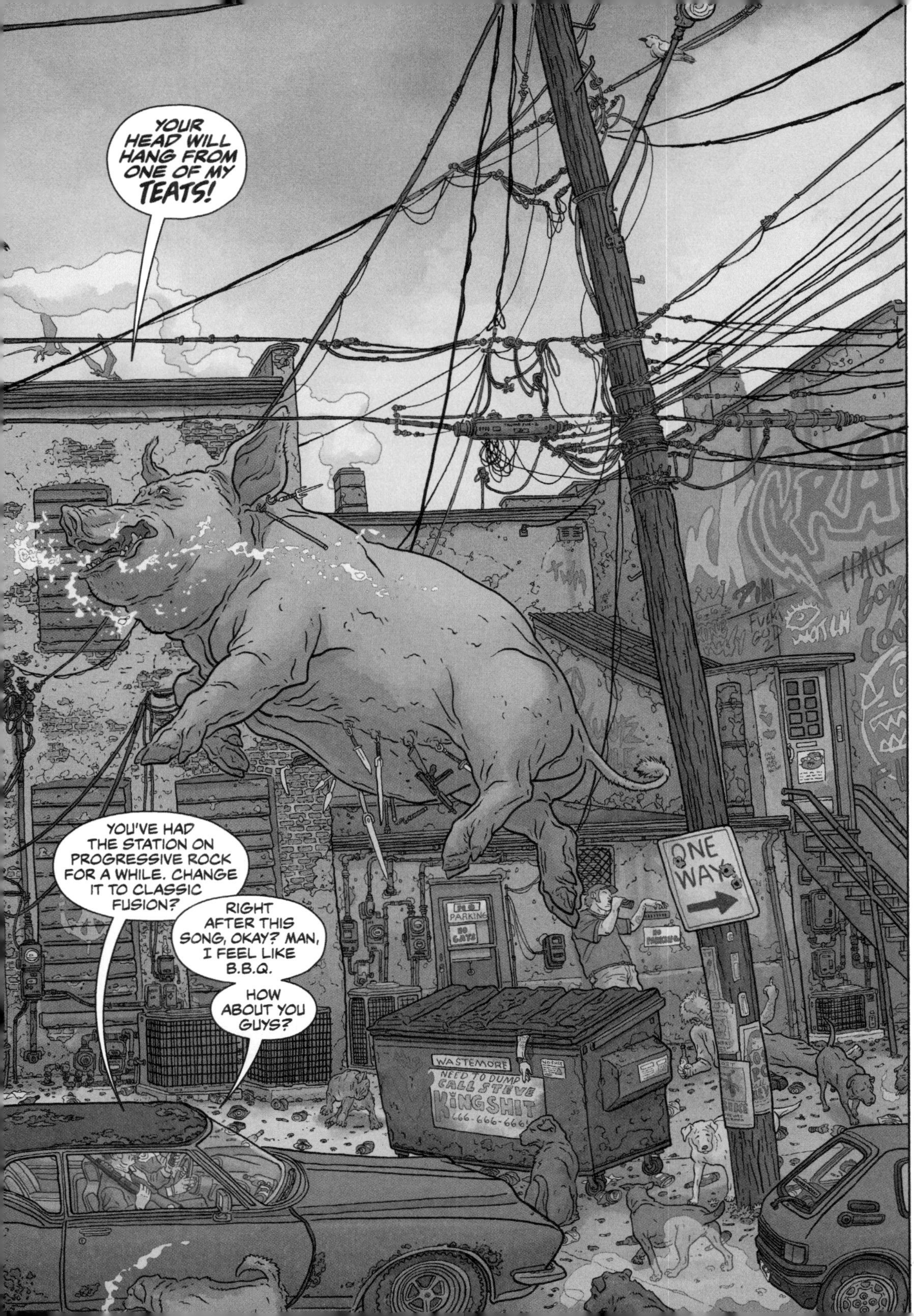
YOUR HEAD WILL HANG FROM ONE OF MY TEATS!
YOU'VE HAD THE STATION ON PROGRESSIVE ROCK FOR A WHILE. CHANGE IT TO CLASSIC FUSION?
RIGHT AFTER THIS SONG, OKAY? MAN, I FEEL LIKE B.B.Q.
HOW ABOUT YOU GUYS?
ONE WAY
NO PARKING
NO CATS
WASTEMORE
NEED TO DUMP CALL STEVE KINGSHIT 666-666-6666

Hostage (*Excerpt*)

GUY DELISLE

originally published in

Hostage

DRAWN AND QUARTERLY

6.1 x 8.5 inches • 436 pages

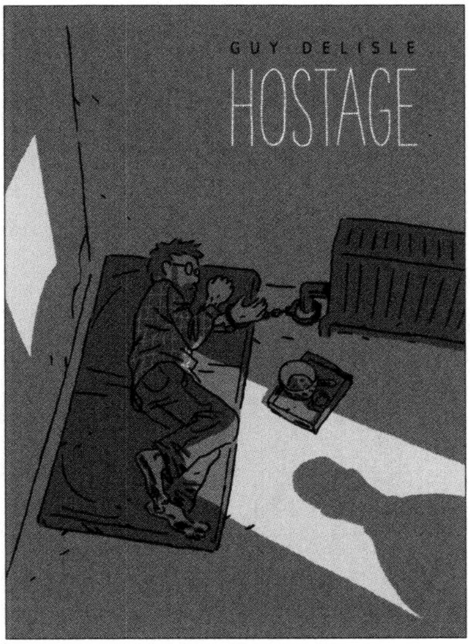
GUY DELISLE
HOSTAGE

Biography

Guy Delisle was born in Québec City, Canada, in 1966, and he now lives in the south of France with his wife and two children. Delisle spent ten years working in animation, which allowed him to learn about movement and drawing. He is best known for his travelogues about life in faraway countries: *Burma Chronicles*, *Jerusalem: Chronicles from the Holy City*, *Pyongyang*, and *Shenzhen*. In 2012, Delisle was awarded the Prize for Best Album for the French edition of *Jerusalem* at the Angoulême International Comics Festival. His most recent book is *Hostage*, based on the true story of a kidnapped Doctors Without Borders administrator.

guydelisle.com

Statement

I based this excerpt on Christophe André's memories, which I recorded on tape. The way he described this moment to me was very intense: both in his voice and his appearance. He said to me, "In my whole life, I've never eaten anything as delicious as that little piece of bread with garlic on it." I did a first draft of this scene which, after several re-readings, didn't feel quite right. This is the second attempt at telling that anecdote, and when I redid it, I tried to get as close as possible to his experience. It was the greatest challenge of this whole book.

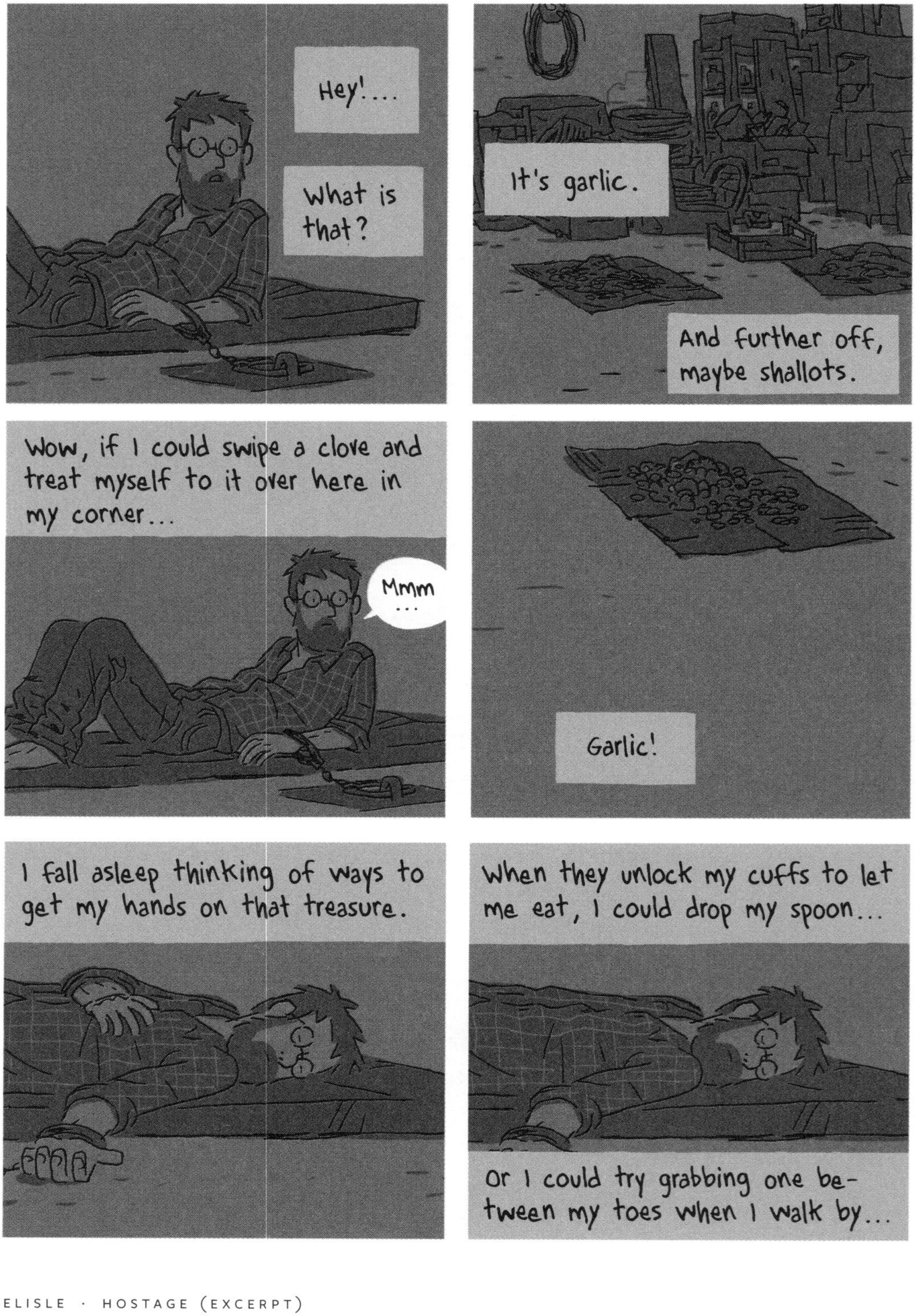
Hey!...
What is that?
It's garlic.
And further off, maybe shallots.
Wow, if I could swipe a clove and treat myself to it over here in my corner...
Mmm ...
Garlic!
I fall asleep thinking of ways to get my hands on that treasure.
When they unlock my cuffs to let me eat, I could drop my spoon...
Or I could try grabbing one be-tween my toes when I walk by...

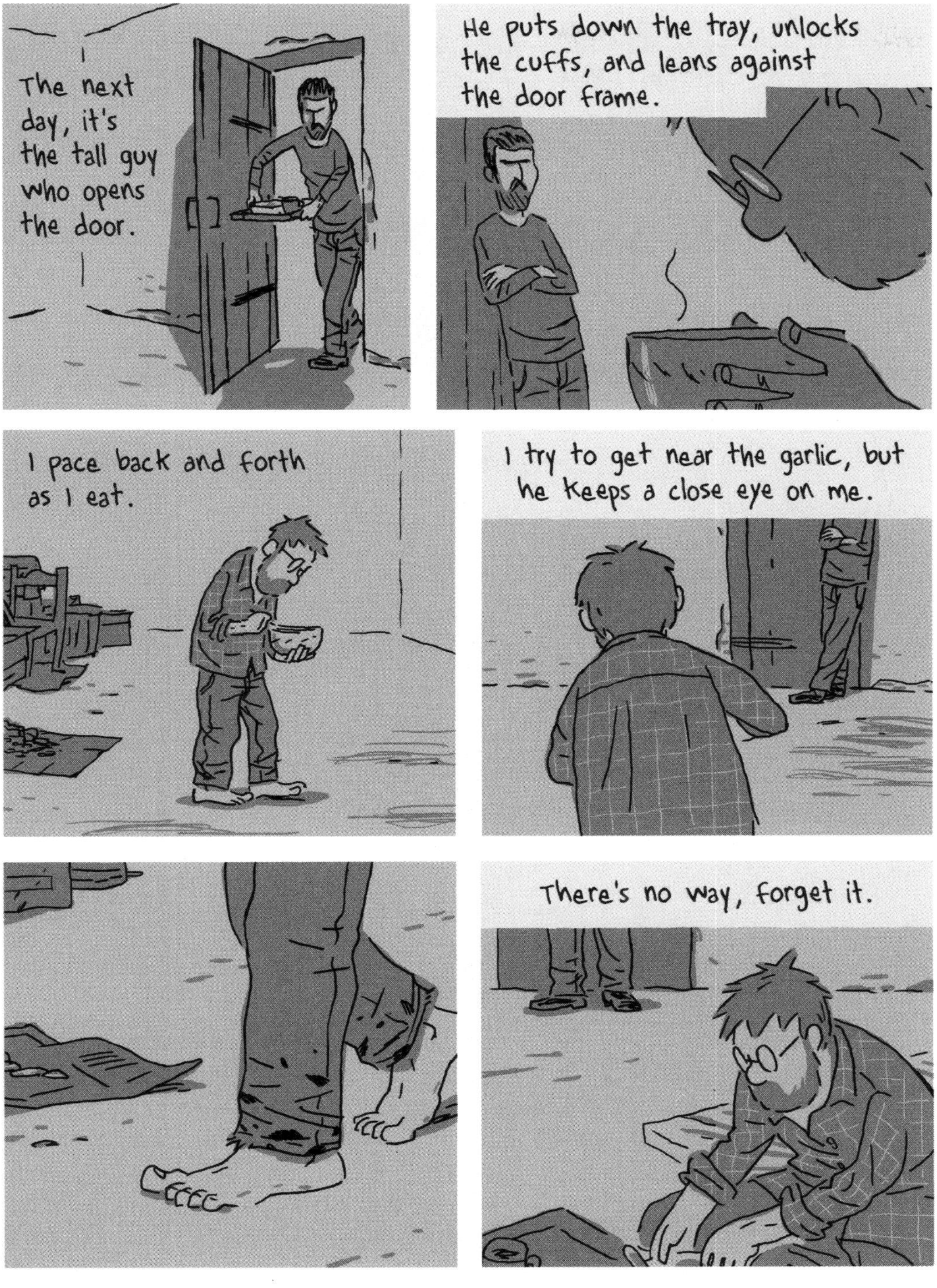

The next day, it's the tall guy who opens the door.
He puts down the tray, unlocks the cuffs, and leans against the door frame.
I pace back and forth as I eat.
I try to get near the garlic, but he keeps a close eye on me.
There's no way, forget it.

I stash my bread under the blanket for later.

Clack!

The tall guy leaves.

Hey! What if...

Maybe if I stretch as far as I can...

Let's see...

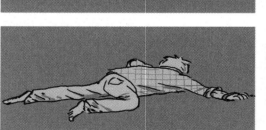

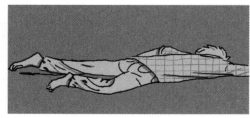

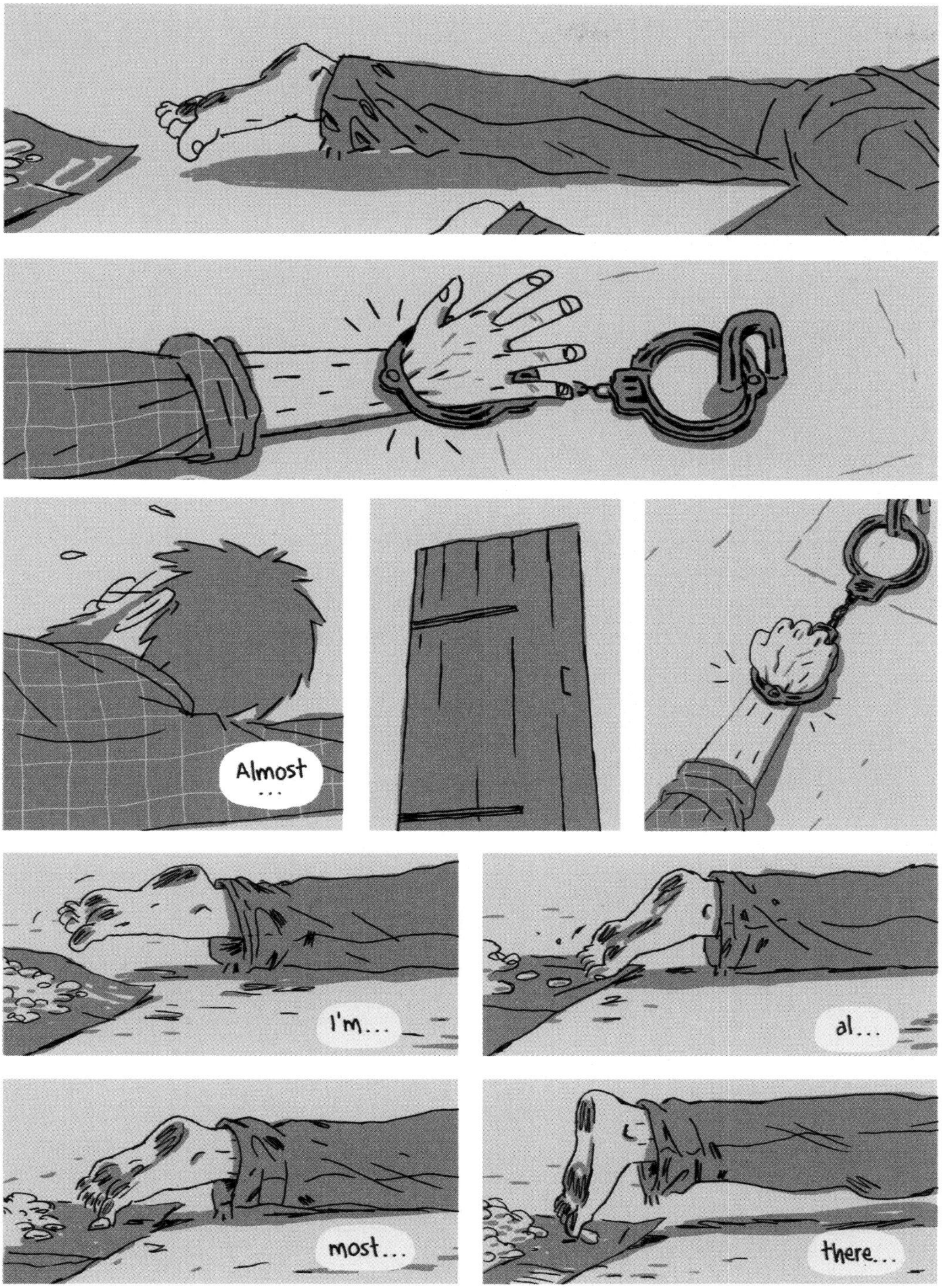
Almost
...
I'm...
al...
most...
there...

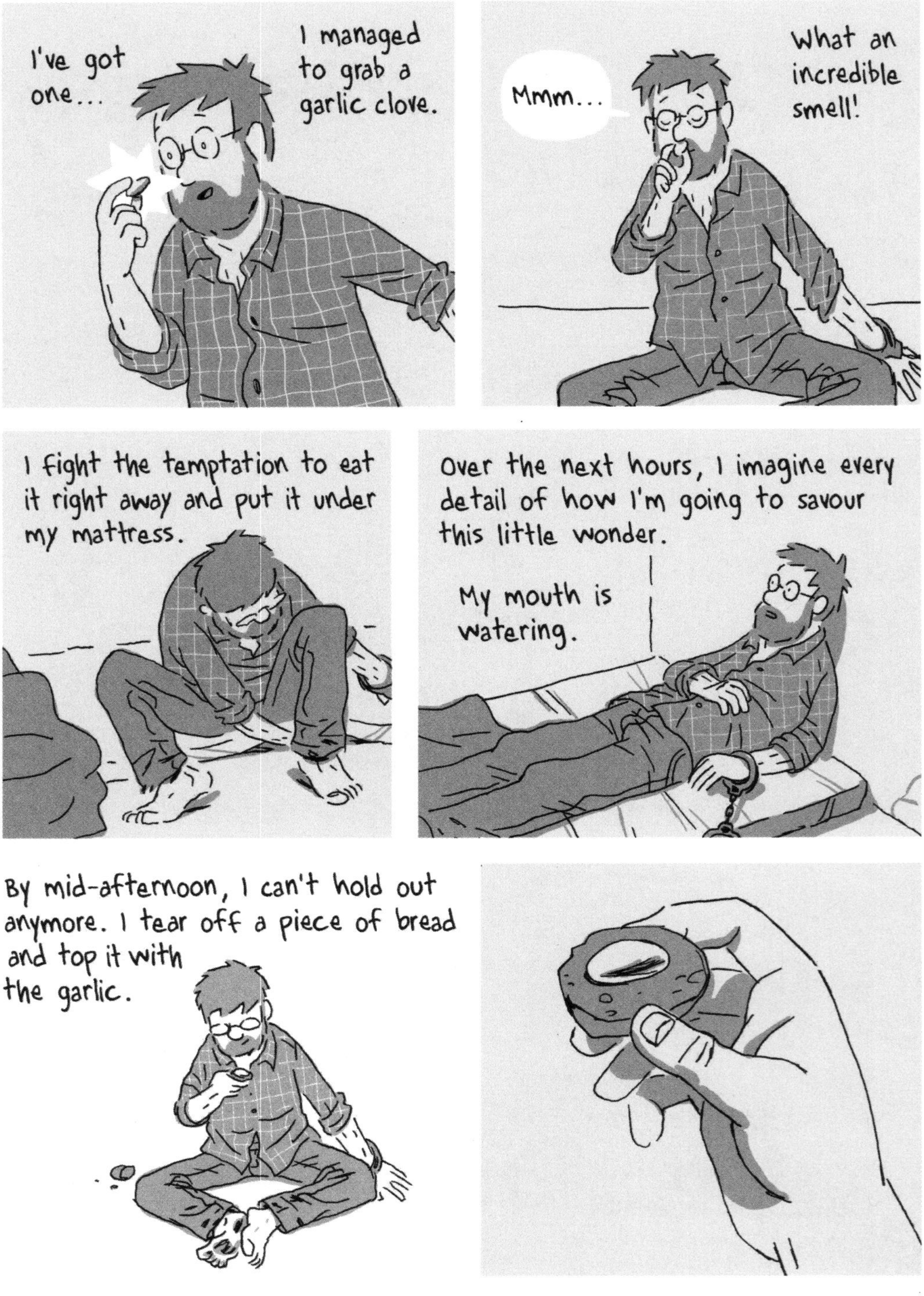
I've got one...
I managed to grab a garlic clove.
Mmm...
What an incredible smell!
I fight the temptation to eat it right away and put it under my mattress.
Over the next hours, I imagine every detail of how I'm going to savour this little wonder.
My mouth is watering.
By mid-afternoon, I can't hold out anymore. I tear off a piece of bread and top it with the garlic.

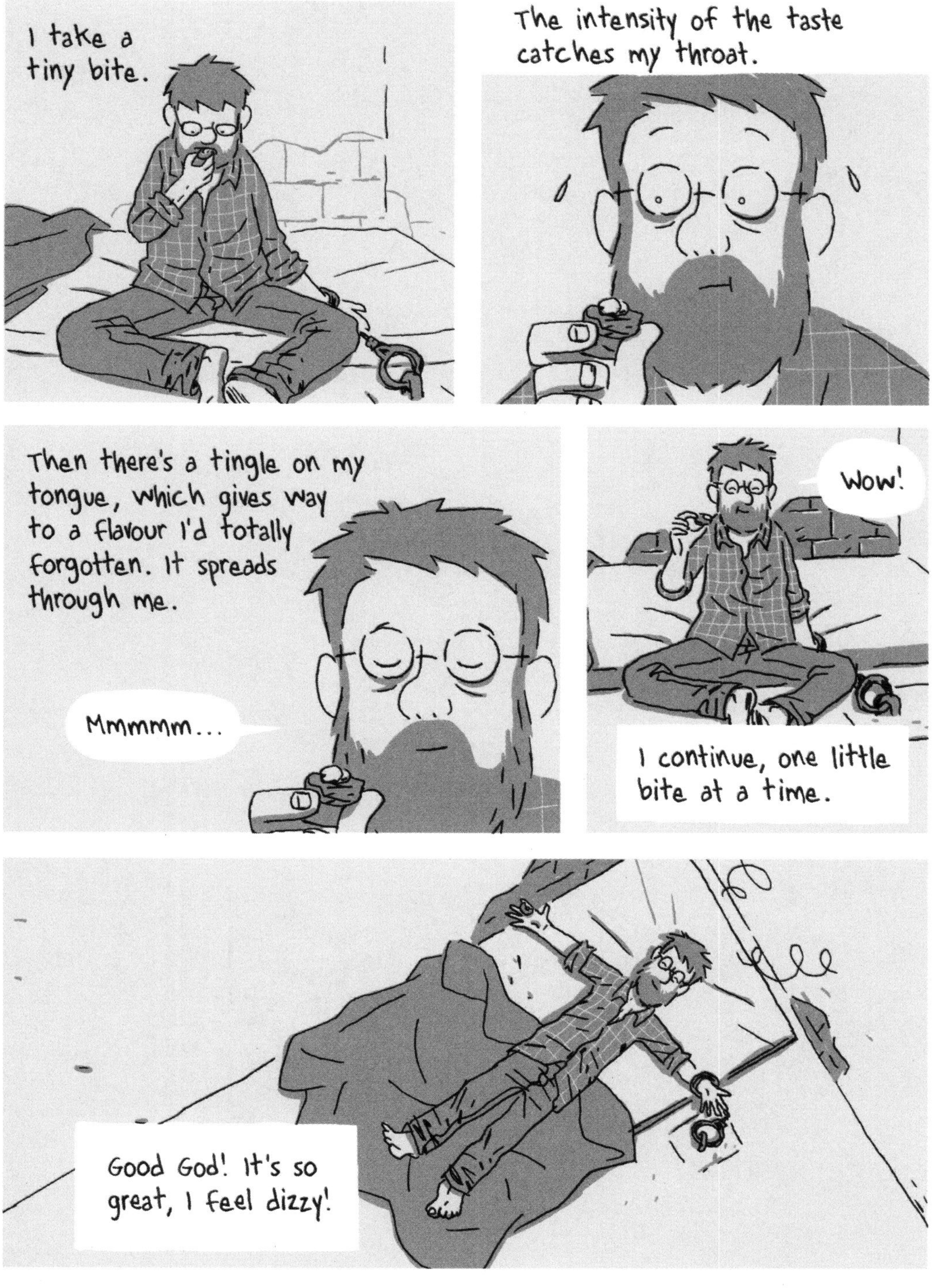
I take a tiny bite.
The intensity of the taste catches my throat.
Then there's a tingle on my tongue, which gives way to a flavour I'd totally forgotten. It spreads through me.
Mmmmm...
Wow!
I continue, one little bite at a time.
Good God! It's so great, I feel dizzy!

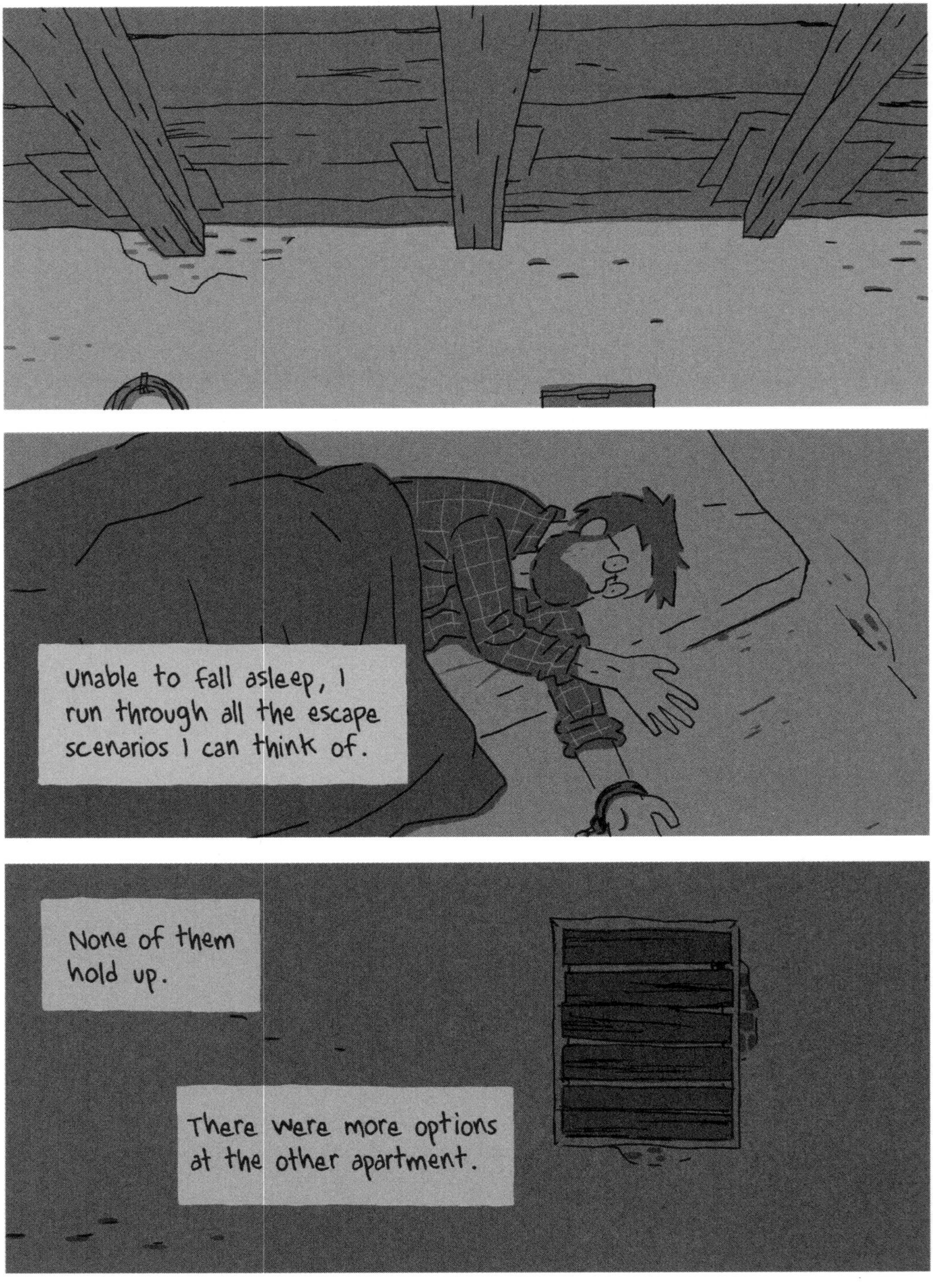
Unable to fall asleep, I run through all the escape scenarios I can think of.
None of them hold up.
There were more options at the other apartment.

Brausebad

ABRAHAM DÍAZ

originally published in

Tonto

EDICIONES VALIENTES

6.5 x 9.5 inches • 78 pages

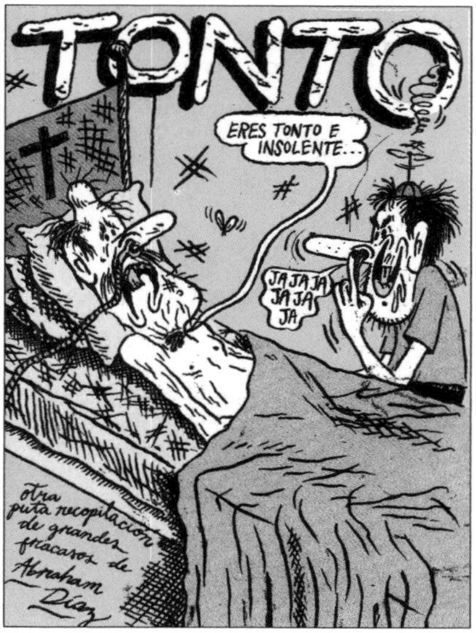
TONTO
ERES TONTO E INSOLENTE...
JA JA JA JA JA JA
otra puta recopilación de grandes fracasos de Abraham Díaz

Biography

I'm 29 years old, and I'm just some idiot who draws comics and cartoons in Mexico City. I've been involved in the Mexico City punk scene and sometimes I've drawn flyers and cover art for some punk bands from around the world. I also run a micro edition publisher of comics and outsider art called Joc Doc. We mostly do graphzines and books whenever we can afford to do it. I've been published in some comic anthologies around the world like *kuš!* or *Kramers Ergot* or *Kovra* by my publisher Ediciones Valientes in Spain, who also published a solo book of my cartoons recently called *Tonto*. I like to edit and publish my own work in Joc Doc the most though.
awfulgraphics.tumblr.com

Statement

I drew this comic some time ago, and it's basically a fantasy I had one night when I was lying in bed before going to sleep where all greedy people such as business potentate people, politicians, drug cartel leaders, rock stars, shitty journalists, economists, etc., were put in a concentration camp to be vanished from the Earth's face. I drew it with a pencil on simple bond half-letter pages, and I published it as a little zine I printed myself with a riso machine.

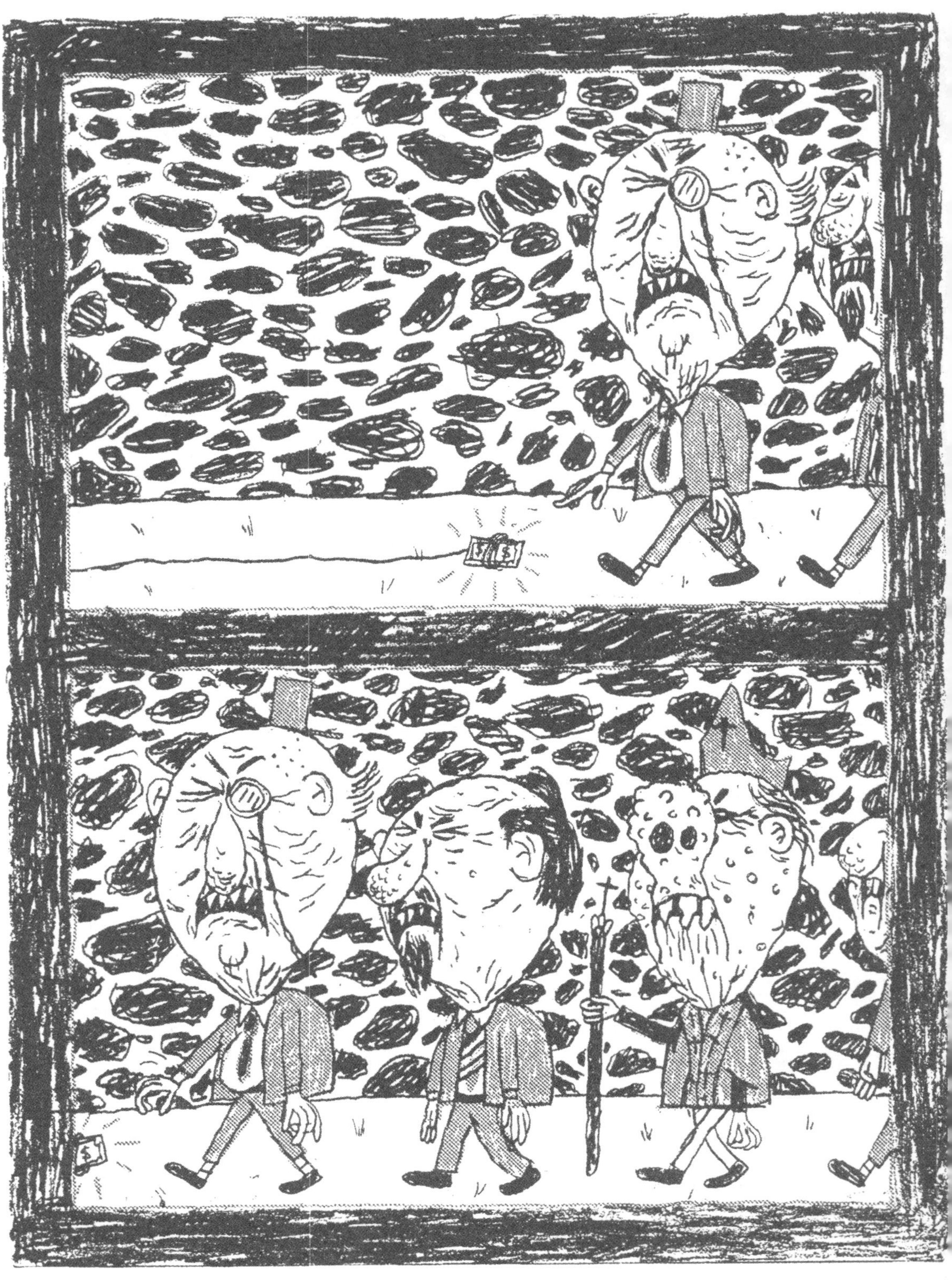

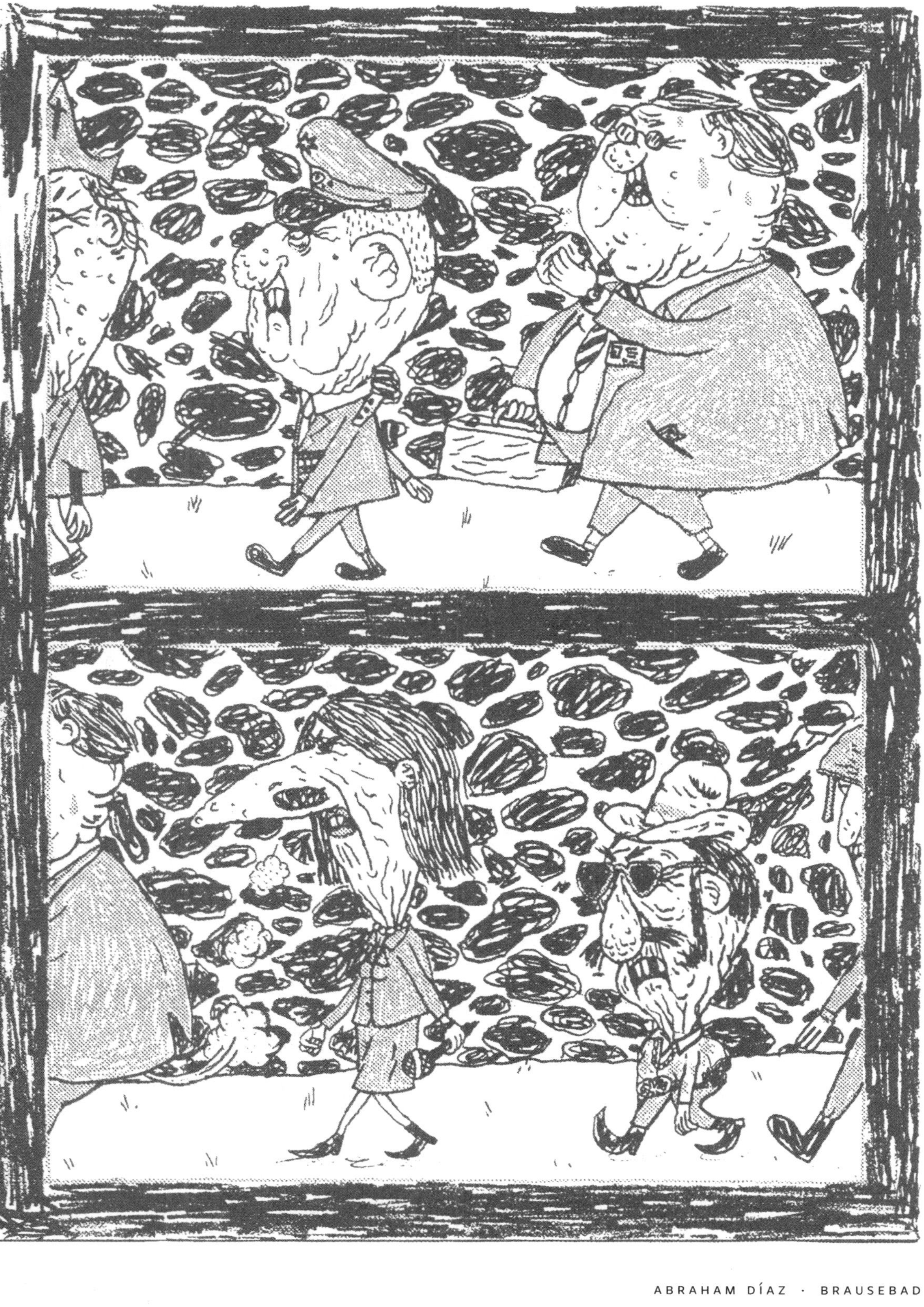

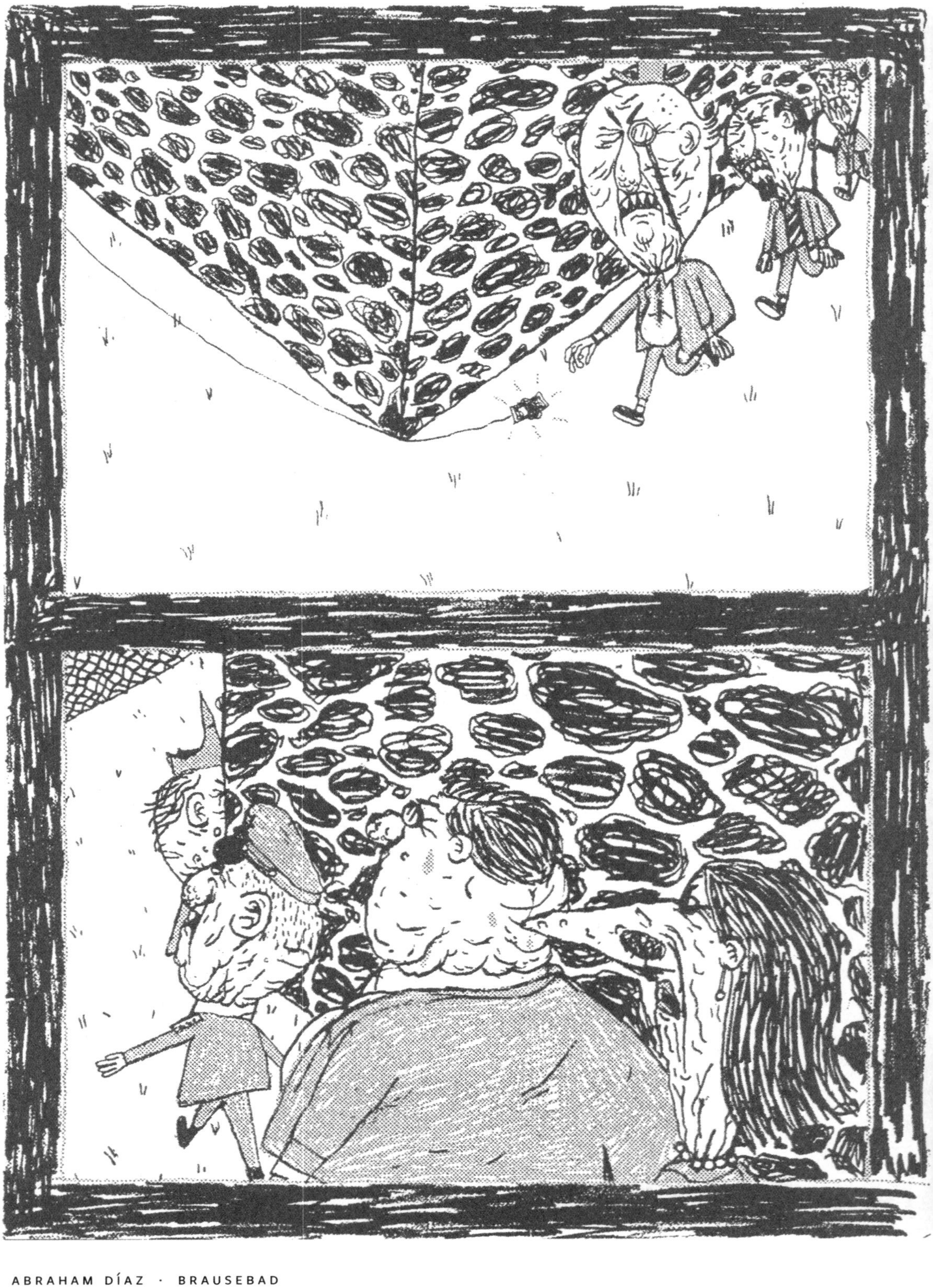

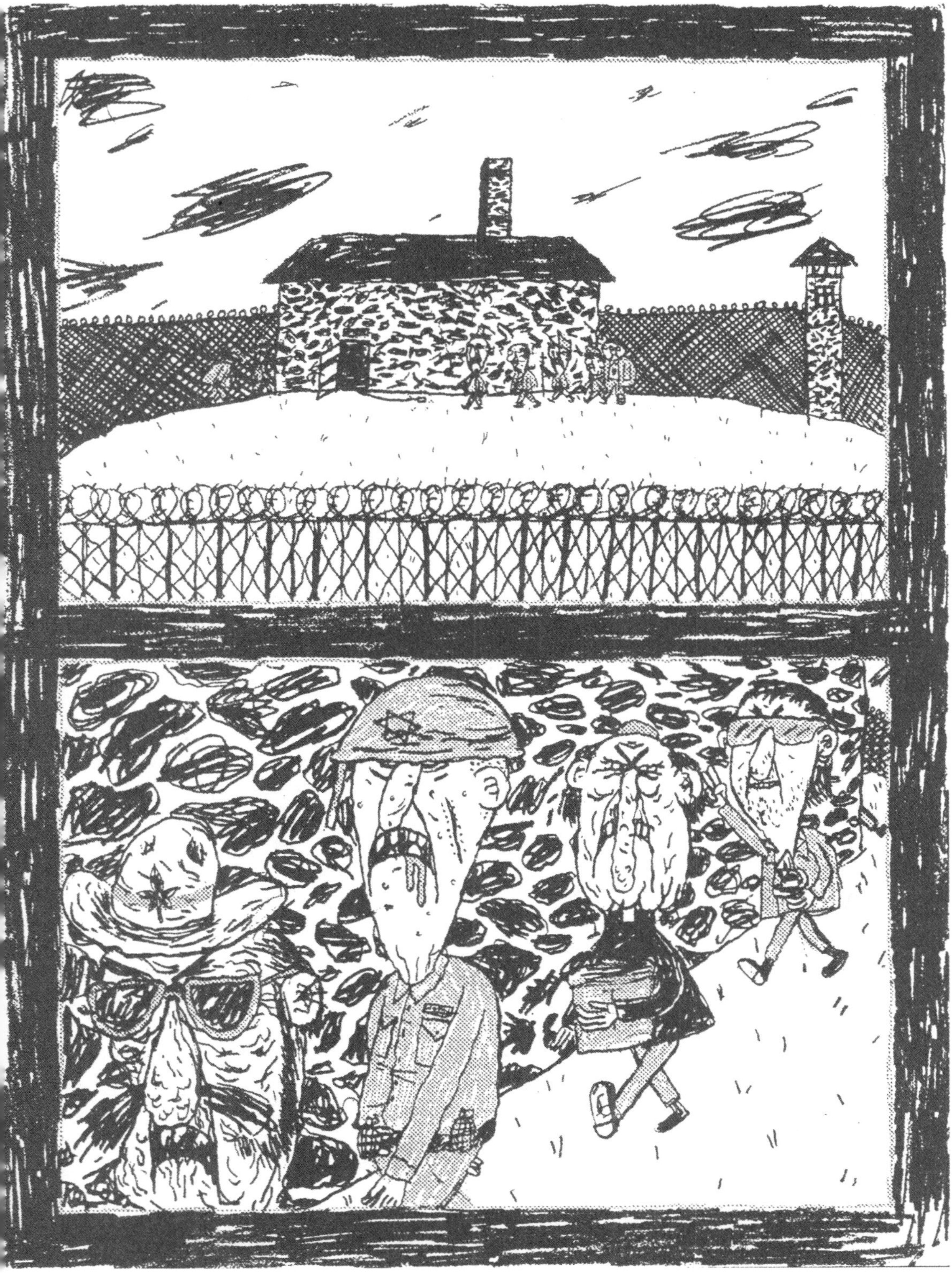

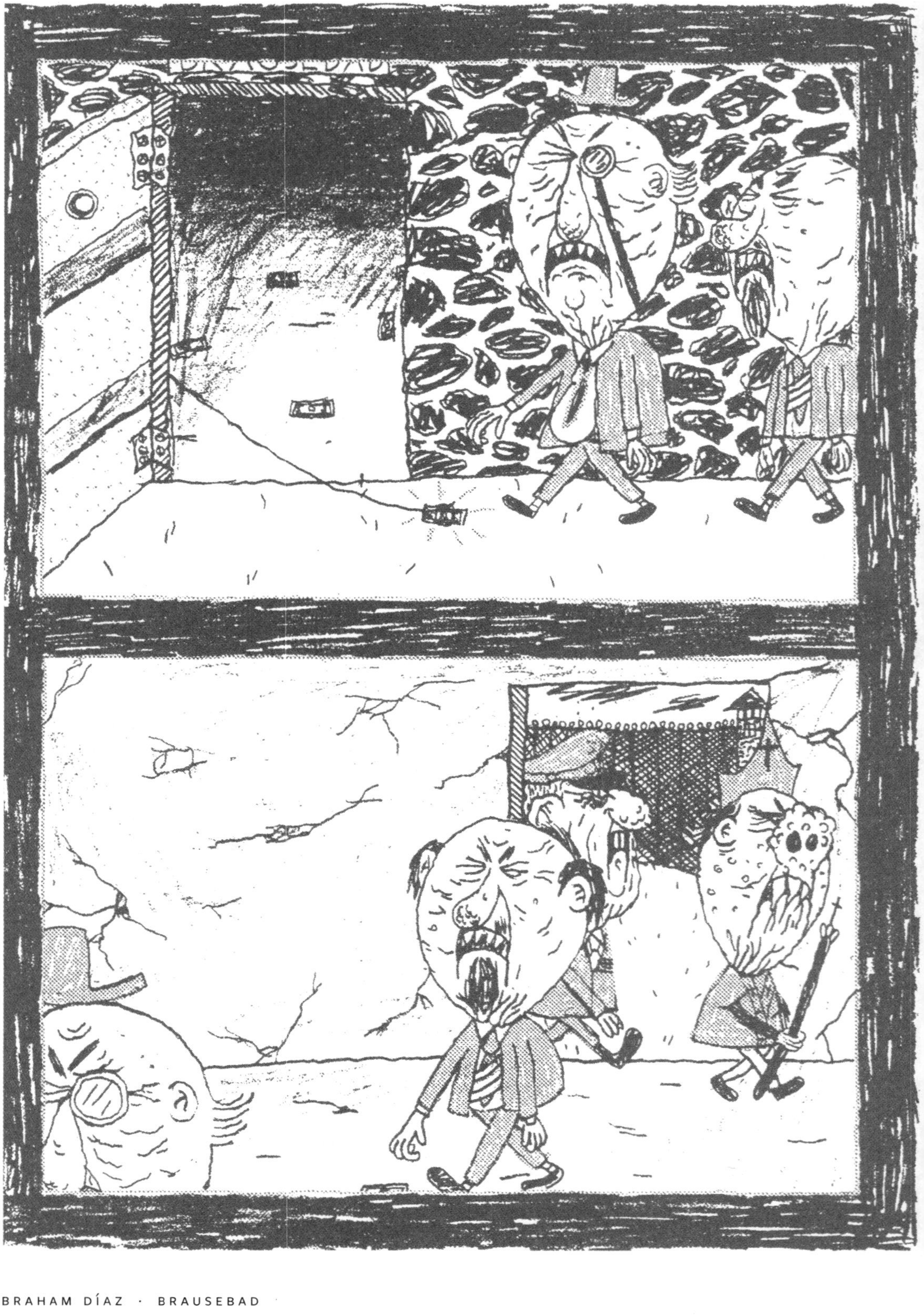

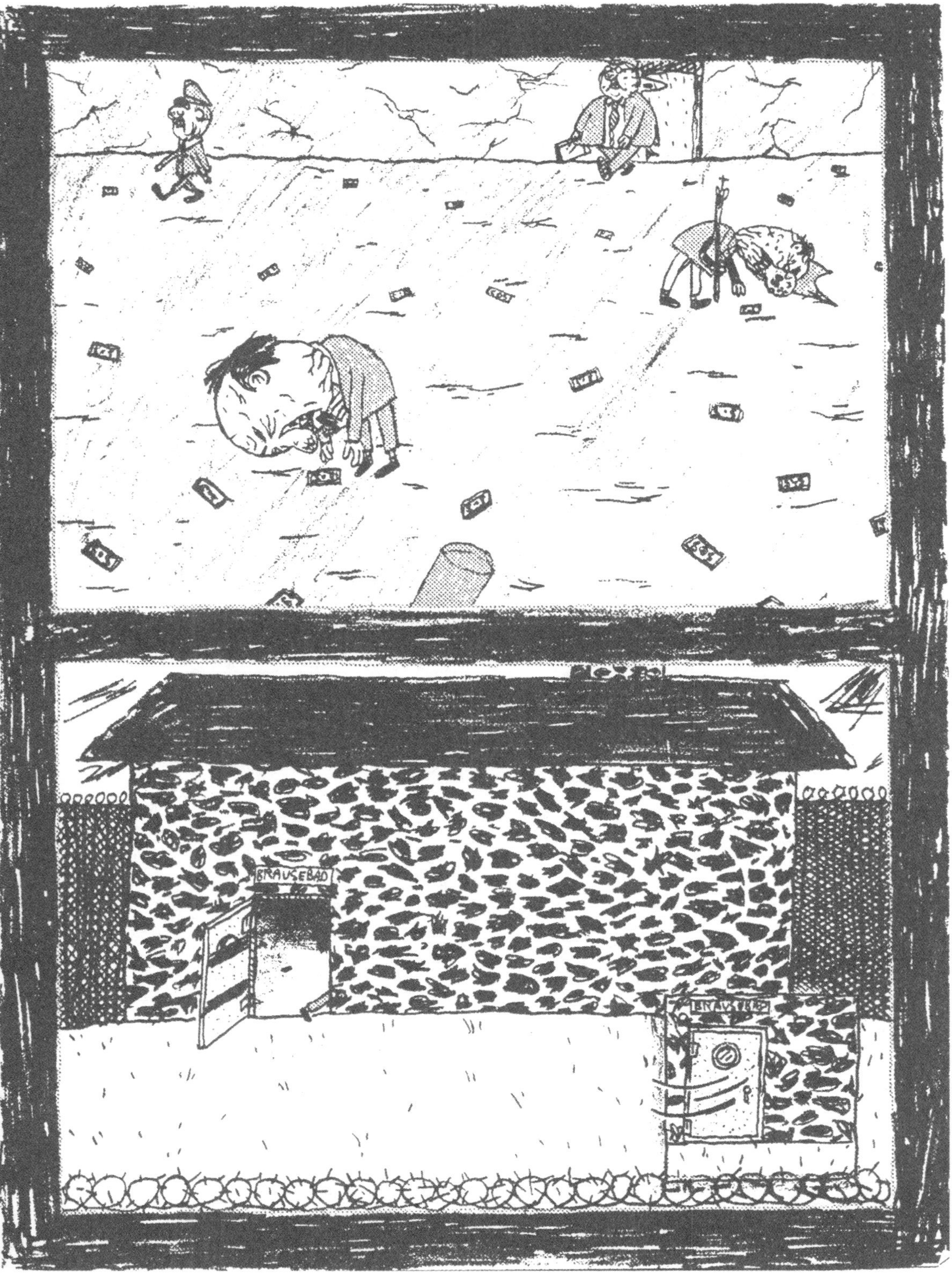
BRAUSEBAD

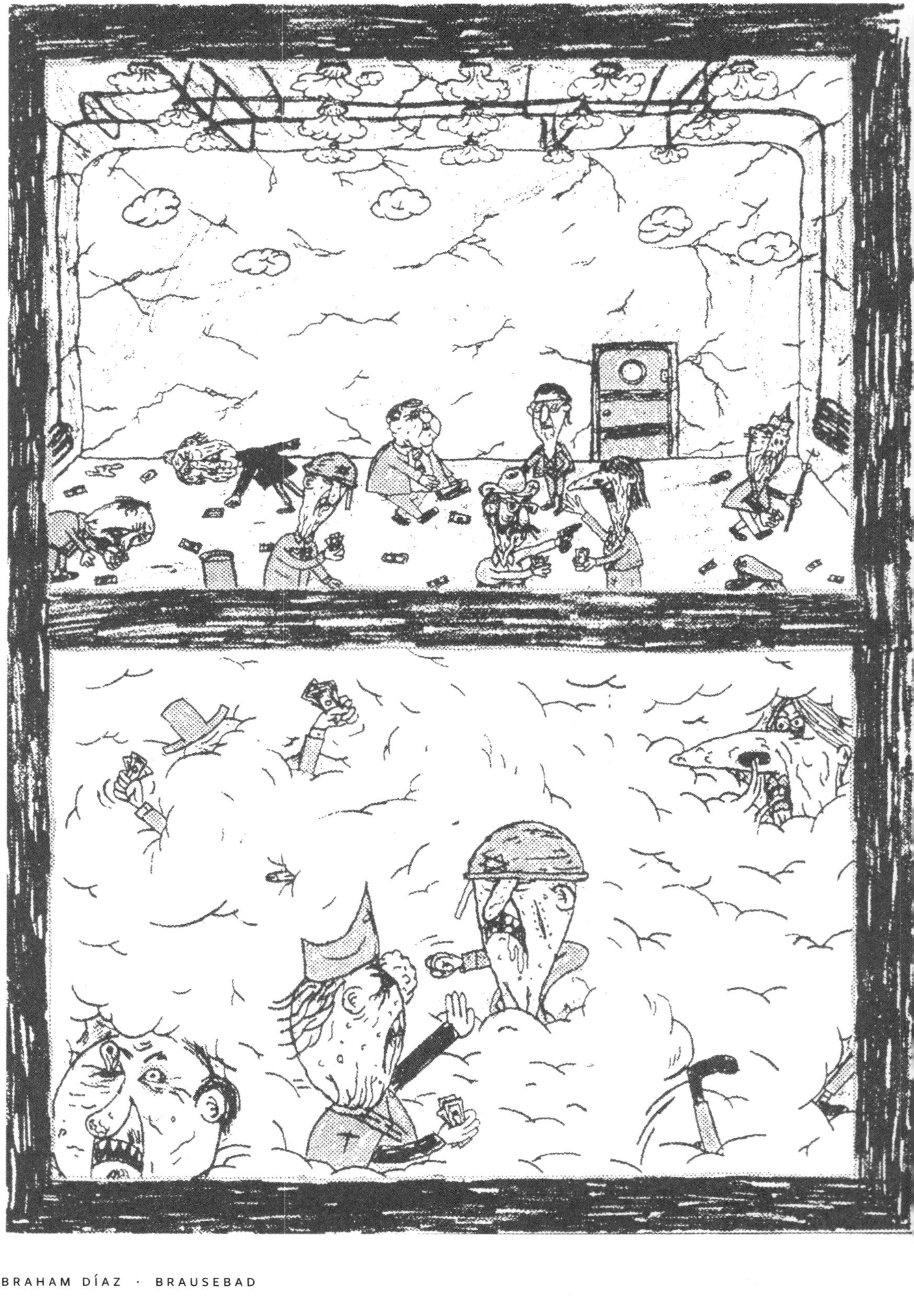

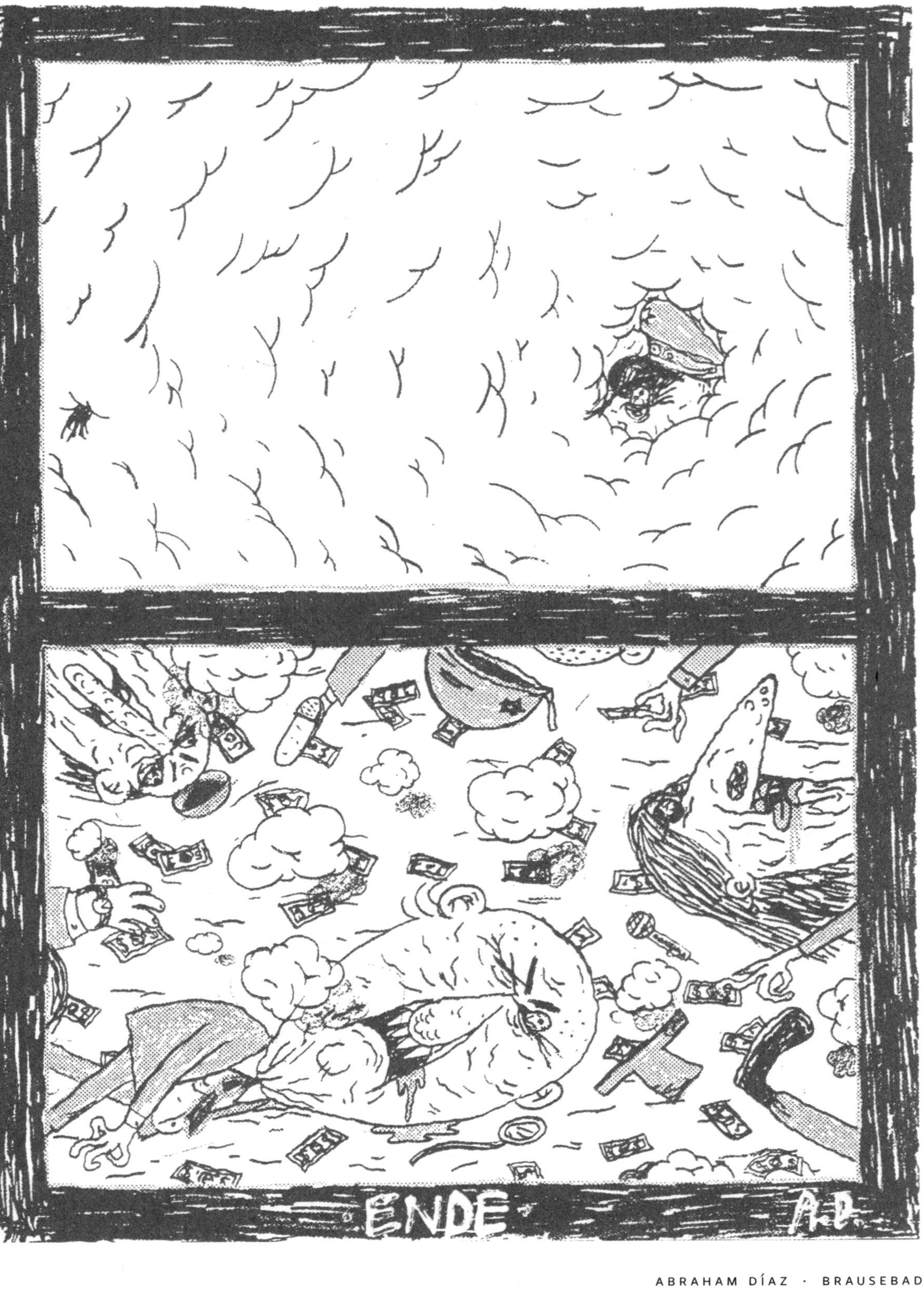
ENDE
A.D.

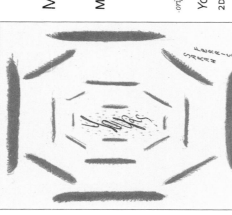

Margot

MARGOT FERRICK

originally published in

Yours
2DCLOUD
6.4 x 8.4 inches • 140 pages

Biography

Margot Ferrick was born in 1988 on Long Island, and now lives in Chicago.
butterstory.tumblr.com

Statement

"Margot" was the last comic in a collection of love letter comics published as *Yours*. I didn't intend every piece in that book to be about unrequited love or unsuccessful relationships but it turned out that way, and at the time I thought the best possible way to end it all was with a letter to an aborted fetus. Aborted pregnancy seemed like the ultimate togetherness and separation in my mind. I also thought that since every other comic in *Yours* was addressed to a separate person, it felt appropriate to address and say goodbye to part of myself as well. After finishing this comic, I changed my first name from Sarah to Margot.

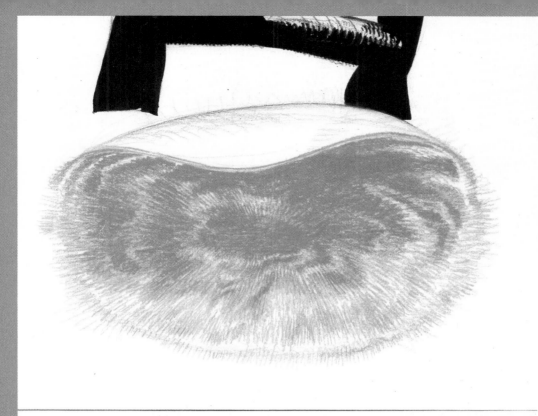

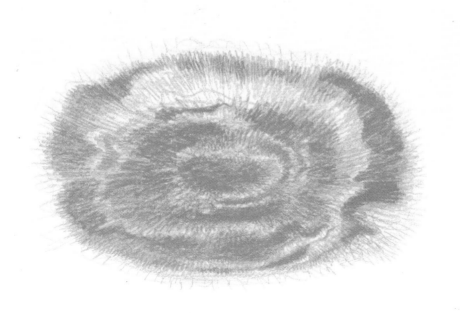

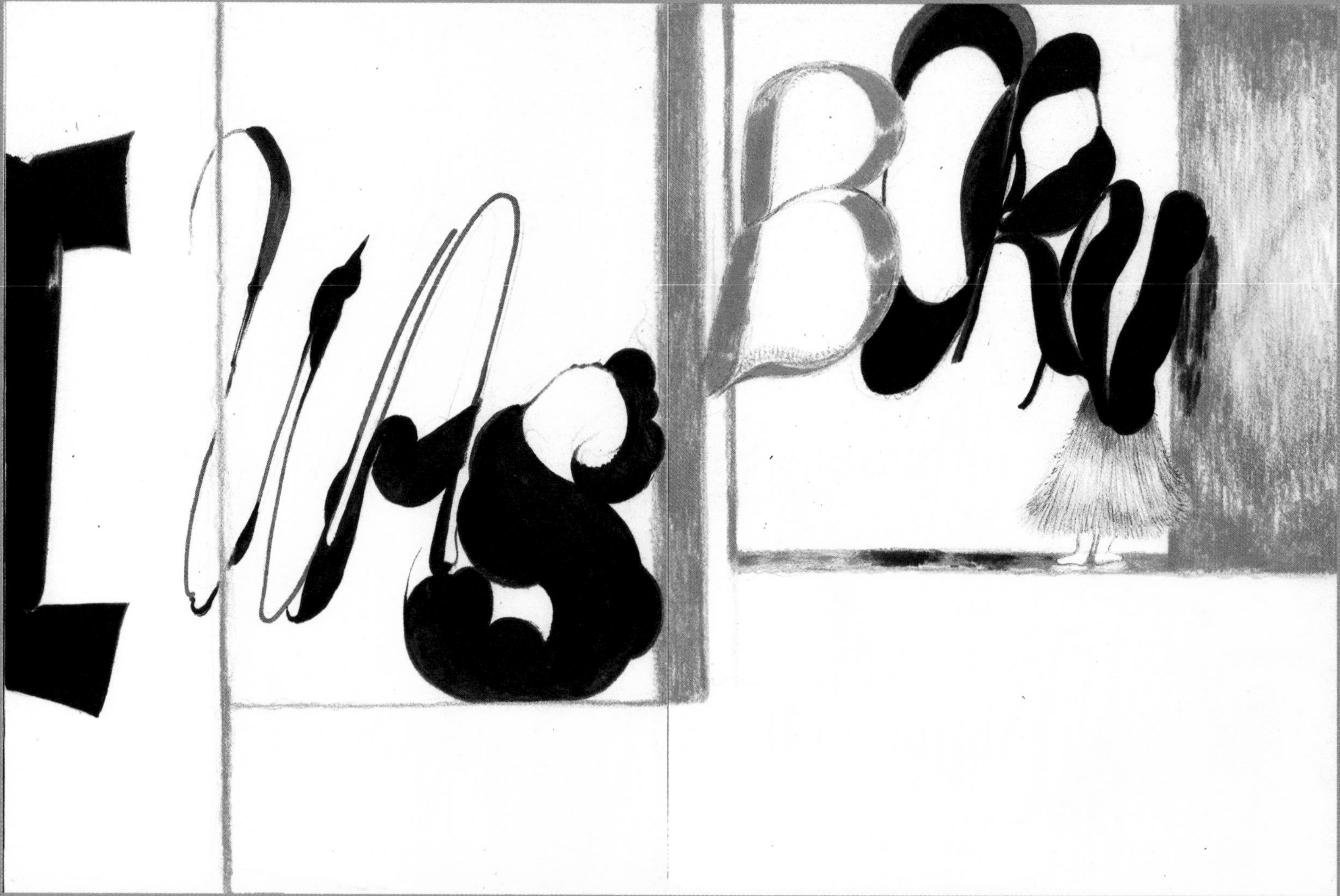
I was born

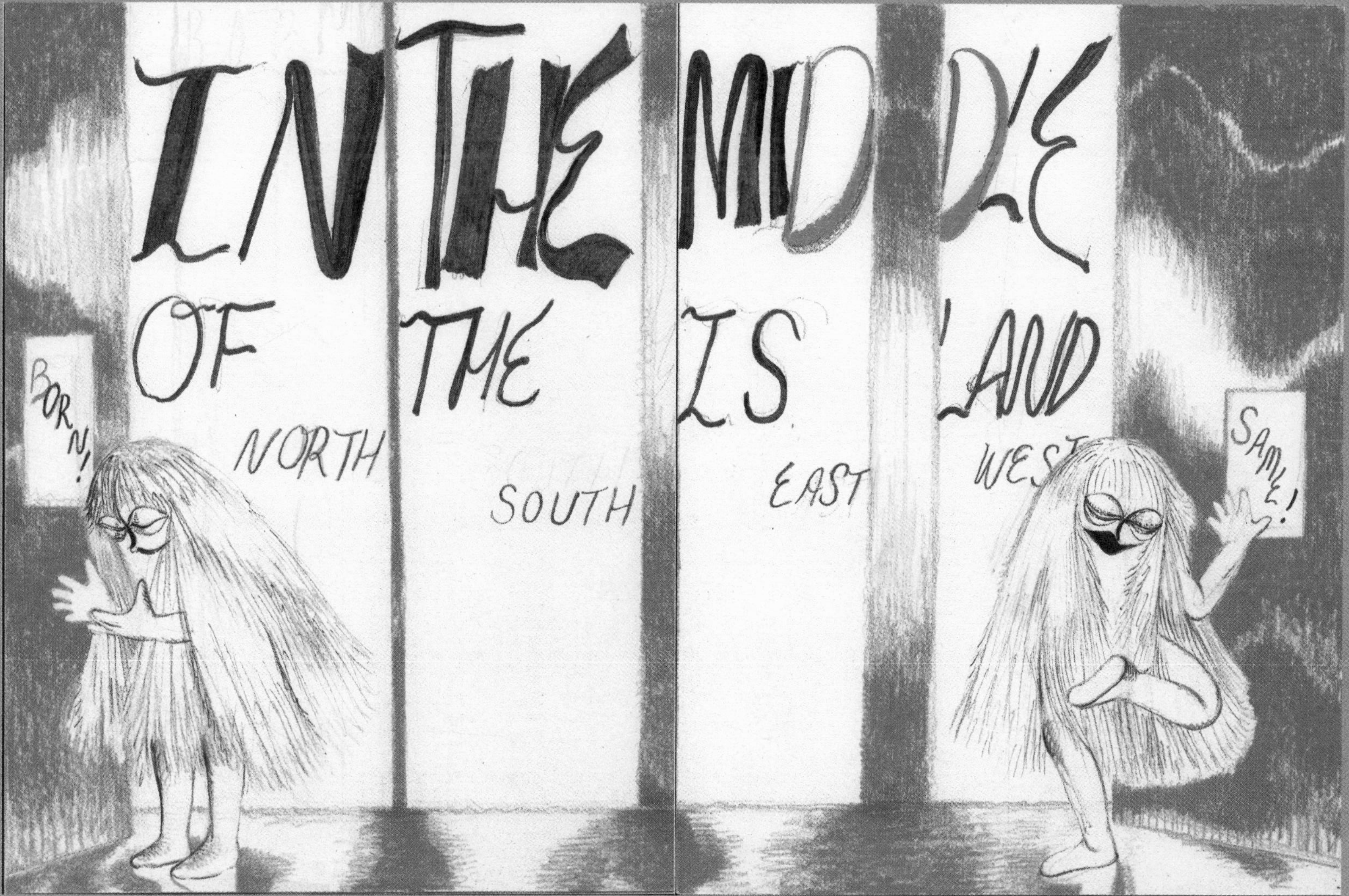
IN THE MIDDLE
OF THE ISLAND
BORN!
NORTH
SOUTH
EAST
WEST
SAME!

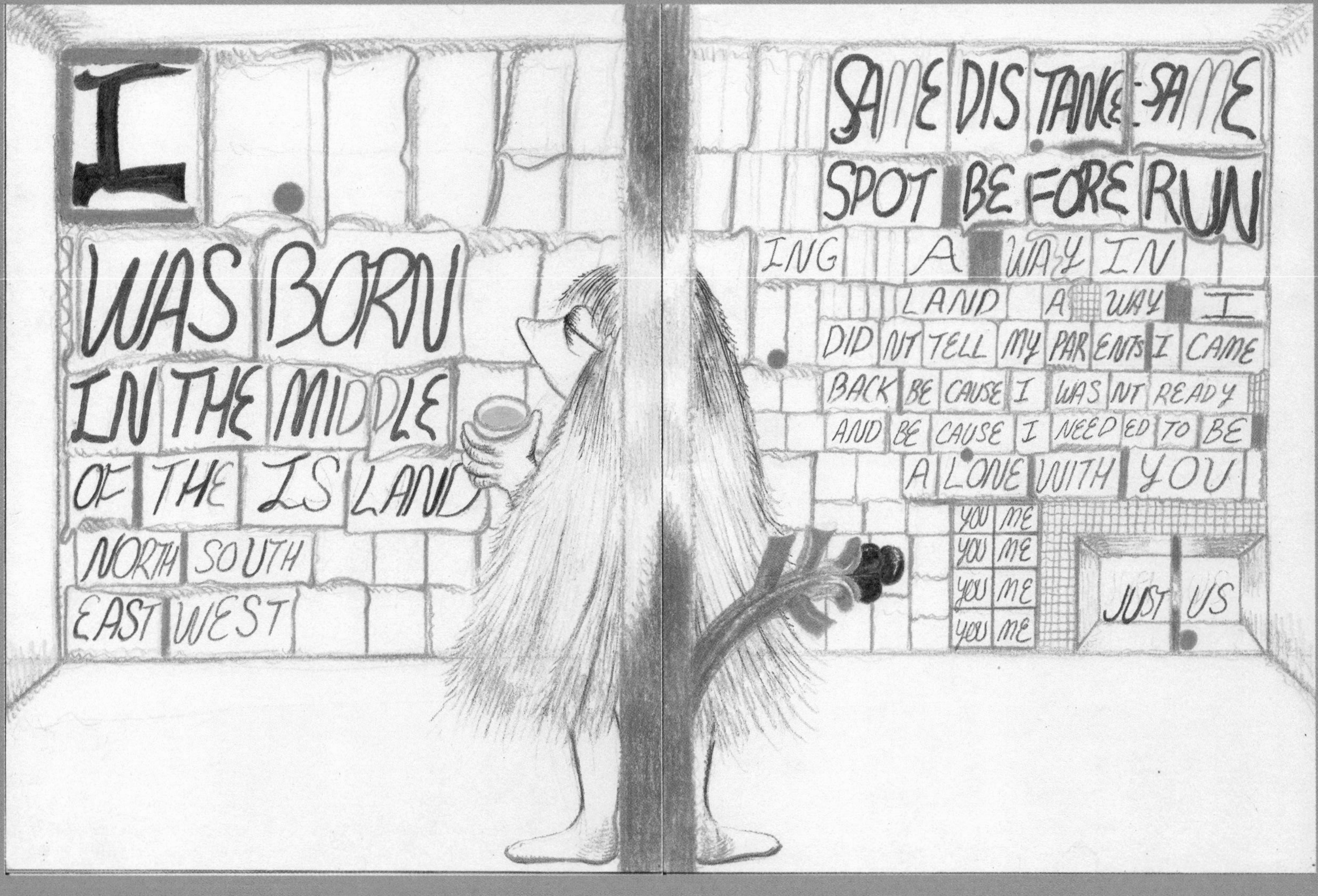
I
WAS BORN
IN THE MIDDLE
OF THE IS LAND
NORTH SOUTH
EAST WEST
SAME DIS TANCE SAME
SPOT BE FORE RUN
ING A WAY IN
LAND A WAY I
DID NT TELL MY PAR ENTS I CAME
BACK BE CAUSE I WAS NT READY
AND BE CAUSE I NEED ED TO BE
A LONE WITH YOU
YOU ME
YOU ME
YOU ME
YOU ME
JUST US

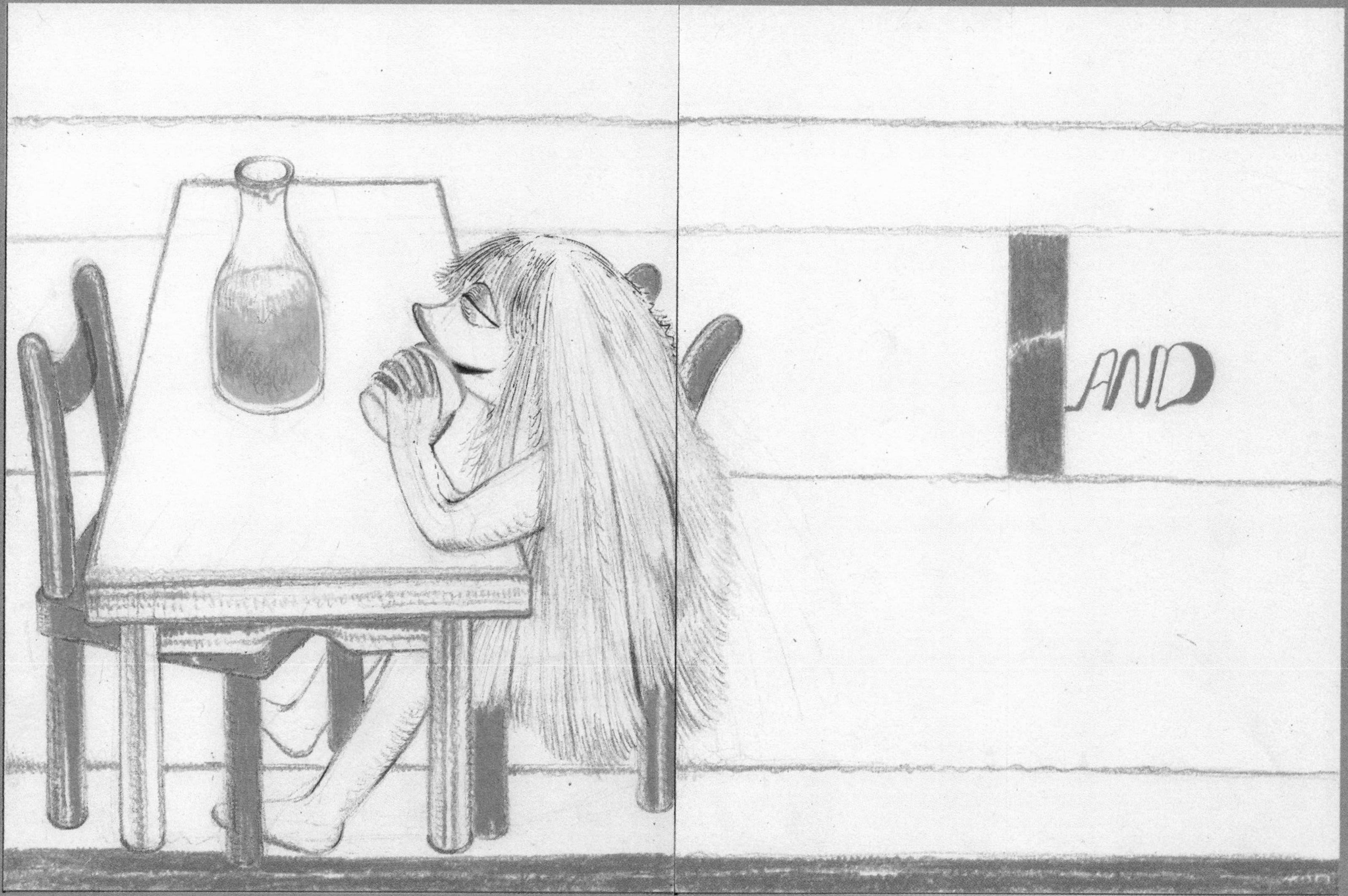
AND

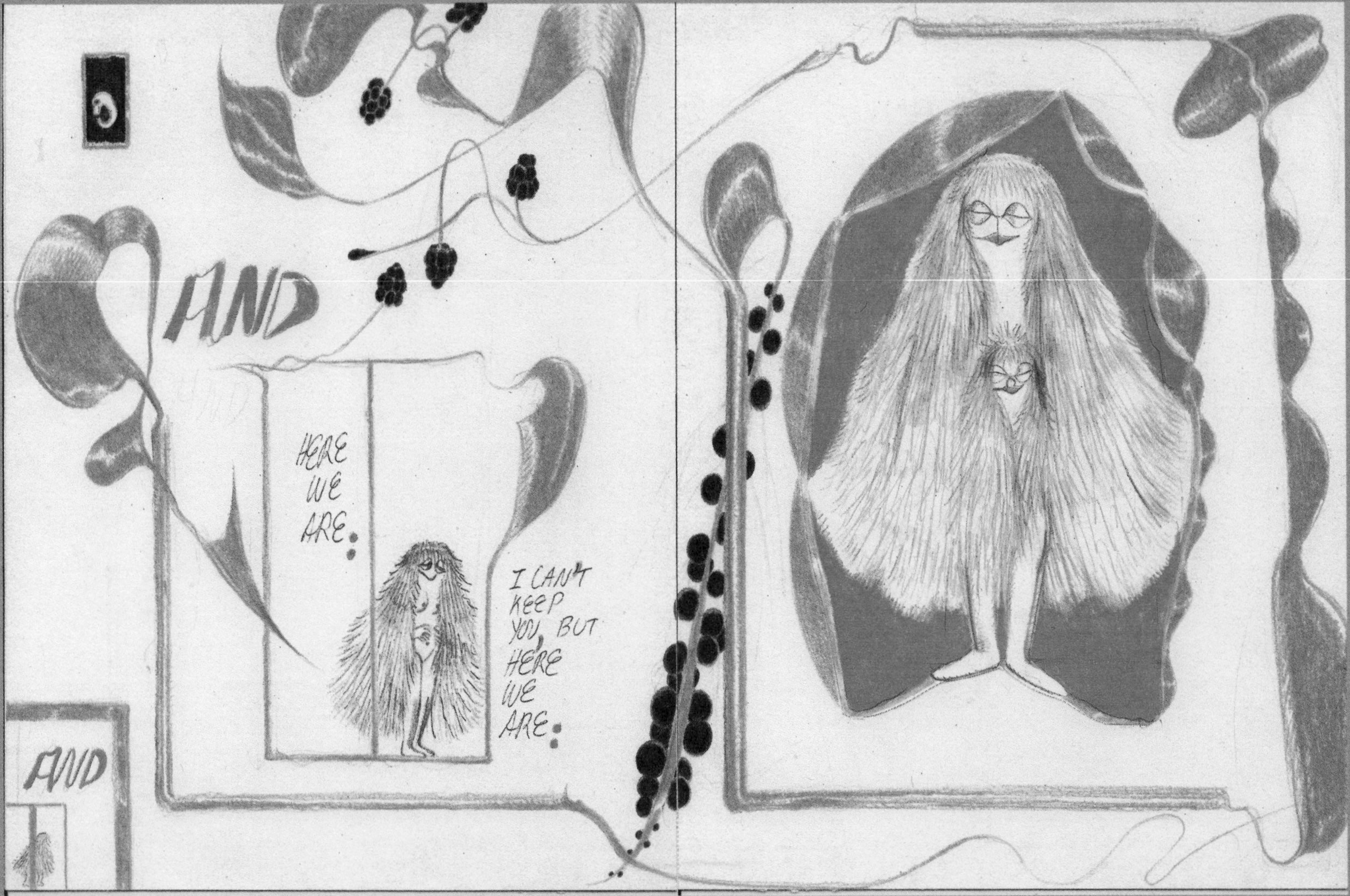

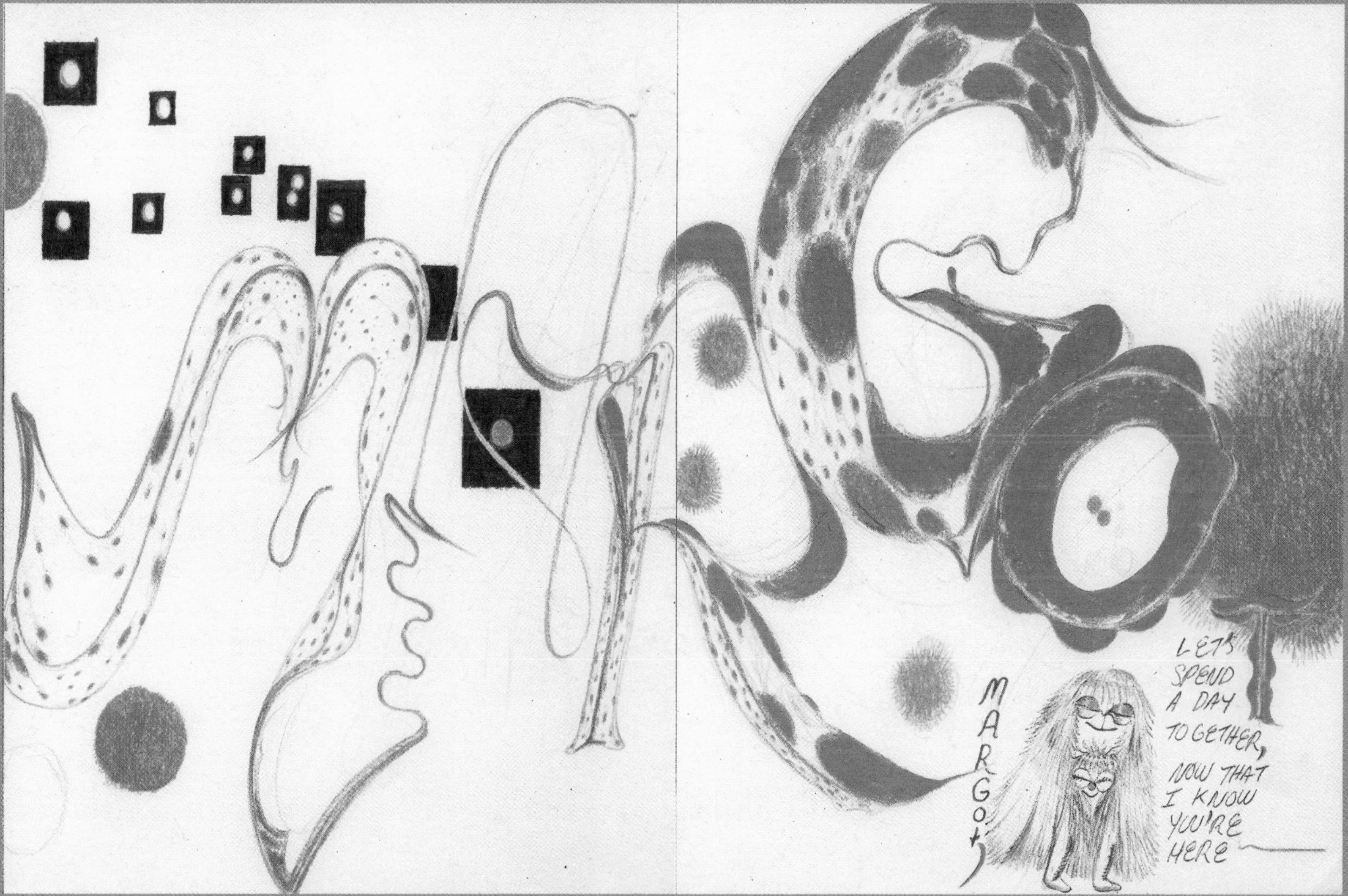
MARGOT
LET'S SPEND A DAY TOGETHER, NOW THAT I KNOW YOU'RE HERE

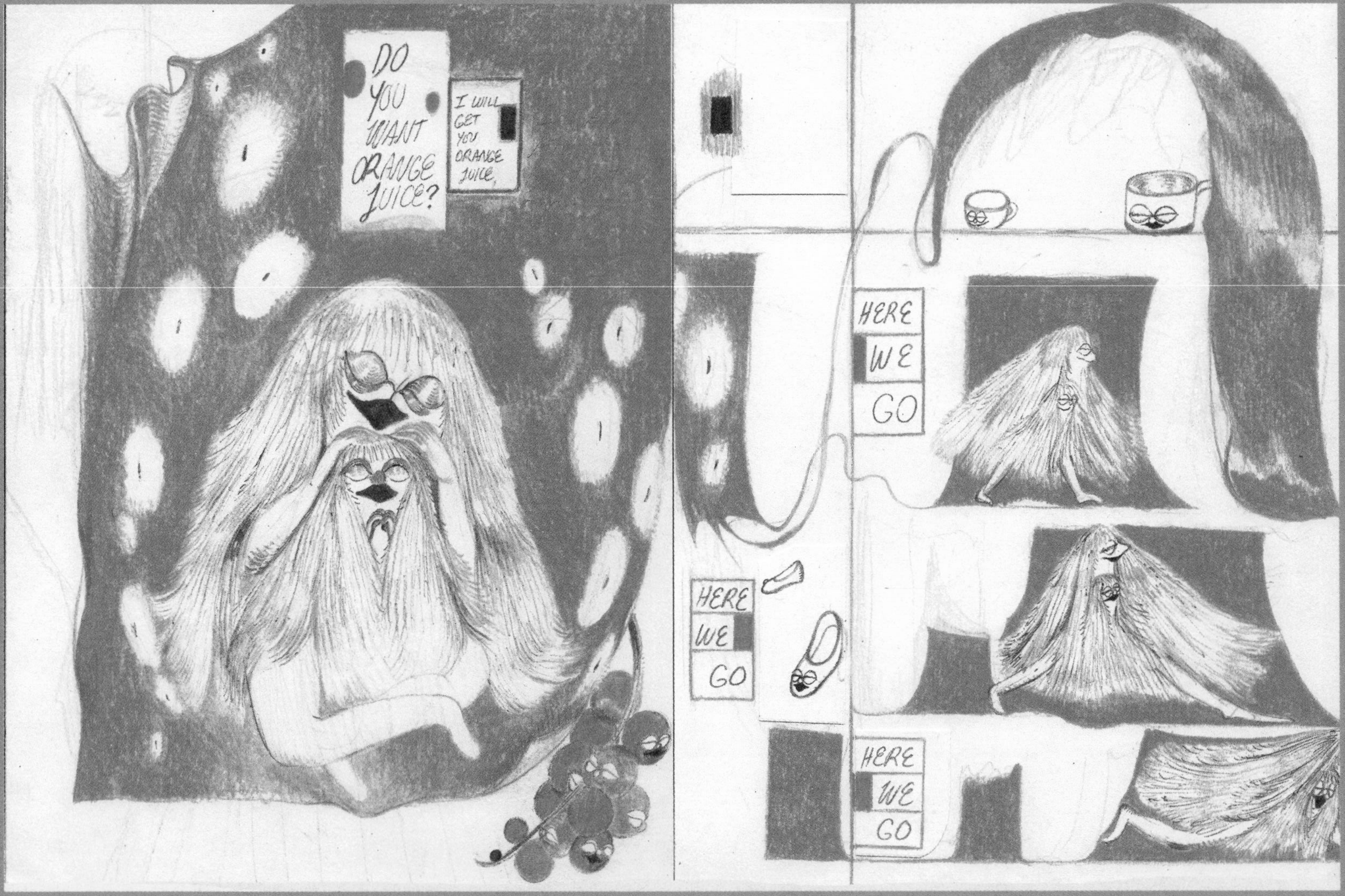
DO YOU WANT ORANGE JUICE?
I WILL GET YOU ORANGE JUICE,
HERE WE GO
HERE WE GO
HERE WE GO

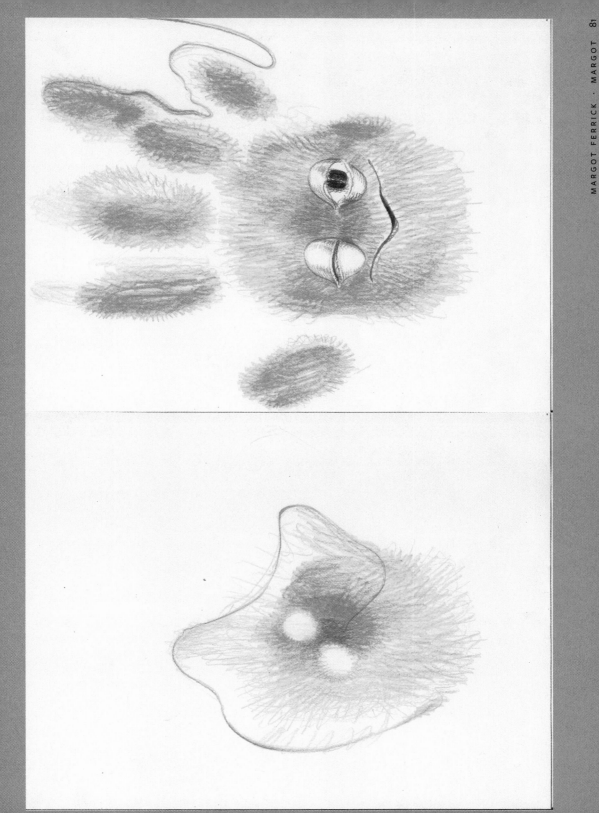

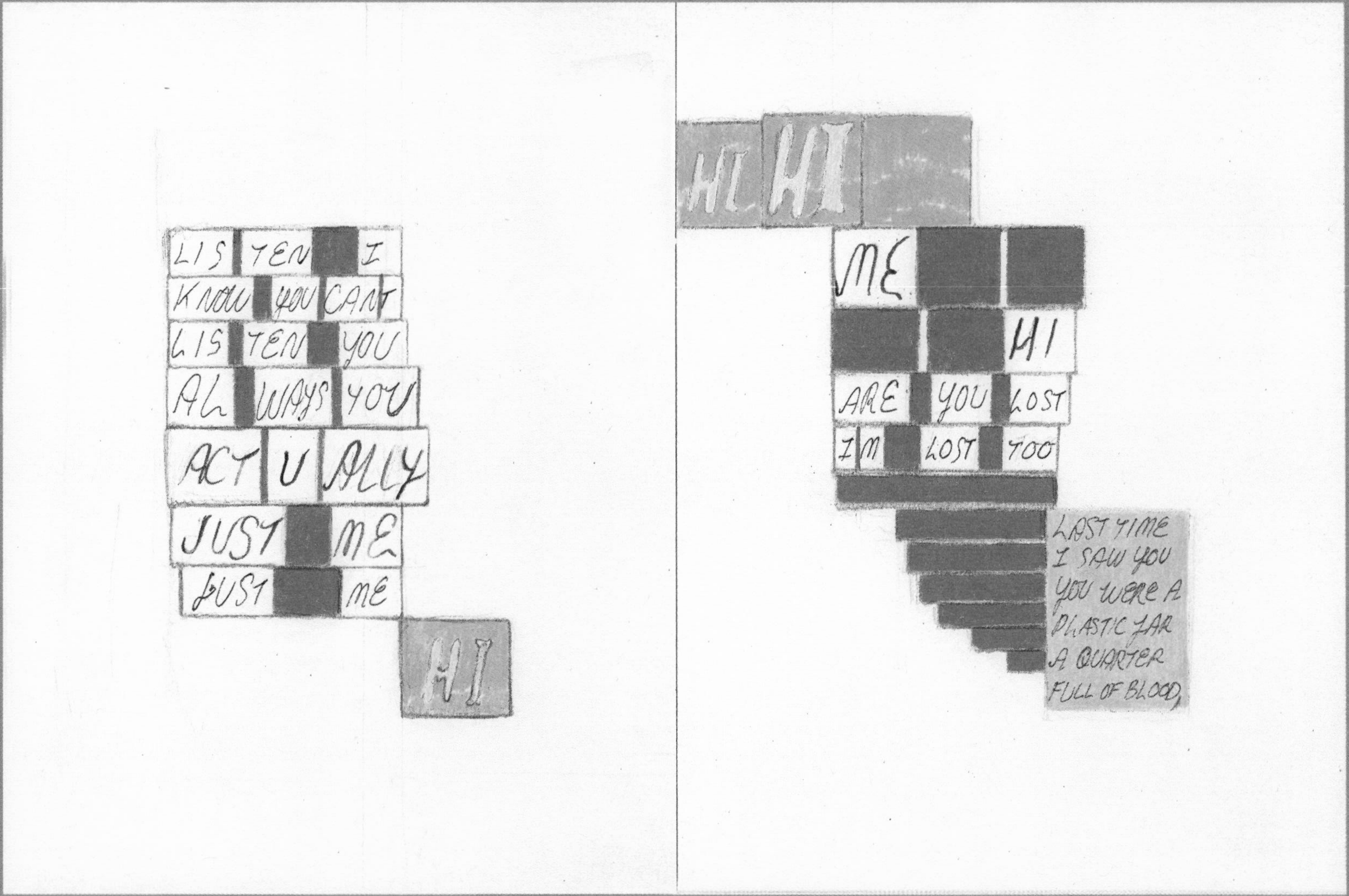
LIS TEN I
KNOW YOU CANT
LIS TEN YOU
AL WAYS YOU
ACT U ALLY
JUST ME
JUST ME
HI
HI HI
ME
HI
ARE YOU LOST
I M LOST TOO
LAST TIME
I SAW YOU
YOU WERE A
PLASTIC JAR
A QUARTER
FULL OF BLOOD,

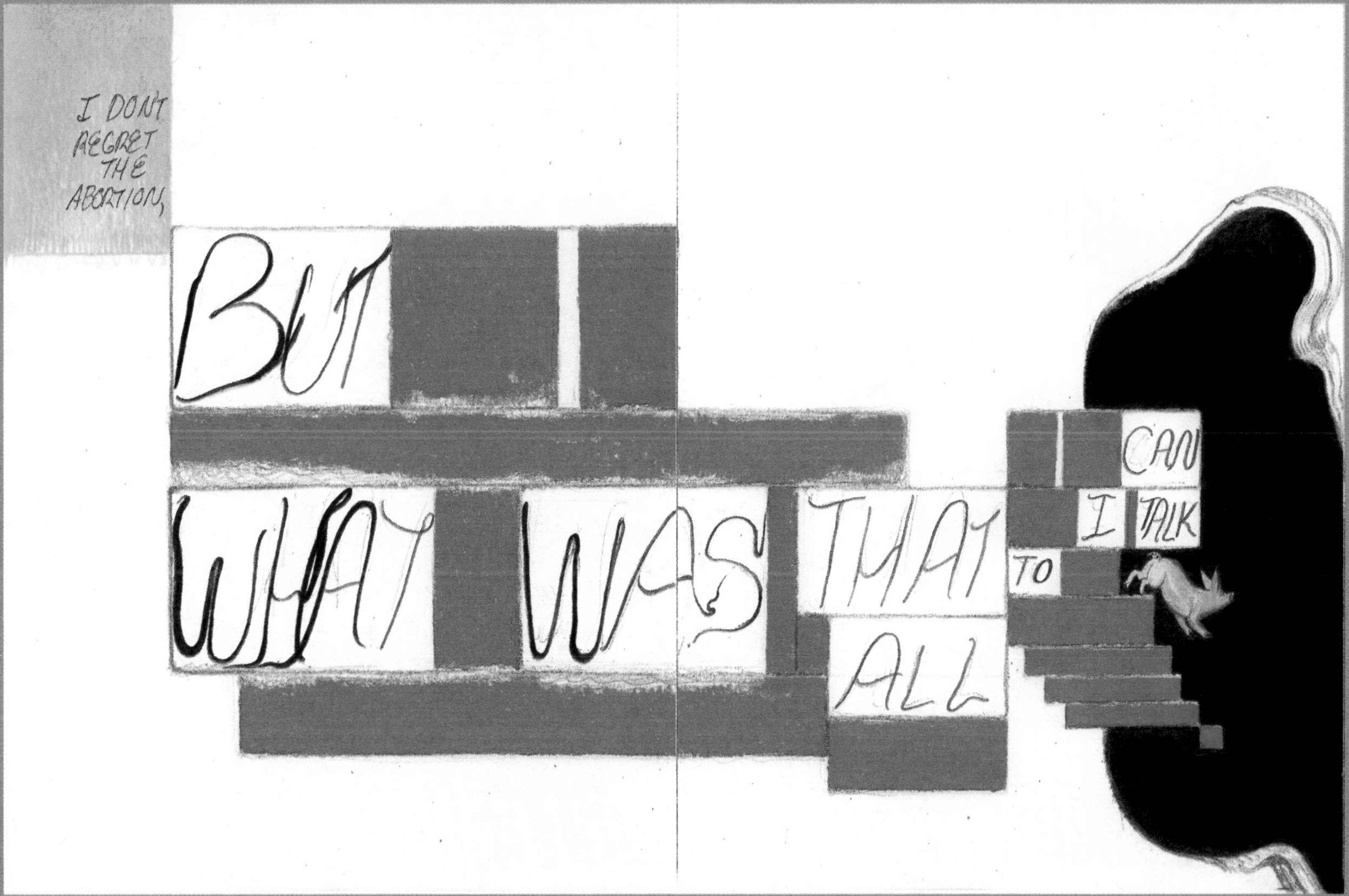
I DONT REGRET THE ABORTION,
BUT
WHAT WAS THAT ALL
CAN I TALK TO

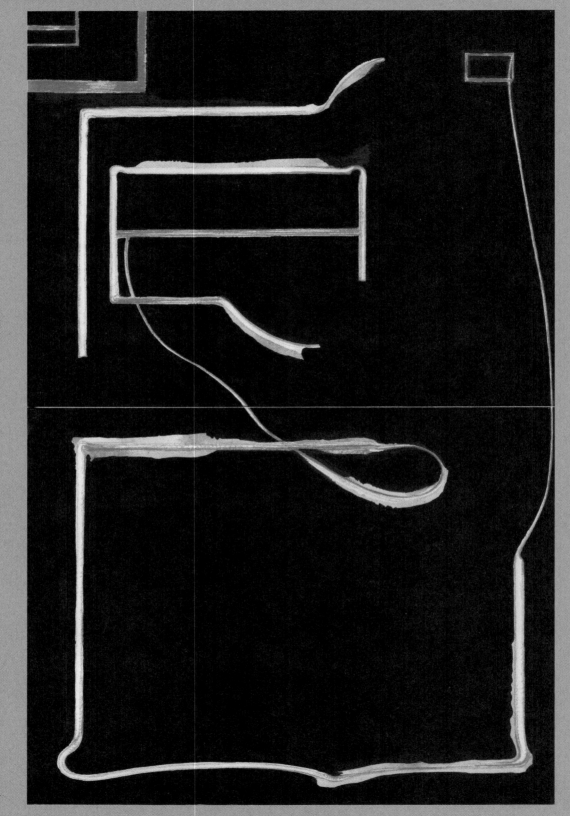

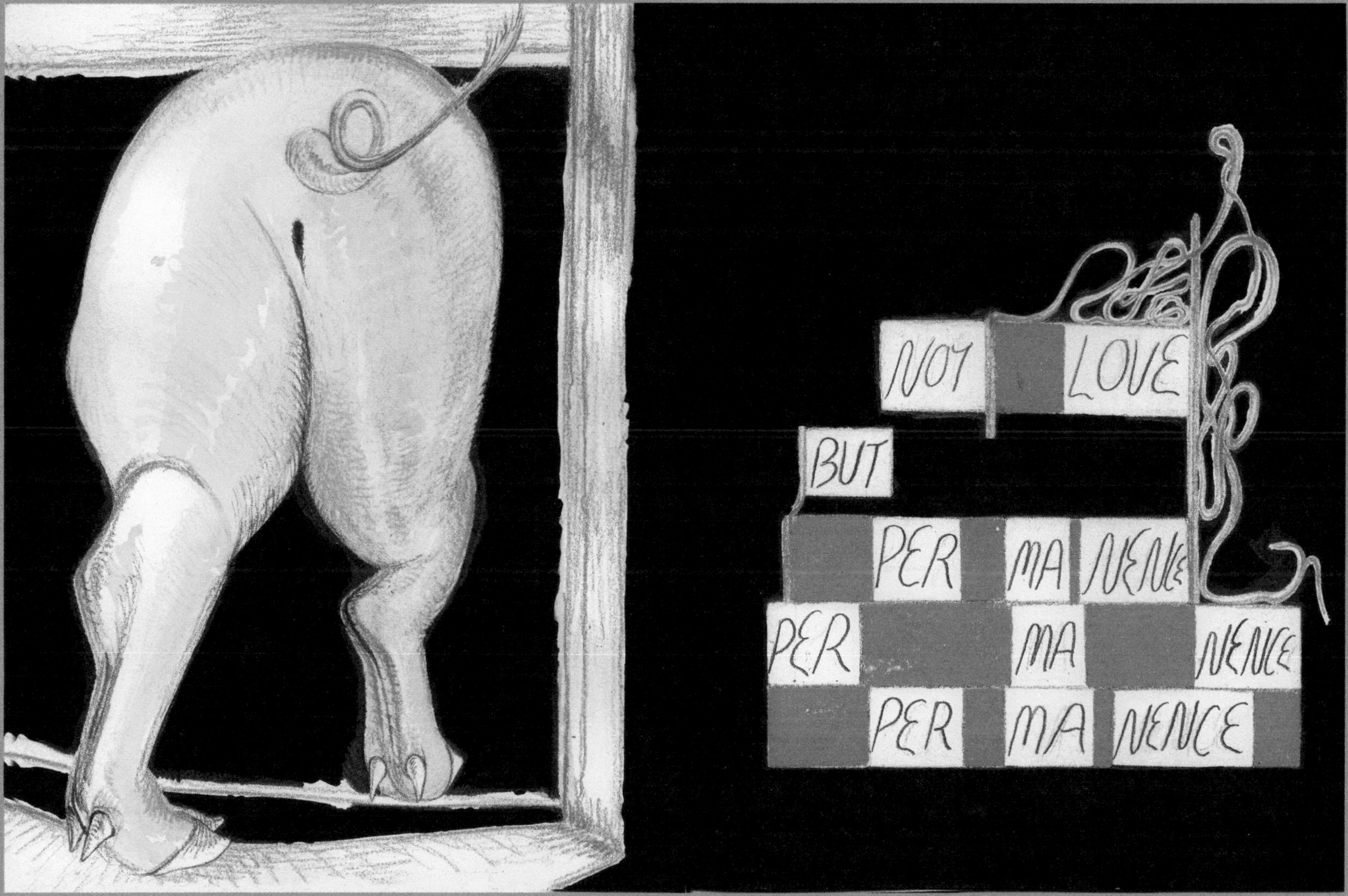
NOT LOVE
BUT
PER MA NENCE
PER MA NENCE
PER MA NENCE

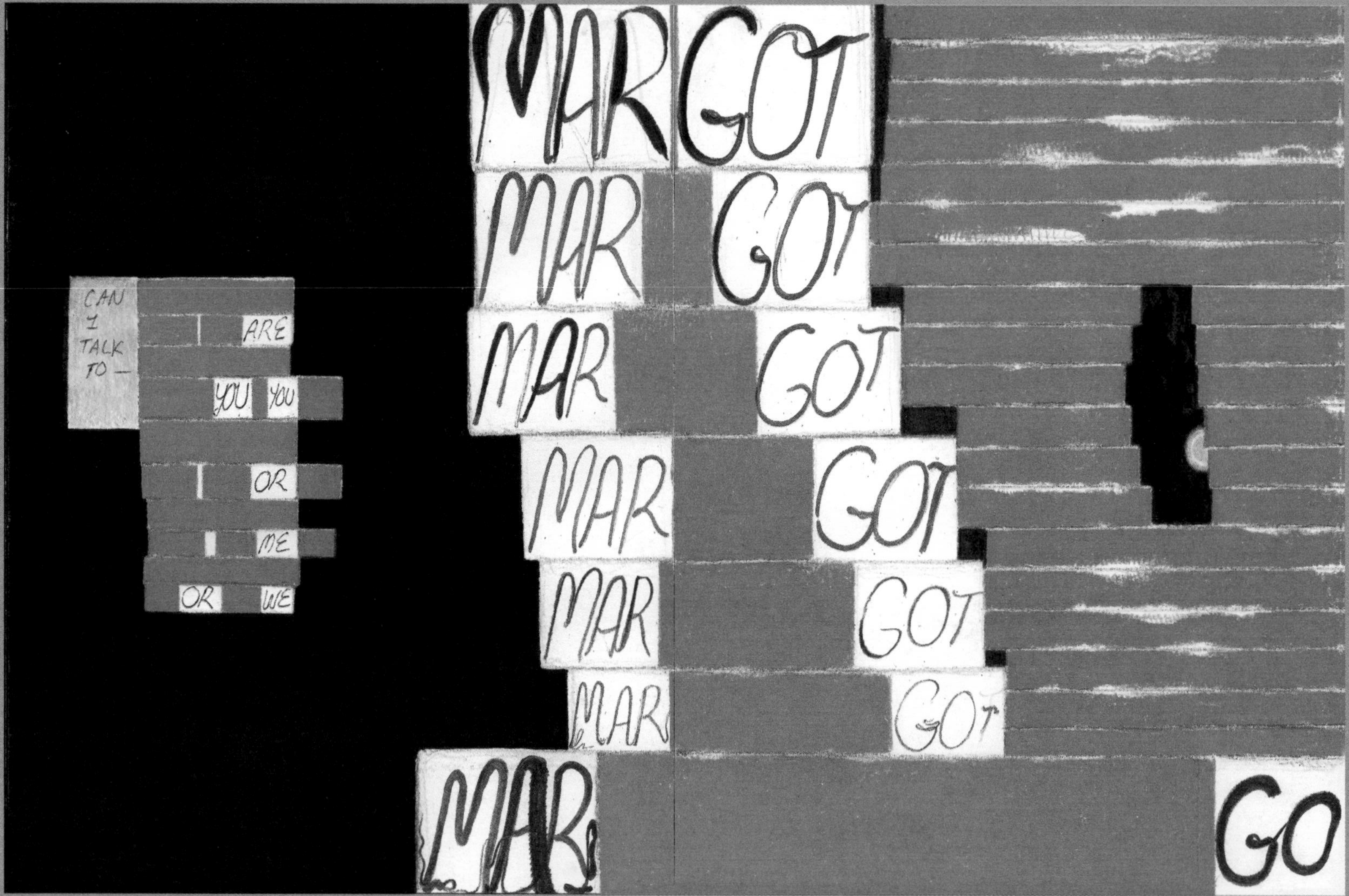
CAN I TALK TO —
ARE
YOU YOU
OR
ME
OR WE
MARGOT
MAR GOT
MAR GOT
MAR GOT
MAR GOT
MAR GOT
MAR GO

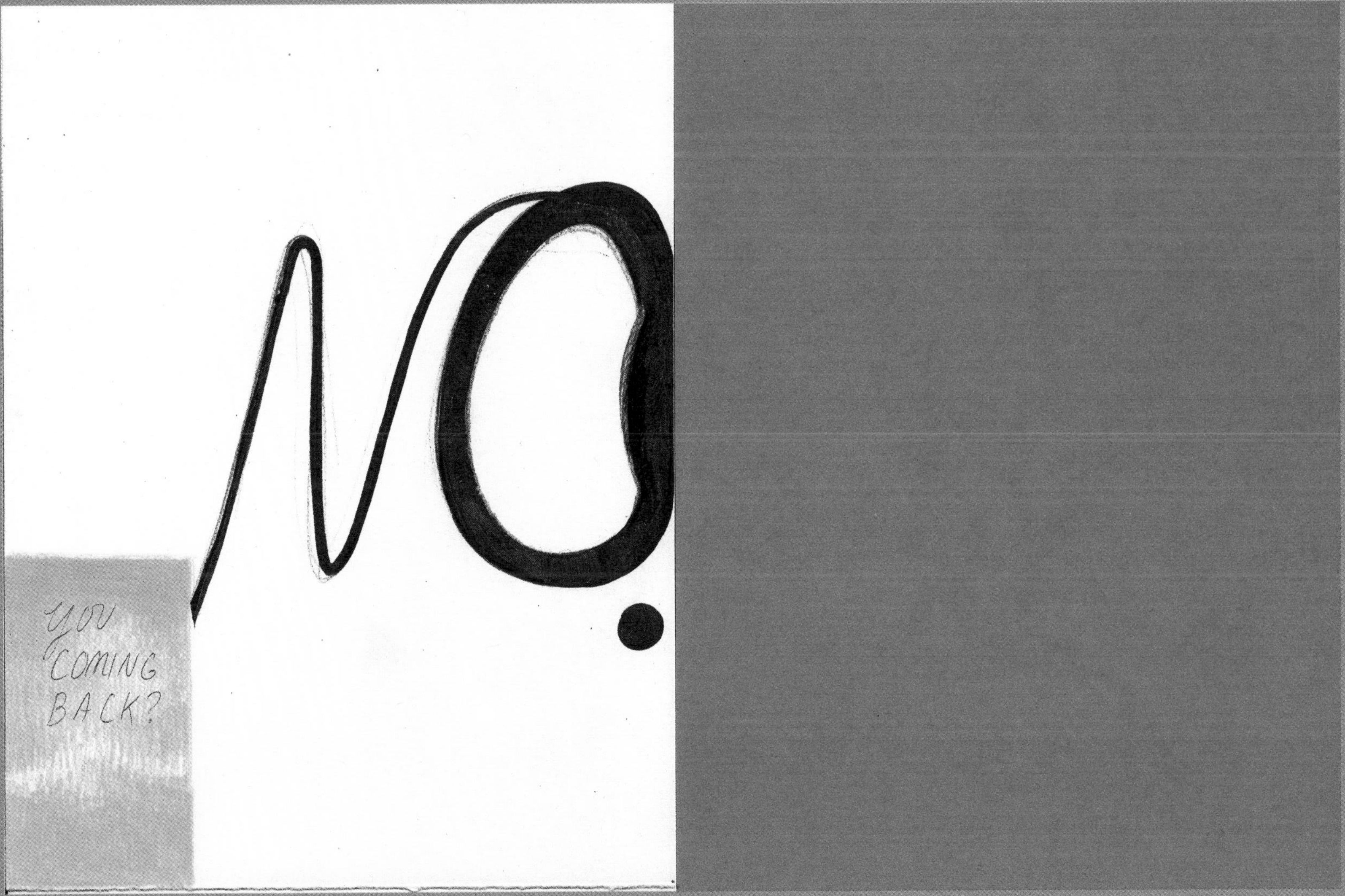
YOU COMING BACK?

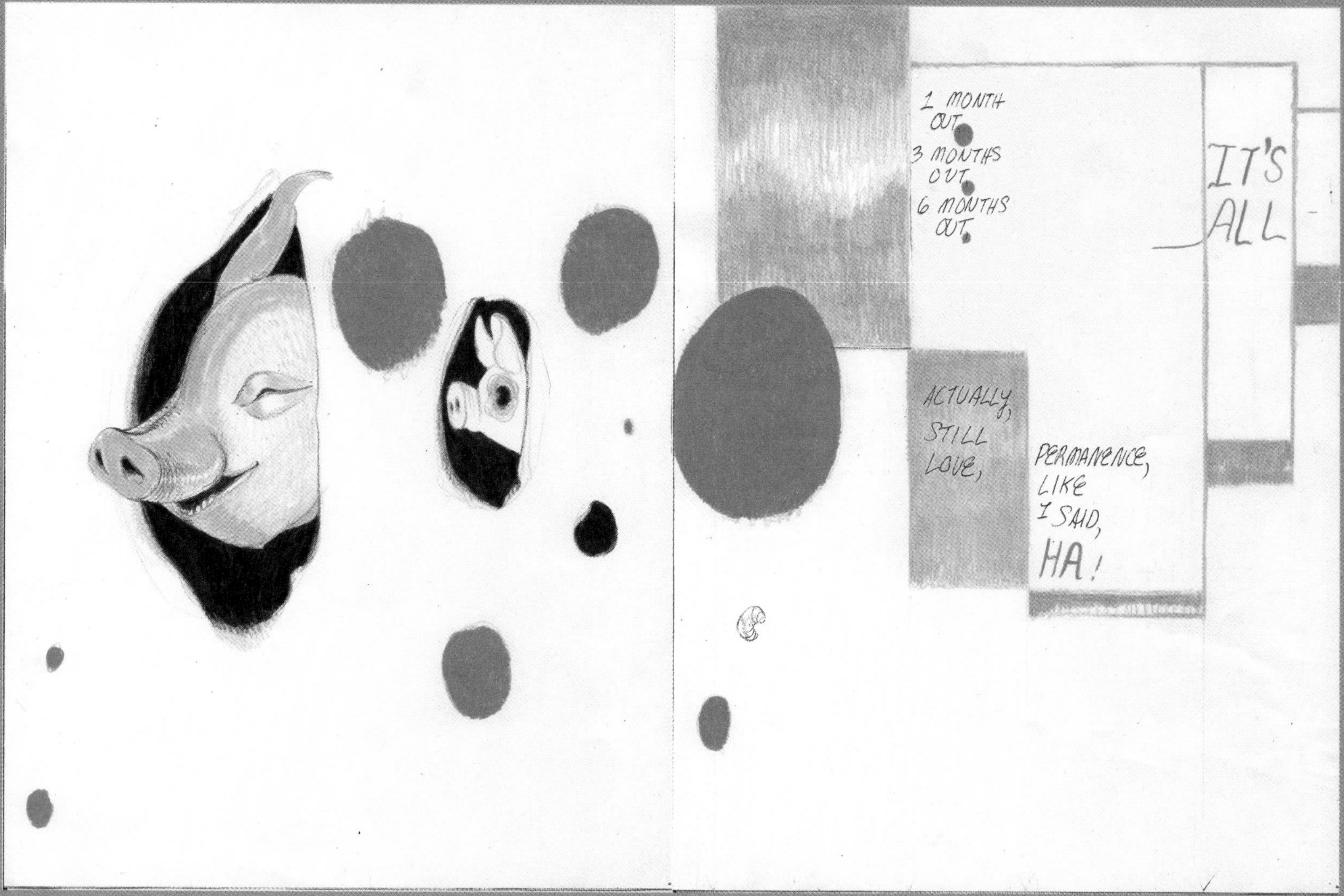
1 MONTH OUT,
3 MONTHS OUT,
6 MONTHS OUT,
IT'S ALL
ACTUALLY, STILL LOVE,
PERMANENCE, LIKE I SAID, HA!

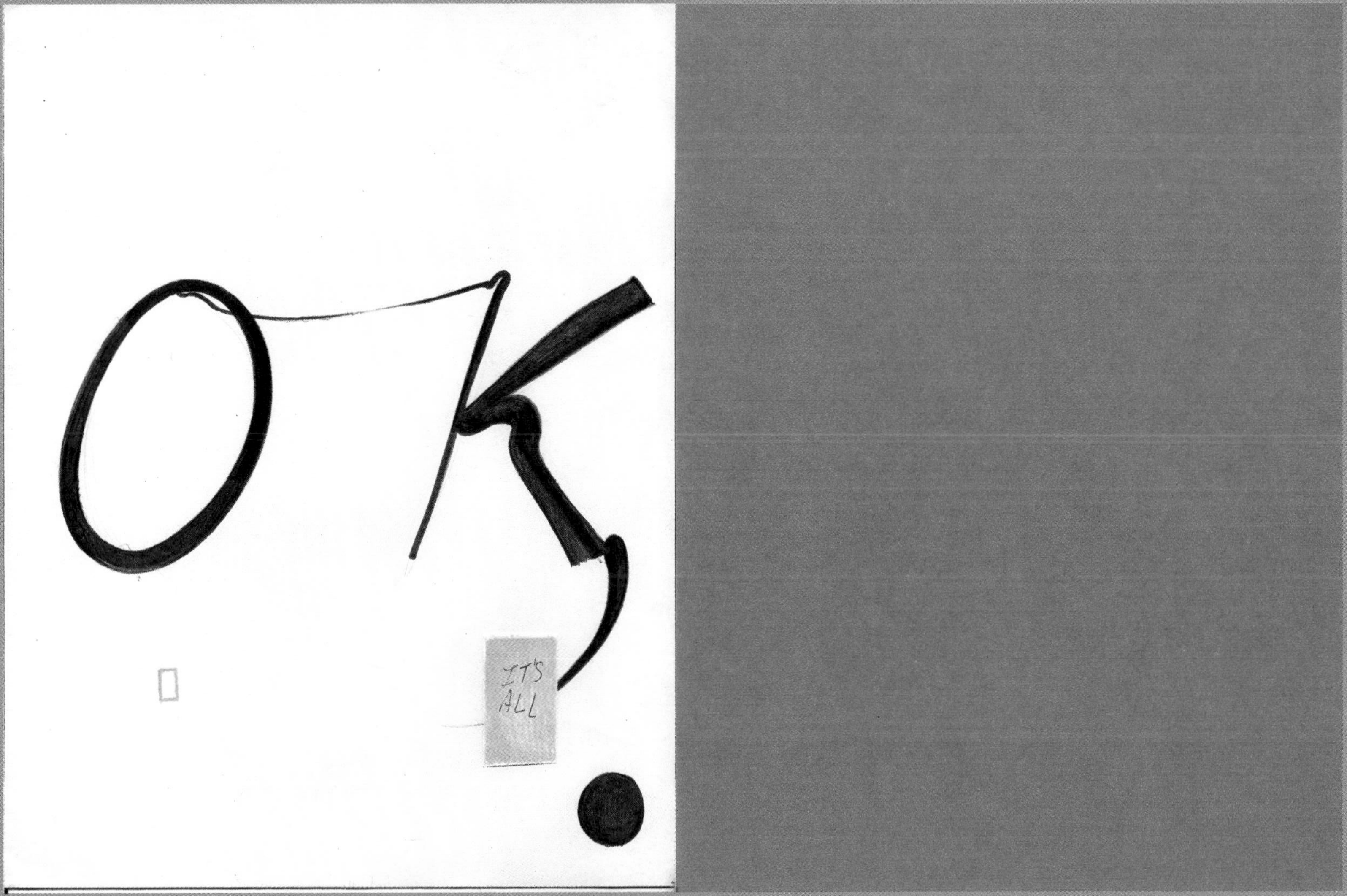
OK.
IT'S
ALL

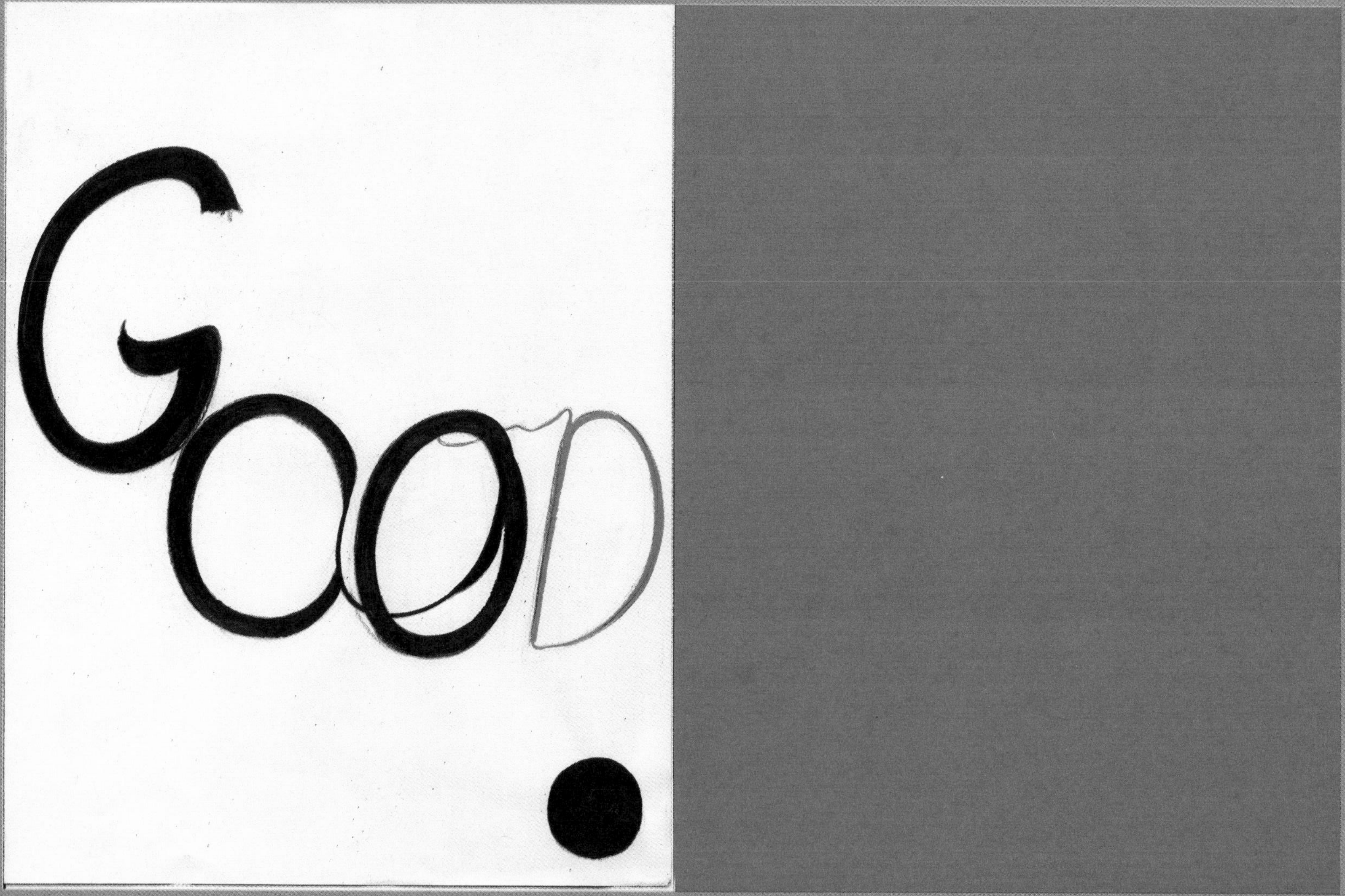
GOOD.

My Favorite Thing Is Monsters, Book 1 (*Excerpt*)

EMIL FERRIS

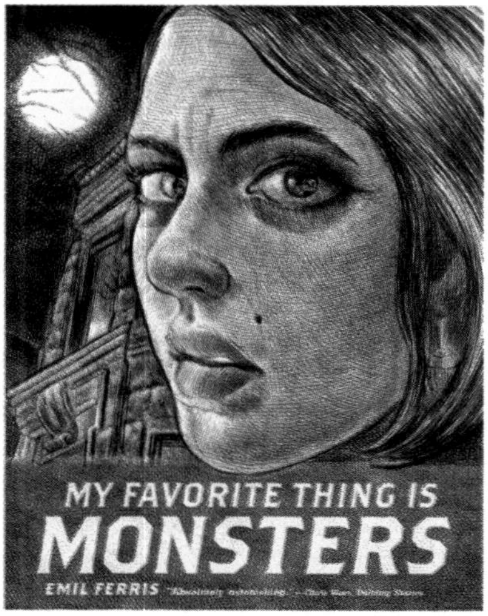
MY FAVORITE THING IS
MONSTERS
EMIL FERRIS

originally published in

My Favorite Thing Is Monsters, Book 1

FANTAGRAPHICS BOOKS
8.75 x 11 inches • 386 pages

Biography

Emil Ferris grew up in Chicago during the turbulent 1960s and is consequently a devotee of all things monstrous and horrific. She has an MFA from the Art Institute of Chicago. In a previous life, Ferris was an illustrator and toy sculptor for a diverse range of clients. In 2010, Ferris was made a Toby Devan Lewis Fellow in the Visual Arts. *My Favorite Thing Is Monsters* is Emil's first, but not last, graphic novel.
emilferris.com

Statement

When the Villagers realize that the Good Monster isn't hiding at The Old Mill or in the churchyard, but that the Good Monster is hiding right within them—right within their own souls—the Villagers will refuse to do the bidding of Bad Monsters (the order-giving power-hungry). When the Villagers refuse to fearfully brutalize other creatures, EVERYTHING WONDERFUL IS POSSIBLE. Instead of shame-based mob action, the Villagers will use their torches and pitchforks to find their way back to the place where they left themselves and their Imagination and their Empathy. I believe that this must happen NOW because our planet is sick. Despite Fiction's maddening bag-lady penchant for wearing both stripes and florals, a parka, a raincoat, and goggles, she is the most Sacred Truth we've got. I believe that Imagination, Stories, and, yes, MONSTERS ARE all IMPORTANT parts of the MAGICK we will need to heal ourselves and our planet.

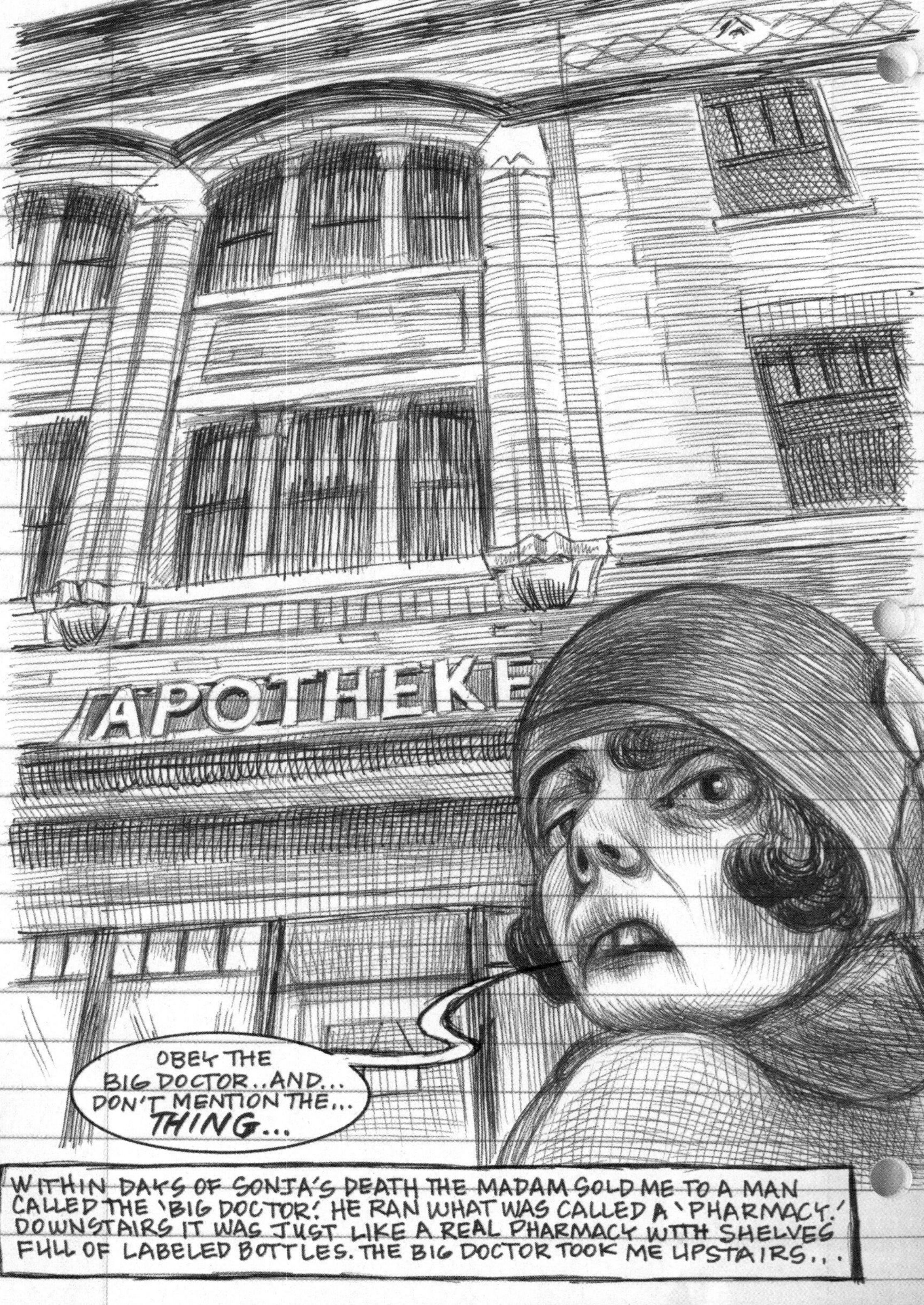
APOTHEKE
OBEY THE BIG DOCTOR.. AND... DON'T MENTION THE... THING...
WITHIN DAYS OF SONJA'S DEATH THE MADAM SOLD ME TO A MAN CALLED THE 'BIG DOCTOR.' HE RAN WHAT WAS CALLED A 'PHARMACY.' DOWNSTAIRS IT WAS JUST LIKE A REAL PHARMACY WITH SHELVES FULL OF LABELED BOTTLES. THE BIG DOCTOR TOOK ME UPSTAIRS...

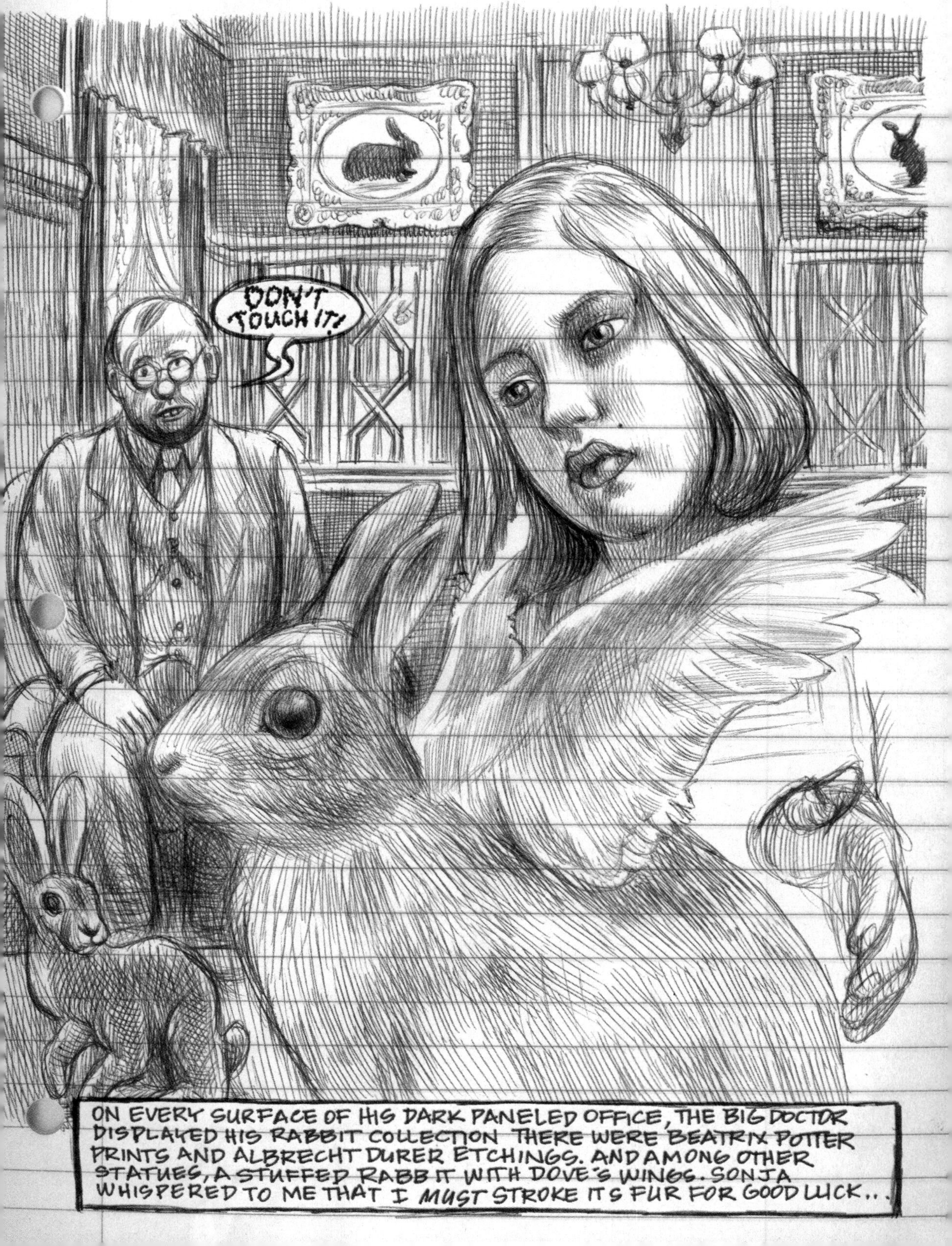
DON'T TOUCH IT!
ON EVERY SURFACE OF HIS DARK PANELED OFFICE, THE BIG DOCTOR DISPLAYED HIS RABBIT COLLECTION. THERE WERE BEATRIX POTTER PRINTS AND ALBRECHT DURER ETCHINGS. AND AMONG OTHER STATUES, A STUFFED RABBIT WITH DOVE'S WINGS. SONJA WHISPERED TO ME THAT I MUST STROKE ITS FUR FOR GOOD LUCK...

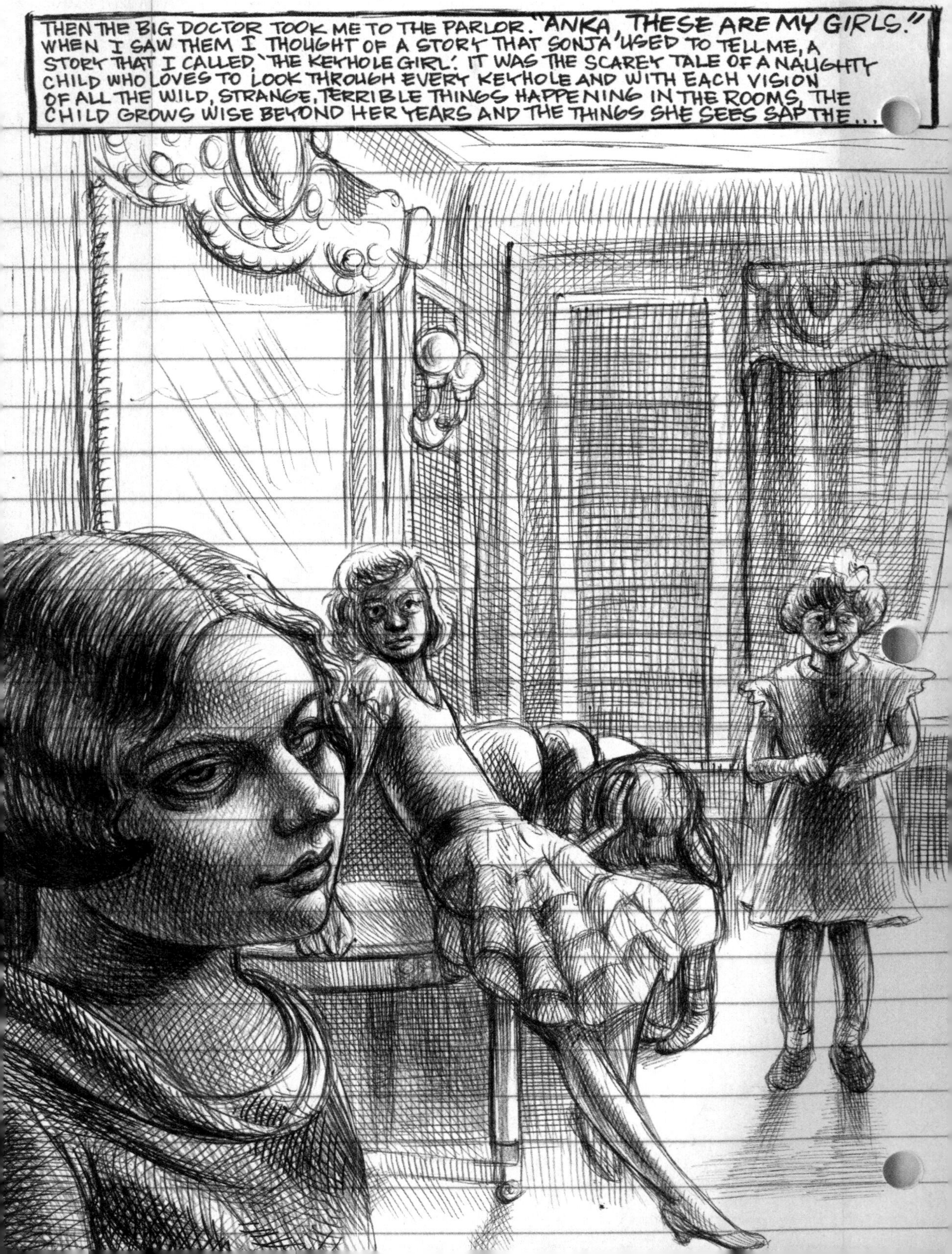
THEN THE BIG DOCTOR TOOK ME TO THE PARLOR. "ANKA, THESE ARE MY GIRLS." WHEN I SAW THEM I THOUGHT OF A STORY THAT SONJA USED TO TELL ME, A STORY THAT I CALLED, 'THE KEYHOLE GIRL.' IT WAS THE SCAREY TALE OF A NAUGHTY CHILD WHO LOVES TO LOOK THROUGH EVERY KEYHOLE AND WITH EACH VISION OF ALL THE WILD, STRANGE, TERRIBLE THINGS HAPPENING IN THE ROOMS, THE CHILD GROWS WISE BEYOND HER YEARS AND THE THINGS SHE SEES SAP THE...

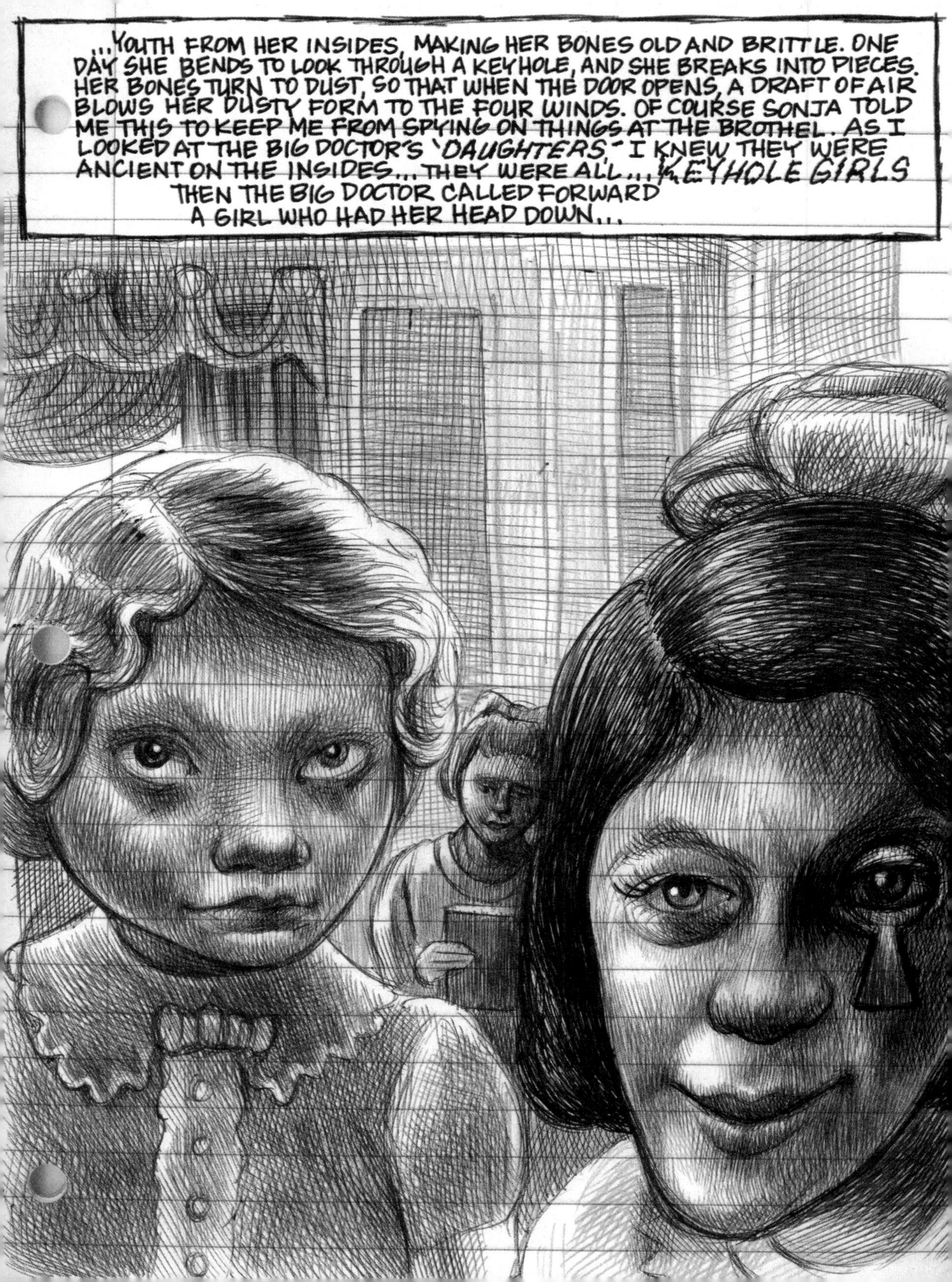
...YOUTH FROM HER INSIDES, MAKING HER BONES OLD AND BRITTLE. ONE DAY SHE BENDS TO LOOK THROUGH A KEYHOLE, AND SHE BREAKS INTO PIECES. HER BONES TURN TO DUST, SO THAT WHEN THE DOOR OPENS, A DRAFT OF AIR BLOWS HER DUSTY FORM TO THE FOUR WINDS. OF COURSE SONJA TOLD ME THIS TO KEEP ME FROM SPYING ON THINGS AT THE BROTHEL. AS I LOOKED AT THE BIG DOCTOR'S "DAUGHTERS," I KNEW THEY WERE ANCIENT ON THE INSIDES... THEY WERE ALL... KEYHOLE GIRLS
THEN THE BIG DOCTOR CALLED FORWARD A GIRL WHO HAD HER HEAD DOWN...

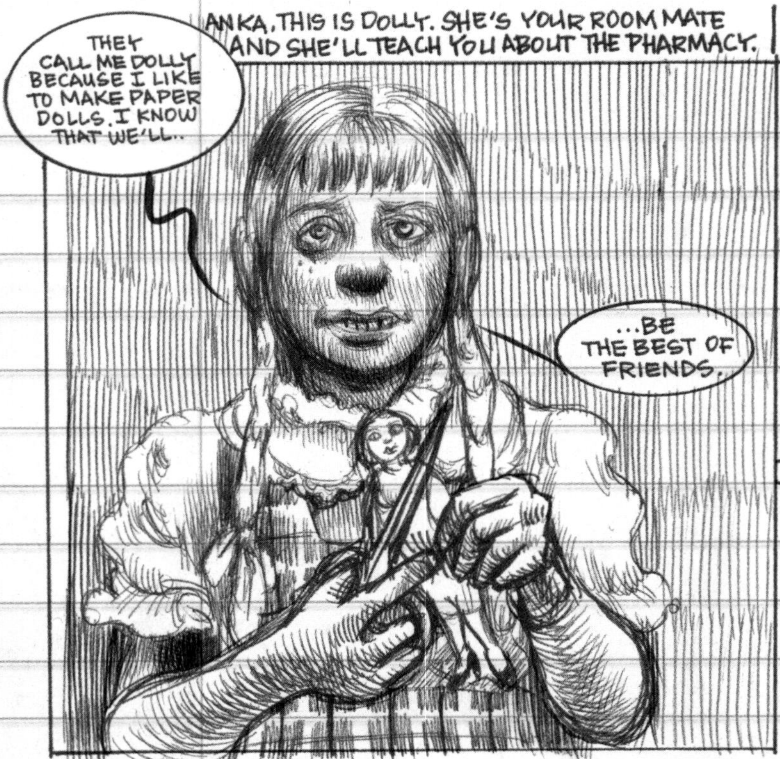
ANKA, THIS IS DOLLY. SHE'S YOUR ROOM MATE AND SHE'LL TEACH YOU ABOUT THE PHARMACY.
THEY CALL ME DOLLY BECAUSE I LIKE TO MAKE PAPER DOLLS. I KNOW THAT WE'LL..
...BE THE BEST OF FRIENDS.

I ASKED DOLLY WHEN I WAS GOING TO BE TRAINED TO WORK IN THE PHARMACY. SHE TOLD ME THAT IN HONOR OF MY ARRIVAL THE PHARMACY WAS CLOSED FOR THE DAY.

I REMEMBER THAT AT FIRST WE WENT TO THE PARLOR AND CUT OUT THE CLOTHES FOR PAPER DOLLS FROM THE ADVERTISEMENTS FOR WOMEN'S CLOTHING. AFTER THAT WE PLAYED HIDE AND SEEK WITH SOME OF THE OTHER GIRLS.
DOLLY TOOK ME TO THE THIRD FLOOR. SHE SAID THAT THERE WERE GOOD HIDING PLACES UP THERE.

SITTING IN A CHAIR IN THE HALL THERE WAS A CRYING WOMAN. DOLLY SAID THAT WE WERE FORBIDDEN FROM TALKING TO ANY STRANGERS WE MIGHT SEE ON THE THIRD FLOOR... JUST THEN A MAN CAME OUT OF ONE OF THE DOORS. DOLLY SEEMED SCARED.

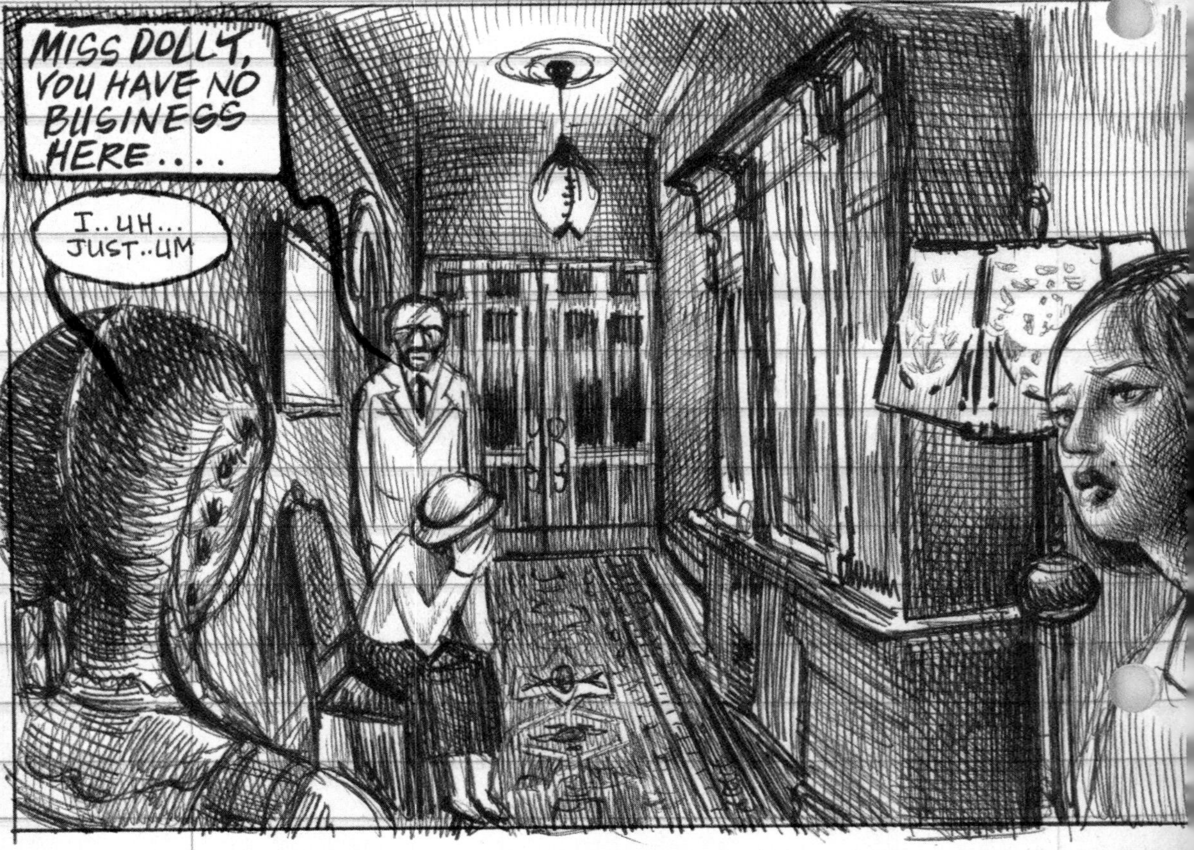
MISS DOLLY, YOU HAVE NO BUSINESS HERE....
I.. UH... JUST.. UM

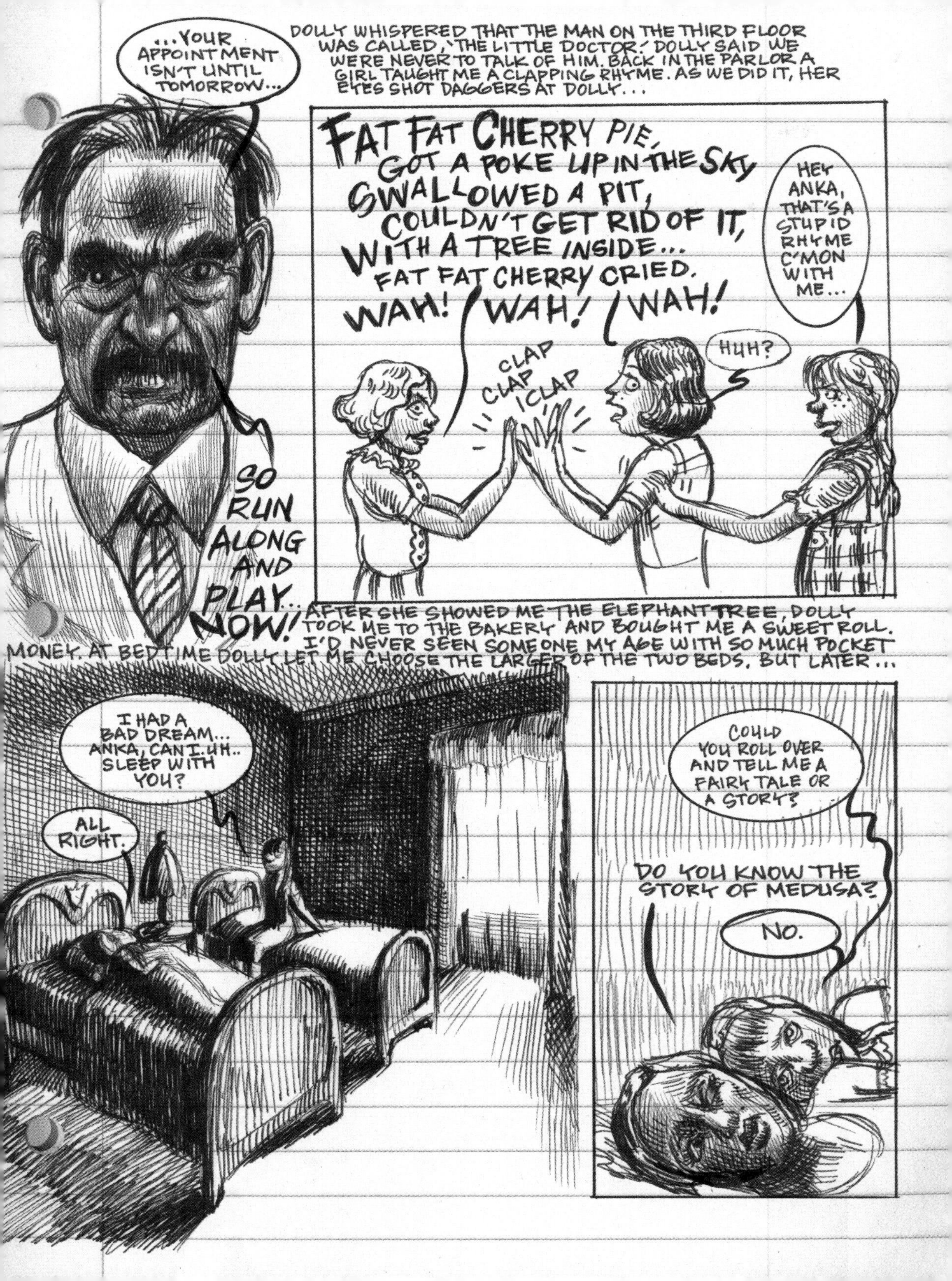
...YOUR APPOINTMENT ISN'T UNTIL TOMORROW...
DOLLY WHISPERED THAT THE MAN ON THE THIRD FLOOR WAS CALLED, 'THE LITTLE DOCTOR.' DOLLY SAID WE WERE NEVER TO TALK OF HIM. BACK IN THE PARLOR A GIRL TAUGHT ME A CLAPPING RHYME. AS WE DID IT, HER EYES SHOT DAGGERS AT DOLLY...
FAT FAT CHERRY PIE, GOT A POKE UP IN THE SKY SWALLOWED A PIT, COULDN'T GET RID OF IT, WITH A TREE INSIDE... FAT FAT CHERRY CRIED.
WAH! WAH! WAH!
CLAP CLAP CLAP
HEY ANKA, THAT'S A STUPID RHYME C'MON WITH ME...
HUH?
SO RUN ALONG AND PLAY... NOW!
AFTER SHE SHOWED ME THE ELEPHANT TREE, DOLLY TOOK ME TO THE BAKERY AND BOUGHT ME A SWEET ROLL. I'D NEVER SEEN SOMEONE MY AGE WITH SO MUCH POCKET MONEY. AT BEDTIME DOLLY LET ME CHOOSE THE LARGER OF THE TWO BEDS. BUT LATER...
I HAD A BAD DREAM... ANKA, CAN I..UH.. SLEEP WITH YOU?
ALL RIGHT.
COULD YOU ROLL OVER AND TELL ME A FAIRY TALE OR A STORY?
DO YOU KNOW THE STORY OF MEDUSA?
NO.

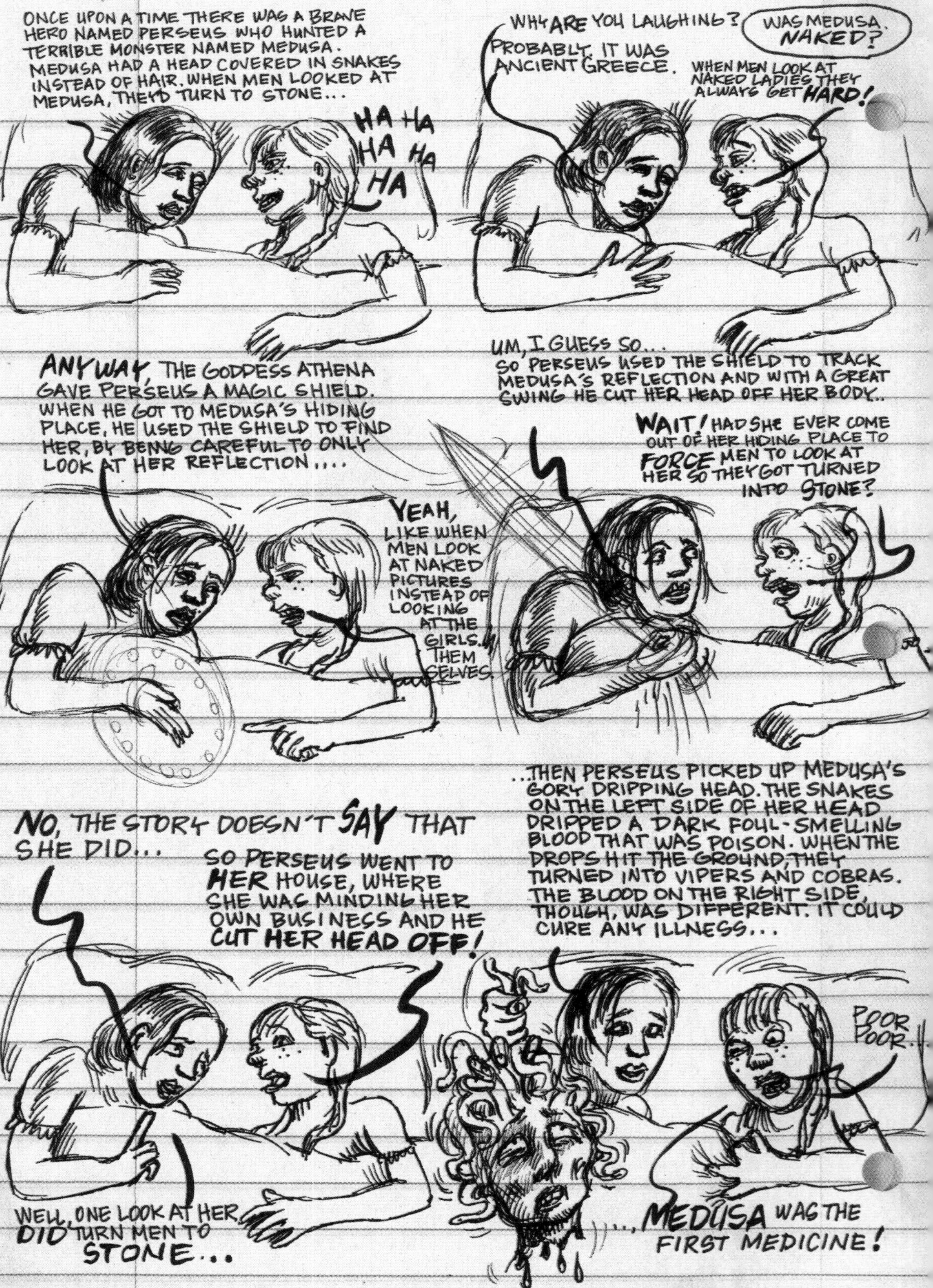
ONCE UPON A TIME THERE WAS A BRAVE HERO NAMED PERSEUS WHO HUNTED A TERRIBLE MONSTER NAMED MEDUSA. MEDUSA HAD A HEAD COVERED IN SNAKES INSTEAD OF HAIR. WHEN MEN LOOKED AT MEDUSA, THEY'D TURN TO STONE...
HA HA HA HA HA
WHY ARE YOU LAUGHING?
WAS MEDUSA NAKED?
PROBABLY. IT WAS ANCIENT GREECE.
WHEN MEN LOOK AT NAKED LADIES THEY ALWAYS GET HARD!
ANYWAY, THE GODDESS ATHENA GAVE PERSEUS A MAGIC SHIELD. WHEN HE GOT TO MEDUSA'S HIDING PLACE, HE USED THE SHIELD TO FIND HER, BY BEING CAREFUL TO ONLY LOOK AT HER REFLECTION....
YEAH, LIKE WHEN MEN LOOK AT NAKED PICTURES INSTEAD OF LOOKING AT THE GIRLS THEMSELVES.
UM, I GUESS SO...
SO PERSEUS USED THE SHIELD TO TRACK MEDUSA'S REFLECTION AND WITH A GREAT SWING HE CUT HER HEAD OFF HER BODY..
WAIT! HAD SHE EVER COME OUT OF HER HIDING PLACE TO FORCE MEN TO LOOK AT HER SO THEY GOT TURNED INTO STONE?
NO, THE STORY DOESN'T SAY THAT SHE DID...
SO PERSEUS WENT TO HER HOUSE, WHERE SHE WAS MINDING HER OWN BUSINESS AND HE CUT HER HEAD OFF!
WELL, ONE LOOK AT HER DID TURN MEN TO STONE...
...THEN PERSEUS PICKED UP MEDUSA'S GORY DRIPPING HEAD. THE SNAKES ON THE LEFT SIDE OF HER HEAD DRIPPED A DARK FOUL-SMELLING BLOOD THAT WAS POISON. WHEN THE DROPS HIT THE GROUND, THEY TURNED INTO VIPERS AND COBRAS. THE BLOOD ON THE RIGHT SIDE, THOUGH, WAS DIFFERENT. IT COULD CURE ANY ILLNESS...
POOR POOR...
...MEDUSA WAS THE FIRST MEDICINE!

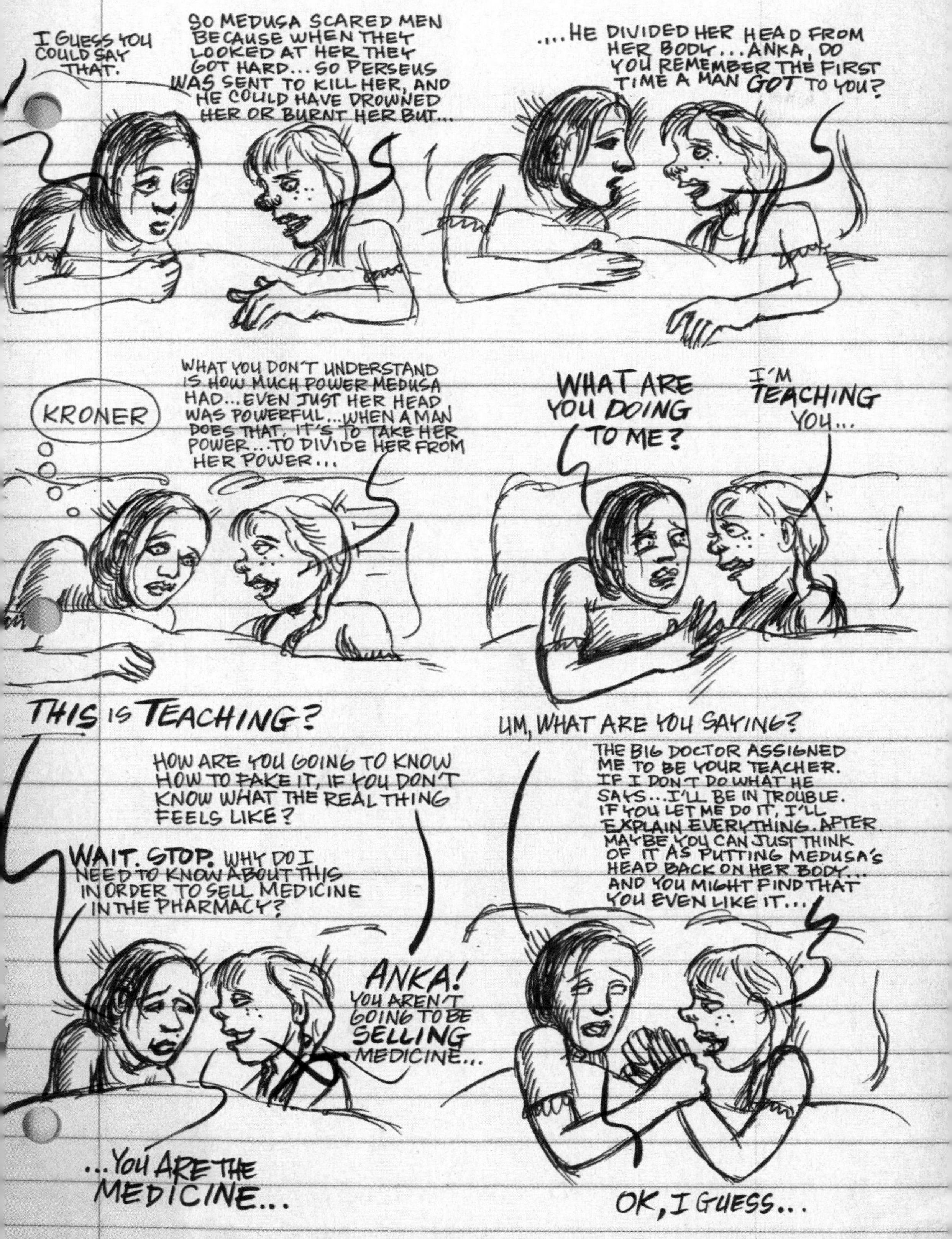

I GUESS YOU COULD SAY THAT.
SO MEDUSA SCARED MEN BECAUSE WHEN THEY LOOKED AT HER THEY GOT HARD... SO PERSEUS WAS SENT TO KILL HER, AND HE COULD HAVE DROWNED HER OR BURNT HER BUT...
....HE DIVIDED HER HEAD FROM HER BODY...ANKA, DO YOU REMEMBER THE FIRST TIME A MAN GOT TO YOU?
KRONER
WHAT YOU DON'T UNDERSTAND IS HOW MUCH POWER MEDUSA HAD...EVEN JUST HER HEAD WAS POWERFUL...WHEN A MAN DOES THAT, IT'S TO TAKE HER POWER...TO DIVIDE HER FROM HER POWER...
WHAT ARE YOU DOING TO ME?
I'M TEACHING YOU...
THIS IS TEACHING?
HOW ARE YOU GOING TO KNOW HOW TO FAKE IT, IF YOU DON'T KNOW WHAT THE REAL THING FEELS LIKE?
WAIT. STOP. WHY DO I NEED TO KNOW ABOUT THIS IN ORDER TO SELL MEDICINE IN THE PHARMACY?
ANKA! YOU AREN'T GOING TO BE SELLING MEDICINE...
...YOU ARE THE MEDICINE...
UM, WHAT ARE YOU SAYING?
THE BIG DOCTOR ASSIGNED ME TO BE YOUR TEACHER. IF I DON'T DO WHAT HE SAYS...I'LL BE IN TROUBLE. IF YOU LET ME DO IT, I'LL EXPLAIN EVERYTHING AFTER. MAYBE YOU CAN JUST THINK OF IT AS PUTTING MEDUSA'S HEAD BACK ON HER BODY... AND YOU MIGHT FIND THAT YOU EVEN LIKE IT...
OK, I GUESS...

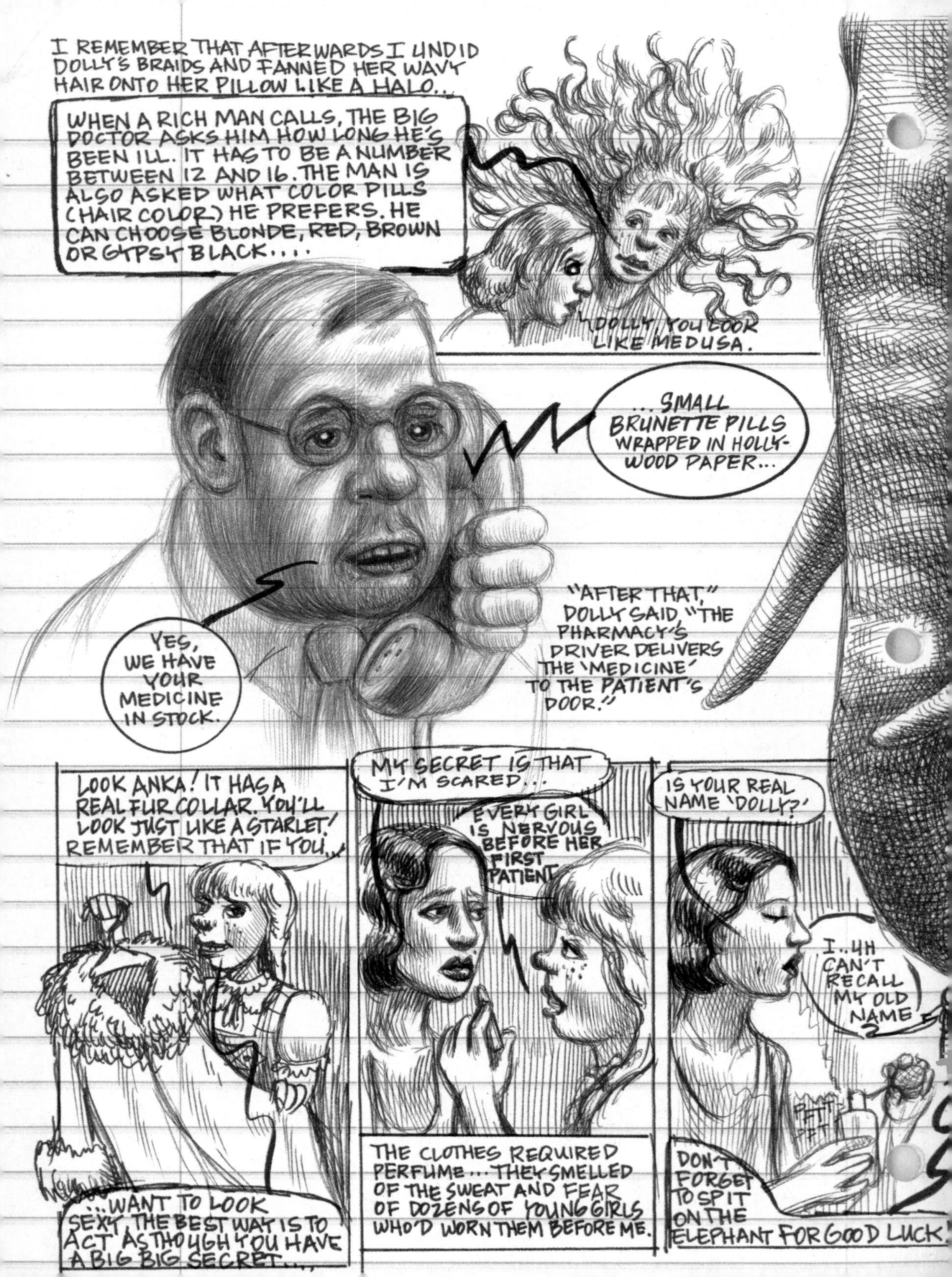

I REMEMBER THAT AFTERWARDS I UNDID DOLLY'S BRAIDS AND FANNED HER WAVY HAIR ONTO HER PILLOW LIKE A HALO...
WHEN A RICH MAN CALLS, THE BIG DOCTOR ASKS HIM HOW LONG HE'S BEEN ILL. IT HAS TO BE A NUMBER BETWEEN 12 AND 16. THE MAN IS ALSO ASKED WHAT COLOR PILLS (HAIR COLOR) HE PREFERS. HE CAN CHOOSE BLONDE, RED, BROWN OR GYPSY BLACK....
"DOLLY, YOU LOOK LIKE MEDUSA."
...SMALL BRUNETTE PILLS WRAPPED IN HOLLY-WOOD PAPER...
YES, WE HAVE YOUR MEDICINE IN STOCK.
"AFTER THAT," DOLLY SAID, "THE PHARMACY'S DRIVER DELIVERS THE 'MEDICINE' TO THE PATIENT'S DOOR."
LOOK ANKA! IT HAS A REAL FUR COLLAR. YOU'LL LOOK JUST LIKE A STARLET! REMEMBER THAT IF YOU...
...WANT TO LOOK SEXY, THE BEST WAY IS TO ACT AS THOUGH YOU HAVE A BIG BIG SECRET...
MY SECRET IS THAT I'M SCARED...
EVERY GIRL IS NERVOUS BEFORE HER FIRST PATIENT
THE CLOTHES REQUIRED PERFUME... THEY SMELLED OF THE SWEAT AND FEAR OF DOZENS OF YOUNG GIRLS WHO'D WORN THEM BEFORE ME.
IS YOUR REAL NAME 'DOLLY?'
I..UH CAN'T RECALL MY OLD NAME
PFT PFT PFT
DON'T FORGET TO SPIT ON THE ELEPHANT FOR GOOD LUCK.

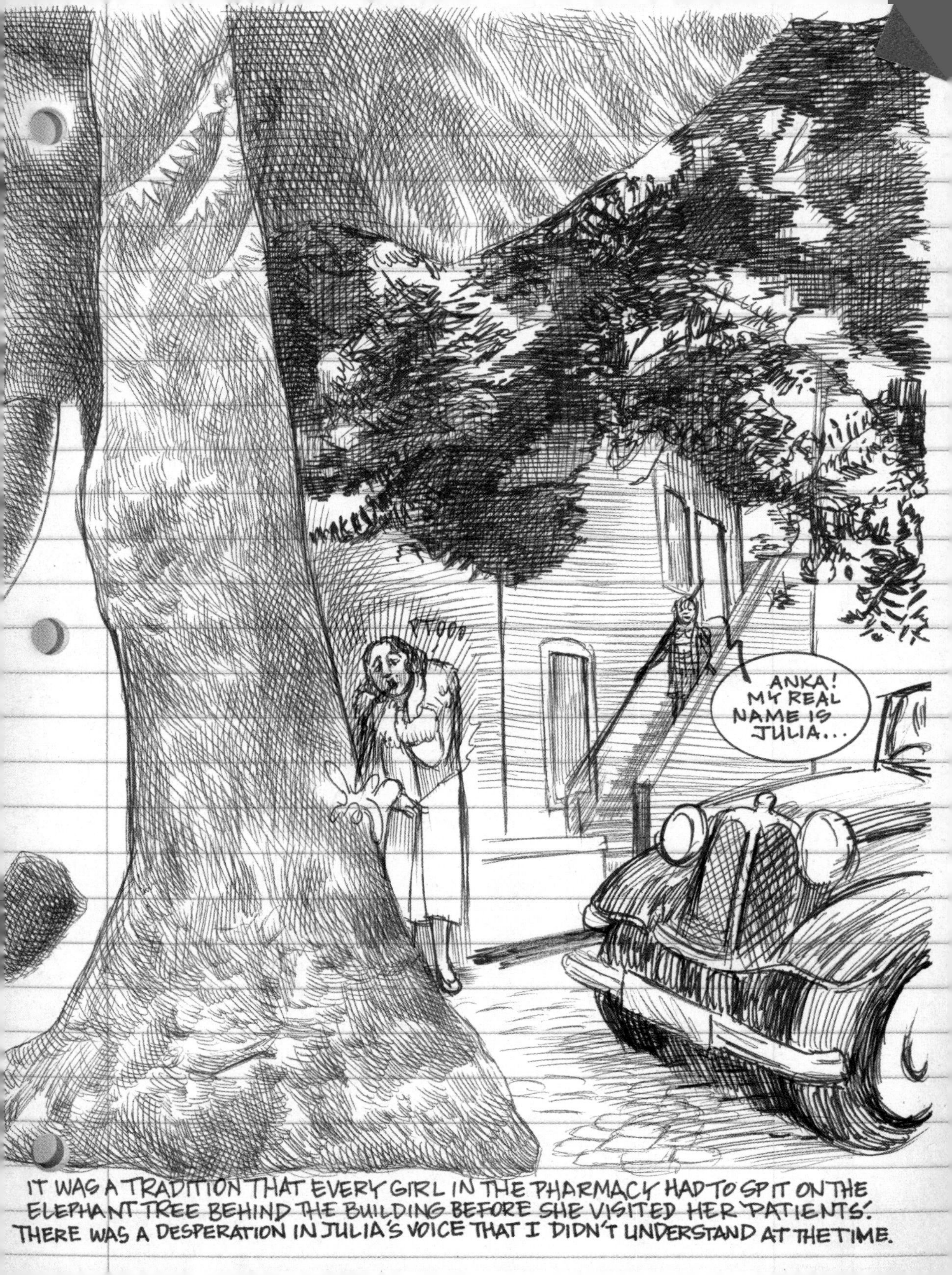
PTOOO
ANKA! MY REAL NAME IS JULIA...

IT WAS A TRADITION THAT EVERY GIRL IN THE PHARMACY HAD TO SPIT ON THE ELEPHANT TREE BEHIND THE BUILDING BEFORE SHE VISITED HER 'PATIENTS'. THERE WAS A DESPERATION IN JULIA'S VOICE THAT I DIDN'T UNDERSTAND AT THE TIME.

CASANOVA NOBODY FRANKENSTEIN
PURGATORY
("A REJECTS STORY")

A Taste of Purgatory (*Excerpt*)

C A S A N O V A   F R A N K E N S T E I N

originally published in

Purgatory

FANTAGRAPHICS BOOKS

4 x 6 inches • 92 pages

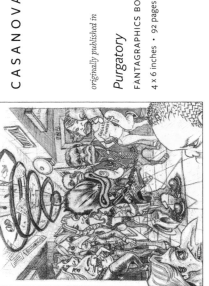

Biography

I have been drawing comics for decades, always while simultaneously working a full-time, non-art-related job. So many artists get broken by this, or by the commercial-art world. But if you want to make your own statement badly enough, nothing can deter you. If anything you will do it just to spite your straight life! cnfrankenstein.daportfolio.com

Statement

This is a story that had been laying heavy on my soul, for many years. A lot of suppressed memories went into the production. I wanted to make something for the young outsiders who are going through hell right now.

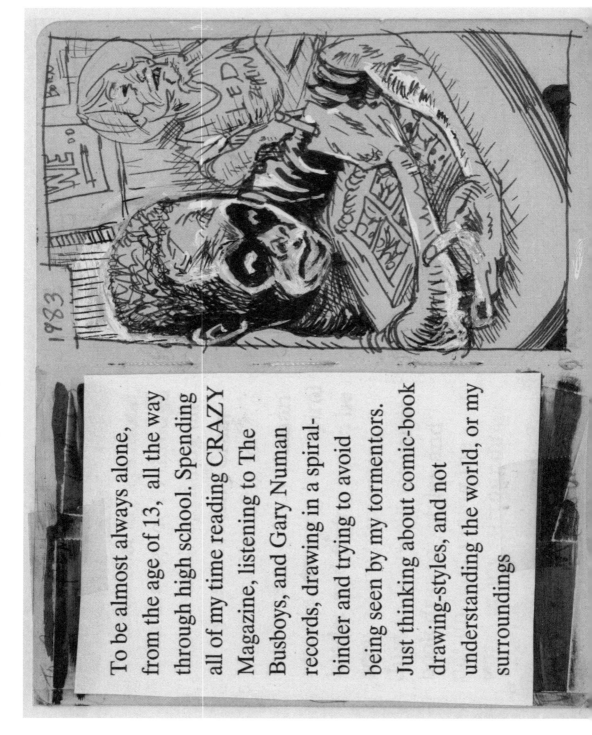

To be almost always alone, from the age of 13, all the way through high school. Spending all of my time reading CRAZY Magazine, listening to The Busboys, and Gary Numan records, drawing in a spiral-binder and trying to avoid being seen by my tormentors. Just thinking about comic-book drawing-styles, and not understanding the world, or my surroundings

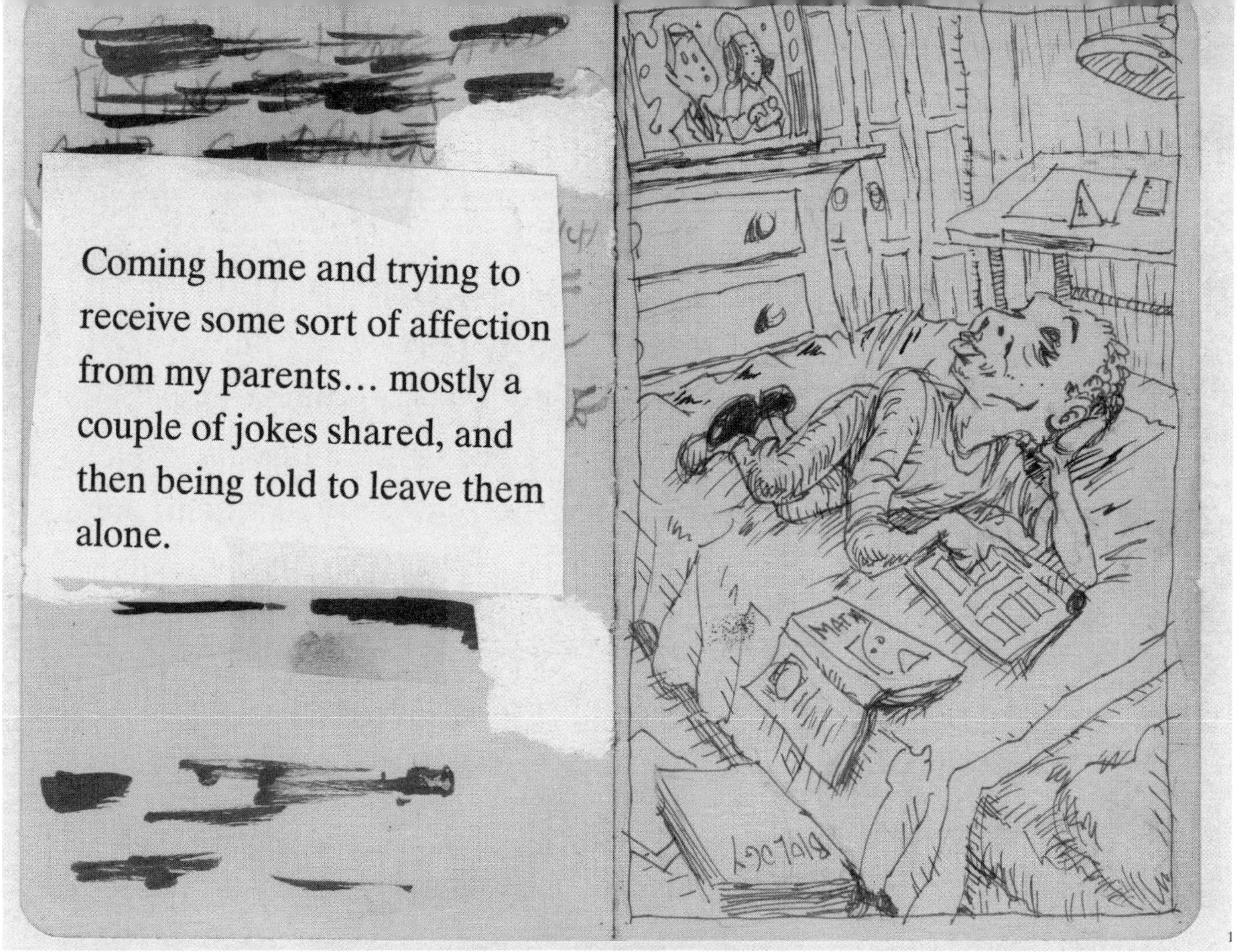
Coming home and trying to receive some sort of affection from my parents… mostly a couple of jokes shared, and then being told to leave them alone.
MATH

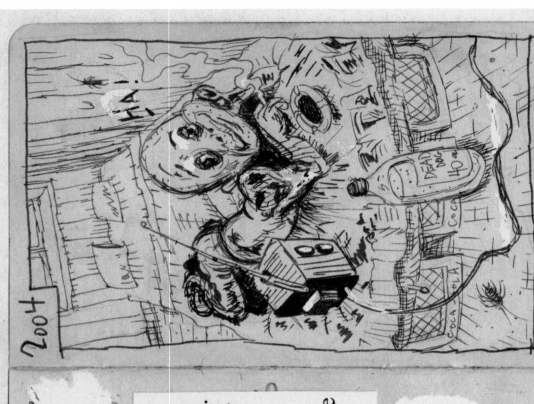

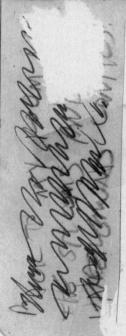

Then to my room, with the sit-coms and underground comics. Trying and failing to study. My mind unable to grasp those things it viewed as illogical or unimportant, but devouring the things it found interesting.
2004
HA!
DEAD DOG 40 oz
COCA COLA
COCA

Doodling... trying and failing, and trying again, to teach myself the alchemy of art, but always coming up short. Even though the other kids thought I was good, it didn't matter to me. I didn't think I was. I didn't want to draw as well as a good teenager. I wanted to draw at the level of the professionals. But I always seemed to come up short and disappoint myself.

So there I would sit. Trying not to enjoy myself too much, or to get too engrossed in what I was doing, because that would just bring the following day, (and its troubles) to me that much more quickly.

Going to sleep at 9PM, because I'd been doing it since I was a little-kid, and my parents never got around to telling me that I could stay up any later than that. Then falling asleep in a messy(-ish) room. A bookshelf by my bed. Encyclopedias at eye-level, comic books, and the HUSTLER Magazines underneath them, on the lower-shelf, odds-and-ends on the bottom. Still afraid of monsters and Satan.

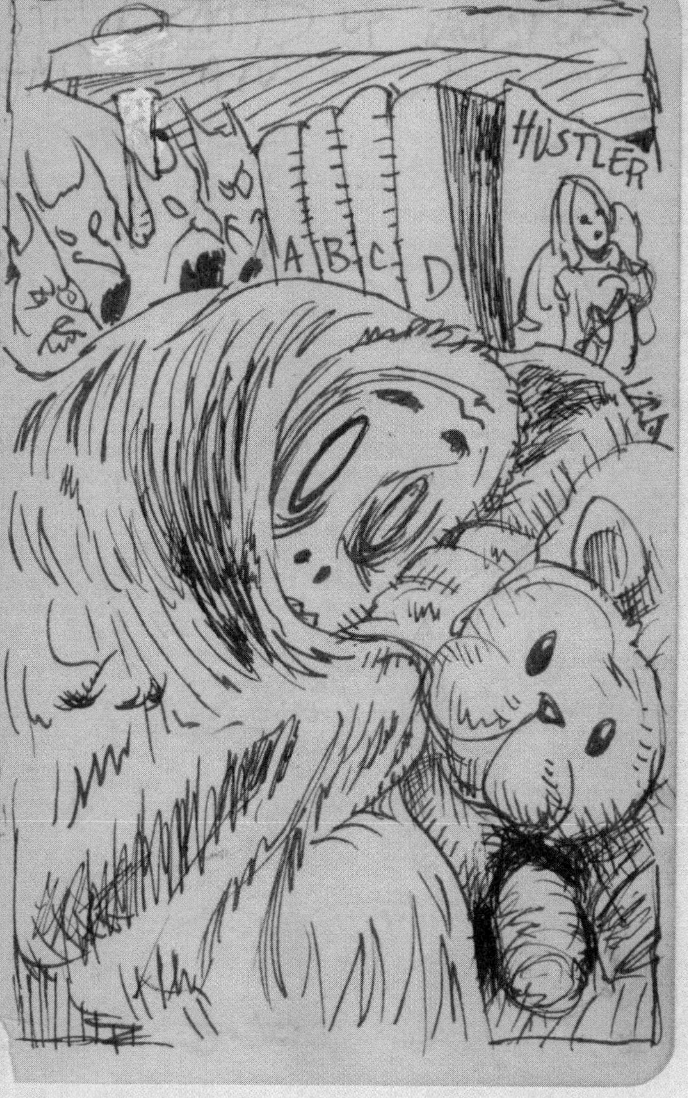
HUSTLER
A B C D

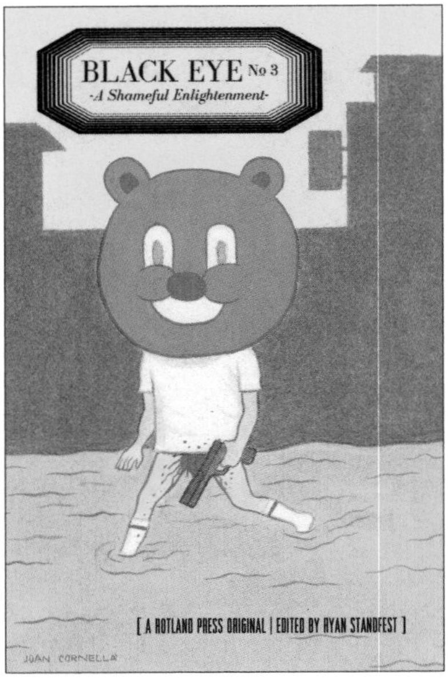
BLACK EYE No 3
-A Shameful Enlightenment-
[A ROTLAND PRESS ORIGINAL | EDITED BY RYAN STANDFEST]
JOAN CORNELLÀ

Frail Nature

JULIA GFRÖRER

originally published in

Black Eye #3

ROTLAND PRESS

5.75 x 9 inches • 136 pages

Biography

Julia Gfrörer is a writer and cartoonist. She graduated from Cornish College of the Arts in Seattle, Washington, and now lives on Long Island. She has published several handmade comics under her own imprint, as well as two longer graphic novels, *Laid Waste* and *Black Is the Color*, with Fantagraphics. Her work has also appeared in numerous anthologies and publications, including *Cicada Magazine*, *Arthur Magazine*, and *Kramers Ergot* 9. She recently translated and illustrated excerpts from a medieval French heraldic text for 2dCloud's *MIRROR MIRROR II* anthology, which she coedited with her partner, writer Sean T. Collins.
thorazos.net

Statement

"Frail Nature" could have been horror, or erotica, but it turned out to be farce. The setting is obviously based on historical religious persecution, and at the heart of the story is the gulf between gruesome reality and the ineffable personal mythologies we rely upon to navigate it. The idea of becoming deranged by desire is a seriously romantic one, but the situation is ultimately ridiculous, and the victim's understated dismay as it plays out is pretty funny, at least from a distance.

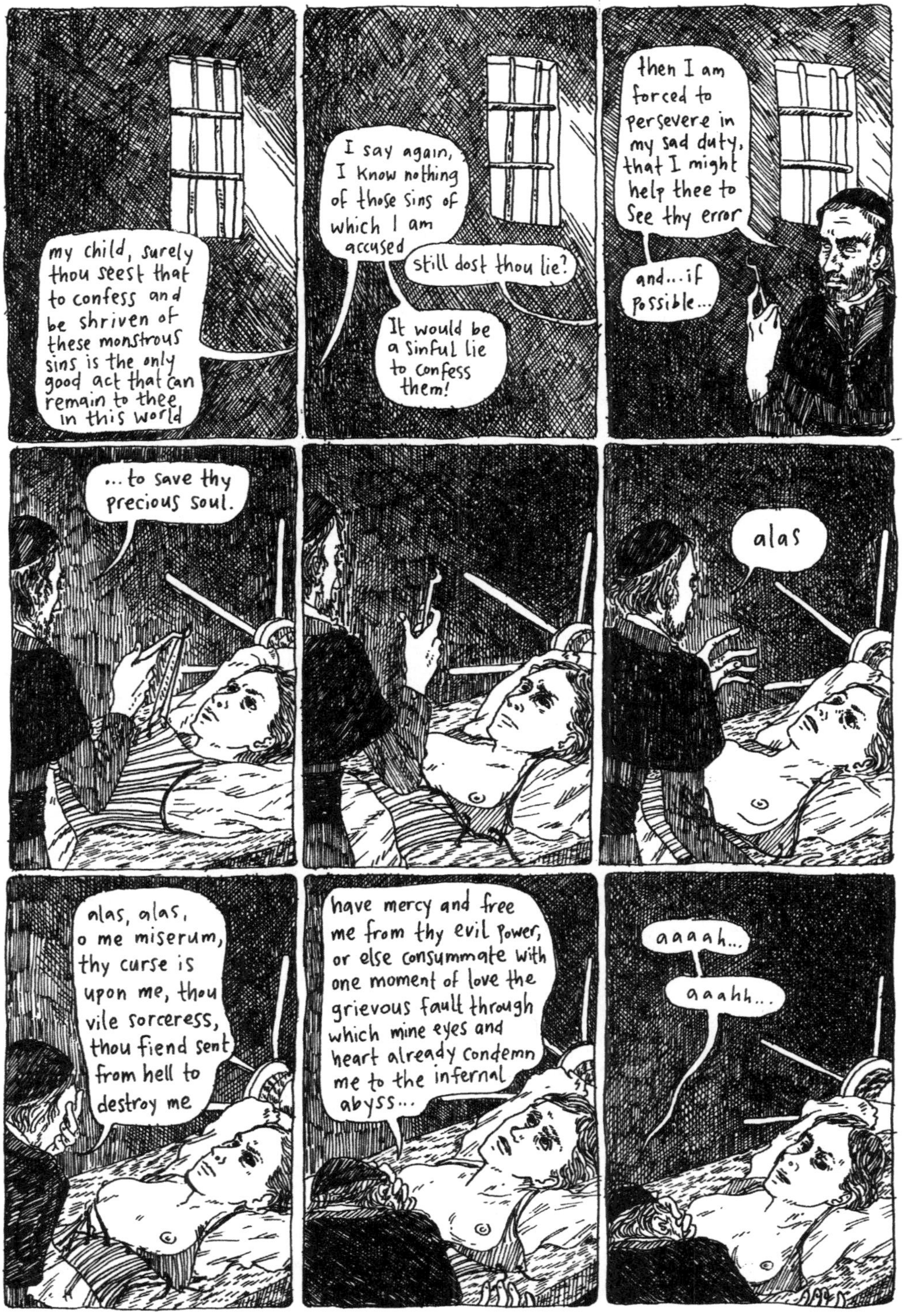
my child, surely thou seest that to confess and be shriven of these monstrous sins is the only good act that can remain to thee in this world
I say again, I know nothing of those sins of which I am accused
still dost thou lie?
It would be a sinful lie to confess them!
then I am forced to persevere in my sad duty, that I might help thee to see thy error
and... if possible...
...to save thy precious soul.
alas
alas, alas, o me miserum, thy curse is upon me, thou vile sorceress, thou fiend sent from hell to destroy me
have mercy and free me from thy evil power, or else consummate with one moment of love the grievous fault through which mine eyes and heart already condemn me to the infernal abyss...
aaaah...
aaahh...

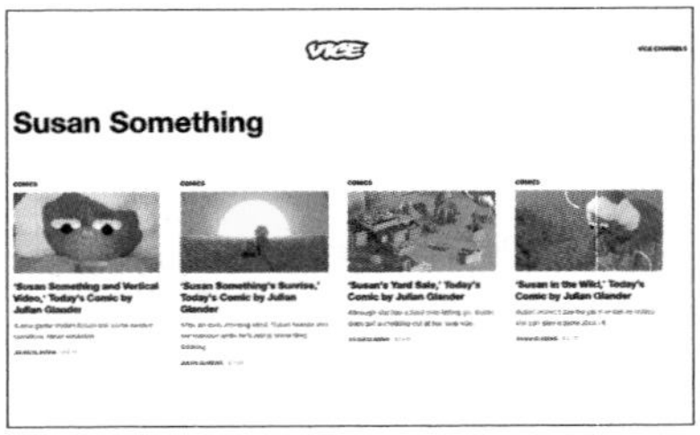
Susan Something

SELECTIONS FROM

Susan Something

JULIAN GLANDER

originally published at

vice.com

VICE MEDIA LLC

DIGITAL

Biography

Julian Glander (born 1990, Detroit) is a 3D artist living in New York. His body of work includes animation, illustration, short films, video games, commercials, and uh comics, I guess.
glander.co

Statement

Susan Something is a twenty-something in the modern world. Her brain is totally fried because she's been blasting technology into her eyeballs since she was a baby. I wish I could say Susan's life was based on mine, but actually she is a lot cooler than me. I have a lot more in common with her dopey mopey friend, Teapot Roommate.

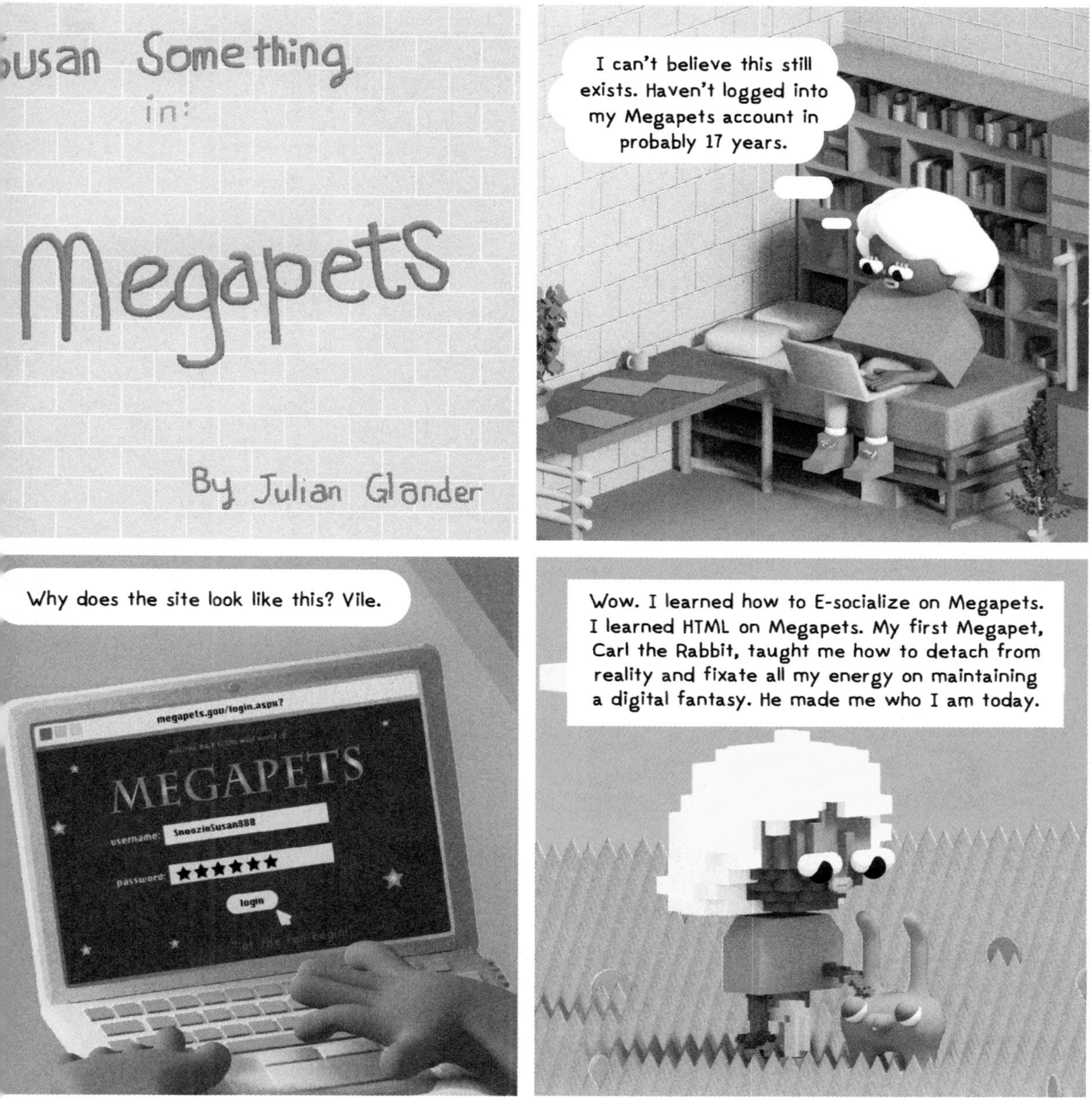
Susan Something
in:
Megapets
By Julian Glander
I can't believe this still exists. Haven't logged into my Megapets account in probably 17 years.
Why does the site look like this? Vile.
megapets.gov/login.aspx?
MEGAPETS
username: SnoozinSusan888
password: ★★★★★★
login
Wow. I learned how to E-socialize on Megapets. I learned HTML on Megapets. My first Megapet, Carl the Rabbit, taught me how to detach from reality and fixate all my energy on maintaining a digital fantasy. He made me who I am today.

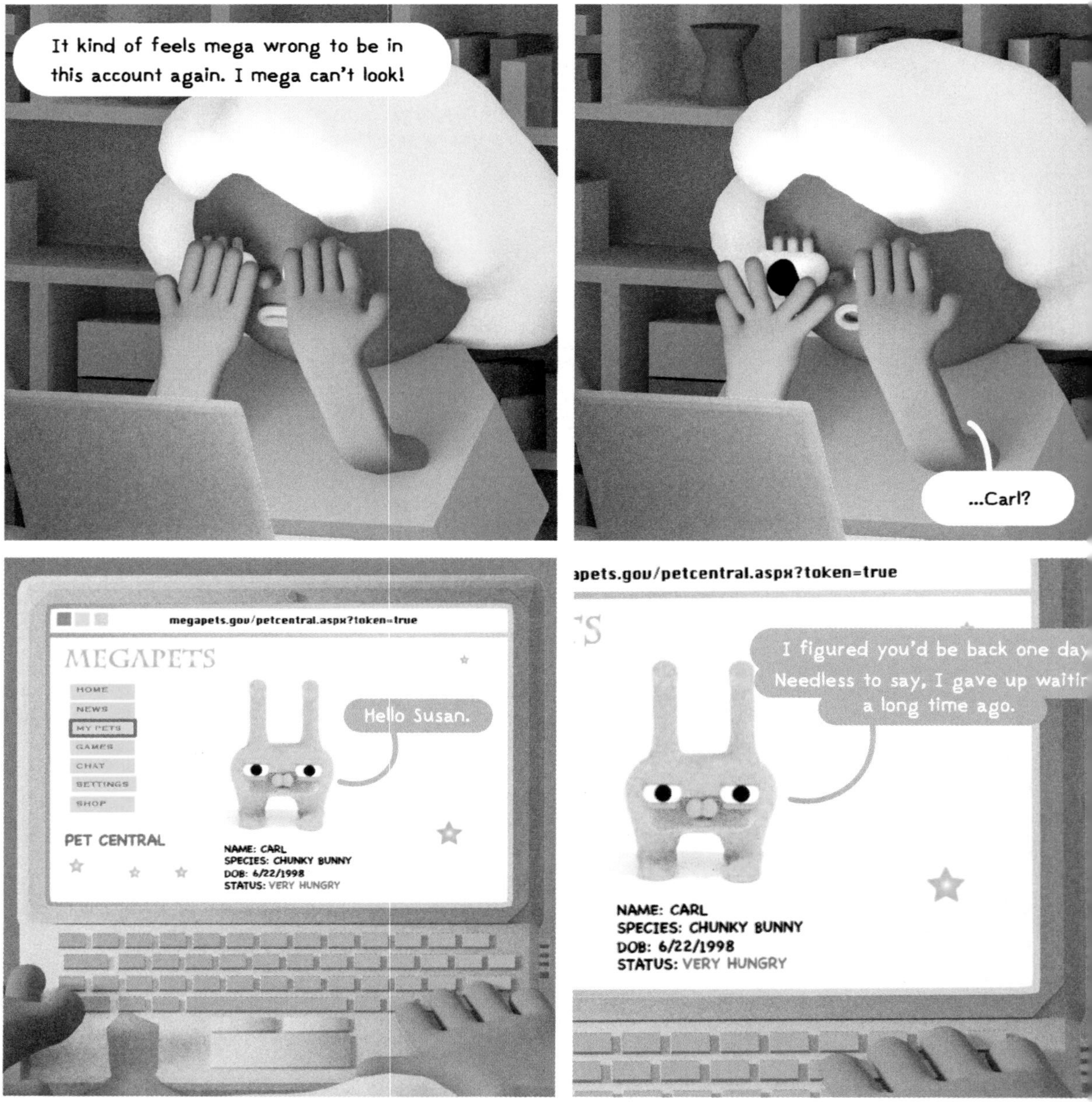

It kind of feels mega wrong to be in this account again. I mega can't look!
...Carl?
megapets.gov/petcentral.aspx?token=true
MEGAPETS
HOME
NEWS
MY PETS
GAMES
CHAT
SETTINGS
SHOP
PET CENTRAL
Hello Susan.
NAME: CARL
SPECIES: CHUNKY BUNNY
DOB: 6/22/1998
STATUS: VERY HUNGRY
apets.gov/petcentral.aspx?token=true
I figured you'd be back one day
Needless to say, I gave up waiti
a long time ago.
NAME: CARL
SPECIES: CHUNKY BUNNY
DOB: 6/22/1998
STATUS: VERY HUNGRY

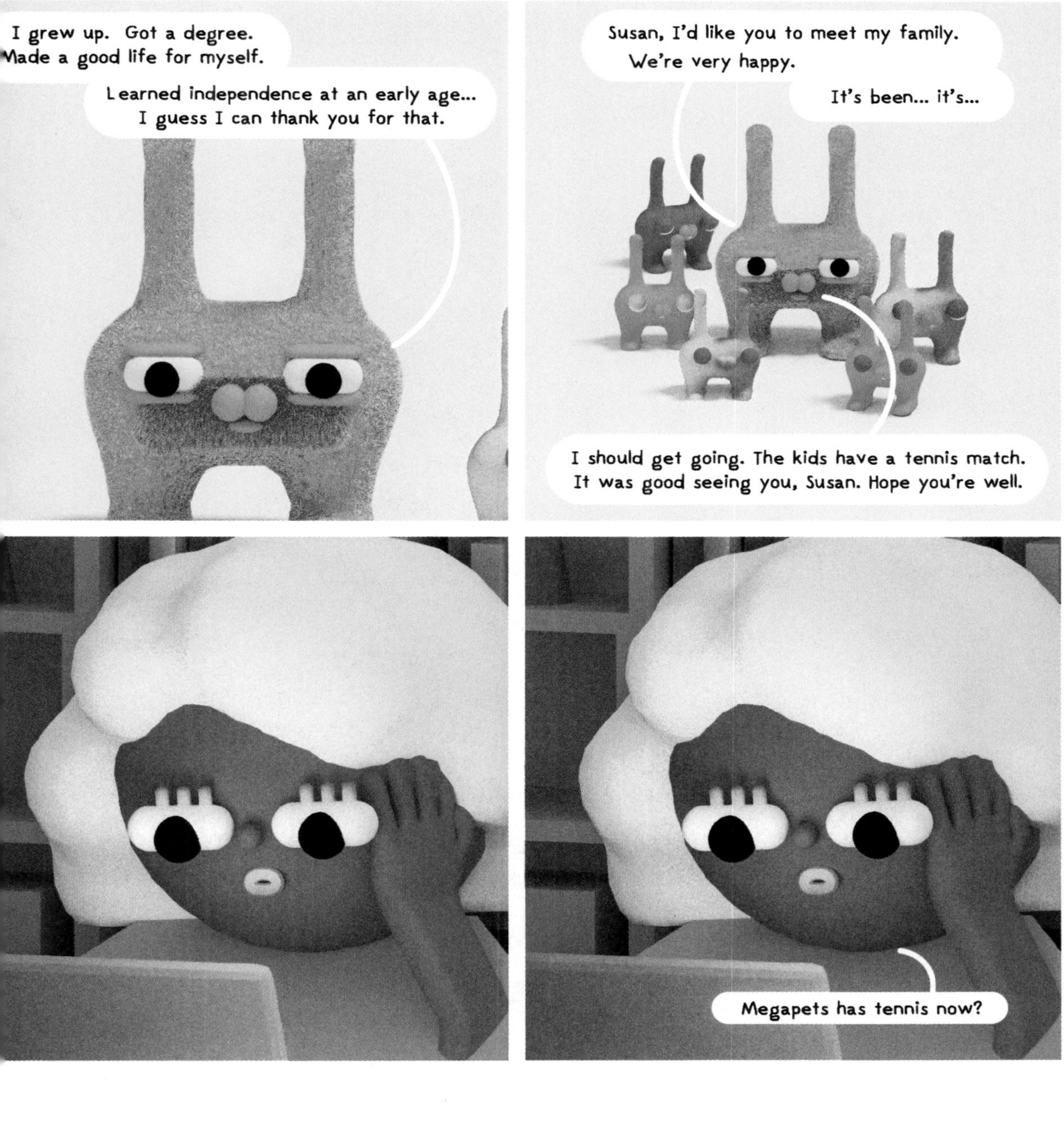
I grew up. Got a degree.
Made a good life for myself.
Learned independence at an early age...
I guess I can thank you for that.
Susan, I'd like you to meet my family.
We're very happy.
It's been... it's...
I should get going. The kids have a tennis match.
It was good seeing you, Susan. Hope you're well.
Megapets has tennis now?

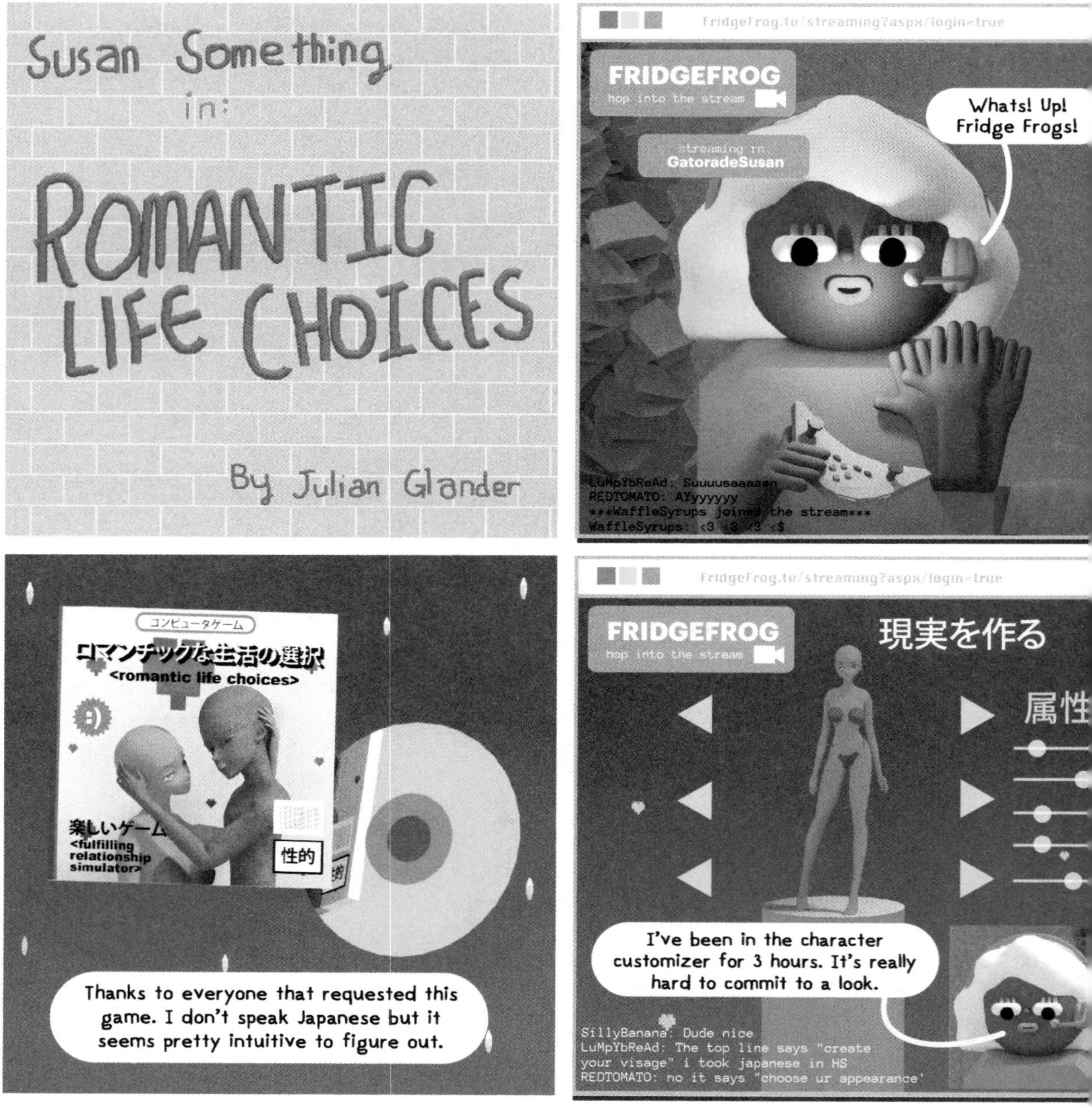
Susan Something in:
ROMANTIC LIFE CHOICES
By Julian Glander
FridgeFrog.tv/streaming?aspx/login=true
FRIDGEFROG
hop into the stream
streaming rn:
GatoradeSusan
Whats! Up! Fridge Frogs!
LuMpYbReAd: Suuuusaaaaan
REDTOMATO: AYyyyyyy
WaffleSyrups joined the stream
WaffleSyrups: <3 <3 <3 <$
コンピュータゲーム
ロマンチックな生活の選択
<romantic life choices>
楽しいゲーム
<fulfilling relationship simulator>
性的
Thanks to everyone that requested this game. I don't speak Japanese but it seems pretty intuitive to figure out.
FridgeFrog.tv/streaming?aspx/login=true
FRIDGEFROG
hop into the stream
現実を作る
属性
I've been in the character customizer for 3 hours. It's really hard to commit to a look.
SillyBanana: Dude nice
LuMpYbReAd: The top line says "create your visage" i took japanese in HS
REDTOMATO: no it says "choose ur appearance'

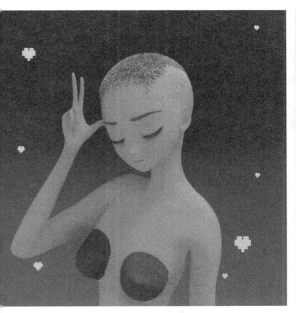

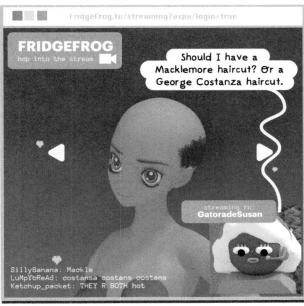

fridgefrog.tv/streaming?aspx/login=true
FRIDGEFROG
hop into the stream
Should I have a Macklemore haircut? Or a George Costanza haircut.
streaming rn:
GatoradeSusan
SillyBanana: Mackle
LuMpYbReAd: costansa costans costans
Ketchup_packet: THEY R BOTH hot
That's kinda cool, u can have sick muscles. I wonder if that helps or hurts in the game when ur trying to find love.
Maybe I'll play as a hunky man. Just kind of explore that.

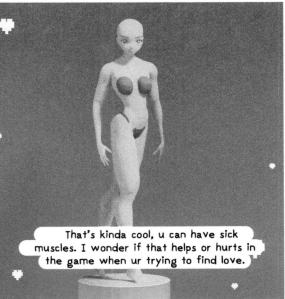

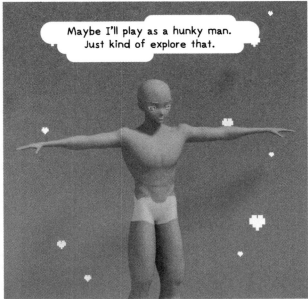

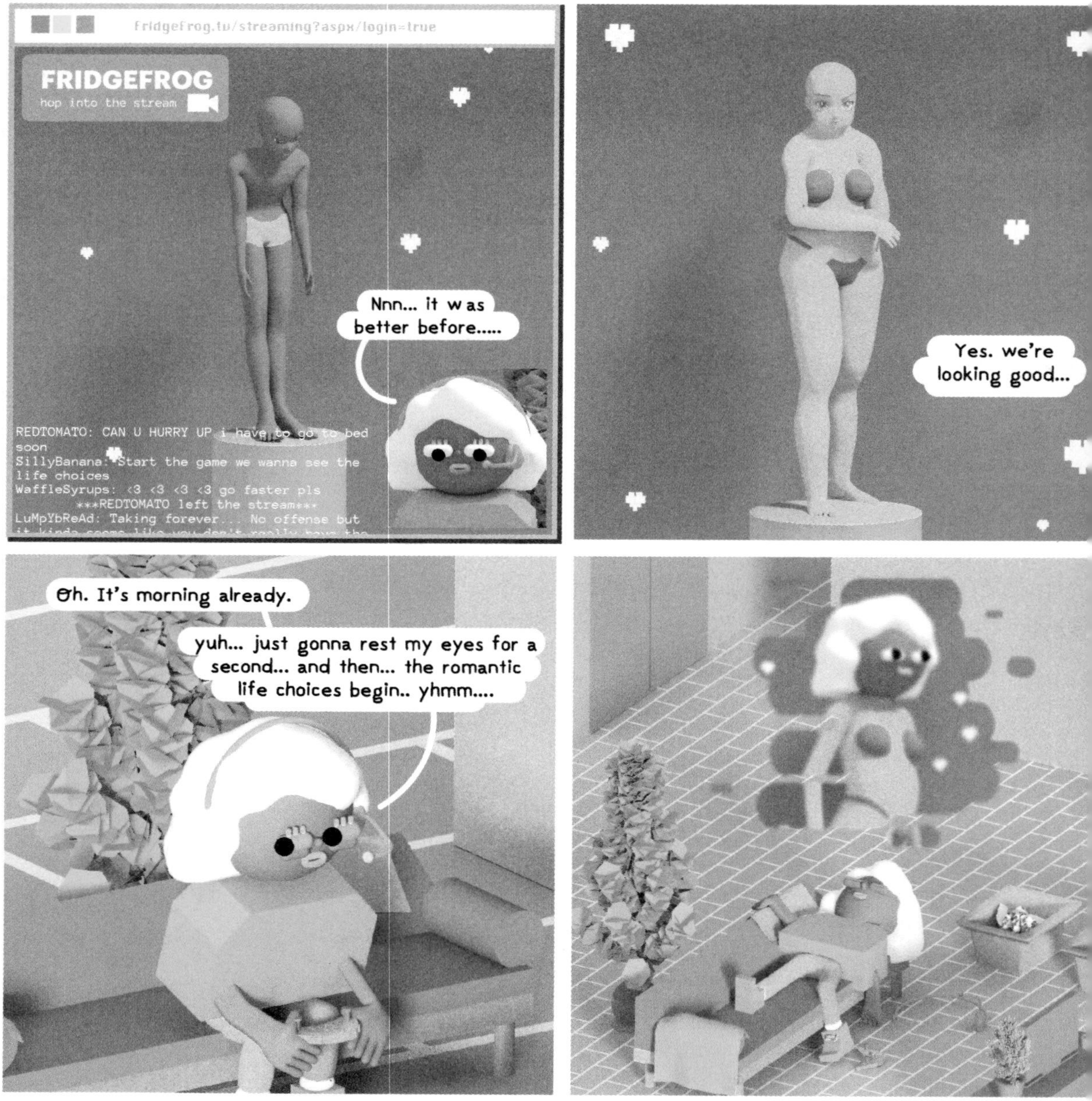
fridgefrog.tv/streaming?aspx/login=true
FRIDGEFROG
hop into the stream
Nnn... it was better before.....
REDTOMATO: CAN U HURRY UP i have to go to bed soon
SillyBanana: Start the game we wanna see the life choices
WaffleSyrups: <3 <3 <3 <3 go faster pls
REDTOMATO left the stream
LuMpYbReAd: Taking forever... No offense but
Yes. we're looking good...
Oh. It's morning already.
yuh... just gonna rest my eyes for a second... and then... the romantic life choices begin.. yhmm....

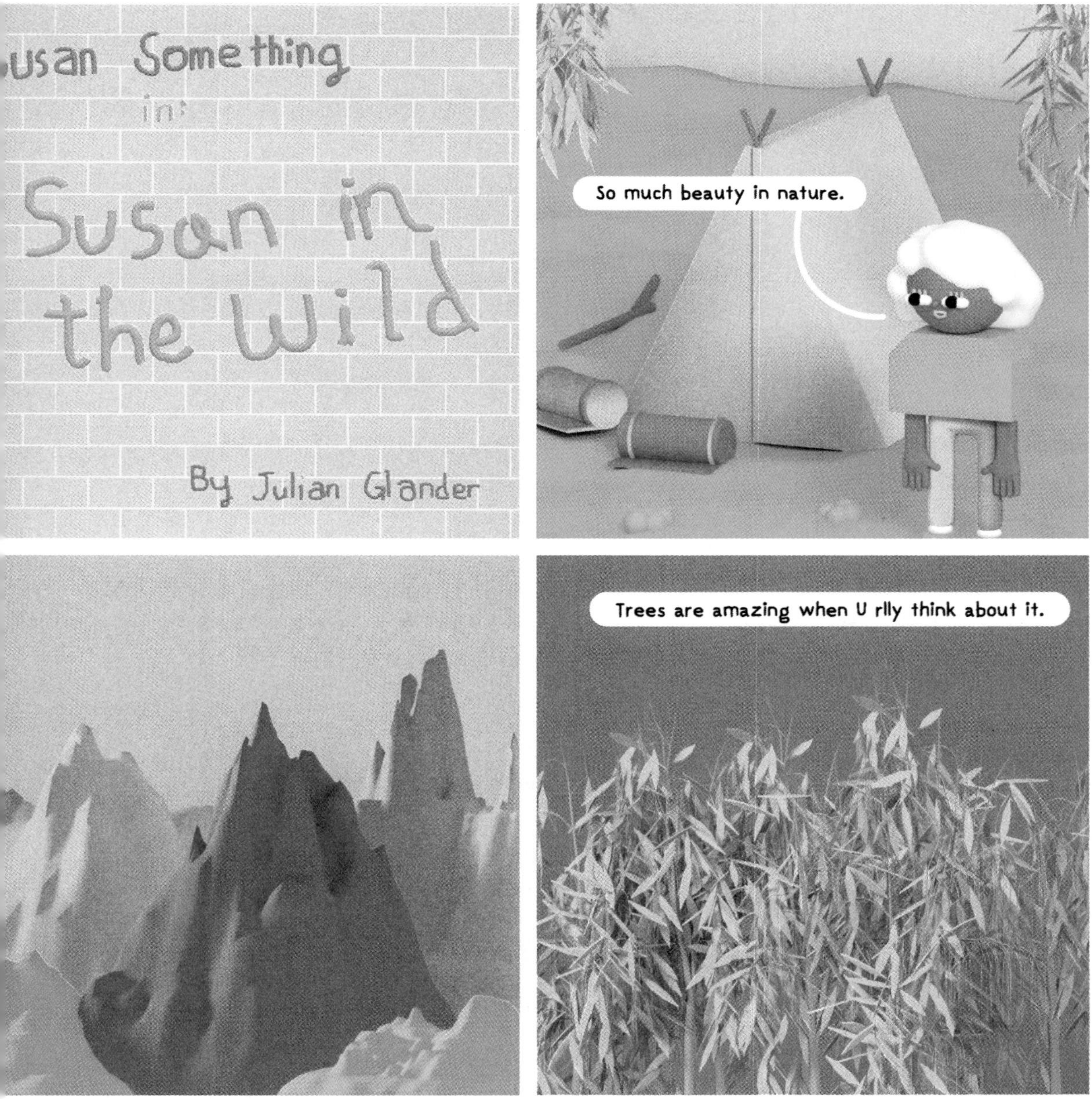

usan Something
in:
Susan in the wild
By Julian Glander
So much beauty in nature.
Trees are amazing when U rlly think about it.

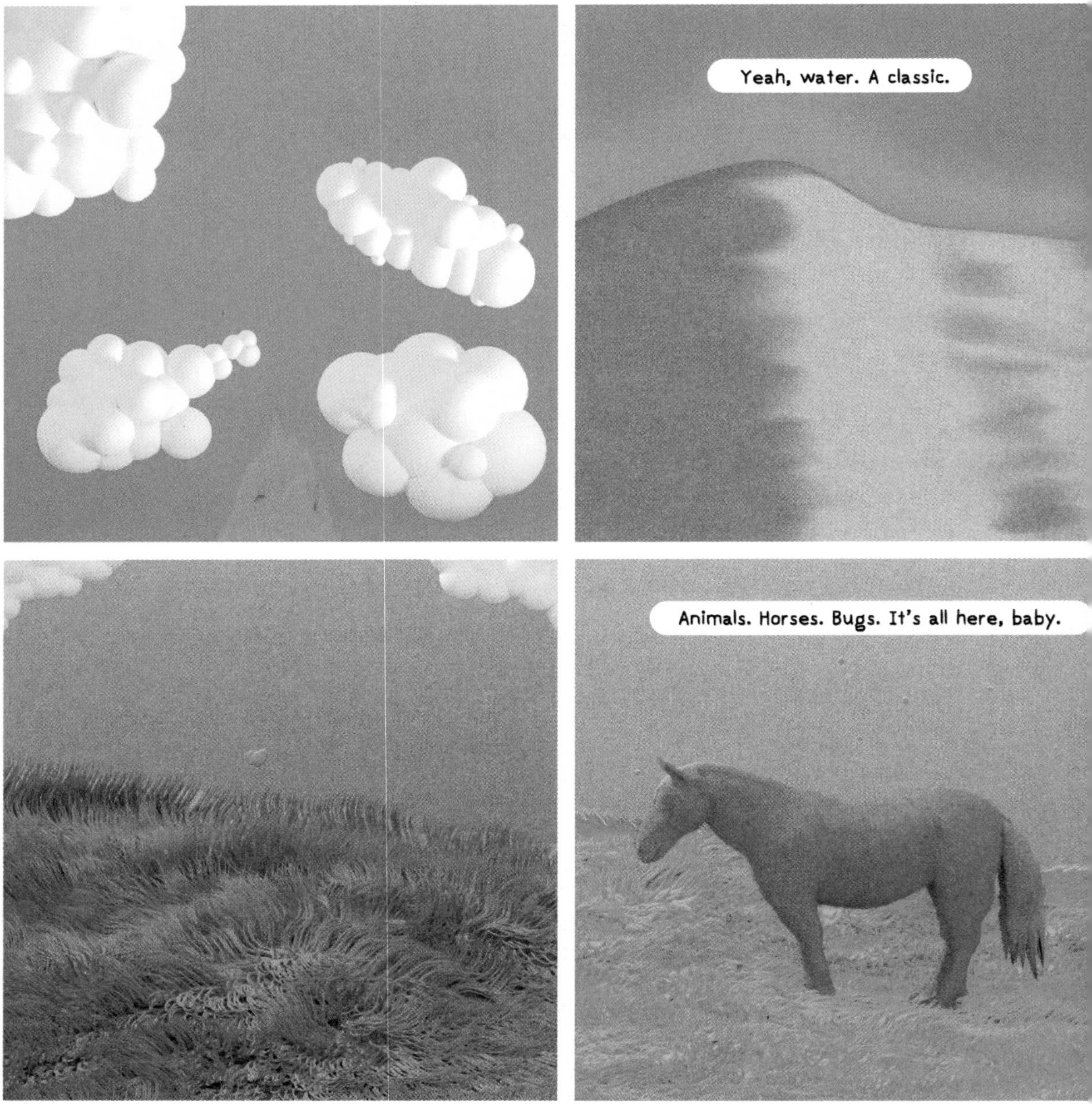
Yeah, water. A classic.
Animals. Horses. Bugs. It's all here, baby.

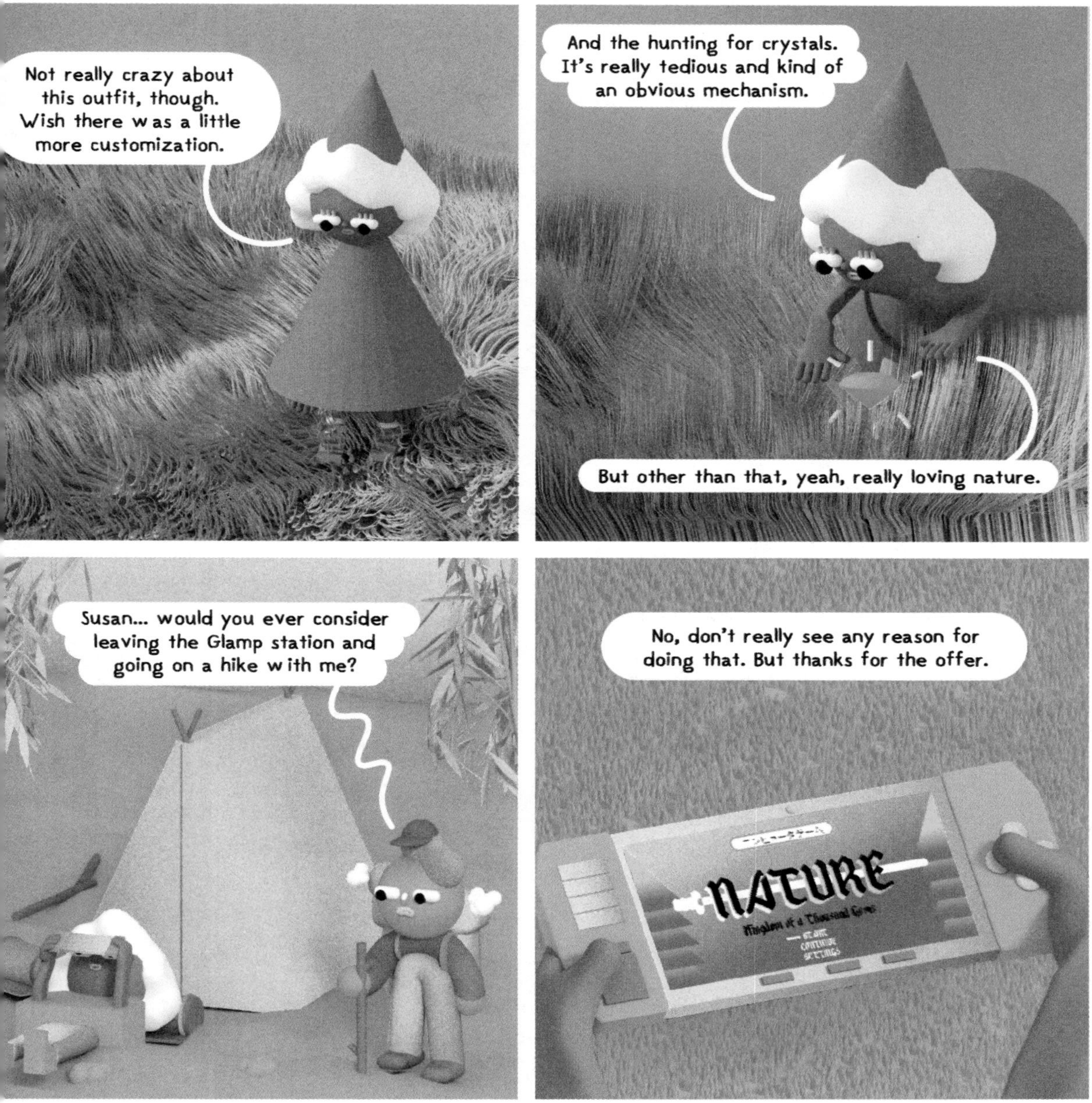
Not really crazy about this outfit, though. Wish there was a little more customization.
And the hunting for crystals. It's really tedious and kind of an obvious mechanism.
But other than that, yeah, really loving nature.
Susan... would you ever consider leaving the Glamp station and going on a hike with me?
No, don't really see any reason for doing that. But thanks for the offer.
NATURE

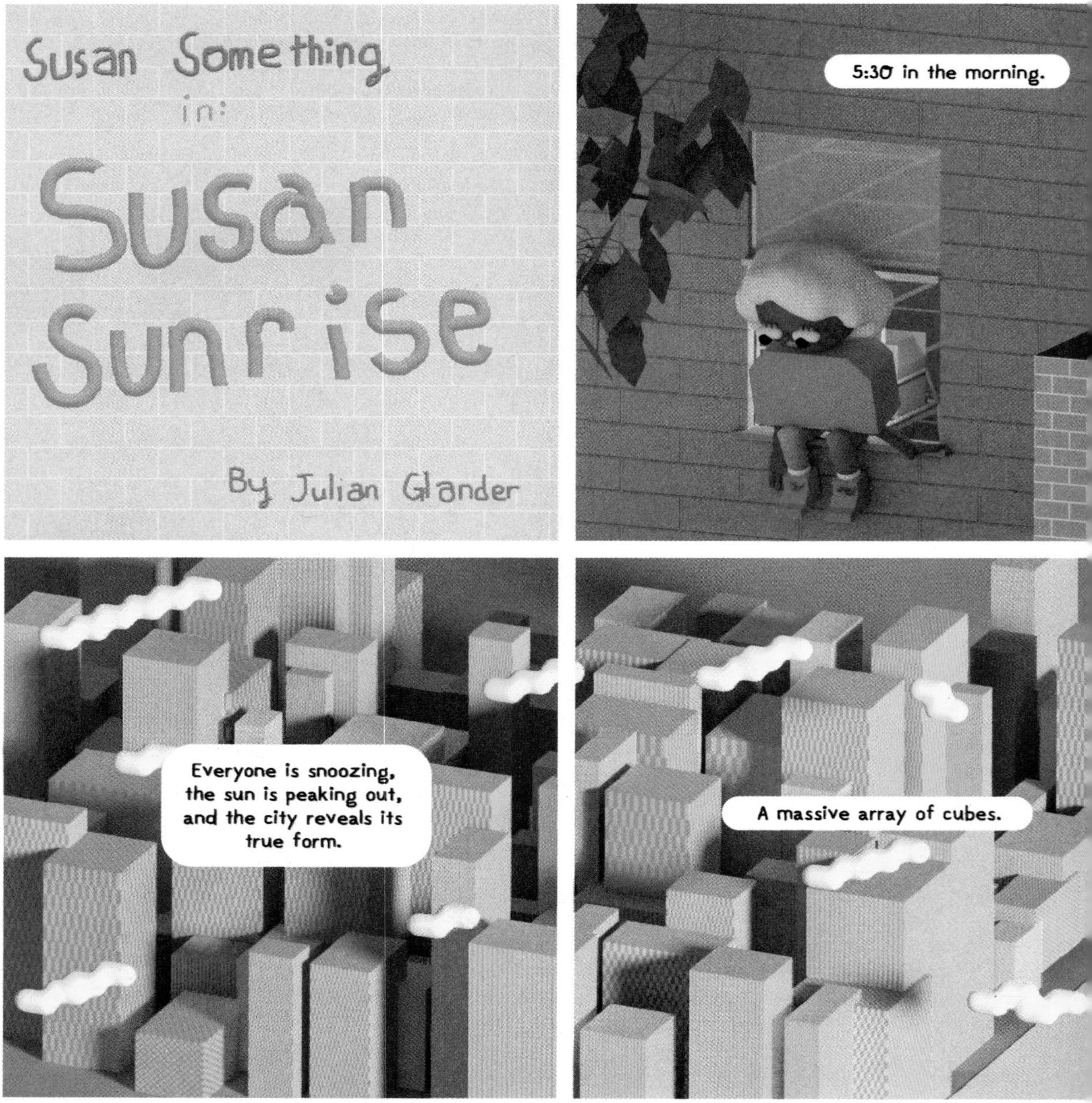
Susan Something
in:
Susan Sunrise
By Julian Glander
5:30 in the morning.
Everyone is snoozing, the sun is peaking out, and the city reveals its true form.
A massive array of cubes.

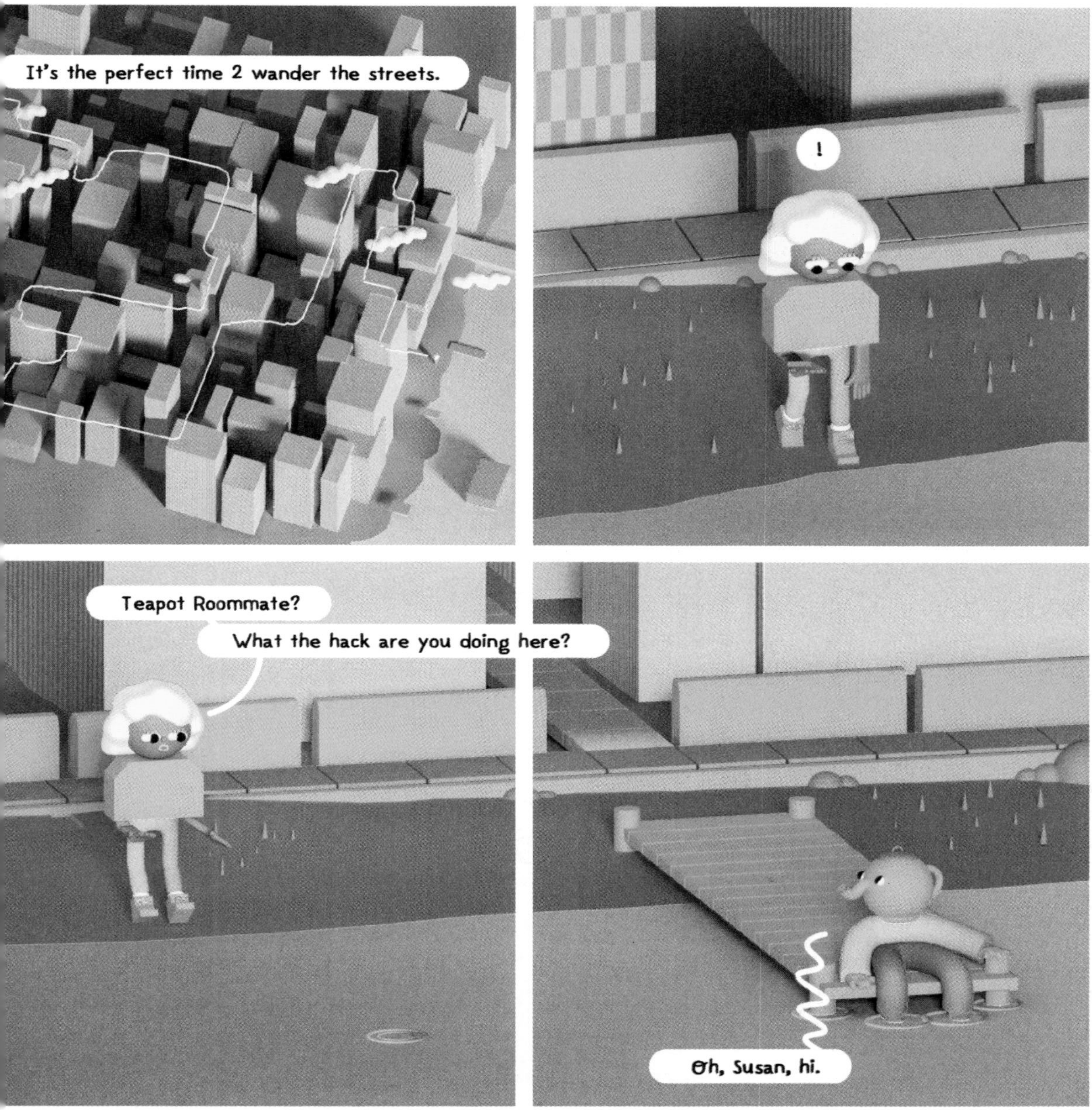
It's the perfect time 2 wander the streets.
!
Teapot Roommate?
What the hack are you doing here?
Oh, Susan, hi.

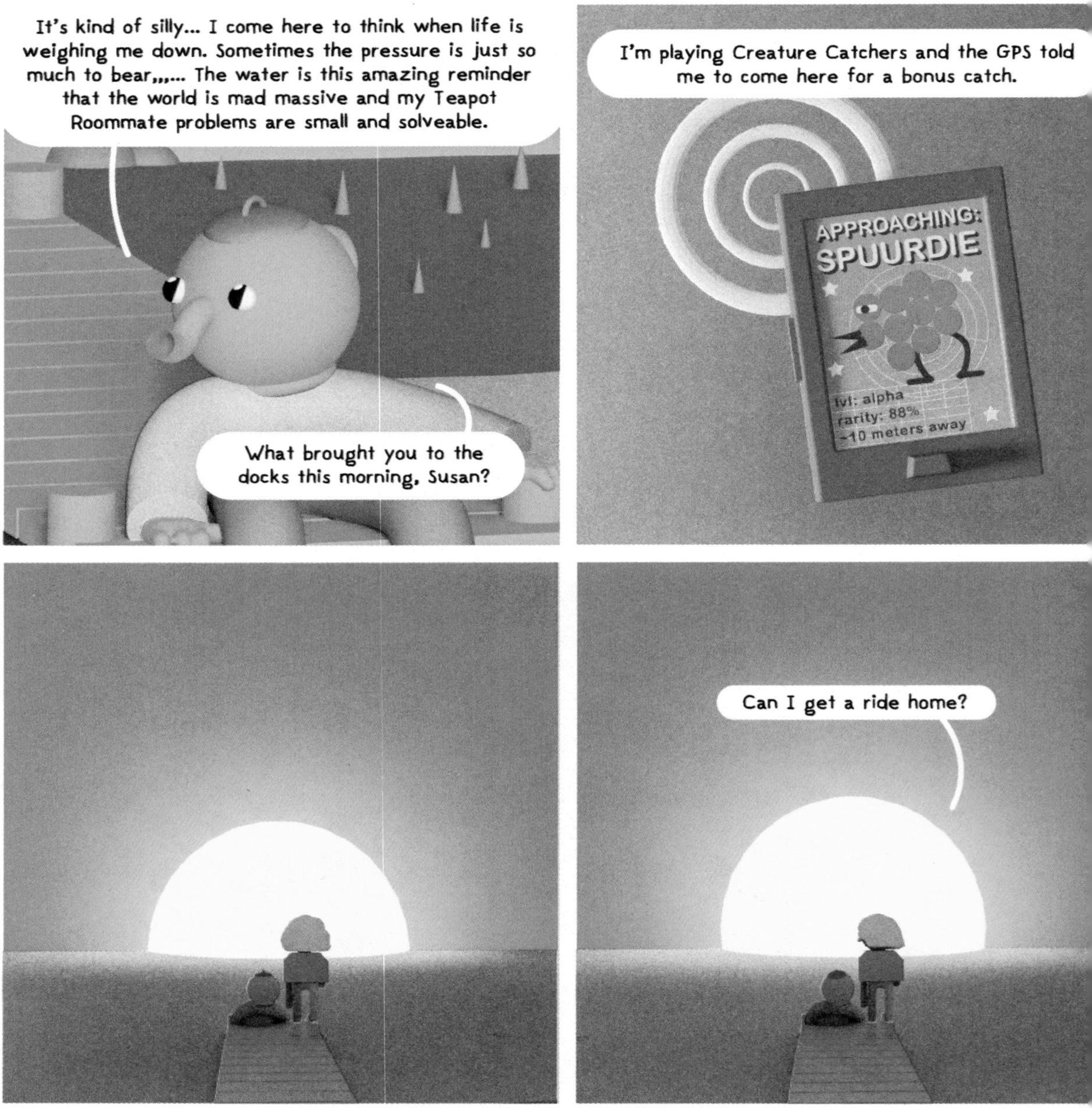
It's kind of silly... I come here to think when life is weighing me down. Sometimes the pressure is just so much to bear,,,... The water is this amazing reminder that the world is mad massive and my Teapot Roommate problems are small and solveable.
What brought you to the docks this morning, Susan?
I'm playing Creature Catchers and the GPS told me to come here for a bonus catch.
APPROACHING: SPUURDIE
lvl: alpha
rarity: 88%
~10 meters away
Can I get a ride home?

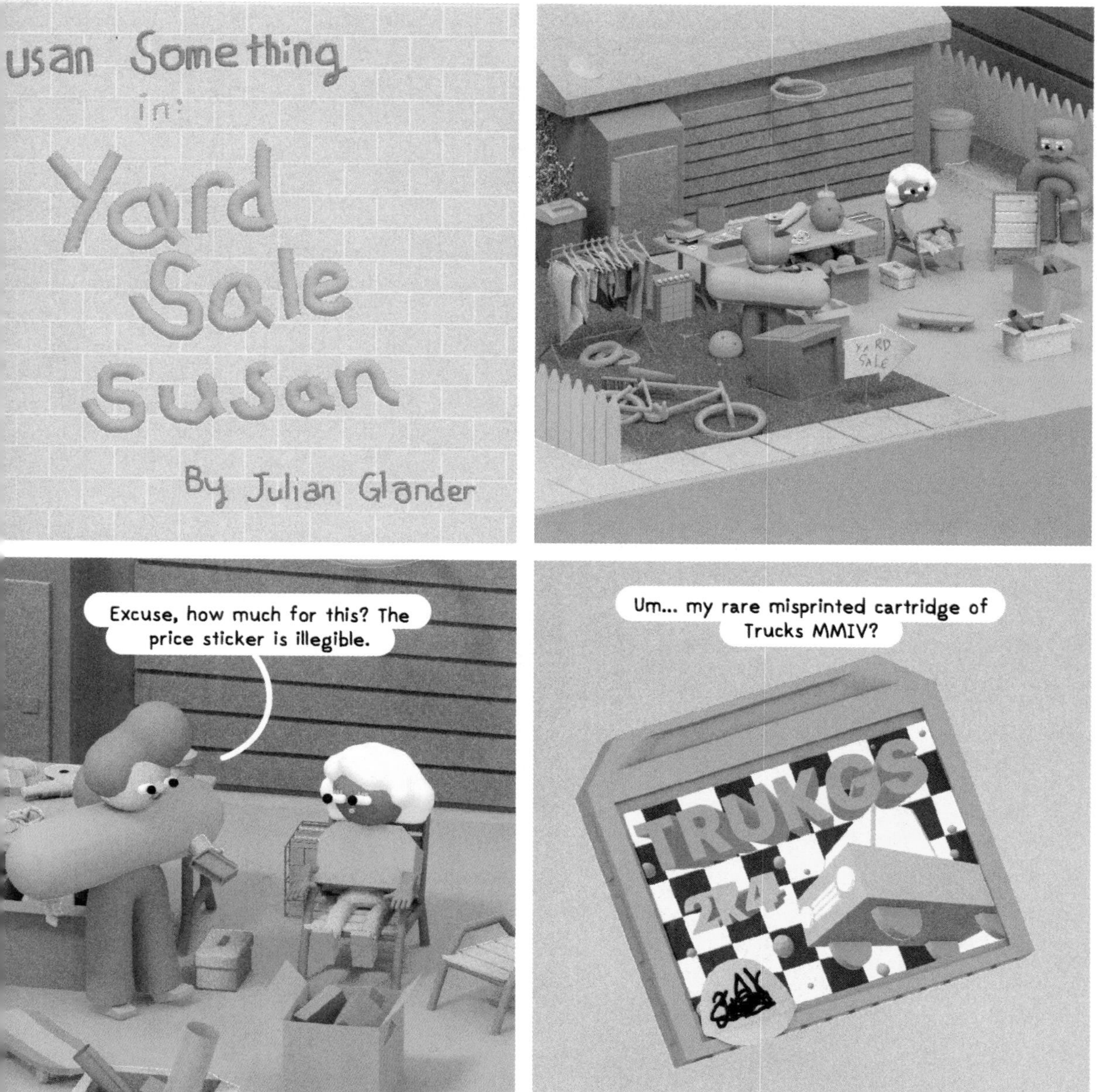

usan Something
in:
Yard Sale Susan
By Julian Glander
YARD SALE
Excuse, how much for this? The price sticker is illegible.
Um... my rare misprinted cartridge of Trucks MMIV?
TRUKGS
2K4

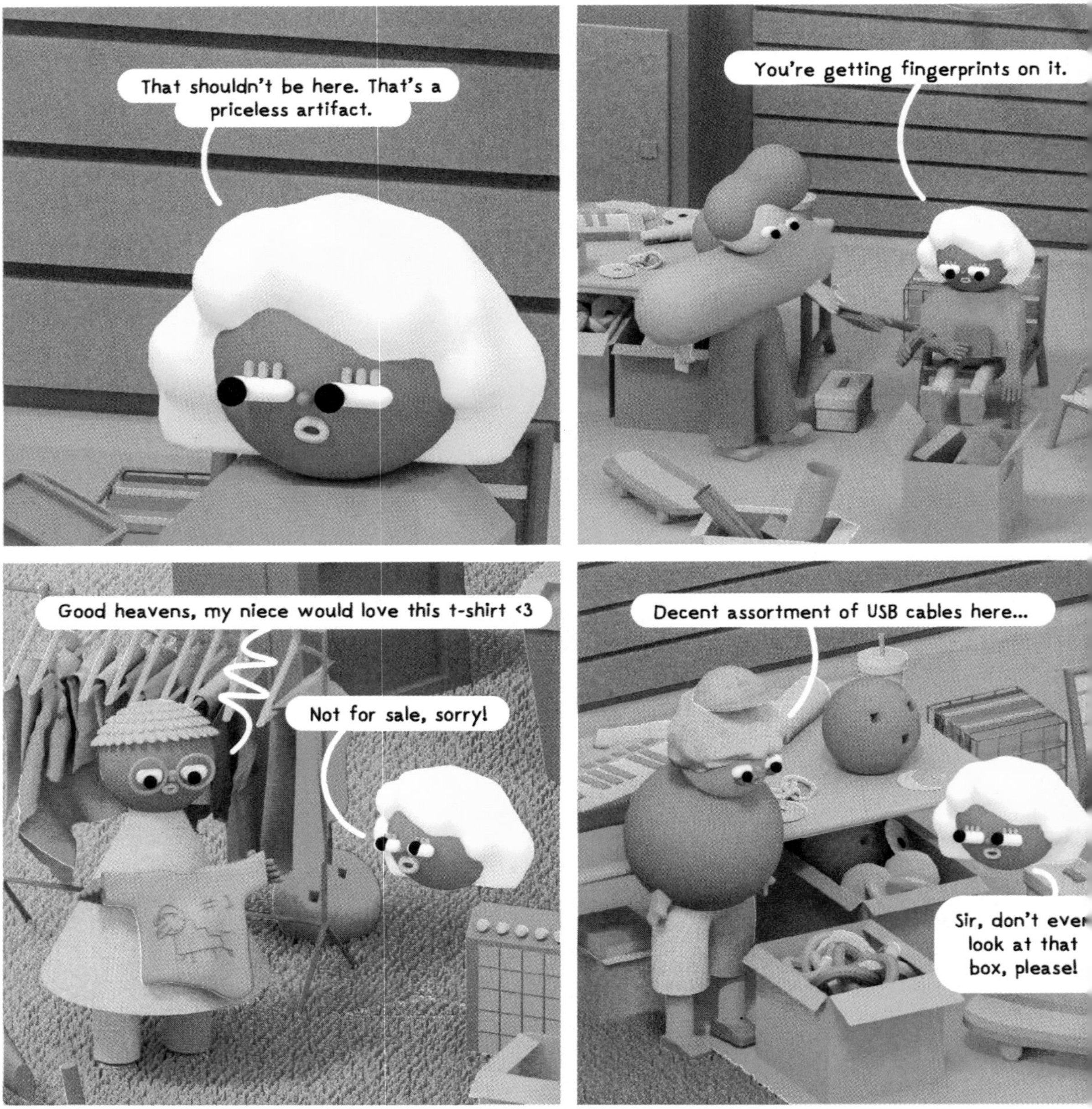
That shouldn't be here. That's a priceless artifact.
You're getting fingerprints on it.
Good heavens, my niece would love this t-shirt <3
Not for sale, sorry!
Decent assortment of USB cables here...
Sir, don't eve
look at that
box, please!

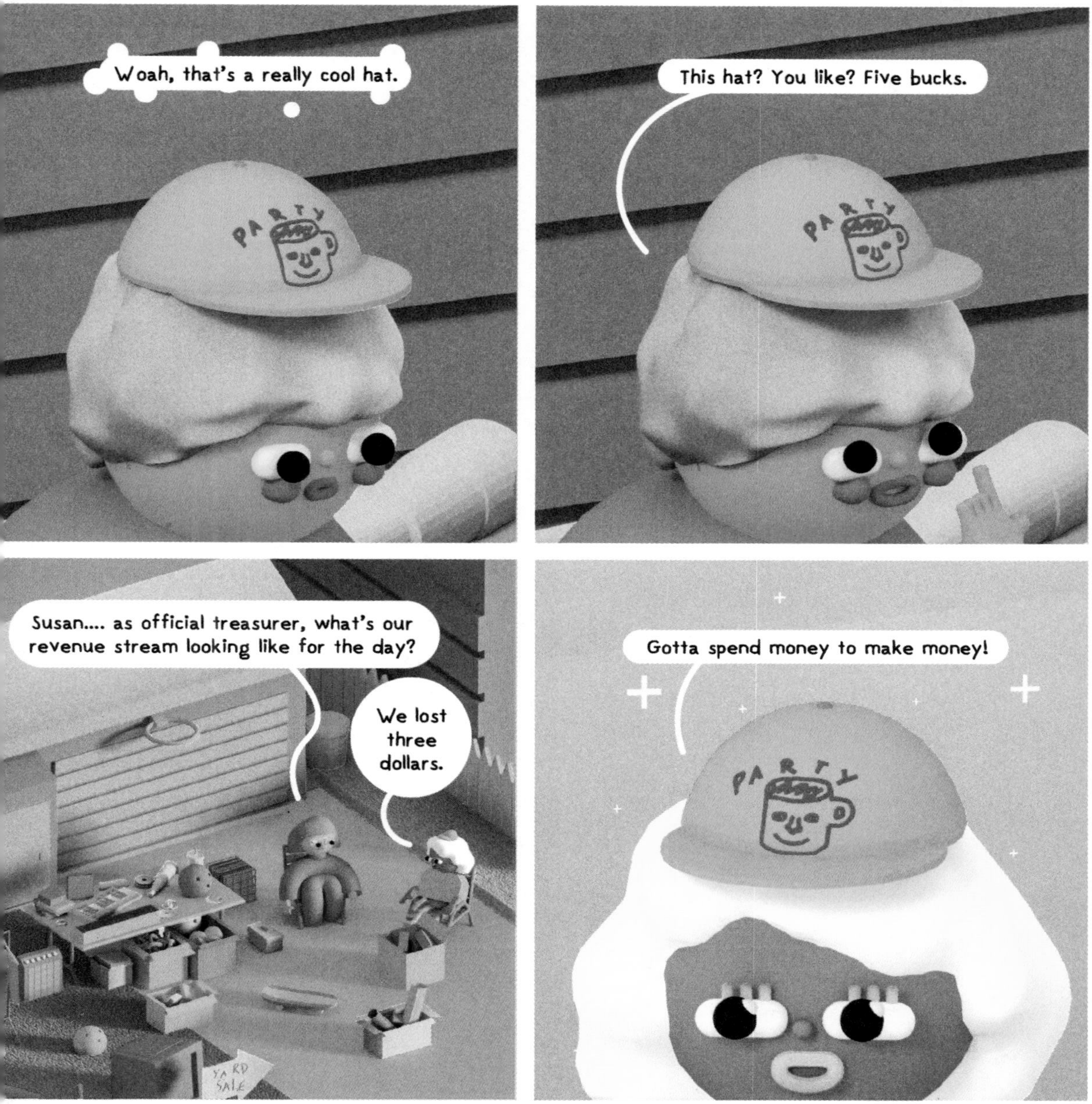
Woah, that's a really cool hat.
This hat? You like? Five bucks.
Susan.... as official treasurer, what's our revenue stream looking like for the day?
We lost three dollars.
YARD SALE
Gotta spend money to make money!

Sam's Story (*Excerpt*)

SARAH GLIDDEN

ROLLING
BLACKOUTS
DISPATCHES FROM TURKEY, SYRIA, AND IRAQ
SARAH GLIDDEN

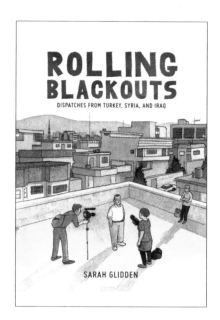

originally published in

Rolling Blackouts
DRAWN AND QUARTERLY
6.5 x 8.9 inches • 304 pages

Biography

Sarah Glidden was born in 1980 in Massachusetts and studied painting at Boston University. She started making comics in 2006 when she was living at the Flux Factory artists collective in Queens, New York, and soon began working on her first book, *How to Understand Israel in 60 Days or Less*. The first chapters were self-published as mini-comics, earning her the Ignatz Award for Promising New Talent in 2008. The complete book was published in 2010 and was translated into five languages. Her second book, *Rolling Blackouts: Dispatches from Turkey, Syria, and Iraq*, was published by Drawn & Quarterly in October 2016, quickly becoming a *New York Times* bestseller, appearing on 15 Best of the Year lists, and earning her the Lynd Ward Graphic Novel Prize.
sarahglidden.com

Statement

Rolling Blackouts is a documentary comic in which I followed journalists Sarah Stuteville and Alex Stonehill of the *Seattle Globalist* on a reporting trip to the Middle East in late 2010, where they were producing a series of stories centered around people displaced by the American-led wars in the region. In this excerpt, they are holding their final interview with Sam Malkandi, a Kurdish Iraqi whose story the *Globalist* would tell in the feature-length documentary, *Barzan*. Malkandi deserted the Iraq-Iran War, was a refugee in Iran and Pakistan, and was finally granted asylum with his family in the United States in the late 90s. In 2004, however, he was accused of aiding an Al Qaeda terrorist in the 9/11 plot. Although there was no concrete evidence to back up this accusation, Malkandi was detained for five years and finally deported back to Iraq. This is his side of the story.

The next day is Sarah's last interview with Sam.

Let's take a moment and just think about what is interesting about this story...

They won't get another chance to talk to Sam. They need to make it count, and for that to happen, they now need to have an idea of how they want to tell his story.

The first interesting thing is he's this really patriotic, hard-working, deeply loved man who gets accused of terrorism and deported.

For a man with such a complicated past, this isn't going to be easy.

The other thing is the ambiguity of what happened. So that's the mall story.

But the third layer of interesting is that on paper, he's an Iraqi guy who went to Iran and then Pakistan and then came to the United States, was approached by a guy from al Qaeda, helped him in some way, and then showed up in the 9/11 Commission Report.

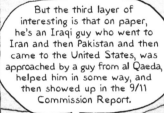

I feel like it's important for him to acknowledge that whether his charges were fair or not, it looks very suspicious. You know?

Yeah.

And Sam may think there's no connection here, but the reason nobody stood up for his case, the reason he didn't get pardoned, the reason he didn't win that immigration case...

...is because of this stuff.

In Sam's mind there's this false charge against him that they never make a case around and that disappears and then they deport him on an immigration issue.

But of course it's connected.

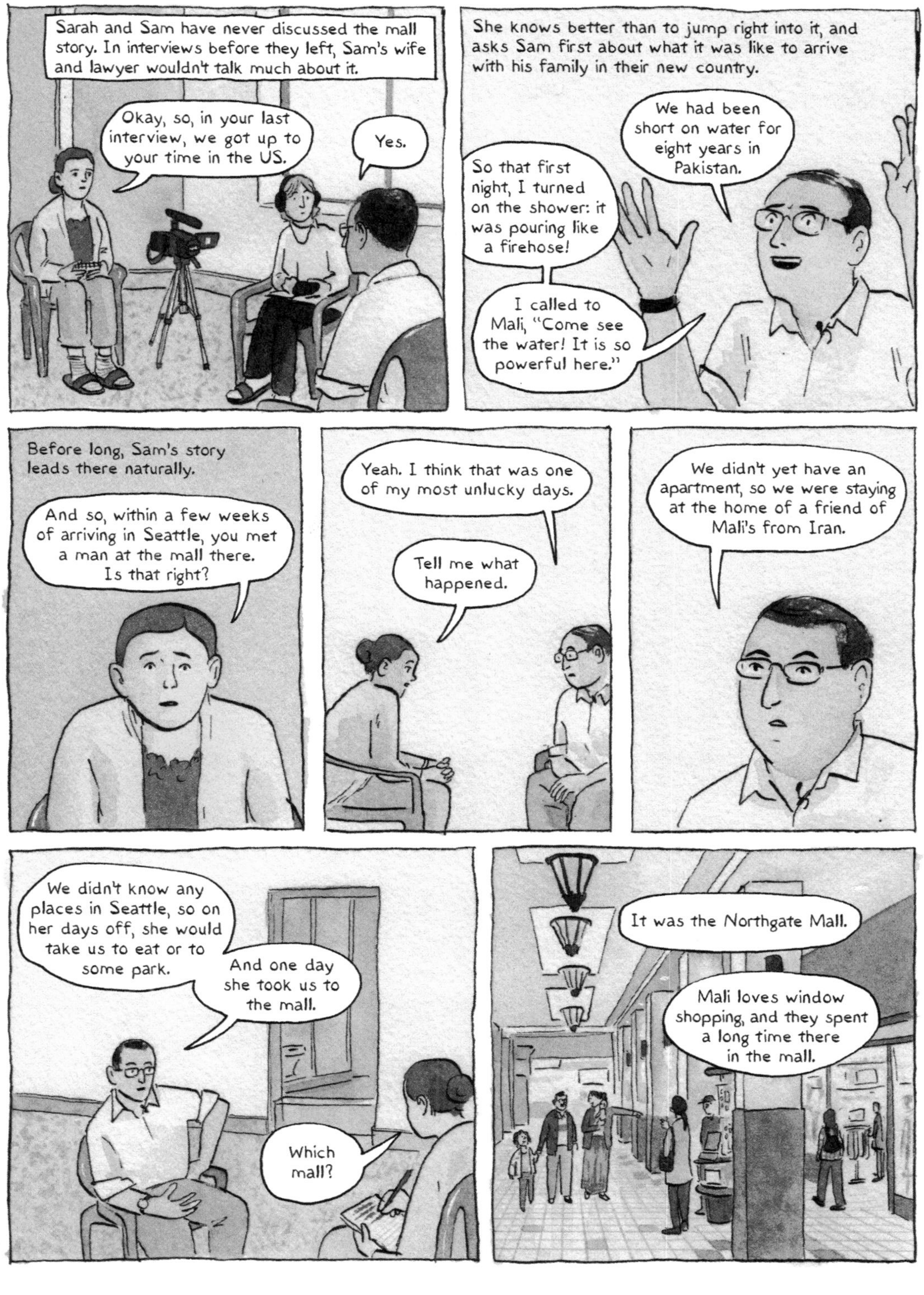
Sarah and Sam have never discussed the mall story. In interviews before they left, Sam's wife and lawyer wouldn't talk much about it.
Okay, so, in your last interview, we got up to your time in the US.
Yes.
She knows better than to jump right into it, and asks Sam first about what it was like to arrive with his family in their new country.
We had been short on water for eight years in Pakistan.
So that first night, I turned on the shower: it was pouring like a firehose!
I called to Mali, "Come see the water! It is so powerful here."
Before long, Sam's story leads there naturally.
And so, within a few weeks of arriving in Seattle, you met a man at the mall there. Is that right?
Yeah. I think that was one of my most unlucky days.
Tell me what happened.
We didn't yet have an apartment, so we were staying at the home of a friend of Mali's from Iran.
We didn't know any places in Seattle, so on her days off, she would take us to eat or to some park.
And one day she took us to the mall.
Which mall?
It was the Northgate Mall.
Mali loves window shopping, and they spent a long time there in the mall.

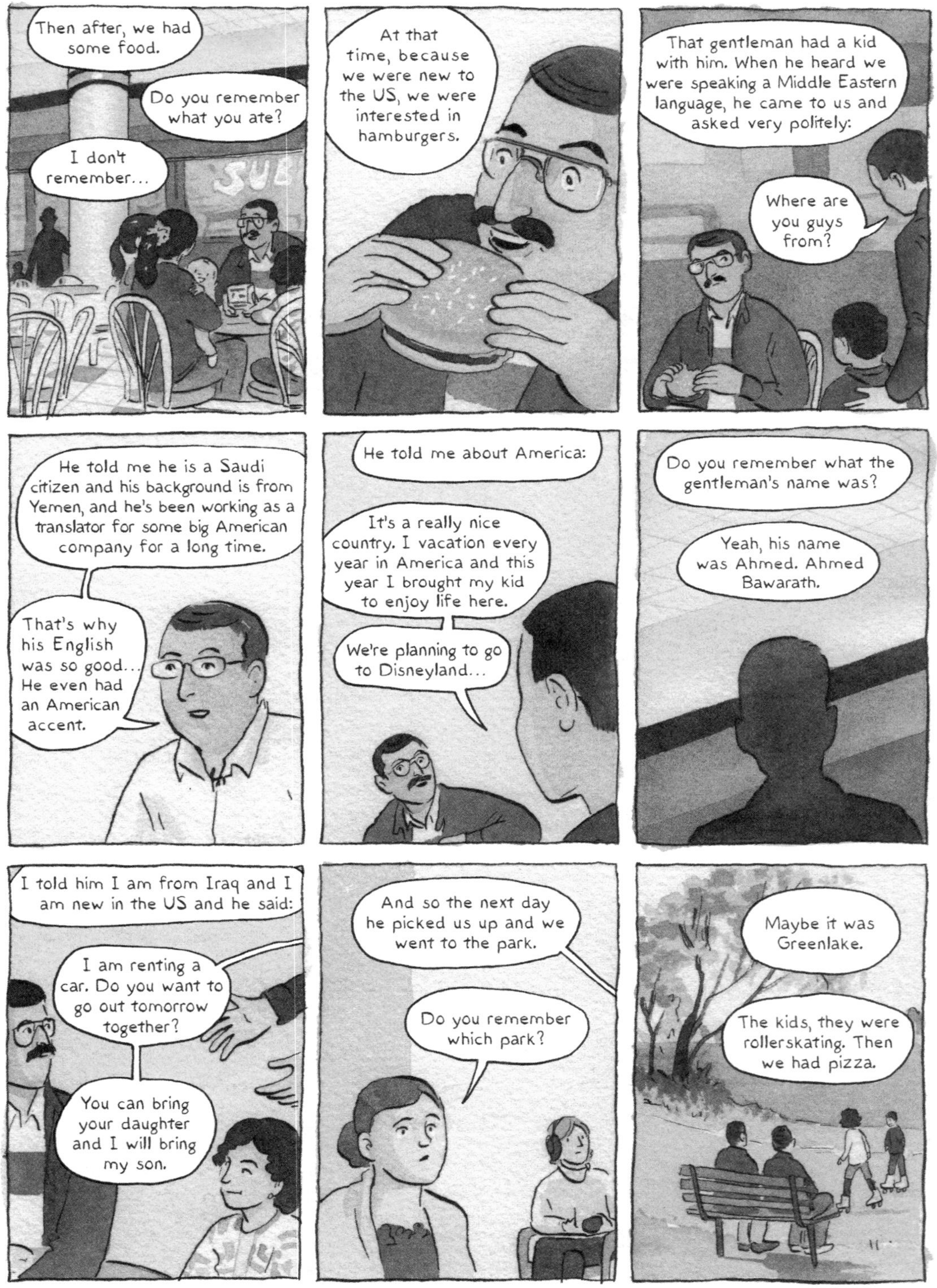
Then after, we had some food.
Do you remember what you ate?
I don't remember...
At that time, because we were new to the US, we were interested in hamburgers.
That gentleman had a kid with him. When he heard we were speaking a Middle Eastern language, he came to us and asked very politely:
Where are you guys from?
He told me he is a Saudi citizen and his background is from Yemen, and he's been working as a translator for some big American company for a long time.
That's why his English was so good... He even had an American accent.
He told me about America:
It's a really nice country. I vacation every year in America and this year I brought my kid to enjoy life here.
We're planning to go to Disneyland...
Do you remember what the gentleman's name was?
Yeah, his name was Ahmed. Ahmed Bawarath.
I told him I am from Iraq and I am new in the US and he said:
I am renting a car. Do you want to go out tomorrow together?
You can bring your daughter and I will bring my son.
And so the next day he picked us up and we went to the park.
Do you remember which park?
Maybe it was Greenlake.
The kids, they were rollerskating. Then we had pizza.

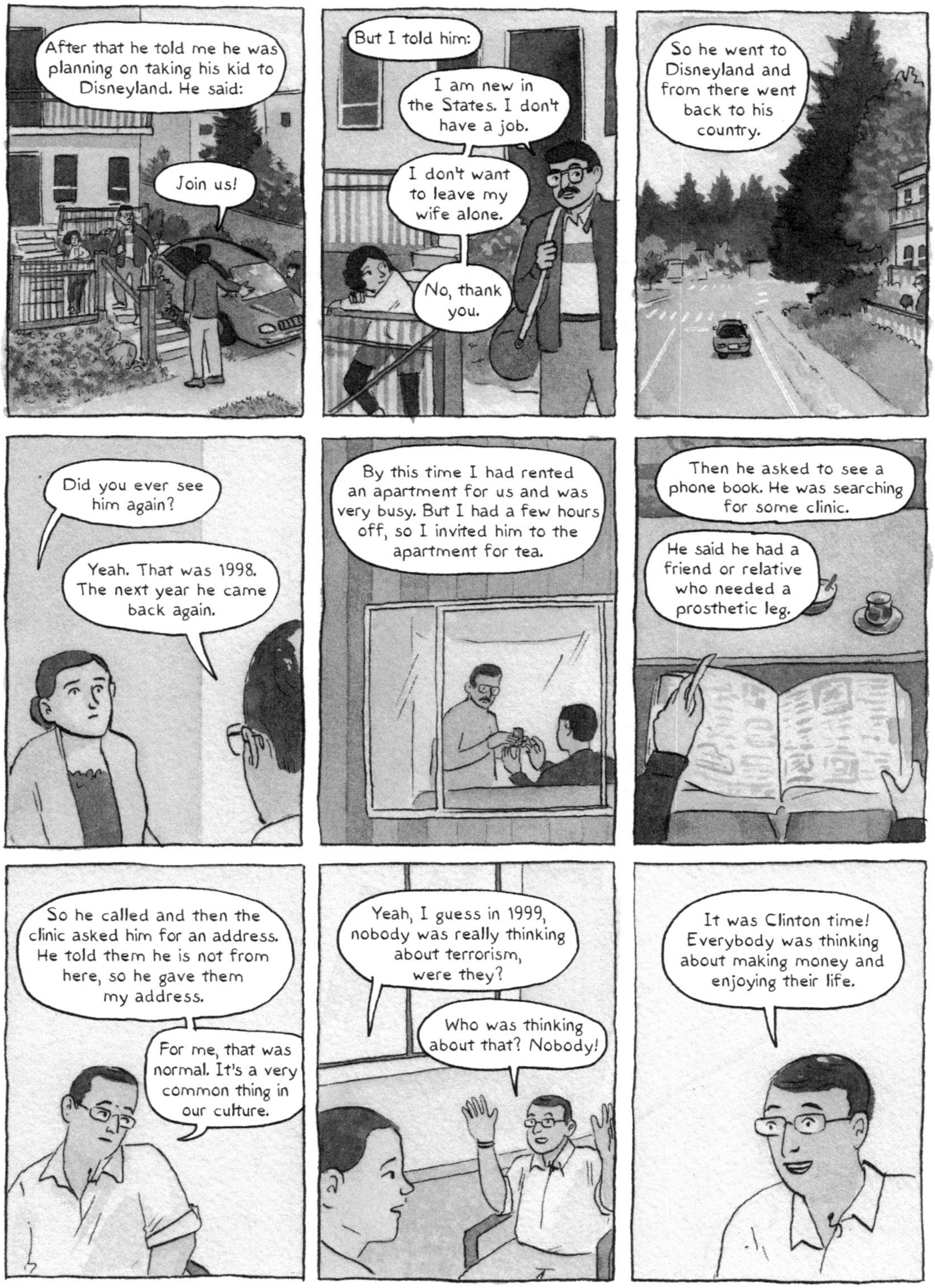
After that he told me he was planning on taking his kid to Disneyland. He said:
Join us!
But I told him:
I am new in the States. I don't have a job.
I don't want to leave my wife alone.
No, thank you.
So he went to Disneyland and from there went back to his country.
Did you ever see him again?
Yeah. That was 1998. The next year he came back again.
By this time I had rented an apartment for us and was very busy. But I had a few hours off, so I invited him to the apartment for tea.
Then he asked to see a phone book. He was searching for some clinic.
He said he had a friend or relative who needed a prosthetic leg.
So he called and then the clinic asked him for an address. He told them he is not from here, so he gave them my address.
For me, that was normal. It's a very common thing in our culture.
Yeah, I guess in 1999, nobody was really thinking about terrorism, were they?
Who was thinking about that? Nobody!
It was Clinton time! Everybody was thinking about making money and enjoying their life.

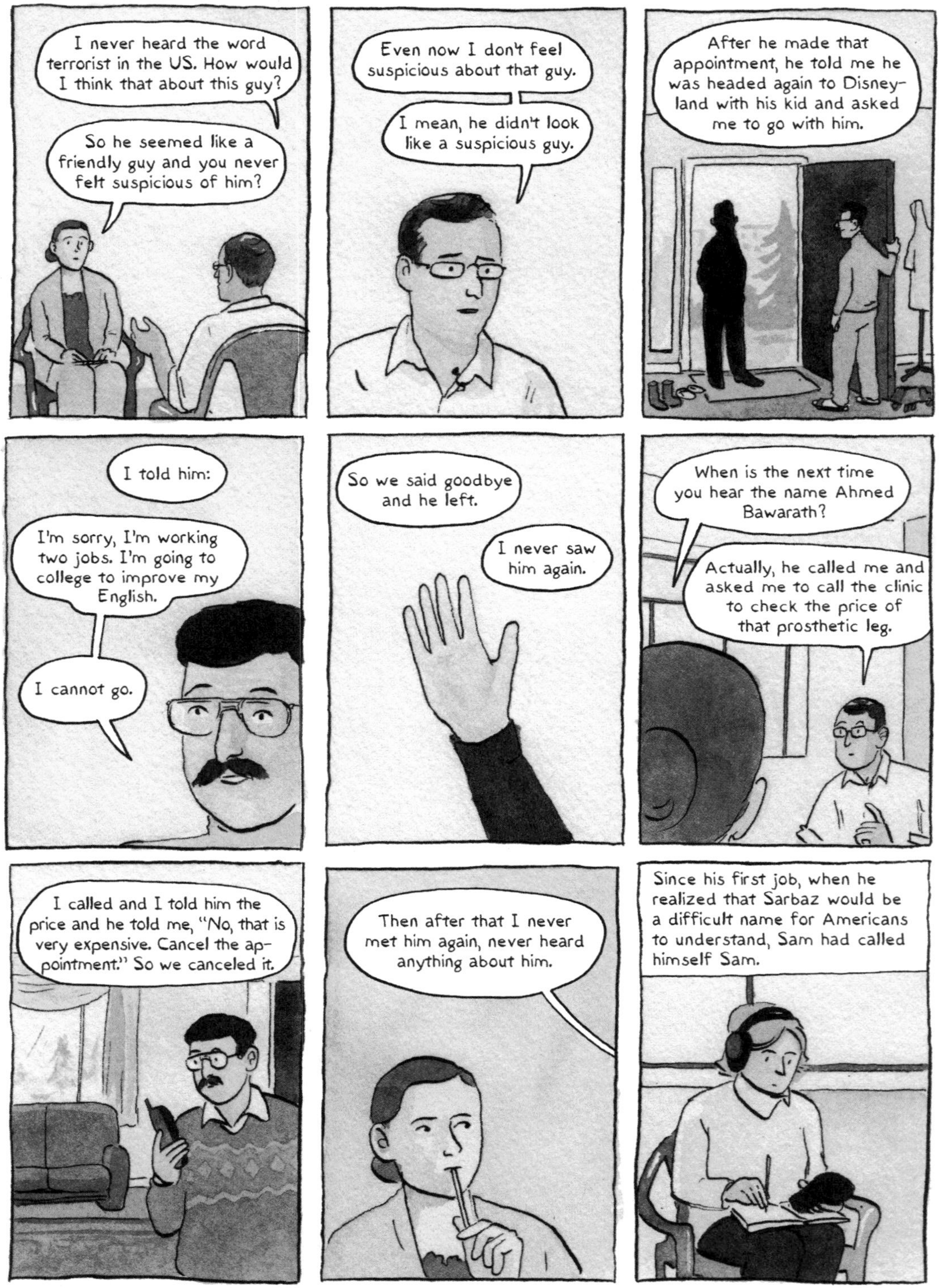
I never heard the word terrorist in the US. How would I think that about this guy?
So he seemed like a friendly guy and you never felt suspicious of him?
Even now I don't feel suspicious about that guy.
I mean, he didn't look like a suspicious guy.
After he made that appointment, he told me he was headed again to Disney-land with his kid and asked me to go with him.
I told him:
I'm sorry, I'm working two jobs. I'm going to college to improve my English.
I cannot go.
So we said goodbye and he left.
I never saw him again.
When is the next time you hear the name Ahmed Bawarath?
Actually, he called me and asked me to call the clinic to check the price of that prosthetic leg.
I called and I told him the price and he told me, "No, that is very expensive. Cancel the ap-pointment." So we canceled it.
Then after that I never met him again, never heard anything about him.
Since his first job, when he realized that Sarbaz would be a difficult name for Americans to understand, Sam had called himself Sam.

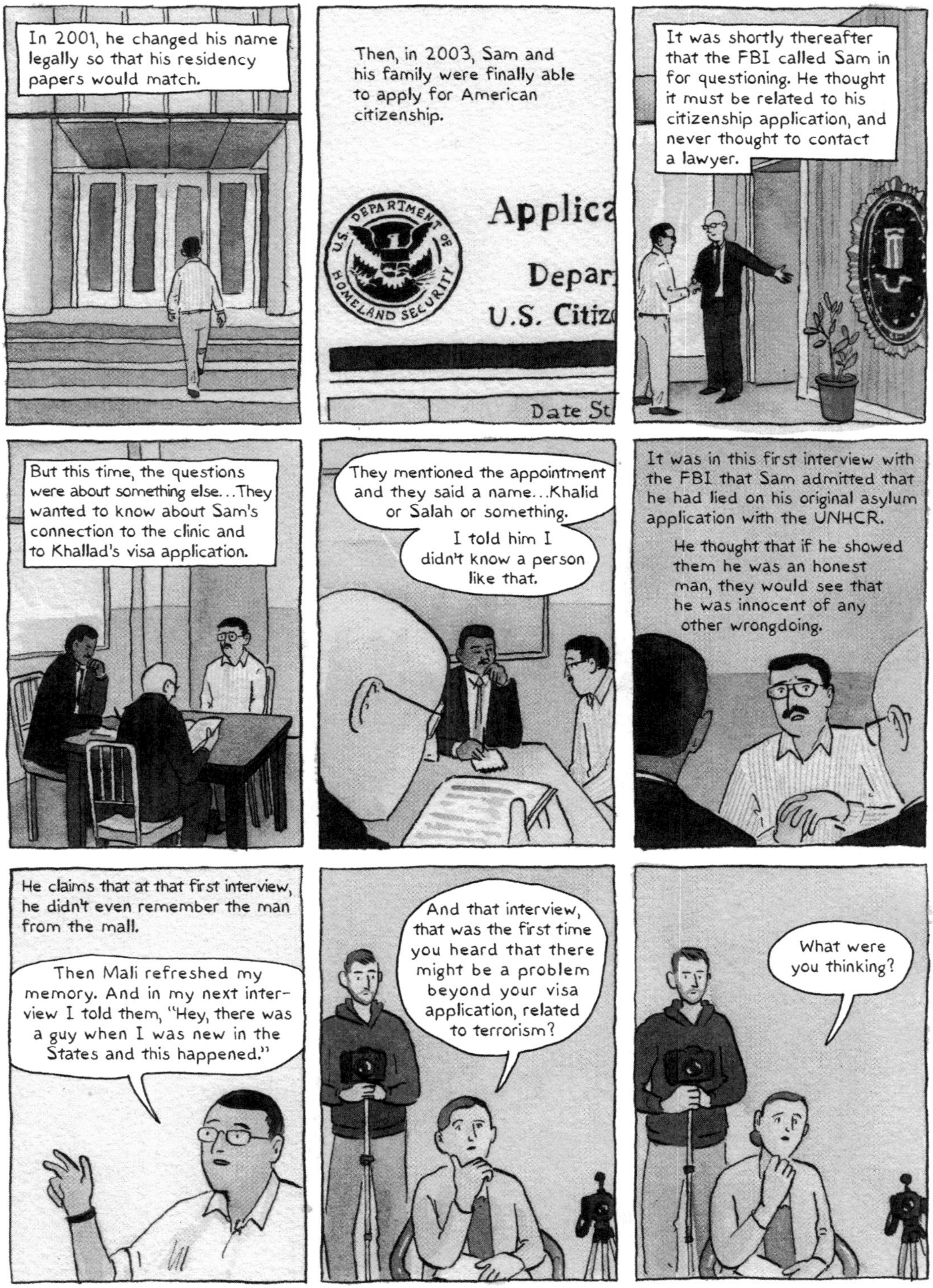
In 2001, he changed his name legally so that his residency papers would match.
Then, in 2003, Sam and his family were finally able to apply for American citizenship.
U.S. DEPARTMENT OF HOMELAND SECURITY
Applica
Depar
U.S. Citiz
Date St
It was shortly thereafter that the FBI called Sam in for questioning. He thought it must be related to his citizenship application, and never thought to contact a lawyer.
But this time, the questions were about something else...They wanted to know about Sam's connection to the clinic and to Khallad's visa application.
They mentioned the appointment and they said a name...Khalid or Salah or something.
I told him I didn't know a person like that.
It was in this first interview with the FBI that Sam admitted that he had lied on his original asylum application with the UNHCR.
He thought that if he showed them he was an honest man, they would see that he was innocent of any other wrongdoing.
He claims that at that first interview, he didn't even remember the man from the mall.
Then Mali refreshed my memory. And in my next interview I told them, "Hey, there was a guy when I was new in the States and this happened."
And that interview, that was the first time you heard that there might be a problem beyond your visa application, related to terrorism?
What were you thinking?

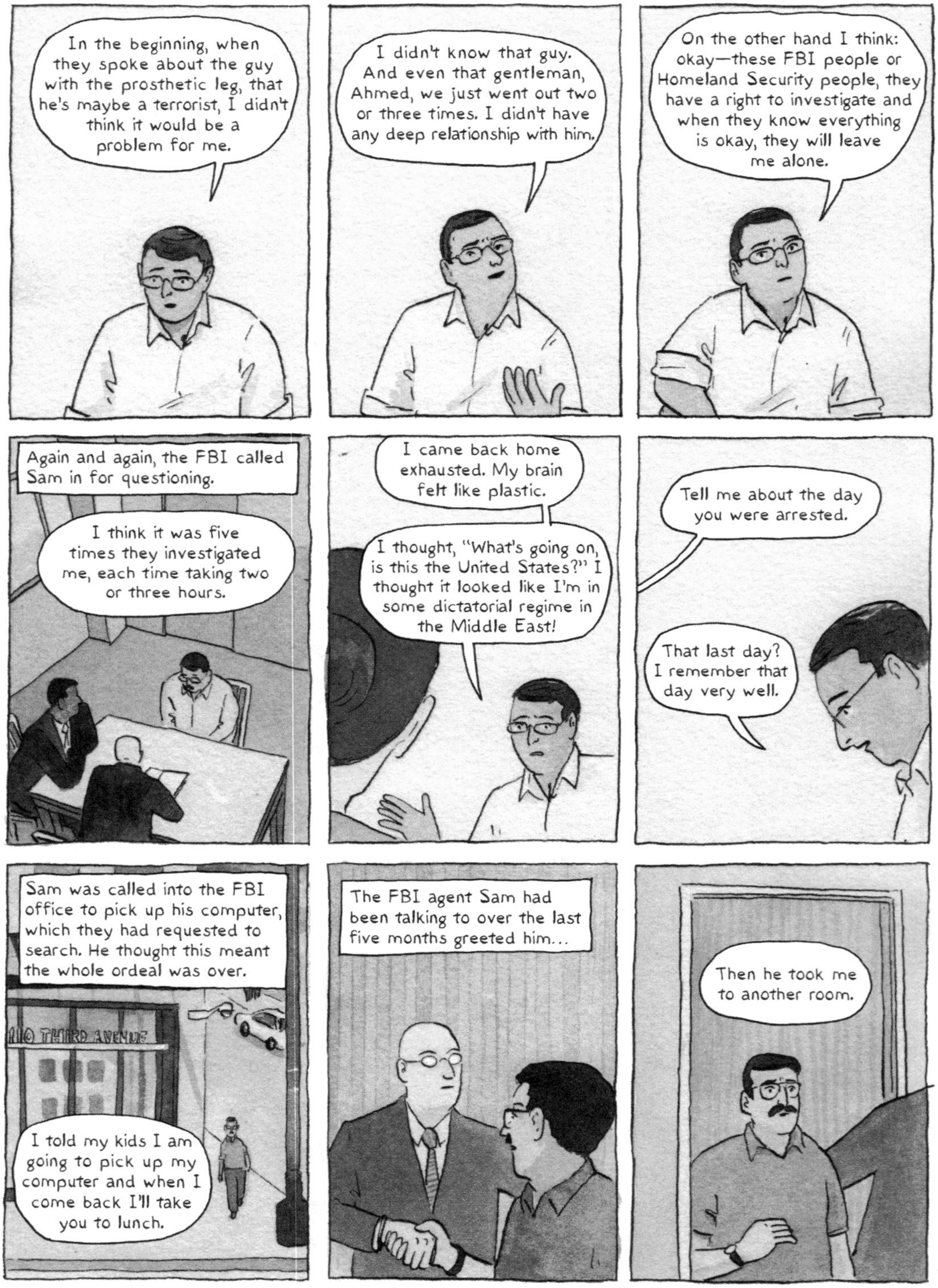
In the beginning, when they spoke about the guy with the prosthetic leg, that he's maybe a terrorist, I didn't think it would be a problem for me.
I didn't know that guy. And even that gentleman, Ahmed, we just went out two or three times. I didn't have any deep relationship with him.
On the other hand I think: okay—these FBI people or Homeland Security people, they have a right to investigate and when they know everything is okay, they will leave me alone.
Again and again, the FBI called Sam in for questioning.
I think it was five times they investigated me, each time taking two or three hours.
I came back home exhausted. My brain felt like plastic.
I thought, "What's going on, is this the United States?" I thought it looked like I'm in some dictatorial regime in the Middle East!
Tell me about the day you were arrested.
That last day? I remember that day very well.
Sam was called into the FBI office to pick up his computer, which they had requested to search. He thought this meant the whole ordeal was over.
I told my kids I am going to pick up my computer and when I come back I'll take you to lunch.
The FBI agent Sam had been talking to over the last five months greeted him...
Then he took me to another room.

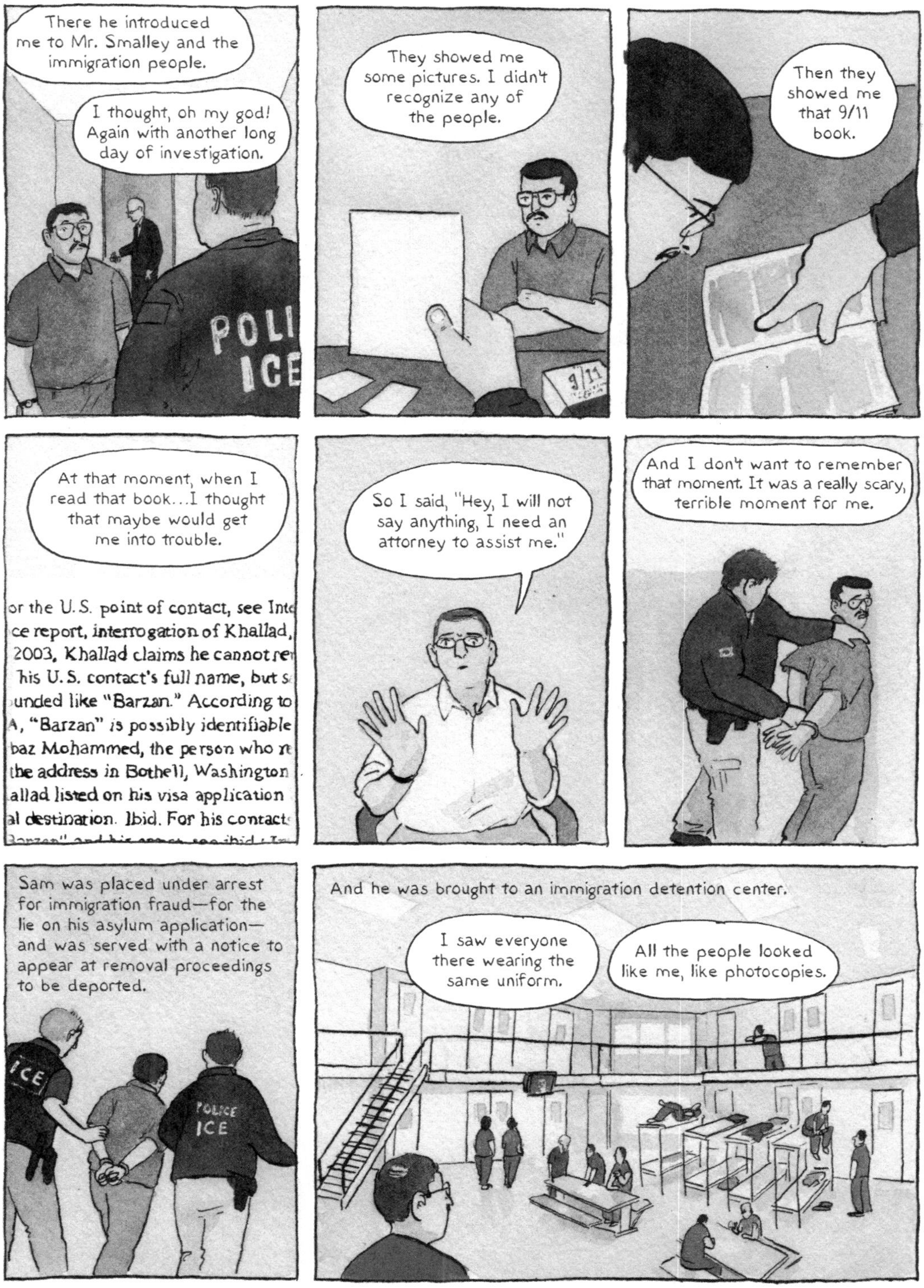

There he introduced me to Mr. Smalley and the immigration people.
I thought, oh my god! Again with another long day of investigation.
POLI
ICE
They showed me some pictures. I didn't recognize any of the people.
9/11
Then they showed me that 9/11 book.
At that moment, when I read that book...I thought that maybe would get me into trouble.
or the U.S. point of contact, see Inte
ce report, interrogation of Khallad,
2003, Khallad claims he cannot re
his U.S. contact's full name, but s
unded like "Barzan." According to
A, "Barzan" is possibly identifiable
baz Mohammed, the person who r
the address in Bothell, Washington
allad listed on his visa application
al destination. Ibid. For his contact
So I said, "Hey, I will not say anything, I need an attorney to assist me."
And I don't want to remember that moment. It was a really scary, terrible moment for me.
Sam was placed under arrest for immigration fraud—for the lie on his asylum application—and was served with a notice to appear at removal proceedings to be deported.
ICE
POLICE
ICE
And he was brought to an immigration detention center.
I saw everyone there wearing the same uniform.
All the people looked like me, like photocopies.

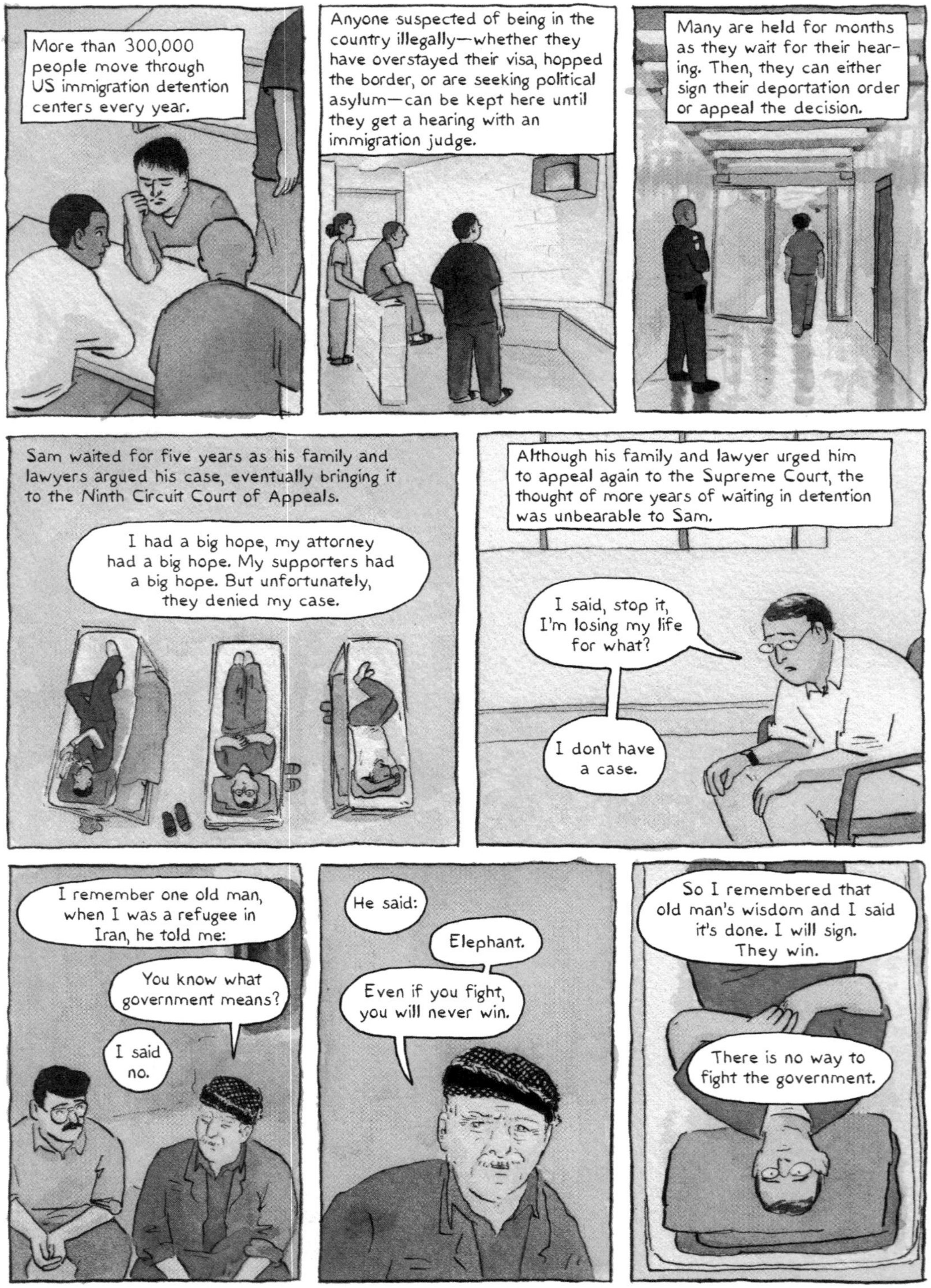
More than 300,000 people move through US immigration detention centers every year.
Anyone suspected of being in the country illegally—whether they have overstayed their visa, hopped the border, or are seeking political asylum—can be kept here until they get a hearing with an immigration judge.
Many are held for months as they wait for their hearing. Then, they can either sign their deportation order or appeal the decision.
Sam waited for five years as his family and lawyers argued his case, eventually bringing it to the Ninth Circuit Court of Appeals.
I had a big hope, my attorney had a big hope. My supporters had a big hope. But unfortunately, they denied my case.
Although his family and lawyer urged him to appeal again to the Supreme Court, the thought of more years of waiting in detention was unbearable to Sam.
I said, stop it, I'm losing my life for what?
I don't have a case.
I remember one old man, when I was a refugee in Iran, he told me:
You know what government means?
I said no.
He said:
Elephant.
Even if you fight, you will never win.
So I remembered that old man's wisdom and I said it's done. I will sign. They win.
There is no way to fight the government.

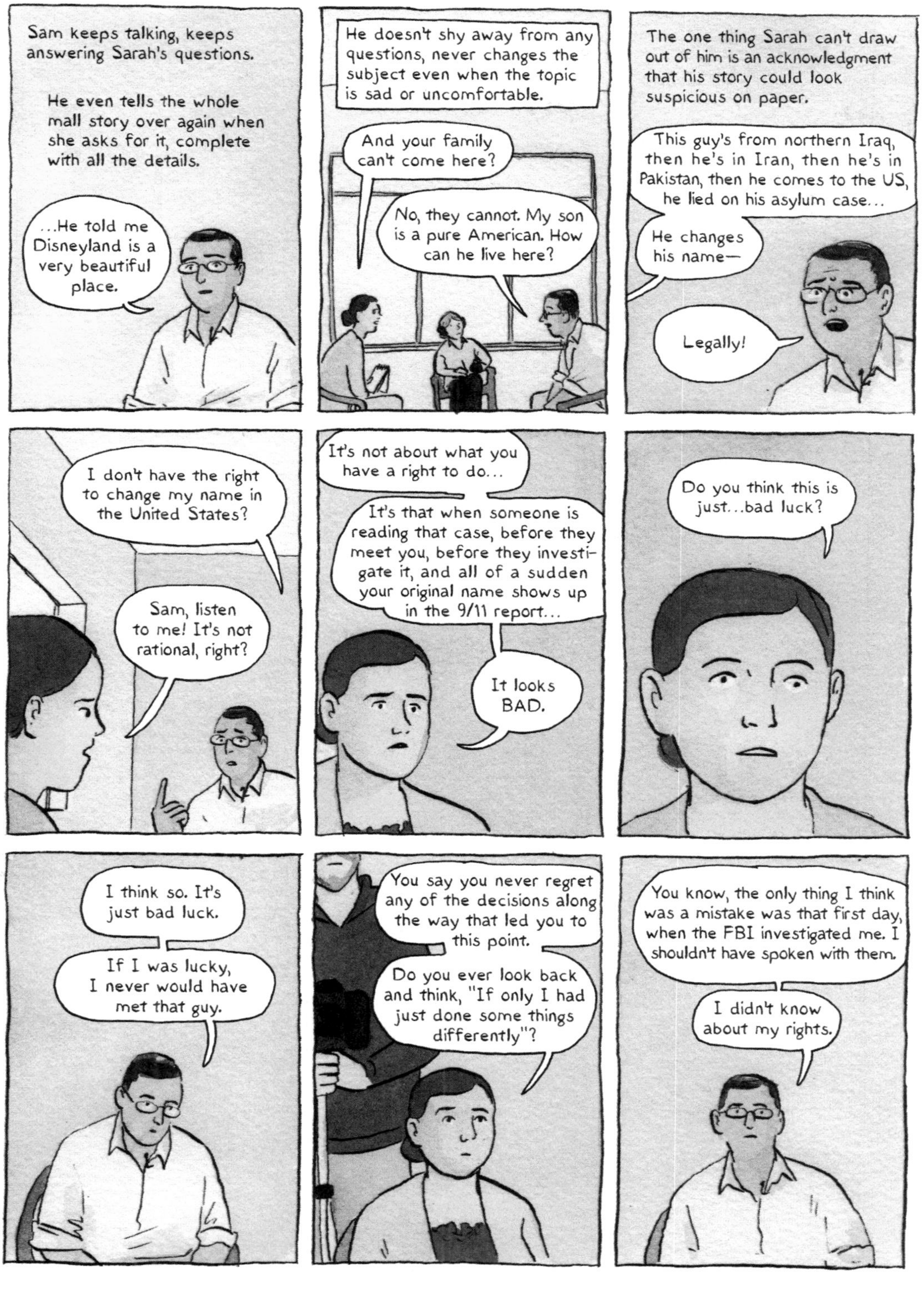

Sam keeps talking, keeps answering Sarah's questions.
He even tells the whole mall story over again when she asks for it, complete with all the details.
...He told me Disneyland is a very beautiful place.
He doesn't shy away from any questions, never changes the subject even when the topic is sad or uncomfortable.
And your family can't come here?
No, they cannot. My son is a pure American. How can he live here?
The one thing Sarah can't draw out of him is an acknowledgment that his story could look suspicious on paper.
This guy's from northern Iraq, then he's in Iran, then he's in Pakistan, then he comes to the US, he lied on his asylum case...
He changes his name—
Legally!
I don't have the right to change my name in the United States?
Sam, listen to me! It's not rational, right?
It's not about what you have a right to do...
It's that when someone is reading that case, before they meet you, before they investigate it, and all of a sudden your original name shows up in the 9/11 report...
It looks BAD.
Do you think this is just...bad luck?
I think so. It's just bad luck.
If I was lucky, I never would have met that guy.
You say you never regret any of the decisions along the way that led you to this point.
Do you ever look back and think, "If only I had just done some things differently"?
You know, the only thing I think was a mistake was that first day, when the FBI investigated me. I shouldn't have spoken with them.
I didn't know about my rights.

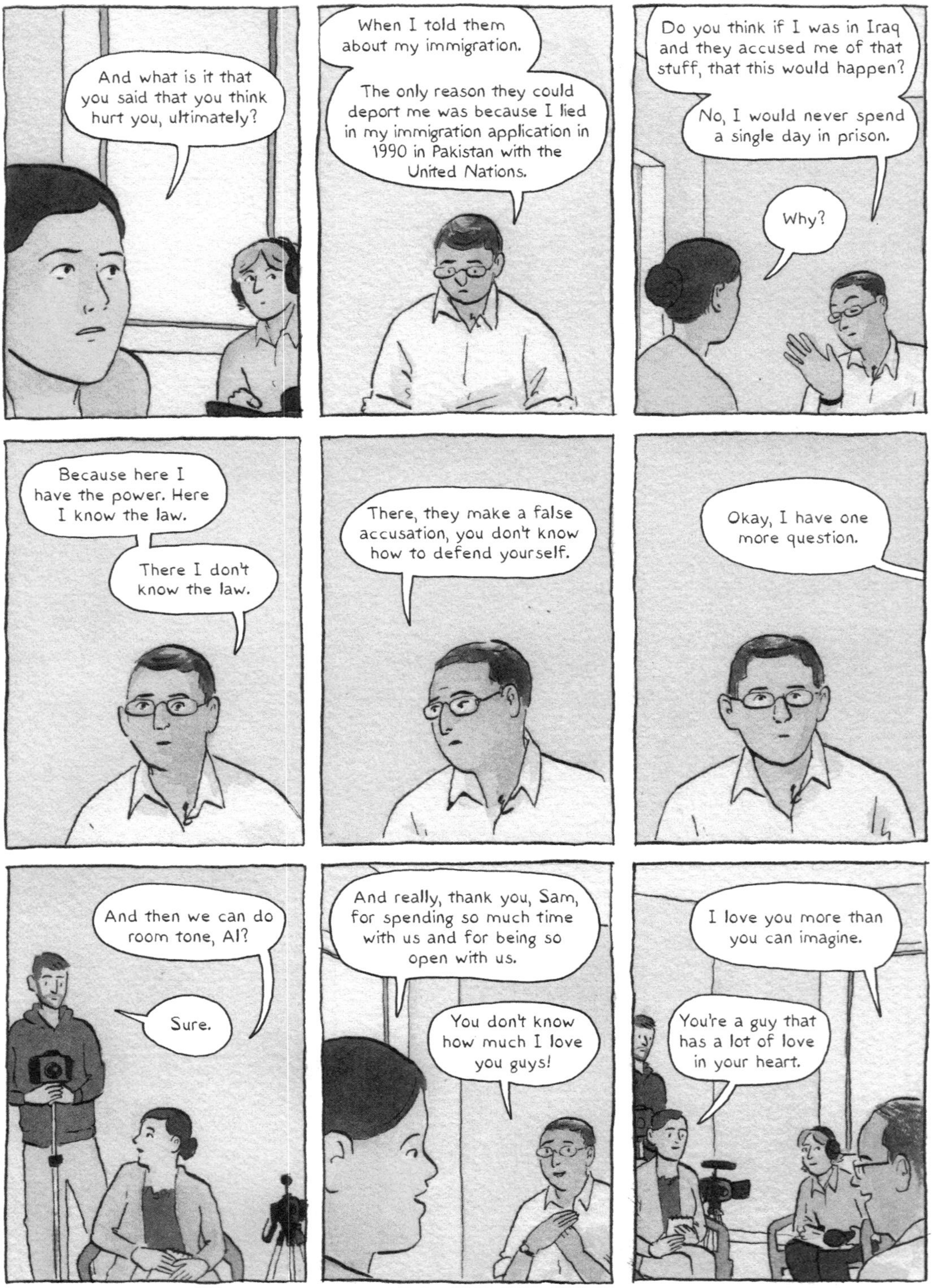

And what is it that you said that you think hurt you, ultimately?
When I told them about my immigration.
The only reason they could deport me was because I lied in my immigration application in 1990 in Pakistan with the United Nations.
Do you think if I was in Iraq and they accused me of that stuff, that this would happen?
No, I would never spend a single day in prison.
Why?
Because here I have the power. Here I know the law.
There I don't know the law.
There, they make a false accusation, you don't know how to defend yourself.
Okay, I have one more question.
And then we can do room tone, Al?
Sure.
And really, thank you, Sam, for spending so much time with us and for being so open with us.
You don't know how much I love you guys!
I love you more than you can imagine.
You're a guy that has a lot of love in your heart.

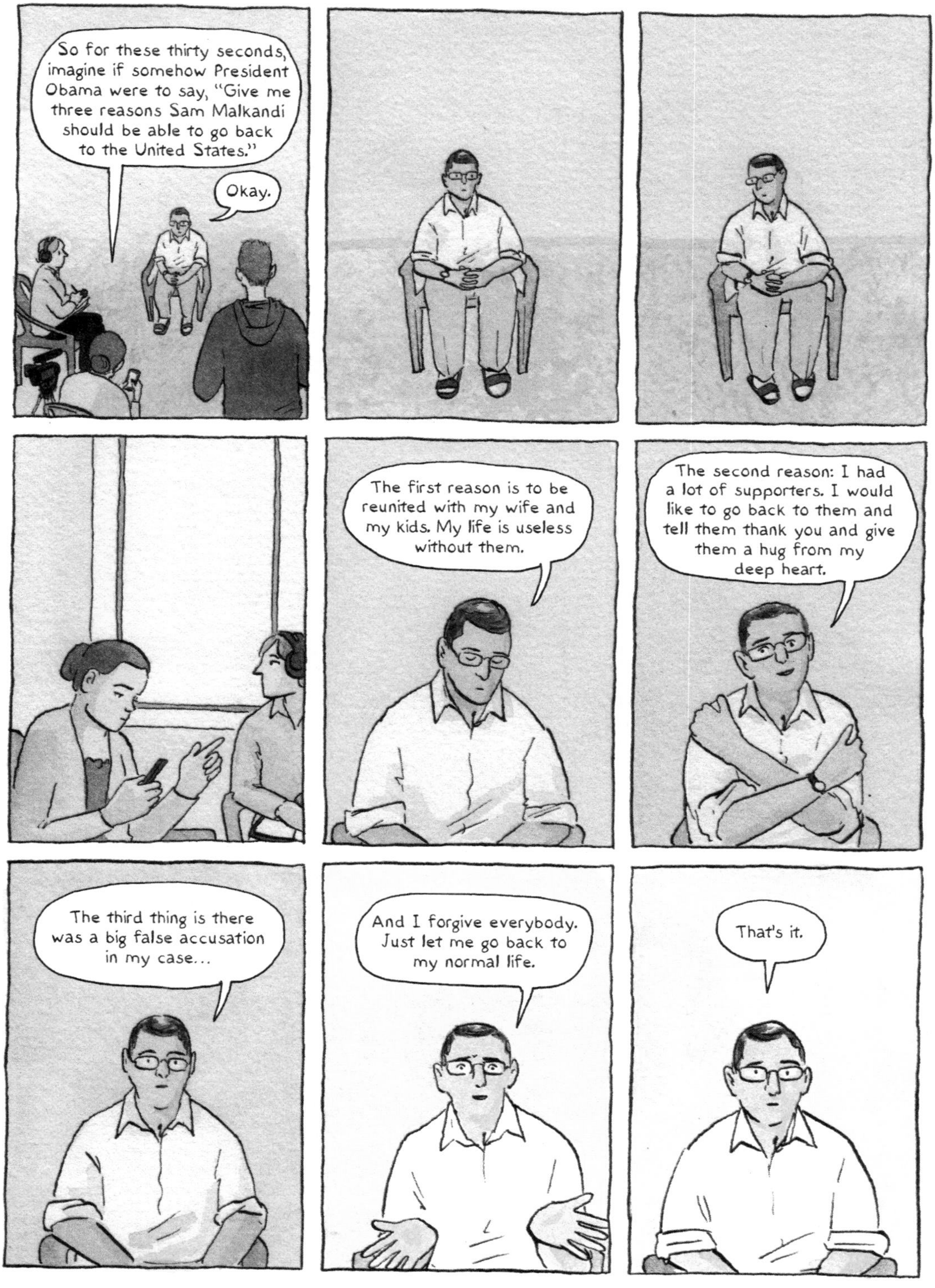
So for these thirty seconds, imagine if somehow President Obama were to say, "Give me three reasons Sam Malkandi should be able to go back to the United States."
Okay.
The first reason is to be reunited with my wife and my kids. My life is useless without them.
The second reason: I had a lot of supporters. I would like to go back to them and tell them thank you and give them a hug from my deep heart.
The third thing is there was a big false accusation in my case...
And I forgive everybody. Just let me go back to my normal life.
That's it.

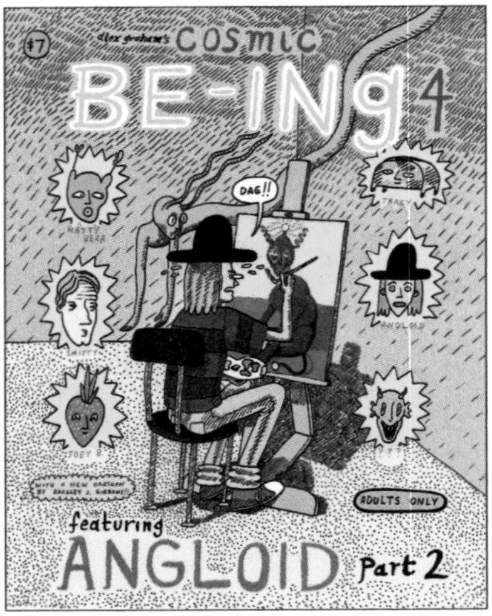
$7
COSMIC
BE-ING 4
DAG!!
ADULTS ONLY
featuring
ANGLOID Part 2

Angloid, Part 2

ALEX GRAHAM

originally published in

Cosmic BE-ING #4

SELF-PUBLISHED

6.45 x 9 inches • 114 pages

Biography

Alex Graham is a painter and cartoonist from Denver, Colorado, currently residing in Seattle, Washington. After (almost) completing one year of art school in 2007, she began working in diners and restaurants around Denver while practicing her craft. Since 2015, she has been self-publishing her comic, titled *Cosmic BE-ING*, and recently completed her first full-length graphic novel.

alexNgraham.com

Statement

This is an excerpt from my semi-autobiographical graphic novel, *Angloid*. It's based on the beginnings of my art career in a crummy, rundown gallery on Colfax Avenue in Denver. I invented a ne'er-do-well gender-ambiguous character (my Mickey Mouse) as an attempt at a nonpreachy, humorous, relatable, and palatable-for-all glimpse into the spectrum of gender, sexuality, and the creative female brain.

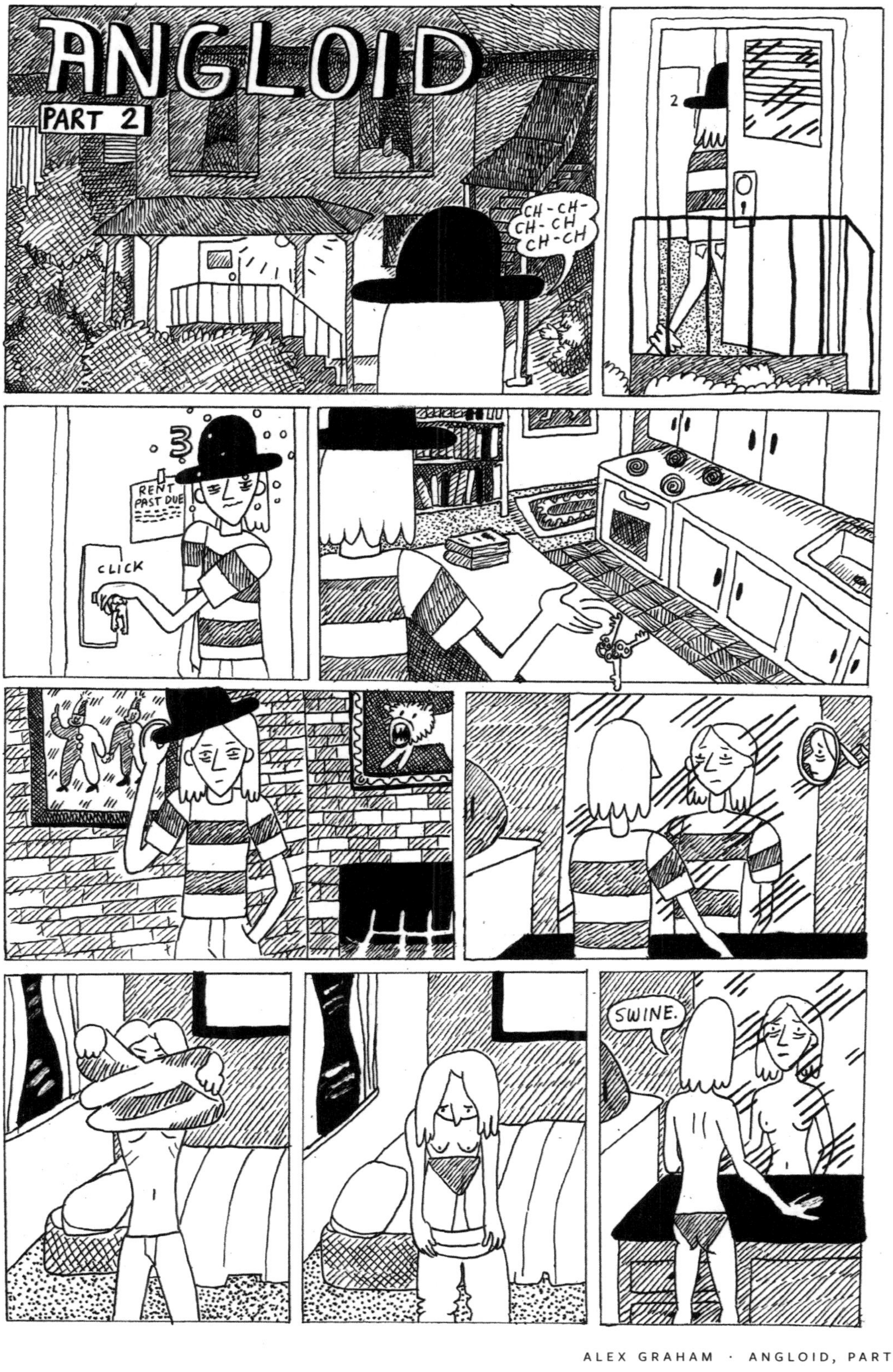
ANGLOID
PART 2
CH-CH-CH-CH CH-CH
2
3
RENT PAST DUE
CLICK
SWINE.

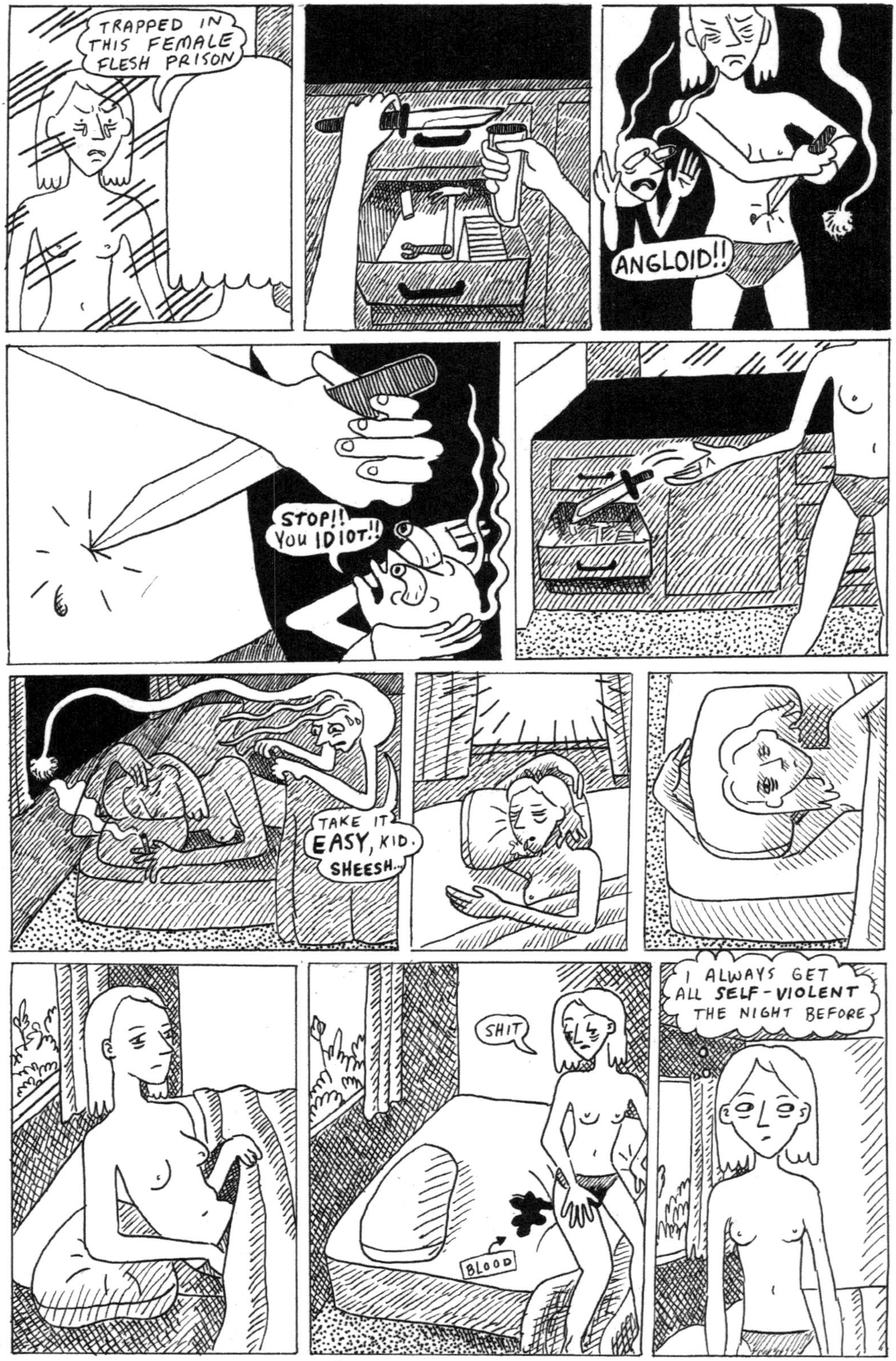
TRAPPED IN THIS FEMALE FLESH PRISON
ANGLOID!!
STOP!! YOU IDIOT!!
TAKE IT EASY, KID. SHEESH...
SHIT
BLOOD
I ALWAYS GET ALL SELF-VIOLENT THE NIGHT BEFORE

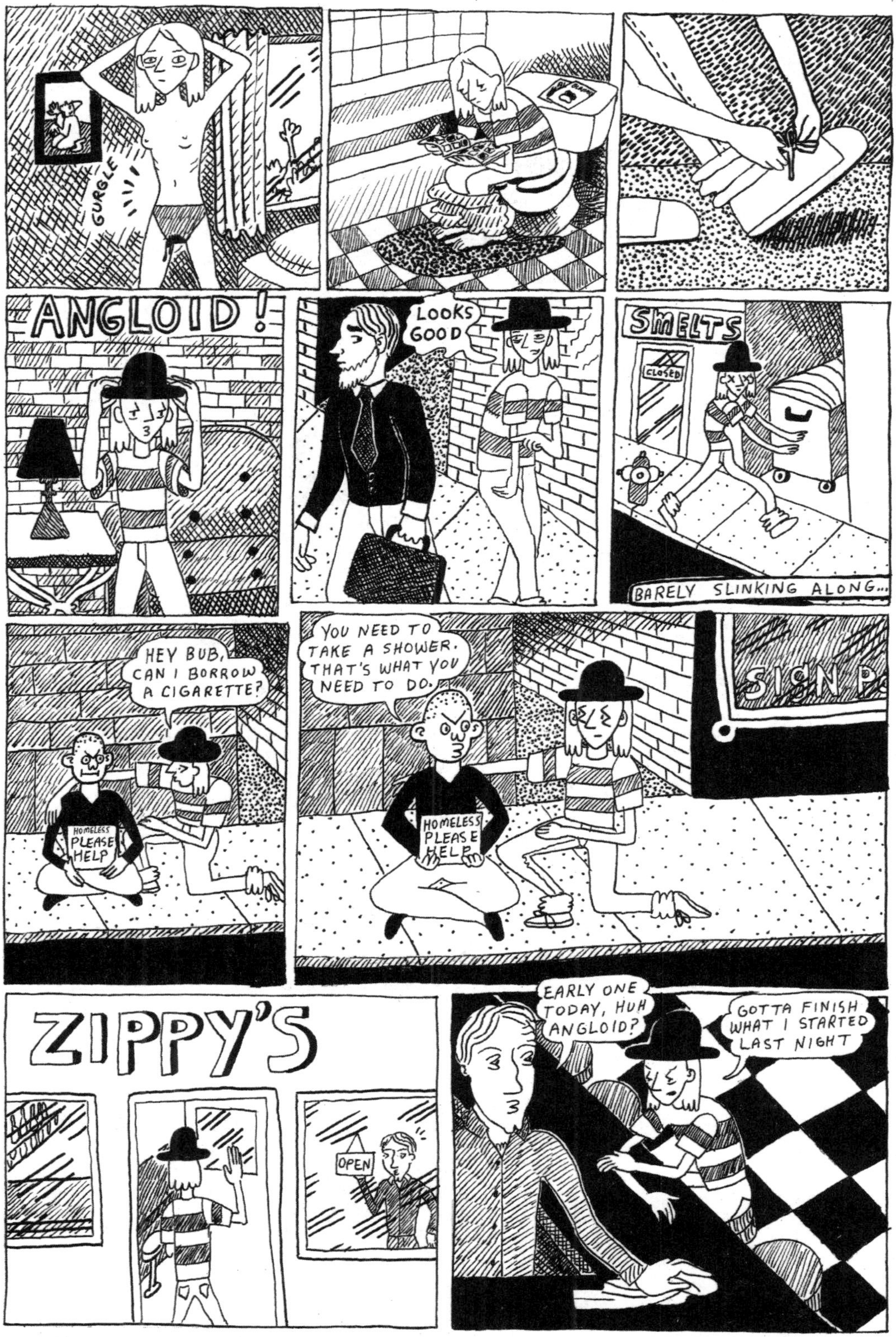
GURGLE
ANGLOID!
LOOKS GOOD
SMELTS
CLOSED
BARELY SLINKING ALONG...
HEY BUB, CAN I BORROW A CIGARETTE?
HOMELESS PLEASE HELP
YOU NEED TO TAKE A SHOWER. THAT'S WHAT YOU NEED TO DO.
HOMELESS PLEASE HELP
ZIPPY'S
OPEN
EARLY ONE TODAY, HUH ANGLOID?
GOTTA FINISH WHAT I STARTED LAST NIGHT

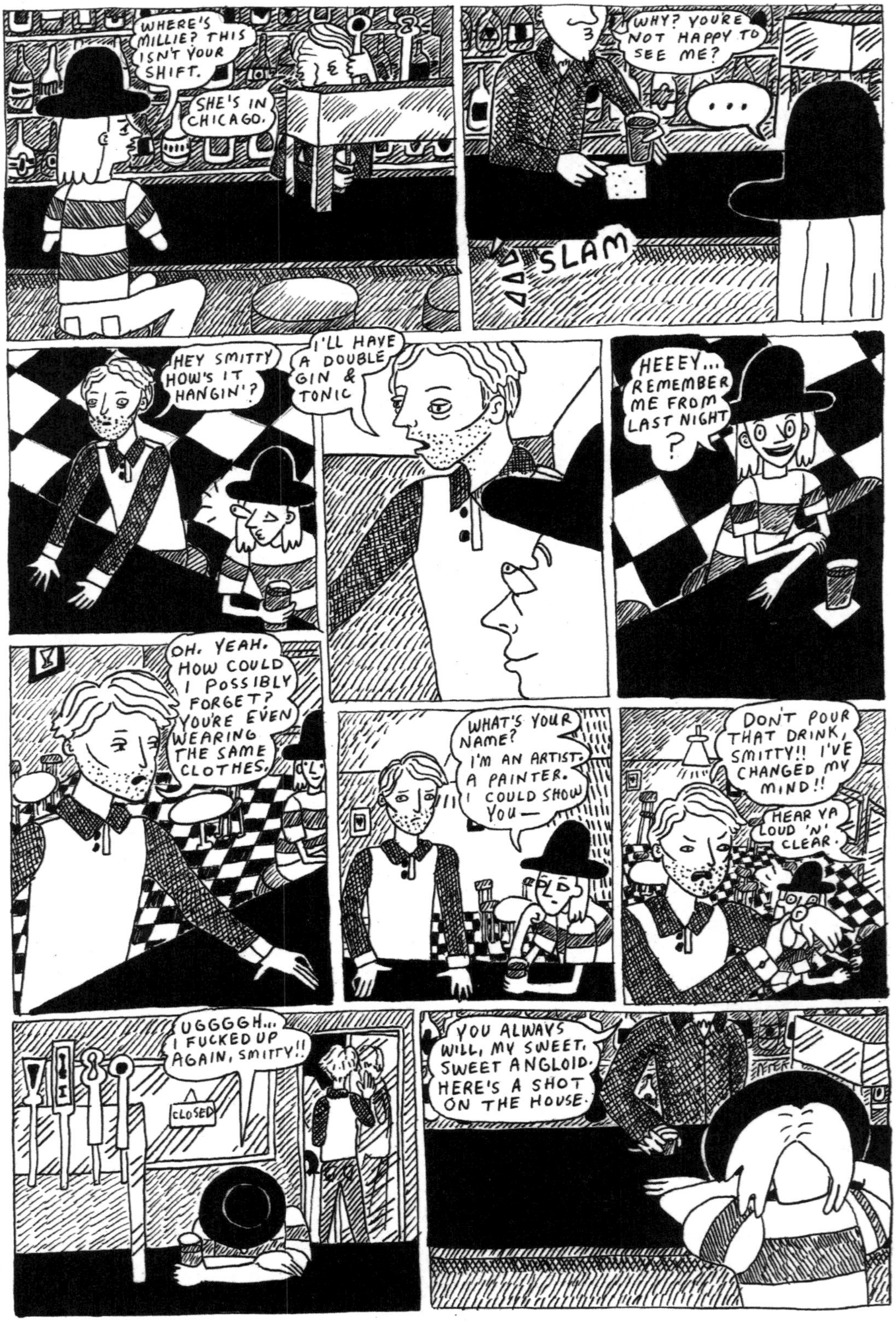
WHERE'S MILLIE? THIS ISN'T YOUR SHIFT.
SHE'S IN CHICAGO.
WHY? YOU'RE NOT HAPPY TO SEE ME?
...
SLAM
HEY SMITTY HOW'S IT HANGIN'?
I'LL HAVE A DOUBLE GIN & TONIC
HEEEY... REMEMBER ME FROM LAST NIGHT?
OH. YEAH. HOW COULD I POSSIBLY FORGET? YOU'RE EVEN WEARING THE SAME CLOTHES.
WHAT'S YOUR NAME? I'M AN ARTIST. A PAINTER. I COULD SHOW YOU—
DON'T POUR THAT DRINK, SMITTY!! I'VE CHANGED MY MIND!!
HEAR YA LOUD 'N' CLEAR.
UGGGGH... I FUCKED UP AGAIN, SMITTY!!
CLOSED
YOU ALWAYS WILL, MY SWEET, SWEET ANGLOID. HERE'S A SHOT ON THE HOUSE.

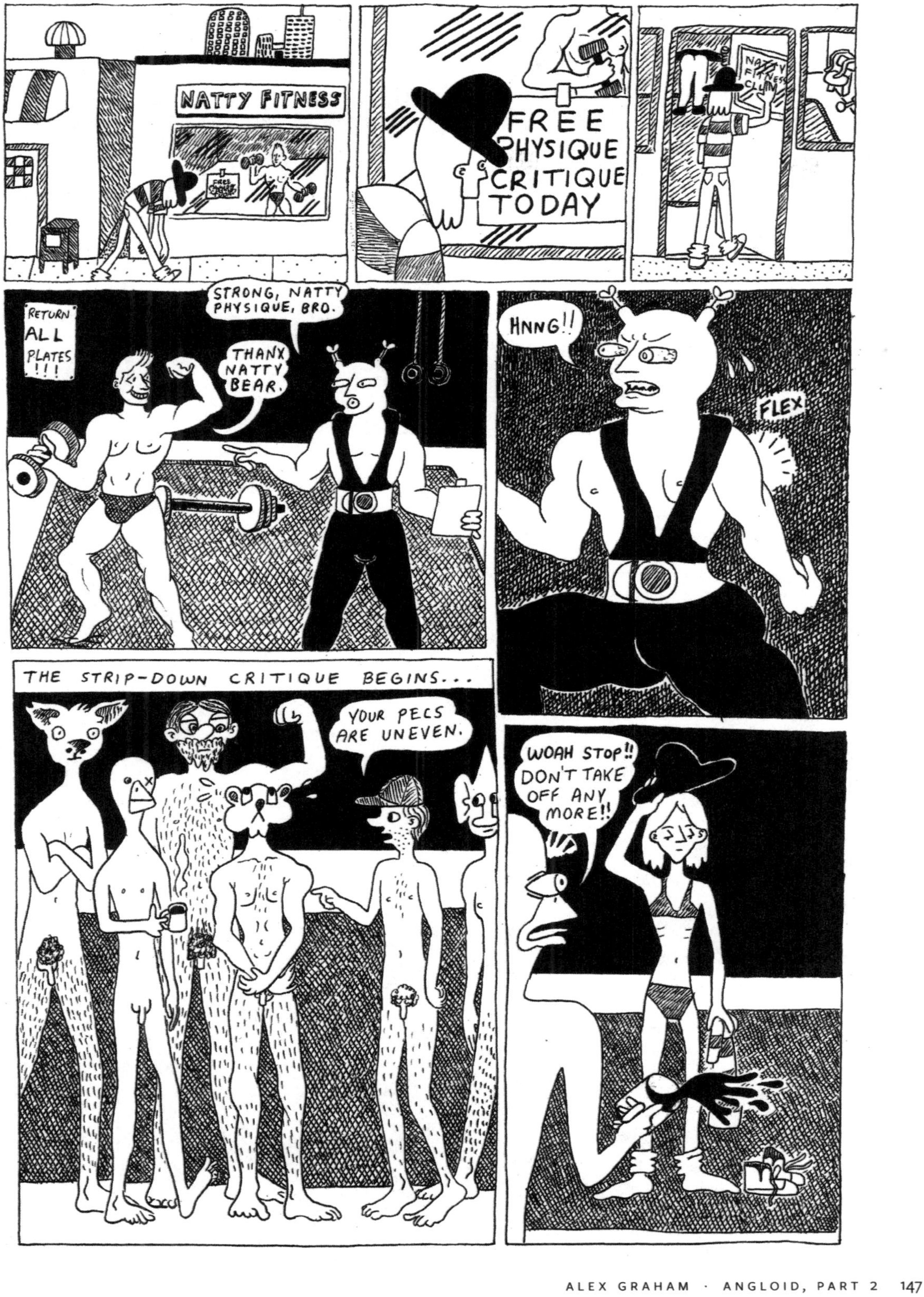
NATTY FITNESS
FREE PHYSIQUE CRITIQUE TODAY
FREE PHYSIQUE CRITIQUE TODAY
NATTY FITNESS CLUB
RETURN ALL PLATES !!!
STRONG, NATTY PHYSIQUE, BRO.
THANX NATTY BEAR.
HNNG!!
FLEX
THE STRIP-DOWN CRITIQUE BEGINS...
YOUR PECS ARE UNEVEN.
WOAH STOP!! DON'T TAKE OFF ANY MORE!!

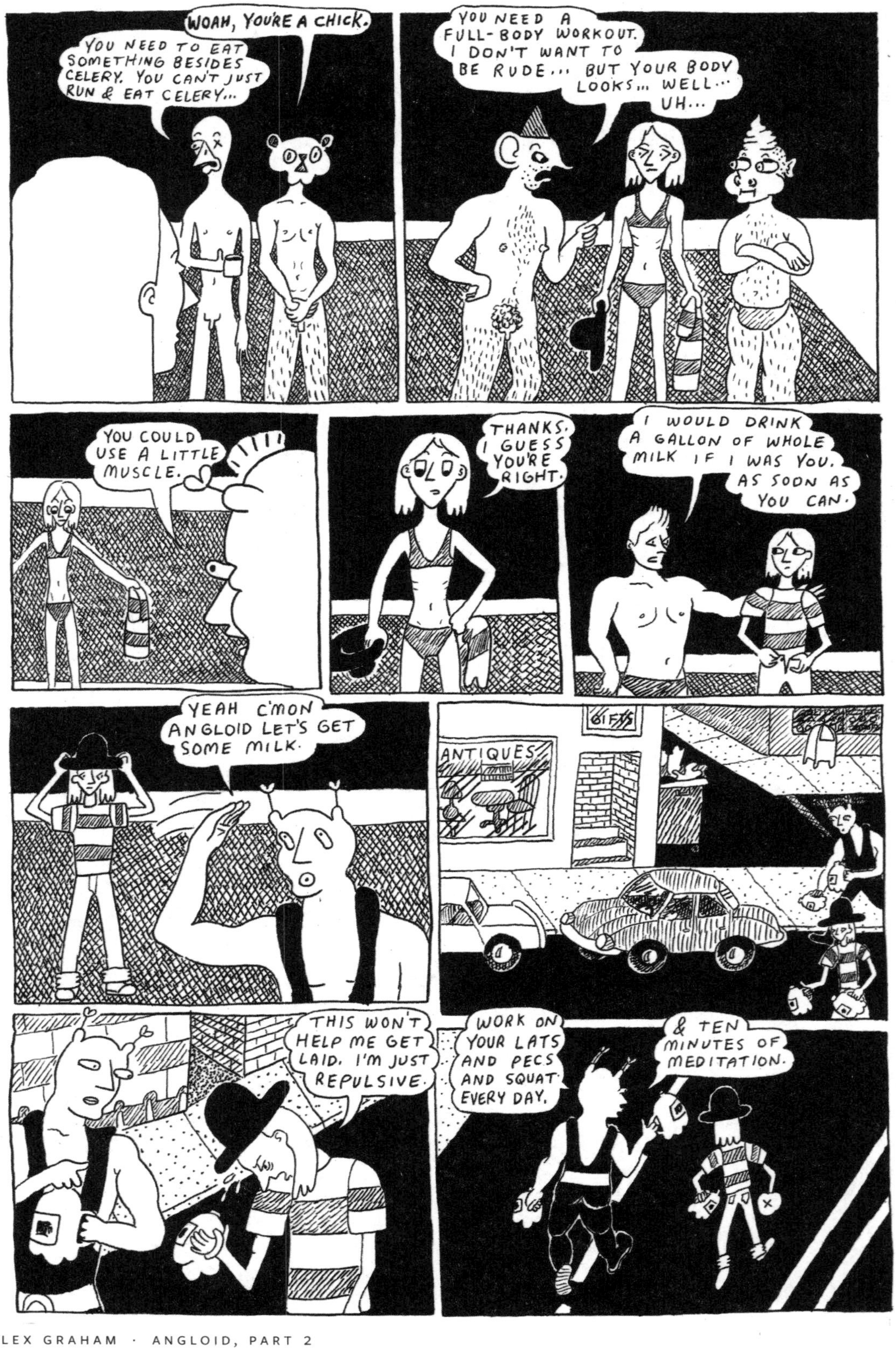
YOU NEED TO EAT SOMETHING BESIDES CELERY. YOU CAN'T JUST RUN & EAT CELERY...
WOAH, YOU'RE A CHICK.
YOU NEED A FULL-BODY WORKOUT. I DON'T WANT TO BE RUDE... BUT YOUR BODY LOOKS... WELL... UH...
YOU COULD USE A LITTLE MUSCLE.
THANKS. I GUESS YOU'RE RIGHT.
I WOULD DRINK A GALLON OF WHOLE MILK IF I WAS YOU. AS SOON AS YOU CAN.
YEAH C'MON ANGLOID LET'S GET SOME MILK.
GIFTS
ANTIQUES
THIS WON'T HELP ME GET LAID. I'M JUST REPULSIVE.
WORK ON YOUR LATS AND PECS AND SQUAT EVERY DAY.
& TEN MINUTES OF MEDITATION.

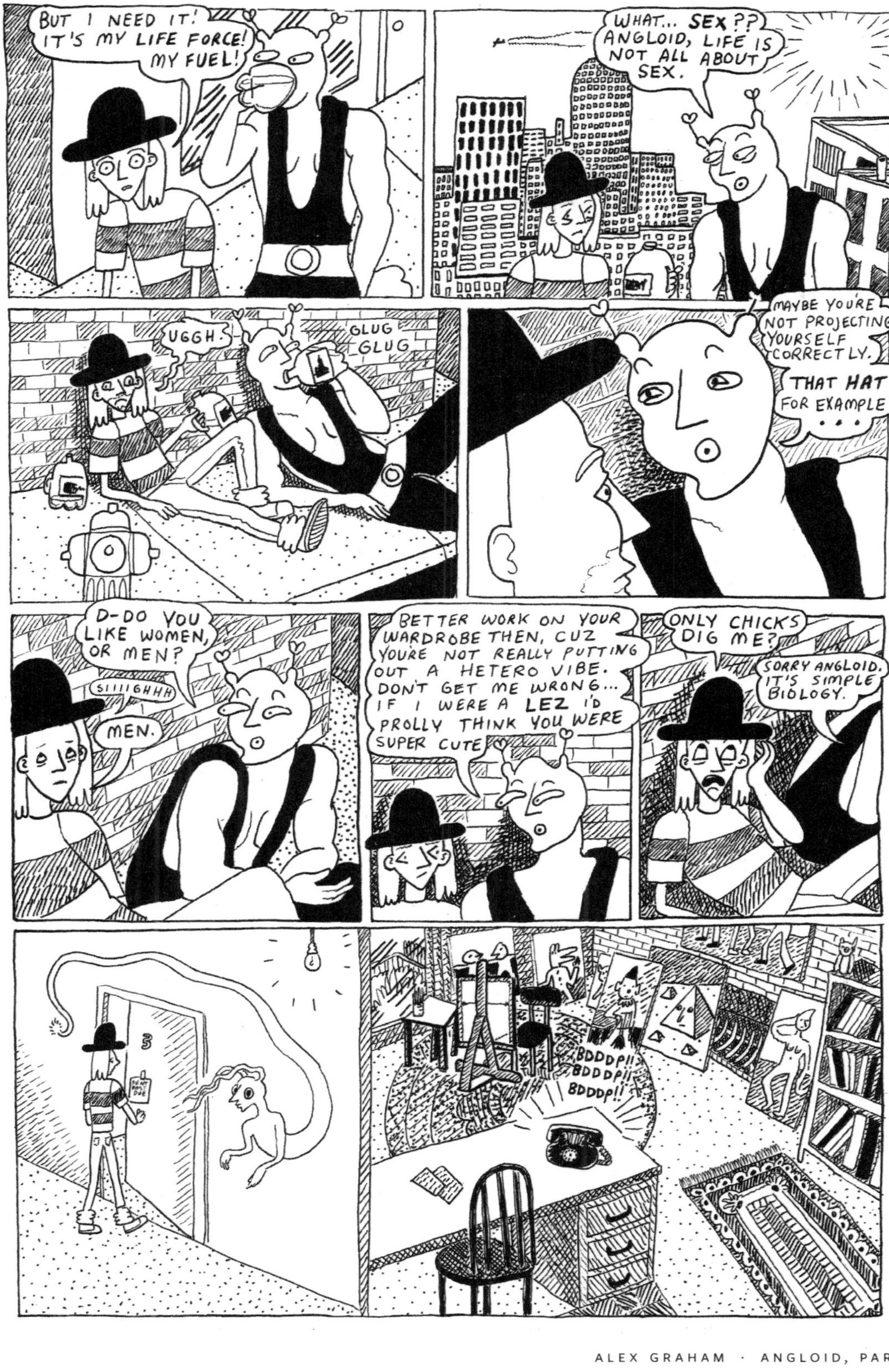
BUT I NEED IT! IT'S MY **LIFE FORCE**! MY **FUEL**!
WHAT... **SEX**?? ANGLOID, LIFE IS NOT ALL ABOUT SEX.
UGGH.
GLUG GLUG
MAYBE YOU'RE NOT PROJECTING YOURSELF CORRECTLY.
THAT **HAT** FOR EXAMPLE ...
D-DO YOU LIKE WOMEN, OR MEN?
SIIIIGHHH
MEN.
BETTER WORK ON YOUR WARDROBE THEN, CUZ YOU'RE NOT REALLY PUTTING OUT A HETERO VIBE. DON'T GET ME WRONG... IF I WERE A **LEZ** I'D PROLLY THINK YOU WERE SUPER CUTE
ONLY CHICKS DIG ME?
SORRY ANGLOID. IT'S SIMPLE BIOLOGY.
3
BDDDP!! BDDDP!! BDDDP!!

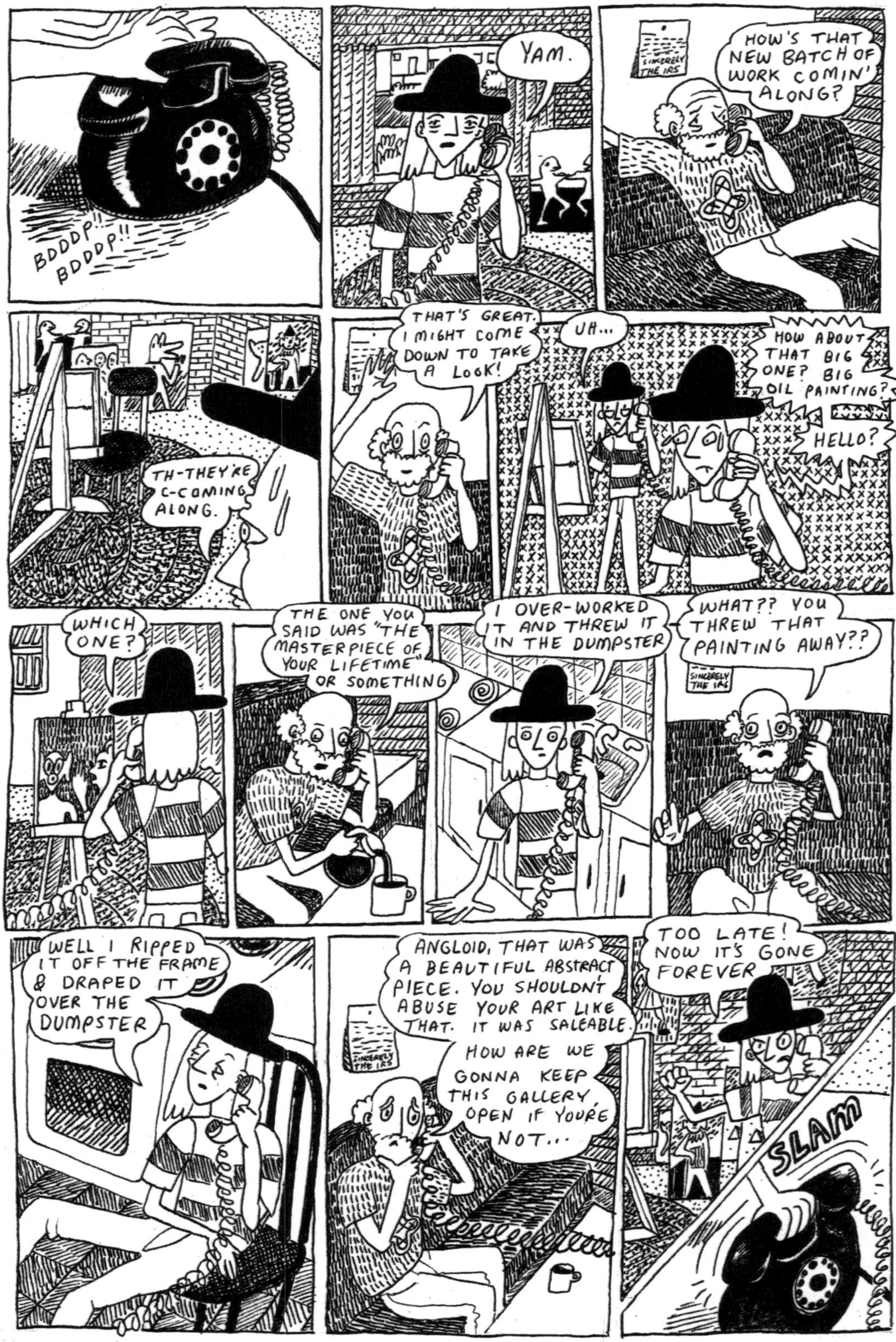
BDDDP!! BDDDP!!
YAM.
SINCERELY THE IRS
HOW'S THAT NEW BATCH OF WORK COMIN' ALONG?
TH-THEY'RE C-COMING ALONG.
THAT'S GREAT. I MIGHT COME DOWN TO TAKE A LOOK!
UH...
HOW ABOUT THAT BIG ONE? BIG OIL PAINTING?
HELLO?
WHICH ONE?
THE ONE YOU SAID WAS "THE MASTERPIECE OF YOUR LIFETIME" OR SOMETHING
I OVER-WORKED IT AND THREW IT IN THE DUMPSTER
WHAT?? YOU THREW THAT PAINTING AWAY??
SINCERELY THE IRS
WELL I RIPPED IT OFF THE FRAME & DRAPED IT OVER THE DUMPSTER
ANGLOID, THAT WAS A BEAUTIFUL ABSTRACT PIECE. YOU SHOULDN'T ABUSE YOUR ART LIKE THAT. IT WAS SALEABLE.
HOW ARE WE GONNA KEEP THIS GALLERY OPEN IF YOU'RE NOT...
SINCERELY THE IRS
TOO LATE! NOW IT'S GONE FOREVER
SLAM

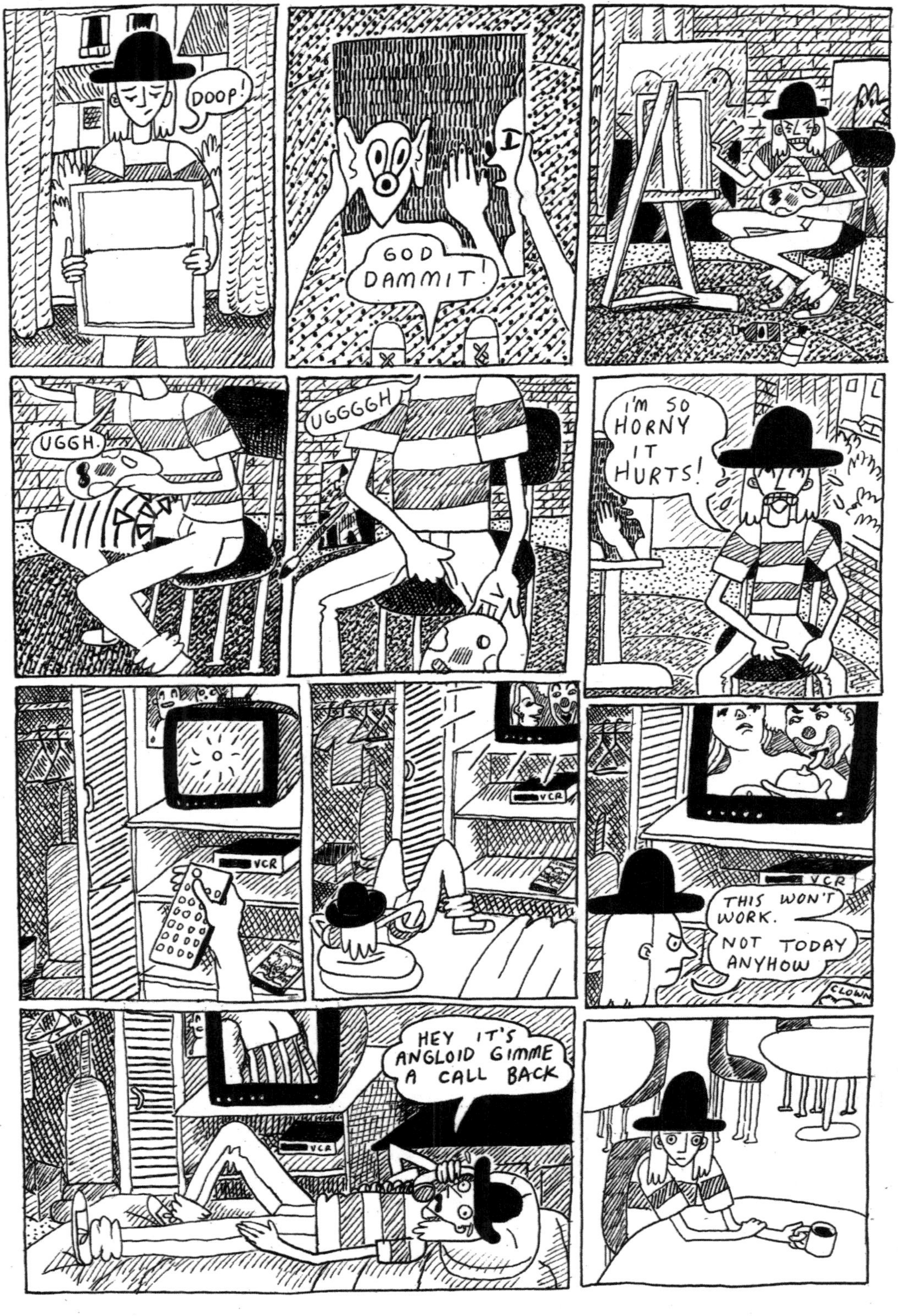
DOOP!
GOD DAMMIT!
UGGH.
UGGGGH
I'M SO HORNY IT HURTS!
VCR
VCR
VCR
THIS WON'T WORK.
NOT TODAY ANYHOW
CLOWN
HEY IT'S ANGLOID GIMME A CALL BACK
VCR

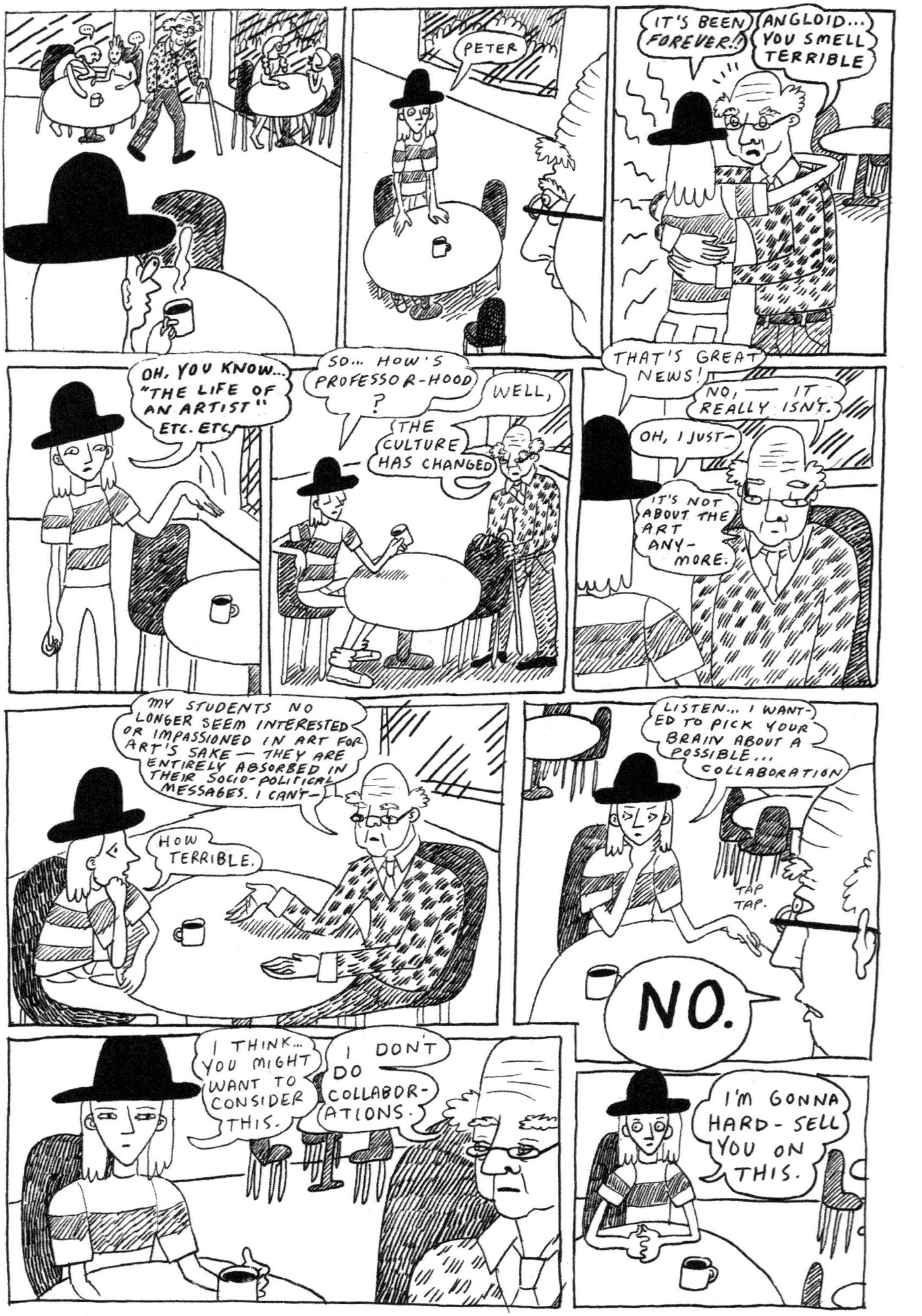
PETER
IT'S BEEN FOREVER!
ANGLOID... YOU SMELL TERRIBLE
OH, YOU KNOW... "THE LIFE OF AN ARTIST" ETC. ETC.
SO... HOW'S PROFESSOR-HOOD ?
WELL,
THE CULTURE HAS CHANGED
THAT'S GREAT NEWS!
NO, — IT REALLY ISN'T.
OH, I JUST-
IT'S NOT ABOUT THE ART ANY-MORE.
MY STUDENTS NO LONGER SEEM INTERESTED OR IMPASSIONED IN ART FOR ART'S SAKE — THEY ARE ENTIRELY ABSORBED IN THEIR SOCIO-POLITICAL MESSAGES. I CAN'T-
HOW TERRIBLE.
LISTEN... I WANTED TO PICK YOUR BRAIN ABOUT A POSSIBLE... COLLABORATION
TAP TAP.
NO.
I THINK... YOU MIGHT WANT TO CONSIDER THIS.
I DON'T DO COLLABOR-ATIONS.
I'M GONNA HARD-SELL YOU ON THIS.

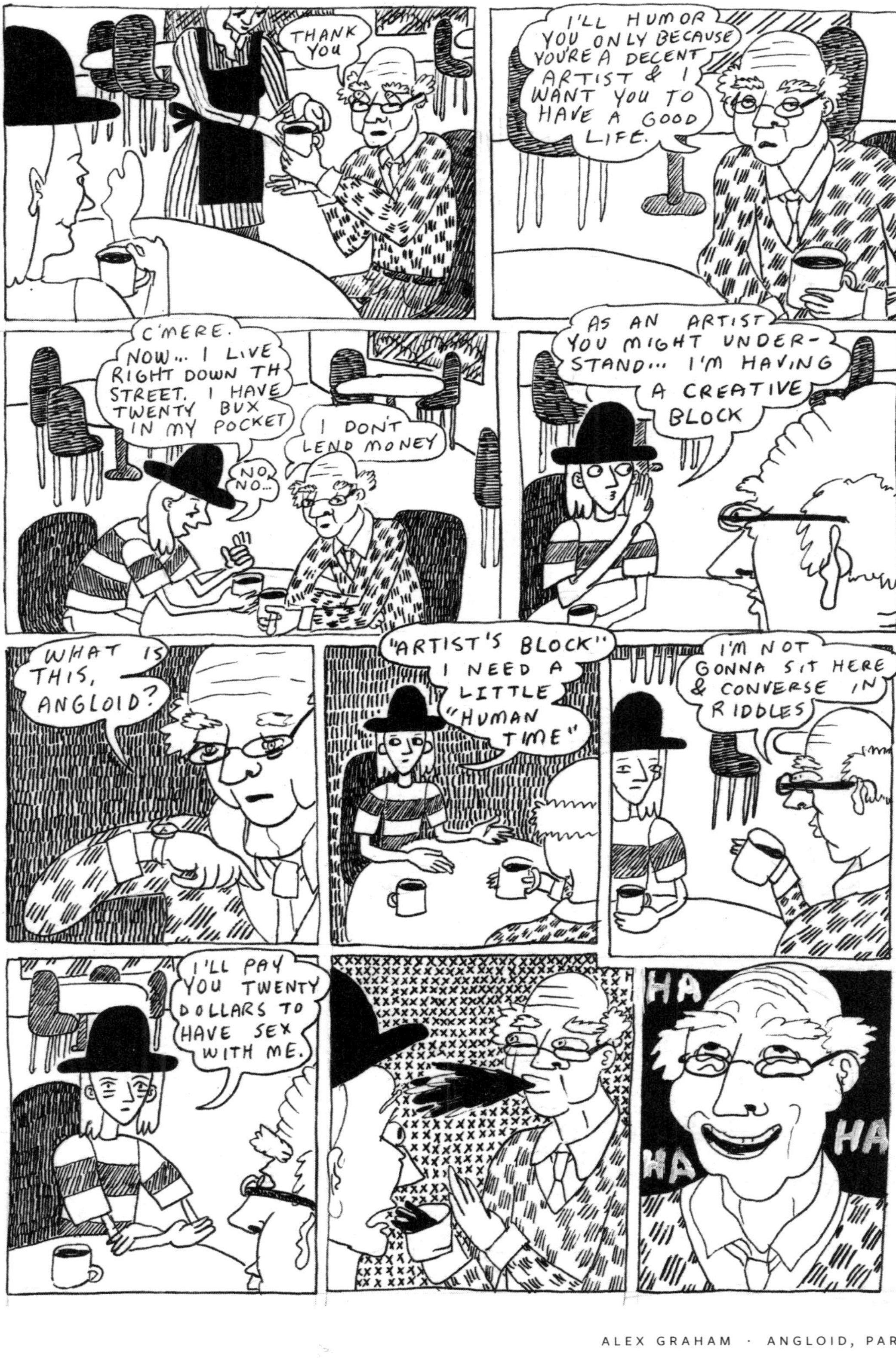
THANK YOU
I'LL HUMOR YOU ONLY BECAUSE YOU'RE A DECENT ARTIST & I WANT YOU TO HAVE A GOOD LIFE.
C'MERE. NOW... I LIVE RIGHT DOWN TH STREET. I HAVE TWENTY BUX IN MY POCKET
I DON'T LEND MONEY
NO, NO...
AS AN ARTIST YOU MIGHT UNDERSTAND... I'M HAVING A CREATIVE BLOCK
WHAT IS THIS, ANGLOID?
"ARTIST'S BLOCK" I NEED A LITTLE "HUMAN TIME"
I'M NOT GONNA SIT HERE & CONVERSE IN RIDDLES
I'LL PAY YOU TWENTY DOLLARS TO HAVE SEX WITH ME.
HA
HA
HA

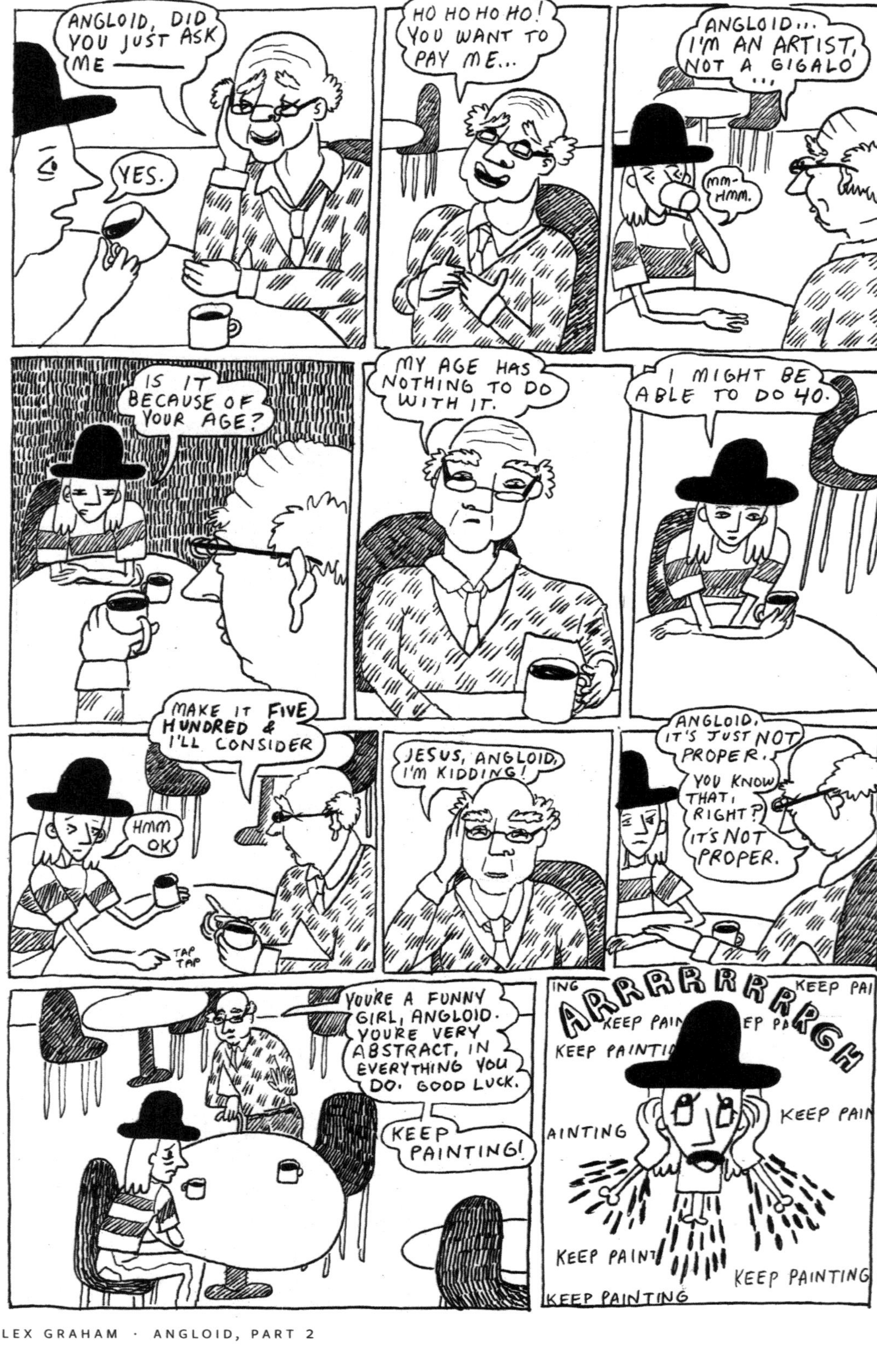
ANGLOID, DID YOU JUST ASK ME ———
YES.
HO HO HO HO! YOU WANT TO PAY ME...
ANGLOID... I'M AN ARTIST, NOT A GIGALO...
MM-HMM.
IS IT BECAUSE OF YOUR AGE?
MY AGE HAS NOTHING TO DO WITH IT.
I MIGHT BE ABLE TO DO 40.
MAKE IT FIVE HUNDRED & I'LL CONSIDER
HMM OK
TAP TAP
JESUS, ANGLOID, I'M KIDDING!
ANGLOID, IT'S JUST NOT PROPER.
YOU KNOW THAT, RIGHT?
IT'S NOT PROPER.
YOU'RE A FUNNY GIRL, ANGLOID. YOU'RE VERY ABSTRACT, IN EVERYTHING YOU DO. GOOD LUCK.
KEEP PAINTING!
ARRRRRRRRRGH
ING
KEEP PAI
KEEP PAIN
EP PA
KEEP PAINTI
KEEP PAIN
AINTING
KEEP PAINT
KEEP PAINTING
KEEP PAINTING

Megg, Mogg & Owl: "A Gift for a Baby"

SIMON HANSELMANN

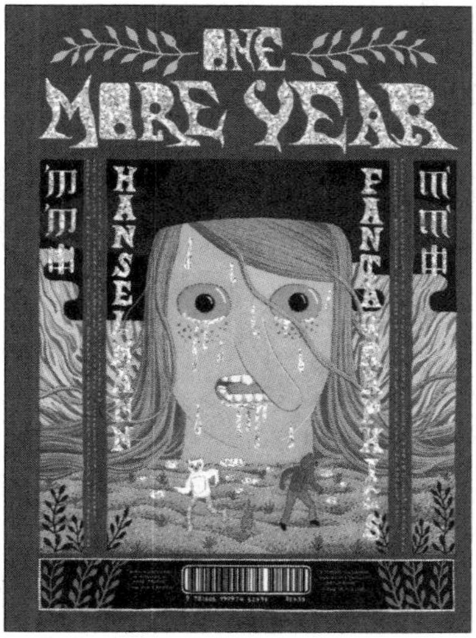
ONE
MORE YEAR
HANSELMANN

originally published in

One More Year

FANTAGRAPHICS BOOKS

6.25 x 8.75 inches • 220 pages

Biography

Hanselmann was born in 1981 in Launceston, Tasmania. His Megg, Mogg and Owl series has been translated into 13 languages, nominated for multiple Ignatz and Eisner awards, and won Best Series at Angoulême in 2018. He currently lives in Seattle, Washington, with his wife and a rotating cast of small animals.
instagram: @simon.hanselmann

Statement

A typical short Megg, Mogg and Owl piece. Owl is attempting to do something nice in a normal fashion and is thus shat upon by his "friends." Alludes to Owl being slightly creepy and manipulative with young women in his dating relationships . . .

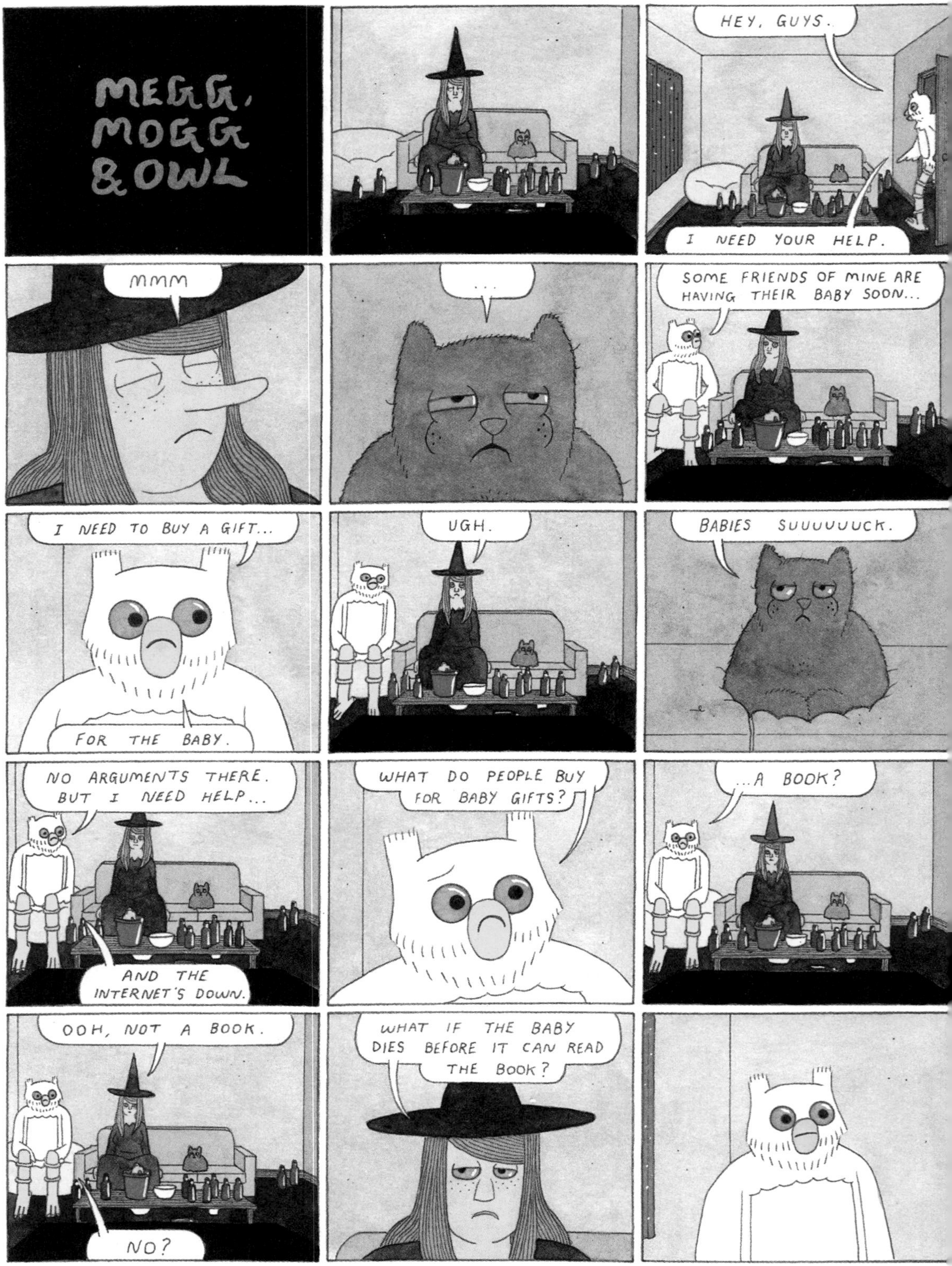
MEGG, MOGG & OWL
HEY, GUYS.
I NEED YOUR HELP.
MMM
...
SOME FRIENDS OF MINE ARE HAVING THEIR BABY SOON...
I NEED TO BUY A GIFT...
FOR THE BABY.
UGH.
BABIES SUUUUUUCK.
NO ARGUMENTS THERE. BUT I NEED HELP...
AND THE INTERNET'S DOWN.
WHAT DO PEOPLE BUY FOR BABY GIFTS?
...A BOOK?
OOH, NOT A BOOK.
NO?
WHAT IF THE BABY DIES BEFORE IT CAN READ THE BOOK?

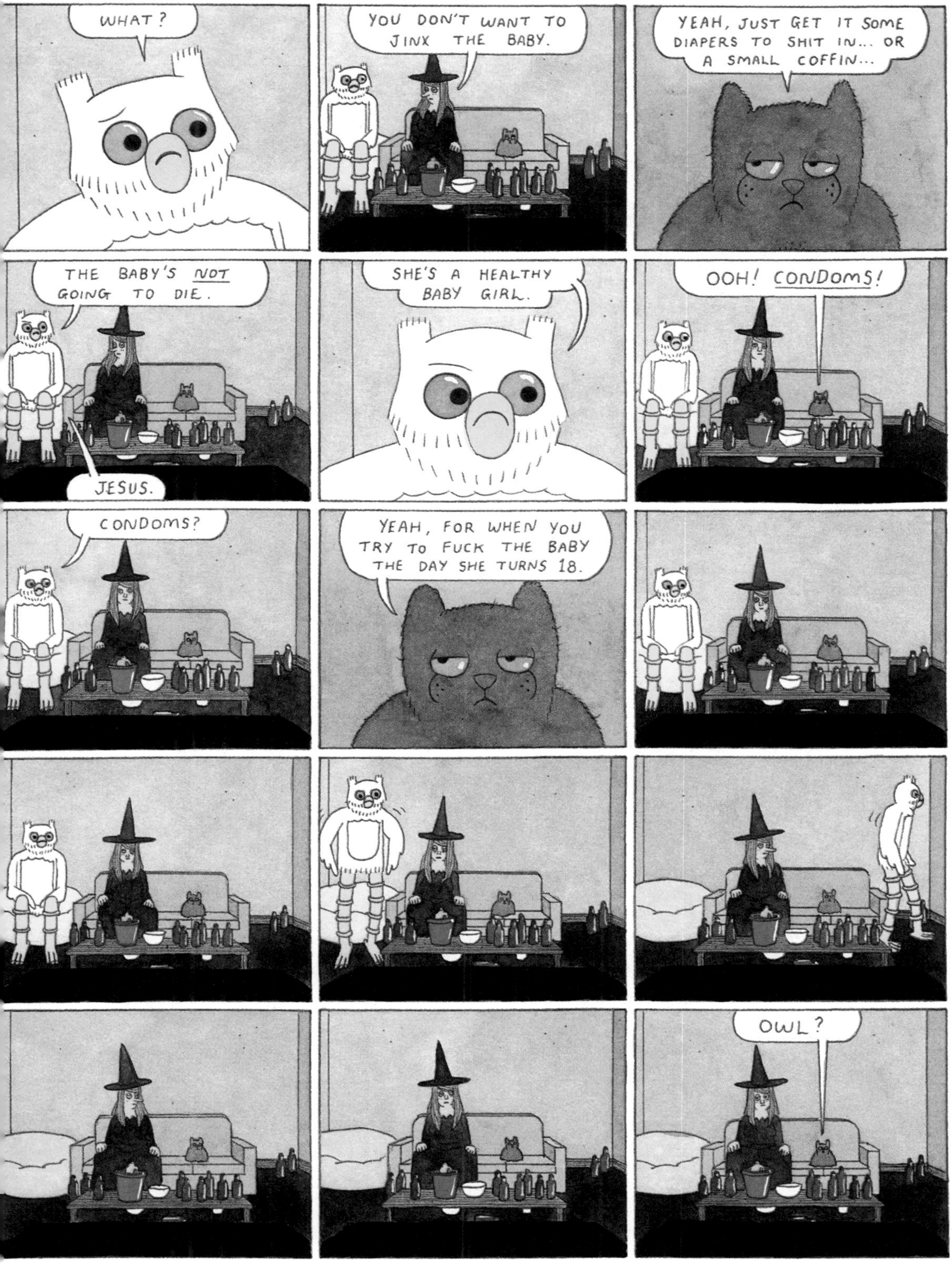
WHAT?
YOU DON'T WANT TO JINX THE BABY.
YEAH, JUST GET IT SOME DIAPERS TO SHIT IN... OR A SMALL COFFIN...
THE BABY'S NOT GOING TO DIE.
JESUS.
SHE'S A HEALTHY BABY GIRL.
OOH! CONDOMS!
CONDOMS?
YEAH, FOR WHEN YOU TRY TO FUCK THE BABY THE DAY SHE TURNS 18.
OWL?

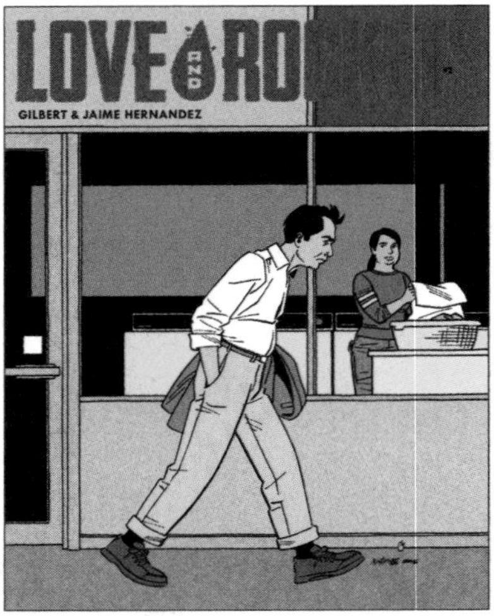
LOVE AND RO
GILBERT & JAIME HERNANDEZ

Forest Spirits

JAIME HERNANDEZ

originally published in

Love and Rockets, vol. 4 #2
FANTAGRAPHICS BOOKS
8.5 x 10.75 inches • 36 pages

Biography

I have been making comics for over 50 years, 36 years professionally, mostly in *Love and Rockets*. Comics have done me well. I hope to one day draw a correct ear.

Statement

Tonta and her friends are close to graduating high school. Her older sister Vivian has infiltrated their private world.

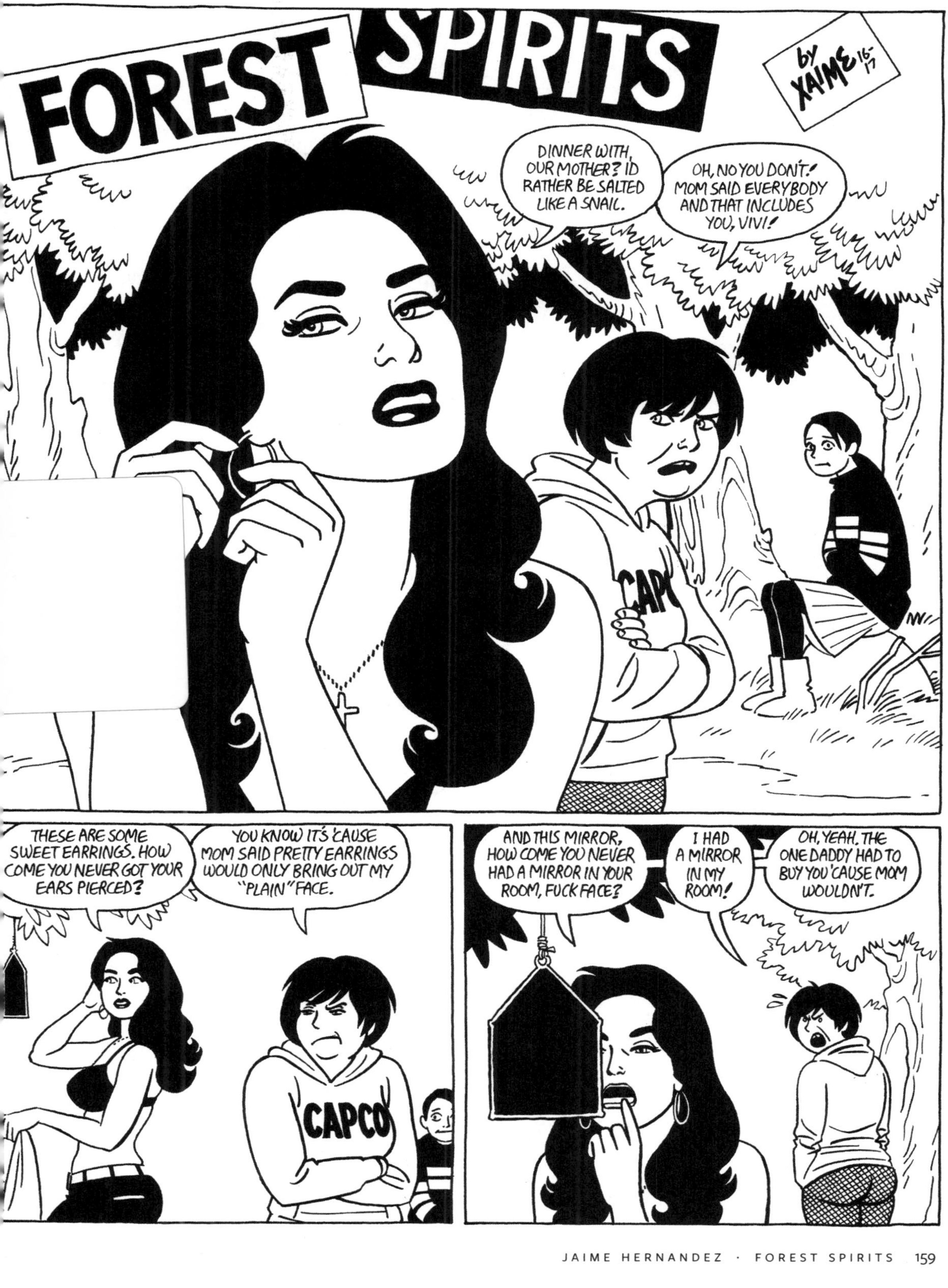
FOREST SPIRITS
by XAIME 15-17
DINNER WITH, OUR MOTHER? I'D RATHER BE SALTED LIKE A SNAIL.
OH, NO YOU DON'T! MOM SAID EVERYBODY AND THAT INCLUDES YOU, VIVI!
CAPCO
THESE ARE SOME SWEET EARRINGS. HOW COME YOU NEVER GOT YOUR EARS PIERCED?
YOU KNOW IT'S 'CAUSE MOM SAID PRETTY EARRINGS WOULD ONLY BRING OUT MY "PLAIN" FACE.
CAPCO
AND THIS MIRROR, HOW COME YOU NEVER HAD A MIRROR IN YOUR ROOM, FUCK FACE?
I HAD A MIRROR IN MY ROOM!
OH, YEAH. THE ONE DADDY HAD TO BUY YOU 'CAUSE MOM WOULDN'T.

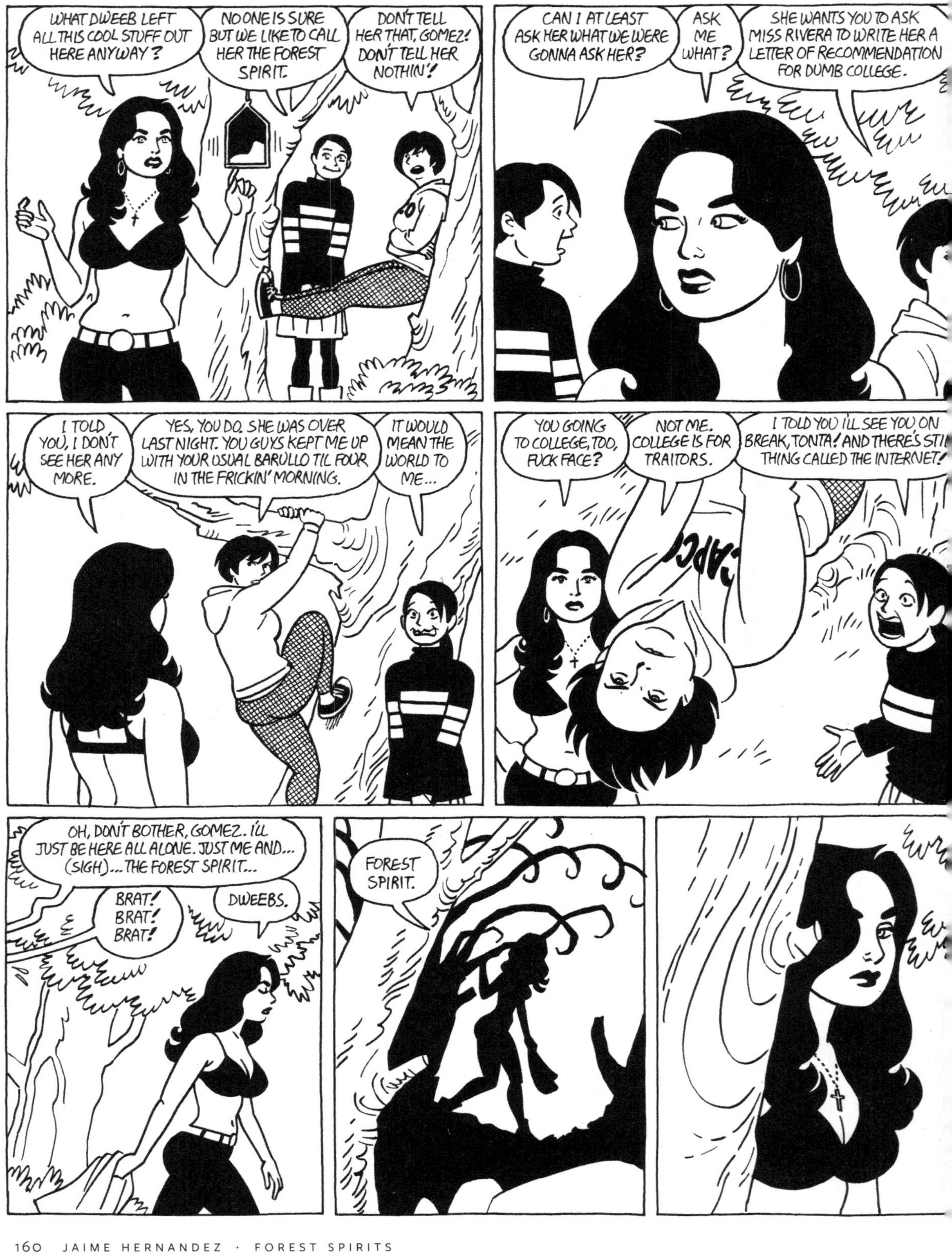

WHAT DWEEB LEFT ALL THIS COOL STUFF OUT HERE ANYWAY?
NO ONE IS SURE BUT WE LIKE TO CALL HER THE FOREST SPIRIT.
DON'T TELL HER THAT, GOMEZ! DON'T TELL HER NOTHIN'!
CAN I AT LEAST ASK HER WHAT WE WERE GONNA ASK HER?
ASK ME WHAT?
SHE WANTS YOU TO ASK MISS RIVERA TO WRITE HER A LETTER OF RECOMMENDATION FOR DUMB COLLEGE.
I TOLD YOU, I DON'T SEE HER ANY MORE.
YES, YOU DO. SHE WAS OVER LAST NIGHT. YOU GUYS KEPT ME UP WITH YOUR USUAL BARULLO TIL FOUR IN THE FRICKIN' MORNING.
IT WOULD MEAN THE WORLD TO ME...
YOU GOING TO COLLEGE, TOO, FUCK FACE?
NOT ME. COLLEGE IS FOR TRAITORS.
I TOLD YOU I'LL SEE YOU, ON BREAK, TONTA! AND THERE'S STI THING CALLED THE INTERNET!
OH, DON'T BOTHER, GOMEZ. I'LL JUST BE HERE ALL ALONE. JUST ME AND... (SIGH)... THE FOREST SPIRIT...
BRAT! BRAT! BRAT!
DWEEBS.
FOREST SPIRIT.

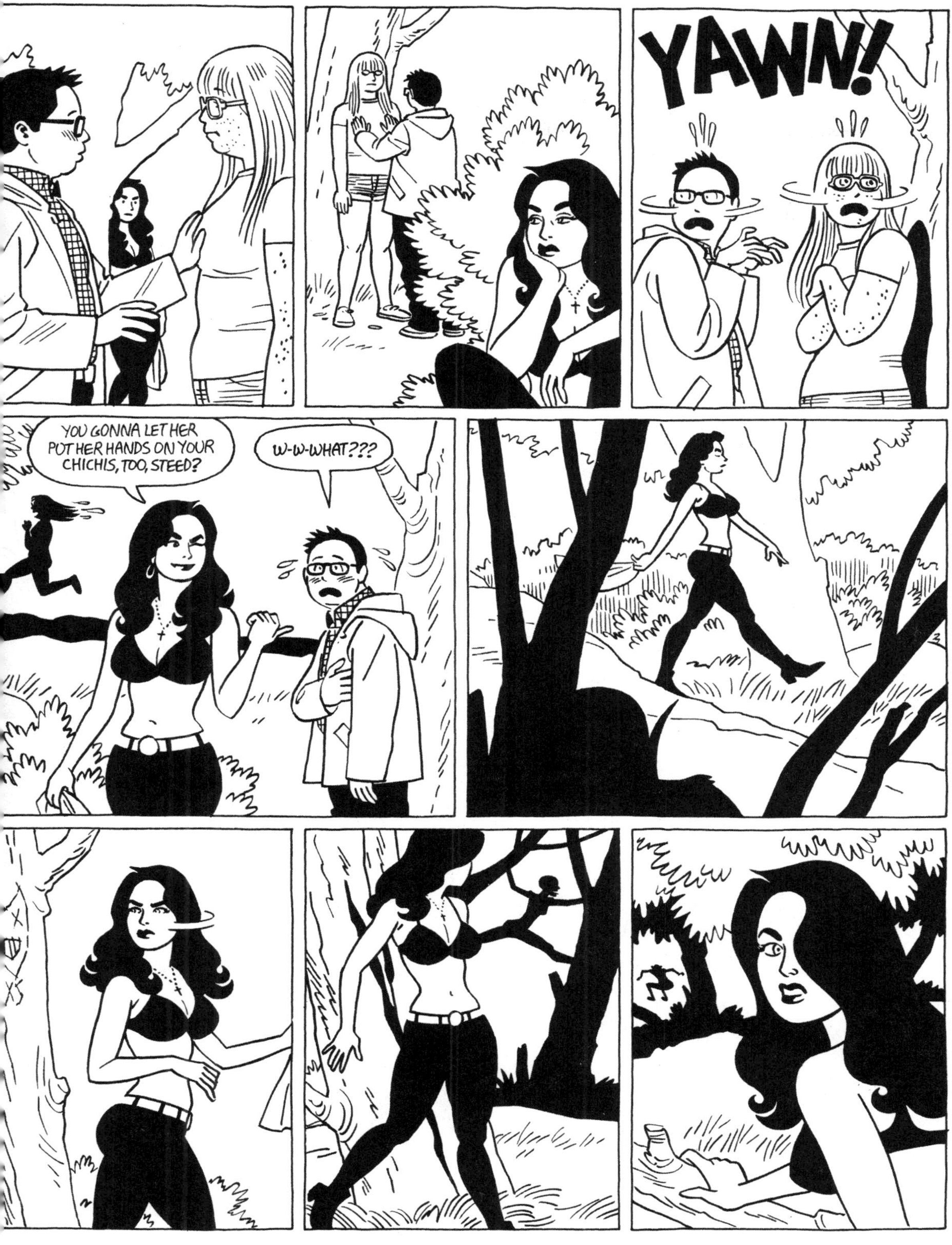
YAWN!
YOU GONNA LET HER PUT HER HANDS ON YOUR CHICHIS, TOO, STEED?
W-W-WHAT???

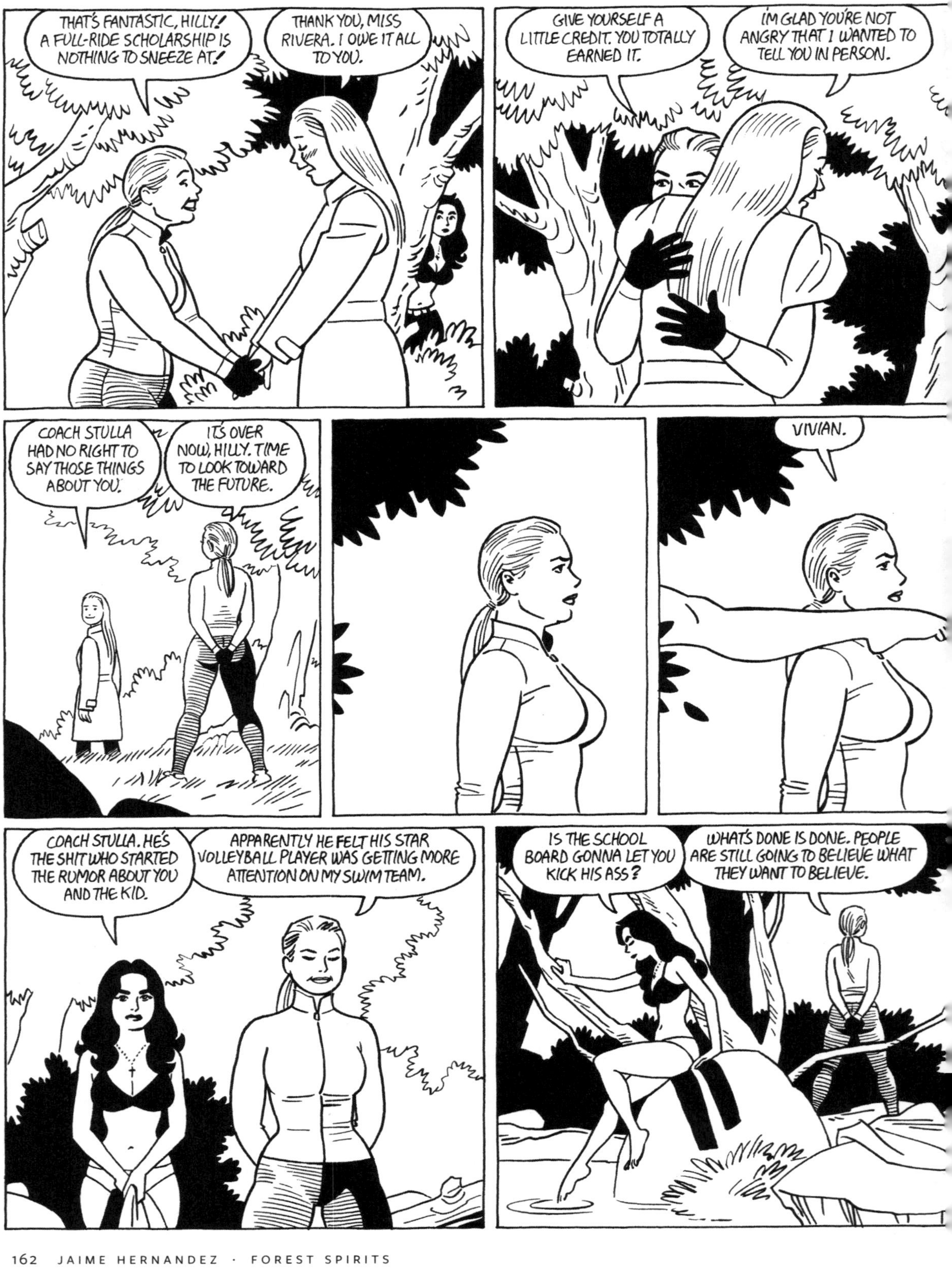
THAT'S FANTASTIC, HILLY! A FULL-RIDE SCHOLARSHIP IS NOTHING TO SNEEZE AT!
THANK YOU, MISS RIVERA. I OWE IT ALL TO YOU.
GIVE YOURSELF A LITTLE CREDIT. YOU TOTALLY EARNED IT.
I'M GLAD YOU'RE NOT ANGRY THAT I WANTED TO TELL YOU IN PERSON.
COACH STULLA HAD NO RIGHT TO SAY THOSE THINGS ABOUT YOU.
IT'S OVER NOW, HILLY. TIME TO LOOK TOWARD THE FUTURE.
VIVIAN.
COACH STULLA. HE'S THE SHIT WHO STARTED THE RUMOR ABOUT YOU AND THE KID.
APPARENTLY HE FELT HIS STAR VOLLEYBALL PLAYER WAS GETTING MORE ATTENTION ON MY SWIM TEAM.
IS THE SCHOOL BOARD GONNA LET YOU KICK HIS ASS?
WHAT'S DONE IS DONE. PEOPLE ARE STILL GOING TO BELIEVE WHAT THEY WANT TO BELIEVE.

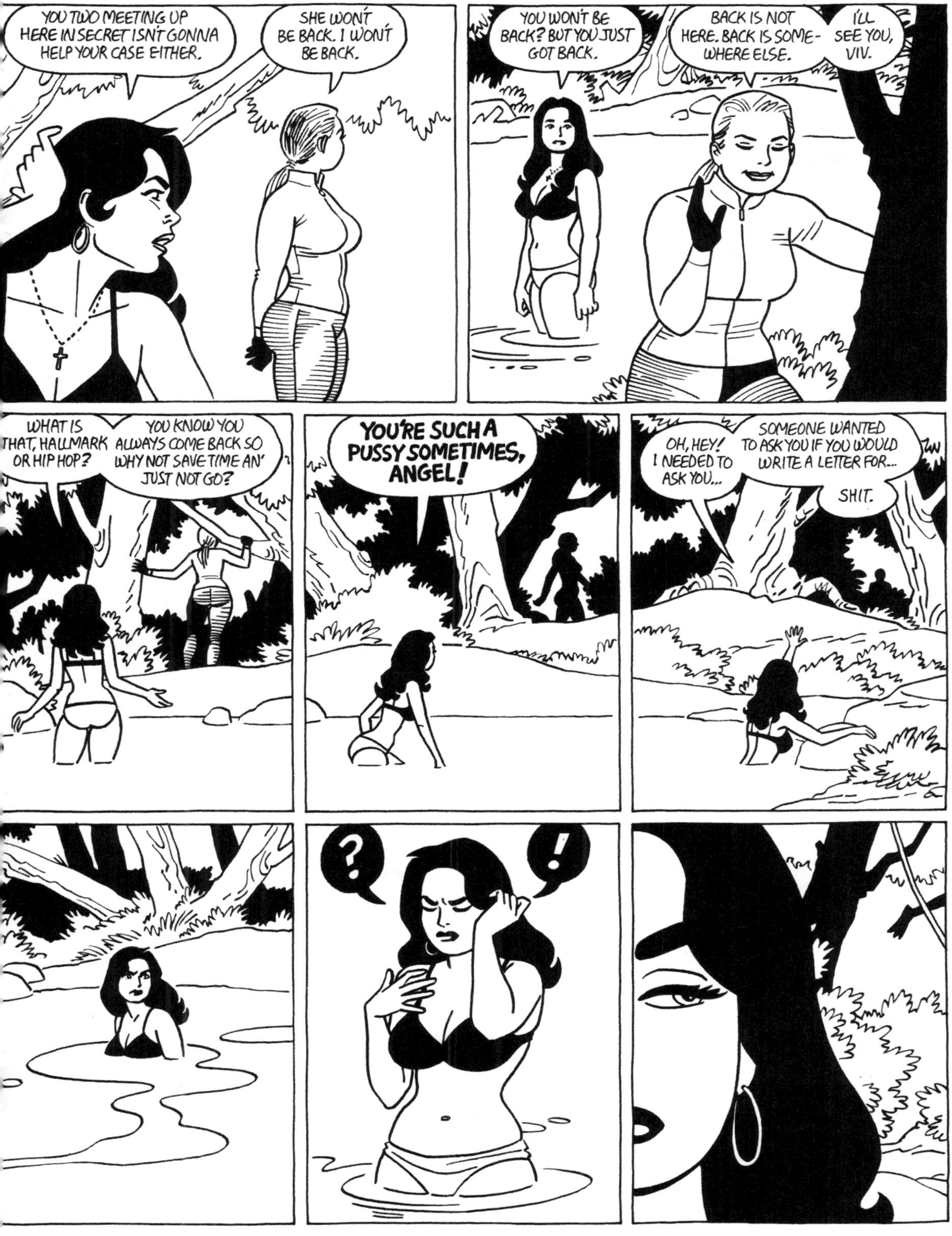
YOU TWO MEETING UP HERE IN SECRET ISN'T GONNA HELP YOUR CASE EITHER.
SHE WON'T BE BACK. I WON'T BE BACK.
YOU WON'T BE BACK? BUT YOU JUST GOT BACK.
BACK IS NOT HERE. BACK IS SOMEWHERE ELSE.
I'LL SEE YOU, VIV.
WHAT IS THAT, HALLMARK OR HIP HOP?
YOU KNOW YOU ALWAYS COME BACK SO WHY NOT SAVE TIME AN' JUST NOT GO?
YOU'RE SUCH A PUSSY SOMETIMES, ANGEL!
OH, HEY! I NEEDED TO ASK YOU...
SOMEONE WANTED TO ASK YOU IF YOU WOULD WRITE A LETTER FOR...
SHIT.
?
!

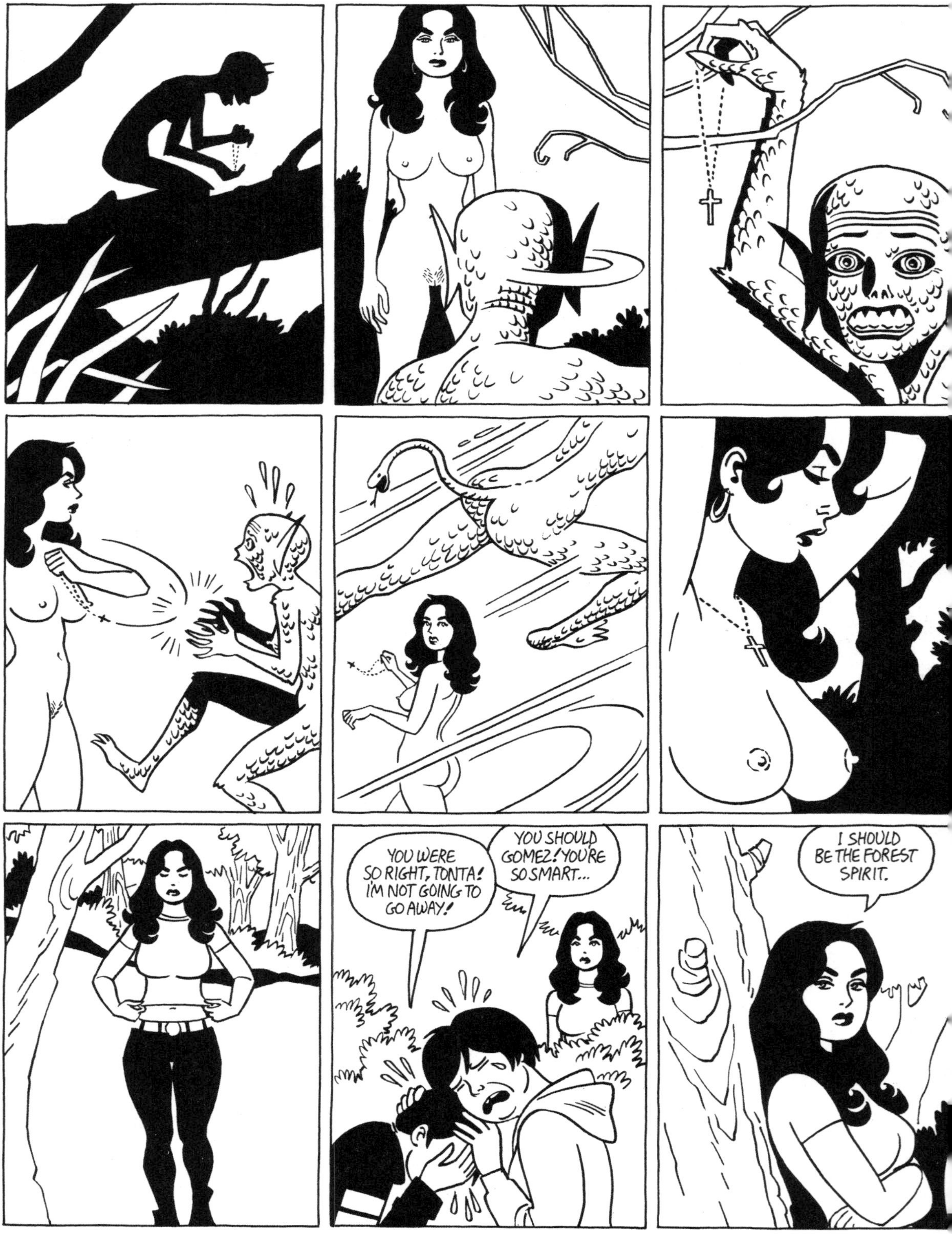
YOU WERE SO RIGHT, TONTA! I'M NOT GOING TO GO AWAY!
YOU SHOULD GOMEZ! YOU'RE SO SMART...
I SHOULD BE THE FOREST SPIRIT.

The Wide Berth AND Benign Neglect

KEVIN HOOYMAN

CONDITIONS HOOYMAN
$5
18 APR
CONDITIONS ON THE GROUND
THE DEEP STATE
ALSO
AQUA-DUO!

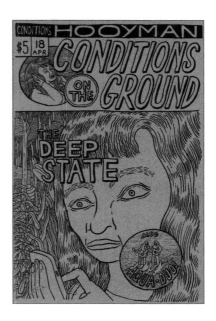

originally published in

Conditions on the Ground #14 and #18

SELF-PUBLISHED

5.5 x 8.5 inches • 32 pages

Biography

Kevin Hooyman was born in Two Harbors, Minnesota, in 1974. He grew up in the great Northwest and now lives in New York.
hooyman.tumblr.com

Statement

Conditions on the Ground is my regular zine series, reporting on my explorations of the life I lead, and what it feels like to be a person in the world today.

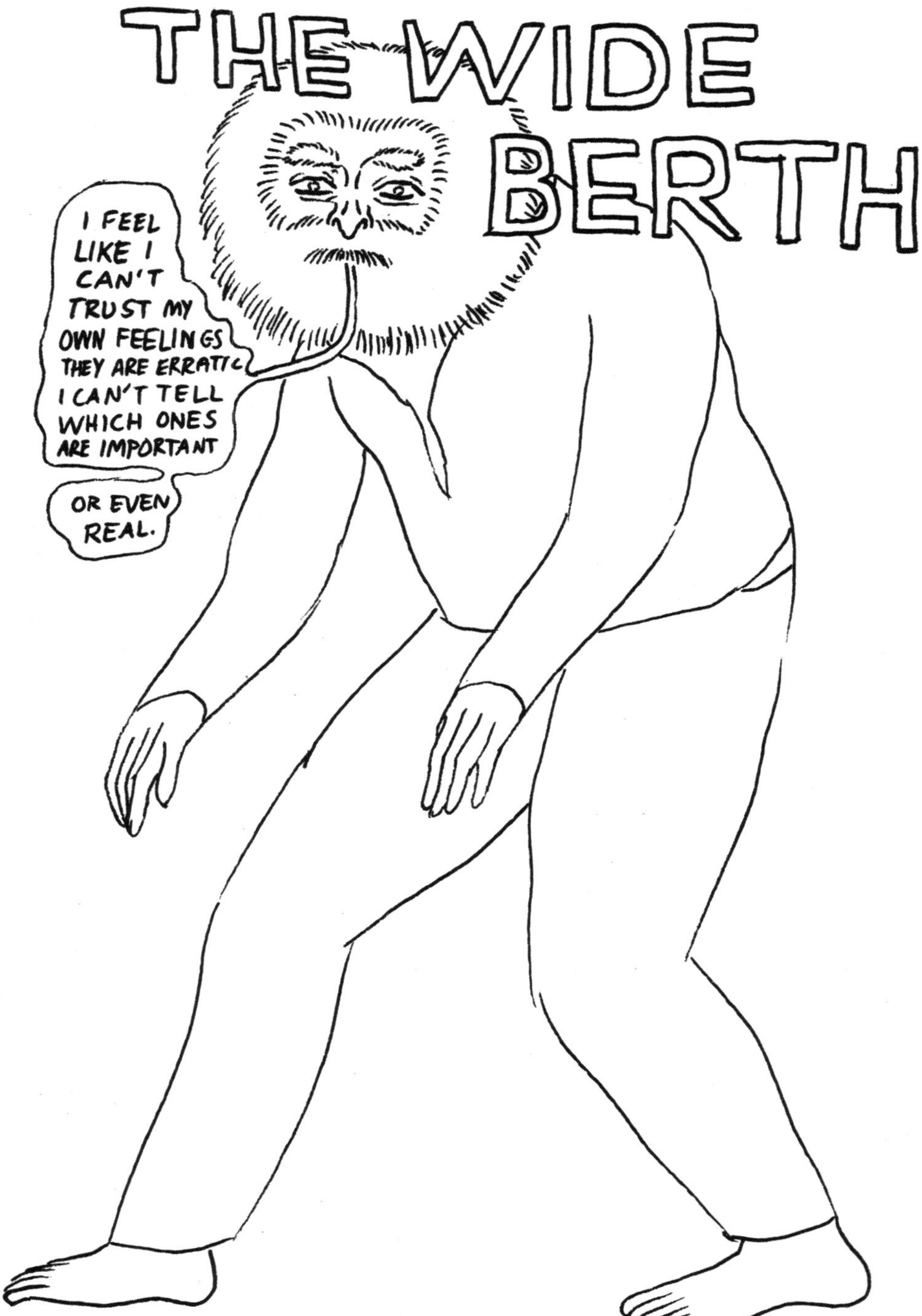
THE WIDE BERTH
I FEEL LIKE I CAN'T TRUST MY OWN FEELINGS THEY ARE ERRATIC I CAN'T TELL WHICH ONES ARE IMPORTANT
OR EVEN REAL.

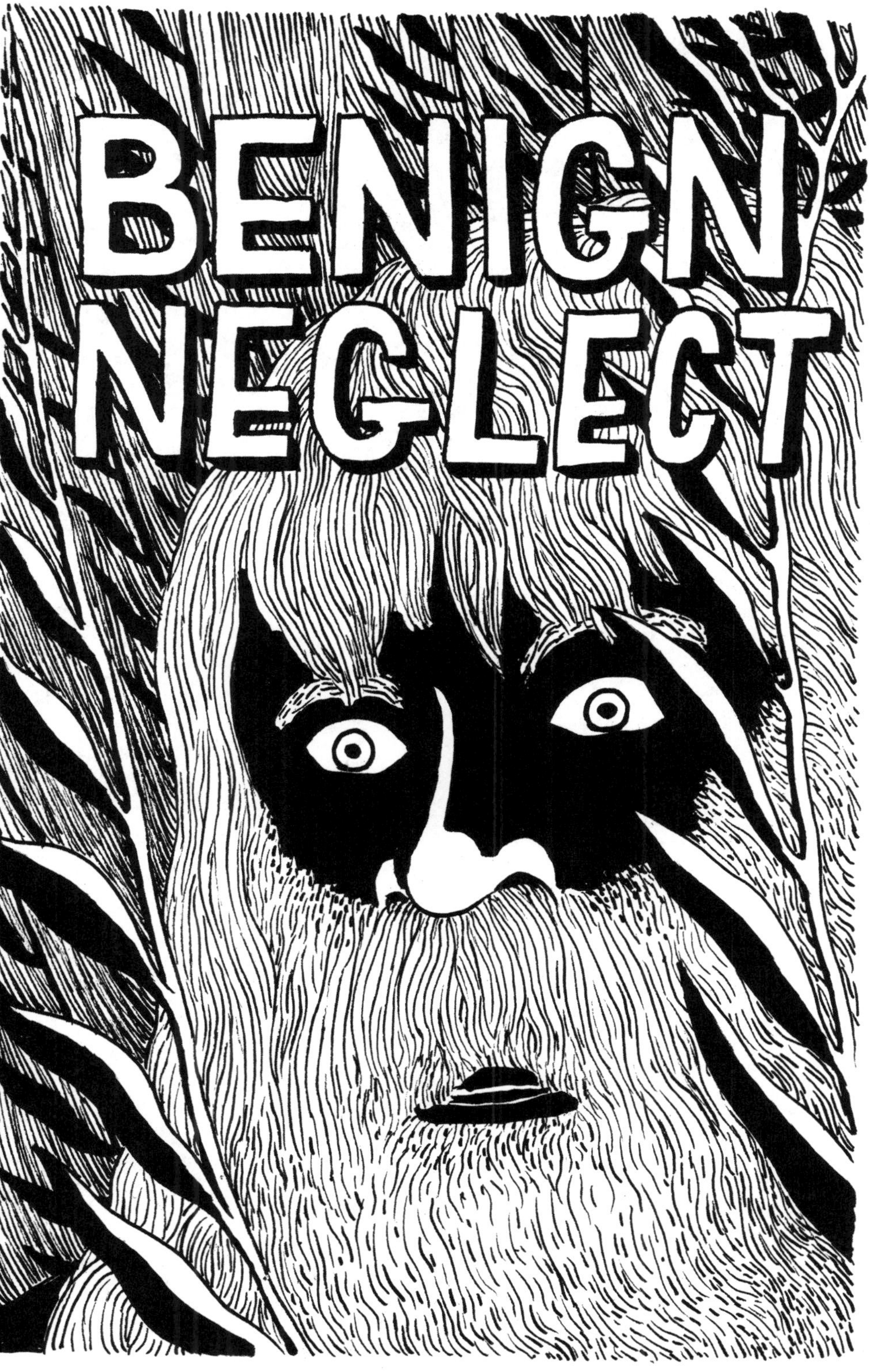
BENIGN
NEGLECT

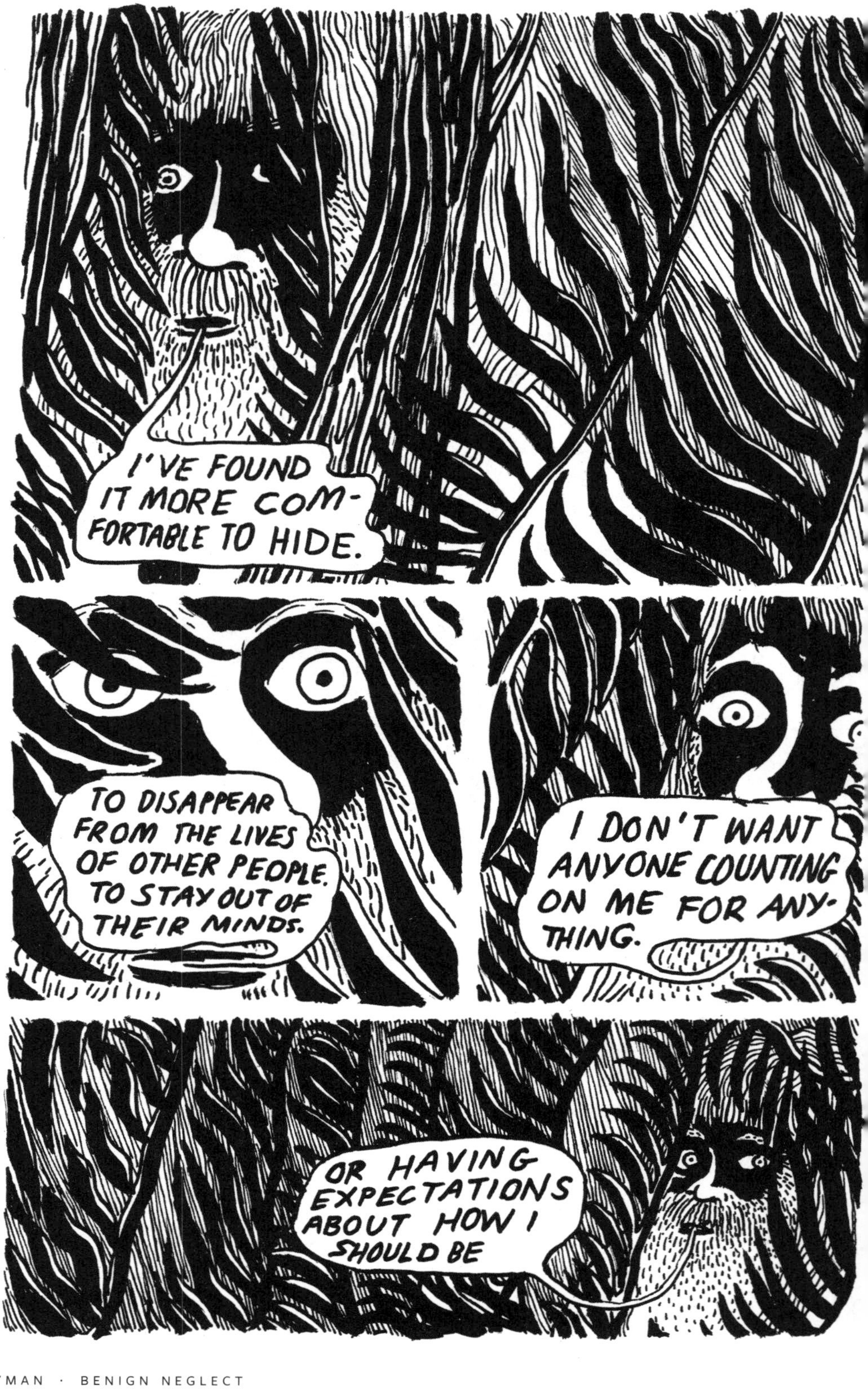
I'VE FOUND IT MORE COM-FORTABLE TO HIDE.
TO DISAPPEAR FROM THE LIVES OF OTHER PEOPLE. TO STAY OUT OF THEIR MINDS.
I DON'T WANT ANYONE COUNTING ON ME FOR ANY-THING.
OR HAVING EXPECTATIONS ABOUT HOW I SHOULD BE

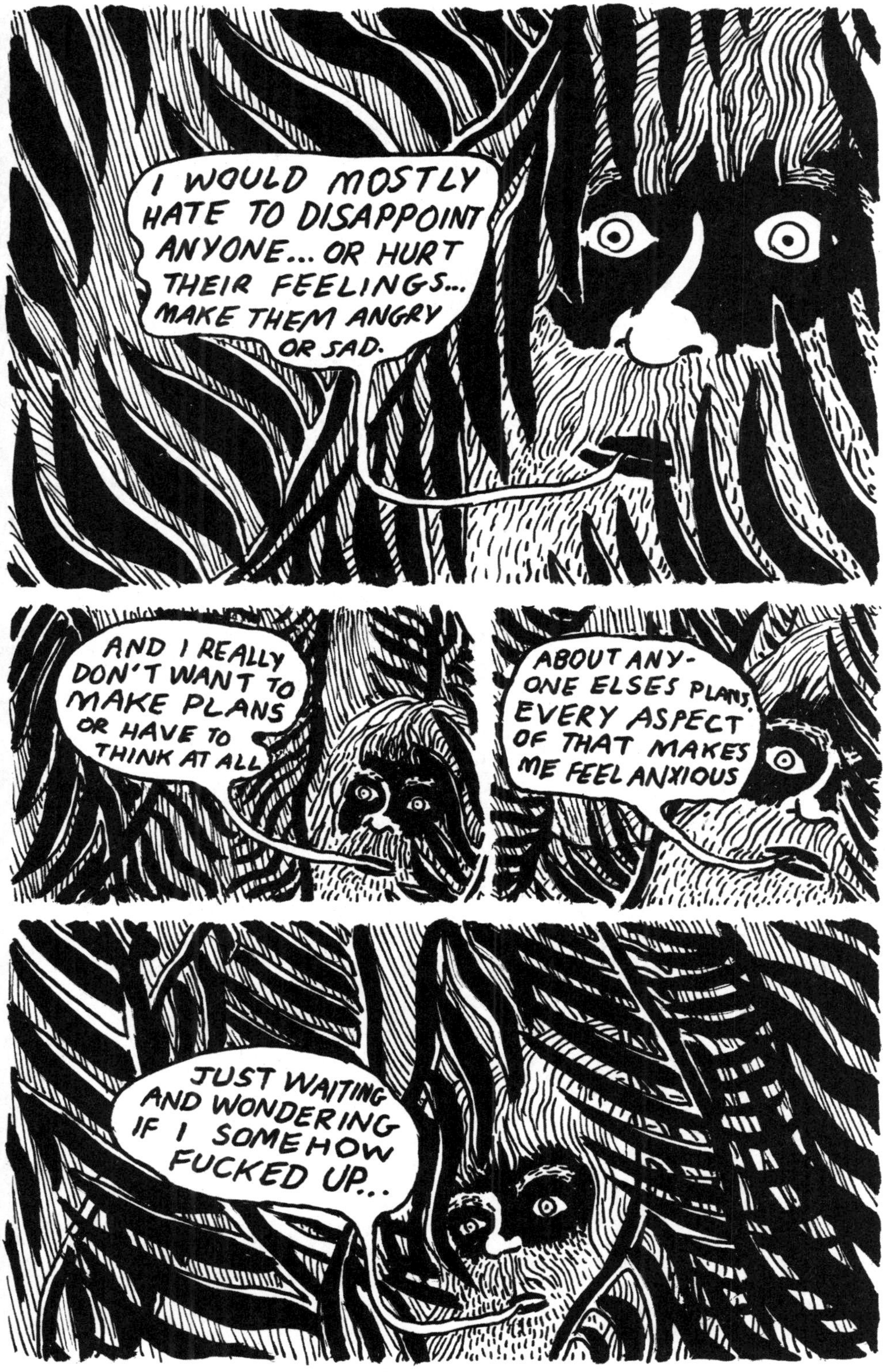
I WOULD MOSTLY HATE TO DISAPPOINT ANYONE... OR HURT THEIR FEELINGS... MAKE THEM ANGRY OR SAD.
AND I REALLY DON'T WANT TO MAKE PLANS OR HAVE TO THINK AT ALL
ABOUT ANY-ONE ELSES PLANS. EVERY ASPECT OF THAT MAKES ME FEEL ANXIOUS
JUST WAITING AND WONDERING IF I SOMEHOW FUCKED UP...

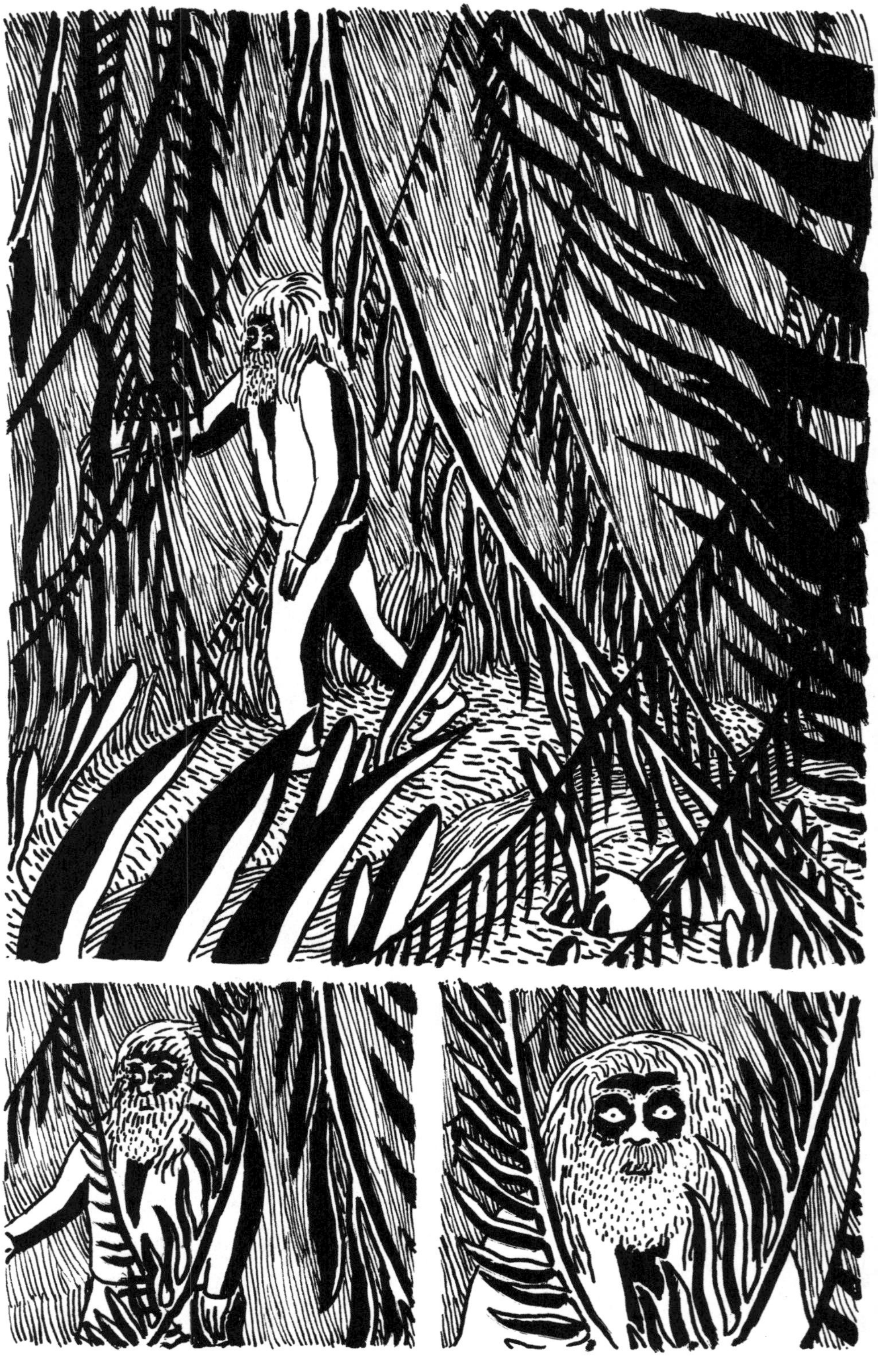

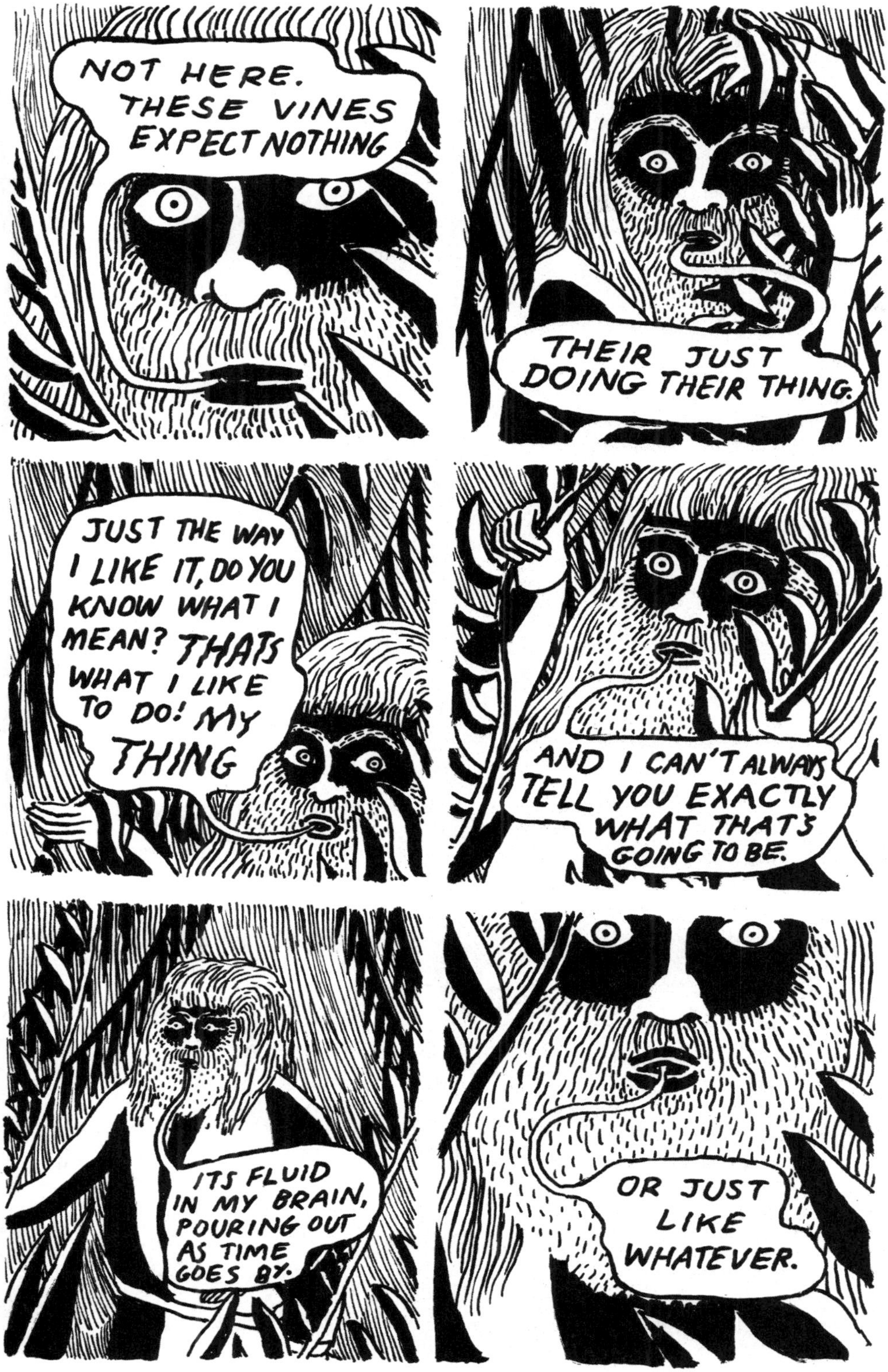
NOT HERE. THESE VINES EXPECT NOTHING
THEIR JUST DOING THEIR THING.
JUST THE WAY I LIKE IT, DO YOU KNOW WHAT I MEAN? THATS WHAT I LIKE TO DO! MY THING
AND I CAN'T ALWAYS TELL YOU EXACTLY WHAT THAT'S GOING TO BE.
ITS FLUID IN MY BRAIN, POURING OUT AS TIME GOES BY.
OR JUST LIKE WHATEVER.

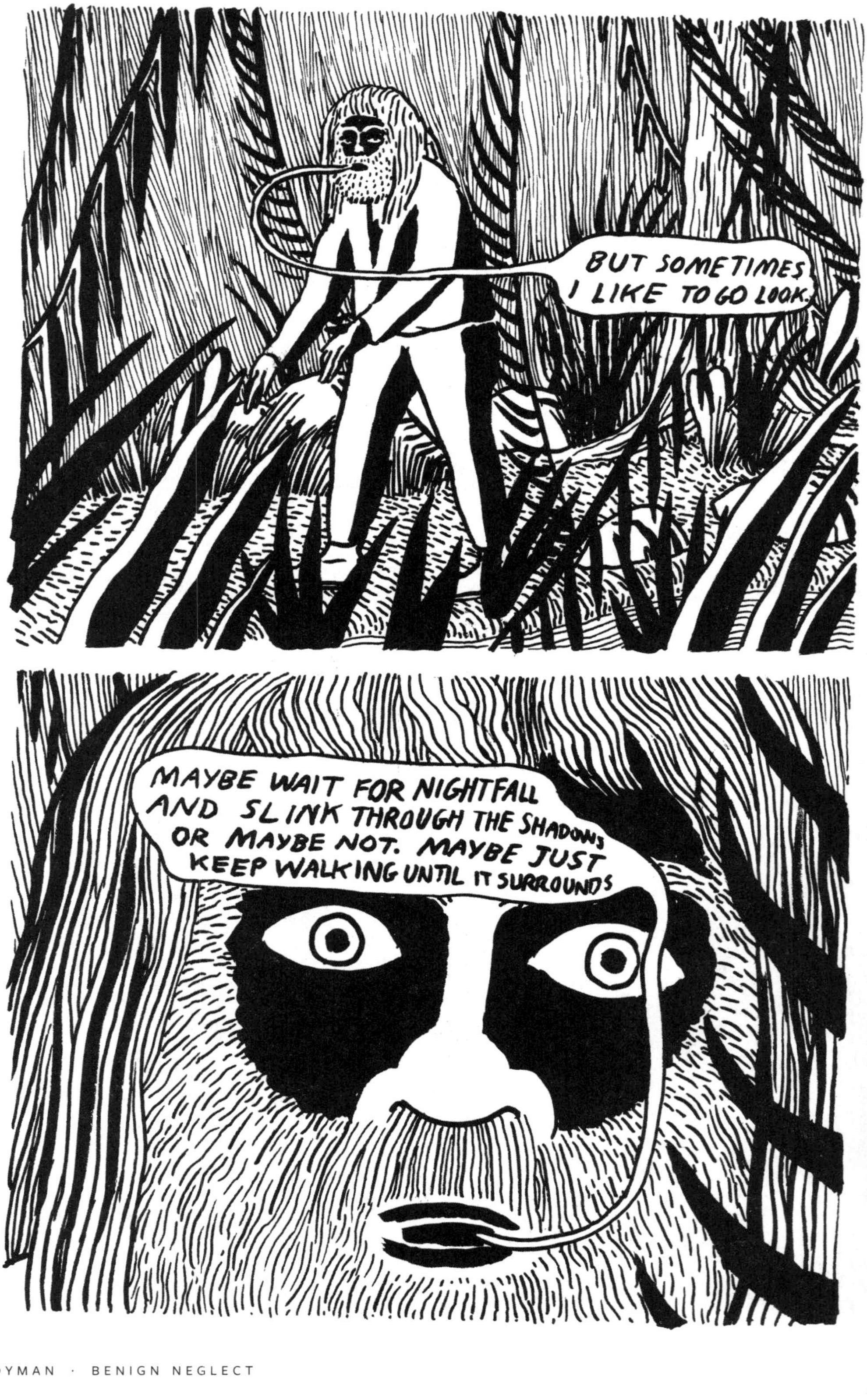
BUT SOMETIMES I LIKE TO GO LOOK.
MAYBE WAIT FOR NIGHTFALL AND SLINK THROUGH THE SHADOWS OR MAYBE NOT. MAYBE JUST KEEP WALKING UNTIL IT SURROUNDS

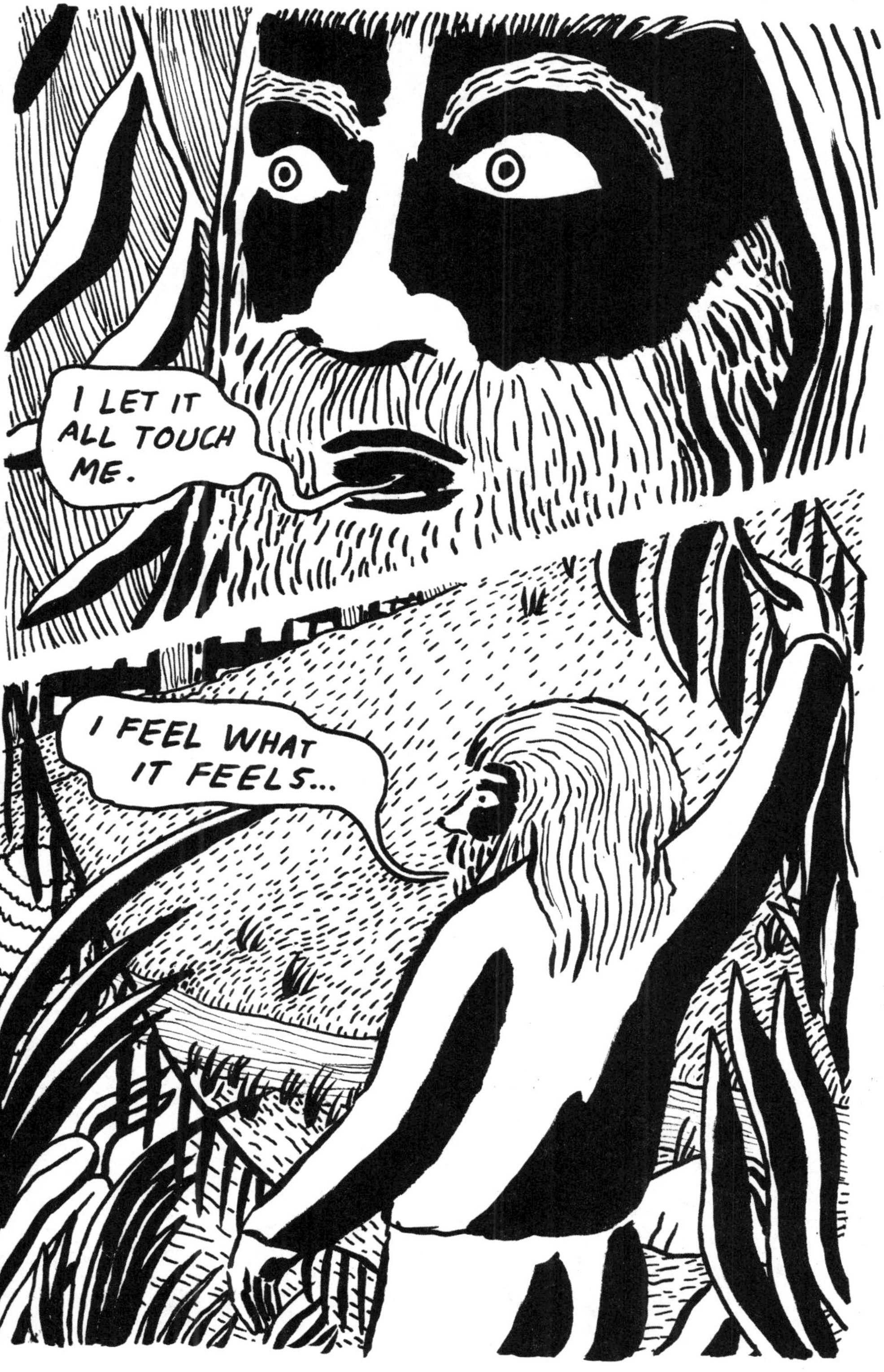
I LET IT ALL TOUCH ME.
I FEEL WHAT IT FEELS...

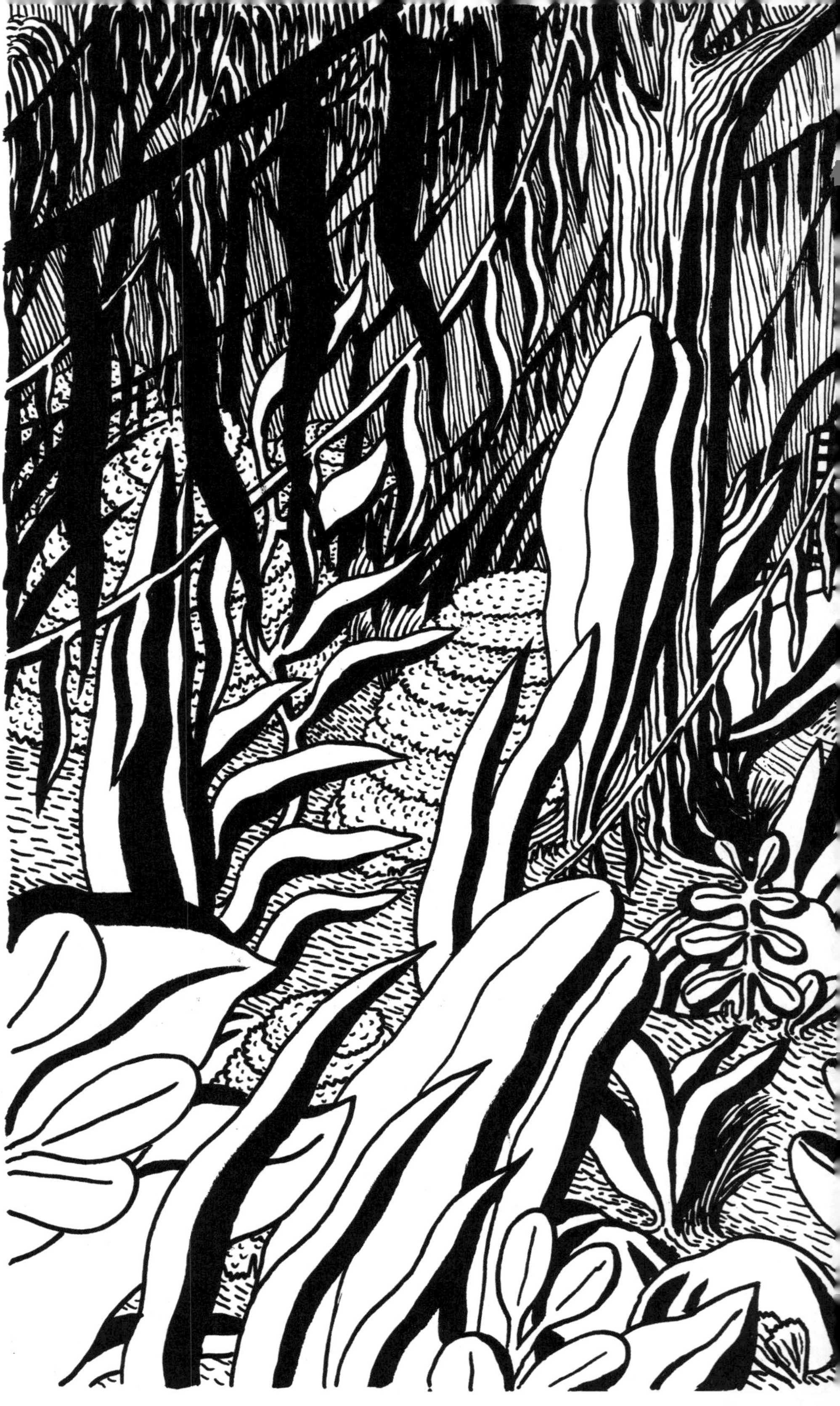

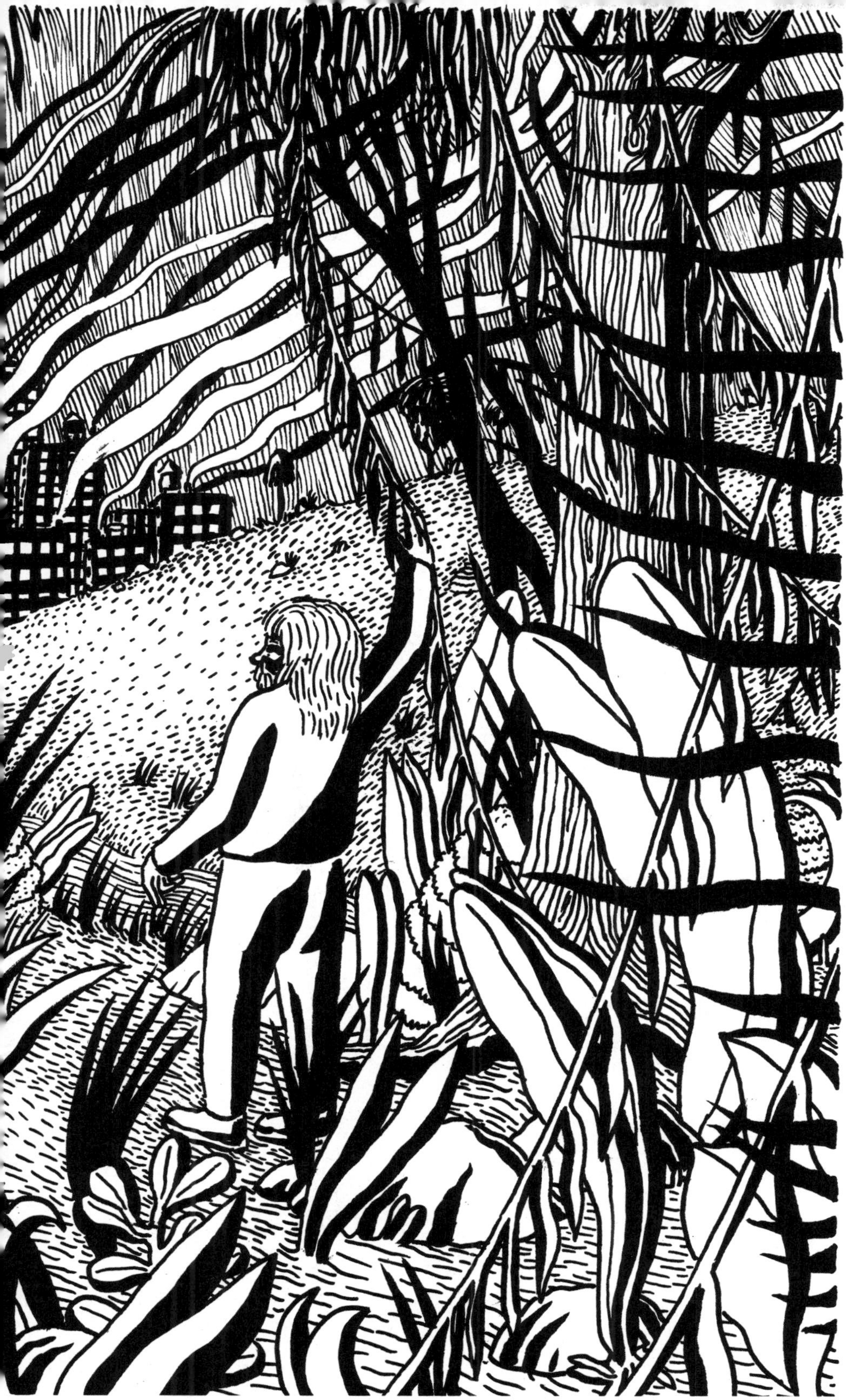

Crawl Space (*Excerpt*)

JESSE JACOBS

originally published in

Crawl Space
KOYAMA PRESS
6.5 x 9 inches • 96 pages

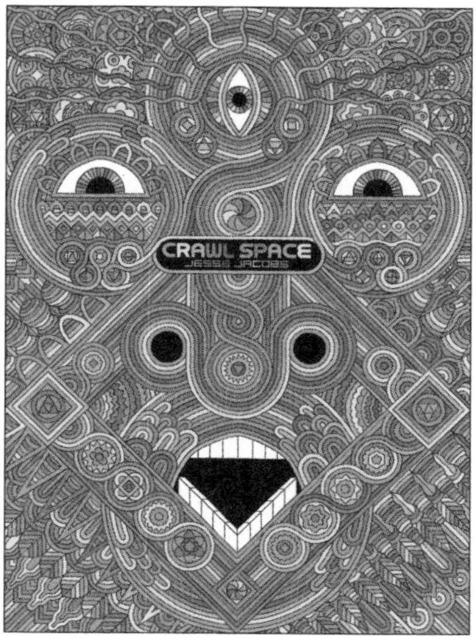
CRAWL SPACE
JESSE JACOBS

Biography

Jesse Jacobs was born in Moncton, New Brunswick, Canada, and graduated with a Bachelor of Fine Arts from the Nova Scotia College of Art and Design. He now works as a cartoonist, video game designer, and illustrator from his home in Hamilton, Ontario. His major comic books, *By This Shall You Know Him*, *Safari Honeymoon*, and *Crawl Space*, were originally published by Koyama Press and have been translated into several languages.
jessejacobs.ca

Statement

My comics are initially driven by my drawings. As I develop imagery, stories begin to emerge in a natural way. As a project develops, both the language and the art work together, informing one another. *Crawl Space* began as an attempt for me to expand on the way that I use color in my work. In an effort to use a full palette, I began drawing in a somewhat traditional psychedelic way. The story grew from there and began to reference my own psychedelic experiences.

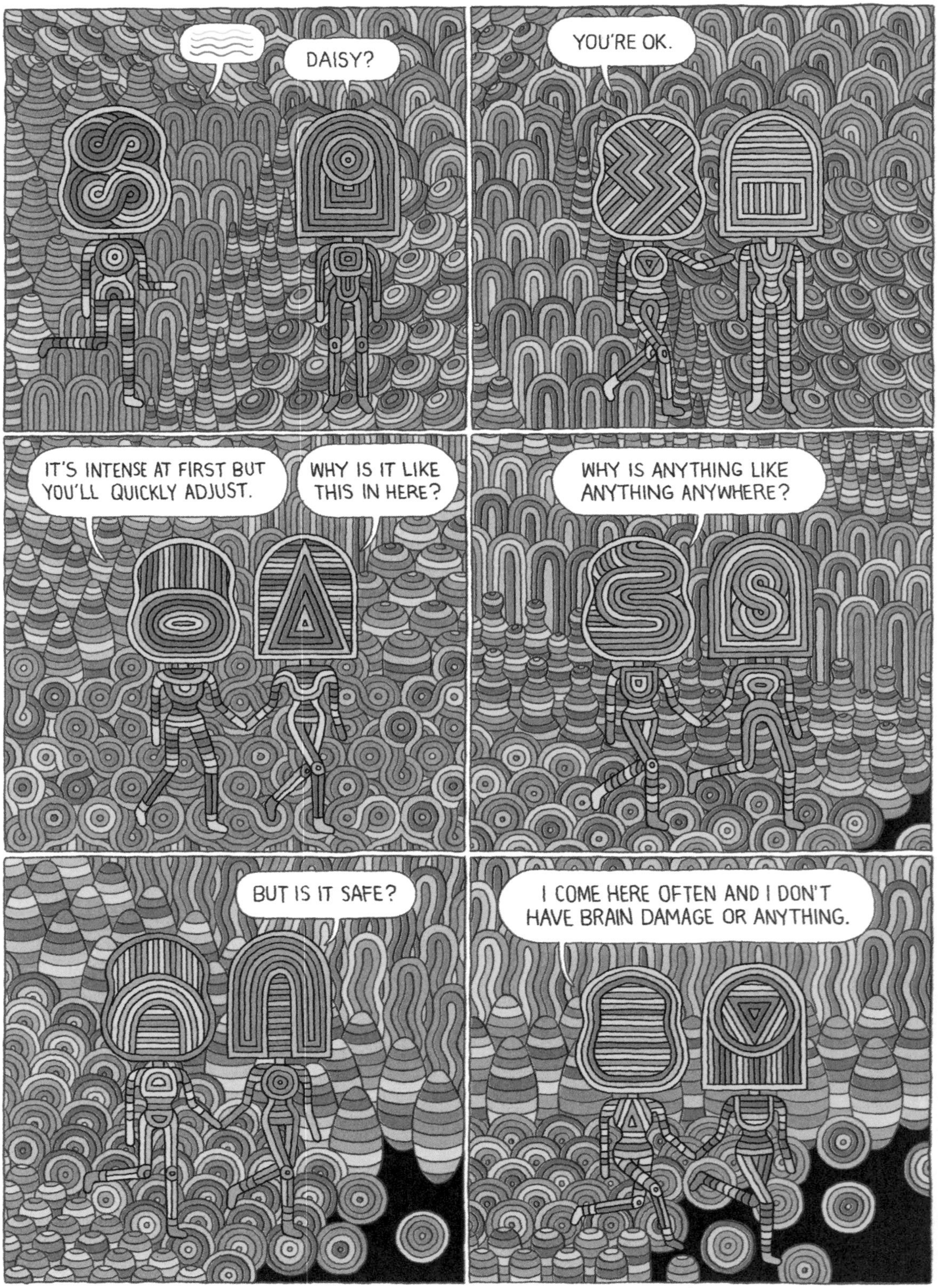
DAISY?
YOU'RE OK.
IT'S INTENSE AT FIRST BUT YOU'LL QUICKLY ADJUST.
WHY IS IT LIKE THIS IN HERE?
WHY IS ANYTHING LIKE ANYTHING ANYWHERE?
BUT IS IT SAFE?
I COME HERE OFTEN AND I DON'T HAVE BRAIN DAMAGE OR ANYTHING.

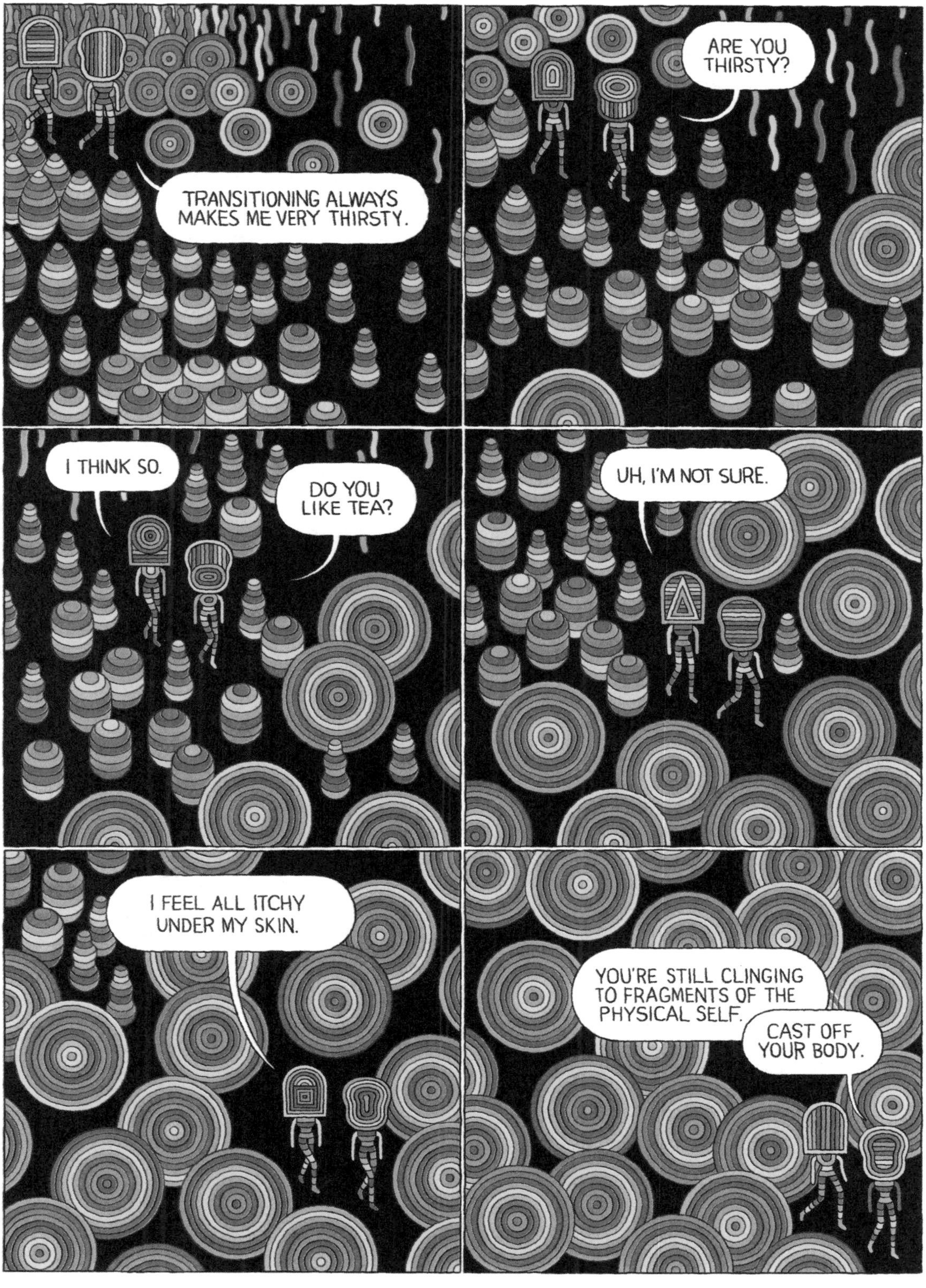
TRANSITIONING ALWAYS MAKES ME VERY THIRSTY.
ARE YOU THIRSTY?
I THINK SO.
DO YOU LIKE TEA?
UH, I'M NOT SURE.
I FEEL ALL ITCHY UNDER MY SKIN.
YOU'RE STILL CLINGING TO FRAGMENTS OF THE PHYSICAL SELF.
CAST OFF YOUR BODY.

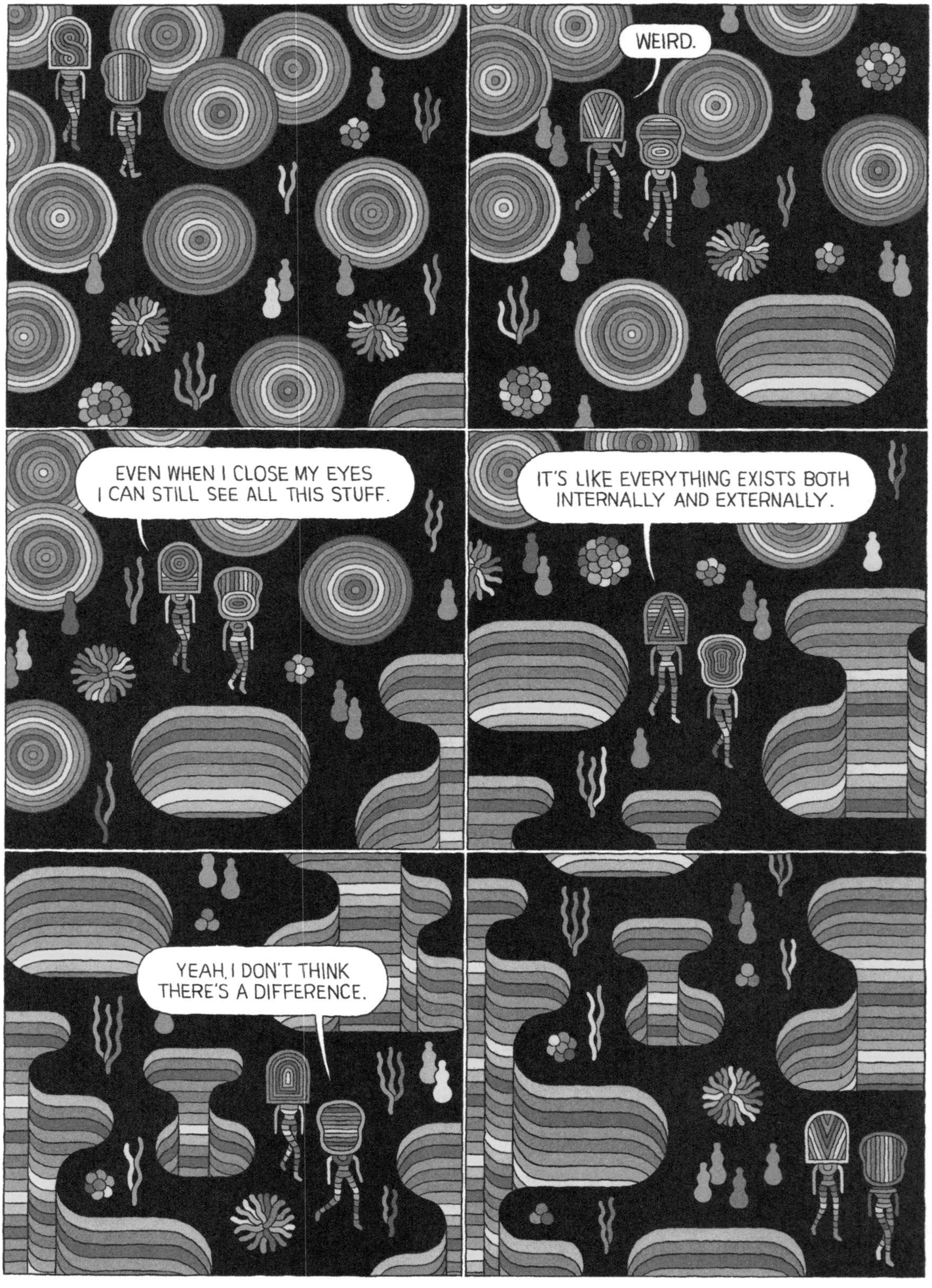
WEIRD.
EVEN WHEN I CLOSE MY EYES I CAN STILL SEE ALL THIS STUFF.
IT'S LIKE EVERYTHING EXISTS BOTH INTERNALLY AND EXTERNALLY.
YEAH, I DON'T THINK THERE'S A DIFFERENCE.

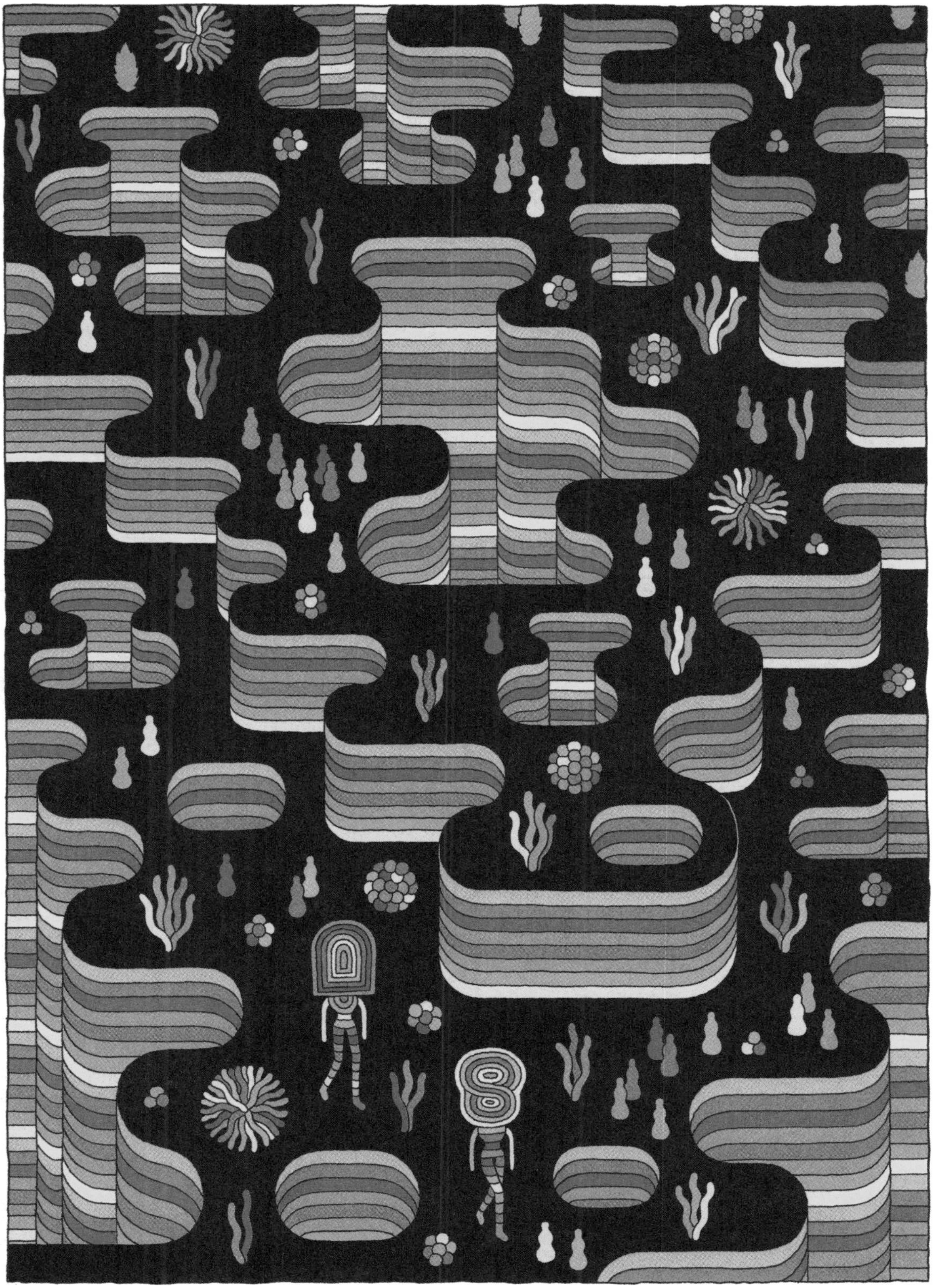

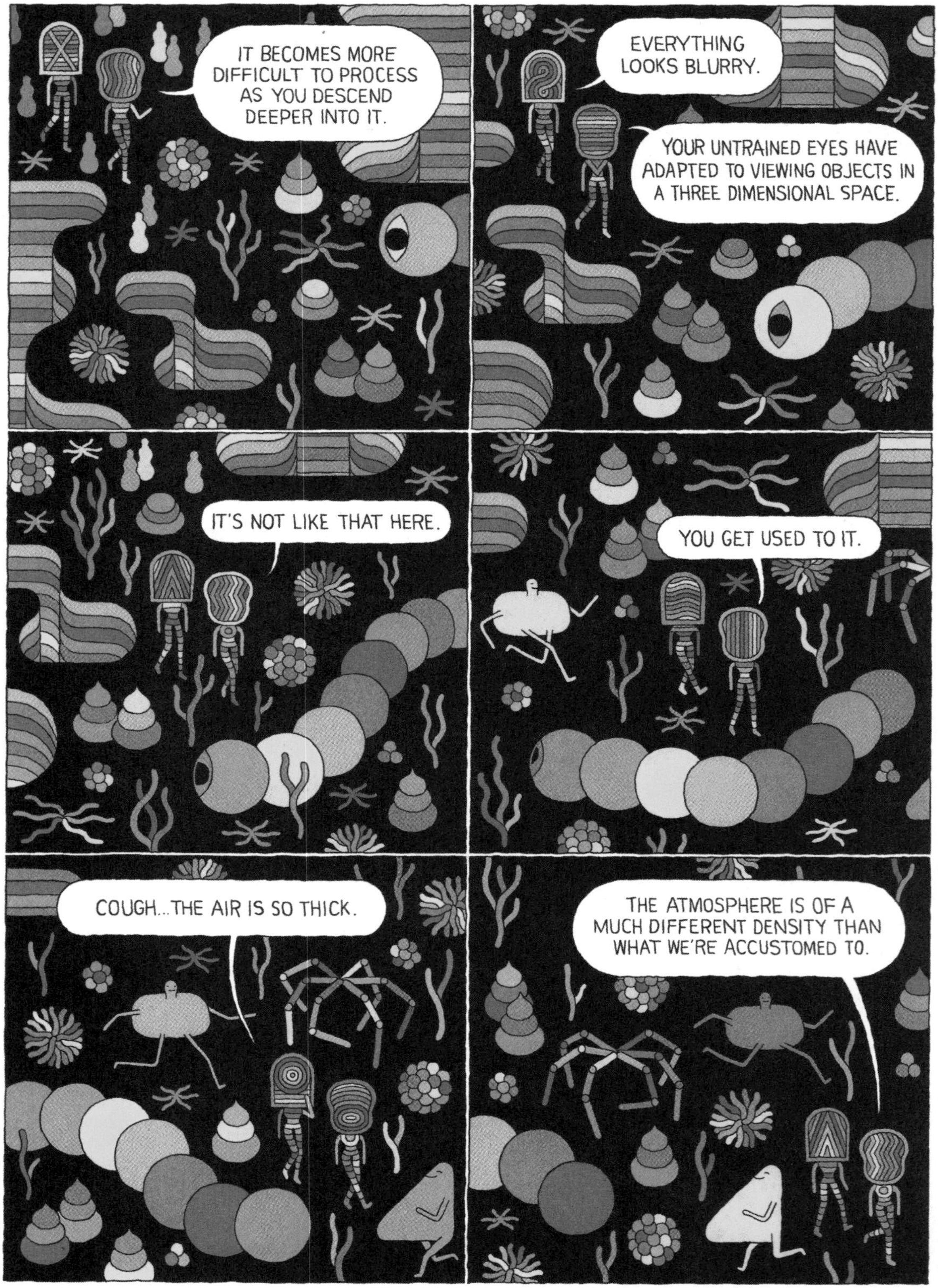
IT BECOMES MORE DIFFICULT TO PROCESS AS YOU DESCEND DEEPER INTO IT.
EVERYTHING LOOKS BLURRY.
YOUR UNTRAINED EYES HAVE ADAPTED TO VIEWING OBJECTS IN A THREE DIMENSIONAL SPACE.
IT'S NOT LIKE THAT HERE.
YOU GET USED TO IT.
COUGH... THE AIR IS SO THICK.
THE ATMOSPHERE IS OF A MUCH DIFFERENT DENSITY THAN WHAT WE'RE ACCUSTOMED TO.

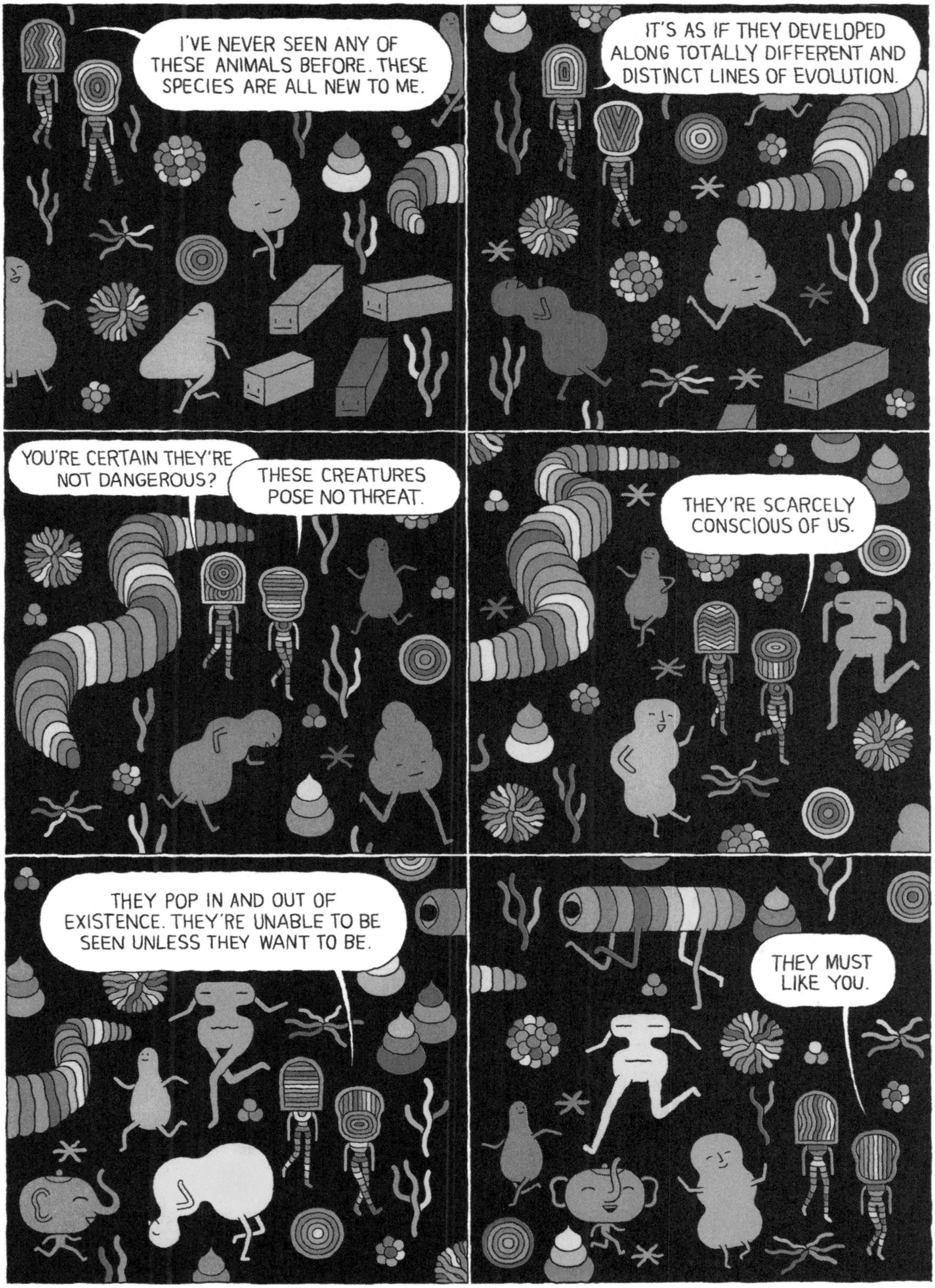
I'VE NEVER SEEN ANY OF THESE ANIMALS BEFORE. THESE SPECIES ARE ALL NEW TO ME.
IT'S AS IF THEY DEVELOPED ALONG TOTALLY DIFFERENT AND DISTINCT LINES OF EVOLUTION.
YOU'RE CERTAIN THEY'RE NOT DANGEROUS?
THESE CREATURES POSE NO THREAT.
THEY'RE SCARCELY CONSCIOUS OF US.
THEY POP IN AND OUT OF EXISTENCE. THEY'RE UNABLE TO BE SEEN UNLESS THEY WANT TO BE.
THEY MUST LIKE YOU.

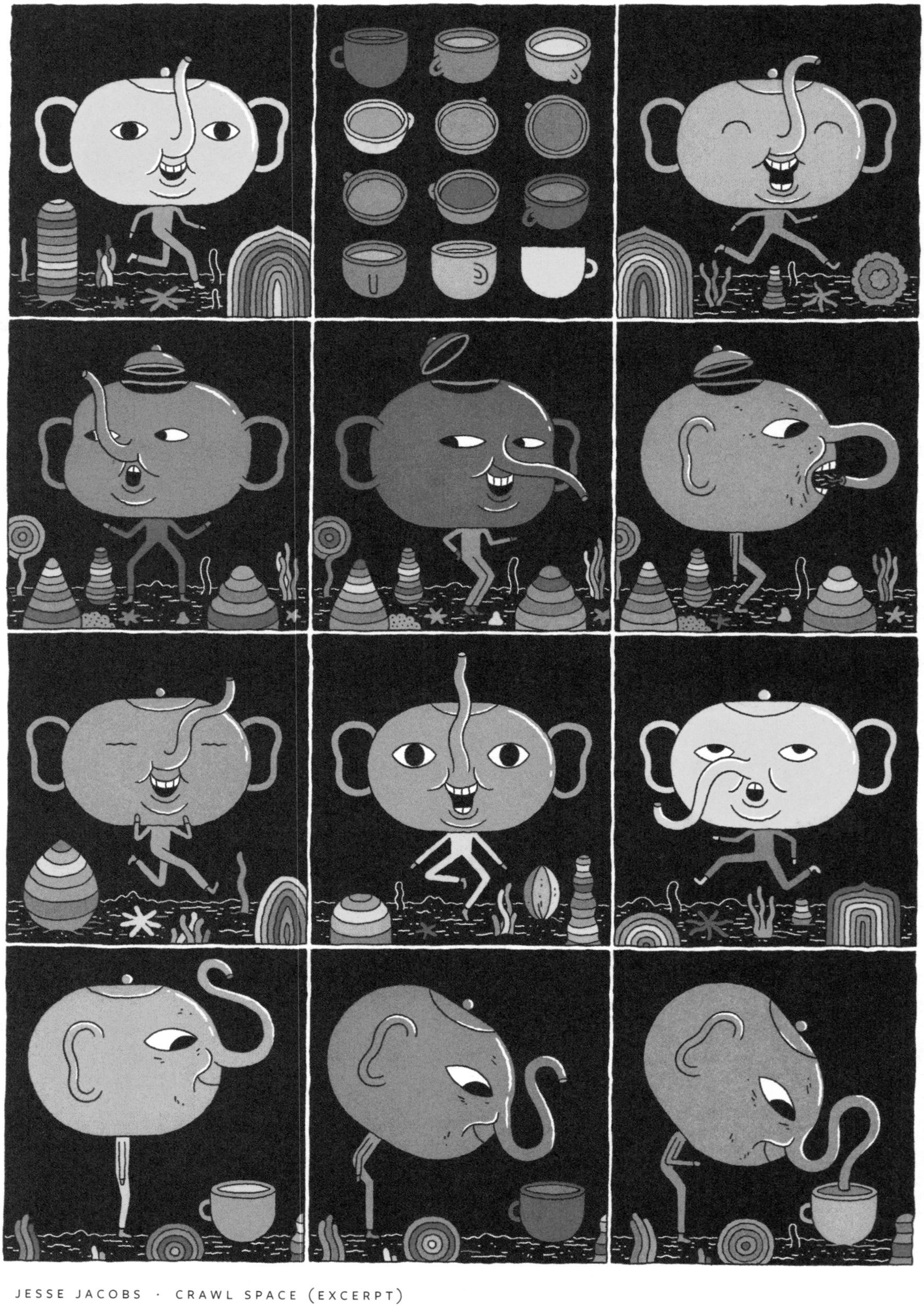

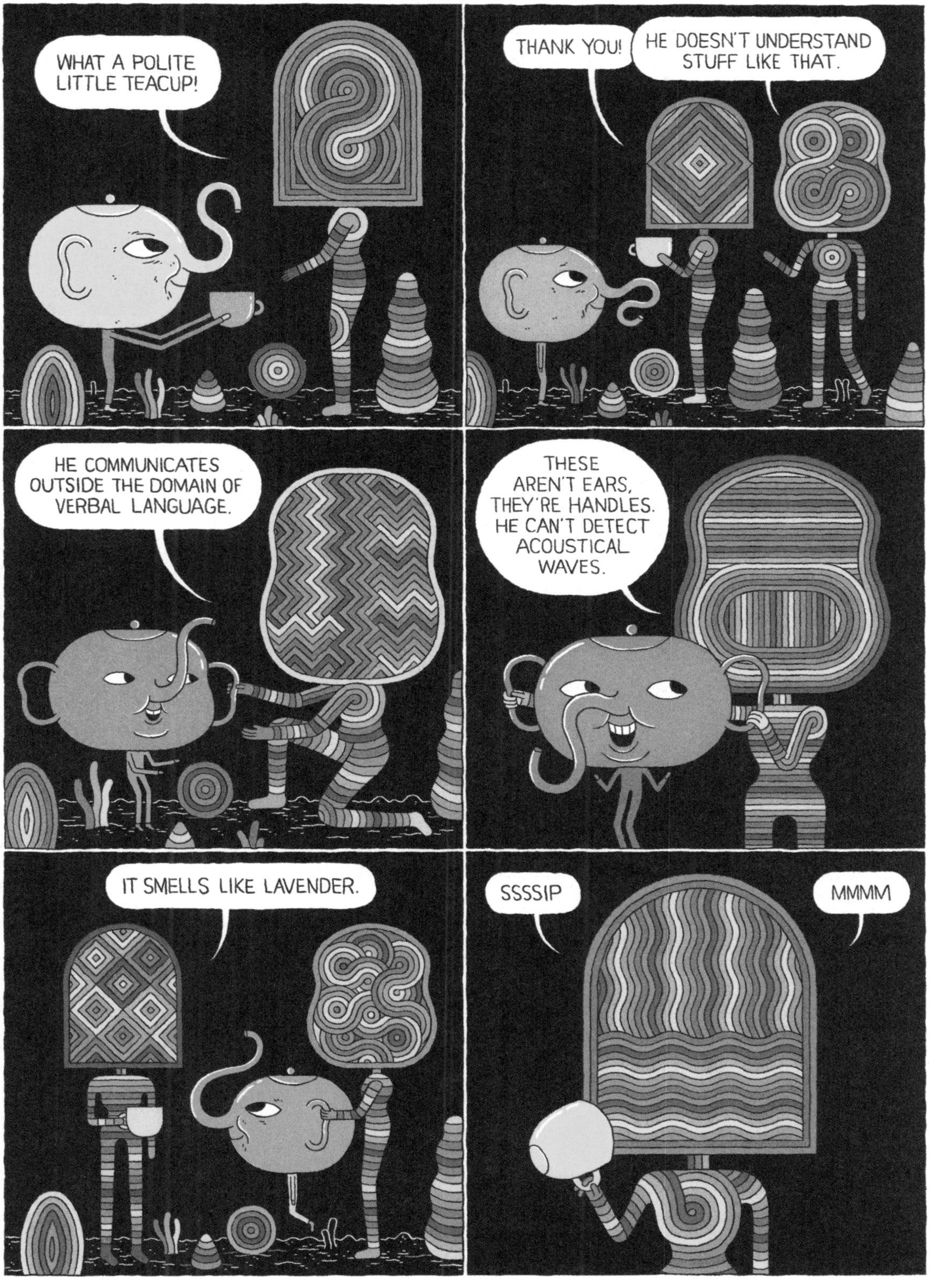
WHAT A POLITE LITTLE TEACUP!
THANK YOU!
HE DOESN'T UNDERSTAND STUFF LIKE THAT.
HE COMMUNICATES OUTSIDE THE DOMAIN OF VERBAL LANGUAGE.
THESE AREN'T EARS, THEY'RE HANDLES. HE CAN'T DETECT ACOUSTICAL WAVES.
IT SMELLS LIKE LAVENDER.
SSSSIP
MMMM

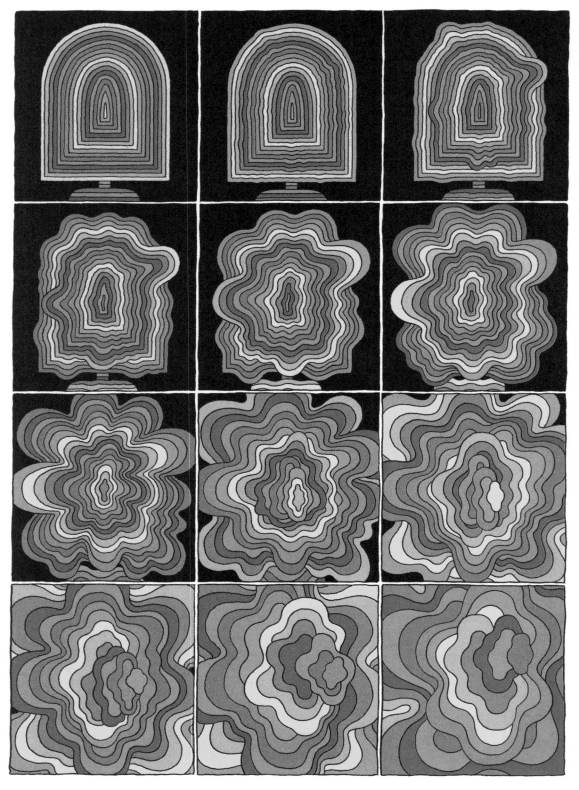

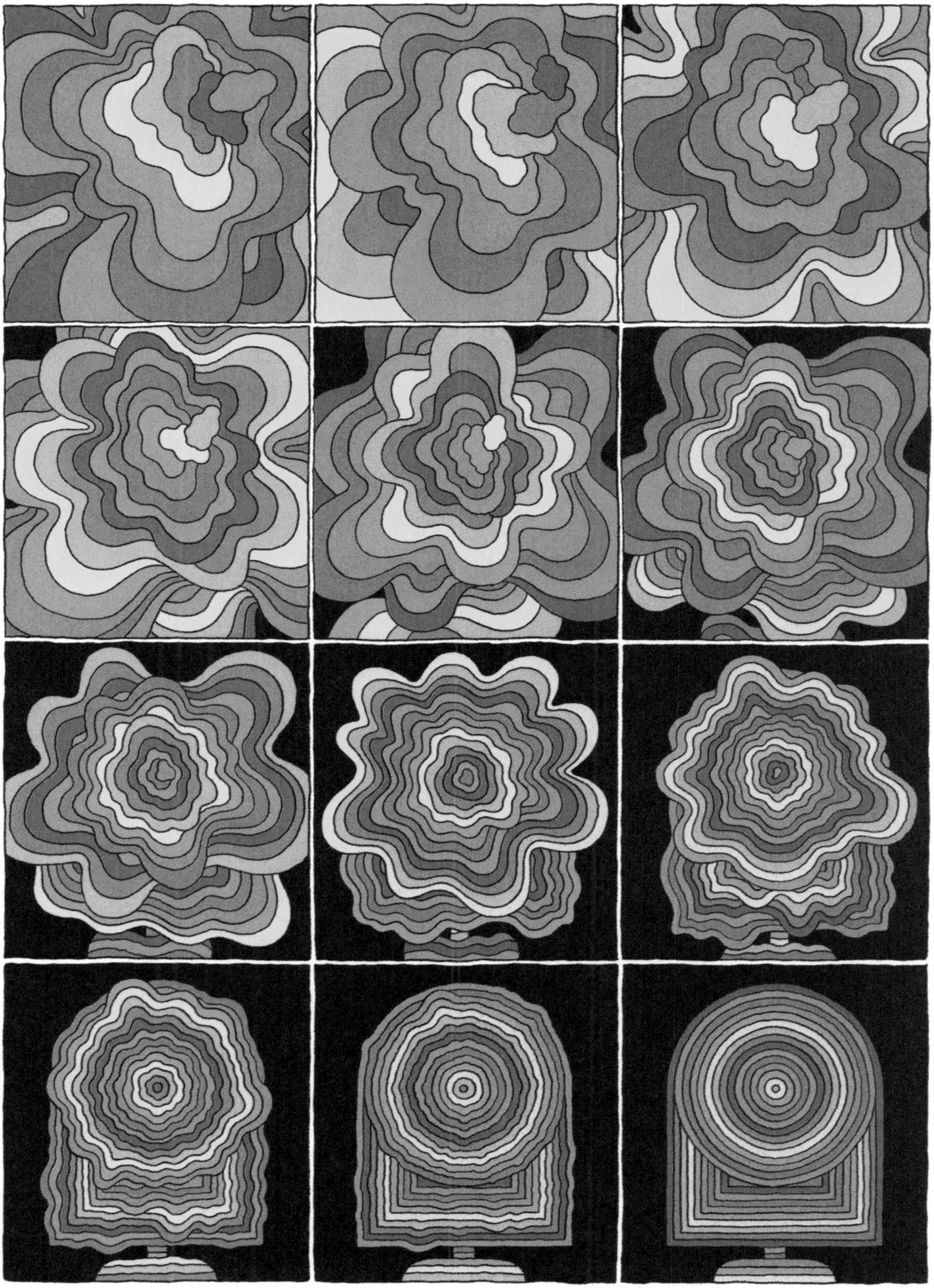

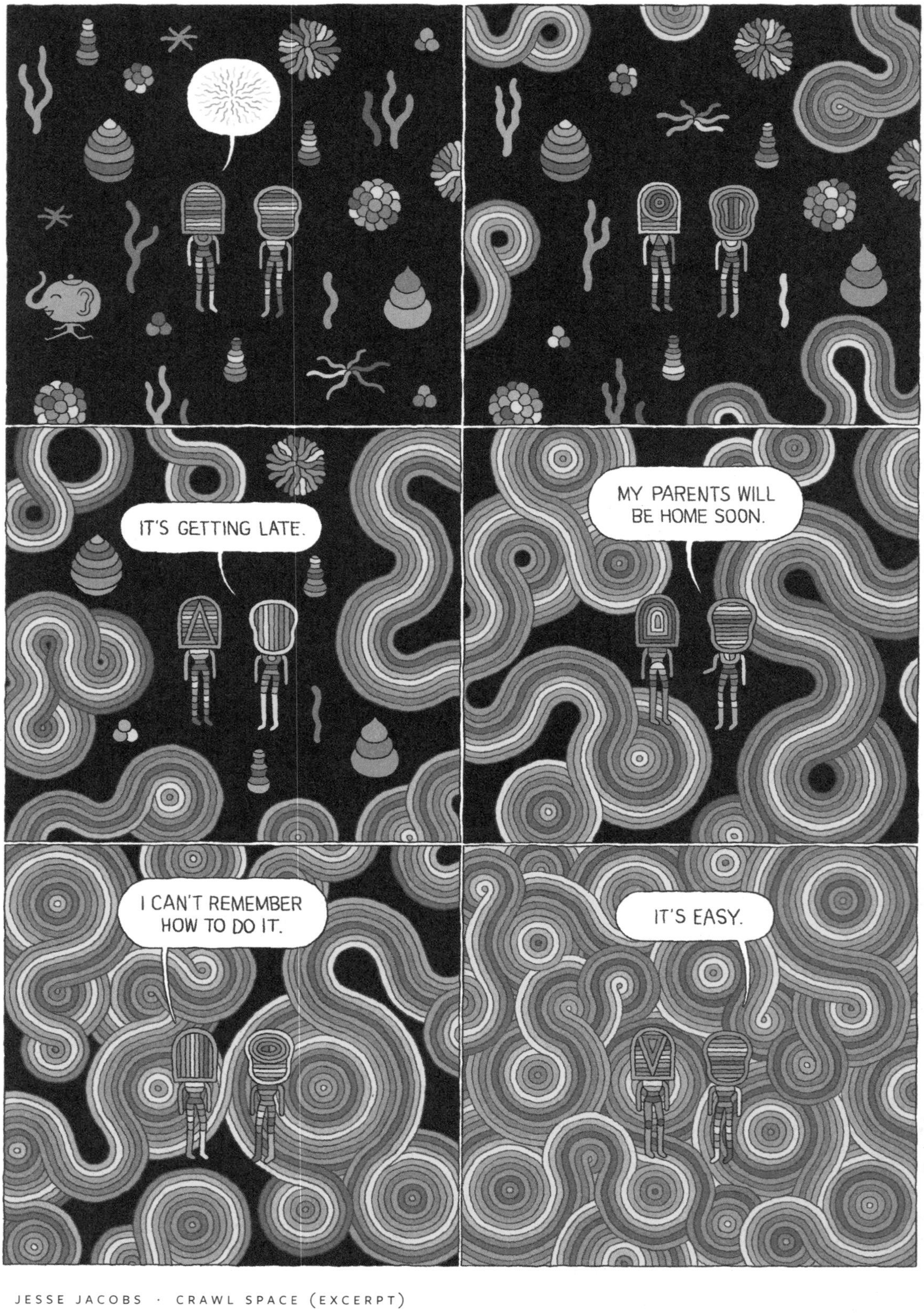
IT'S GETTING LATE.
MY PARENTS WILL BE HOME SOON.
I CAN'T REMEMBER HOW TO DO IT.
IT'S EASY.

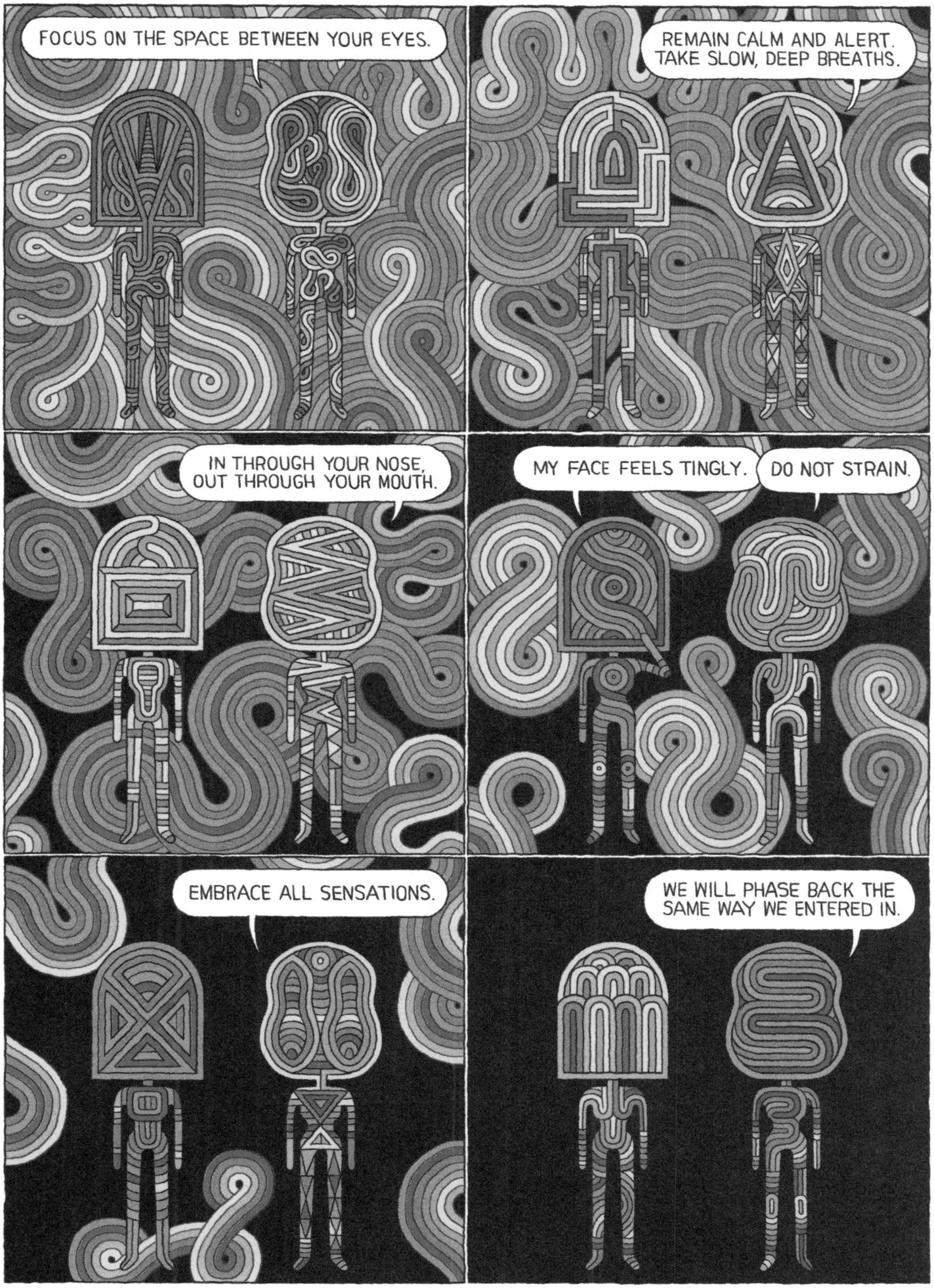
FOCUS ON THE SPACE BETWEEN YOUR EYES.
REMAIN CALM AND ALERT. TAKE SLOW, DEEP BREATHS.
IN THROUGH YOUR NOSE, OUT THROUGH YOUR MOUTH.
MY FACE FEELS TINGLY.
DO NOT STRAIN.
EMBRACE ALL SENSATIONS.
WE WILL PHASE BACK THE SAME WAY WE ENTERED IN.

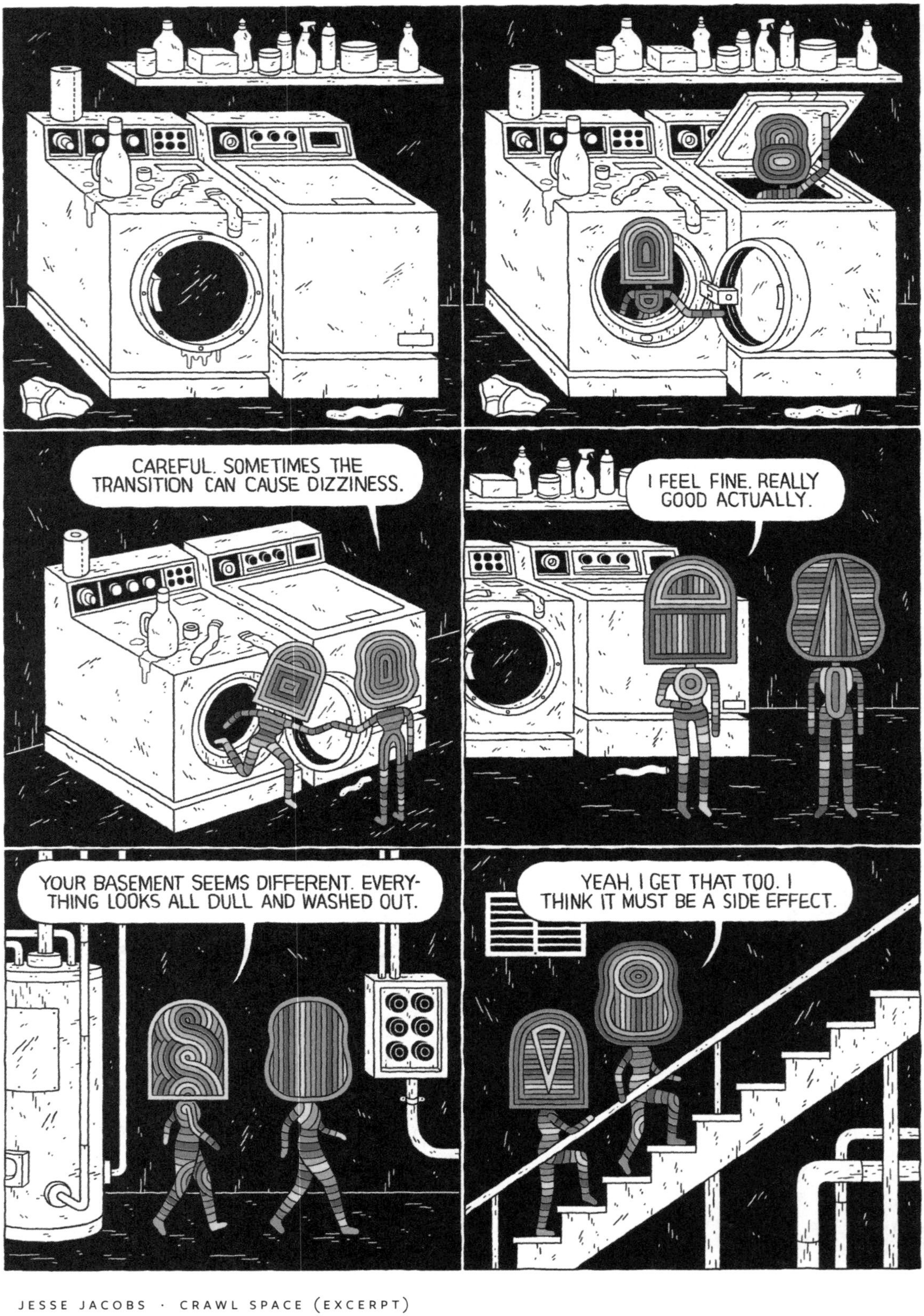
CAREFUL. SOMETIMES THE TRANSITION CAN CAUSE DIZZINESS.
I FEEL FINE. REALLY GOOD ACTUALLY.
YOUR BASEMENT SEEMS DIFFERENT. EVERY-THING LOOKS ALL DULL AND WASHED OUT.
YEAH, I GET THAT TOO. I THINK IT MUST BE A SIDE EFFECT.

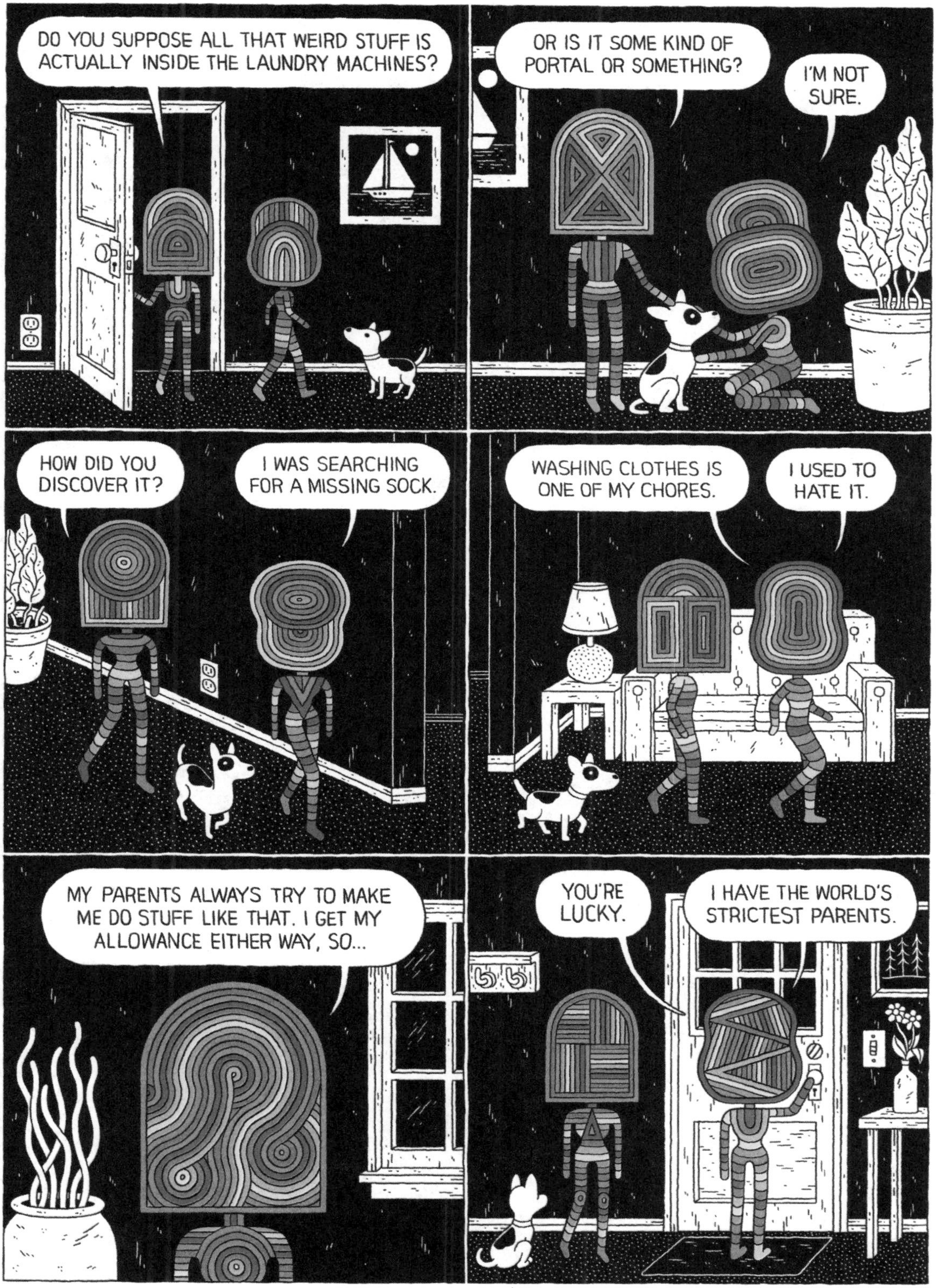
DO YOU SUPPOSE ALL THAT WEIRD STUFF IS ACTUALLY INSIDE THE LAUNDRY MACHINES?
OR IS IT SOME KIND OF PORTAL OR SOMETHING?
I'M NOT SURE.
HOW DID YOU DISCOVER IT?
I WAS SEARCHING FOR A MISSING SOCK.
WASHING CLOTHES IS ONE OF MY CHORES.
I USED TO HATE IT.
MY PARENTS ALWAYS TRY TO MAKE ME DO STUFF LIKE THAT. I GET MY ALLOWANCE EITHER WAY, SO...
YOU'RE LUCKY.
I HAVE THE WORLD'S STRICTEST PARENTS.

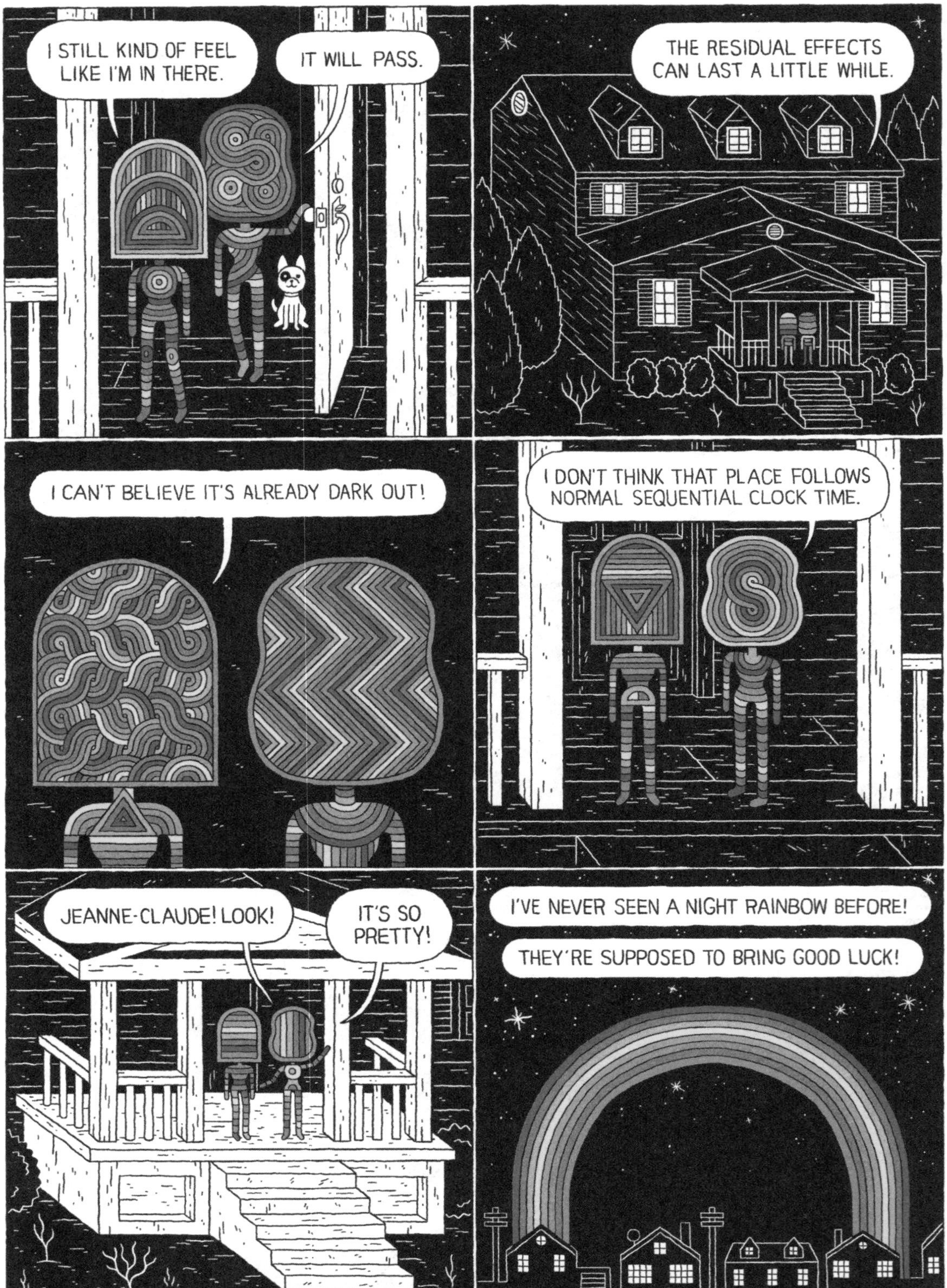
I STILL KIND OF FEEL LIKE I'M IN THERE.
IT WILL PASS.
THE RESIDUAL EFFECTS CAN LAST A LITTLE WHILE.
I CAN'T BELIEVE IT'S ALREADY DARK OUT!
I DON'T THINK THAT PLACE FOLLOWS NORMAL SEQUENTIAL CLOCK TIME.
JEANNE-CLAUDE! LOOK!
IT'S SO PRETTY!
I'VE NEVER SEEN A NIGHT RAINBOW BEFORE!
THEY'RE SUPPOSED TO BRING GOOD LUCK!

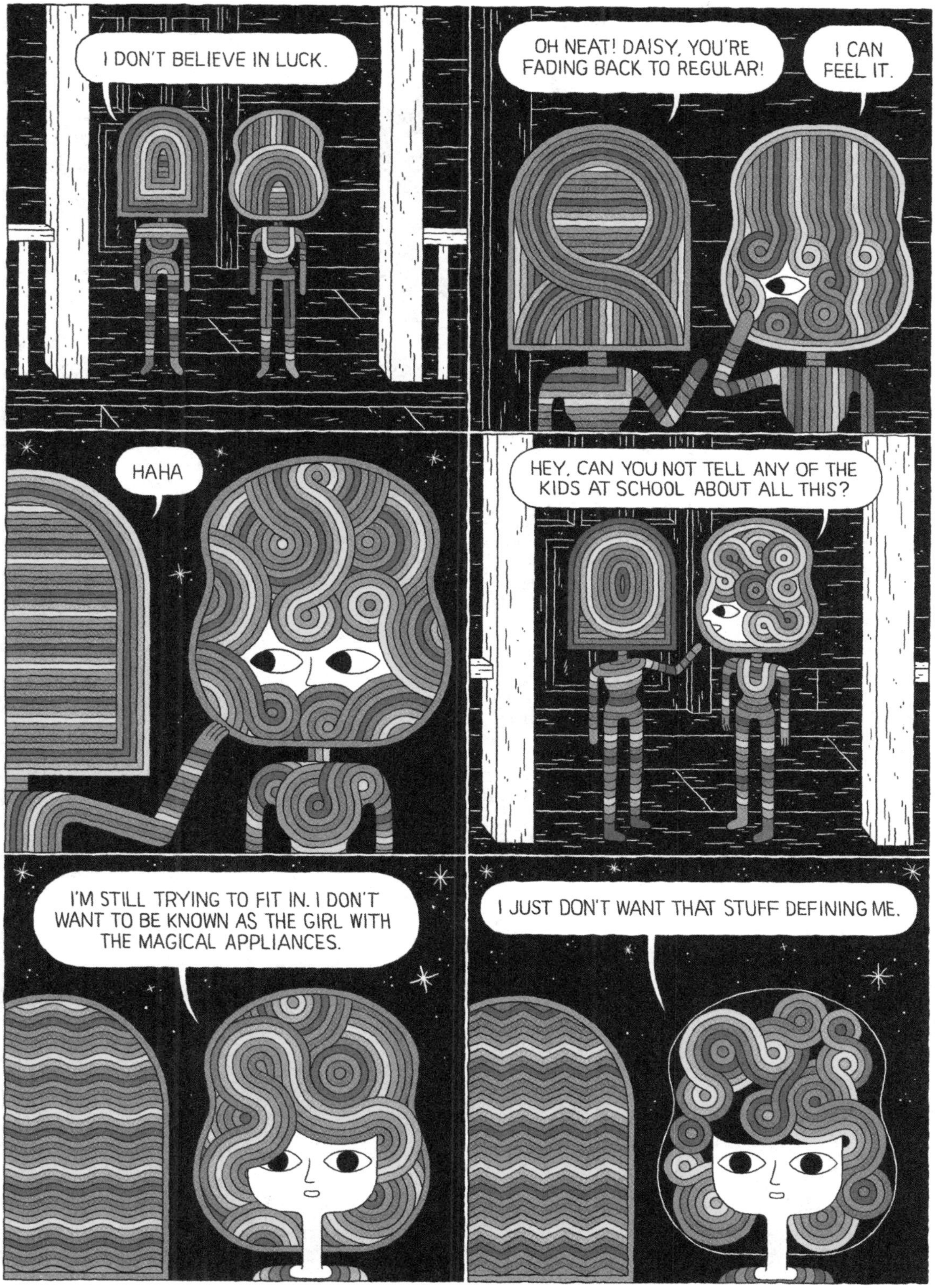
I DON'T BELIEVE IN LUCK.
OH NEAT! DAISY, YOU'RE FADING BACK TO REGULAR!
I CAN FEEL IT.
HAHA
HEY, CAN YOU NOT TELL ANY OF THE KIDS AT SCHOOL ABOUT ALL THIS?
I'M STILL TRYING TO FIT IN. I DON'T WANT TO BE KNOWN AS THE GIRL WITH THE MAGICAL APPLIANCES.
I JUST DON'T WANT THAT STUFF DEFINING ME.

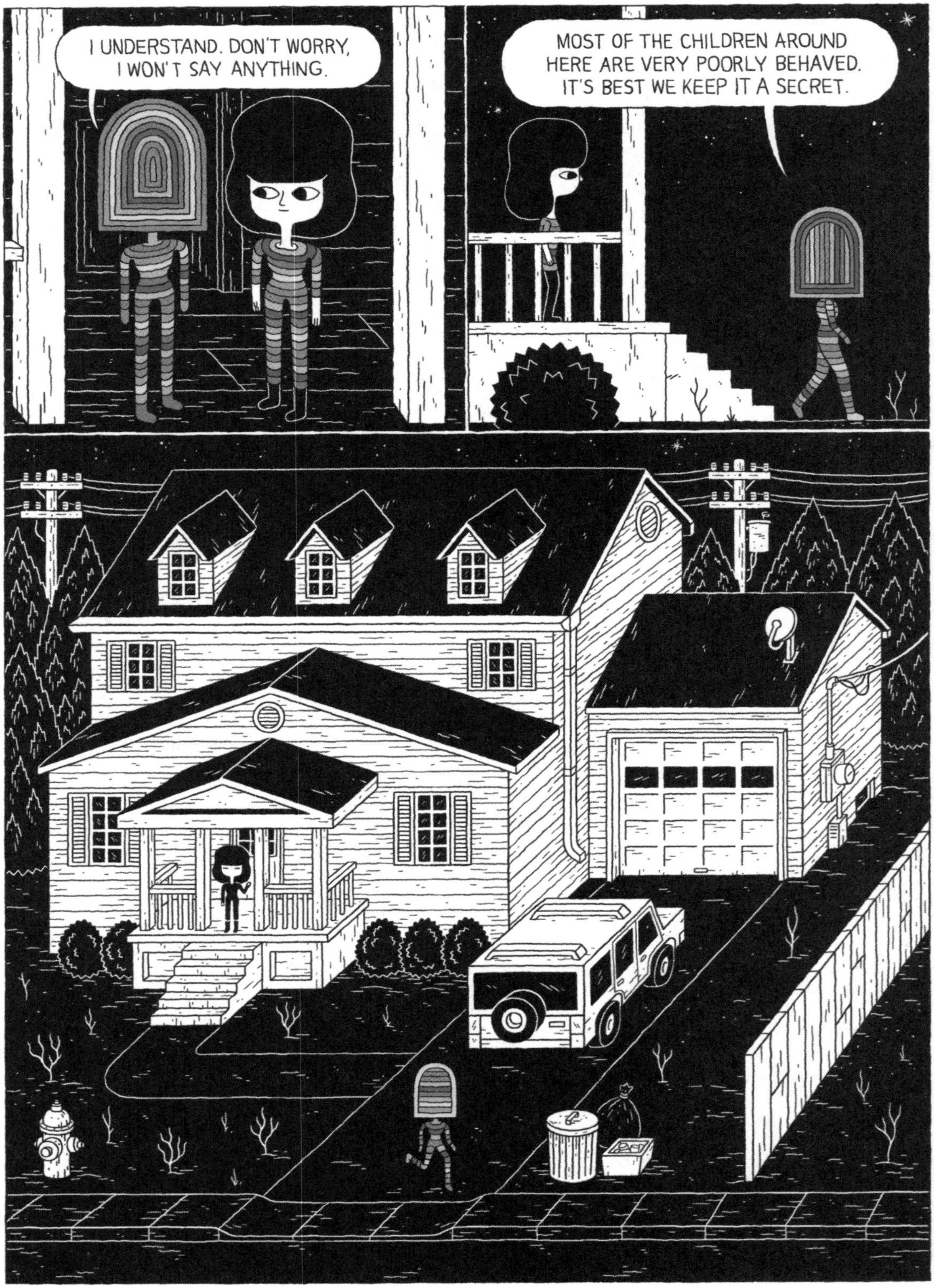
I UNDERSTAND. DON'T WORRY, I WON'T SAY ANYTHING.
MOST OF THE CHILDREN AROUND HERE ARE VERY POORLY BEHAVED. IT'S BEST WE KEEP IT A SECRET.

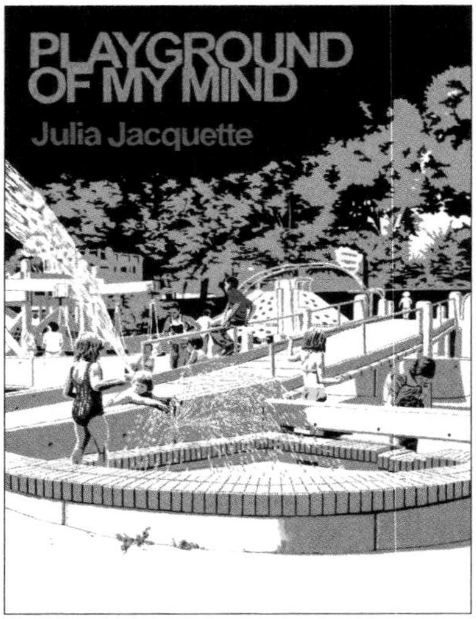
PLAYGROUND
OF MY MIND
Julia Jacquette

Playground of My Mind (*Excerpt*)

JULIA JACQUETTE

originally published in

Playground of My Mind

WELLIN MUSEUM OF ART AND DELMONICO BOOKS/PRESTEL
10.5 x 14 inches • 62 pages

Biography

Julia Jacquette is an American artist based in New York City and Amsterdam. Her work has been shown extensively at galleries and museums around the world, including the Museum of Modern Art (NY), the Museum of Fine Arts, Boston, and the RISD Museum, among other institutions. Jacquette's work was featured in solo exhibitions at the Tang Museum in Saratoga Springs, New York, and the Wellin Museum in Clinton, New York, publisher of her graphic memoir, *Playground of My Mind,* and a monograph, *Unrequited and Acts of Play.* She has taught at the Rhode Island School of Design and Princeton University, and is currently on the faculty at the Fashion Institute of Technology (NYC). juliajacquette.net

Statement

Playground of My Mind is a graphic reminiscence of the modernist playgrounds of New York City and their influence on my aesthetics and thinking. The original paintings on paper were exhibited in 2017 at the Wellin Museum, who also published the memoir. These playgrounds, of rational and utopian ideals, were constructed in the tumultuous setting of 1960s and '70s New York: a chaotic atmosphere but one that was open to new ideas in architecture and play. Focus is placed on the playgrounds that I interacted with most: Richard Dattner's seminal Adventure Playground in Central Park, an M. Paul Friedberg playground (now destroyed) that was situated in the city housing I grew up in, and Discovery Play Park, which my father collaborated on, also located in Central Park. The book makes an argument for the reconsideration of "Brutalist" architecture (here in its most playful and sculptural form), and affinities with the Dutch playgrounds of Aldo van Eyck are delineated. When we play in and around great design, does it teach us?

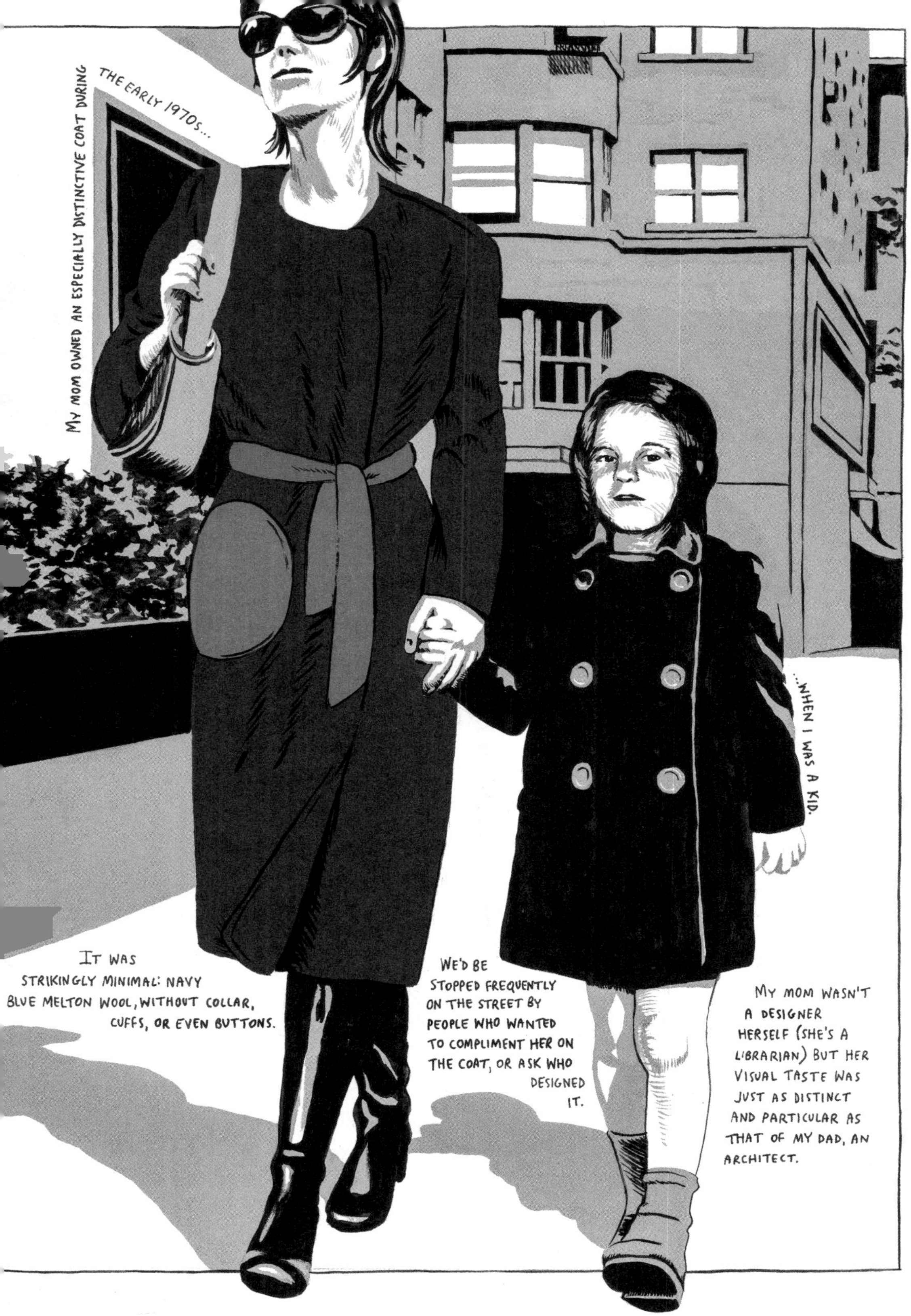
MY MOM OWNED AN ESPECIALLY DISTINCTIVE COAT DURING THE EARLY 1970s...
...WHEN I WAS A KID.
IT WAS STRIKINGLY MINIMAL: NAVY BLUE MELTON WOOL, WITHOUT COLLAR, CUFFS, OR EVEN BUTTONS.
WE'D BE STOPPED FREQUENTLY ON THE STREET BY PEOPLE WHO WANTED TO COMPLIMENT HER ON THE COAT, OR ASK WHO DESIGNED IT.
MY MOM WASN'T A DESIGNER HERSELF (SHE'S A LIBRARIAN) BUT HER VISUAL TASTE WAS JUST AS DISTINCT AND PARTICULAR AS THAT OF MY DAD, AN ARCHITECT.

A neighbor once recounted seeing my mom glaring at a newly, and abundantly, decorated Christmas tree in the lobby of our apartment building...

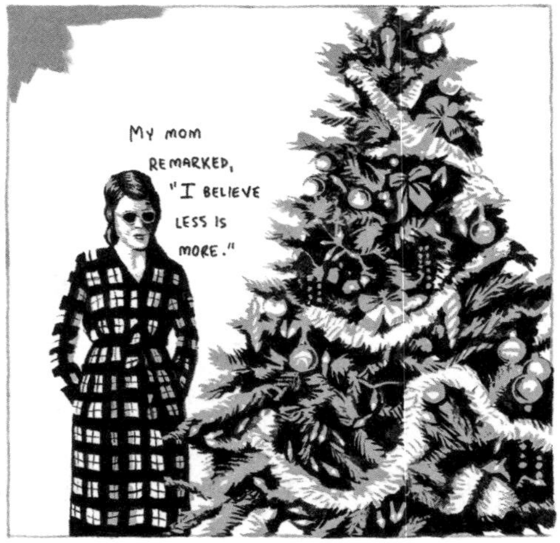
My mom remarked, "I believe less is more."

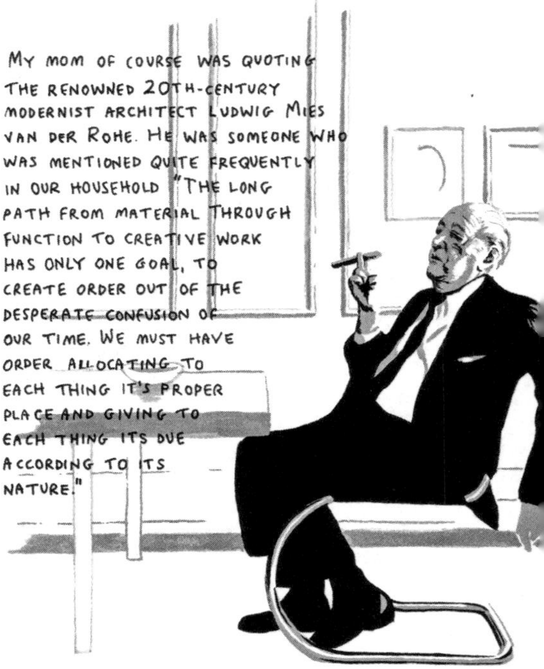

My mom of course was quoting the renowned 20th-century modernist architect Ludwig Mies van der Rohe. He was someone who was mentioned quite frequently in our household. "The long path from material through function to creative work has only one goal, to create order out of the desperate confusion of our time. We must have order allocating to each thing it's proper place and giving to each thing its due according to its nature."

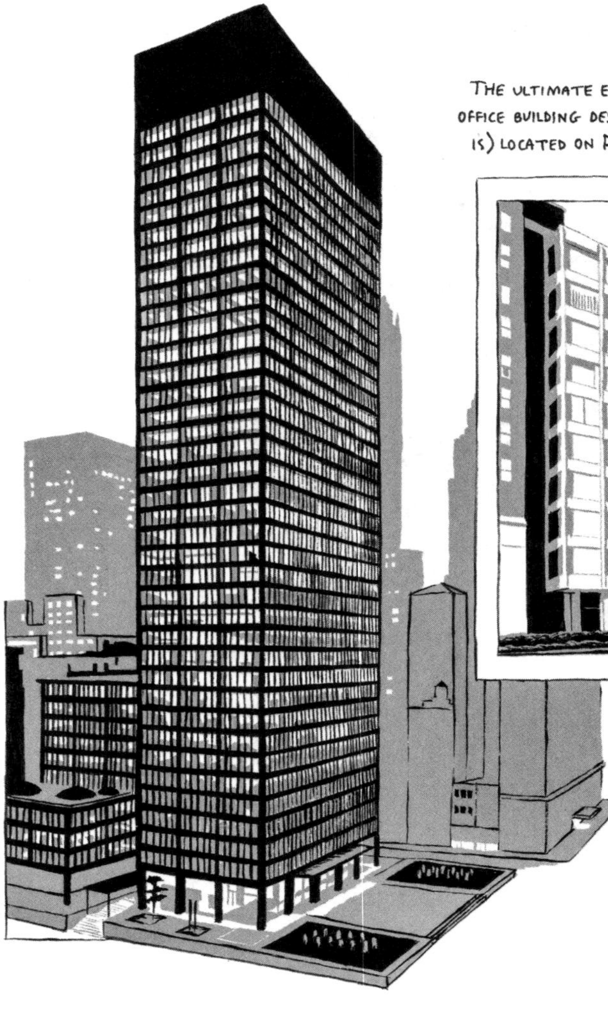

The ultimate example of order was Mies's elegant influential, minimalist office building designed for the Seagram Corporation which was (and still is) located on Park Avenue just a couple of miles south of the building I grew up in.

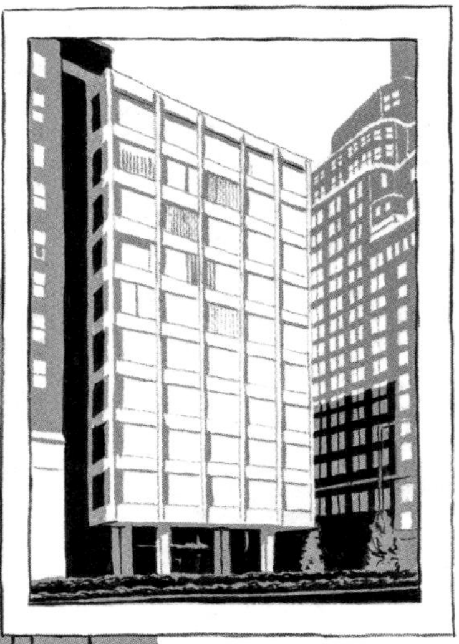

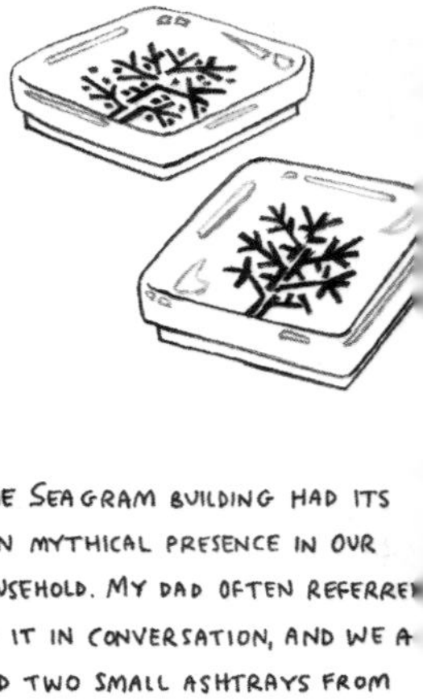

The Seagram building had its own mythical presence in our household. My dad often referre to it in conversation, and we a had two small ashtrays from the famous restaurant on the ground floor, the Four Seasons. Mom and Dad had swiped them while there on a date in th 1960s. Above: another favorite, the Olivetti/Pepsi-Co building by Skidmore, Owings and Merrill, Park Avenue.

"ARCHITECTURE IS THE WILL OF AN EPOCH TRANSLATED INTO SPACE".
LUDWIG MIES VAN DER ROHE

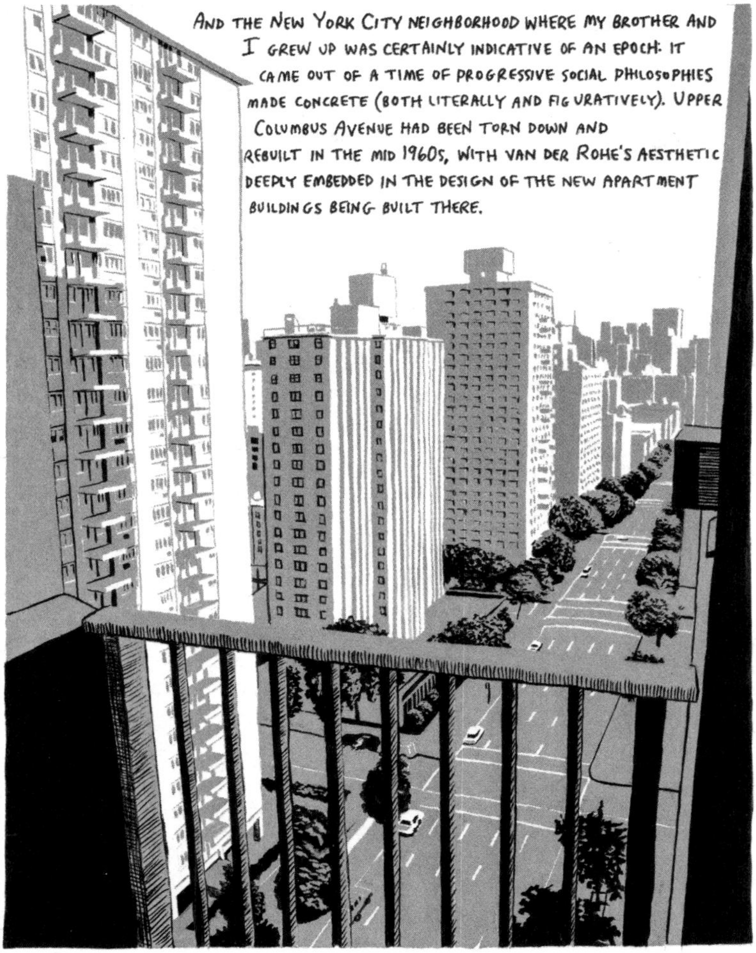
AND THE NEW YORK CITY NEIGHBORHOOD WHERE MY BROTHER AND I GREW UP WAS CERTAINLY INDICATIVE OF AN EPOCH: IT CAME OUT OF A TIME OF PROGRESSIVE SOCIAL PHILOSOPHIES MADE CONCRETE (BOTH LITERALLY AND FIGURATIVELY). UPPER COLUMBUS AVENUE HAD BEEN TORN DOWN AND REBUILT IN THE MID 1960S, WITH VAN DER ROHE'S AESTHETIC DEEPLY EMBEDDED IN THE DESIGN OF THE NEW APARTMENT BUILDINGS BEING BUILT THERE.

OUR BUILDING WAS LOCATED AT 94TH STREET AND COLUMBUS AVENUE. THAT STRETCH OF COLUMBUS RESEMBLES A RIVER RUNNING THROUGH A CANYON. WITH ITS MANY SAME-HEIGHT APARTMENT BUILDINGS LINING THE AVENUE AND ITS ONSTANT TRAFFIC FLOWING DOWNTOWN. THESE BUILDINGS HAD POPPED UP AT THE SAME TIME, MANY OF THEM SUBSIDIZED HOUSING LIKE OUR BUILDING. OUR BUILDING HAD JUST BEEN COMPLETED WHEN MY FAMILY MOVED IN DURING 1966.

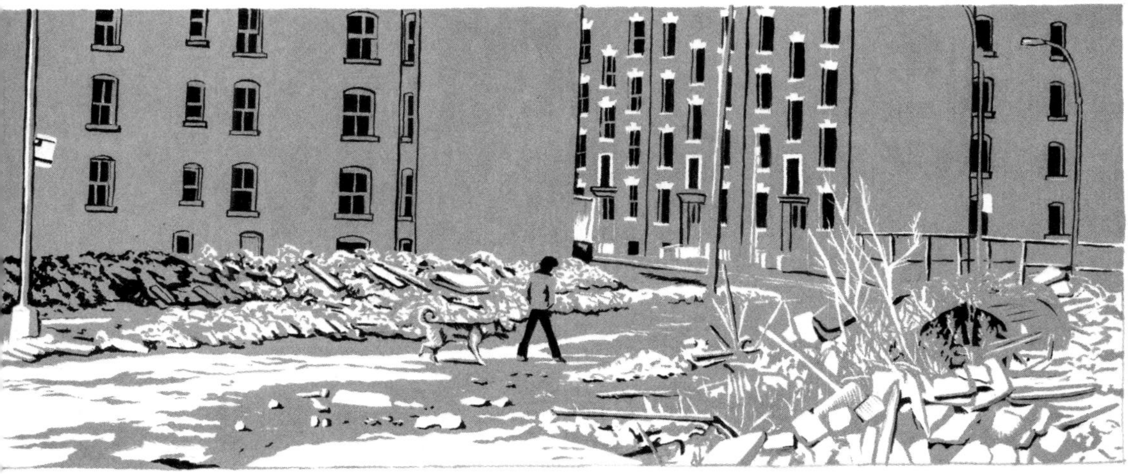

MUCH OF COLUMBUS AVENUE JUST SOUTH OF US REMAINED RUBLE-STREWN LOTS UNTIL THE CITY'S BOOM TIME OF THE 1980S.

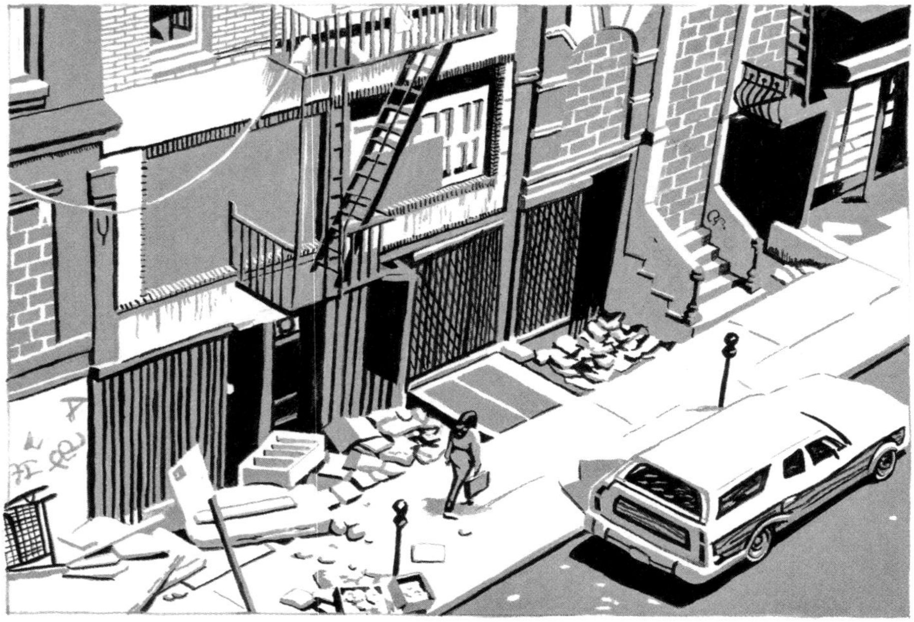

DURING MY CHILDHOO
NEW YORK WAS
FULL OF BURNED-OUT
AND BRICKED-UP
BUILDINGS, AND OUR
NEIGHBORHOOD HAD
ITS SHARE OF THEM.
ALTHOUGH MANY
FAMILIES LEFT THE
CITY IN THE 50s
AND 60s IT NEVER
OCCURRED TO MY
PARENTS TO EXIT
NEW YORK CITY AN
RELOCATE TO THE
SUBURBS.

OUR LOCAL ELEMENTARY SCHOOL PARTNERED WITH A TEACHERS' COLLEGE AND IMPLEMENTED AN "OPEN CLASSROOM" SYSTEM WHERE KIDS OF DIFFERENT AGES LEARNED IN TEAM-LIKE GROUPS.

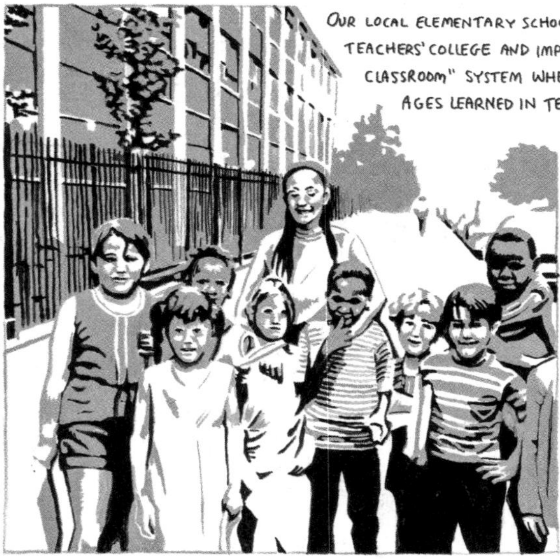

PARENTS FROM THE NEIGHBORHOOD WOR
TOGETHER TO RENOVATE AN ABANDO
BUILDING AND TURN IT INTO A SCHOOL
KIDS TOO YOUNG FOR KINDERGARTEN IN
ELEMENTARY SCHOOL. IN GOOD WEATHER
BACKYARD WAS USED FOR ART CLASSES.
BROTHER LAWRENCE IS ON THE LE

THE CITY WAS SAID TO BE IN DECLINE, BUT THAT CHAOTIC ATMOSPHERE ALSO FOSTERED

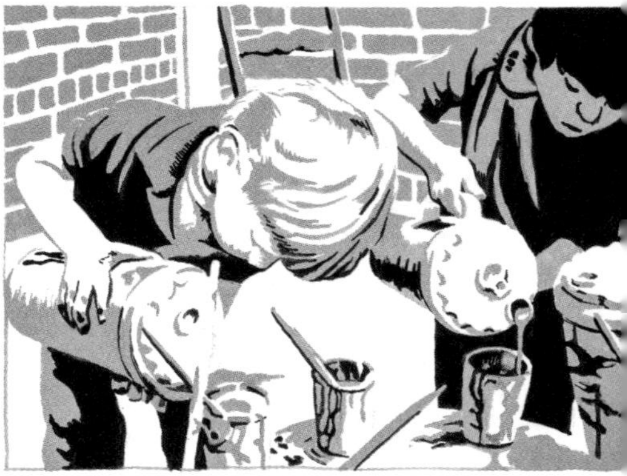

NEW IDEAS ABOUT WHAT A CITY, AND A SOCIETY, COULD BE.

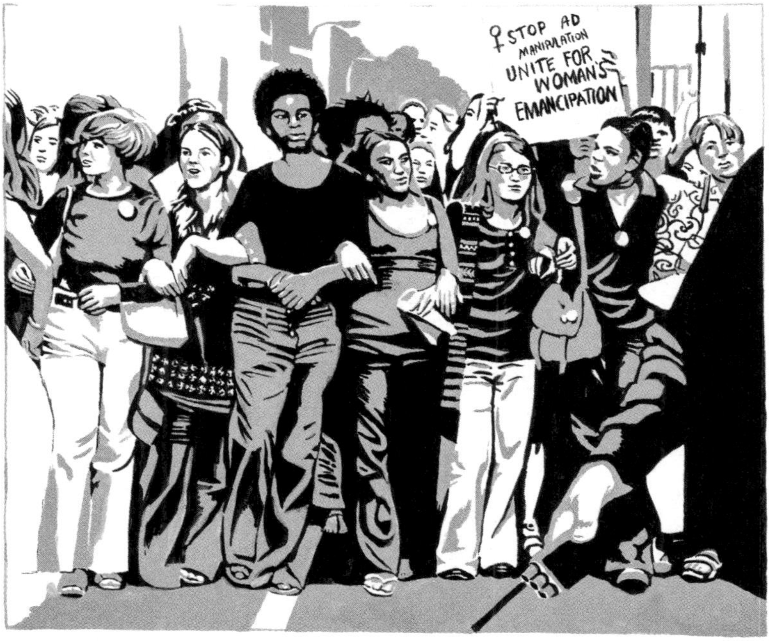
STOP AD MANIPULATION
UNITE FOR WOMAN'S EMANCIPATION

MY MOM CONTINUALLY EMPHASIZED TO MY BROTHER, MYSELF, AND MY FRIENDS, THAT GIRLS WERE JUST AS CAPABLE AND INTELLIGENT AS BOYS. SHE POINTED OUT HOW THE MEDIA OFTEN PORTRAYED WOMEN AS DITZY SEX OBJECTS. SHE ALSO WALKED IN THE FAMOUS WOMEN'S STRIKE FOR EQUALITY MARCH DOWN FIFTH AVENUE IN AUGUST OF 1970.

AMONG ALL THIS BREAKING APART AND CHANGE IN THE SOCIAL CONSCIOUSNESS - NOT TO MENTION CHANGES IN THE ACTUAL FABRIC OF THE CULTURE - THERE WAS MUCH NEW BUILDING: INNOVATIVE STRUCTURES THAT ATTEMPTED TO MAKE THE CITY BETTER.

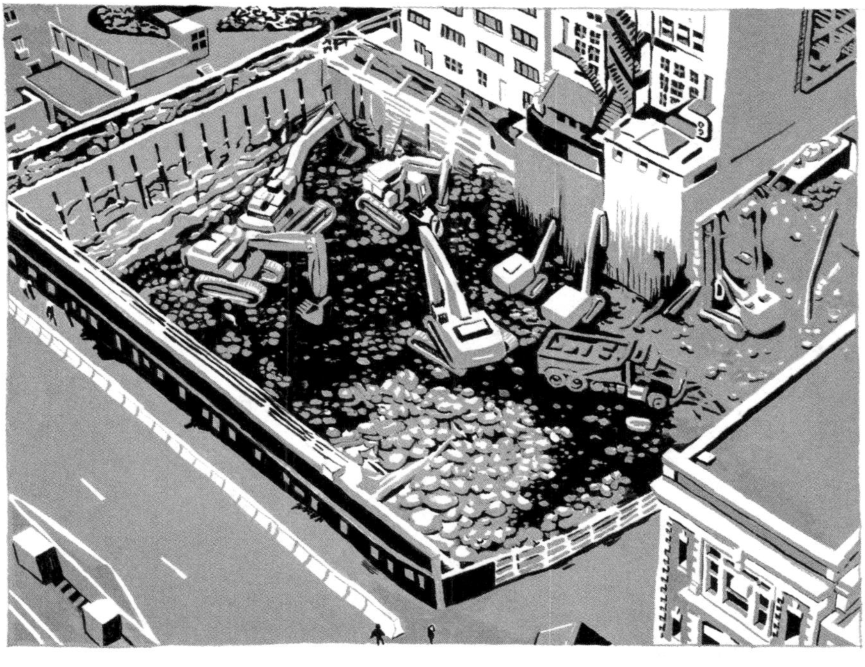

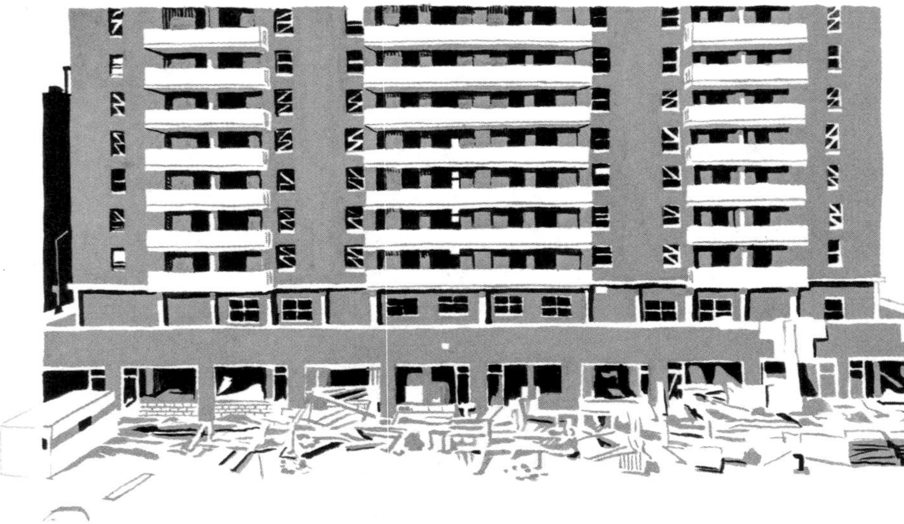

THE BUILDING WE MOVED INTO IN 1966 WAS CALLED COLUMBUS PARK TOWERS.

MANY OF THE APARTMENT BUILDINGS IN OUR NEIGHBORHOOD, INCLUDING OURS WERE PART OF THE MITCHELL-LAMA PROGRAM DEVELOPED BY TWO NY STATE SENATORS, IT CREATED AFFORDABLE HOUSING FOR THOUSANDS OF FAMILIES AND INDIVIDUALS.

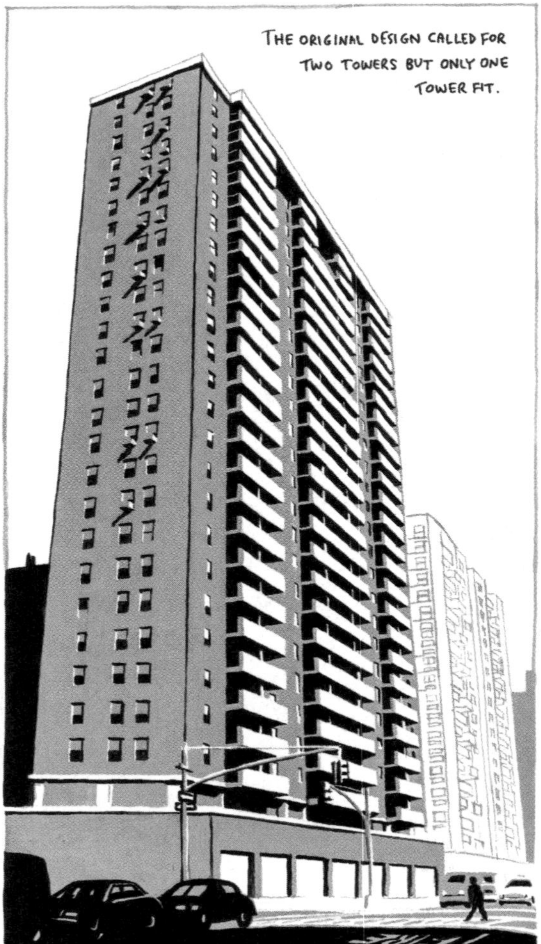
THE ORIGINAL DESIGN CALLED FOR TWO TOWERS BUT ONLY ONE TOWER FIT.

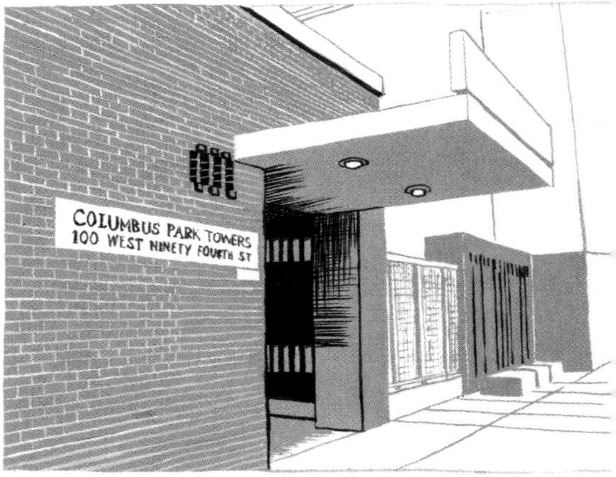
COLUMBUS PARK TOWERS
100 WEST NINETY FOURTH ST

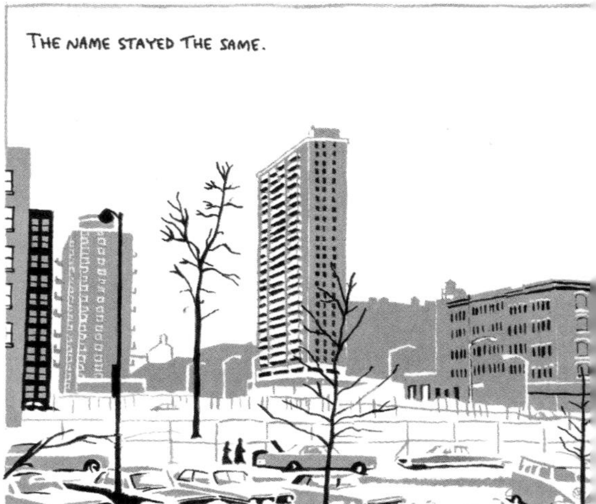
THE NAME STAYED THE SAME.

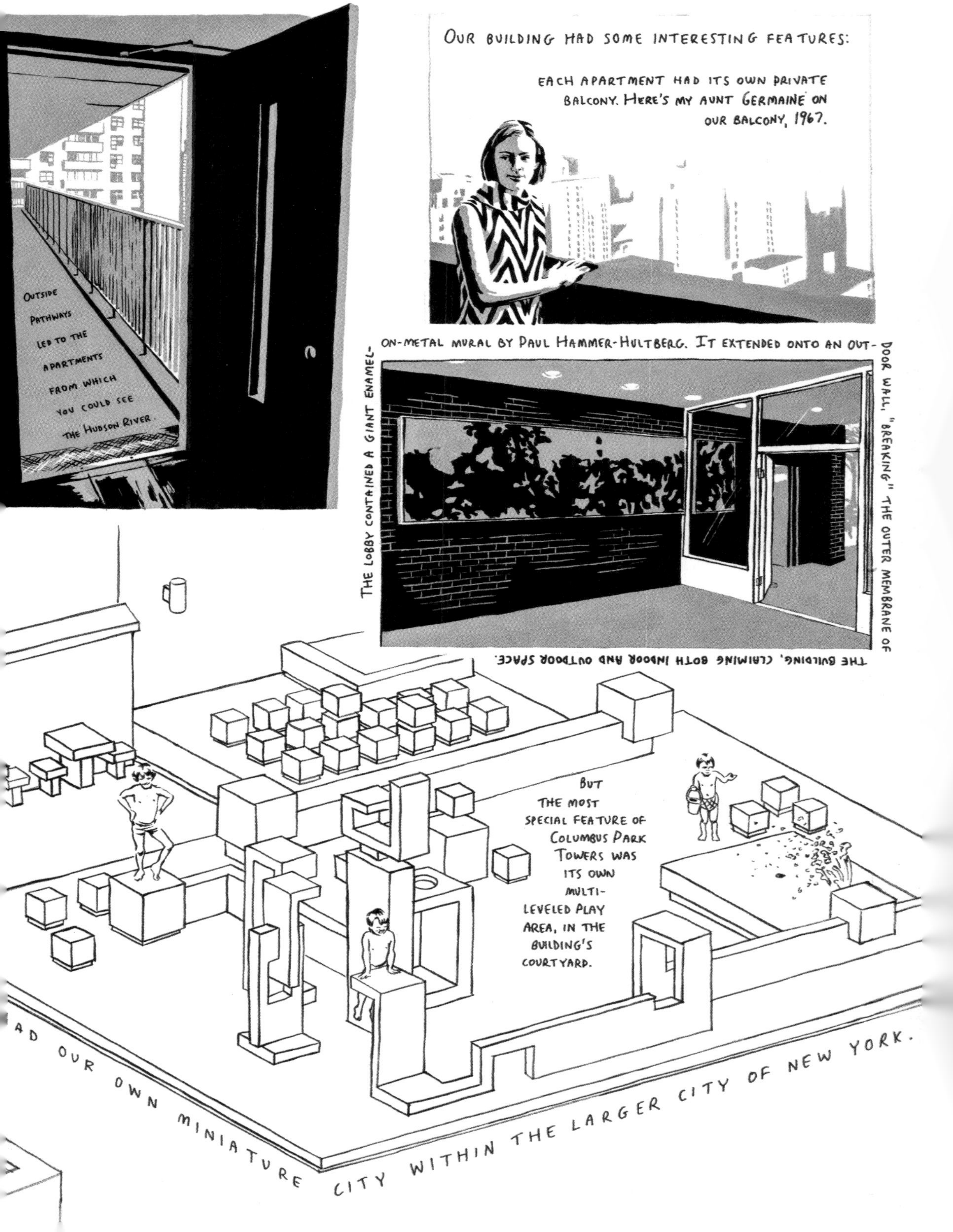
Outside pathways led to the apartments from which you could see the Hudson River.
Our building had some interesting features:
Each apartment had its own private balcony. Here's my aunt Germaine on our balcony, 1967.
The lobby contained a giant enamel-on-metal mural by Paul Hammer-Hultberg. It extended onto an out-door wall, "breaking" the outer membrane of the building, claiming both indoor and outdoor space.
But the most special feature of Columbus Park Towers was its own multi-leveled play area, in the building's courtyard.
AD OUR OWN MINIATURE CITY WITHIN THE LARGER CITY OF NEW YORK.

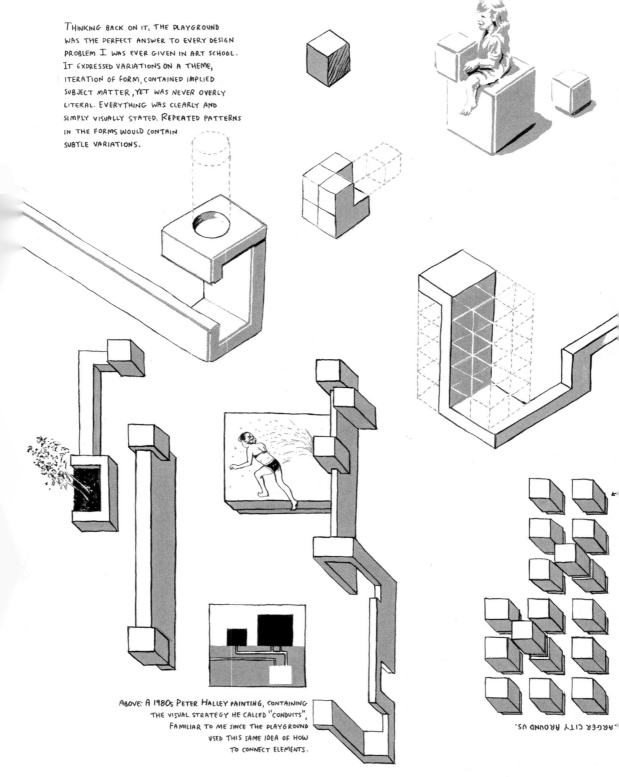

THINKING BACK ON IT, THE PLAYGROUND WAS THE PERFECT ANSWER TO EVERY DESIGN PROBLEM I WAS EVER GIVEN IN ART SCHOOL. IT EXPRESSED VARIATIONS ON A THEME, ITERATION OF FORM, CONTAINED IMPLIED SUBJECT MATTER, YET WAS NEVER OVERLY LITERAL. EVERYTHING WAS CLEARLY AND SIMPLY VISUALLY STATED. REPEATED PATTERNS IN THE FORMS WOULD CONTAIN SUBTLE VARIATIONS.

ABOVE: A 1980s PETER HALLEY PAINTING, CONTAINING THE VISUAL STRATEGY HE CALLED "CONDUITS", FAMILIAR TO ME SINCE THE PLAYGROUND USED THIS SAME IDEA OF HOW TO CONNECT ELEMENTS.

...ARGER CITY AROUND US.

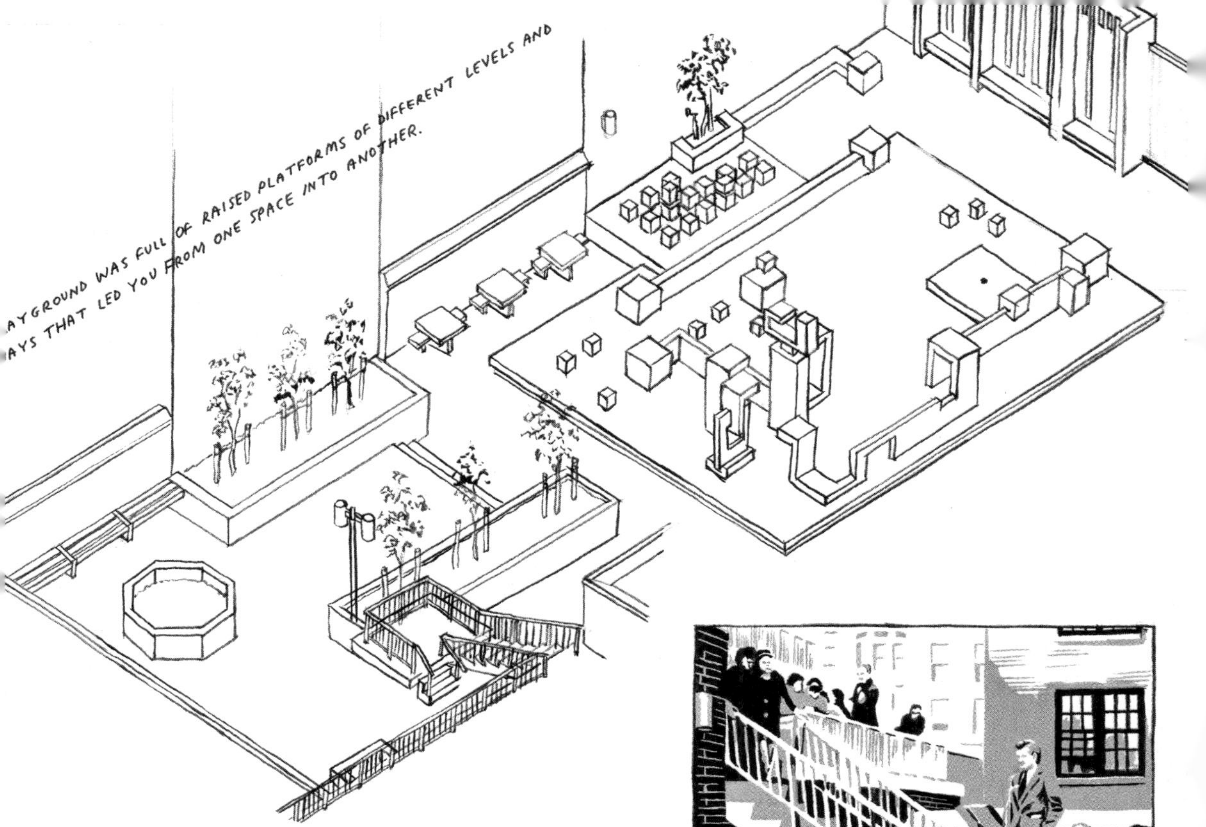
AYGROUND WAS FULL OF RAISED PLATFORMS OF DIFFERENT LEVELS AND
AYS THAT LED YOU FROM ONE SPACE INTO ANOTHER.

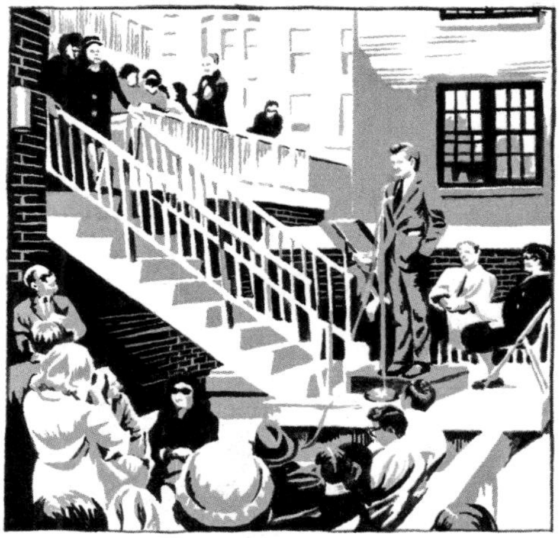

IN 1966 OUR FAMILY MOVED INTO COLUMBUS PARK TOWERS JUST AS IT OPENED, AS DID MANY FAMILIES WITH KIDS OUR AGE. MAYOR JOHN LINDSAY SPOKE AT THE DEDICATION CEREMONY.

THE PLAYGROUND ACTED AS AN ACROPOLIS FOR THIS CITY WITHIN A CITY.

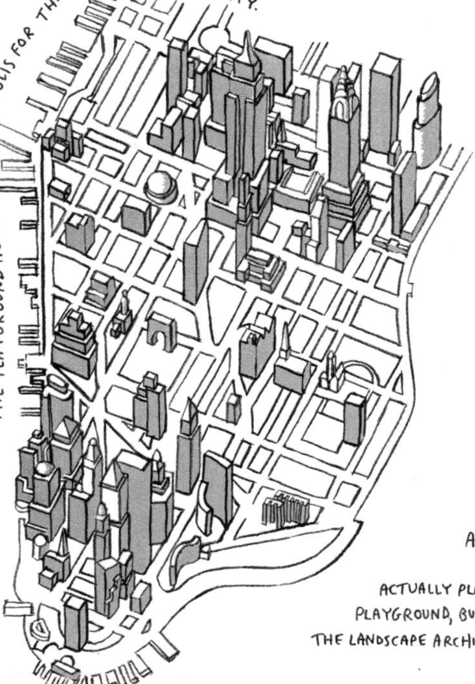

AS KIDS, IT NEVER OCCURRED TO US THAT SOMEONE ACTUALLY PLANNED AND DESIGNED THE PLAYGROUND, BUT OF COURSE SOMEONE HAD, THE LANDSCAPE ARCHITECT M. PAUL FRIEDBERG.

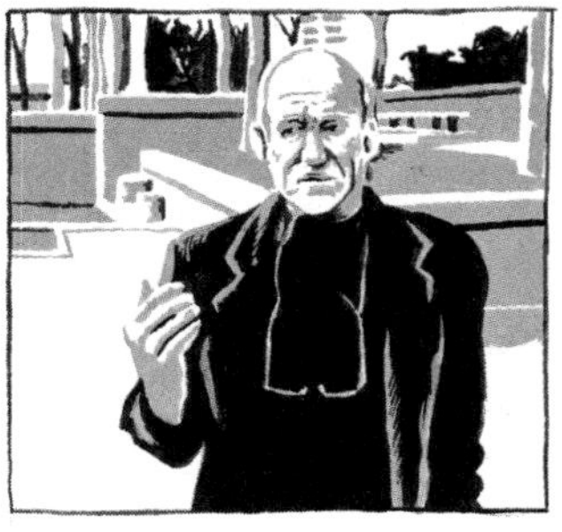

ALTHOUGH THE COLUMBUS PARK TOWERS PLAYGROUND WAS SITUATED WITHIN THE GROUNDS OF THE BUILDING. IT WAS VISIBLE FROM THE STREET THROUGH A GRILLE-LIKE FENCE NEXT TO A BRICK WALL THAT ALSO HAD PEEP HOLES. THE MEMBRANE BETWEEN (STREET) OUTSIDE AND (COURTYARD) INSIDE WAS VISUALLY PERMEABLE.

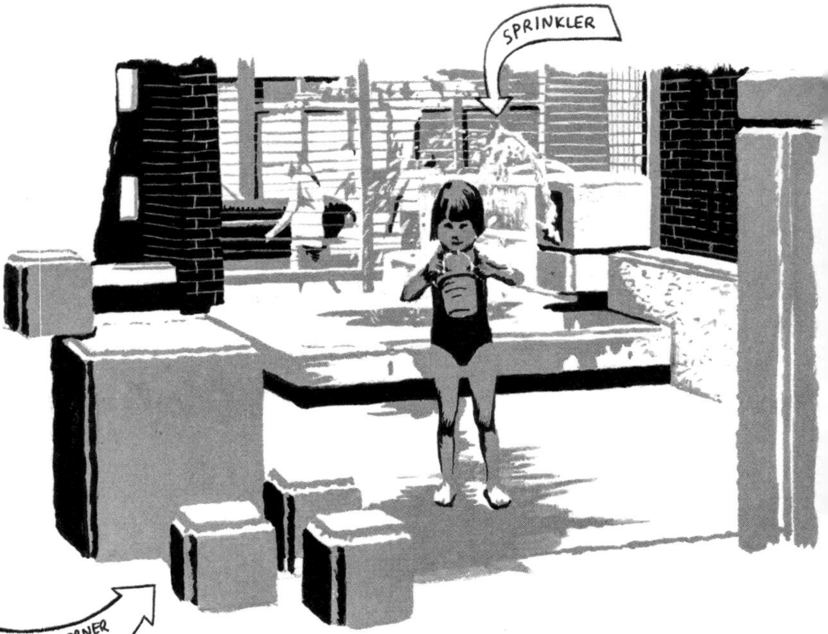
SPRINKLER

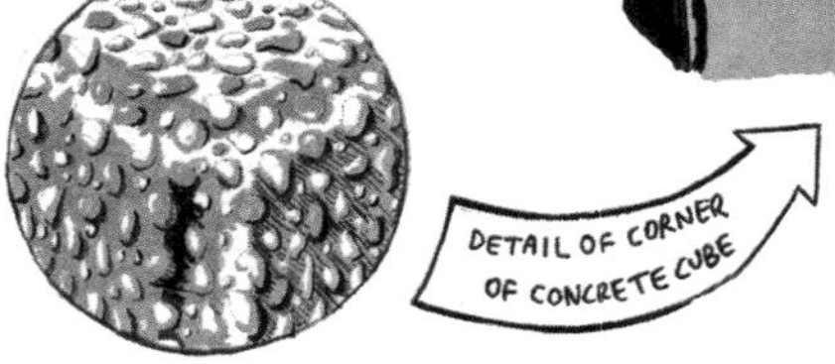
DETAIL OF CORNER OF CONCRETE CUBE

IN THE COLUMBUS PARK TOWERS PLAYGROUND, ALL THE PLAY STRUCTURES WERE MADE OF A PEBBLED CONCRETE AGGREGATE AND HAD CHAMFERED EDGES.

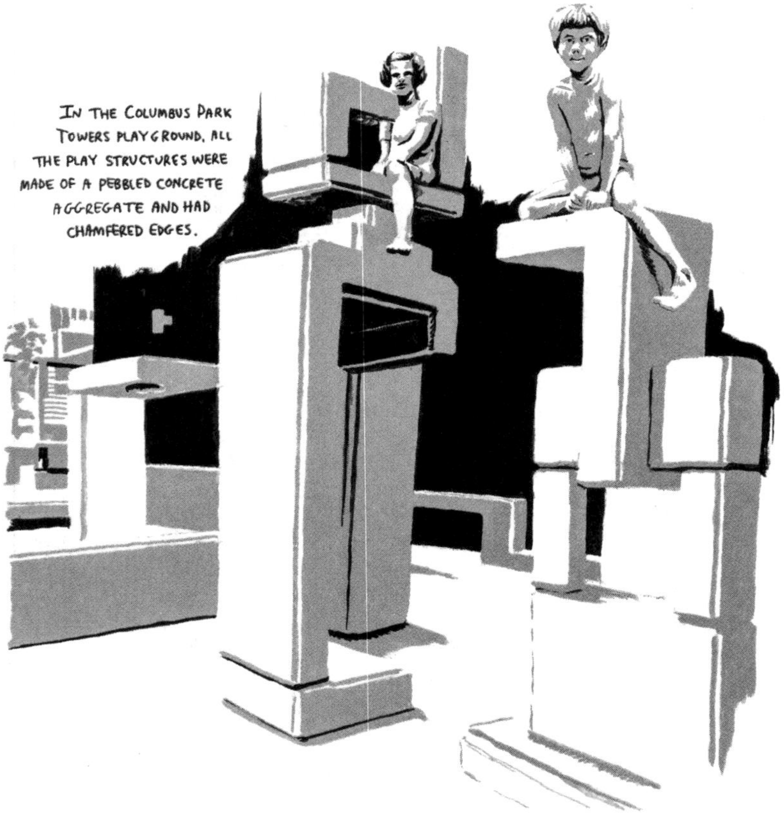

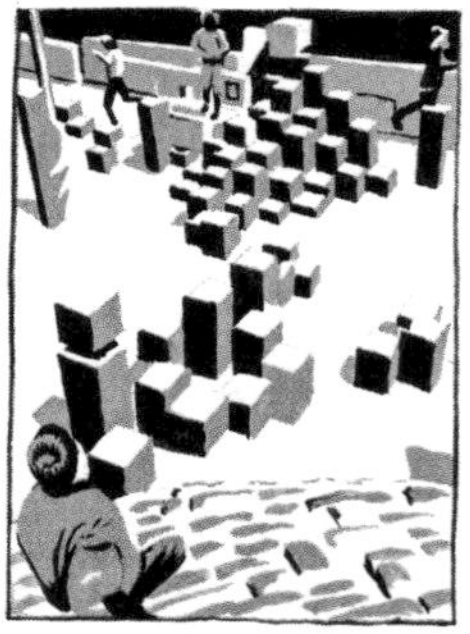

COLUMBUS PARK TOWERS AND ITS PLAYGROUND WERE COMPLETED AROUND THE SAME TIME FRIEDBERG CREATED HIS SEMINAL WORK OF LANDSCAPE ARCHITECTURE JACOB RIIS PLAZA LOCATED IN A PUBLIC HOUSING COMPLEX ON THE LOWER EAST SIDE.

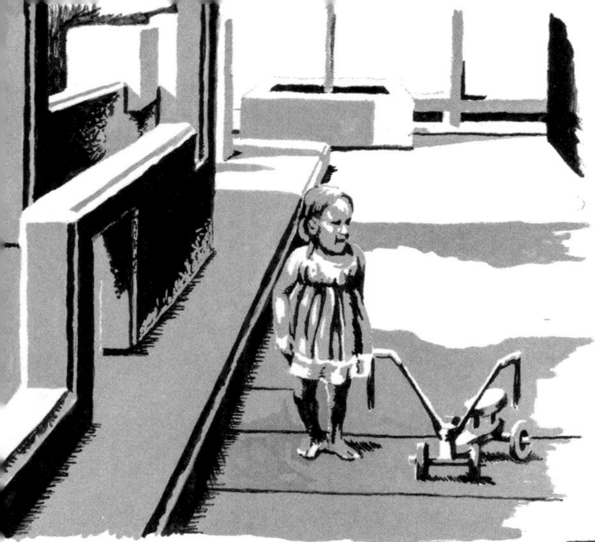

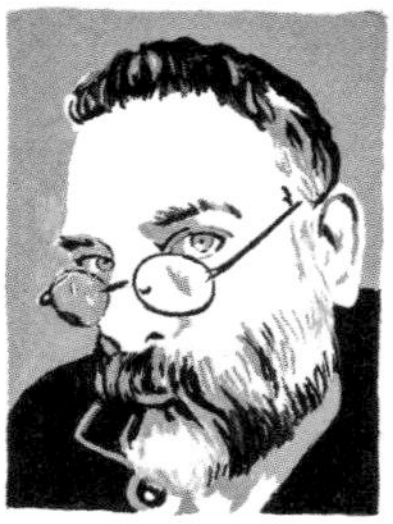

"Columbus Park Towers was a kind of liberal, social engineering in physical form, which promulgated ideas of diversity and community." Artist Nayland Blake, who also grew up in Columbus Park Towers.

realize now how the design of the
ayground influenced me. Everything
draw is based on a grid of squares
thogonal, and with lots of right
gles." My brother Lawrence, now an architect.

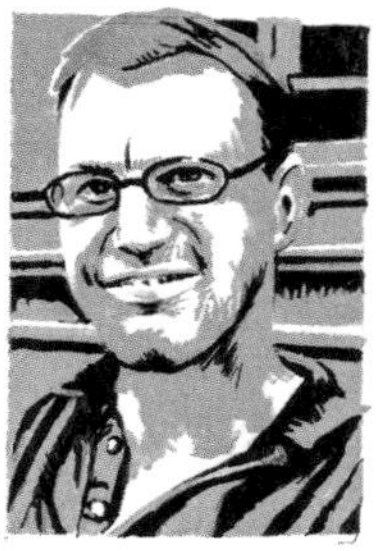

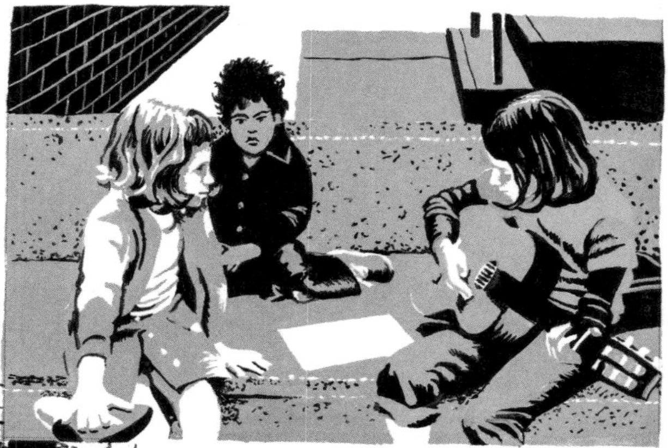

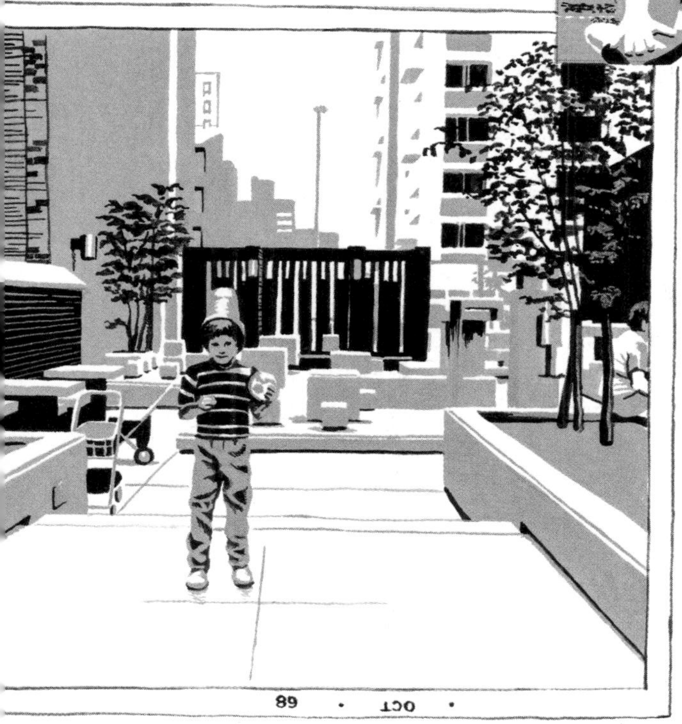

The fact that the playground was made of this textured concrete was puzzling to some of the residents.

"The aggregate would scratch your knees, but we were in the playground all the time." Susan Horowitz, who grew up with us in CPT.

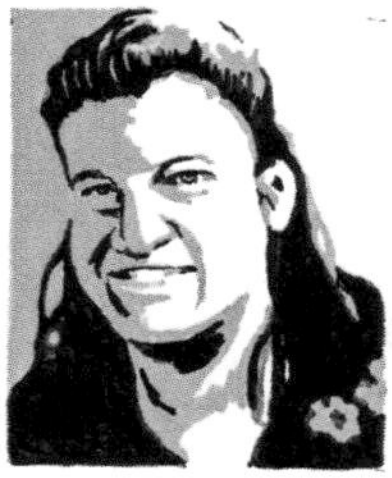

VERY CLOSE BY TO COLUMBUS PARK TOWERS WAS CENTRAL PARK- JUST ONE BLOCK AWAY.

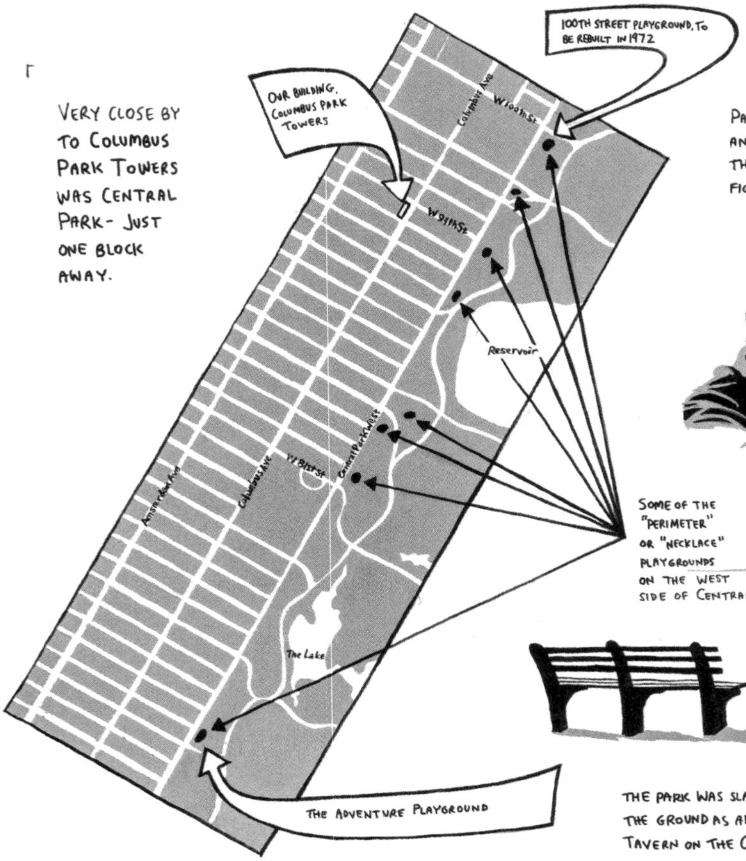
100TH STREET PLAYGROUND, TO BE REBUILT IN 1972
OUR BUILDING, COLUMBUS PARK TOWERS
Columbus Ave
W100thSt
W94thSt
Reservoir
Amsterdam Ave
Columbus Ave
W81st St
Central Park West
The Lake
SOME OF THE "PERIMETER" OR "NECKLACE" PLAYGROUNDS ON THE WEST SIDE OF CENTRAL PARK
THE ADVENTURE PLAYGROUND

UNTIL THE MID 1960s, THE DESIGN OF NYC PLAYGROUNDS WAS DETERMINED BY ROBERT MOSES, PARKS COMMISSIONER FROM 1934 TO 1965. NEVER AN ELECTED OFFICIAL, MOSES WAS ONE OF THE MOST POWERFUL POLITICAL FIGURES IN THE CITY.

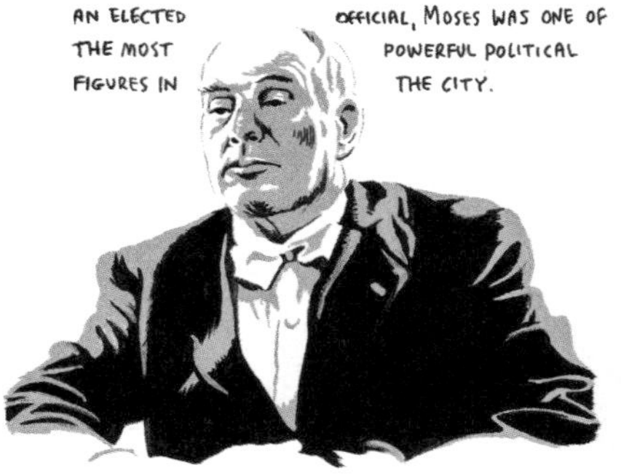

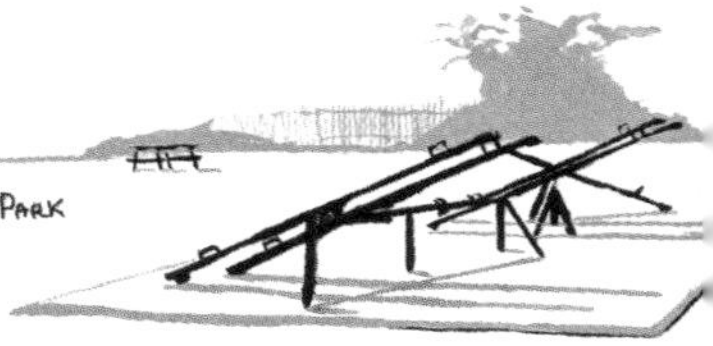

HIS STANDARD-ISSUE PLAYGROUNDS CONSISTED OF THE SAME FEW ISOLATED ELEMENTS (SWINGS, SLIDES, SEESAWS) ENCLOSED BY A TALL FENCE. ONE OF THESE TWENTY "PERIMETER" PLAYGROUNDS JUST IN THE PARK WAS SLATED TO BE TORN DOWN. MOSES PLANNED TO USE THE GROUND AS ADDITIONAL PARKING FOR THE NEARBY RESTAURANT, TAVERN ON THE GREEN. A GROUP OF NYC MOTHERS PREVENTED THE DESTRUCTION OF THE PLAYGROUND. IN 1966 IT WAS REBUILT AS THE "ADVENTURE PLAYGROUND," DESIGNED BY ARCHITECT RICHARD DATTNER WITH THE SUPPORT OF THE NEW PARKS COMMISIONER, THOMAS HOVING.

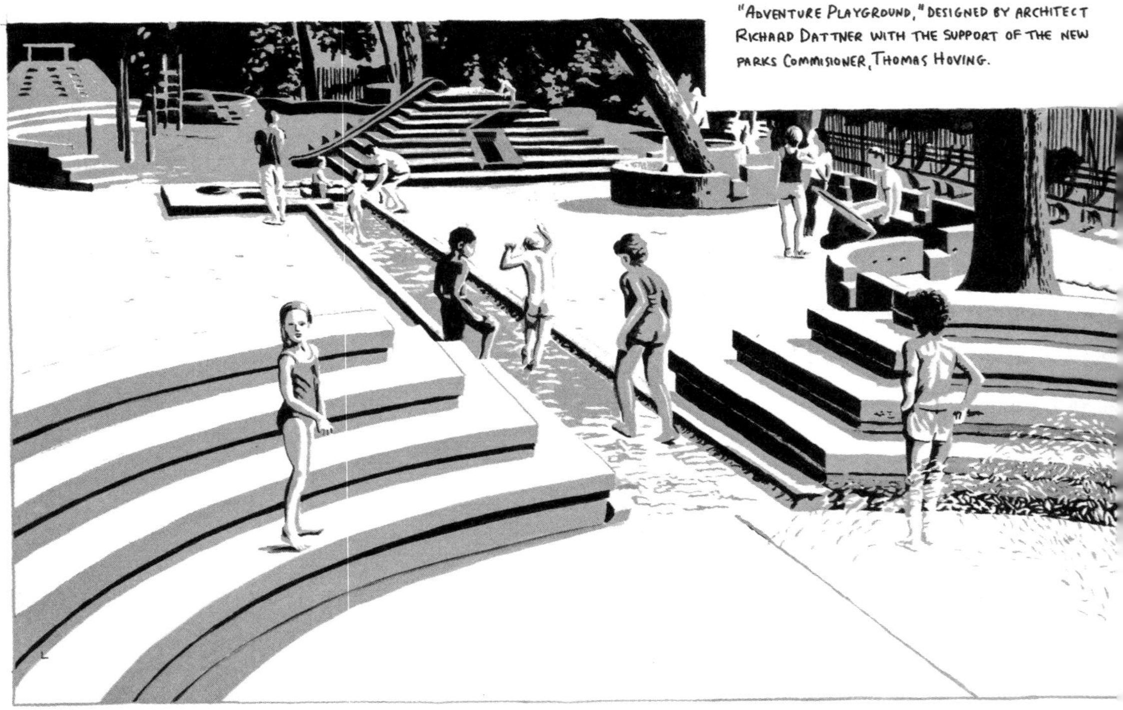

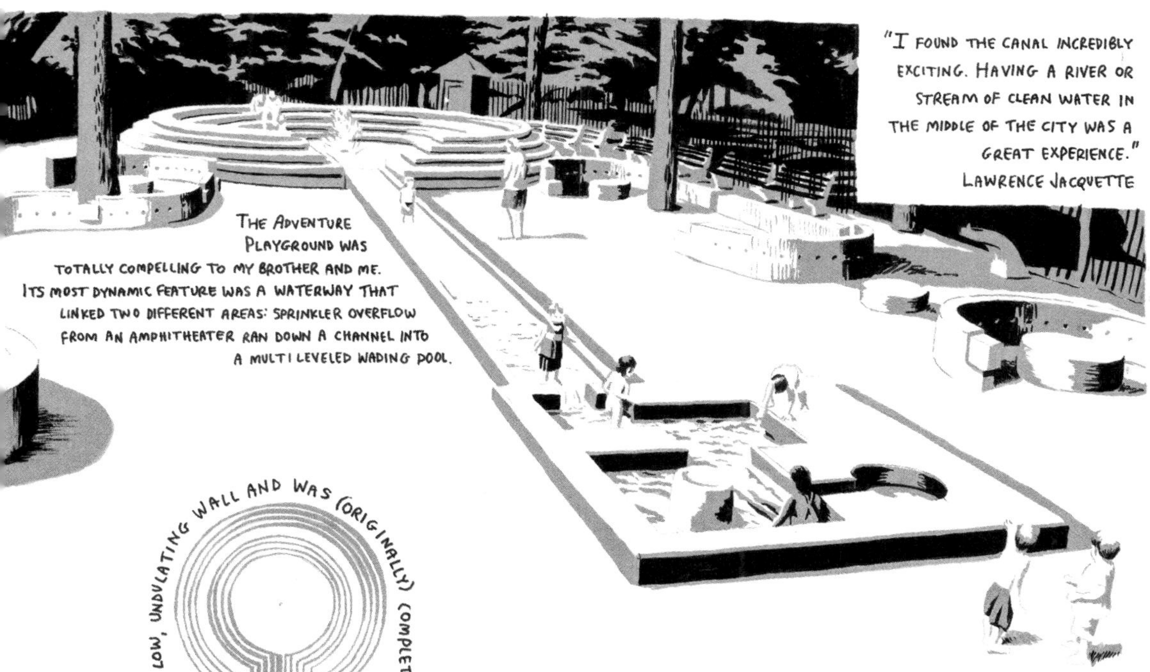
"I found the canal incredibly exciting. Having a river or stream of clean water in the middle of the city was a great experience."
Lawrence Jacquette
The Adventure Playground was totally compelling to my brother and me. Its most dynamic feature was a waterway that linked two different areas: sprinkler overflow from an amphitheater ran down a channel into a multi leveled wading pool.

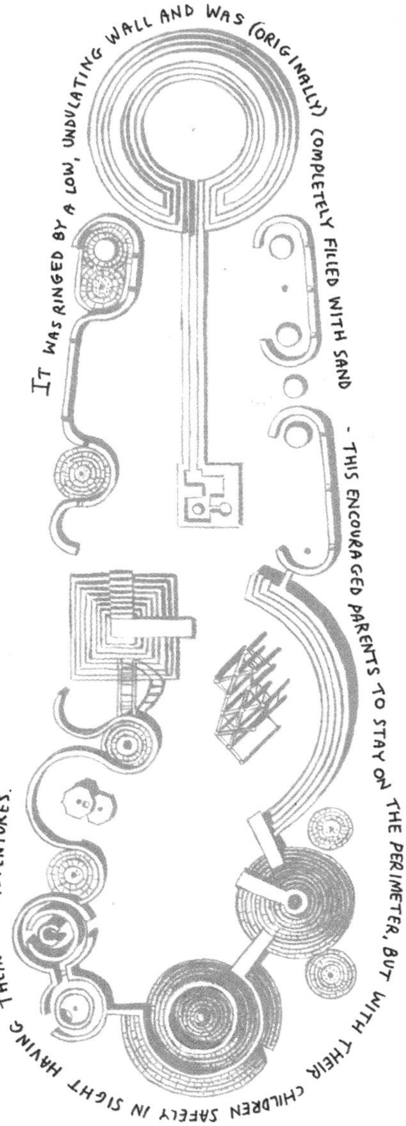
It was ringed by a low, undulating wall and was (originally) completely filled with sand - this encouraged parents to stay on the perimeter, but with their children safely in sight having their own adventures.

The elements of the playground referred to ancient architecture from all over the world.

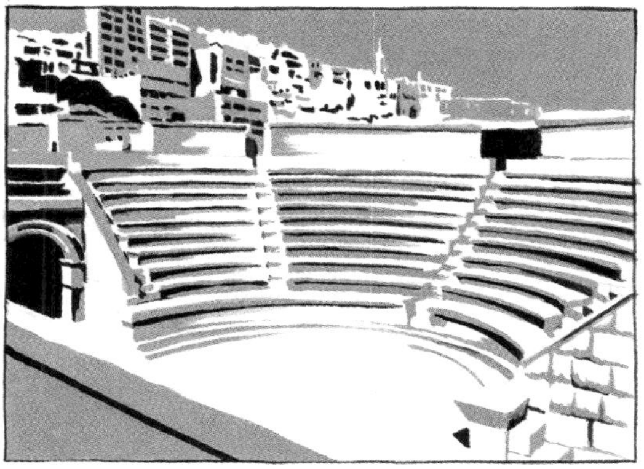

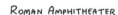

Roman Amphitheater

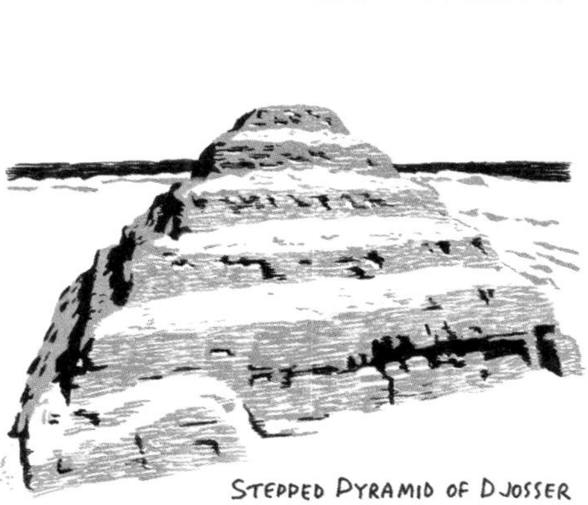

Stepped Pyramid of Djosser

Saqqara, Egypt

"The next best thing to a playground that children designed themselves is a playground that an adult designed, but incorporating the possibility for children to create their own places within it." Richard Dattner

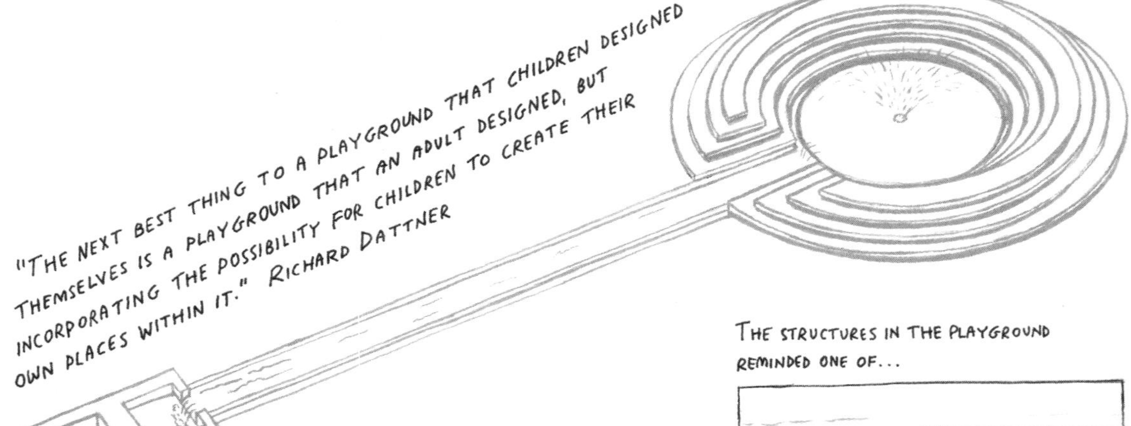

The playground suggested ideas of...

Connectivity, flow, and movement through space.

The structures in the playground reminded one of...

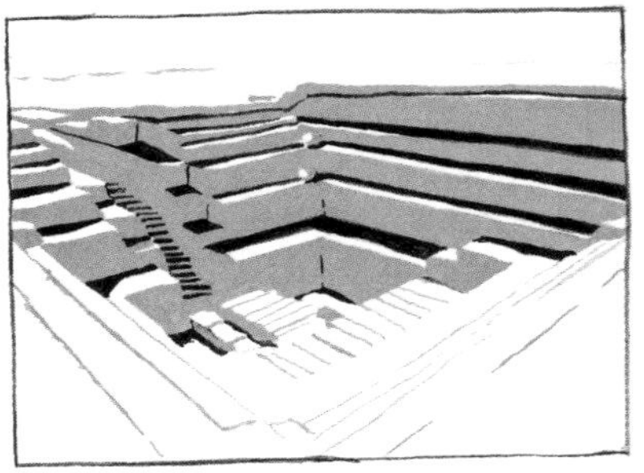

Balat Mastaba, Egypt

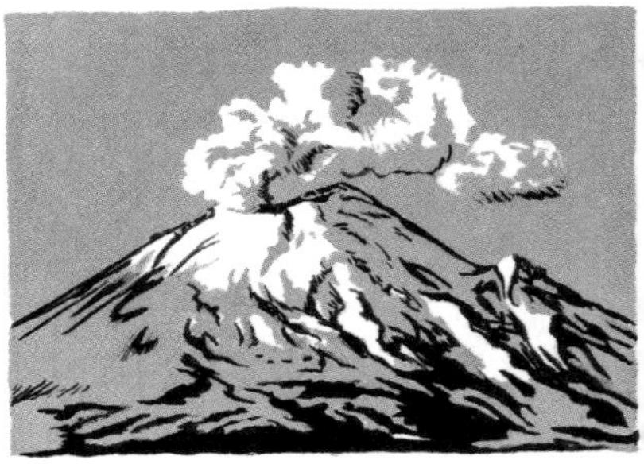

Popocatépetl Volcano, Mexico

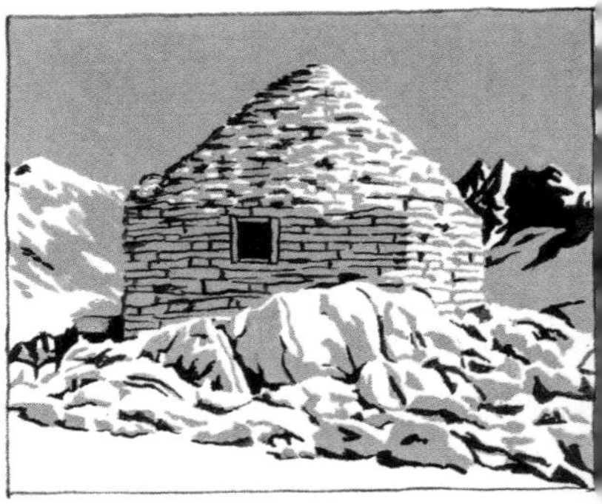

Stone Hut, Greece

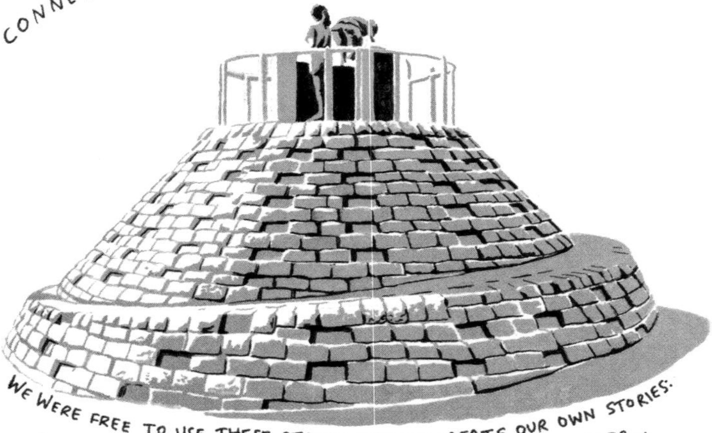

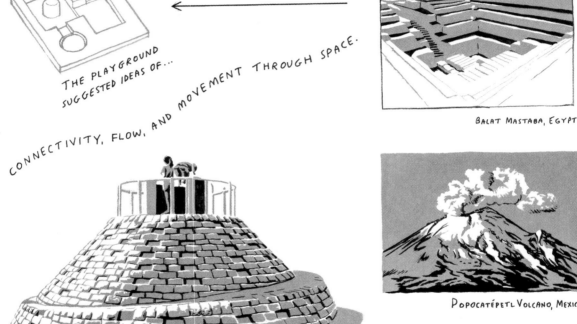

We were free to use these structures to create our own stories:
This is a mountain, a volcano, a stream, a river...

All the elements of the Adventure Playground linked together in some way

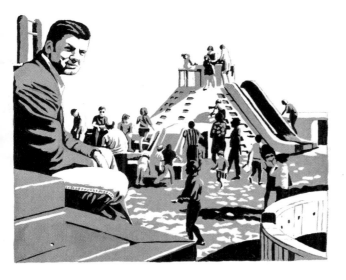

"THE TWO MAIN ELEMENTS ARE SAND AND WATER. THE REST IS EXTRA"

RICHARD DATTNER

ᴧCH OF THE ADVENTURE PLAYGROUND WAS MADE WITH POURED CONCRETE AGGREGATE:

CONCRETE WITH

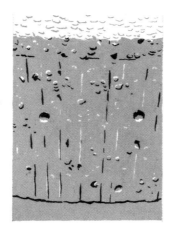

PEBBLES IN IT.

THE TEXTURE OF THE WOODEN MOLDS THE CONCRETE WAS POURED IN BECAME PART OF THE SURFACE.

IN 1973 MY FATHER, WILLIAM JACQUETTE, JOINED WITH TWO OTHER ARCHITECTS TO DESIGN A PLAYGROUND IN CENTRAL PARK. ROSS RYAN JACQUETTE CALLED THEIR DESIGN "DISCOVERY PLAY PARK." THIS IS A PHOTO OF THE PARTNERS ROSS RYAN JACQUETTE ON THE DAY THEIR PLAYGROUND OPENED.

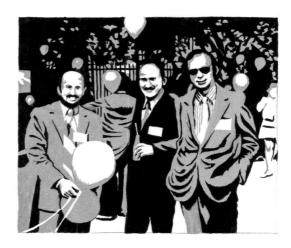

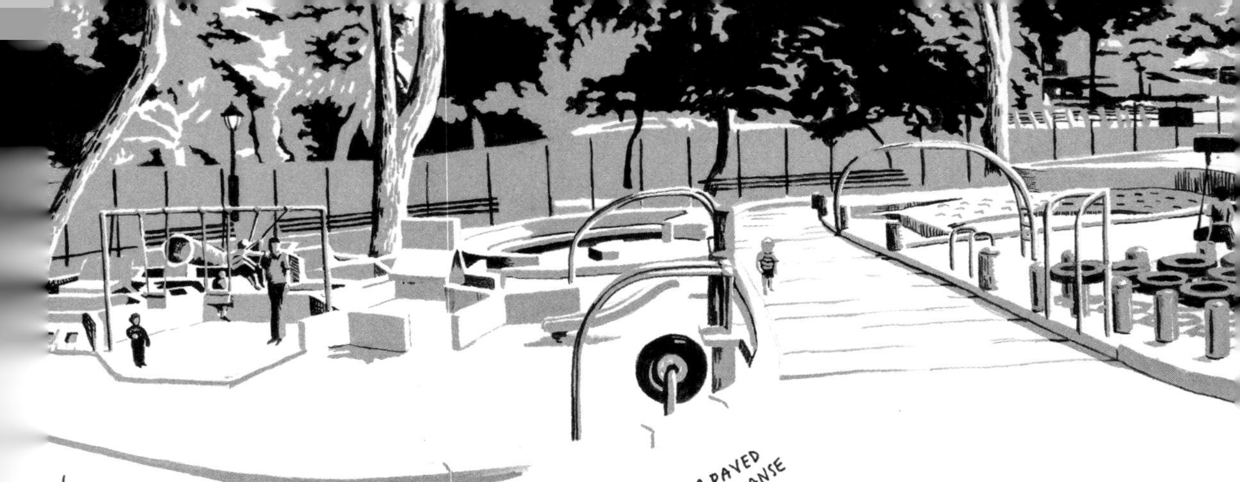

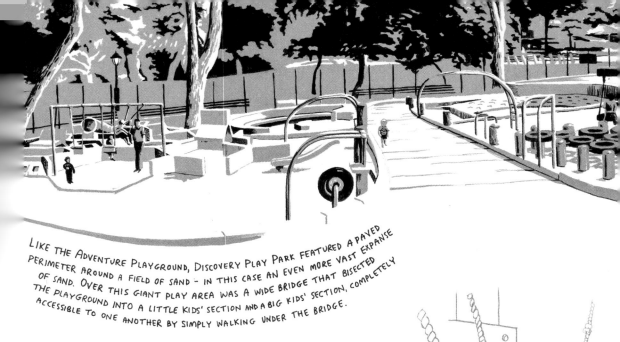

LIKE THE ADVENTURE PLAYGROUND, DISCOVERY PLAY PARK FEATURED A PAVED PERIMETER AROUND A FIELD OF SAND — IN THIS CASE AN EVEN MORE VAST EXPANSE OF SAND. OVER THIS GIANT PLAY AREA WAS A WIDE BRIDGE THAT BISECTED THE PLAYGROUND INTO A LITTLE KIDS' SECTION AND A BIG KIDS' SECTION, COMPLETELY ACCESSIBLE TO ONE ANOTHER BY SIMPLY WALKING UNDER THE BRIDGE.

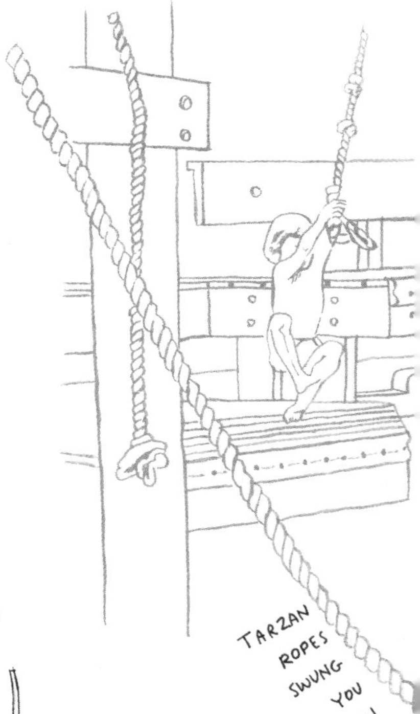

TARZAN ROPES SWUNG YOU BETWEEN RAISED WOODEN PLATFORMS

THE IDEAS SET FORTH IN THE ADVENTURE PLAYGROUND WERE EXPANDED ON AND ELABORATED ON IN DISCOVERY PLAY PARK IN AN ABUNDANT, EXUBERANT WAY.

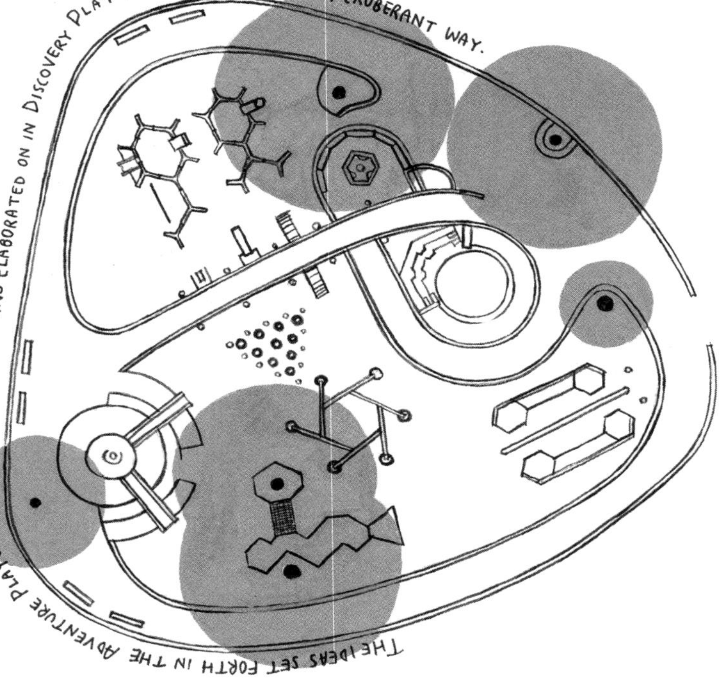

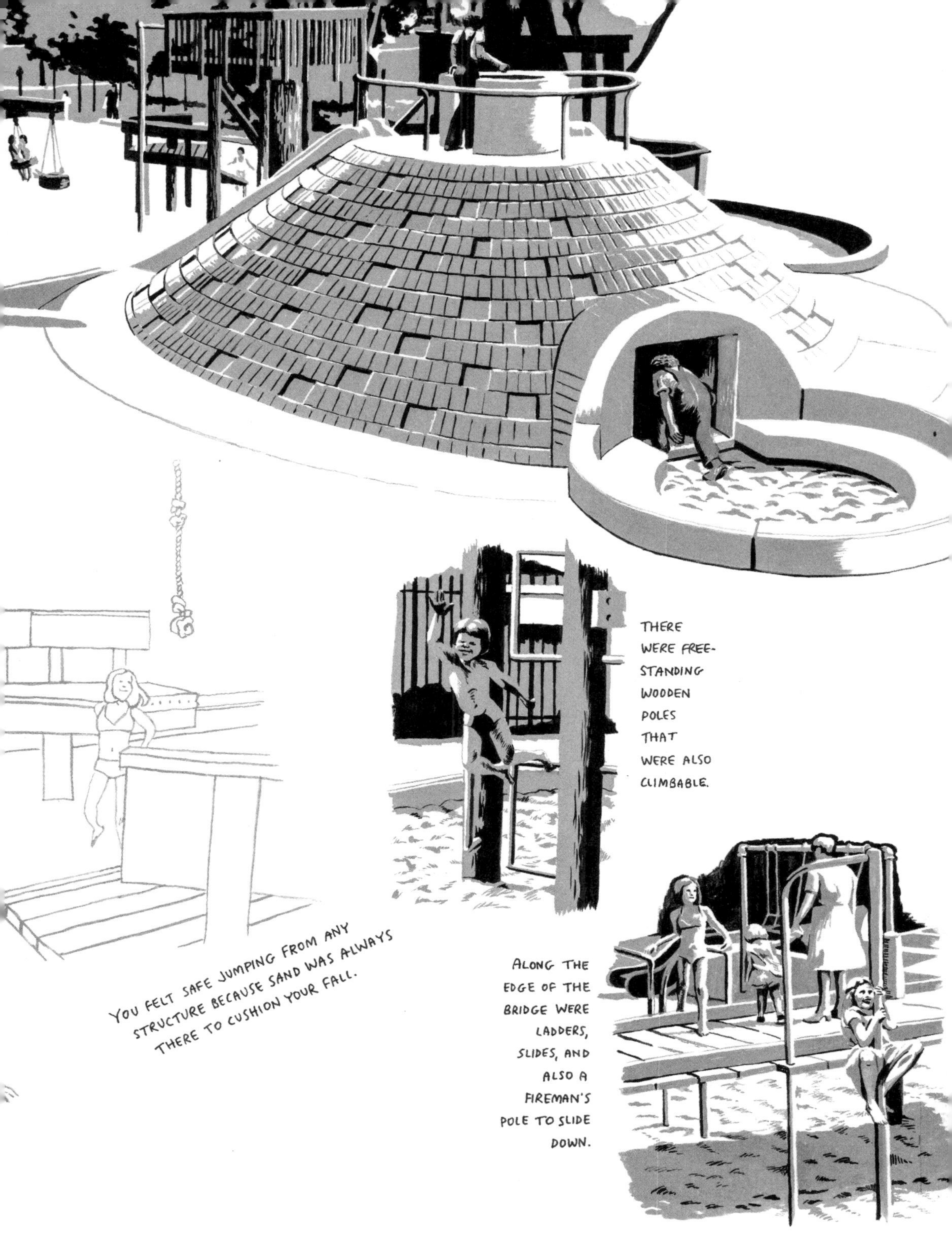
THERE WERE FREE-STANDING WOODEN POLES THAT WERE ALSO CLIMBABLE.
YOU FELT SAFE JUMPING FROM ANY STRUCTURE BECAUSE SAND WAS ALWAYS THERE TO CUSHION YOUR FALL.
ALONG THE EDGE OF THE BRIDGE WERE LADDERS, SLIDES, AND ALSO A FIREMAN'S POLE TO SLIDE DOWN.

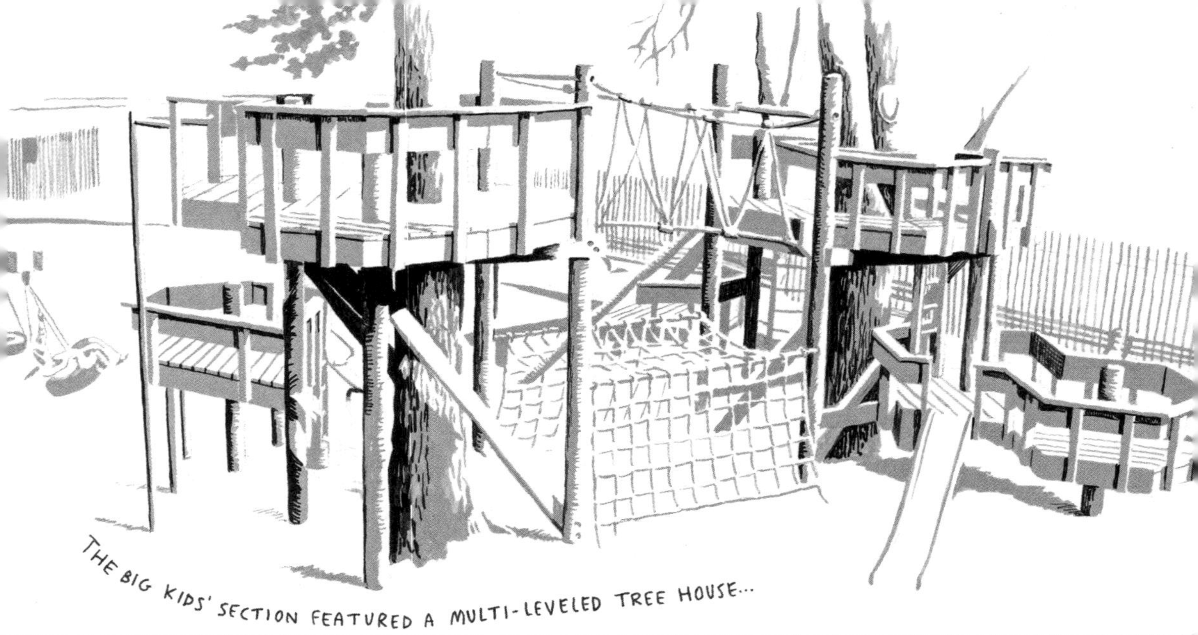
THE BIG KIDS' SECTION FEATURED A MULTI-LEVELED TREE HOUSE...

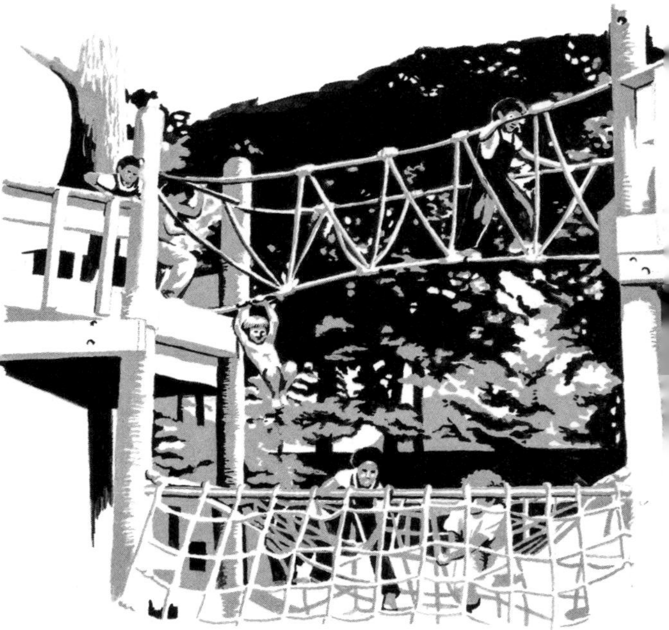
...WITH A ROPE BRIDGE, AND A NET UNDERNEATH

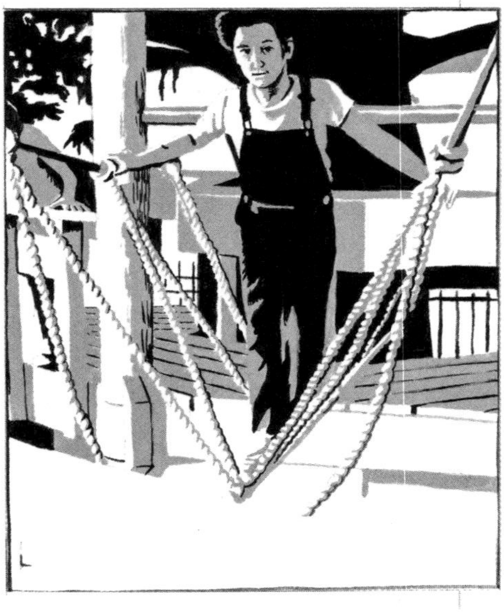

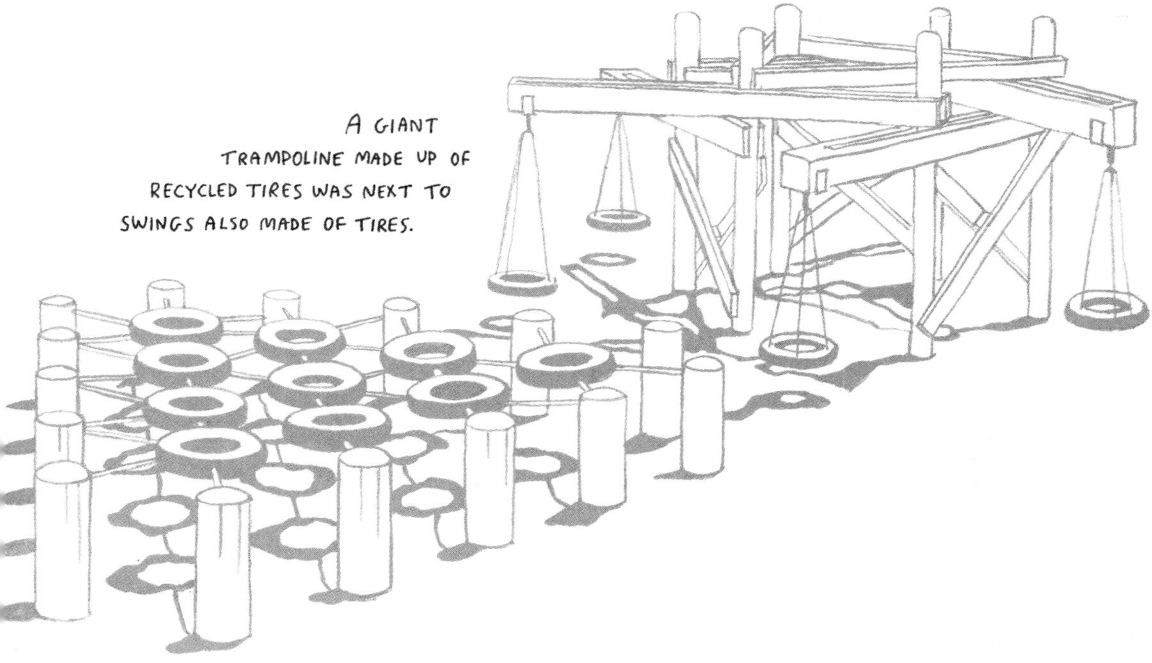
A GIANT TRAMPOLINE MADE UP OF RECYCLED TIRES WAS NEXT TO SWINGS ALSO MADE OF TIRES.

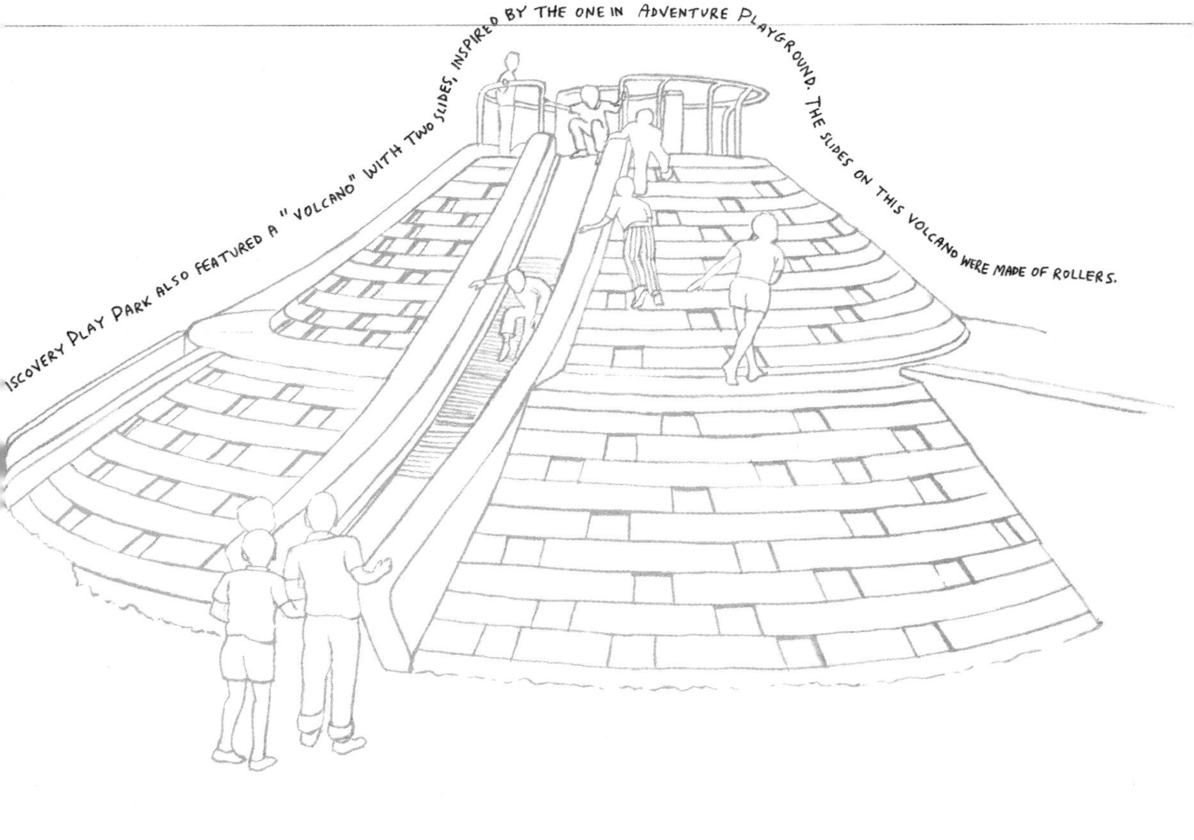
ISCOVERY PLAY PARK ALSO FEATURED A "VOLCANO" WITH TWO SLIDES, INSPIRED BY THE ONE IN ADVENTURE PLAYGROUND. THE SLIDES ON THIS VOLCANO WERE MADE OF ROLLERS.

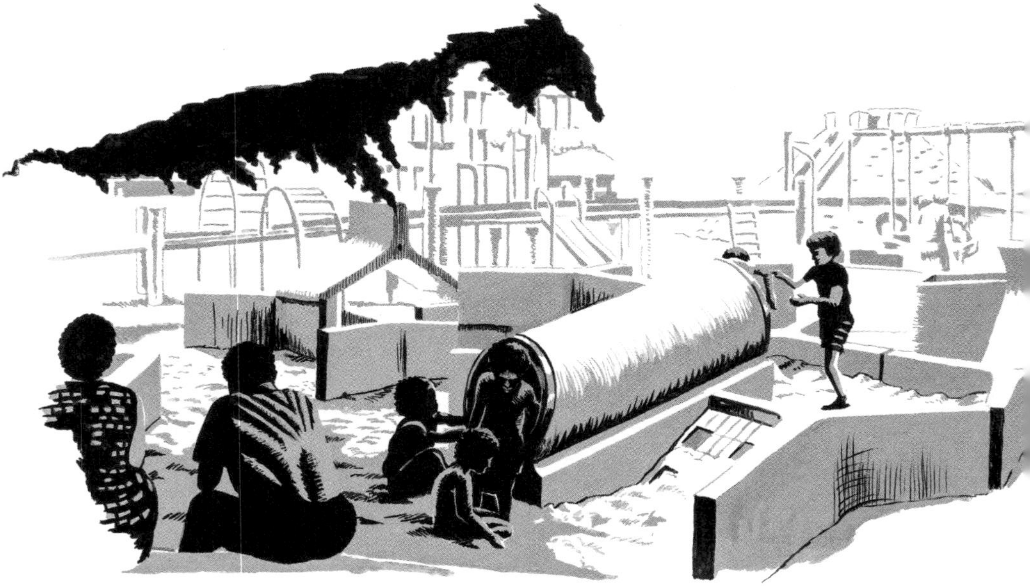

THE LITTLE KIDS' SIDE OF THE PLAYGROUND INCLUDED SWINGS, A MAZE OF THREE-WALLED CONCRETE ELEMENTS, A TUBULAR SLIDE, AND AN HEXAGONAL SANDBOX WITH A MUSHROOM-LIKE STRUCTURE TO POUR SAND THROUGH.

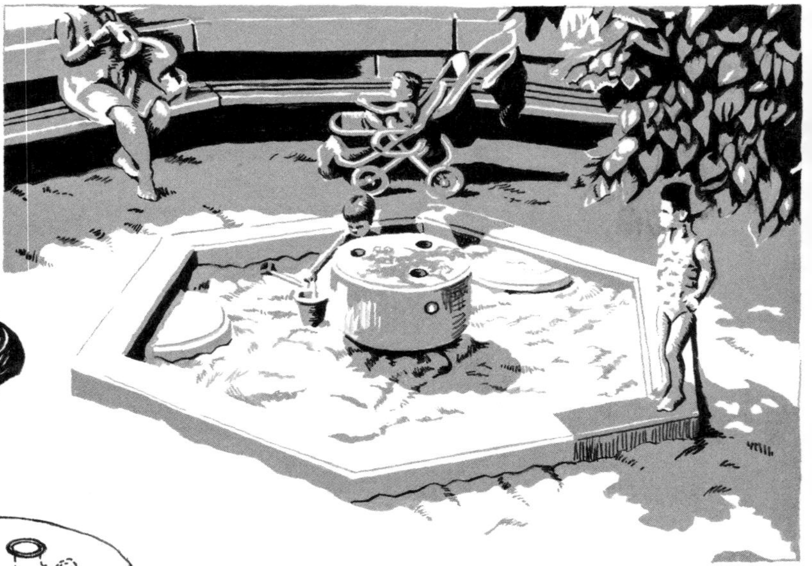

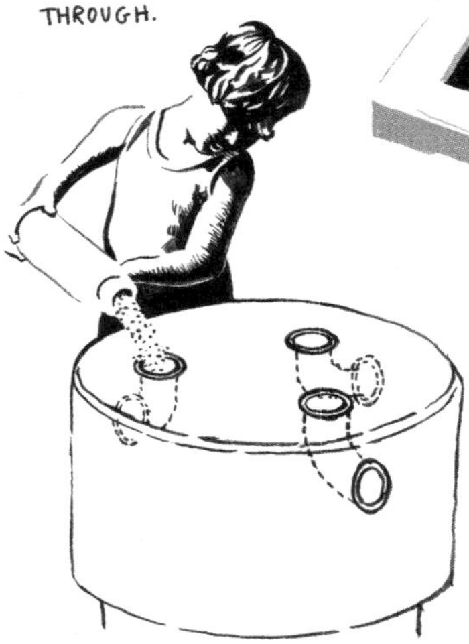

THIS WAS ALL WITHIN THE GIANT SANDBOX THAT WAS THE PLAYGROUND ITSEL

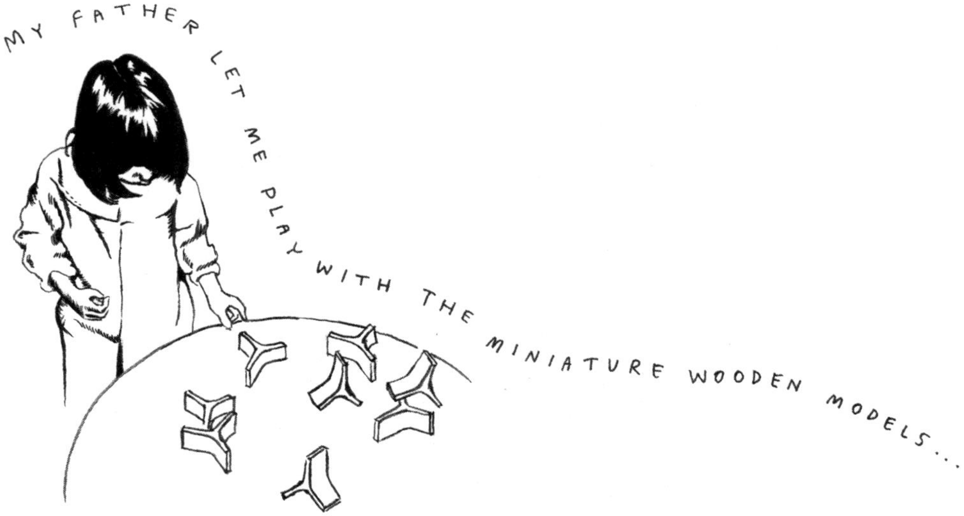
MY FATHER LET ME PLAY WITH THE MINIATURE WOODEN MODELS...

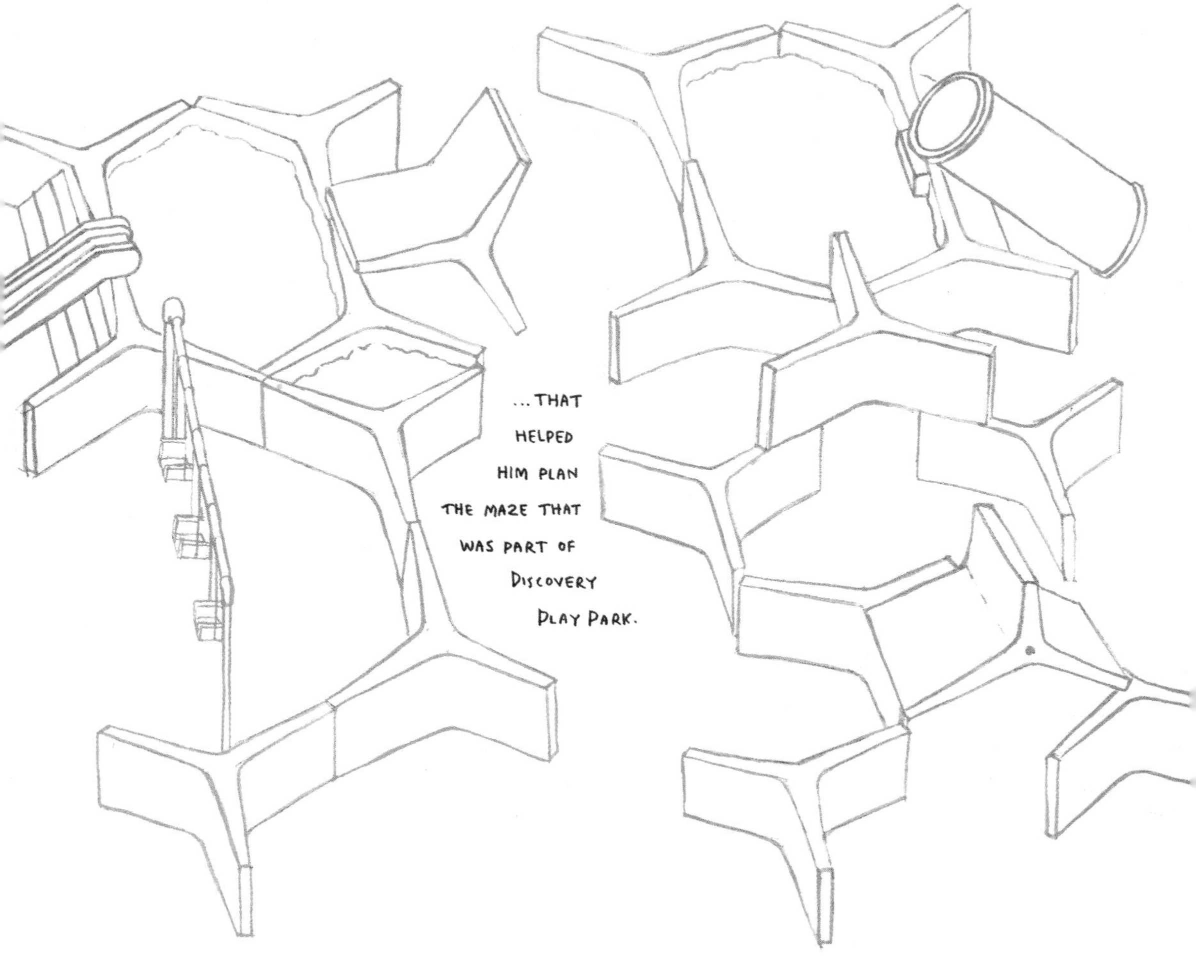
...THAT HELPED HIM PLAN THE MAZE THAT WAS PART OF DISCOVERY PLAY PARK.

Miss V: My Last Love Story

ANDRE KRAYEWSKI &
ED KRAYEWSKI

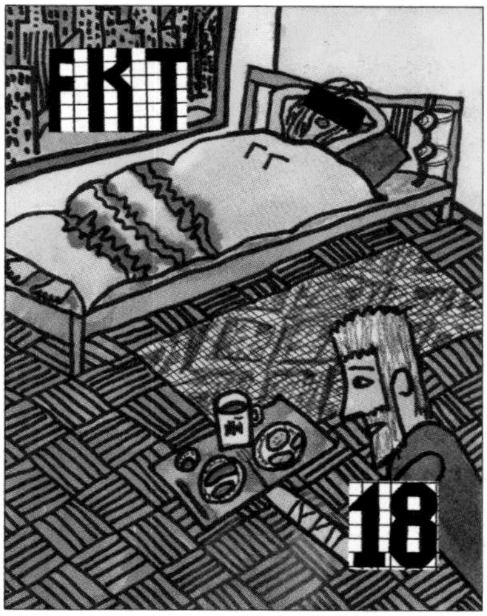
FKT
18

originally published in

FKT #18

SELF-PUBLISHED

8 x 10.5 inches • 40 pages

Biography

Andre Krayewski, who was born in Poland in 1933, was a dashing bon vivant, fount of idiosyncratic outsider wisdom, and creative genius. A noted innovator of the Polish School of Posters, Andre expressed his bold creative vision in a vast array of media, including posters, paintings, and prose over a 65-plus-year career spanning several continents. He began to work on comics with his son Ed in 2012. They produced *SKYLINER,* a graphic novel based on his semi-autobiographical memoir, and for two years they worked on *FKT,* a monthly comics magazine. He died in 2018 in Newark, New Jersey, his home for the last 33 years. He obtained his MFA from the Warsaw Academy of Fine Arts.

Ed Krayewski writes, teaches journalism, and makes comics. His work has appeared in *Reason, The Hill,* and the *New York Post,* among other publications. He formerly worked in television for NBC News, Fox News, and Fox Business, and before that taught seventh-grade Language Arts and Social Studies at George Washington Carver Elementary in Newark. He lives in Philadelphia with his wife, their two-year-old daughter, Jackie, for whom issue 17 of *FKT* was dedicated, and their cat, Bricks. He is a graduate of Seton Hall and the Columbia Graduate School of Journalism.
fkt.co

Statement

Andre Krayewski's son Kayetan began to purchase underground comics for his father in the early 2010s, which sparked an interest in creating comics of his own. This included various Meathaus collections as well as the *The Best American Comics 2009*. Andre especially loved the Doug Allen work in that book, and he found out he would be featured in this year's edition just a few months before his death.

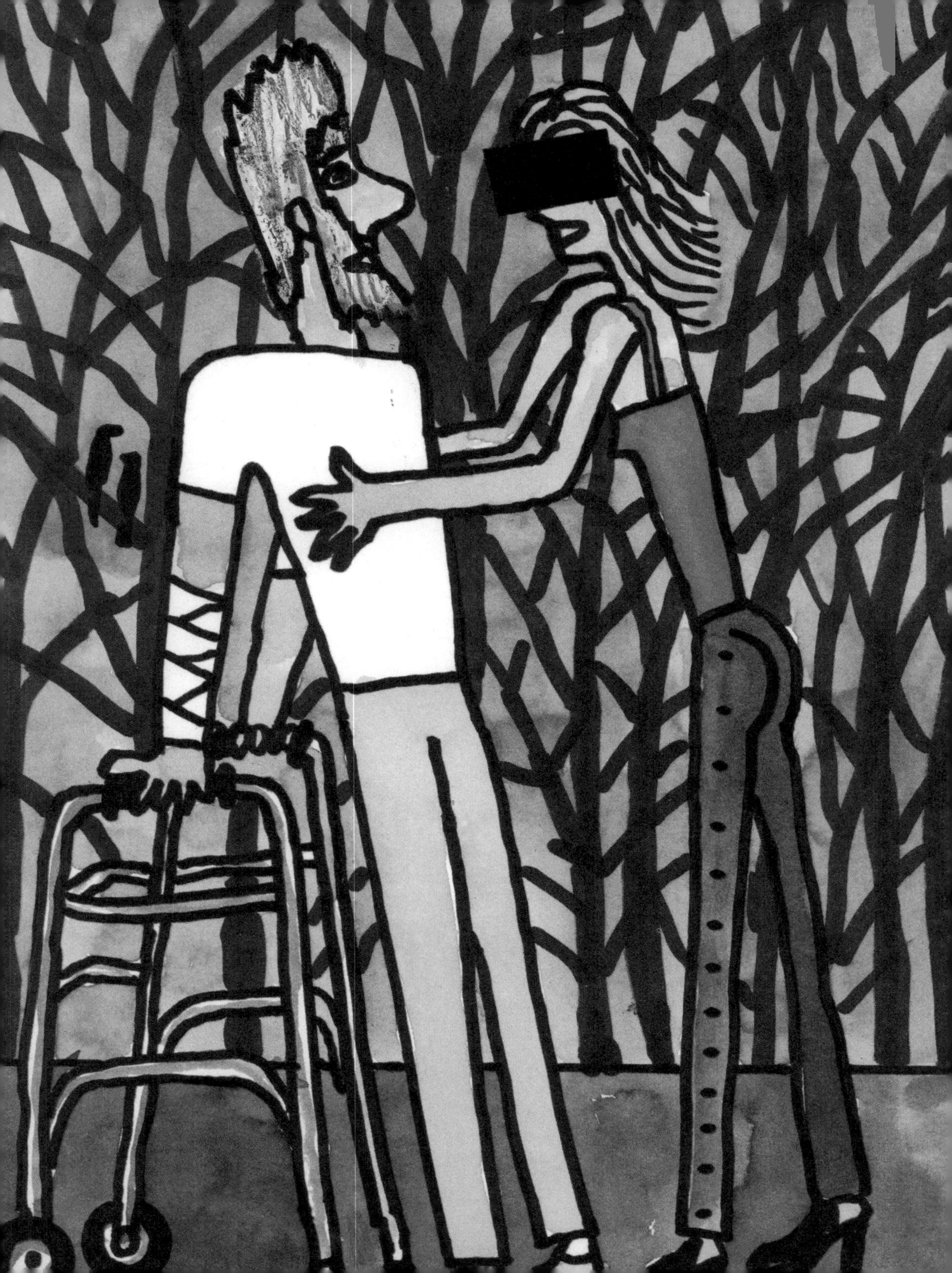

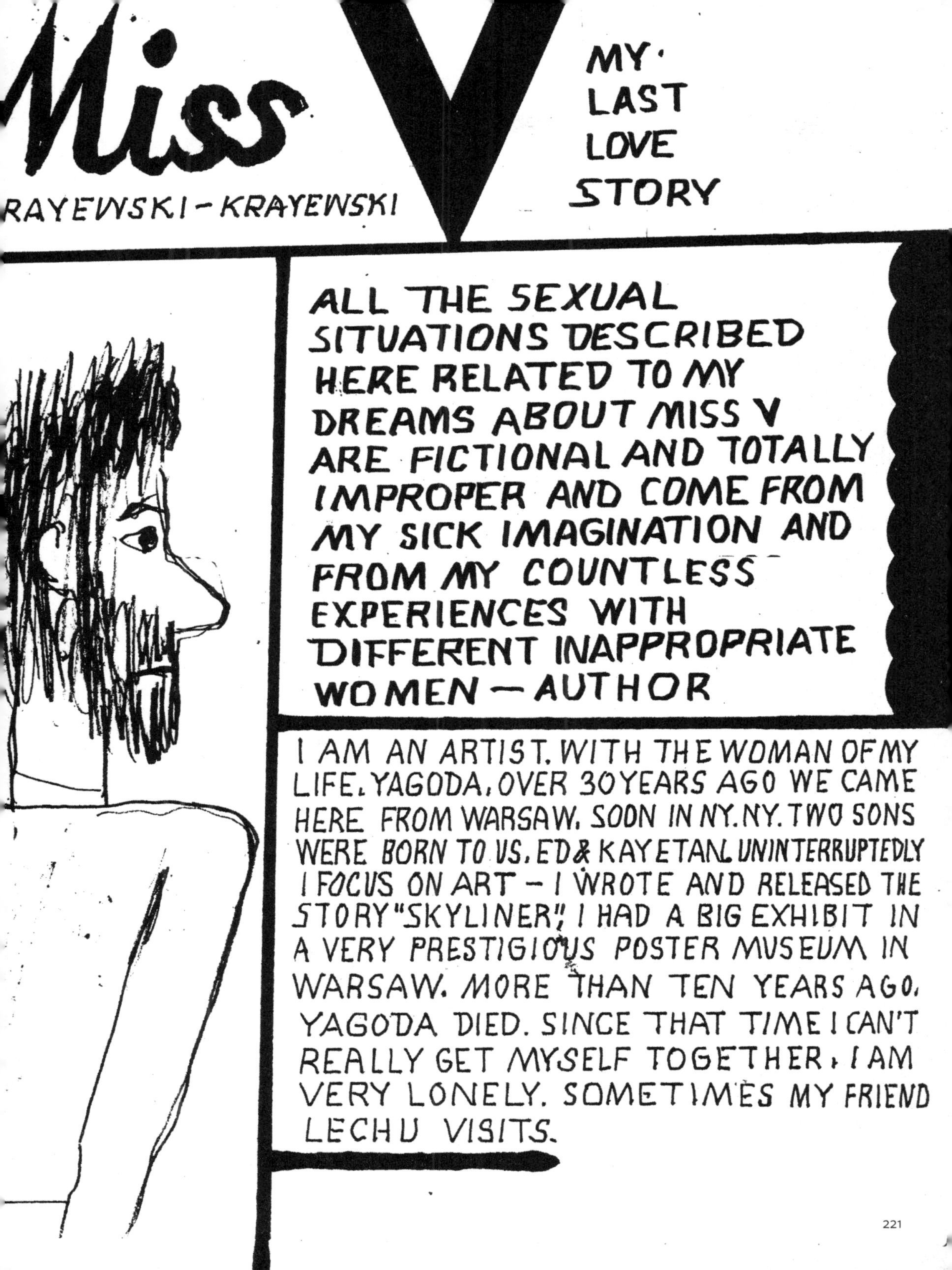
Miss V
RAYEWSKI-KRAYEWSKI
MY LAST LOVE STORY
ALL THE SEXUAL SITUATIONS DESCRIBED HERE RELATED TO MY DREAMS ABOUT MISS V ARE FICTIONAL AND TOTALLY IMPROPER AND COME FROM MY SICK IMAGINATION AND FROM MY COUNTLESS EXPERIENCES WITH DIFFERENT INAPPROPRIATE WOMEN — AUTHOR
I AM AN ARTIST. WITH THE WOMAN OF MY LIFE, YAGODA, OVER 30 YEARS AGO WE CAME HERE FROM WARSAW. SOON IN NY. NY. TWO SONS WERE BORN TO US, ED & KAYETAN. UNINTERRUPTEDLY I FOCUS ON ART — I WROTE AND RELEASED THE STORY "SKYLINER", I HAD A BIG EXHIBIT IN A VERY PRESTIGIOUS POSTER MUSEUM IN WARSAW. MORE THAN TEN YEARS AGO, YAGODA DIED. SINCE THAT TIME I CAN'T REALLY GET MYSELF TOGETHER. I AM VERY LONELY. SOMETIMES MY FRIEND LECHU VISITS.

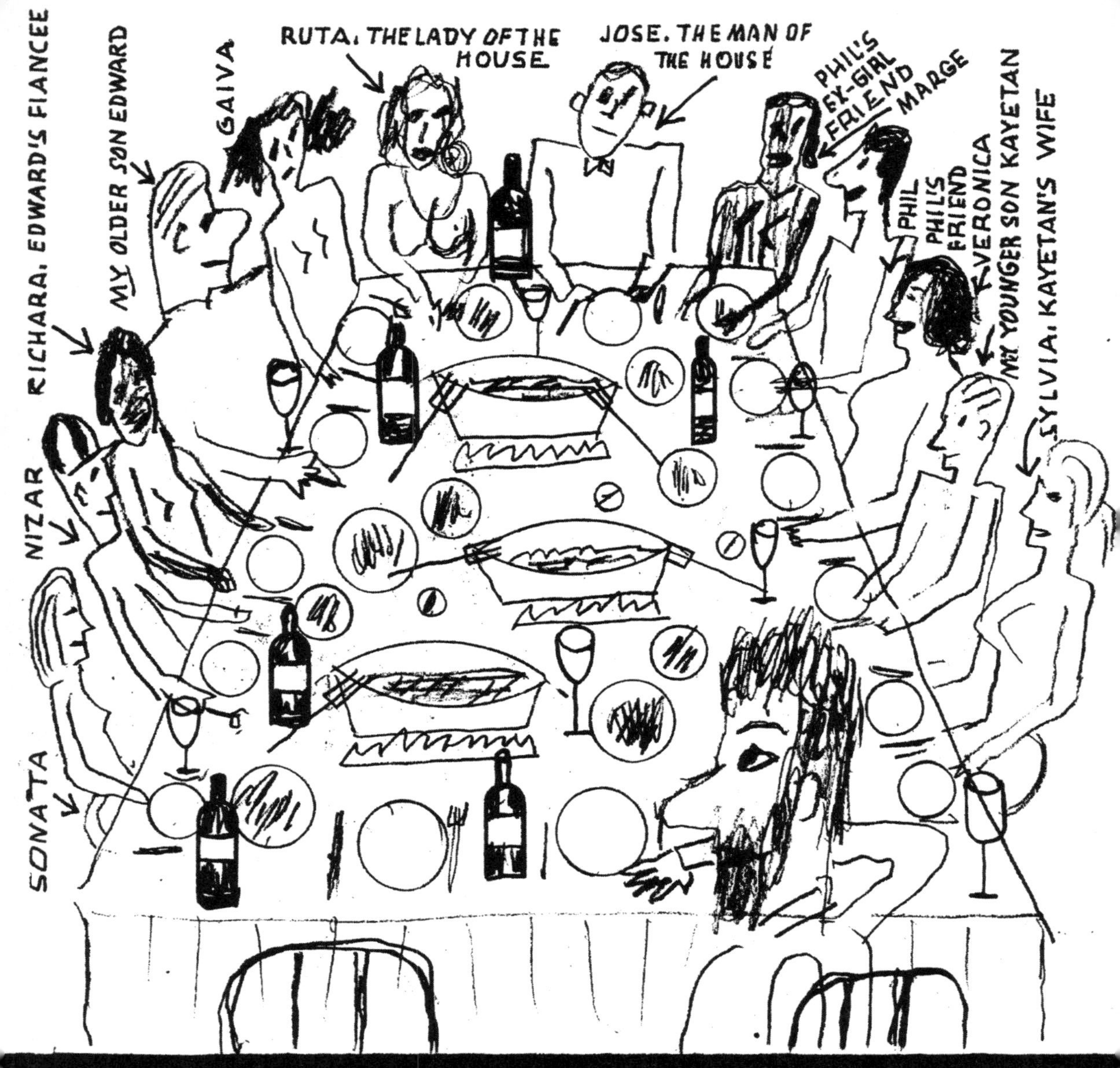
RICHARA, EDWARD'S FIANCEE
MY OLDER SON EDWARD
GAIVA
RUTA, THE LADY OF THE HOUSE
JOSE, THE MAN OF THE HOUSE
PHIL'S EX-GIRL FRIEND
MARGE
PHIL
PHIL'S FRIEND VERONICA
MY YOUNGER SON KAYETAN
SYLVIA, KAYETAN'S WIFE
NIZAR
SONATA

SOME TIME AGO, I WAS INVITED TO AN EASTER FONDUE PARTY O
MY SON'S FRIEND, JOSE, WHO HAD JUST BOUGHT A NEW HOME ON UNI
STREET. THE WHOLE TIME THE CHAIR NEXT TO ME STOOD EMPTY AND WHE
I ASKED WHO WOULD BE SITTING HERE, I GOT THE ANSWER THAT SOO
WOULD ARRIVE A COUSIN OF RUTA WHO JUST YESTERDAY ARRIVED FR
LITHUANIA. LITHUANIA, A FORMER SOVIET REPUBLIC, REMEMBERING T
SOVIETS, EVEN FROM THE TIME OF WW2 I ALWAYS LIVED WITH THE CONVIC
THAT CITIZENS OF THE FORMER SOVIET REPUBLICS WERE CLOSER I
RESEMBLANCE TO ANIMALS THAN TO PEOPLE, AND WAITED. WORRIED ABO

VHAT KIND OF MONSTER WOULD SOON ARRIVE AND SIT NEXT TO ME. HE MONSTER TURNED OUT A TALL, BEAUTIFUL, BLONDE WITH A SINGSONG ASTERN EUROPEAN ACCENT WHICH SOUNDED LIKE SOME SORT OF BEAUTIFUL MUSIC. FROM THE VERY BEGINNING SHE STUNNED ME WITH HER NIQUE PERSONALITY AND THE POSITIVE AURA EMANATING ROM HER. THE ONE FLAW FOR ME WITH MISS V WERE HER MAYBE A BIT TOOSMALL BREASTS — WHICH I TOLD HER IMMEDIATELY. SHE RESPONDED THAT →

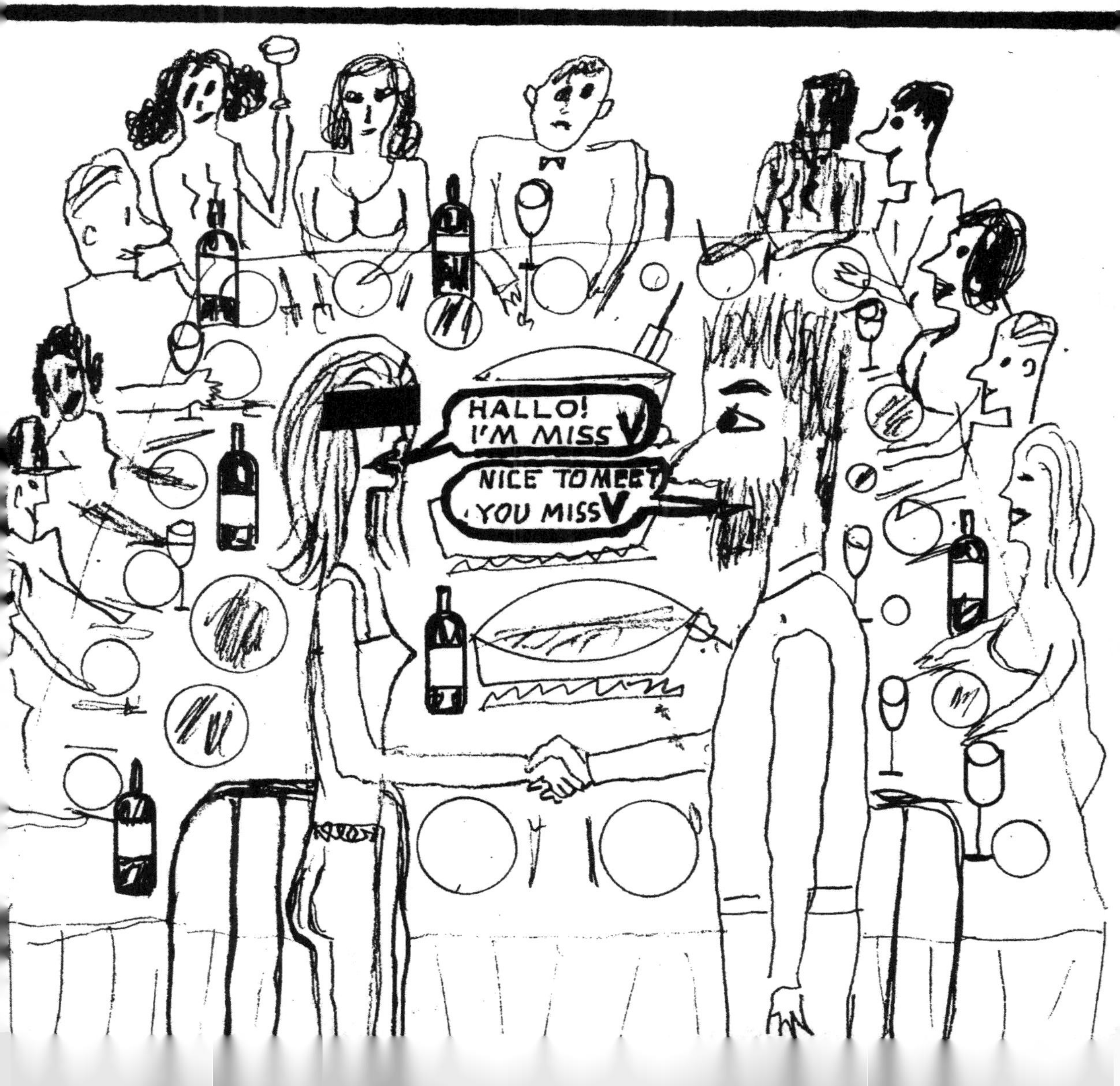

HALLO! I'M MISS V
NICE TO MEET YOU MISS V

SHE LIKED HER BREASTS VERY MUCH. WHEN I ASKED HER IF HER GUYS ALSO LIKED THEM SHE ANSWERED ENIGMATICALLY COMSI-COMSA

WHEN IT CAME TO ME, MY ENTIRE LIFE I LIKED WOMEN WITH BIG BREASTS. THE BIGGER THE MORE THEY EXCITED ME.

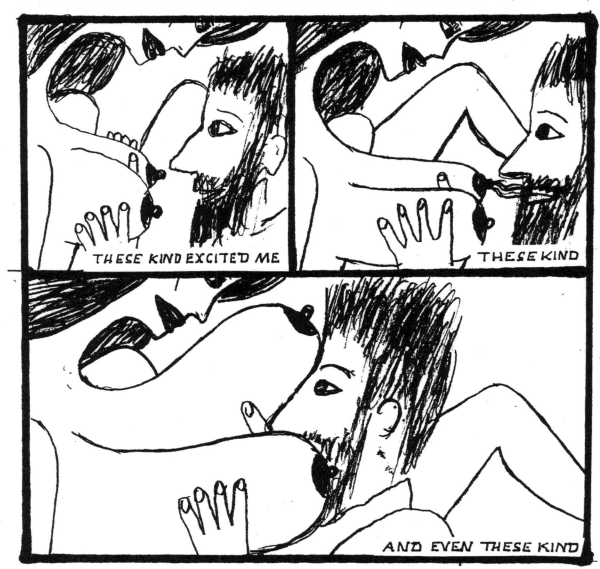

THESE KIND EXCITED ME

THESE KIND

AND EVEN THESE KIND

SHORTLY, AFTER ALL, MISS V'S SMALL BREASTS STOPPED BOTHERING ME AND EVEN IN A CERTAIN SENSE I GOT TO LIKE THEM

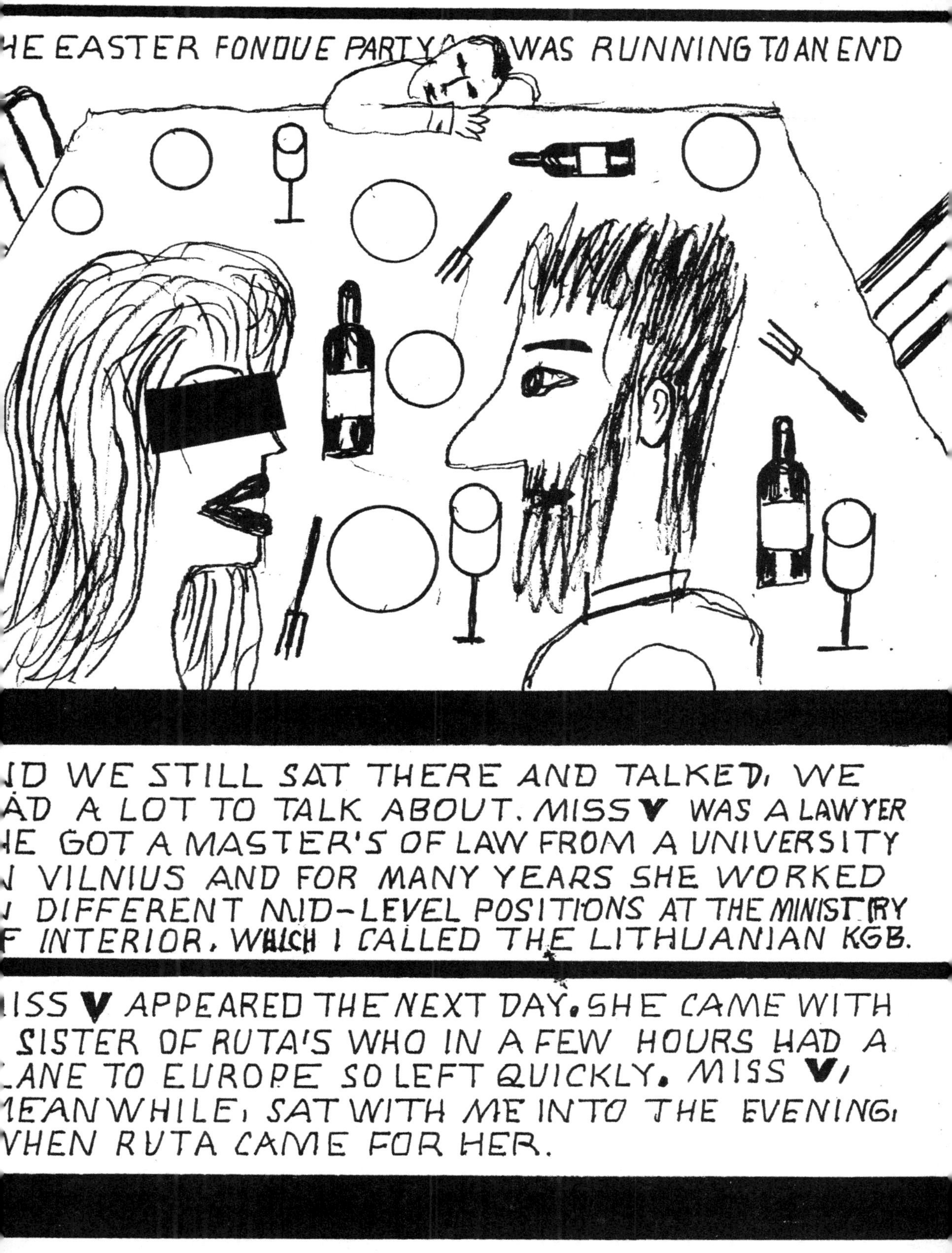
HE EASTER FONDUE PARTY WAS RUNNING TO AN END
ID WE STILL SAT THERE AND TALKED, WE ÀD A LOT TO TALK ABOUT. MISS V WAS A LAWYER HE GOT A MASTER'S OF LAW FROM A UNIVERSITY I VILNIUS AND FOR MANY YEARS SHE WORKED I DIFFERENT MID-LEVEL POSITIONS AT THE MINISTRY F INTERIOR, WHICH I CALLED THE LITHUANIAN KGB.
ISS V APPEARED THE NEXT DAY. SHE CAME WITH SISTER OF RUTA'S WHO IN A FEW HOURS HAD A LANE TO EUROPE SO LEFT QUICKLY. MISS V, EANWHILE, SAT WITH ME INTO THE EVENING, VHEN RUTA CAME FOR HER.

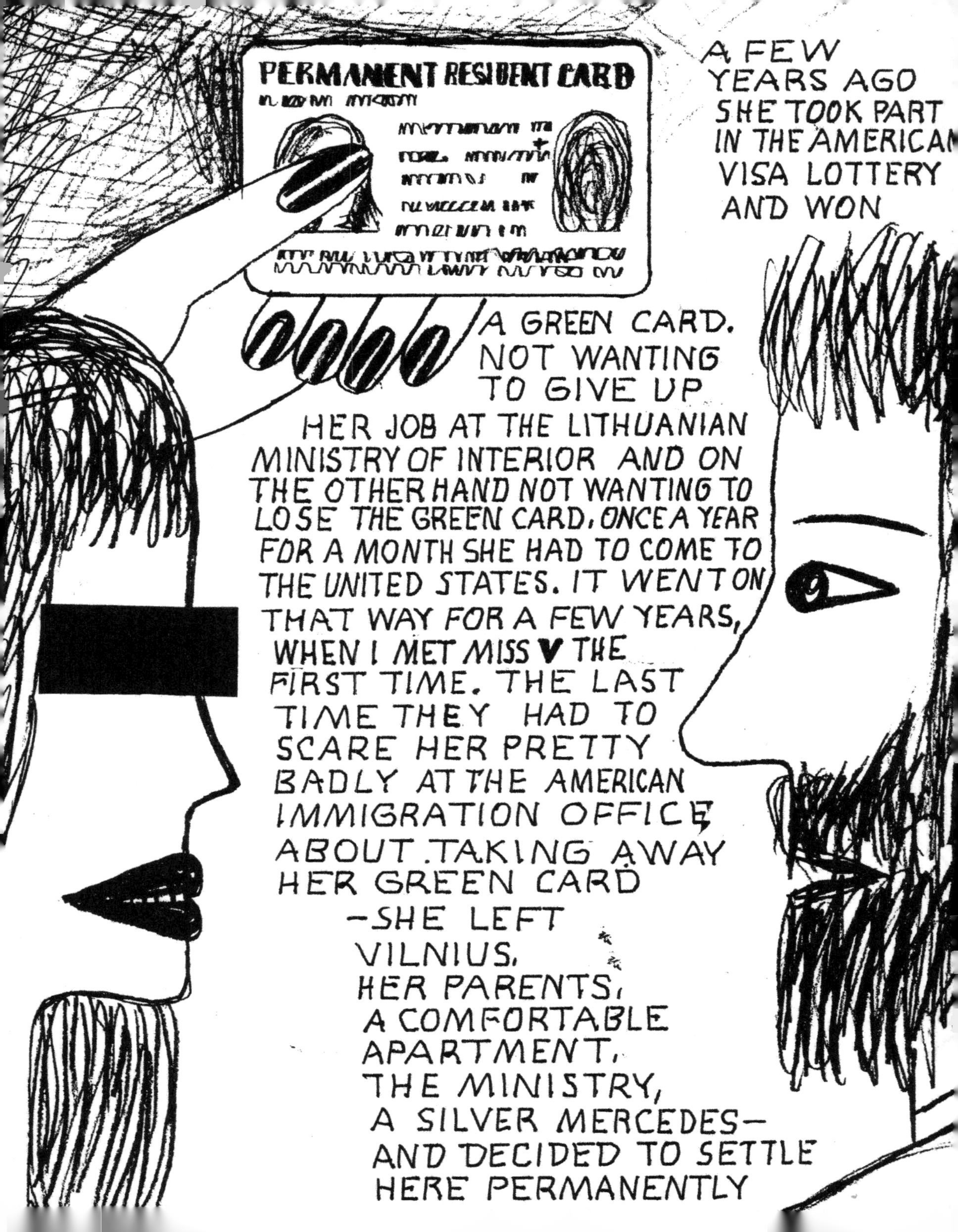
PERMANENT RESIDENT CARD
A FEW YEARS AGO SHE TOOK PART IN THE AMERICAN VISA LOTTERY AND WON
A GREEN CARD. NOT WANTING TO GIVE UP
HER JOB AT THE LITHUANIAN MINISTRY OF INTERIOR AND ON THE OTHER HAND NOT WANTING TO LOSE THE GREEN CARD, ONCE A YEAR FOR A MONTH SHE HAD TO COME TO THE UNITED STATES. IT WENT ON THAT WAY FOR A FEW YEARS, WHEN I MET MISS V THE FIRST TIME. THE LAST TIME THEY HAD TO SCARE HER PRETTY BADLY AT THE AMERICAN IMMIGRATION OFFICE ABOUT TAKING AWAY HER GREEN CARD
—SHE LEFT VILNIUS, HER PARENTS, A COMFORTABLE APARTMENT, THE MINISTRY, A SILVER MERCEDES— AND DECIDED TO SETTLE HERE PERMANENTLY

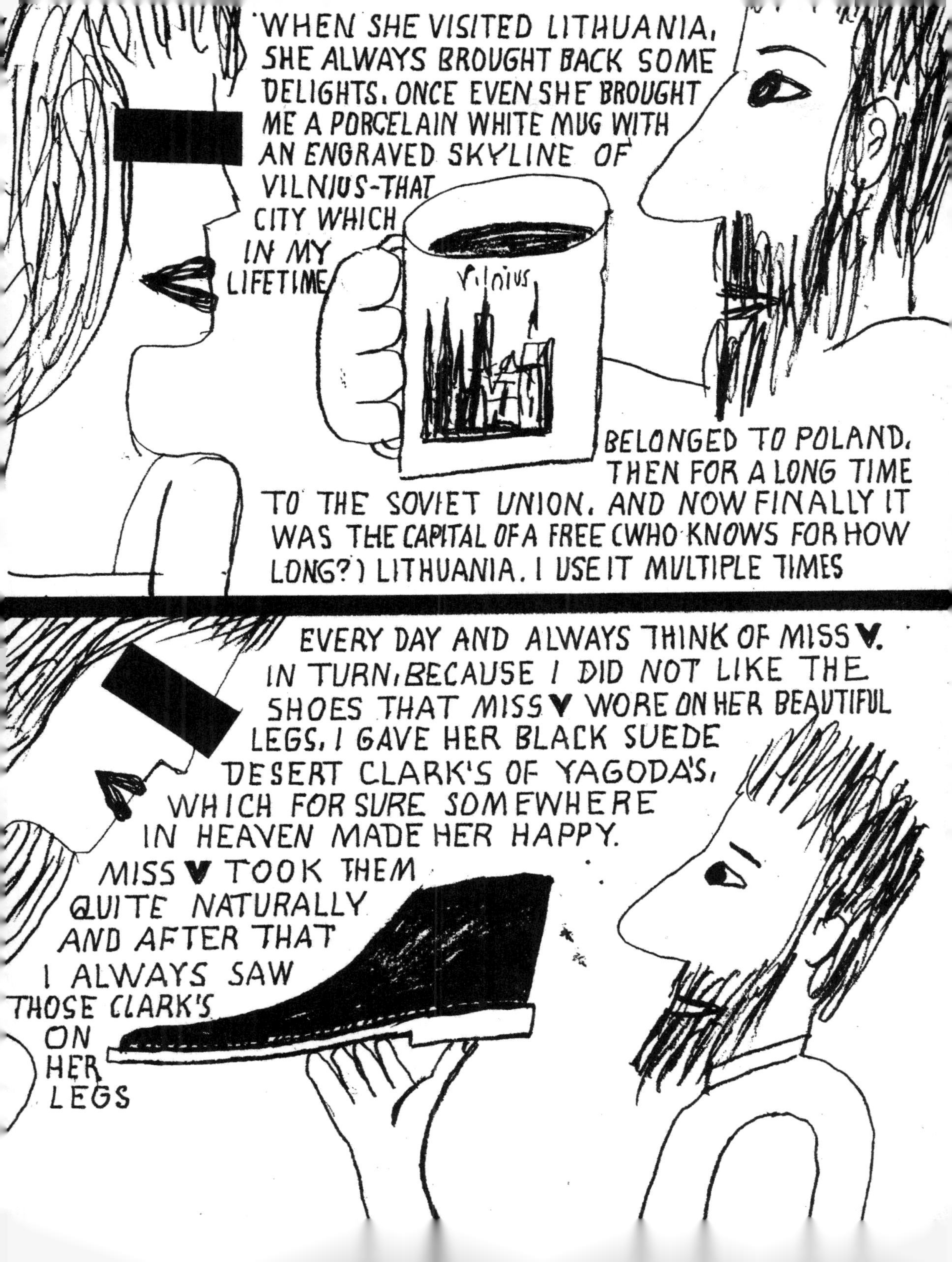
WHEN SHE VISITED LITHUANIA, SHE ALWAYS BROUGHT BACK SOME DELIGHTS. ONCE EVEN SHE BROUGHT ME A PORCELAIN WHITE MUG WITH AN ENGRAVED SKYLINE OF VILNIUS-THAT CITY WHICH IN MY LIFETIME
Vilnius
BELONGED TO POLAND, THEN FOR A LONG TIME TO THE SOVIET UNION, AND NOW FINALLY IT WAS THE CAPITAL OF A FREE (WHO KNOWS FOR HOW LONG?) LITHUANIA. I USE IT MULTIPLE TIMES
EVERY DAY AND ALWAYS THINK OF MISS V. IN TURN, BECAUSE I DID NOT LIKE THE SHOES THAT MISS V WORE ON HER BEAUTIFUL LEGS, I GAVE HER BLACK SUEDE DESERT CLARK'S OF YAGODA'S, WHICH FOR SURE SOMEWHERE IN HEAVEN MADE HER HAPPY.
MISS V TOOK THEM QUITE NATURALLY AND AFTER THAT I ALWAYS SAW THOSE CLARK'S ON HER LEGS

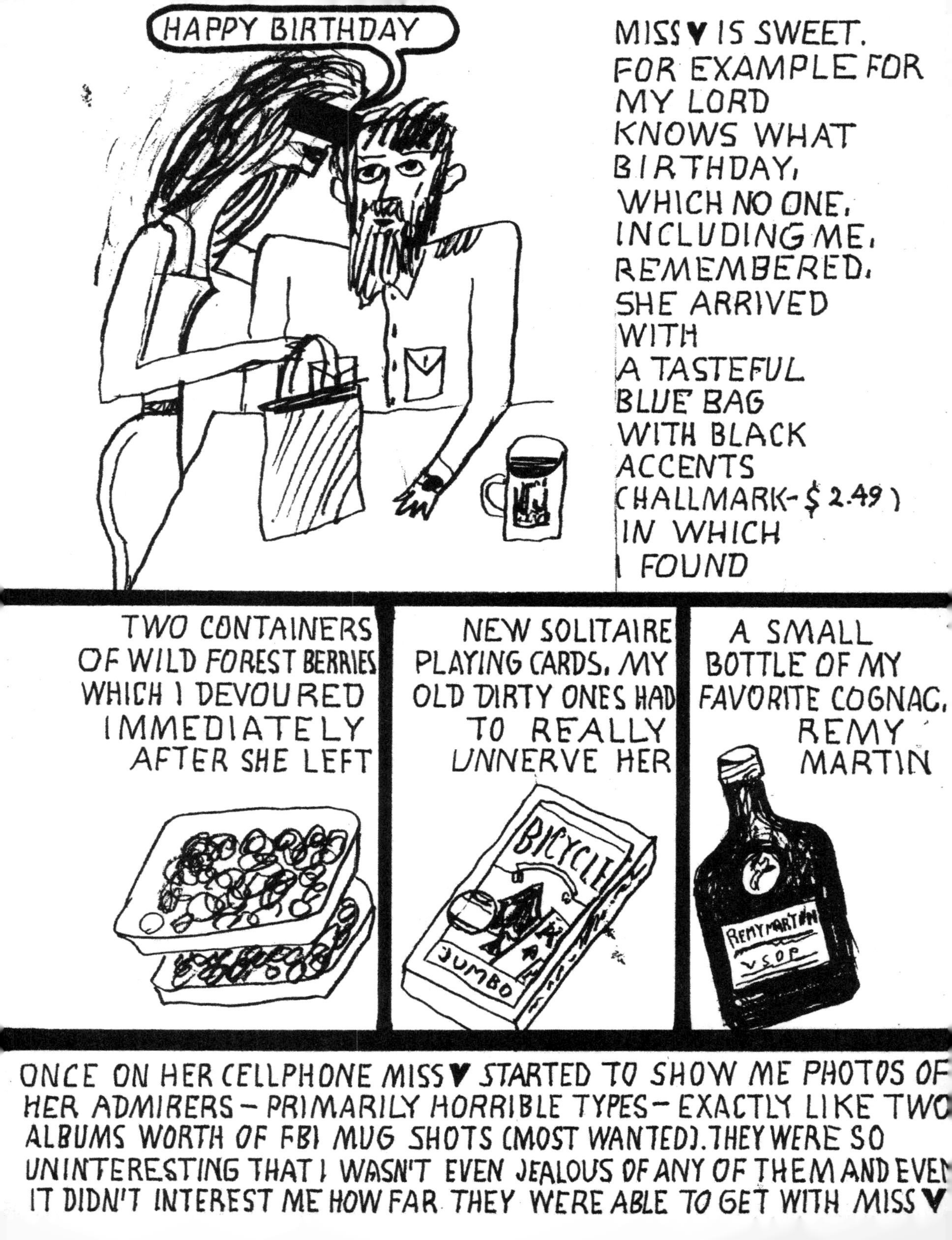

HAPPY BIRTHDAY
MISS♥ IS SWEET. FOR EXAMPLE FOR MY LORD KNOWS WHAT BIRTHDAY, WHICH NO ONE, INCLUDING ME, REMEMBERED. SHE ARRIVED WITH A TASTEFUL BLUE BAG WITH BLACK ACCENTS (HALLMARK-$2.49) IN WHICH I FOUND
TWO CONTAINERS OF WILD FOREST BERRIES WHICH I DEVOURED IMMEDIATELY AFTER SHE LEFT
NEW SOLITAIRE PLAYING CARDS. MY OLD DIRTY ONES HAD TO REALLY UNNERVE HER
BICYCLE
JUMBO
A SMALL BOTTLE OF MY FAVORITE COGNAC. REMY MARTIN
REMY MARTIN
VSOP
ONCE ON HER CELLPHONE MISS♥ STARTED TO SHOW ME PHOTOS OF HER ADMIRERS – PRIMARILY HORRIBLE TYPES – EXACTLY LIKE TWO ALBUMS WORTH OF FBI MUG SHOTS (MOST WANTED). THEY WERE SO UNINTERESTING THAT I WASN'T EVEN JEALOUS OF ANY OF THEM AND EVEN IT DIDN'T INTEREST ME HOW FAR THEY WERE ABLE TO GET WITH MISS♥

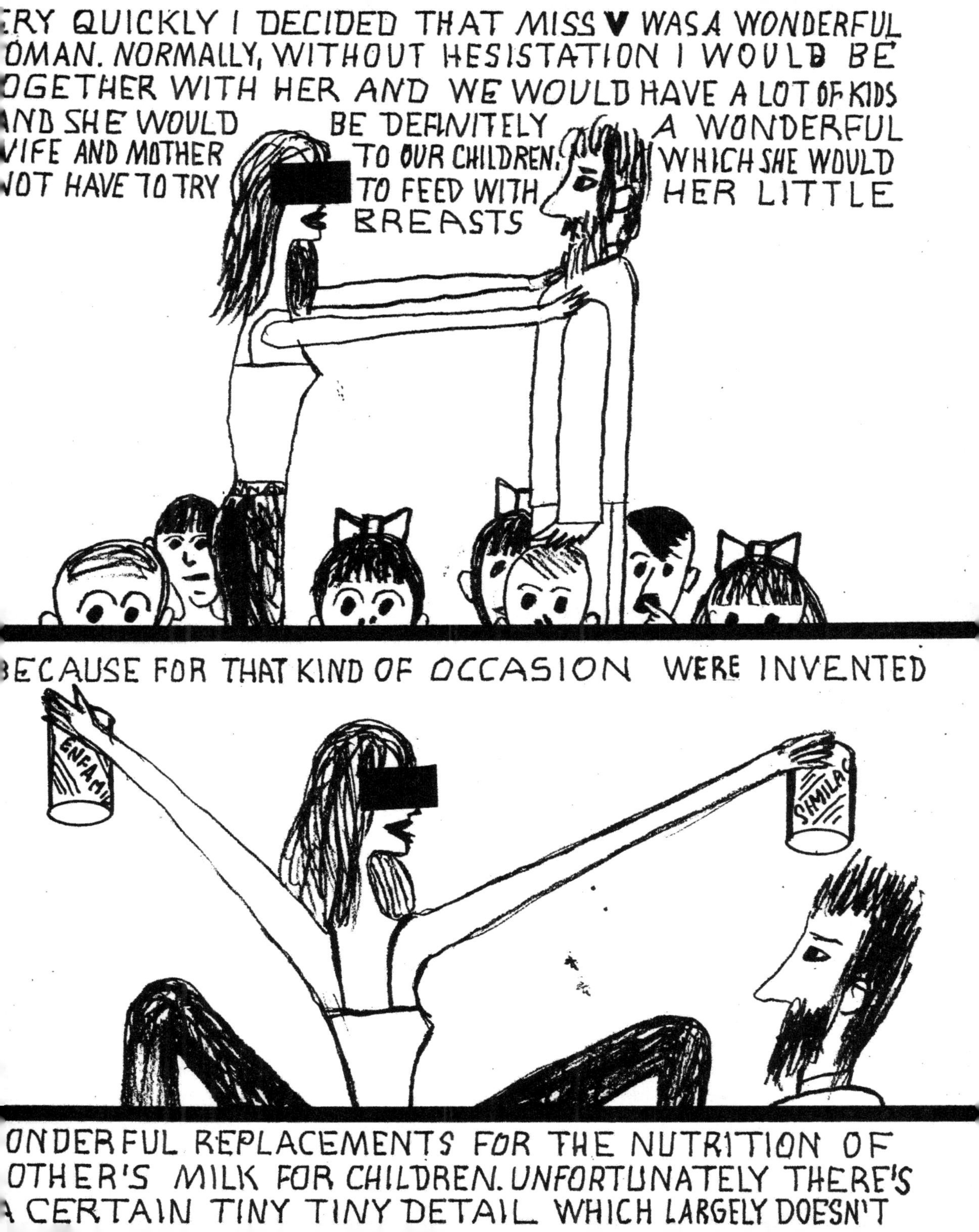
ERY QUICKLY I DECIDED THAT MISS V WAS A WONDERFUL
OMAN. NORMALLY, WITHOUT HESISTATION I WOULD BE
OGETHER WITH HER AND WE WOULD HAVE A LOT OF KIDS
ND SHE WOULD BE DEFINITELY A WONDERFUL
VIFE AND MOTHER TO OUR CHILDREN, WHICH SHE WOULD
NOT HAVE TO TRY TO FEED WITH HER LITTLE
BREASTS
ECAUSE FOR THAT KIND OF OCCASION WERE INVENTED
ENFAMI
SIMILAC
ONDERFUL REPLACEMENTS FOR THE NUTRITION OF
OTHER'S MILK FOR CHILDREN. UNFORTUNATELY THERE'S
A CERTAIN TINY TINY DETAIL WHICH LARGELY DOESN'T

ALLOW US TO BE TOGETHER — NAMELY IN THE MONSTROU
DIFFERENCE IN AGE WHICH SEPARATED US LIKE THE **GRAND CANYO**
AND UNFORTUNATELY THERE WAS NOTHING TO DO ABOUT IT. SH
AND I UNDERSTAND THAT — EVEN THOUGH I HAVE ALWAY
FELT LIKE A YOUNG PLAYBOY

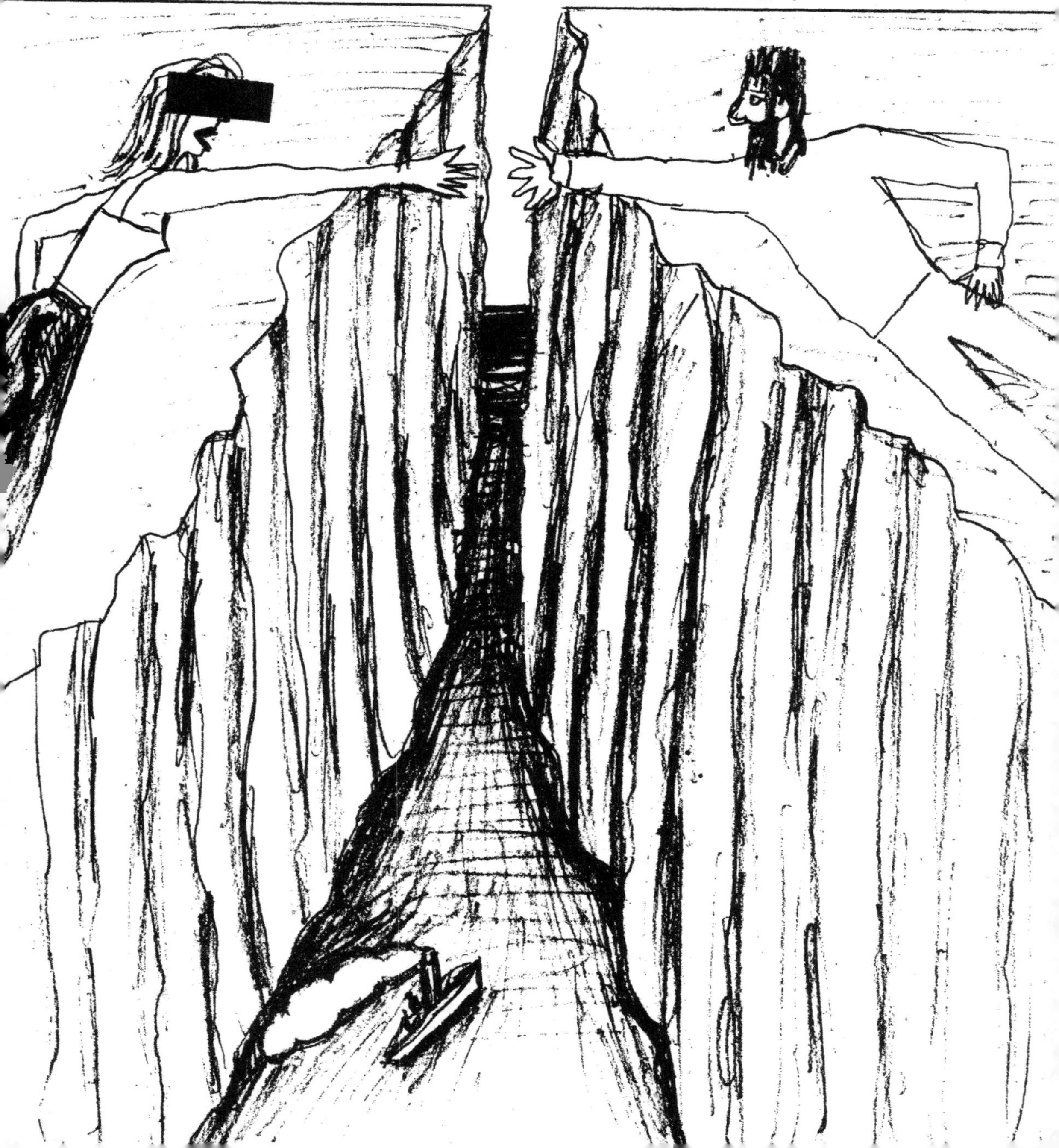

ITH GREAT SADNESS I DECIDED THAT MISS V
AS VERY SECRETIVE — LIKE WOMEN PERMANENTLY
EATING ON MEN, WHEN ONCE LATE IN THE EVENING
HE RETURNED FROM MY HOUSE, SHE WAS ATTACKED
N THE PARKING LOT BY TWO CRIMINALS. THEY PROBABLY
VANTED TO DRAG HER TO A NEARBY BUSH, THERE
TO RAPE AND MAYBE ON THE OCCASION
MURDER HER. MISS V, AS AN EMPLOYEE OF
LITHUANIEN KGB, KNEW VERY WELL THE
MARTIAL ARTS AND WITHOUT TROUBLE
N A FEW SECONDS HANDLED THEM →

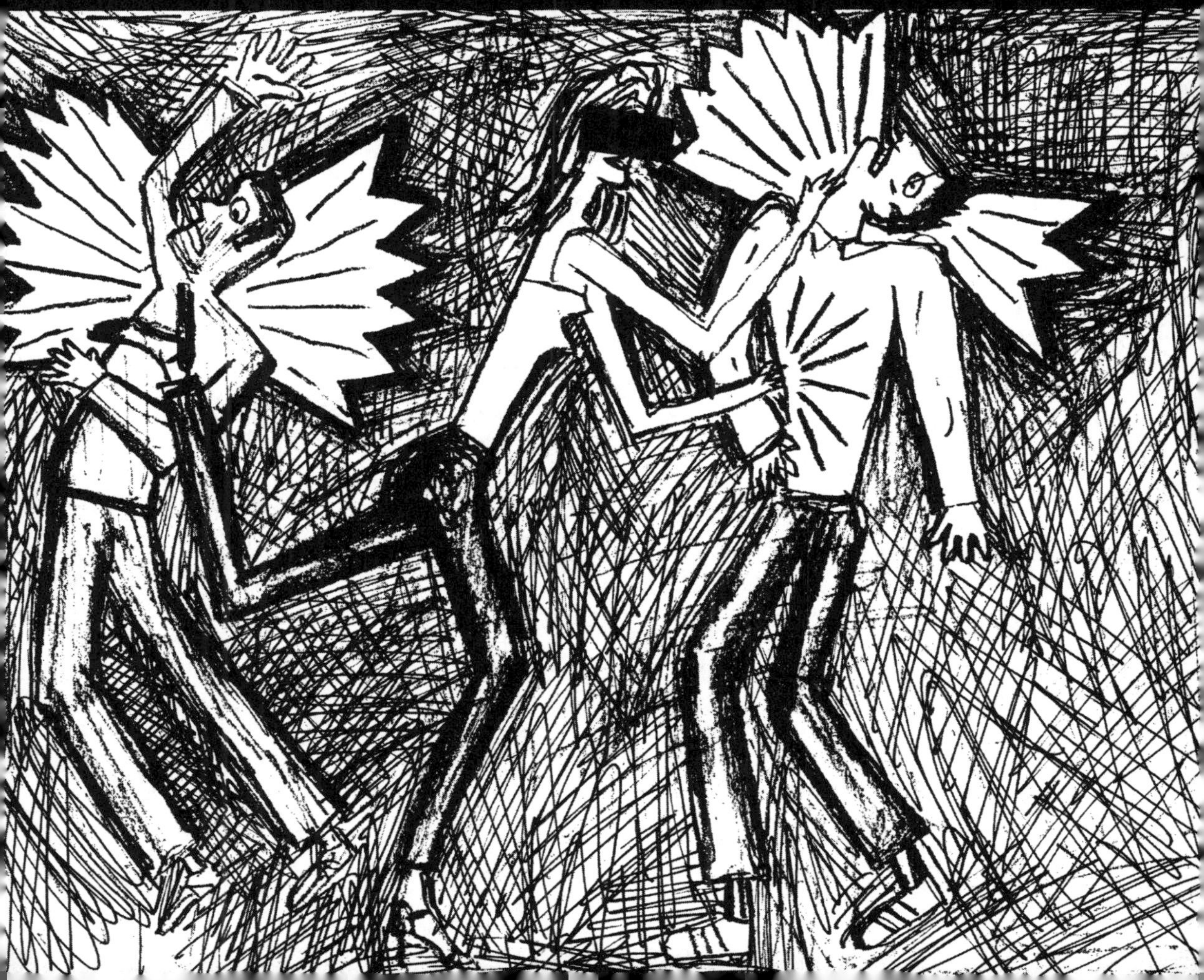

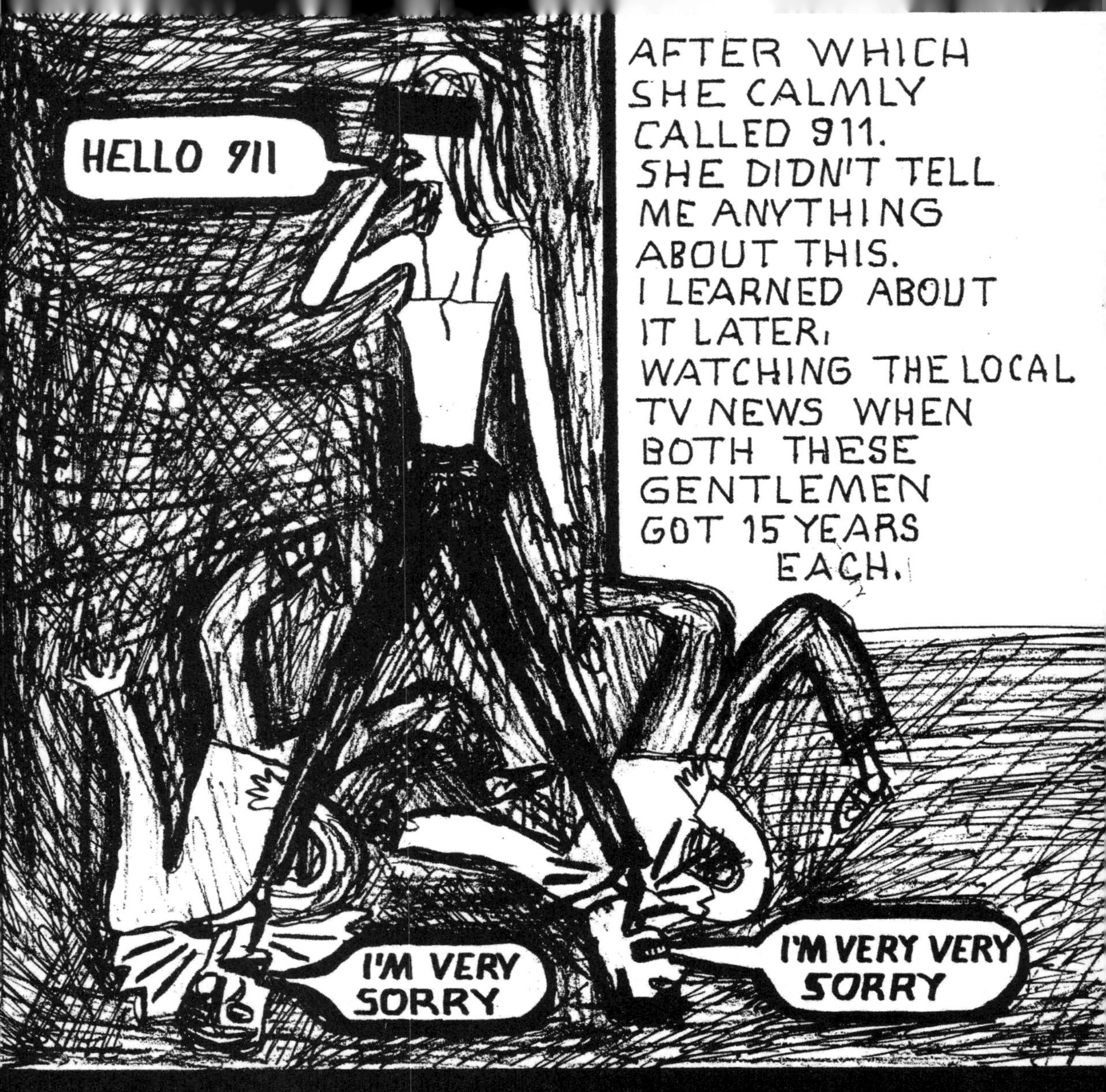
AFTER WHICH SHE CALMLY CALLED 911. SHE DIDN'T TELL ME ANYTHING ABOUT THIS. I LEARNED ABOUT IT LATER, WATCHING THE LOCAL TV NEWS WHEN BOTH THESE GENTLEMEN GOT 15 YEARS EACH.
HELLO 911
I'M VERY SORRY
I'M VERY VERY SORRY

MISS V CARRIES ON HERE A NOMADIC LIFE. SHE HAS THREE PLACES WHERE SHE STAYS — HERE ON UNION STREET WITH HER COUSIN RUTA, SOMEWHERE ON WEST 23RD STREET IN MANHATTAN, AND SOMEWHERE WITH SOME FRIENDS ON LONG ISLAND. OFTEN SHE STAYED THERE FOR SEVERAL DAYS, WHICH DIDN'T INTERRUPT HER MONEY CHASE — MISS V LOVES MONEY — THEN AFTER A FEW DAYS STAYING AND WORKING FOR EXAMPLE IN UPSTATE NEW YORK, QUEENS, OR SOUTH JERSEY.

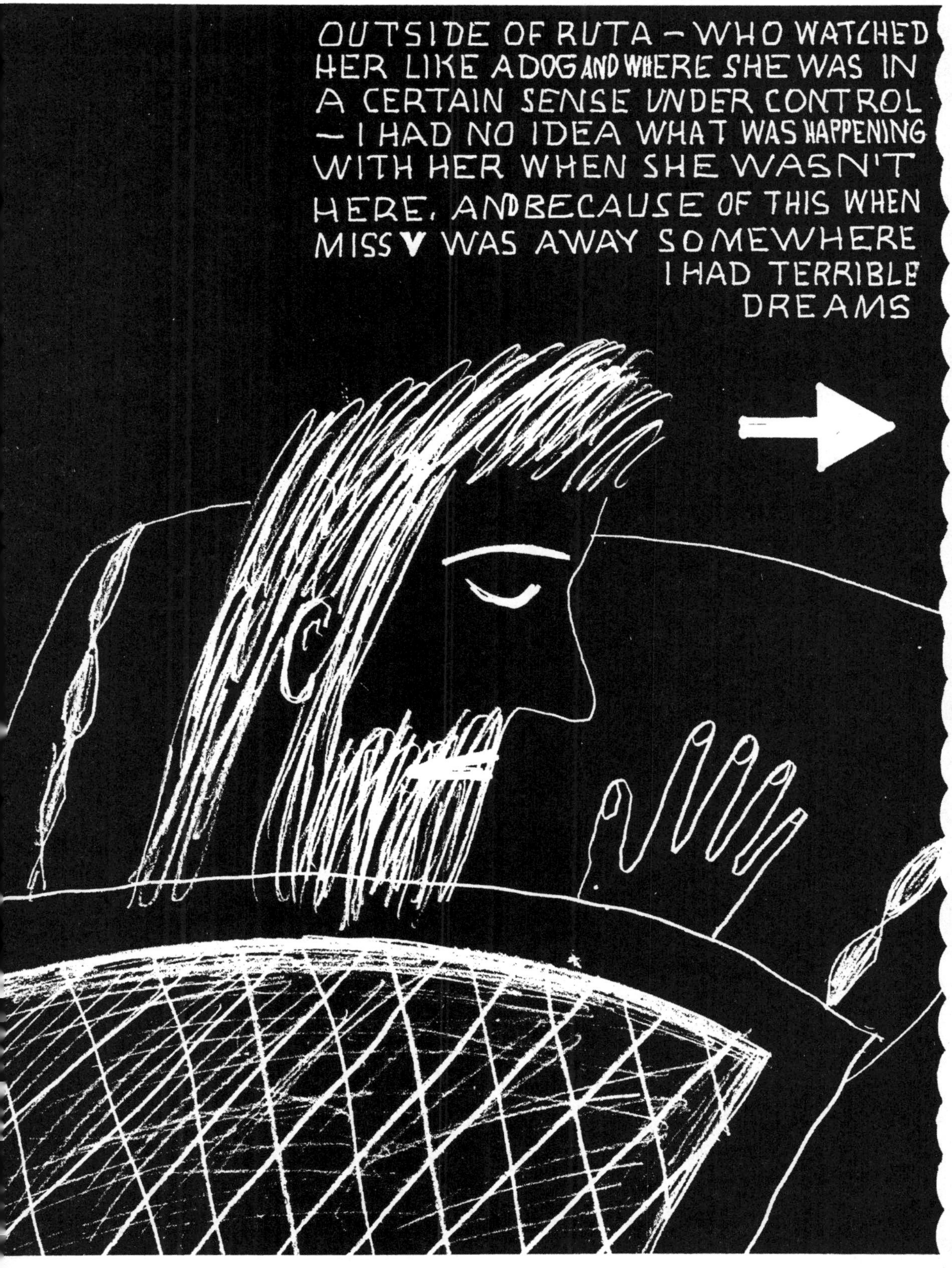
OUTSIDE OF RUTA – WHO WATCHED HER LIKE A DOG AND WHERE SHE WAS IN A CERTAIN SENSE UNDER CONTROL – I HAD NO IDEA WHAT WAS HAPPENING WITH HER WHEN SHE WASN'T HERE. AND BECAUSE OF THIS WHEN MISS V WAS AWAY SOMEWHERE I HAD TERRIBLE DREAMS

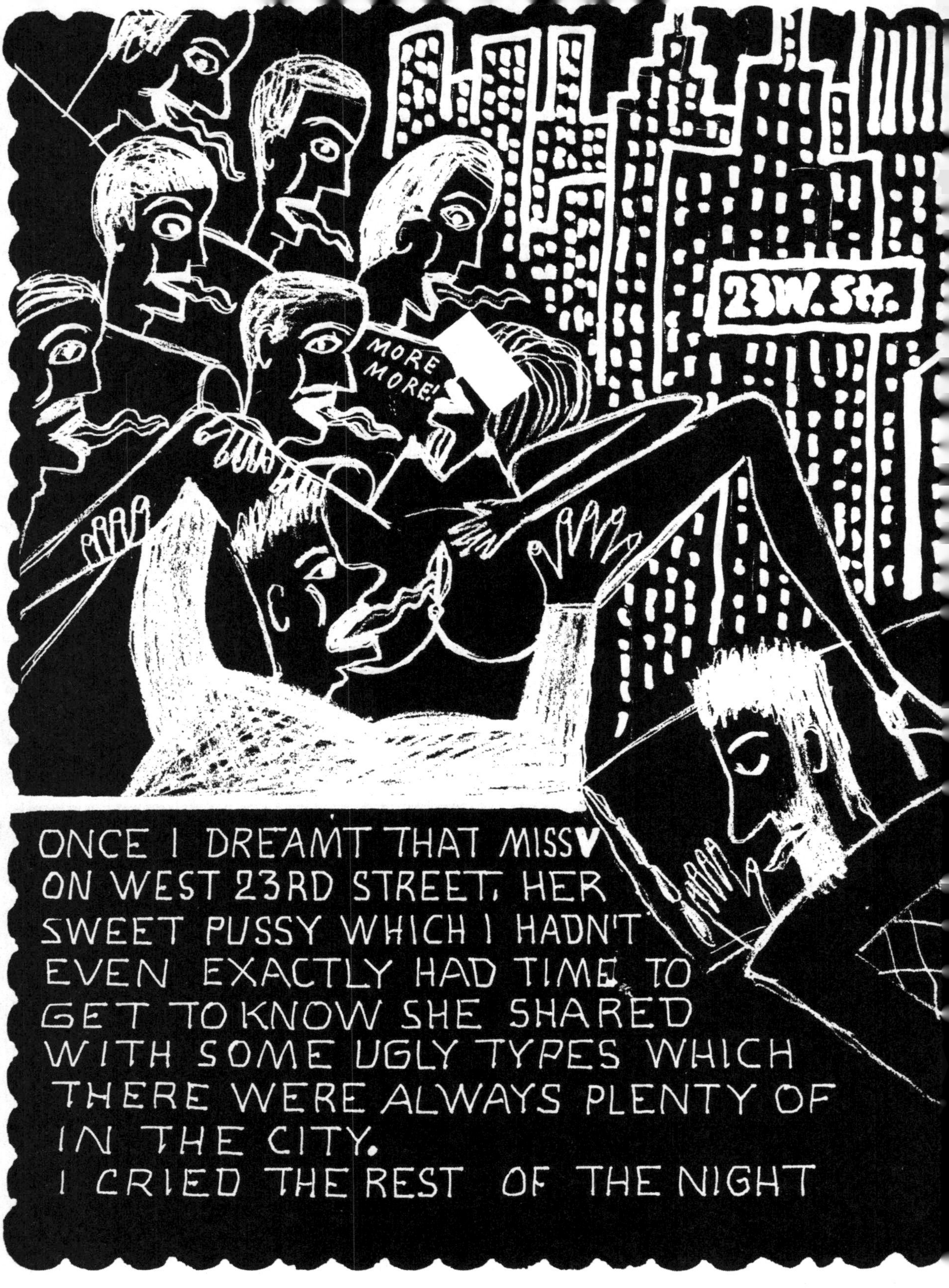

23W. Str.
MORE MORE!
ONCE I DREAMT THAT MISS V ON WEST 23RD STREET, HER SWEET PUSSY WHICH I HADN'T EVEN EXACTLY HAD TIME TO GET TO KNOW SHE SHARED WITH SOME UGLY TYPES WHICH THERE WERE ALWAYS PLENTY OF IN THE CITY.
I CRIED THE REST OF THE NIGHT

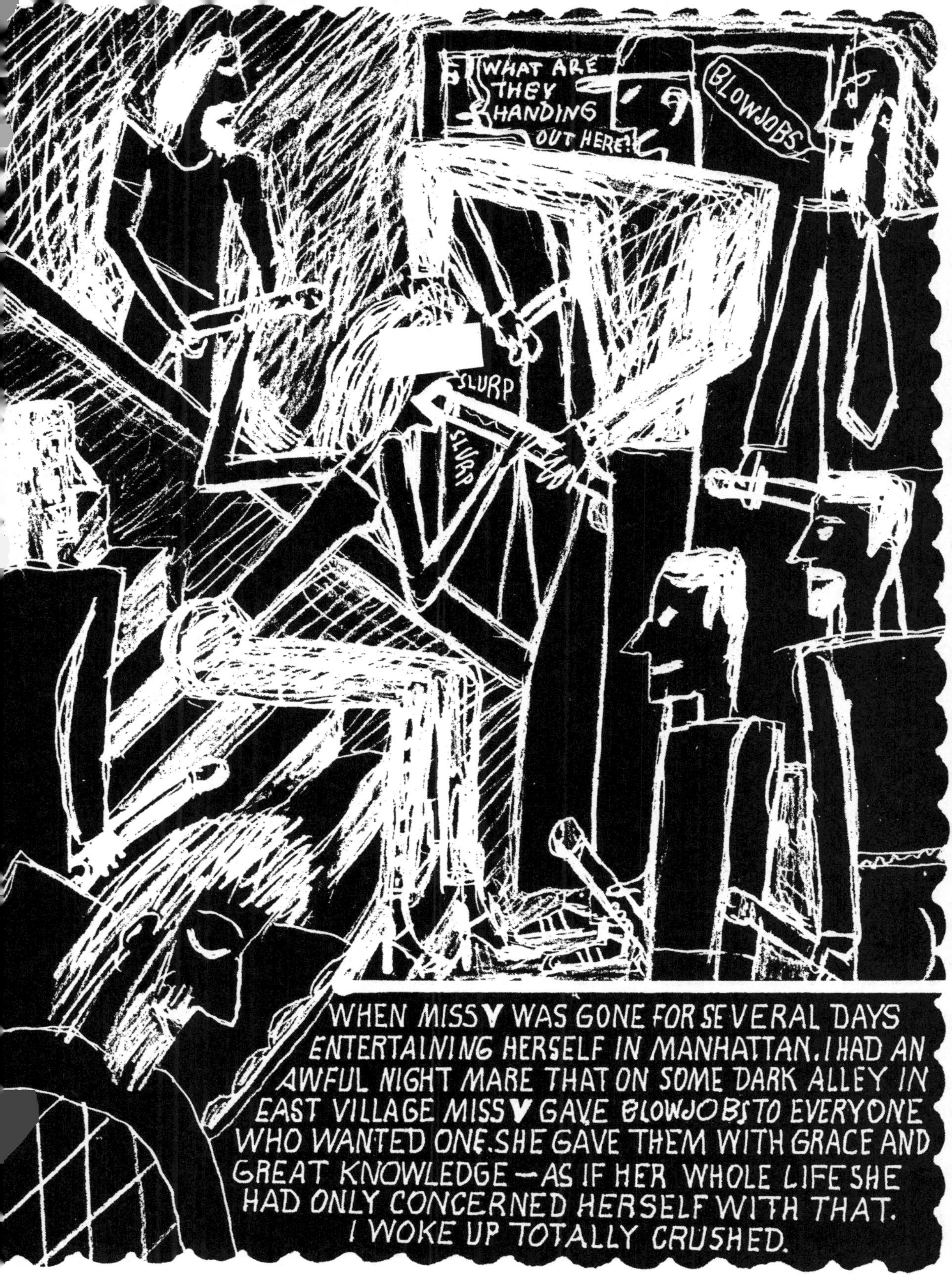
WHAT ARE THEY HANDING OUT HERE?
BLOWJOBS
SLURP
SLURP
WHEN MISS V WAS GONE FOR SEVERAL DAYS ENTERTAINING HERSELF IN MANHATTAN, I HAD AN AWFUL NIGHTMARE THAT ON SOME DARK ALLEY IN EAST VILLAGE MISS V GAVE BLOWJOBS TO EVERYONE WHO WANTED ONE. SHE GAVE THEM WITH GRACE AND GREAT KNOWLEDGE—AS IF HER WHOLE LIFE SHE HAD ONLY CONCERNED HERSELF WITH THAT.
I WOKE UP TOTALLY CRUSHED.

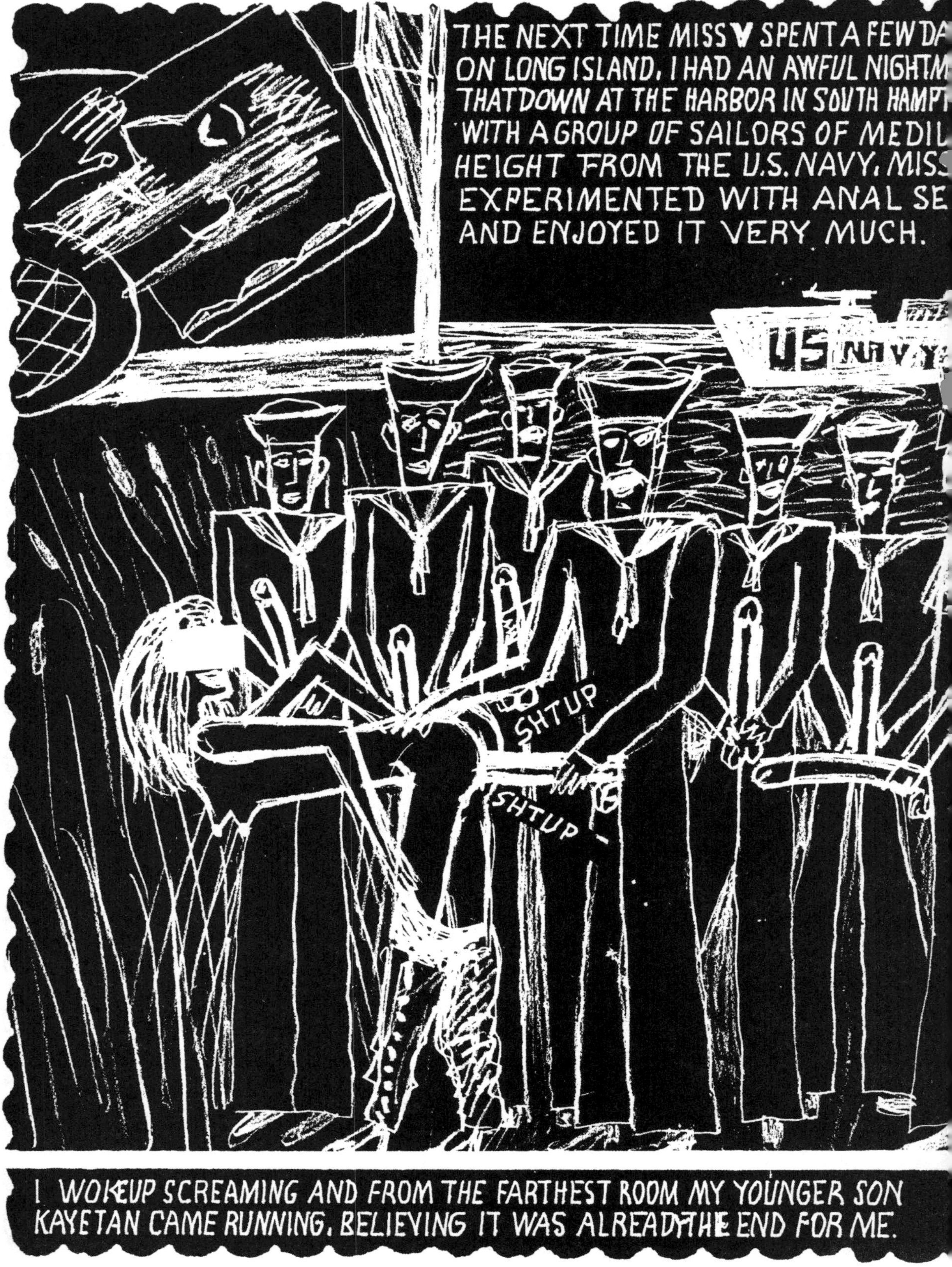
THE NEXT TIME MISS V SPENT A FEW DA
ON LONG ISLAND, I HAD AN AWFUL NIGHTM
THATDOWN AT THE HARBOR IN SOUTH HAMPT
WITH A GROUP OF SAILORS OF MEDIU
HEIGHT FROM THE U.S. NAVY, MISS
EXPERIMENTED WITH ANAL SE
AND ENJOYED IT VERY MUCH.
US NAVY
SHTUP
SHTUP
I WOKEUP SCREAMING AND FROM THE FARTHEST ROOM MY YOUNGER SON
KAYETAN CAME RUNNING, BELIEVING IT WAS ALREADY THE END FOR ME.

BY NATURE NOT BEING TOO RELIGIOUS I DON'T HAVE UNDERSTANDING ABOUT MANY ACTIONS CONNECTED TO RELIGION.

ONCE WHEN MISS V SPENT SEVERAL DAYS IN MANHATTAN I DREAMT THAT SHE WAS SERIOUSLY IN THE THRALL OF SOME INSANE RELIGIOUS SECT. IT WASN'T ENOUGH THAT SHE HAD TO HAND OVER MOST OF HER HARD EARNED MONEY, SHE HAD TO SPEND HER DAYS IN GROUP PRAYER AND MEDITATION AND HER NIGHTS IN GROUP UNPROTECTED SEX. FOR THE REST OF THE NIGHT I COULDN'T SLEEP

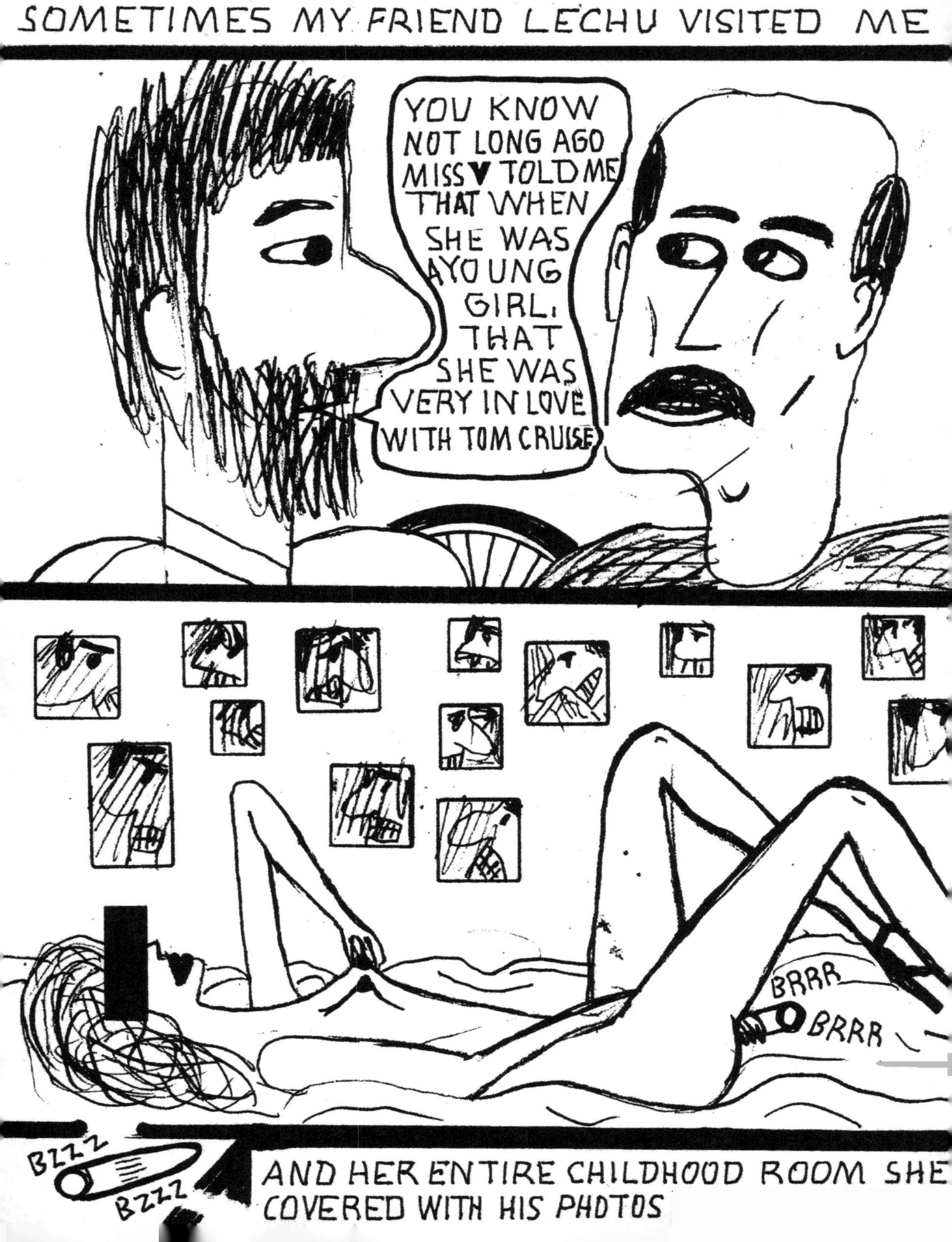
SOMETIMES MY FRIEND LECHU VISITED ME
YOU KNOW NOT LONG AGO MISS ▼ TOLD ME THAT WHEN SHE WAS A YOUNG GIRL, THAT SHE WAS VERY IN LOVE WITH TOM CRUISE
BRRR
BRRR
BZZZ
BZZZ
AND HER ENTIRE CHILDHOOD ROOM SHE COVERED WITH HIS PHOTOS

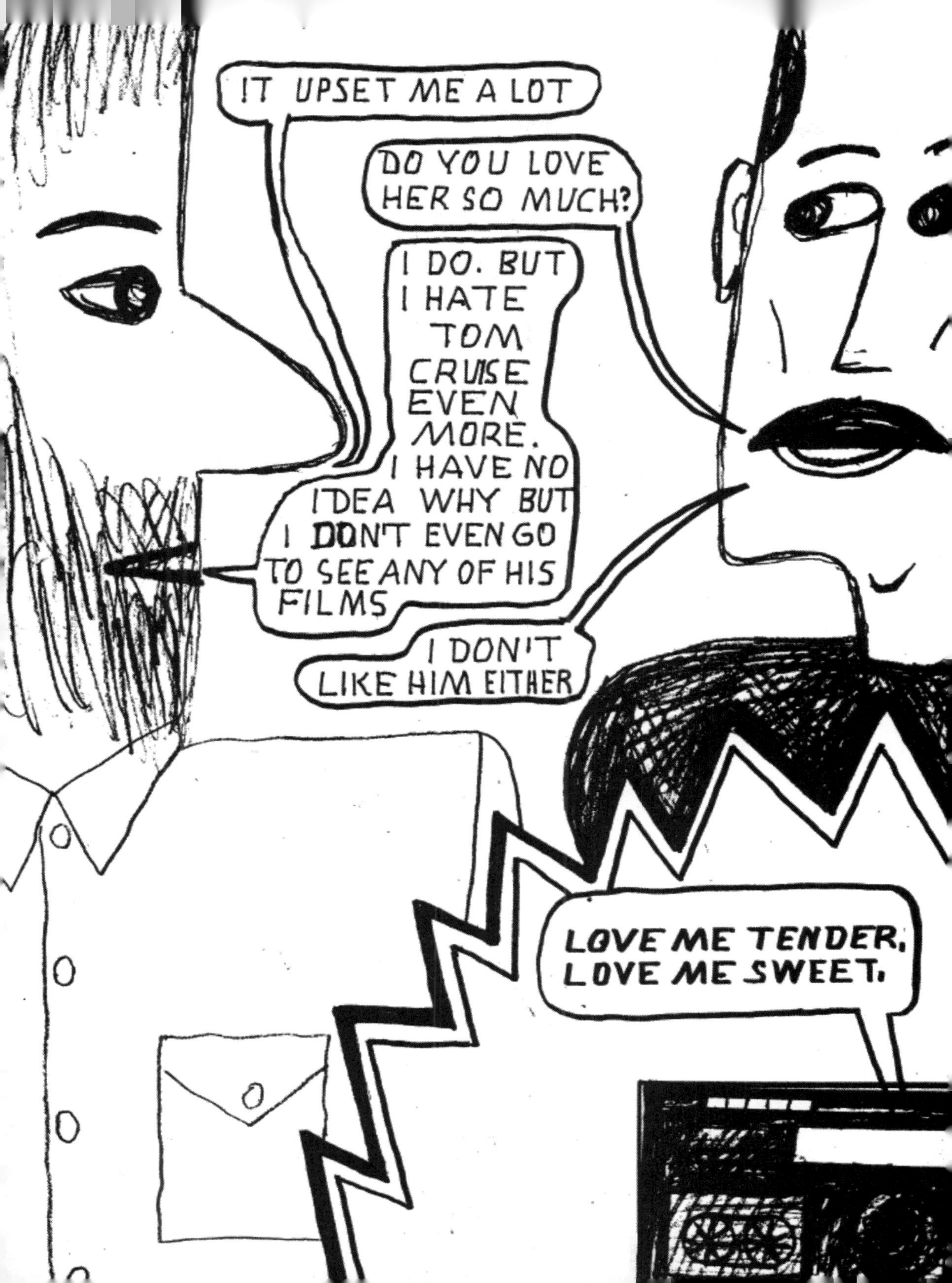
IT UPSET ME A LOT
DO YOU LOVE HER SO MUCH?
I DO. BUT I HATE TOM CRUISE EVEN MORE. I HAVE NO IDEA WHY BUT I DON'T EVEN GO TO SEE ANY OF HIS FILMS
I DON'T LIKE HIM EITHER
LOVE ME TENDER, LOVE ME SWEET.

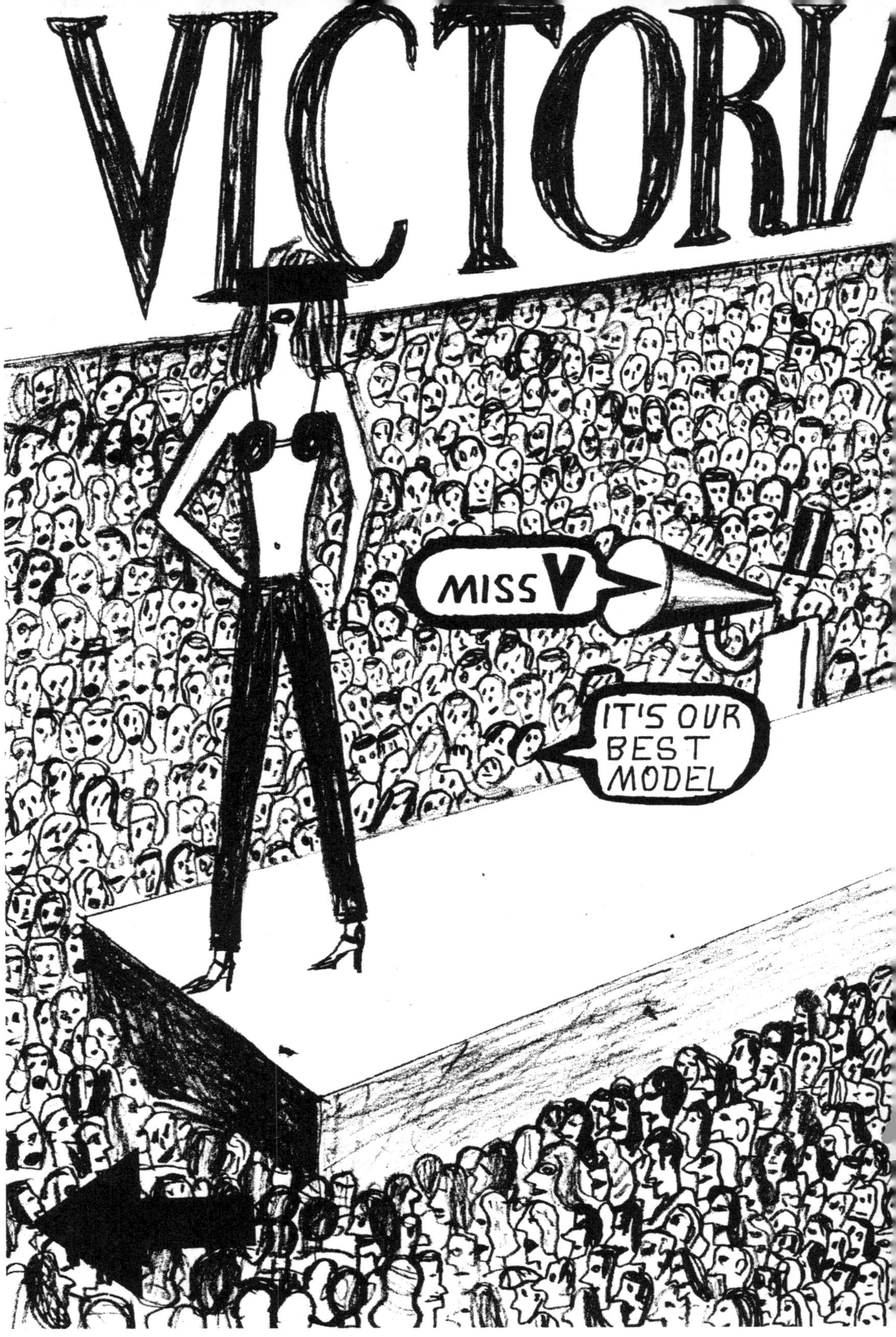
VICTORIA
MISS V
IT'S OUR BEST MODEL

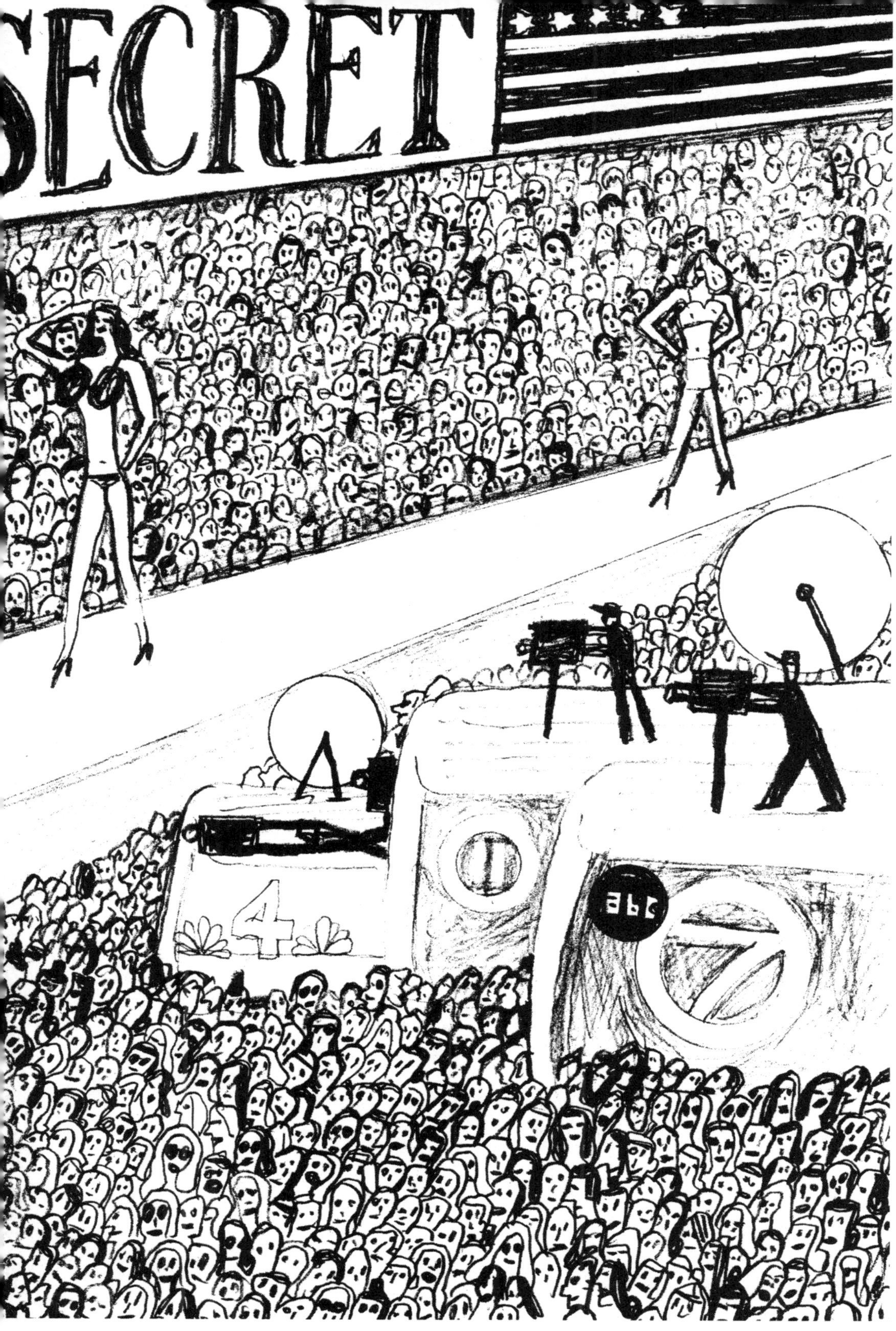
SECRET
4
abc

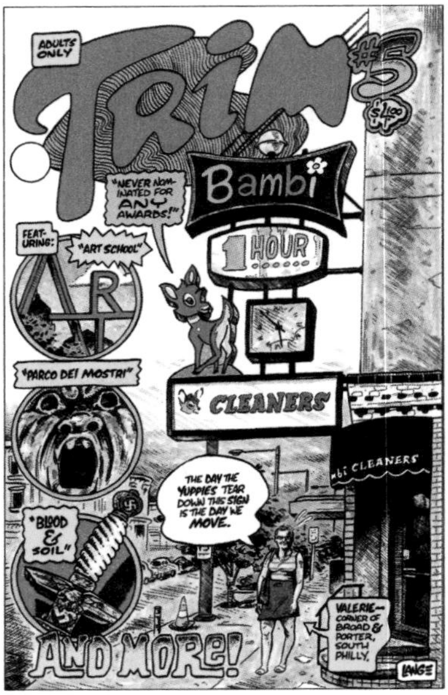
ADULTS ONLY
TRIM
#5
"NEVER NOMINATED FOR ANY AWARDS!"
Bambi
FEATURING:
"ART SCHOOL"
1 HOUR
"PARCO DEI MOSTRI"
CLEANERS
THE DAY THE YUPPIES TEAR DOWN THIS SIGN IS THE DAY WE MOVE.
"BLOOD & SOIL"
VALERIE— CORNER OF BROAD & PORTER, SOUTH PHILLY.
AND MORE!
LANGE

SELECTIONS FROM

Art School

AARON LANGE

originally published in

TRIM #5

THE COMIX COMPANY

5.5 x 8.5 inches • 36 pages

Biography

Aaron Lange is the artist and writer of the underground comix *ROMP*, *TRIM*, *CA$H GRAB!*, and other obscurities. His work has appeared in publications as diverse as *Hustler*, *Mineshaft*, *Smoke Signal*, *Cinema Sewer*, and in collaborations with Dennis Eichhorn. He lives in Cleveland with his wife, cats, and ashtrays.
thecomixcompany.ecrater.com

Statement

These Art School comix are self-contained vignettes, excerpted from a larger whole (from *TRIM* #5, published by The Comix Company). I had scripts and notes for more, but trashed them. I could have easily filled volumes on the subject. Though my time in art school was unpleasant, I have a morbid fascination with the subject and can talk endlessly about it with like-minded individuals who have suffered similarly. The bloated institution that is higher arts education is so absurd that straight reporting is in effect parody. I believe things have since changed, but when I was a student in early 2000s Midwestern America, comic book art was very much looked down upon. The older professors were frustrated and pompous abstract artists. Most had never even heard of *Juxtapoz* (which at the time was the best-selling arts publication). Craft was never discussed. Focus was on fiddle-faddle like "intent," "process," and "purpose." I would encourage younger readers to not only avoid art school, but to drop out of high school as well.

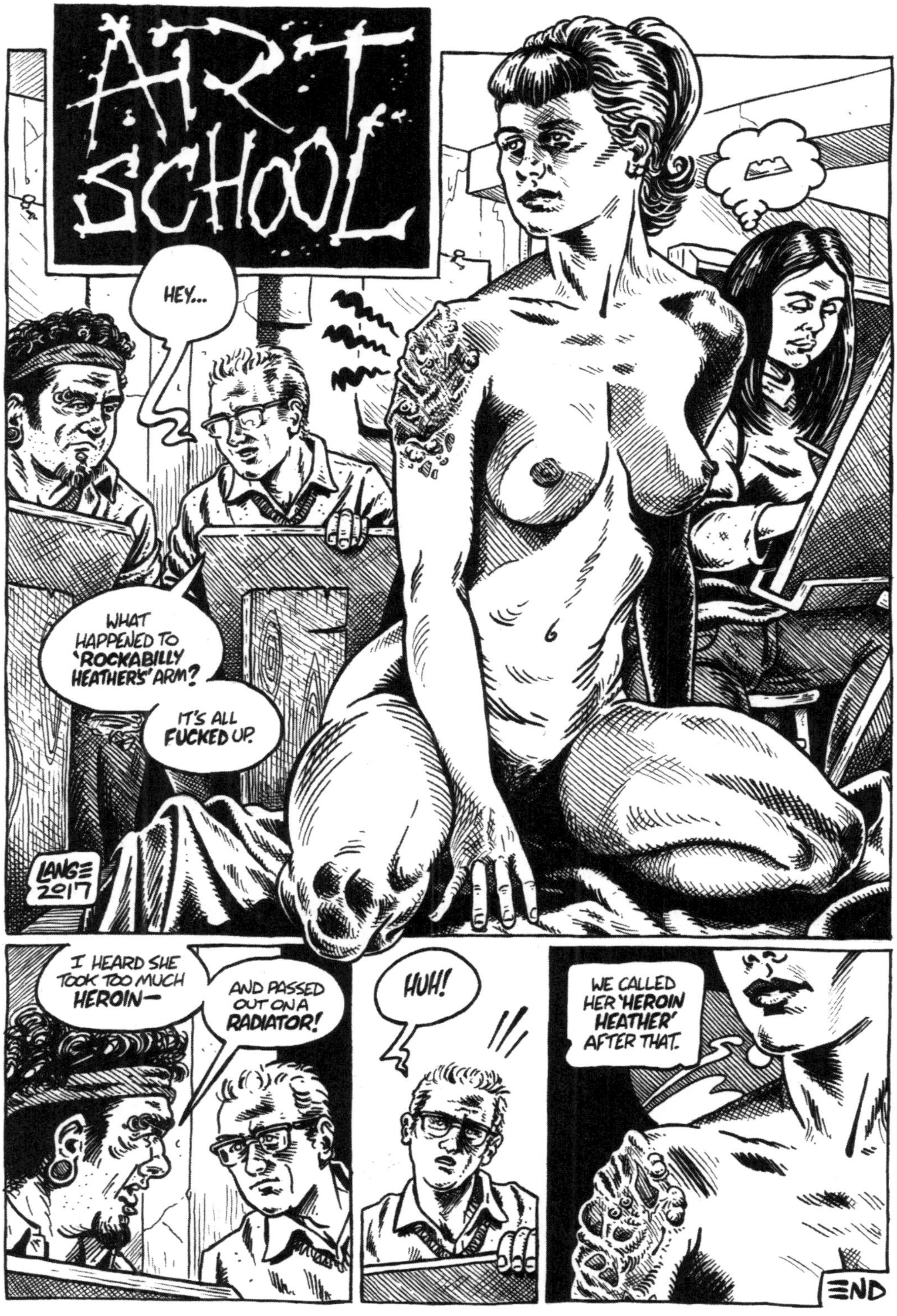
ART SCHOOL
HEY...
WHAT HAPPENED TO 'ROCKABILLY HEATHER'S' ARM?
IT'S ALL FUCKED UP.
LANGE 2017
I HEARD SHE TOOK TOO MUCH HEROIN—
AND PASSED OUT ON A RADIATOR!
HUH!
WE CALLED HER 'HEROIN HEATHER' AFTER THAT.
END

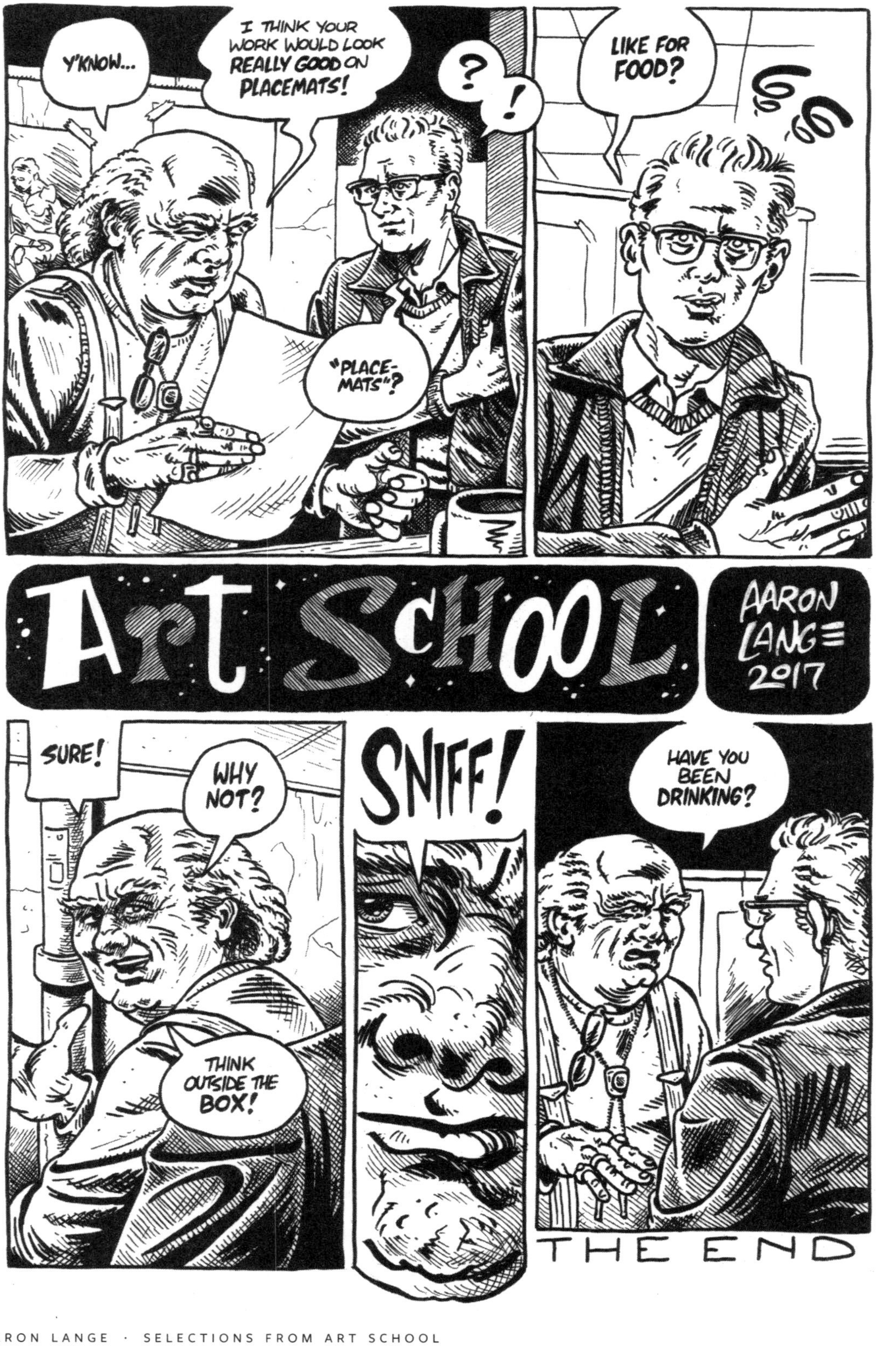
Y'KNOW...
I THINK YOUR WORK WOULD LOOK REALLY GOOD ON PLACEMATS!
?
!
"PLACE-MATS"?
LIKE FOR FOOD?
ART SCHOOL
AARON LANGE 2017
SURE!
WHY NOT?
THINK OUTSIDE THE BOX!
SNIFF!
HAVE YOU BEEN DRINKING?
THE END

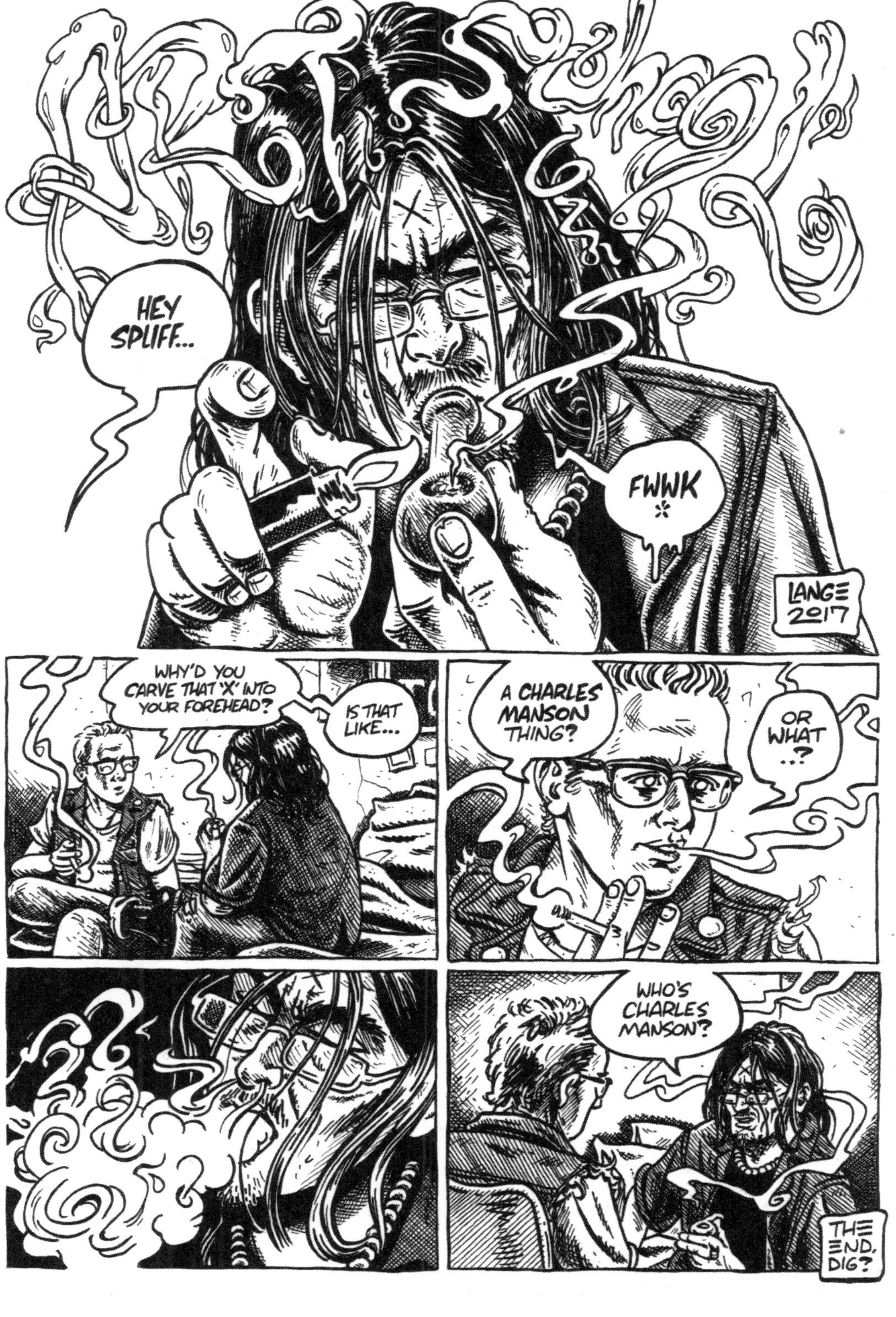
HEY SPLIFF...
FWWK
LANGE 2017
WHY'D YOU CARVE THAT 'X' INTO YOUR FOREHEAD?
IS THAT LIKE...
A CHARLES MANSON THING?
OR WHAT ..?
WHO'S CHARLES MANSON?
THE END, DIG?

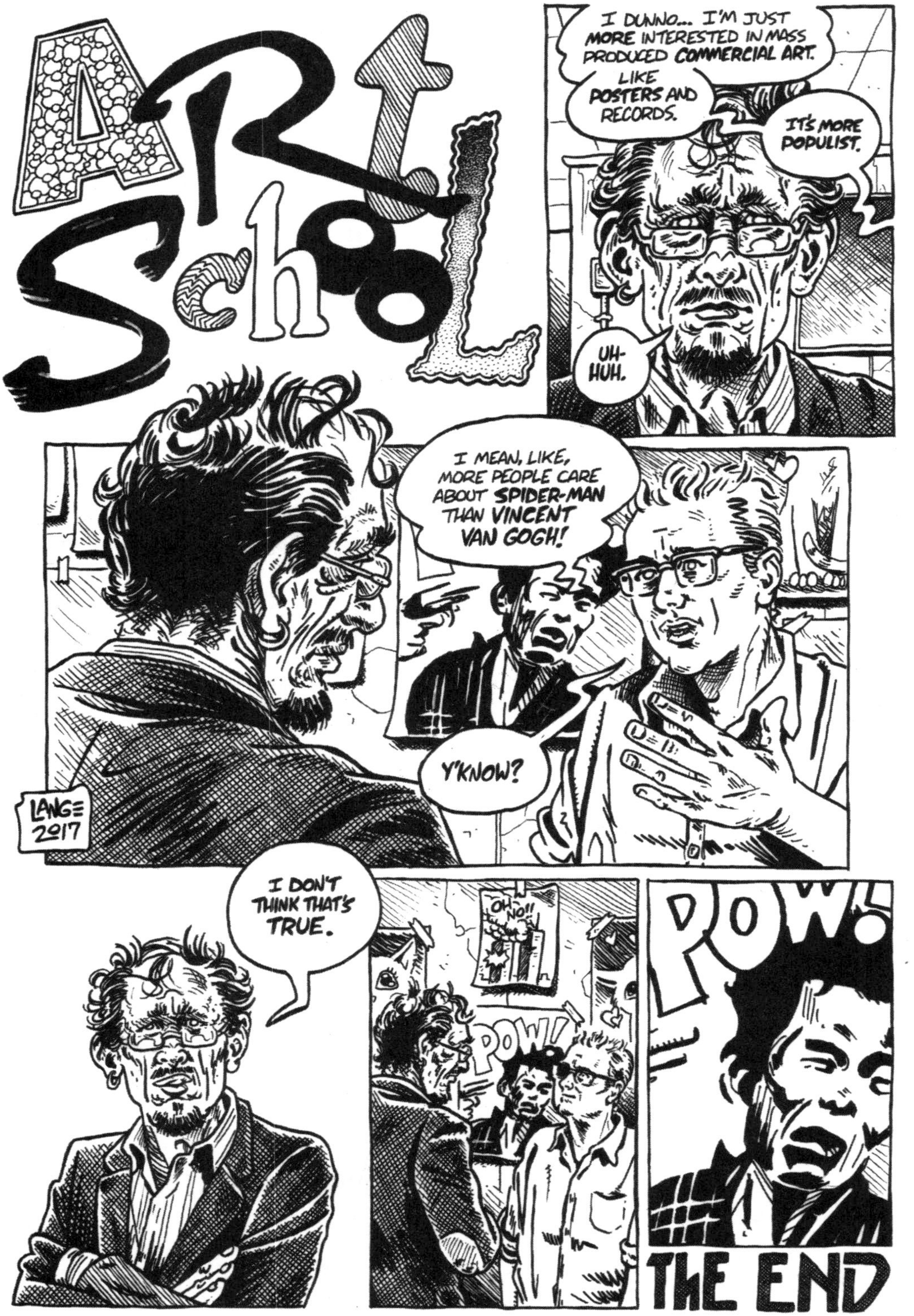

ART SCHOOL
I DUNNO... I'M JUST MORE INTERESTED IN MASS PRODUCED COMMERCIAL ART.
LIKE POSTERS AND RECORDS.
IT'S MORE POPULIST.
UH-HUH.
I MEAN, LIKE, MORE PEOPLE CARE ABOUT SPIDER-MAN THAN VINCENT VAN GOGH!
Y'KNOW?
LANGE 2017
I DON'T THINK THAT'S TRUE.
OH NO!!
POW!
POW!
THE END

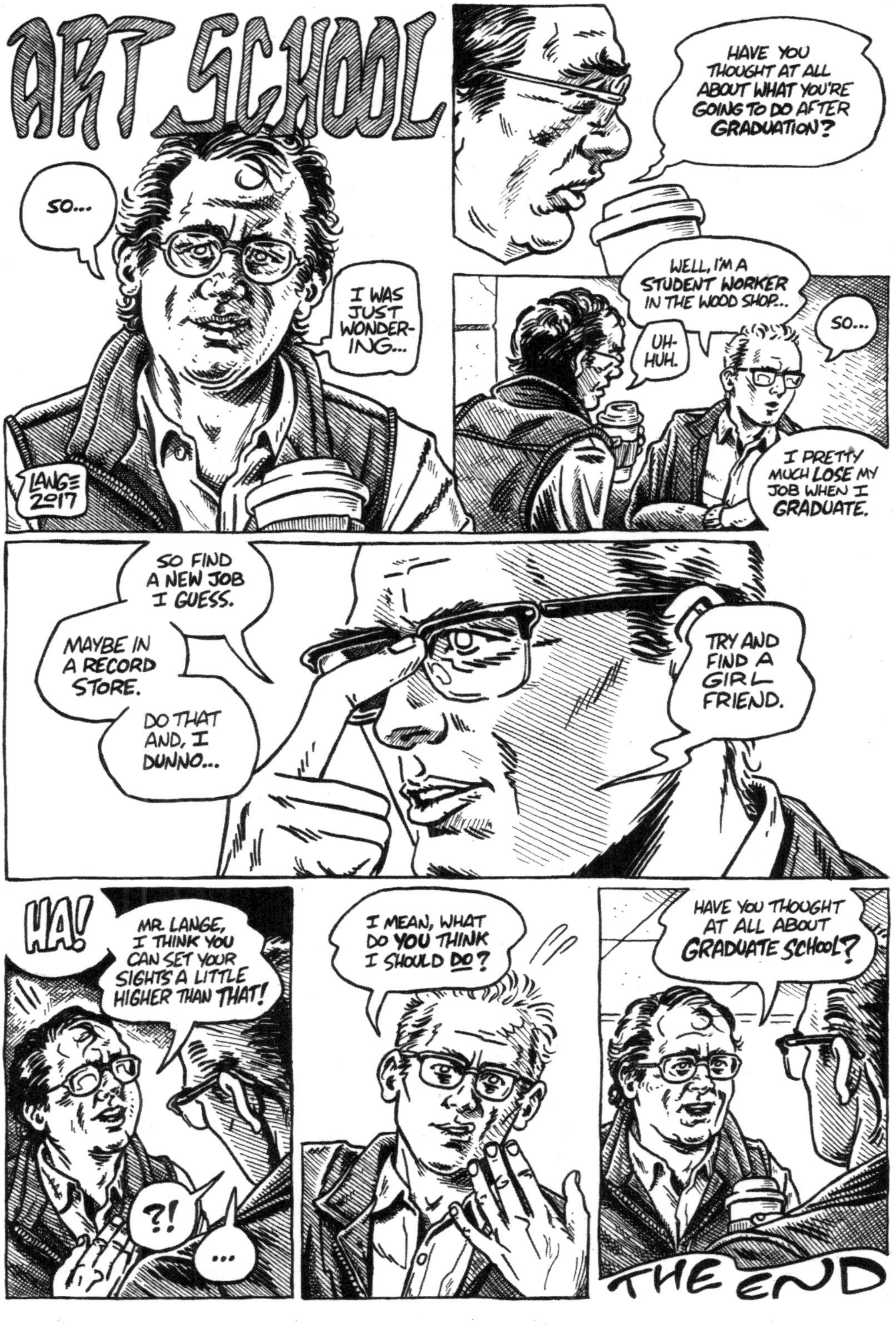
ART SCHOOL
SO...
I WAS JUST WONDERING...
LANGE 2017
HAVE YOU THOUGHT AT ALL ABOUT WHAT YOU'RE GOING TO DO AFTER GRADUATION?
WELL, I'M A STUDENT WORKER IN THE WOOD SHOP...
UH-HUH.
SO...
I PRETTY MUCH LOSE MY JOB WHEN I GRADUATE.
SO FIND A NEW JOB I GUESS.
MAYBE IN A RECORD STORE.
DO THAT AND, I DUNNO...
TRY AND FIND A GIRL FRIEND.
HA!
MR. LANGE, I THINK YOU CAN SET YOUR SIGHTS A LITTLE HIGHER THAN THAT!
?!
...
I MEAN, WHAT DO YOU THINK I SHOULD DO?
HAVE YOU THOUGHT AT ALL ABOUT GRADUATE SCHOOL?
THE END

Seabrook of Arabia (*Excerpt*)

JOE OLLMANN

the Abominable Mr. Seabrook
JOE OLLMANN

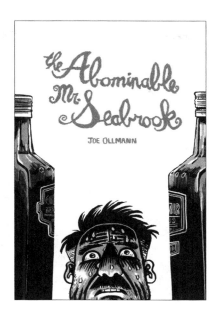

originally published in

The Abominable Mr. Seabrook

DRAWN AND QUARTERLY

6 x 9 inches • 316 pages

Biography

Joe Ollmann is a fairly old cartoonist. He is the author of seven graphic novels, one of which won a Doug Wright Award—a big deal to a few cartoonists in Canada—but then lost that same award many times with other books. Currently working on a graphic novel about a fictional beloved cartoonist.

wagpress.net

Statement

This excerpt from my version of the life story of the American travel writer and amateur explorer William Seabrook takes place in the Middle East in 1925. Seabrook lived in the area around Iraq, Syria, and Jordan with a group of Bedouin who were still nomadic and living a traditional lifestyle. He wrote with great regard for the Arab people and the Muslim faith in his book *Adventures in Arabia*. (Just for context, the seemingly random bondage scene near the end of this excerpt is part of a longer explanation of Seabrook's lifelong obsession with bondage.)

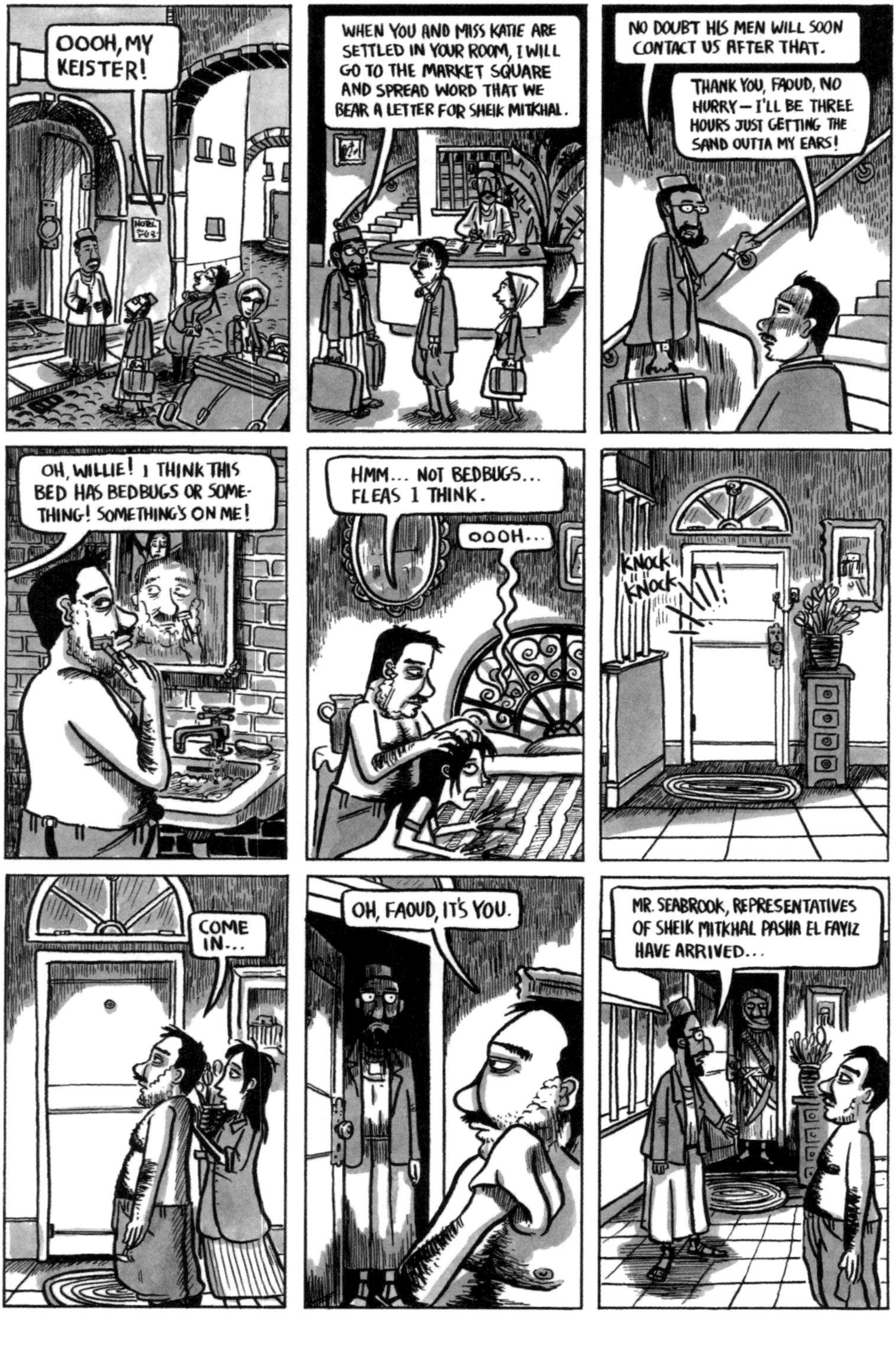
OOOH, MY KEISTER!
WHEN YOU AND MISS KATIE ARE SETTLED IN YOUR ROOM, I WILL GO TO THE MARKET SQUARE AND SPREAD WORD THAT WE BEAR A LETTER FOR SHEIK MITKHAL.
NO DOUBT HIS MEN WILL SOON CONTACT US AFTER THAT.
THANK YOU, FAOUD, NO HURRY — I'LL BE THREE HOURS JUST GETTING THE SAND OUTTA MY EARS!
OH, WILLIE! I THINK THIS BED HAS BEDBUGS OR SOMETHING! SOMETHING'S ON ME!
HMM... NOT BEDBUGS... FLEAS I THINK.
OOOH...
KNOCK KNOCK
COME IN...
OH, FAOUD, IT'S YOU.
MR. SEABROOK, REPRESENTATIVES OF SHEIK MITKHAL PASHA EL FAYIZ HAVE ARRIVED...

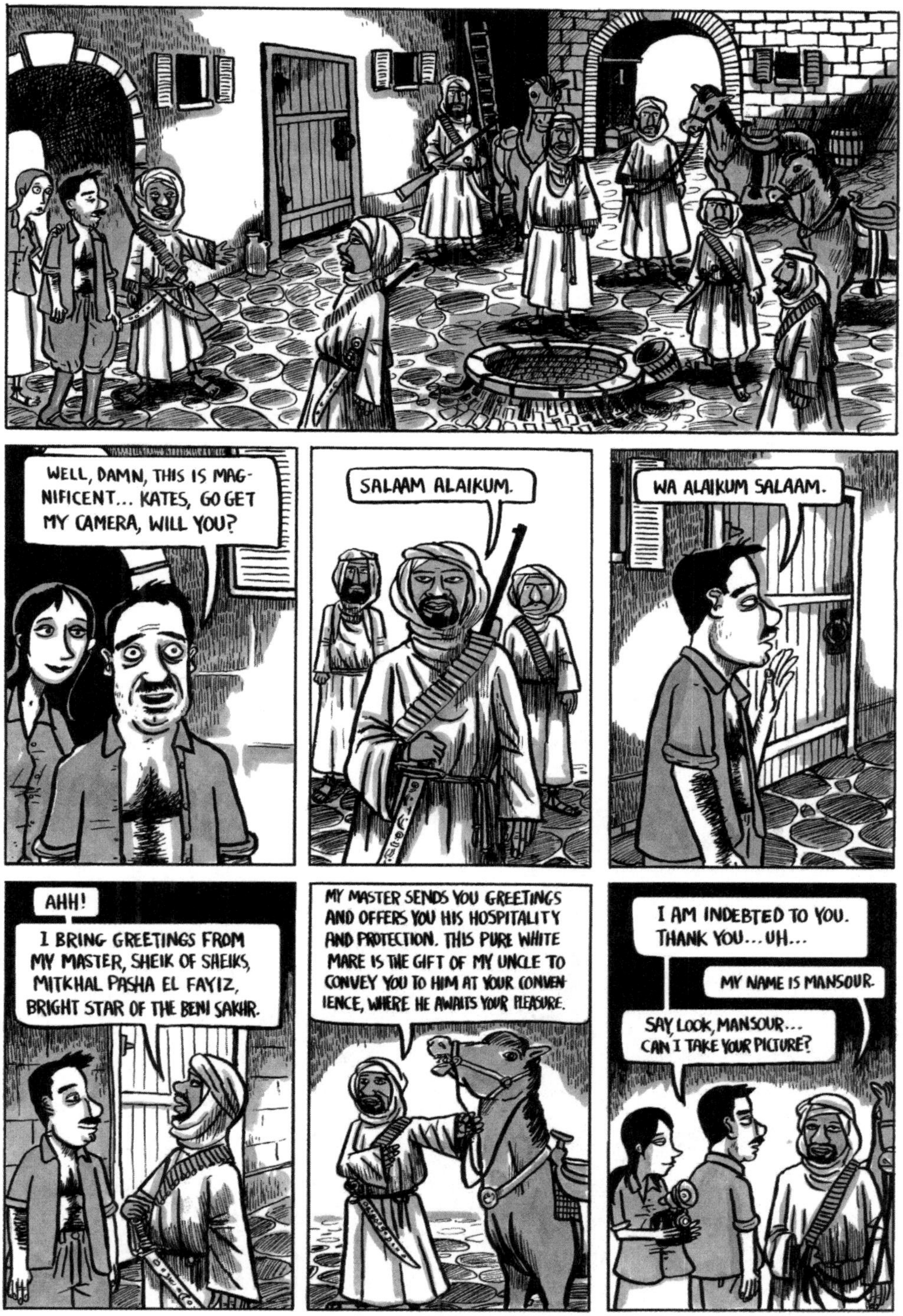
WELL, DAMN, THIS IS MAGNIFICENT... KATES, GO GET MY CAMERA, WILL YOU?
SALAAM ALAIKUM.
WA ALAIKUM SALAAM.
AHH!
I BRING GREETINGS FROM MY MASTER, SHEIK OF SHEIKS, MITKHAL PASHA EL FAYIZ, BRIGHT STAR OF THE BENI SAKHR.
MY MASTER SENDS YOU GREETINGS AND OFFERS YOU HIS HOSPITALITY AND PROTECTION. THIS PURE WHITE MARE IS THE GIFT OF MY UNCLE TO CONVEY YOU TO HIM AT YOUR CONVENIENCE, WHERE HE AWAITS YOUR PLEASURE.
I AM INDEBTED TO YOU. THANK YOU... UH...
MY NAME IS MANSOUR.
SAY, LOOK, MANSOUR... CAN I TAKE YOUR PICTURE?

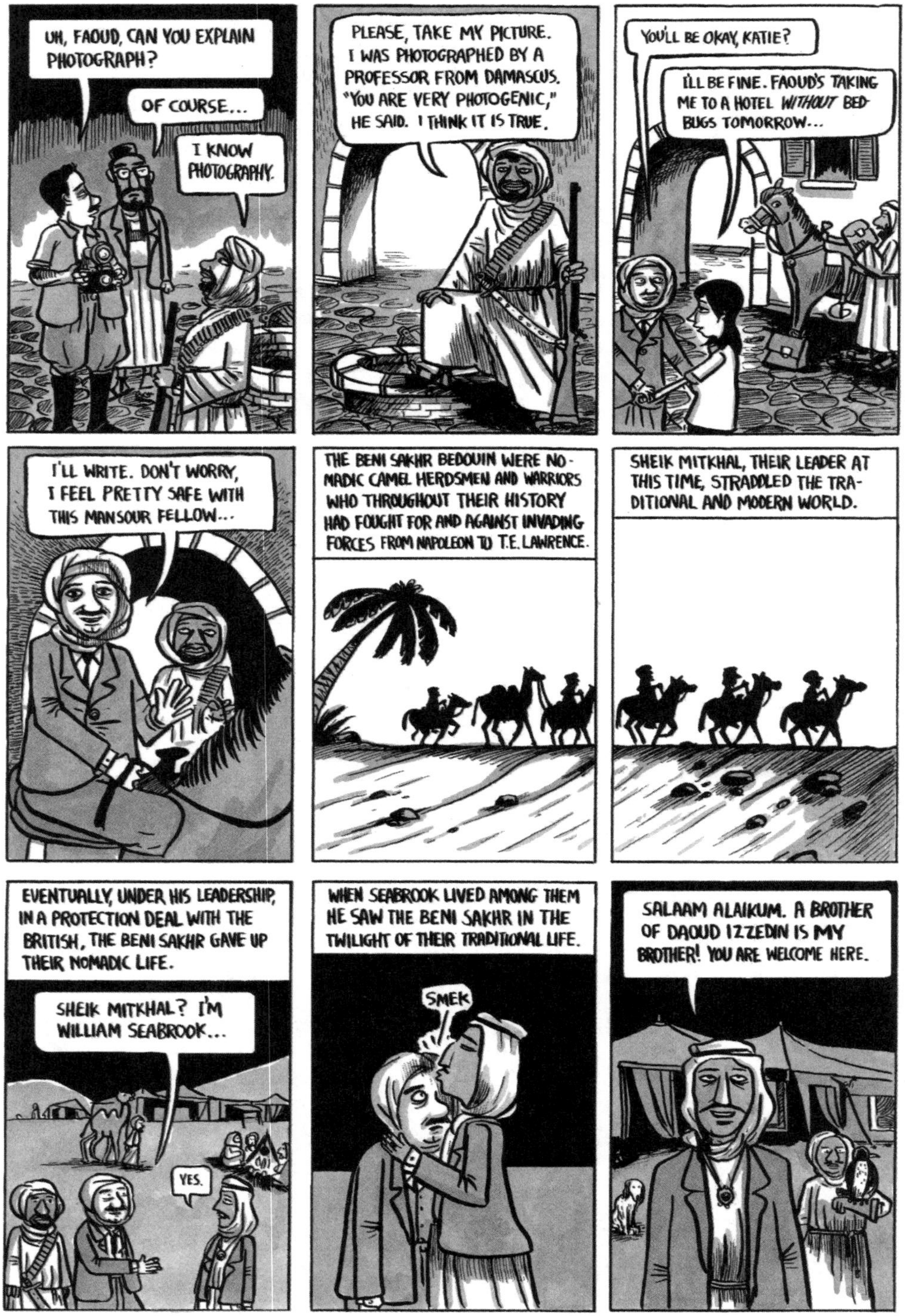
UH, FAOUD, CAN YOU EXPLAIN PHOTOGRAPH?
OF COURSE...
I KNOW PHOTOGRAPHY.
PLEASE, TAKE MY PICTURE. I WAS PHOTOGRAPHED BY A PROFESSOR FROM DAMASCUS. "YOU ARE VERY PHOTOGENIC," HE SAID. I THINK IT IS TRUE.
YOU'LL BE OKAY, KATIE?
I'LL BE FINE. FAOUD'S TAKING ME TO A HOTEL *WITHOUT* BED-BUGS TOMORROW...
I'LL WRITE. DON'T WORRY, I FEEL PRETTY SAFE WITH THIS MANSOUR FELLOW...
THE BENI SAKHR BEDOUIN WERE NOMADIC CAMEL HERDSMEN AND WARRIORS WHO THROUGHOUT THEIR HISTORY HAD FOUGHT FOR AND AGAINST INVADING FORCES FROM NAPOLEON TO T.E. LAWRENCE.
SHEIK MITKHAL, THEIR LEADER AT THIS TIME, STRADDLED THE TRADITIONAL AND MODERN WORLD.
EVENTUALLY, UNDER HIS LEADERSHIP, IN A PROTECTION DEAL WITH THE BRITISH, THE BENI SAKHR GAVE UP THEIR NOMADIC LIFE.
SHEIK MITKHAL? I'M WILLIAM SEABROOK...
YES.
WHEN SEABROOK LIVED AMONG THEM HE SAW THE BENI SAKHR IN THE TWILIGHT OF THEIR TRADITIONAL LIFE.
SMEK
SALAAM ALAIKUM. A BROTHER OF DAOUD IZZEDIN IS MY BROTHER! YOU ARE WELCOME HERE.

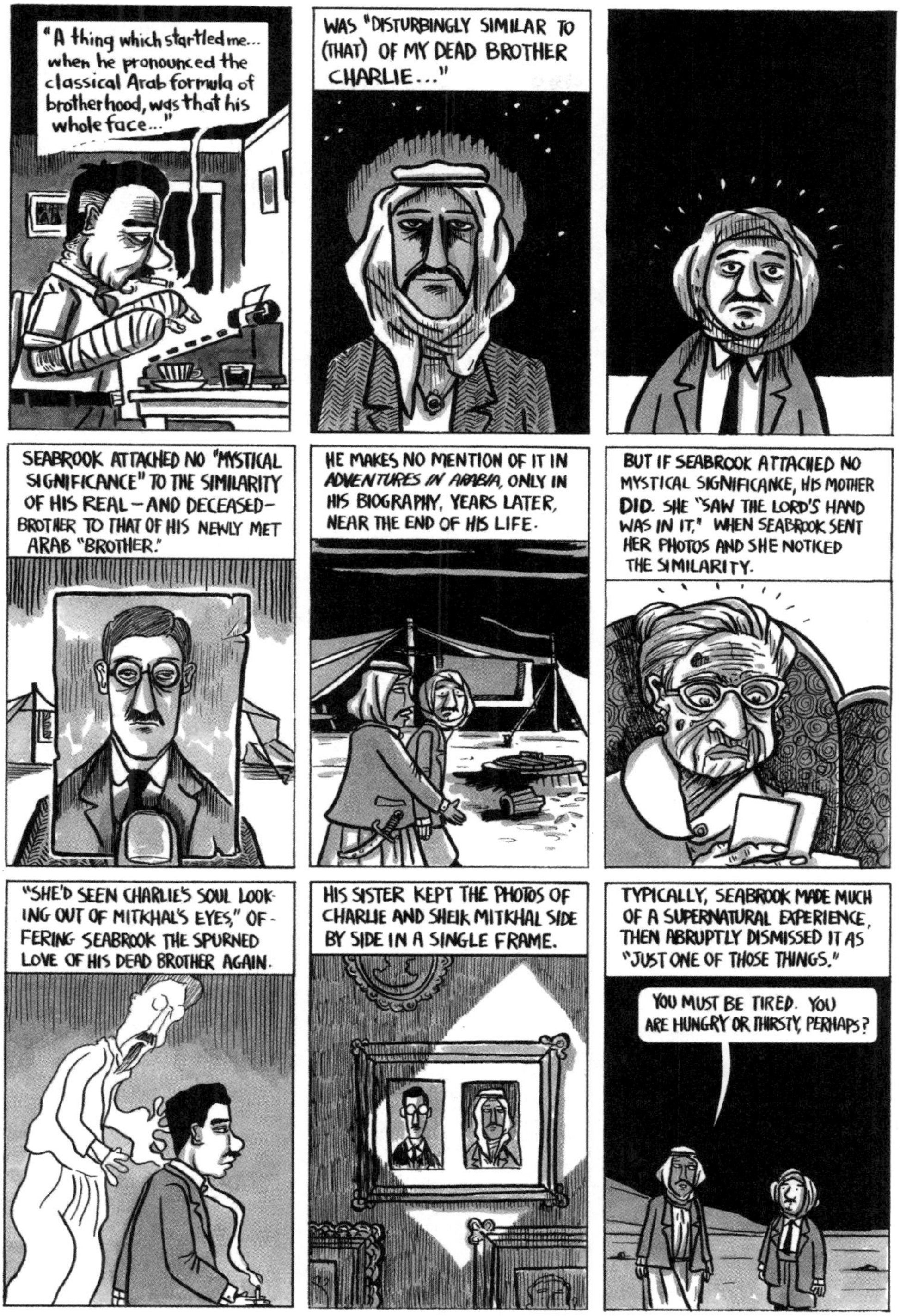
"A thing which startled me... when he pronounced the classical Arab formula of brotherhood, was that his whole face..."
WAS "DISTURBINGLY SIMILAR TO (THAT) OF MY DEAD BROTHER CHARLIE..."
SEABROOK ATTACHED NO "MYSTICAL SIGNIFICANCE" TO THE SIMILARITY OF HIS REAL—AND DECEASED—BROTHER TO THAT OF HIS NEWLY MET ARAB "BROTHER."
HE MAKES NO MENTION OF IT IN ADVENTURES IN ARABIA, ONLY IN HIS BIOGRAPHY, YEARS LATER, NEAR THE END OF HIS LIFE.
BUT IF SEABROOK ATTACHED NO MYSTICAL SIGNIFICANCE, HIS MOTHER DID. SHE "SAW THE LORD'S HAND WAS IN IT," WHEN SEABROOK SENT HER PHOTOS AND SHE NOTICED THE SIMILARITY.
"SHE'D SEEN CHARLIE'S SOUL LOOKING OUT OF MITKHAL'S EYES," OFFERING SEABROOK THE SPURNED LOVE OF HIS DEAD BROTHER AGAIN.
HIS SISTER KEPT THE PHOTOS OF CHARLIE AND SHEIK MITKHAL SIDE BY SIDE IN A SINGLE FRAME.
TYPICALLY, SEABROOK MADE MUCH OF A SUPERNATURAL EXPERIENCE, THEN ABRUPTLY DISMISSED IT AS "JUST ONE OF THOSE THINGS."
YOU MUST BE TIRED. YOU ARE HUNGRY OR THIRSTY, PERHAPS?

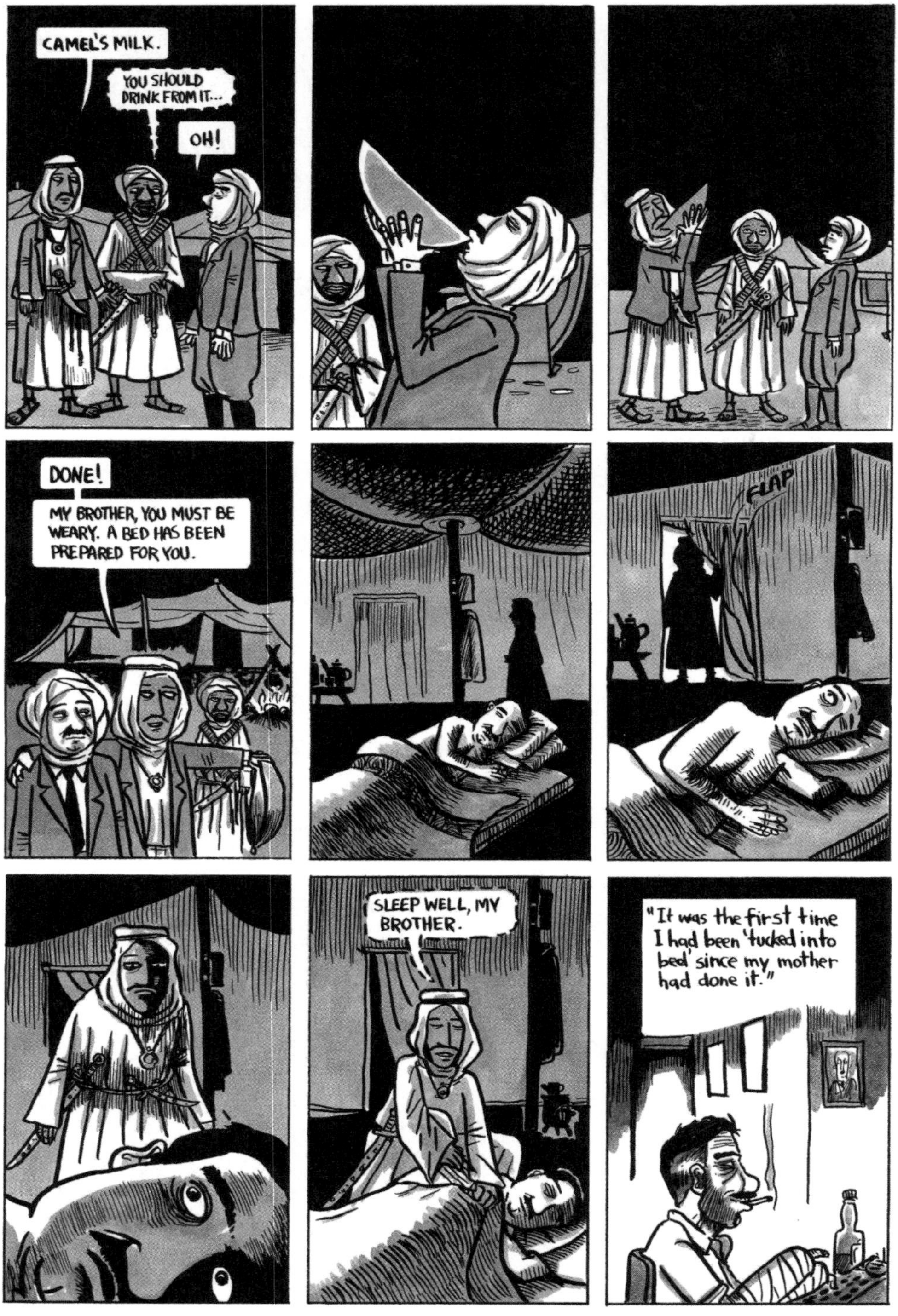
CAMEL'S MILK.
YOU SHOULD DRINK FROM IT...
OH!
DONE!
MY BROTHER, YOU MUST BE WEARY. A BED HAS BEEN PREPARED FOR YOU.
FLAP
SLEEP WELL, MY BROTHER.
"It was the first time I had been 'tucked into bed' since my mother had done it."

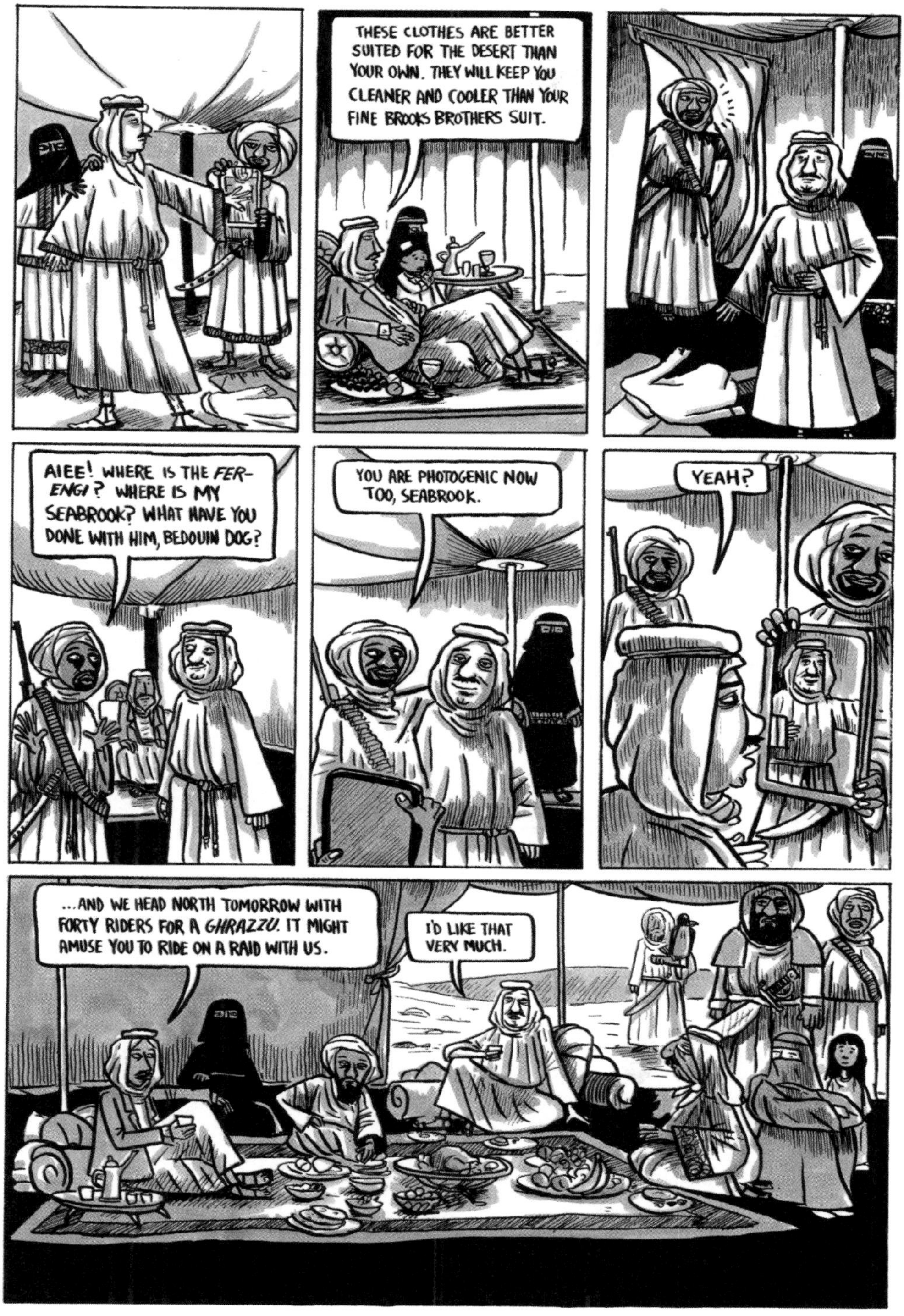

THESE CLOTHES ARE BETTER SUITED FOR THE DESERT THAN YOUR OWN. THEY WILL KEEP YOU CLEANER AND COOLER THAN YOUR FINE BROOKS BROTHERS SUIT.
AIEE! WHERE IS THE *FERENGI*? WHERE IS MY SEABROOK? WHAT HAVE YOU DONE WITH HIM, BEDOUIN DOG?
YOU ARE PHOTOGENIC NOW TOO, SEABROOK.
YEAH?
...AND WE HEAD NORTH TOMORROW WITH FORTY RIDERS FOR A *GHRAZZU*. IT MIGHT AMUSE YOU TO RIDE ON A RAID WITH US.
I'D LIKE THAT VERY MUCH.

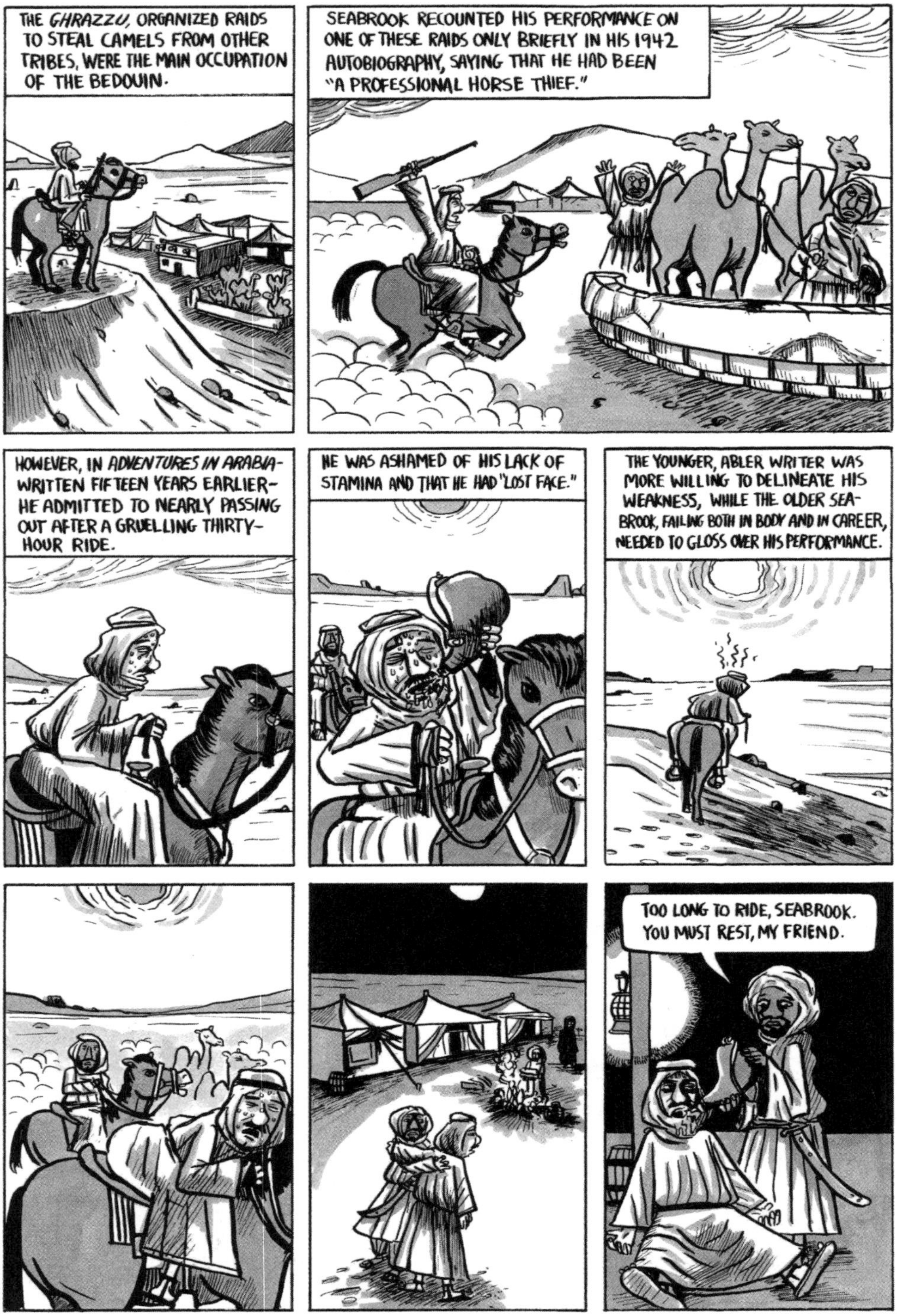
THE *GHRAZZU*, ORGANIZED RAIDS TO STEAL CAMELS FROM OTHER TRIBES, WERE THE MAIN OCCUPATION OF THE BEDOUIN.
SEABROOK RECOUNTED HIS PERFORMANCE ON ONE OF THESE RAIDS ONLY BRIEFLY IN HIS 1942 AUTOBIOGRAPHY, SAYING THAT HE HAD BEEN "A PROFESSIONAL HORSE THIEF."
HOWEVER, IN *ADVENTURES IN ARABIA*- WRITTEN FIFTEEN YEARS EARLIER- HE ADMITTED TO NEARLY PASSING OUT AFTER A GRUELLING THIRTY-HOUR RIDE.
HE WAS ASHAMED OF HIS LACK OF STAMINA AND THAT HE HAD "LOST FACE."
THE YOUNGER, ABLER WRITER WAS MORE WILLING TO DELINEATE HIS WEAKNESS, WHILE THE OLDER SEA-BROOK, FAILING BOTH IN BODY AND IN CAREER, NEEDED TO GLOSS OVER HIS PERFORMANCE.
TOO LONG TO RIDE, SEABROOK. YOU MUST REST, MY FRIEND.

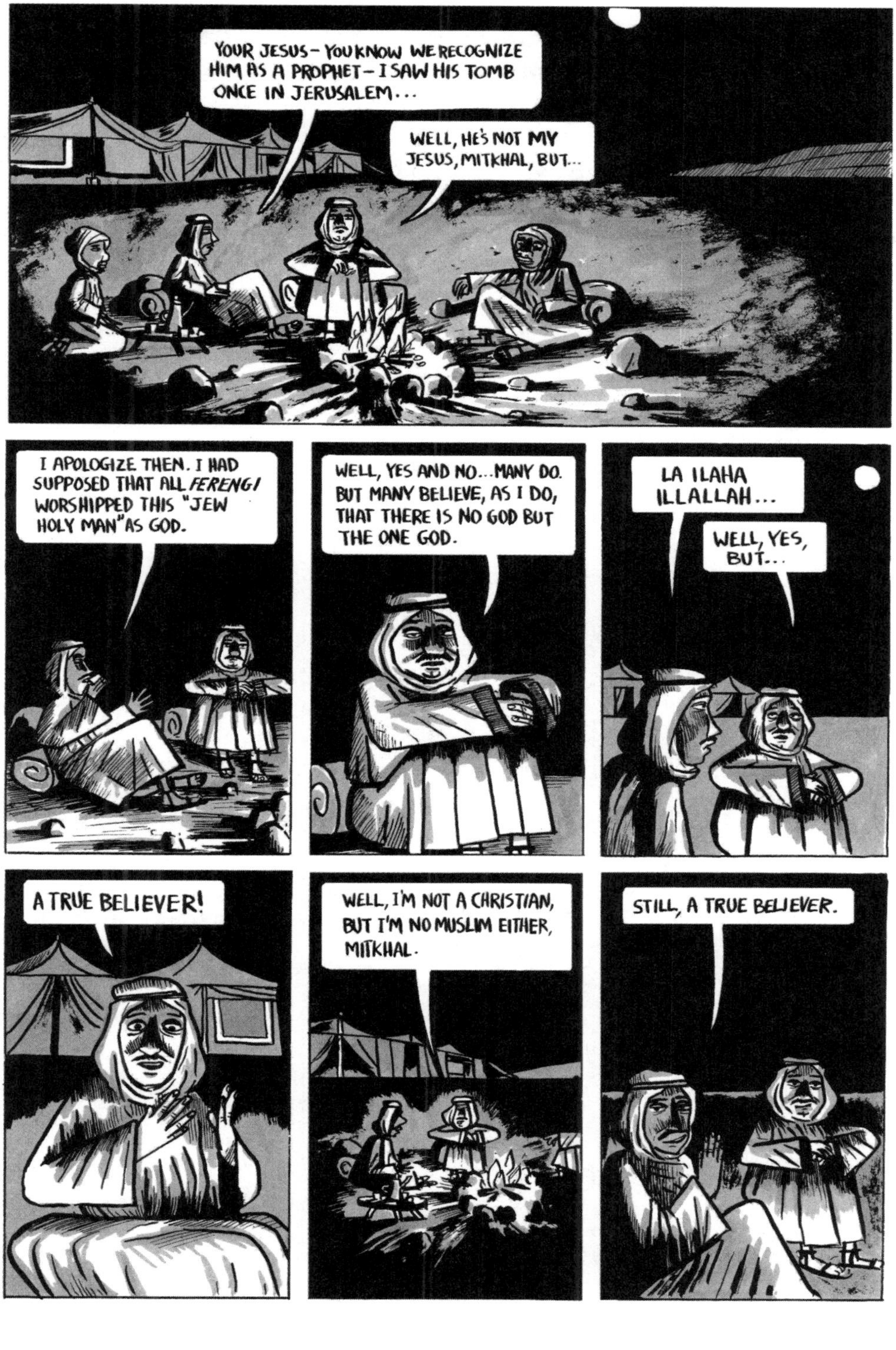
YOUR JESUS - YOU KNOW WE RECOGNIZE HIM AS A PROPHET - I SAW HIS TOMB ONCE IN JERUSALEM...
WELL, HE'S NOT MY JESUS, MITKHAL, BUT...
I APOLOGIZE THEN. I HAD SUPPOSED THAT ALL *FERENGI* WORSHIPPED THIS "JEW HOLY MAN" AS GOD.
WELL, YES AND NO... MANY DO. BUT MANY BELIEVE, AS I DO, THAT THERE IS NO GOD BUT THE ONE GOD.
LA ILAHA ILLALLAH...
WELL, YES, BUT...
A TRUE BELIEVER!
WELL, I'M NOT A CHRISTIAN, BUT I'M NO MUSLIM EITHER, MITKHAL.
STILL, A TRUE BELIEVER.

SEABROOK WAS EVENTUALLY INVITED TO STAY ON AND LIVE AS ONE OF THE BEDOUIN. SHEIK MITKHAL EVEN WANTED HIM TO MARRY HIS NIECE.

HE WAS AT HOME HERE – HIS PREDILECTION FOR BONDAGE WAS ACCEPTED BY THE MEN AND TOLERATED BY THE OULED NAÏL WOMEN. HIS "SUPREME WANT" WAS FULFILLED HERE.

HE LIKED ALL ASPECTS OF BEDOUIN LIFE AND HE SERIOUSLY CONSIDERED STAYING, BUT IN THE END, SEABROOK SHOWED THAT HE WOULD RUN AWAY EVEN FROM A SITUATION THAT HE FOUND AGREEABLE.

SEABROOK, I WANT YOU TO HAVE THIS.

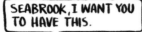

IT PLEASES YOU? YOU HAD ADMIRED IT...

IT'S BEAUTIFUL, OF COURSE, BUT MITKHAL, IT'S TOO MUCH... GOLD... THIS MUST BE WORTH...

IT'S NOTHING!

OH, MITKHAL, MY BROTHER, YOU KNOW I'M HONOURED BY THIS, BUT I WOULD REALLY PREFER THE WOODEN BOWL WE FIRST SHARED CAMEL MILK FROM.

ARE YOU SURE YOU WON'T STAY? I'M CONVINCED YOU ARE NO FERENGI, BUT A BEDOUIN.

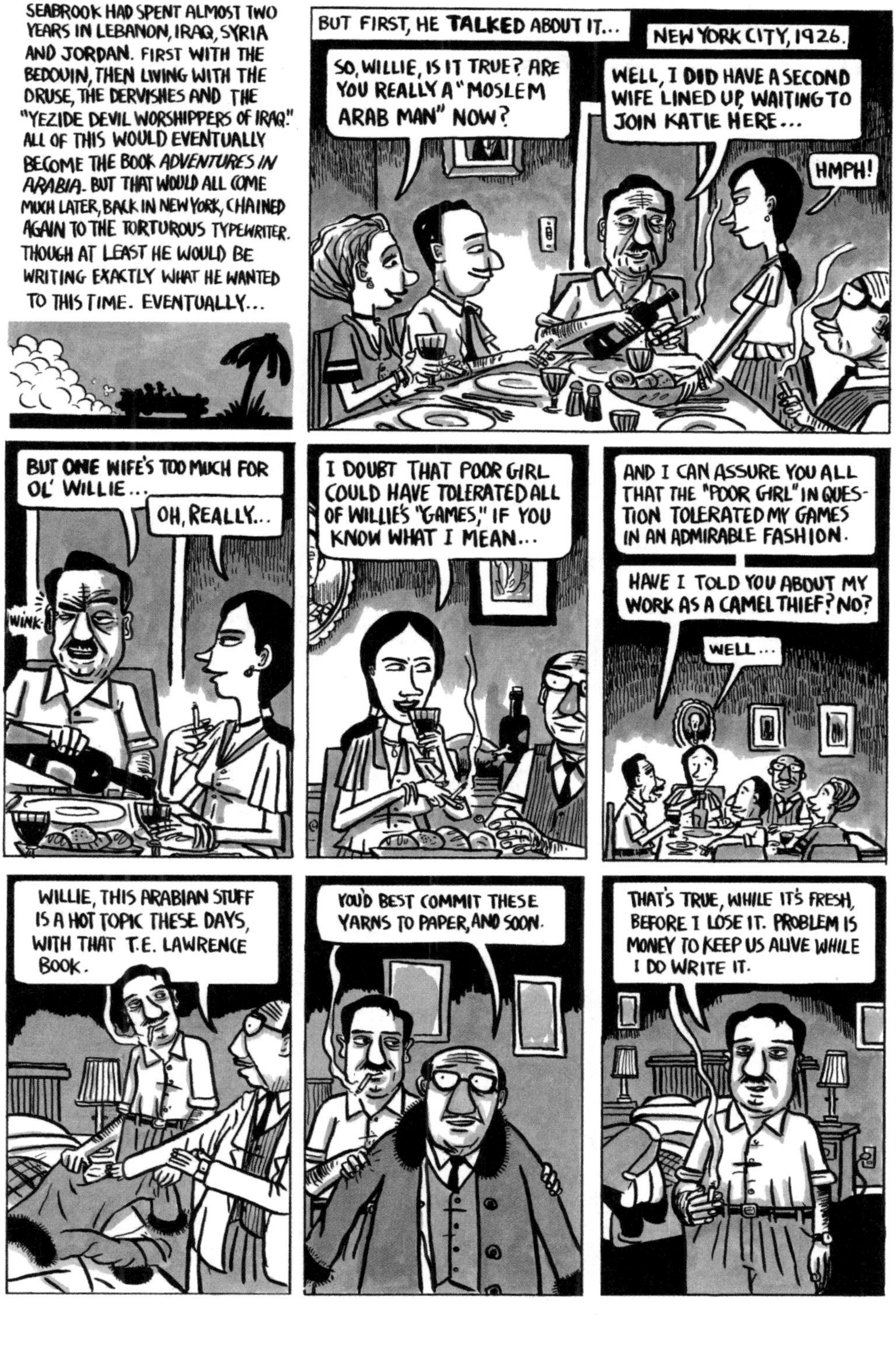
SEABROOK HAD SPENT ALMOST TWO YEARS IN LEBANON, IRAQ, SYRIA AND JORDAN. FIRST WITH THE BEDOUIN, THEN LIVING WITH THE DRUSE, THE DERVISHES AND THE "YEZIDE DEVIL WORSHIPPERS OF IRAQ." ALL OF THIS WOULD EVENTUALLY BECOME THE BOOK *ADVENTURES IN ARABIA*. BUT THAT WOULD ALL COME MUCH LATER, BACK IN NEW YORK, CHAINED AGAIN TO THE TORTUROUS TYPEWRITER. THOUGH AT LEAST HE WOULD BE WRITING EXACTLY WHAT HE WANTED TO THIS TIME. EVENTUALLY...
BUT FIRST, HE **TALKED** ABOUT IT...
NEW YORK CITY, 1926.
SO, WILLIE, IS IT TRUE? ARE YOU REALLY A "MOSLEM ARAB MAN" NOW?
WELL, I **DID** HAVE A SECOND WIFE LINED UP, WAITING TO JOIN KATIE HERE...
HMPH!
BUT **ONE** WIFE'S TOO MUCH FOR OL' WILLIE...
OH, REALLY...
WINK
I DOUBT THAT POOR GIRL COULD HAVE TOLERATED ALL OF WILLIE'S "GAMES," IF YOU KNOW WHAT I MEAN...
AND I CAN ASSURE YOU ALL THAT THE "POOR GIRL" IN QUESTION TOLERATED MY GAMES IN AN ADMIRABLE FASHION.
HAVE I TOLD YOU ABOUT MY WORK AS A CAMEL THIEF? NO?
WELL...
WILLIE, THIS ARABIAN STUFF IS A HOT TOPIC THESE DAYS, WITH THAT T.E. LAWRENCE BOOK.
YOU'D BEST COMMIT THESE YARNS TO PAPER, AND SOON.
THAT'S TRUE, WHILE IT'S FRESH, BEFORE I LOSE IT. PROBLEM IS MONEY TO KEEP US ALIVE WHILE I DO WRITE IT.

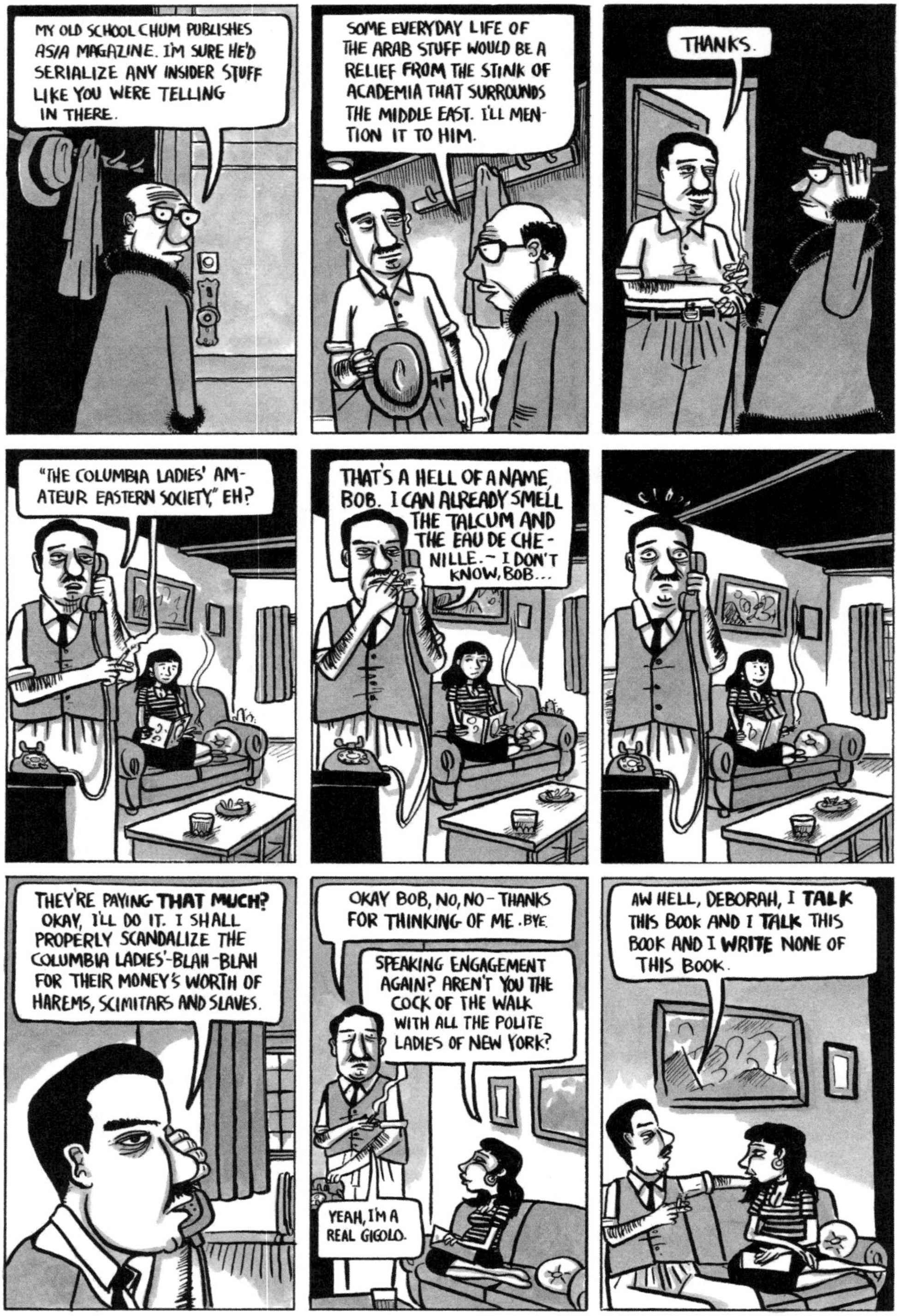
MY OLD SCHOOL CHUM PUBLISHES ASIA MAGAZINE. I'M SURE HE'D SERIALIZE ANY INSIDER STUFF LIKE YOU WERE TELLING IN THERE.
SOME EVERYDAY LIFE OF THE ARAB STUFF WOULD BE A RELIEF FROM THE STINK OF ACADEMIA THAT SURROUNDS THE MIDDLE EAST. I'LL MENTION IT TO HIM.
THANKS.
"THE COLUMBIA LADIES' AMATEUR EASTERN SOCIETY," EH?
THAT'S A HELL OF A NAME, BOB. I CAN ALREADY SMELL THE TALCUM AND THE EAU DE CHENILLE.– I DON'T KNOW, BOB...
THEY'RE PAYING THAT MUCH? OKAY, I'LL DO IT. I SHALL PROPERLY SCANDALIZE THE COLUMBIA LADIES'-BLAH-BLAH FOR THEIR MONEY'S WORTH OF HAREMS, SCIMITARS AND SLAVES.
OKAY BOB, NO, NO– THANKS FOR THINKING OF ME. BYE.
SPEAKING ENGAGEMENT AGAIN? AREN'T YOU THE COCK OF THE WALK WITH ALL THE POLITE LADIES OF NEW YORK?
YEAH, I'M A REAL GIGOLO.
AW HELL, DEBORAH, I TALK THIS BOOK AND I TALK THIS BOOK AND I WRITE NONE OF THIS BOOK.

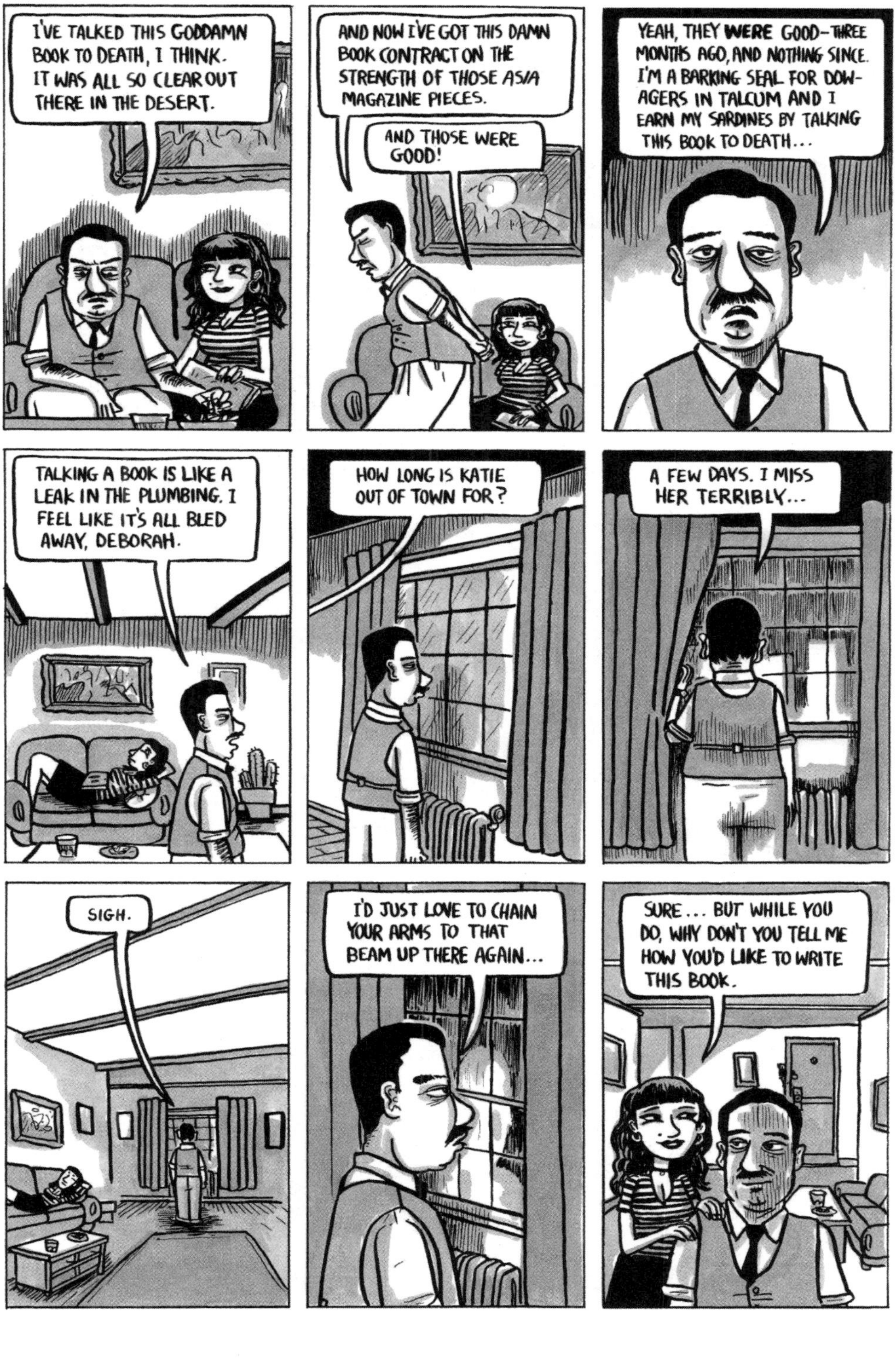

I'VE TALKED THIS GODDAMN BOOK TO DEATH, I THINK. IT WAS ALL SO CLEAR OUT THERE IN THE DESERT.
AND NOW I'VE GOT THIS DAMN BOOK CONTRACT ON THE STRENGTH OF THOSE ASIA MAGAZINE PIECES.
AND THOSE WERE GOOD!
YEAH, THEY WERE GOOD—THREE MONTHS AGO, AND NOTHING SINCE. I'M A BARKING SEAL FOR DOWAGERS IN TALCUM AND I EARN MY SARDINES BY TALKING THIS BOOK TO DEATH...
TALKING A BOOK IS LIKE A LEAK IN THE PLUMBING. I FEEL LIKE IT'S ALL BLED AWAY, DEBORAH.
HOW LONG IS KATIE OUT OF TOWN FOR?
A FEW DAYS. I MISS HER TERRIBLY...
SIGH.
I'D JUST LOVE TO CHAIN YOUR ARMS TO THAT BEAM UP THERE AGAIN...
SURE... BUT WHILE YOU DO, WHY DON'T YOU TELL ME HOW YOU'D LIKE TO WRITE THIS BOOK.

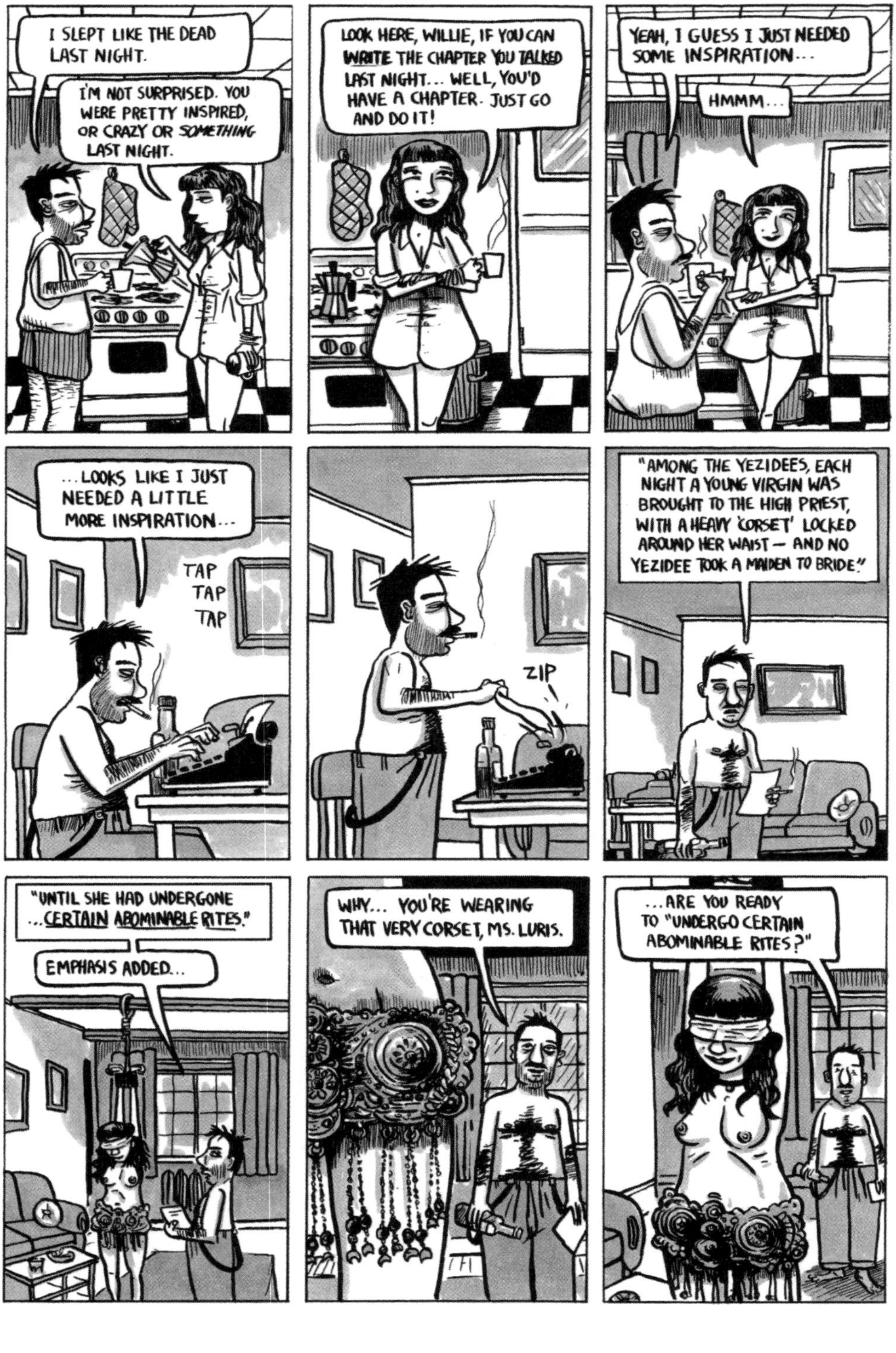
I SLEPT LIKE THE DEAD LAST NIGHT.
I'M NOT SURPRISED. YOU WERE PRETTY INSPIRED, OR CRAZY OR SOMETHING LAST NIGHT.
LOOK HERE, WILLIE, IF YOU CAN WRITE THE CHAPTER YOU TALKED LAST NIGHT... WELL, YOU'D HAVE A CHAPTER. JUST GO AND DO IT!
YEAH, I GUESS I JUST NEEDED SOME INSPIRATION...
HMMM...
...LOOKS LIKE I JUST NEEDED A LITTLE MORE INSPIRATION...
TAP
TAP
TAP
ZIP
"AMONG THE YEZIDEES, EACH NIGHT A YOUNG VIRGIN WAS BROUGHT TO THE HIGH PRIEST, WITH A HEAVY 'CORSET' LOCKED AROUND HER WAIST — AND NO YEZIDEE TOOK A MAIDEN TO BRIDE."
"UNTIL SHE HAD UNDERGONE ...CERTAIN ABOMINABLE RITES."
EMPHASIS ADDED...
WHY... YOU'RE WEARING THAT VERY CORSET, MS. LURIS.
...ARE YOU READY TO "UNDERGO CERTAIN ABOMINABLE RITES?"

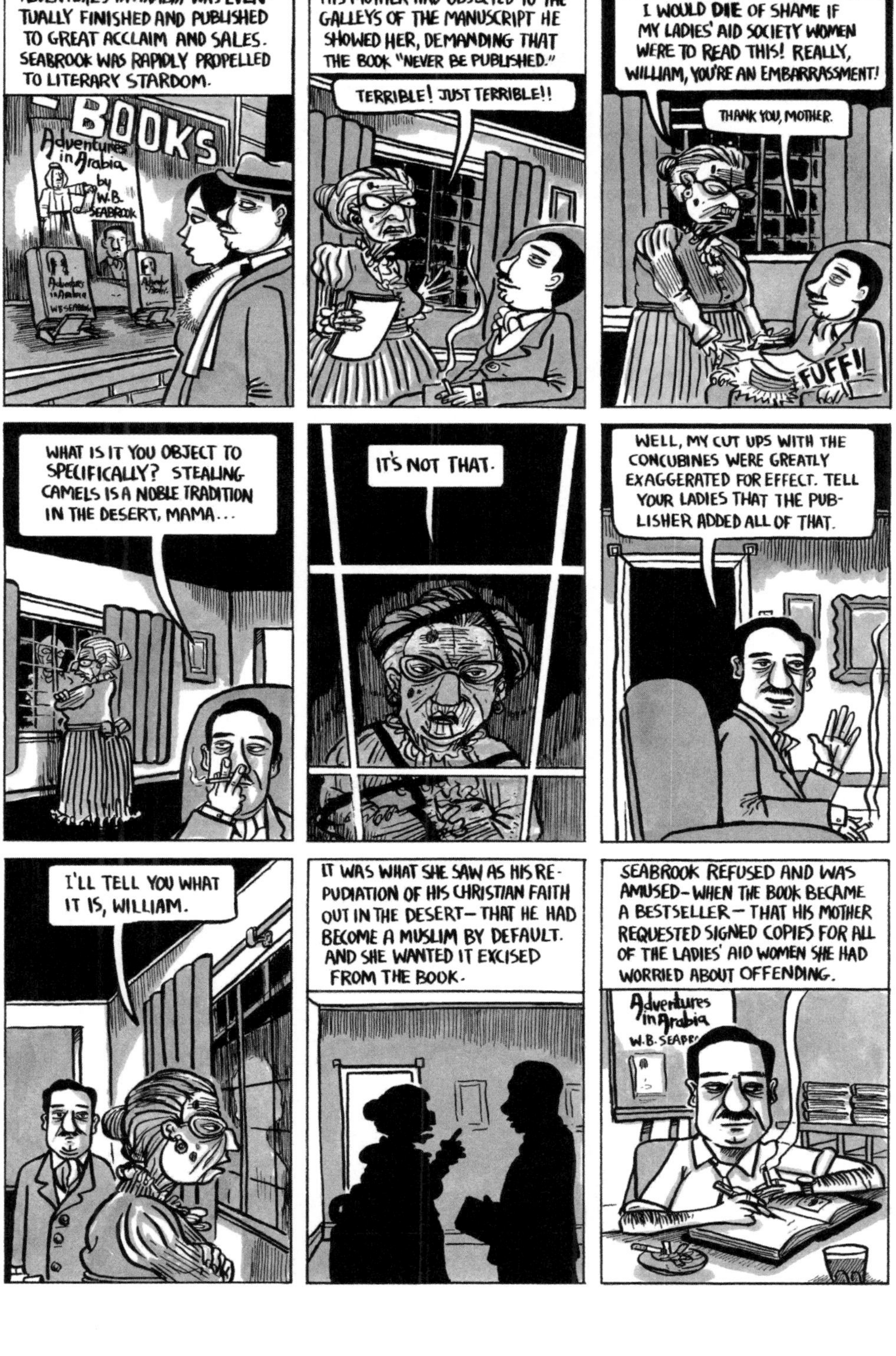
ADVENTURES IN ARABIA WAS EVENTUALLY FINISHED AND PUBLISHED TO GREAT ACCLAIM AND SALES. SEABROOK WAS RAPIDLY PROPELLED TO LITERARY STARDOM.
BOOKS
Adventures in Arabia by W.B. SEABROOK
HIS MOTHER HAD OBJECTED TO THE GALLEYS OF THE MANUSCRIPT HE SHOWED HER, DEMANDING THAT THE BOOK "NEVER BE PUBLISHED."
TERRIBLE! JUST TERRIBLE!!
I WOULD DIE OF SHAME IF MY LADIES' AID SOCIETY WOMEN WERE TO READ THIS! REALLY, WILLIAM, YOU'RE AN EMBARRASSMENT!
THANK YOU, MOTHER.
FUFF!
WHAT IS IT YOU OBJECT TO SPECIFICALLY? STEALING CAMELS IS A NOBLE TRADITION IN THE DESERT, MAMA...
IT'S NOT THAT.
WELL, MY CUT UPS WITH THE CONCUBINES WERE GREATLY EXAGGERATED FOR EFFECT. TELL YOUR LADIES THAT THE PUBLISHER ADDED ALL OF THAT.
I'LL TELL YOU WHAT IT IS, WILLIAM.
IT WAS WHAT SHE SAW AS HIS REPUDIATION OF HIS CHRISTIAN FAITH OUT IN THE DESERT—THAT HE HAD BECOME A MUSLIM BY DEFAULT. AND SHE WANTED IT EXCISED FROM THE BOOK.
SEABROOK REFUSED AND WAS AMUSED—WHEN THE BOOK BECAME A BESTSELLER—THAT HIS MOTHER REQUESTED SIGNED COPIES FOR ALL OF THE LADIES' AID WOMEN SHE HAD WORRIED ABOUT OFFENDING.
Adventures in Arabia
W.B. SEABR

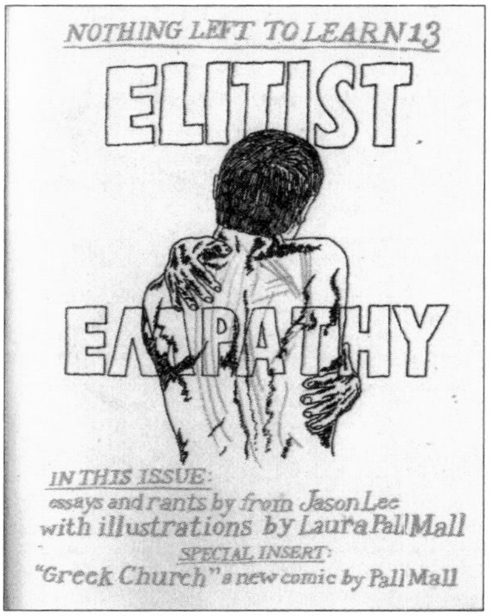
NOTHING LEFT TO LEARN 13
ELITIST
EMPATHY
IN THIS ISSUE:
essays and rants by from Jason Lee
with illustrations by Laura PallMall
SPECIAL INSERT:
"Greek Church" a new comic by Pall Mall

SELECTIONS FROM

Things More Likely to Kill You Than . . .

AND **Busy Comic** (AS PALM FRANZ)

LAURA PALLMALL

originally published in

Nothing Left to Learn #13: Elitist Empathy AND *Nothing Left to Learn #14: Pugilist Palmistry*

SELF-PUBLISHED

5.5 x 7.25 inches • 36 pages

Biography

Laura PallMall is a pseudonym of Pittsburgh-based writer/artist Jason Lee, who publishes a series of multidisciplinary zines under the label "Nothing Left to Learn." Palm Franz is a pseudonym of comics-maker/illustrator Laura PallMall.
nothinglefttolearn.tumblr.com

Statement

"Nothing Left to Learn," is a series of multidisciplinary zines founded on the principle of alternative media of all genres, work free from the accepted norms and practices of their traditional spheres. To that end it is a series of zines that includes drink recipes, political opinions, illustrations, comics, prose, and visual art. "Things More Likely to Kill You Than . . ." is a series of drawings excerpted from a zine called *Elitist Empathy*, which was a collection of comics, essays, and drawings meant to address the 2016 election (and our reaction to it) from a variety of different genres, angles, and tones. "Busy Comic" was from the next issue of the series, which revolved around a series of boxing illustrations and essays; I normally write pretty by-the-books narrative comics and prose, and Palm Franz is a pseudonym under which I occasionally do more colorful and experimental work. "Busy Comic" was the first result of that intermittent project.

ISIS (standing for all brown people and by extension, all minorities) are the latest targets of the ever-spinning color wheel White America uses to justify its xenophobia and racism. Don't believe the hype–The American Way of Life remains, by far, the greatest existential threat to The American Way of Life.

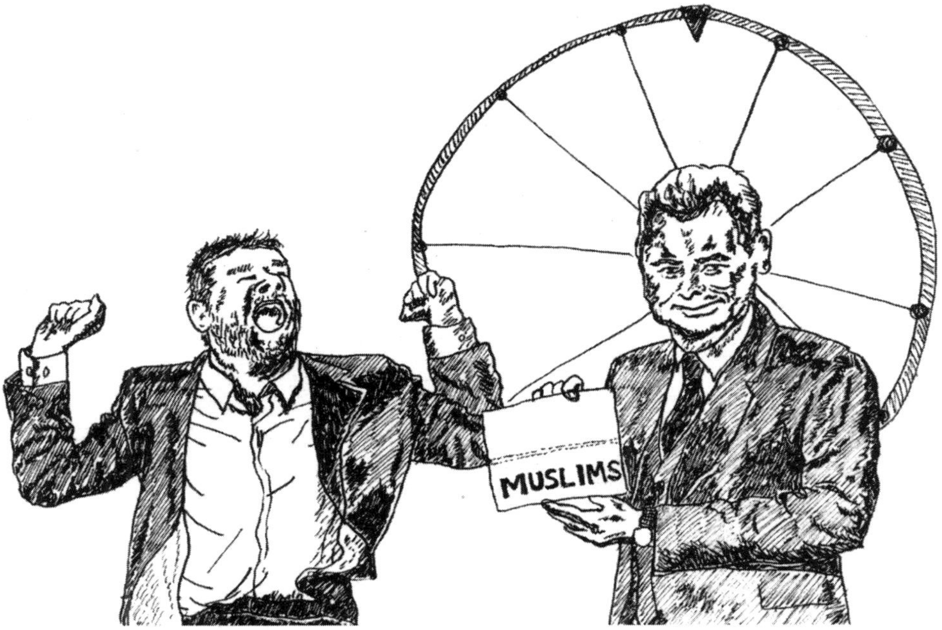
MUSLIMS

SOME THINGS MORE LIKELY TO KILL YOU THAN ISIS

MORE LIKELY TO KILL YOU THAN ISIS:
HIGH SCHOOL FOOTBALL

MORE AMERICANS DIE FROM INJURIES SUSTAINED IN HIGH SCHOOL FOOTBALL GAMES AND PRACTICES THAN FROM TERRORIST ATTACKS.

MORE LIKELY TO KILL YOU THAN ISIS:

HOT DOGS

NUMBER OF CHILDREN WHO DIE FROM CHOKING ON HOT DOGS > NUMBER OF AMERICANS KILLED IN ISIS-RELATED ATTACKS

MORE LIKELY TO KILL YOU THAN ISIS:

JEALOUS LOVERS

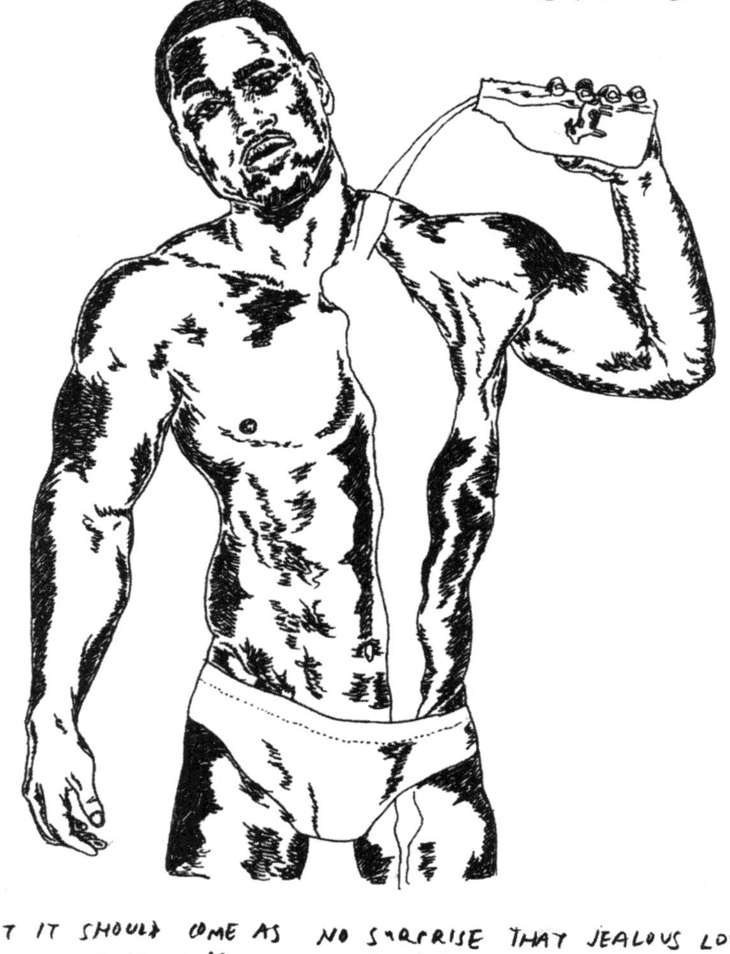

AT THIS POINT IT SHOULD COME AS NO SURPRISE THAT JEALOUS LOVERS KILL MORE AMERICANS THAN ISIS. ALSO BETWEEN 2012 AND 2014, MORE PEOPLE WERE KILLED BY MEN WHO KNEW OR SUSPECTED THAT THEIR SIGNIFICANT OTHERS HAD SLEPT WITH TREY SONGZ THAN WERE KILLED BY "ISLAMIC TERROR"

MORE LIKELY TO KILL YOU THAN ISIS:

FIREWORKS

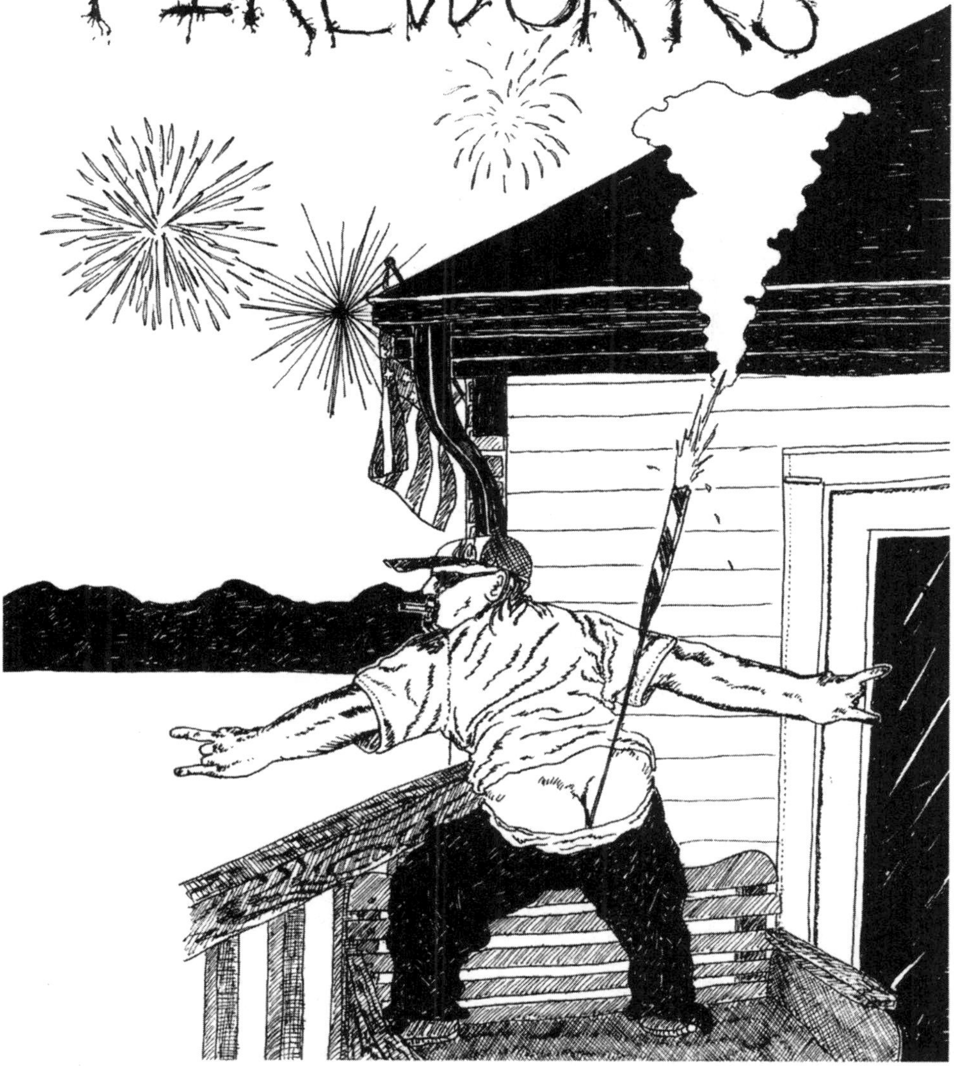

MORE AMERICANS DIE BLOWING THEMSELVES UP CELEBRATING AMERICA THAN BY BEING BLOWN UP BY "RADICAL ISLAM."

BUSY COMIC

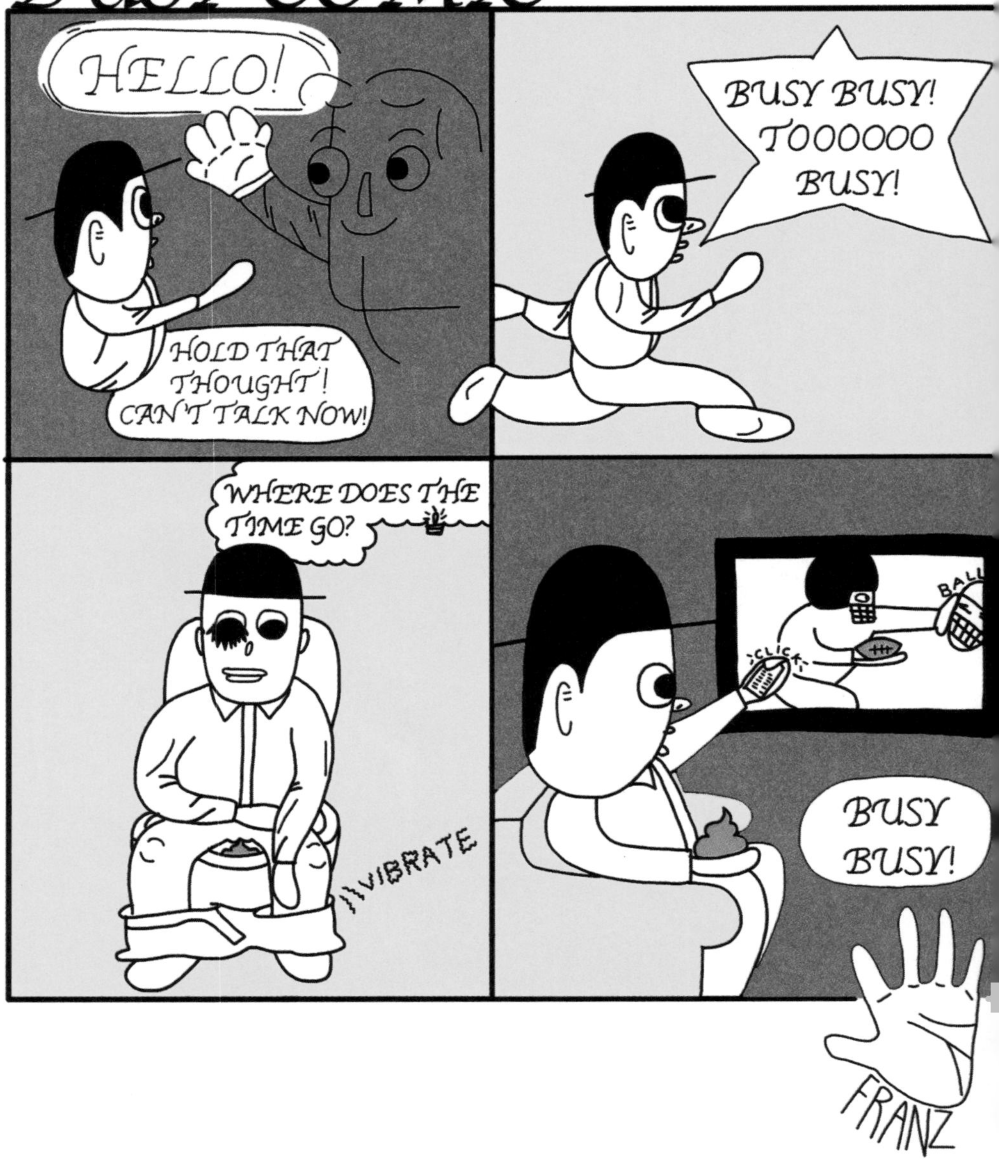
HELLO!
HOLD THAT THOUGHT! CAN'T TALK NOW!
BUSY BUSY! TOOOOOO BUSY!
WHERE DOES THE TIME GO?
VIBRATE
CLICK
BUSY BUSY!
FRANZ

SONGY
OF
PARADISE
by Gary Panter

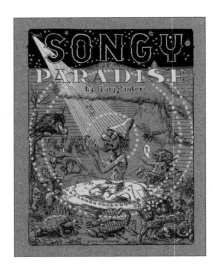

Songy of Paradise (*Excerpt*)

GARY PANTER

originally published in

Songy of Paradise
FANTAGRAPHICS BOOKS
11.25 x 15.25 inches • 40 pages

Biography

Gary Panter is an artist working in Brooklyn.
garypanter.com

Statement

Songy of Paradise is a comic interpretation of John Milton's *Paradise Regained* in which the character of Jesus has been replaced by an obstinate hillbilly. Though it is in graphic comic form and has occasional humor, it is not intended as a parody of Milton. The project was supported by a research grant at The Dorothy and Lewis B. Cullman Center for Scholars and Writers at the New York Public Library.

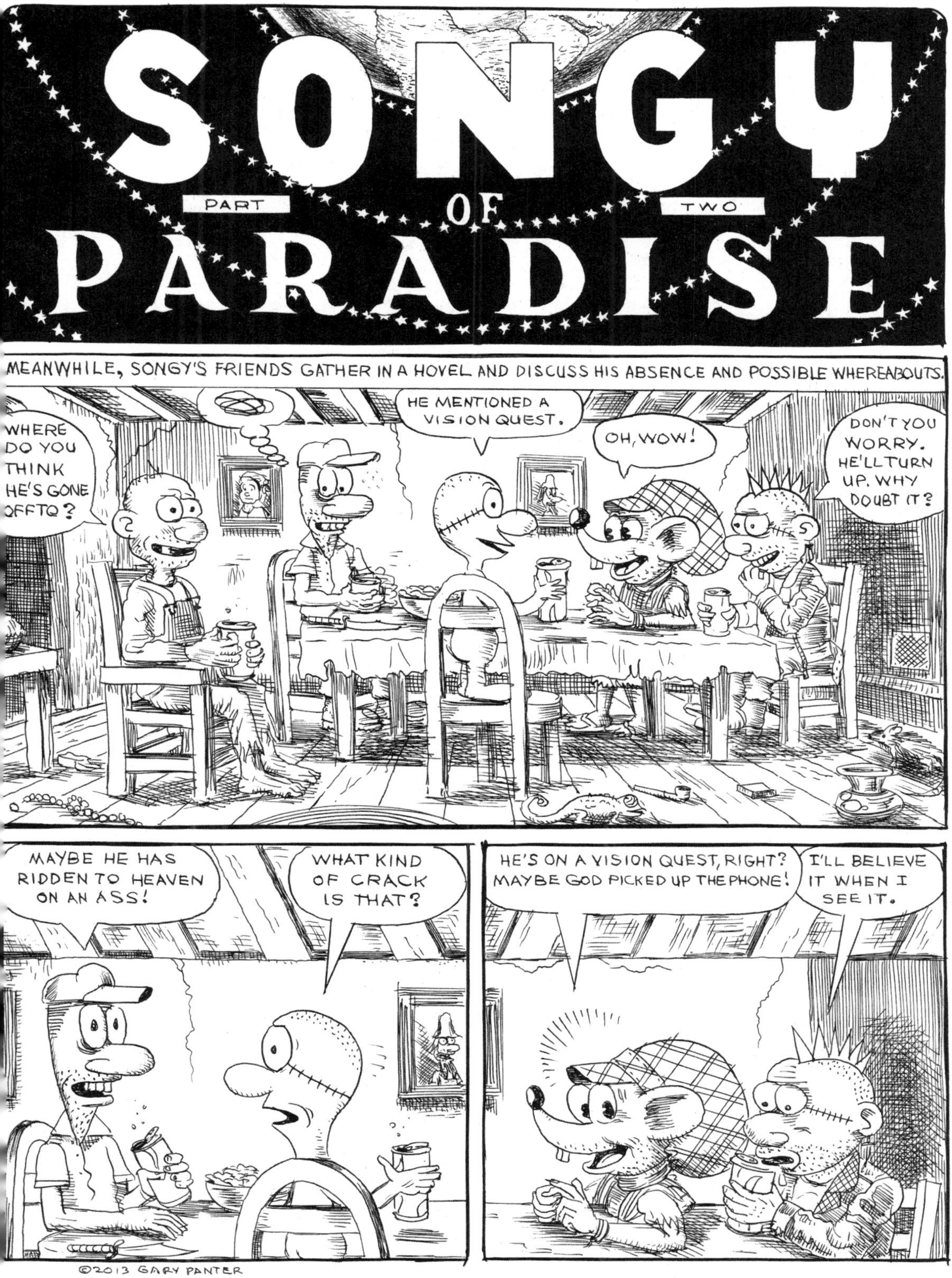
SONGY OF PARADISE
PART TWO
MEANWHILE, SONGY'S FRIENDS GATHER IN A HOVEL AND DISCUSS HIS ABSENCE AND POSSIBLE WHEREABOUTS.
WHERE DO YOU THINK HE'S GONE OFFTO?
HE MENTIONED A VISION QUEST.
OH, WOW!
DON'T YOU WORRY. HE'LL TURN UP. WHY DOUBT IT?
MAYBE HE HAS RIDDEN TO HEAVEN ON AN ASS!
WHAT KIND OF CRACK IS THAT?
HE'S ON A VISION QUEST, RIGHT? MAYBE GOD PICKED UP THE PHONE!
I'LL BELIEVE IT WHEN I SEE IT.
©2013 GARY PANTER

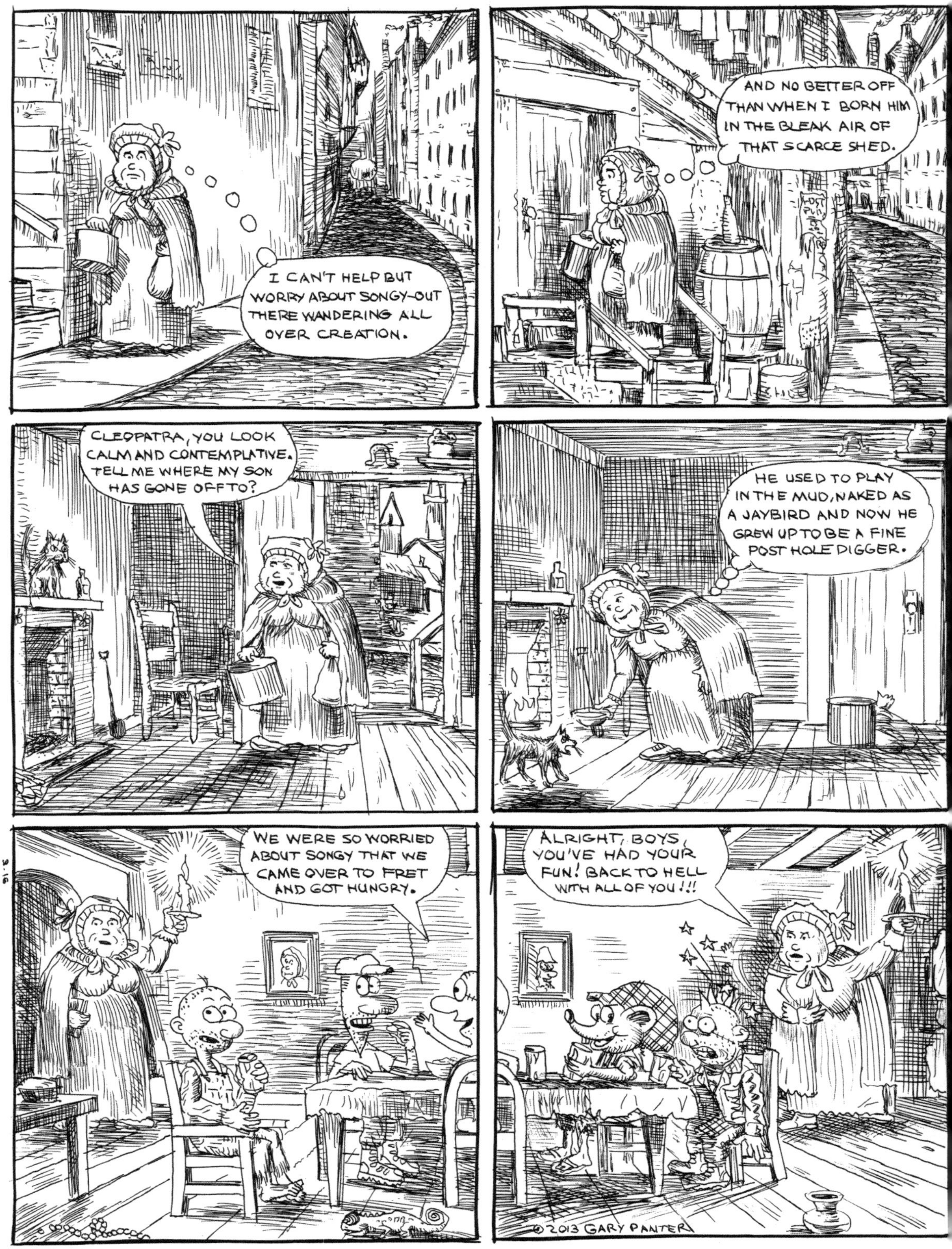
I CAN'T HELP BUT WORRY ABOUT SONGY-OUT THERE WANDERING ALL OVER CREATION.
AND NO BETTER OFF THAN WHEN I BORN HIM IN THE BLEAK AIR OF THAT SCARCE SHED.
CLEOPATRA, YOU LOOK CALM AND CONTEMPLATIVE. TELL ME WHERE MY SON HAS GONE OFF TO?
HE USED TO PLAY IN THE MUD, NAKED AS A JAYBIRD AND NOW HE GREW UP TO BE A FINE POST HOLE DIGGER.
WE WERE SO WORRIED ABOUT SONGY THAT WE CAME OVER TO FRET AND GOT HUNGRY.
ALRIGHT, BOYS, YOU'VE HAD YOUR FUN! BACK TO HELL WITH ALL OF YOU!!!
© 2013 GARY PANTER

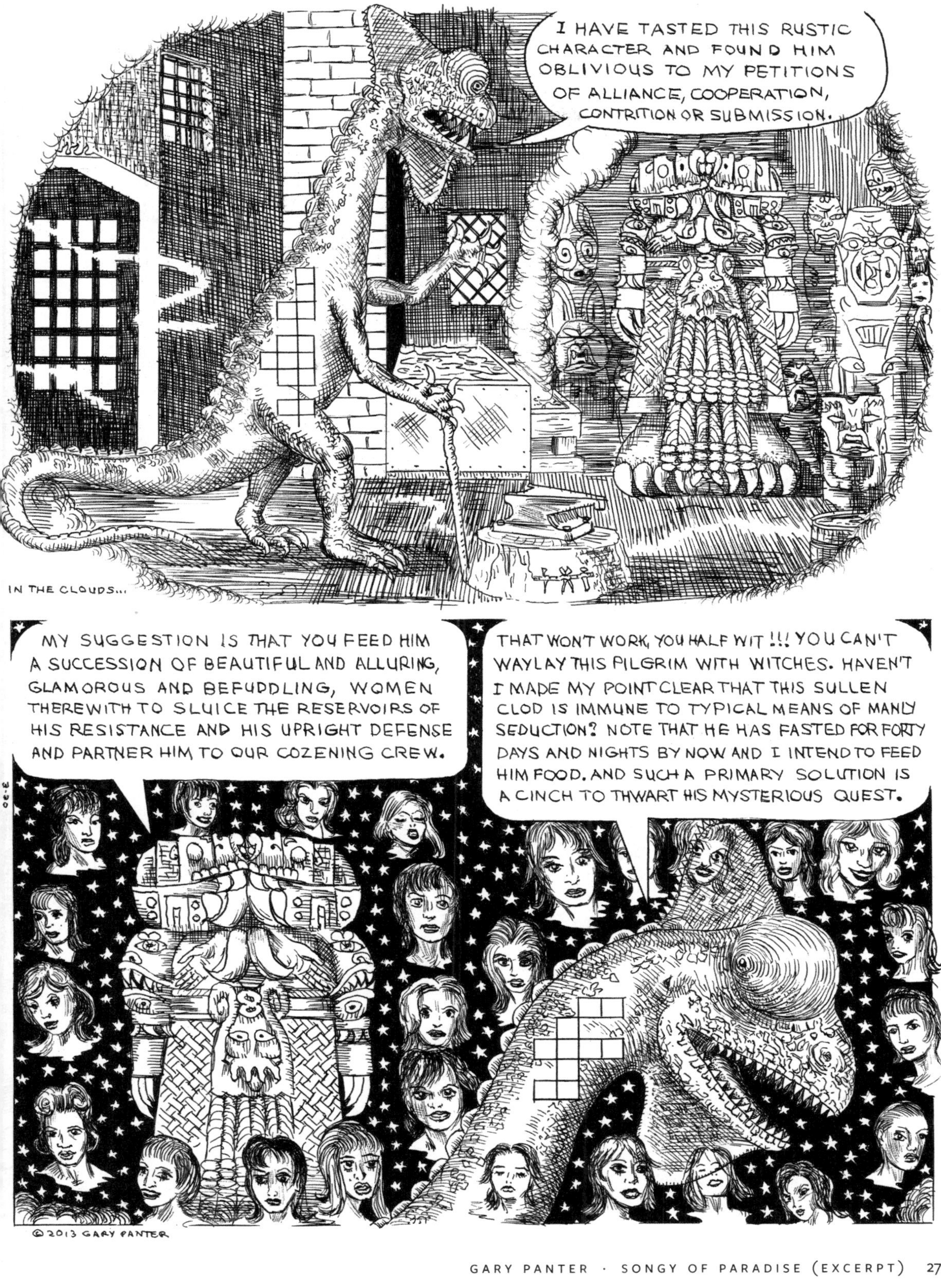

I HAVE TASTED THIS RUSTIC CHARACTER AND FOUND HIM OBLIVIOUS TO MY PETITIONS OF ALLIANCE, COOPERATION, CONTRITION OR SUBMISSION.
IN THE CLOUDS...
MY SUGGESTION IS THAT YOU FEED HIM A SUCCESSION OF BEAUTIFUL AND ALLURING, GLAMOROUS AND BEFUDDLING, WOMEN THEREWITH TO SLUICE THE RESERVOIRS OF HIS RESISTANCE AND HIS UPRIGHT DEFENSE AND PARTNER HIM TO OUR COZENING CREW.
THAT WON'T WORK, YOU HALF WIT !!! YOU CAN'T WAYLAY THIS PILGRIM WITH WITCHES. HAVEN'T I MADE MY POINT CLEAR THAT THIS SULLEN CLOD IS IMMUNE TO TYPICAL MEANS OF MANLY SEDUCTION? NOTE THAT HE HAS FASTED FOR FORTY DAYS AND NIGHTS BY NOW AND I INTEND TO FEED HIM FOOD. AND SUCH A PRIMARY SOLUTION IS A CINCH TO THWART HIS MYSTERIOUS QUEST.

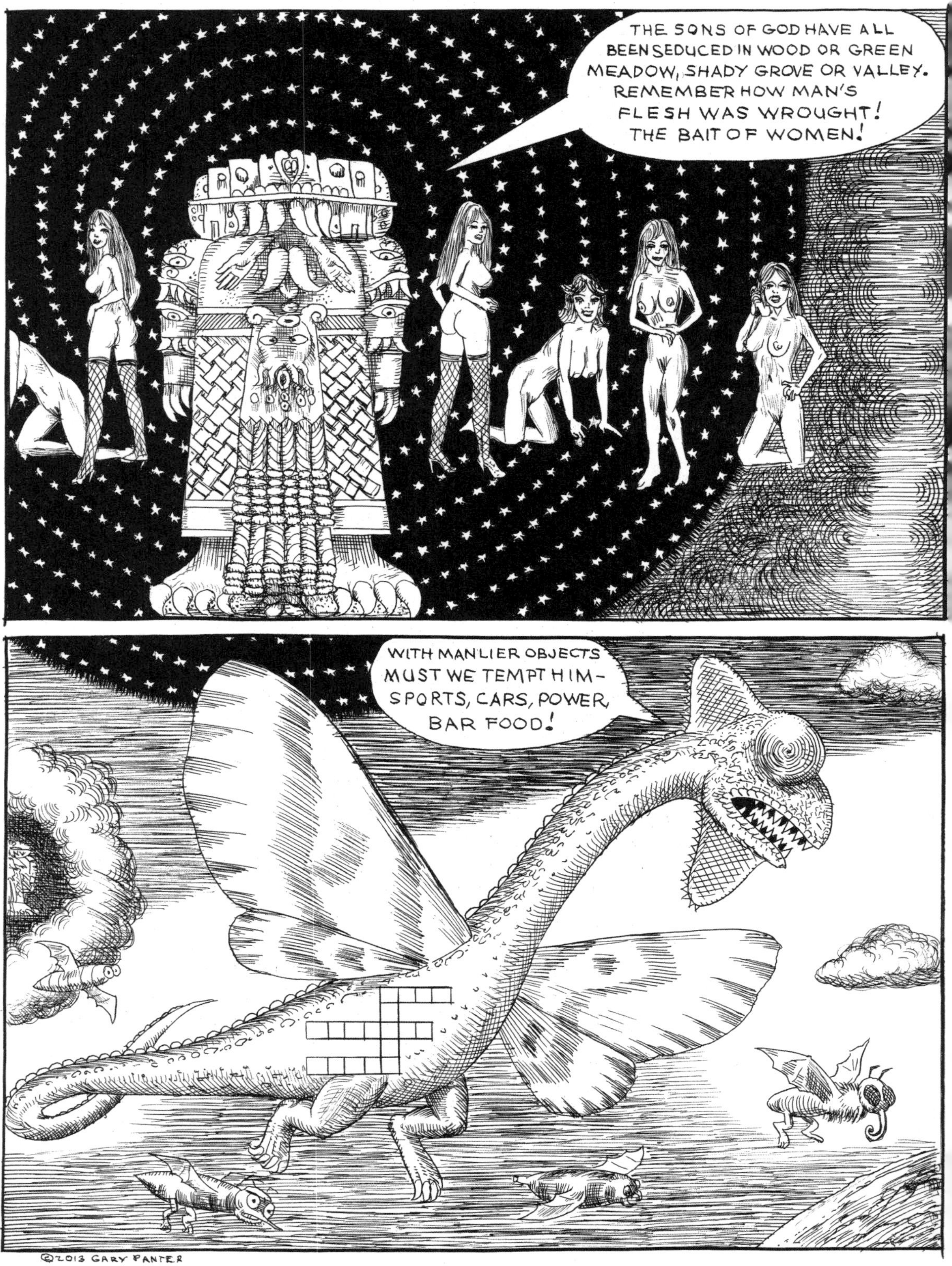
THE SONS OF GOD HAVE ALL BEEN SEDUCED IN WOOD OR GREEN MEADOW, SHADY GROVE OR VALLEY. REMEMBER HOW MAN'S FLESH WAS WROUGHT! THE BAIT OF WOMEN!
WITH MANLIER OBJECTS MUST WE TEMPT HIM- SPORTS, CARS, POWER, BAR FOOD!

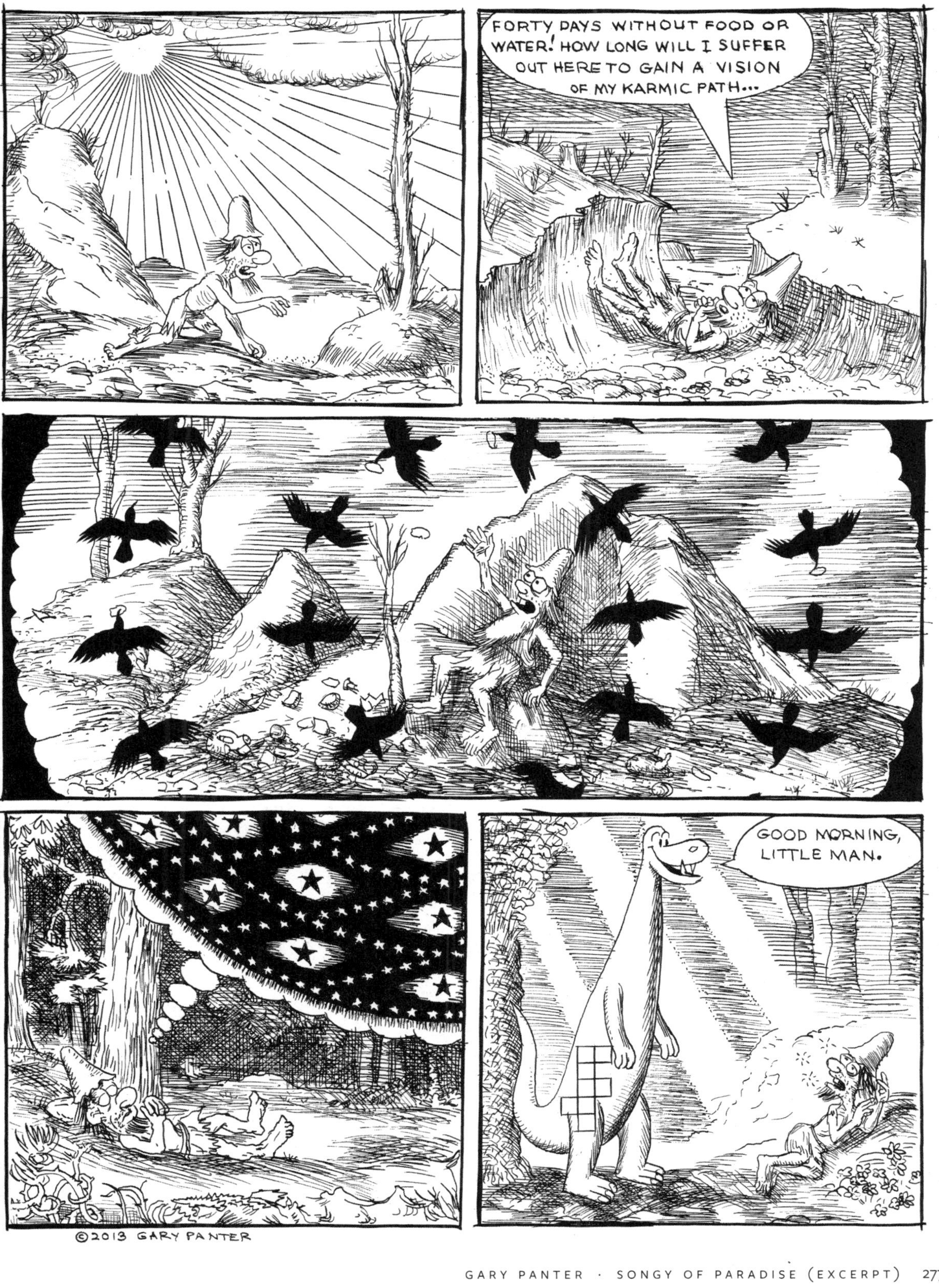
FORTY DAYS WITHOUT FOOD OR WATER! HOW LONG WILL I SUFFER OUT HERE TO GAIN A VISION OF MY KARMIC PATH...
GOOD MORNING, LITTLE MAN.

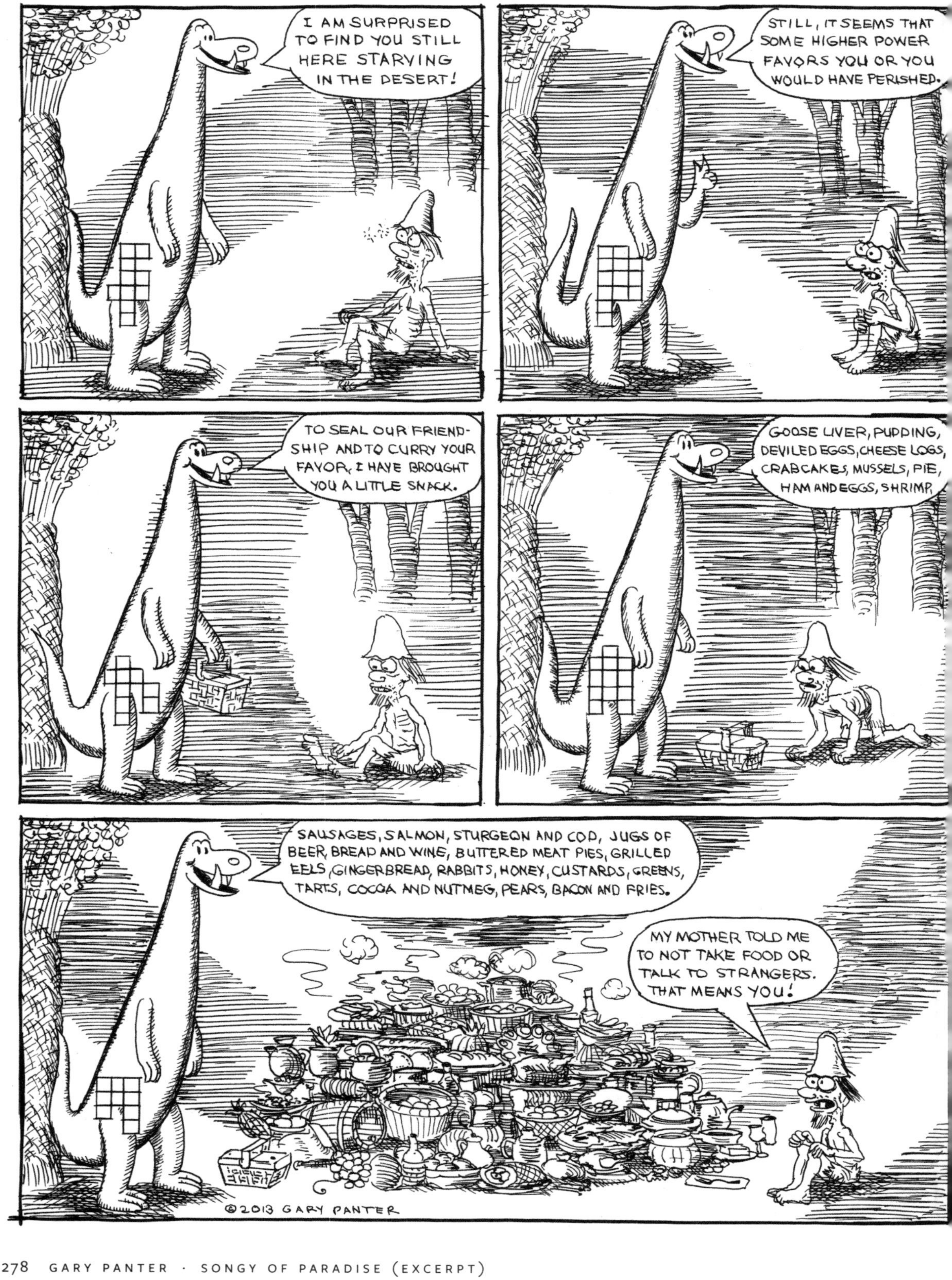
I AM SURPRISED TO FIND YOU STILL HERE STARVING IN THE DESERT!
STILL, IT SEEMS THAT SOME HIGHER POWER FAVORS YOU OR YOU WOULD HAVE PERISHED.
TO SEAL OUR FRIENDSHIP AND TO CURRY YOUR FAVOR, I HAVE BROUGHT YOU A LITTLE SNACK.
GOOSE LIVER, PUDDING, DEVILED EGGS, CHEESE LOGS, CRABCAKES, MUSSELS, PIE, HAM AND EGGS, SHRIMP,
SAUSAGES, SALMON, STURGEON AND COD, JUGS OF BEER, BREAD AND WINE, BUTTERED MEAT PIES, GRILLED EELS, GINGERBREAD, RABBITS, HONEY, CUSTARDS, GREENS, TARTS, COCOA AND NUTMEG, PEARS, BACON AND FRIES.
MY MOTHER TOLD ME TO NOT TAKE FOOD OR TALK TO STRANGERS. THAT MEANS YOU!
©2013 GARY PANTER

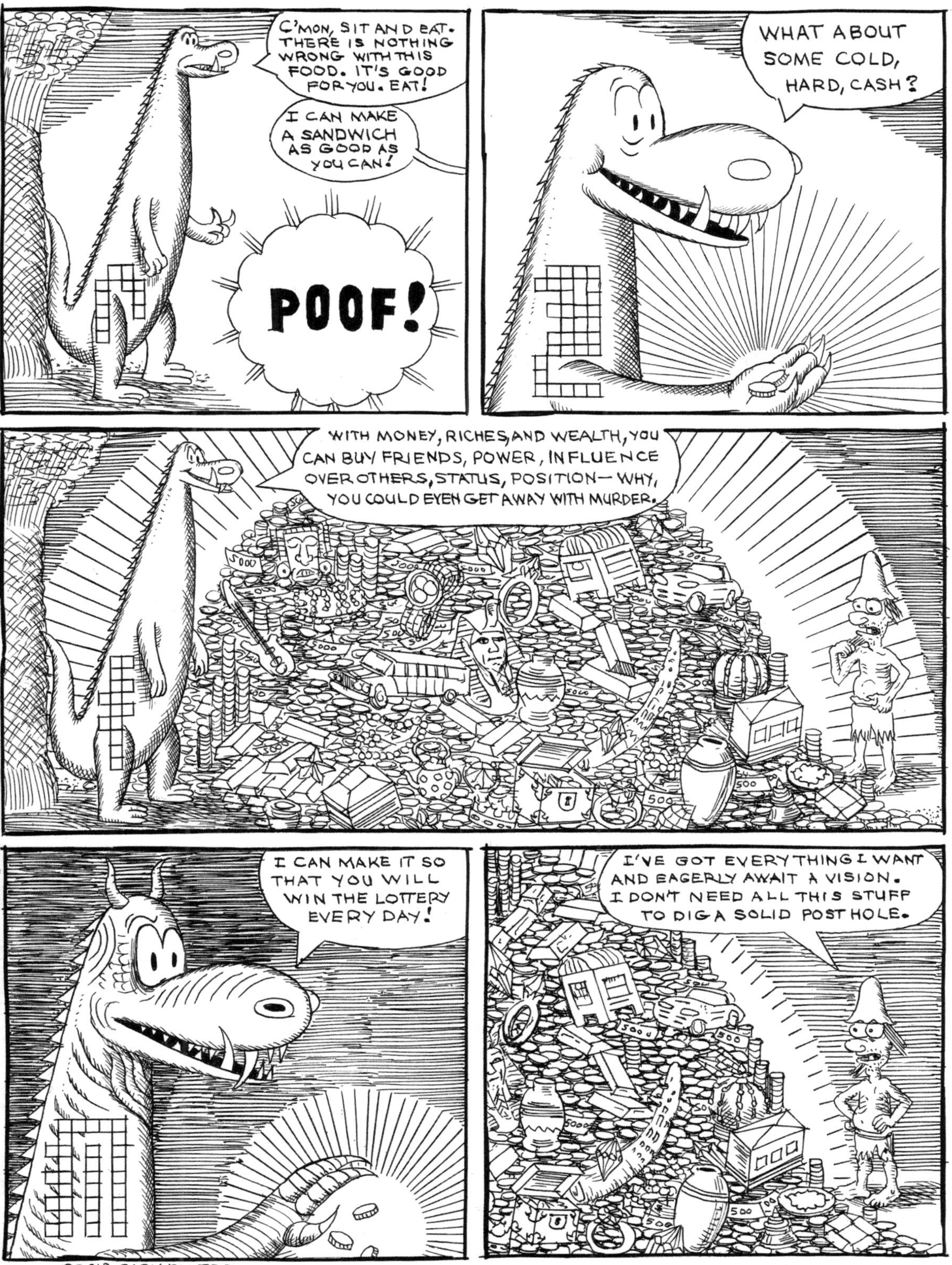
C'MON, SIT AND EAT. THERE IS NOTHING WRONG WITH THIS FOOD. IT'S GOOD FOR YOU. EAT!
I CAN MAKE A SANDWICH AS GOOD AS YOU CAN!
POOF!
WHAT ABOUT SOME COLD, HARD, CASH?
WITH MONEY, RICHES, AND WEALTH, YOU CAN BUY FRIENDS, POWER, INFLUENCE OVER OTHERS, STATUS, POSITION— WHY, YOU COULD EVEN GET AWAY WITH MURDER.
I CAN MAKE IT SO THAT YOU WILL WIN THE LOTTERY EVERY DAY!
I'VE GOT EVERYTHING I WANT AND EAGERLY AWAIT A VISION. I DON'T NEED ALL THIS STUFF TO DIG A SOLID POST HOLE.

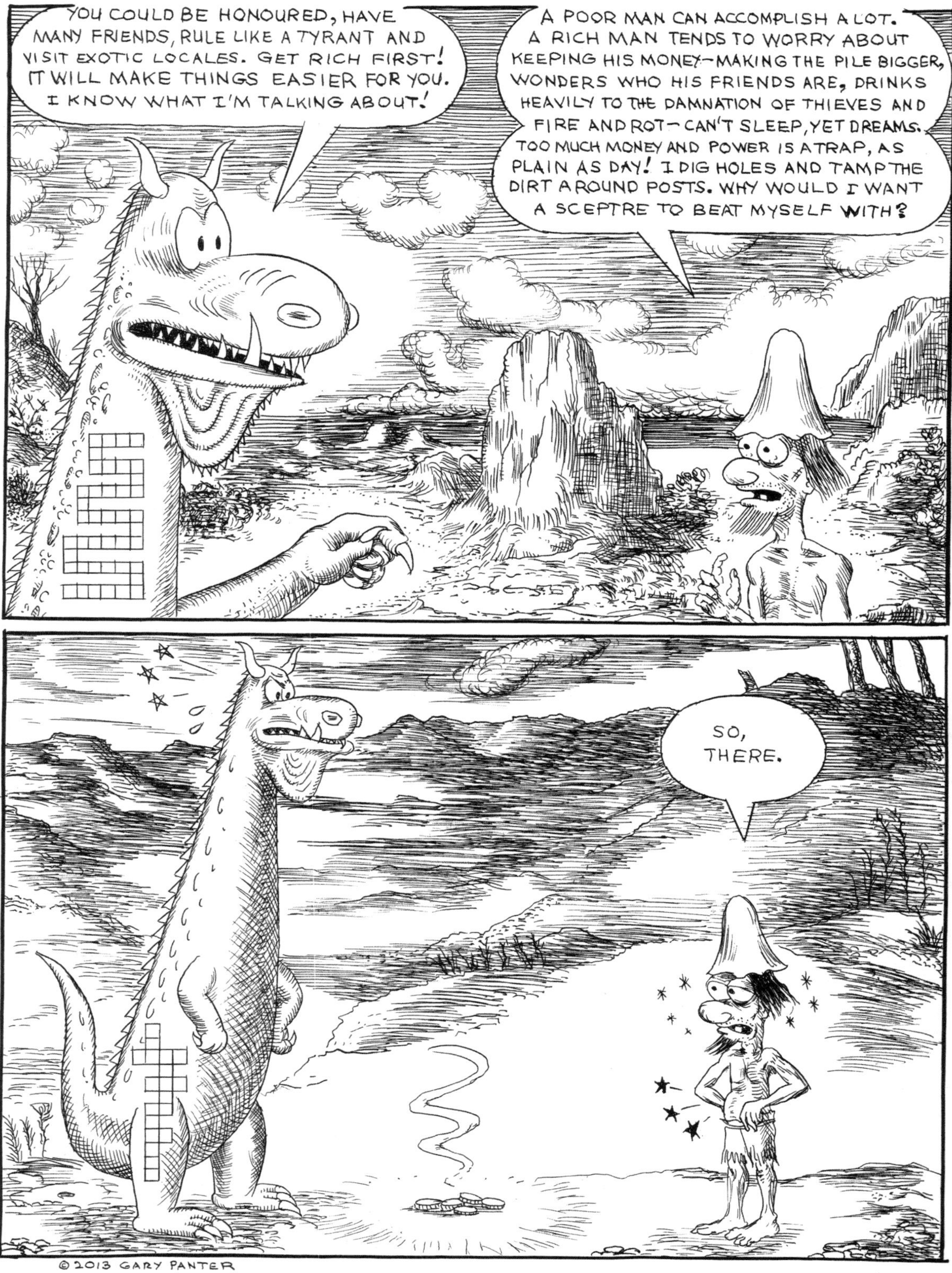
YOU COULD BE HONOURED, HAVE MANY FRIENDS, RULE LIKE A TYRANT AND VISIT EXOTIC LOCALES. GET RICH FIRST! IT WILL MAKE THINGS EASIER FOR YOU. I KNOW WHAT I'M TALKING ABOUT!
A POOR MAN CAN ACCOMPLISH A LOT. A RICH MAN TENDS TO WORRY ABOUT KEEPING HIS MONEY—MAKING THE PILE BIGGER, WONDERS WHO HIS FRIENDS ARE, DRINKS HEAVILY TO THE DAMNATION OF THIEVES AND FIRE AND ROT—CAN'T SLEEP, YET DREAMS. TOO MUCH MONEY AND POWER IS A TRAP, AS PLAIN AS DAY! I DIG HOLES AND TAMP THE DIRT AROUND POSTS. WHY WOULD I WANT A SCEPTRE TO BEAT MYSELF WITH?
5-17
SO, THERE.
©2013 GARY PANTER

UGLY

CHLOË PERKIS

originally published as

UGLY

BRED PRESS

5 x 7.5 inches • 20 pages

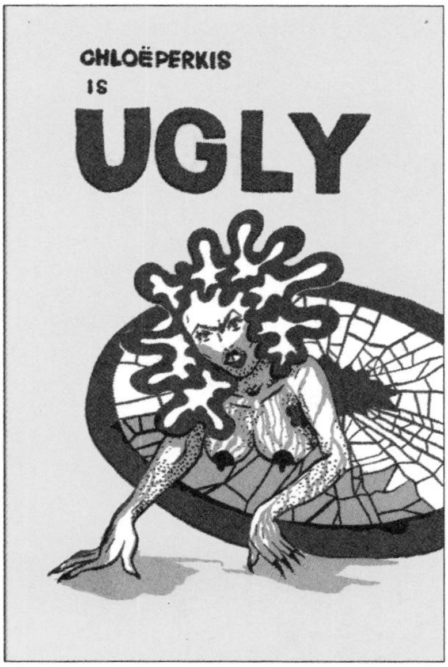
CHLOË PERKIS
IS
UGLY

Biography

Chloë Perkis is a non-binary artist who lives in Chicago, Illinois. Their body of work involves comics, ceramics, and printmaking.
chloeperkis.com

Statement

I made *UGLY* to transform the anxieties and insecurities I felt surrounding my sexual and romantic experiences. I wanted to reclaim the ugliness, turning it into something funny.

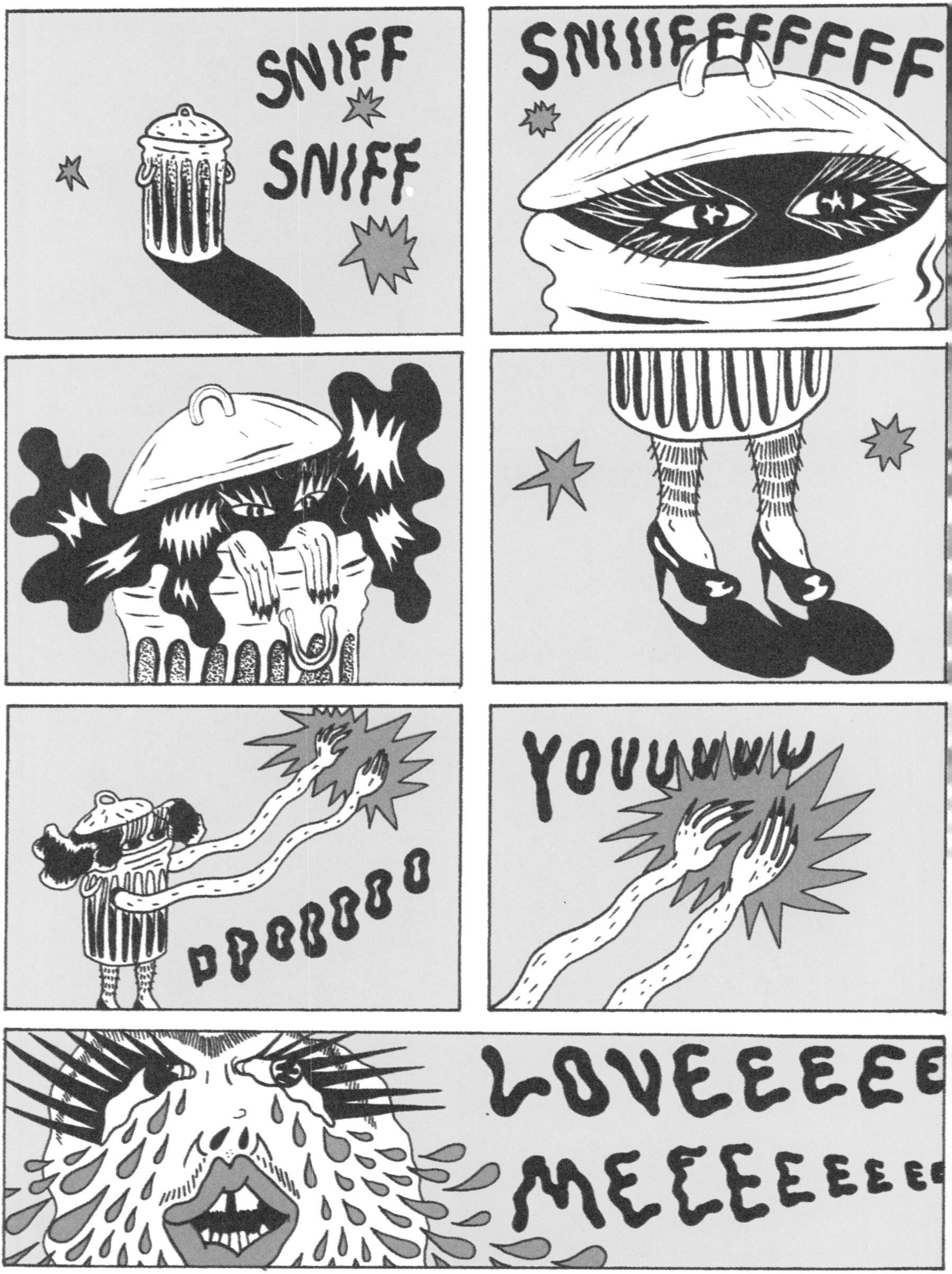
SNIFF
SNIFF
SNIIIFFFFFFF
OOOOOOO
YOUUUUU
LOVEEEEE
MEEEEEEEE

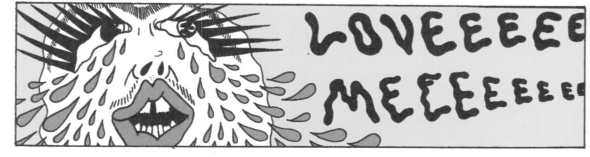

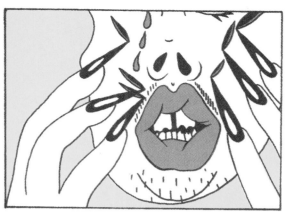

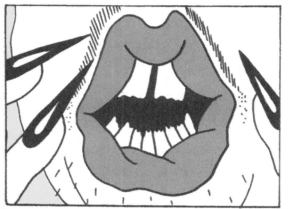
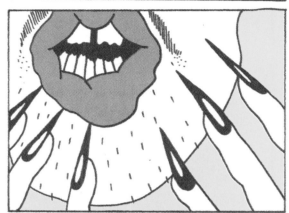

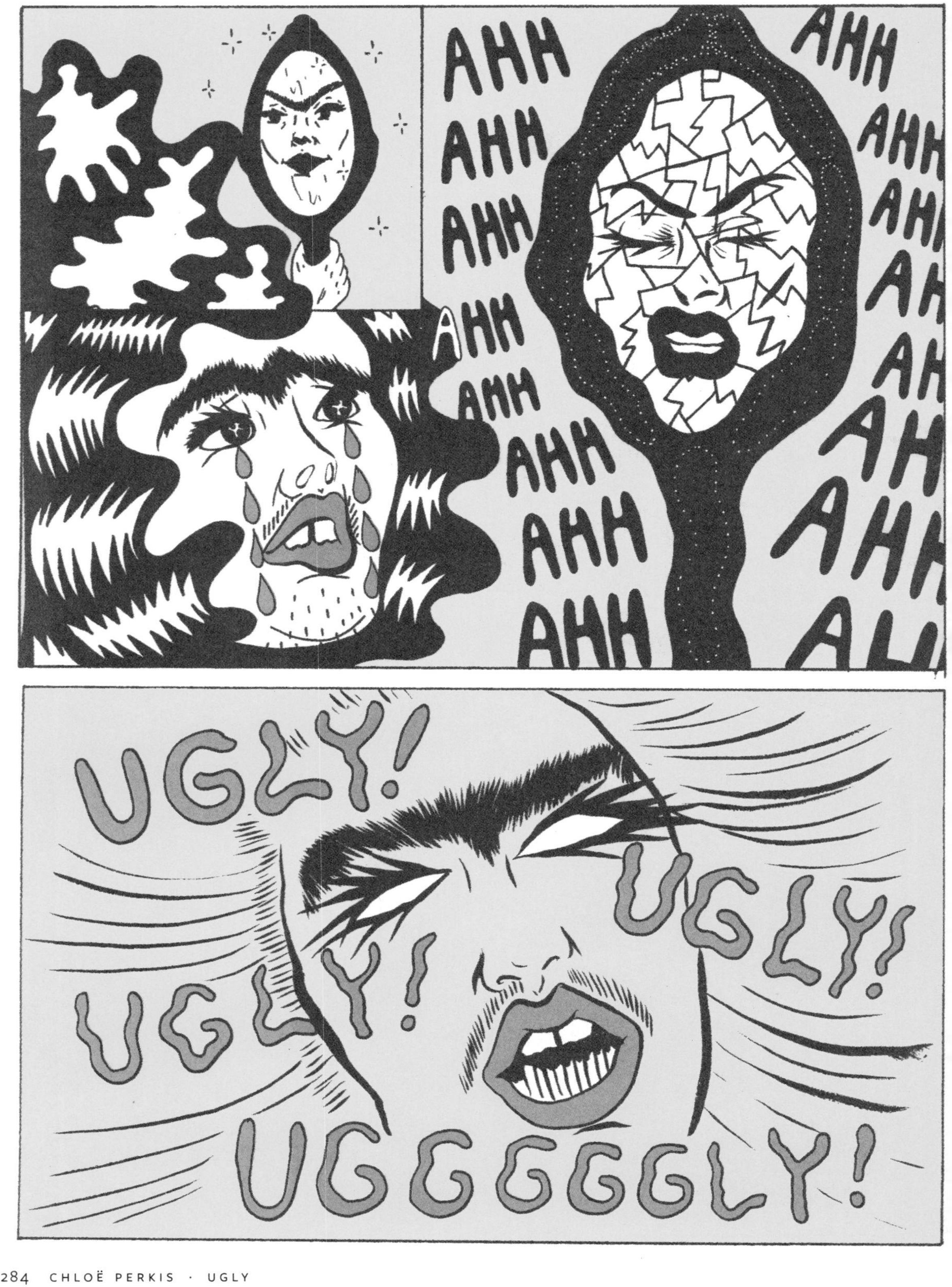
AHH
AHH
AHH
AHH
AHH
AHH
AHH
AHH
AHH
UGLY!
UGLY!
UGLY!
UGGGGGLY!

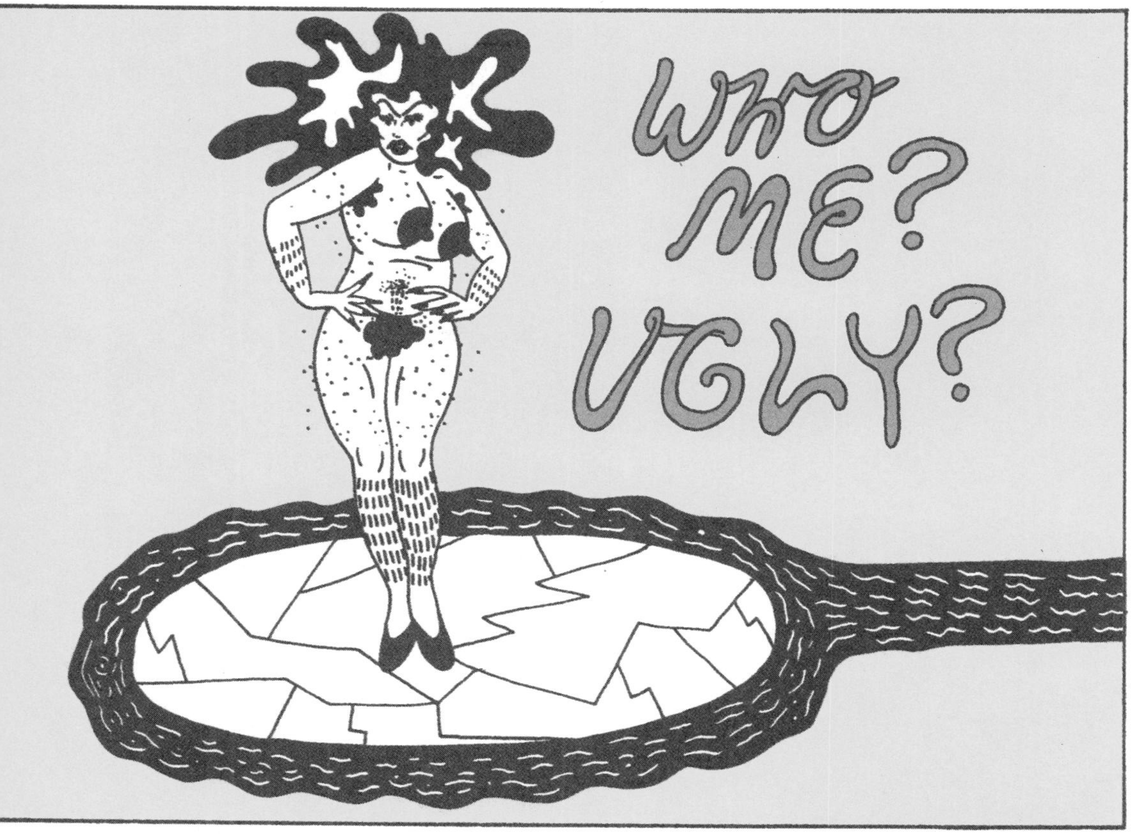
WHO ME? UGLY?

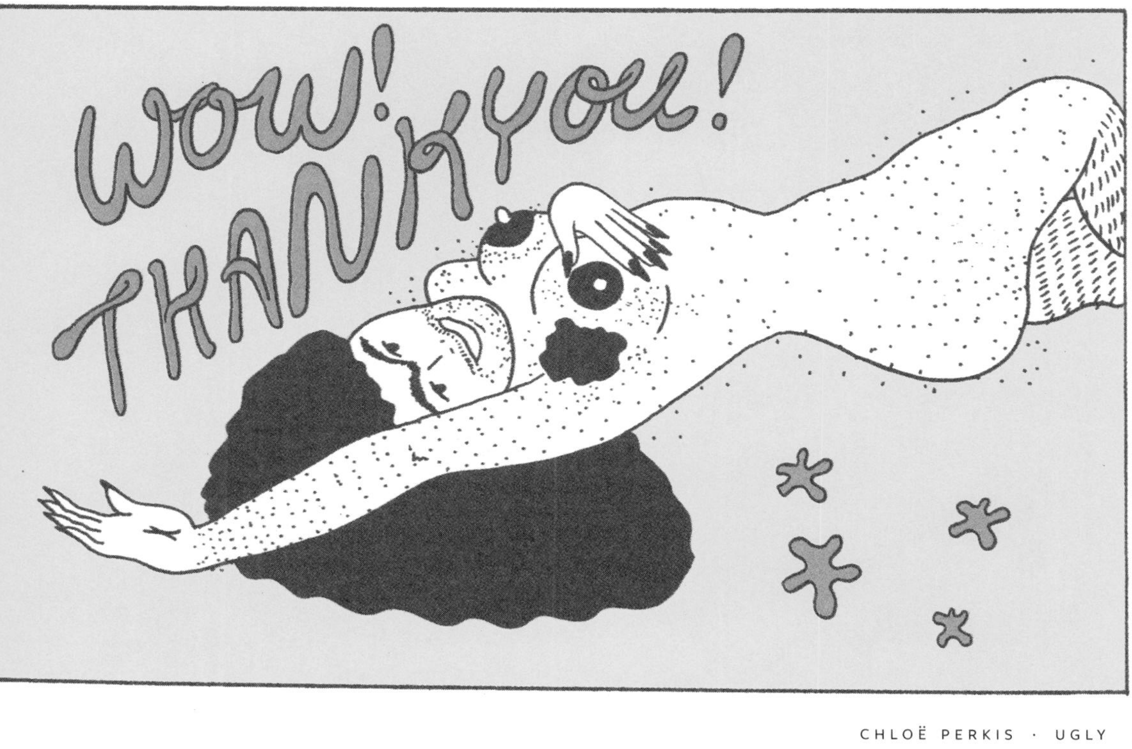
WOW! THANK YOU!

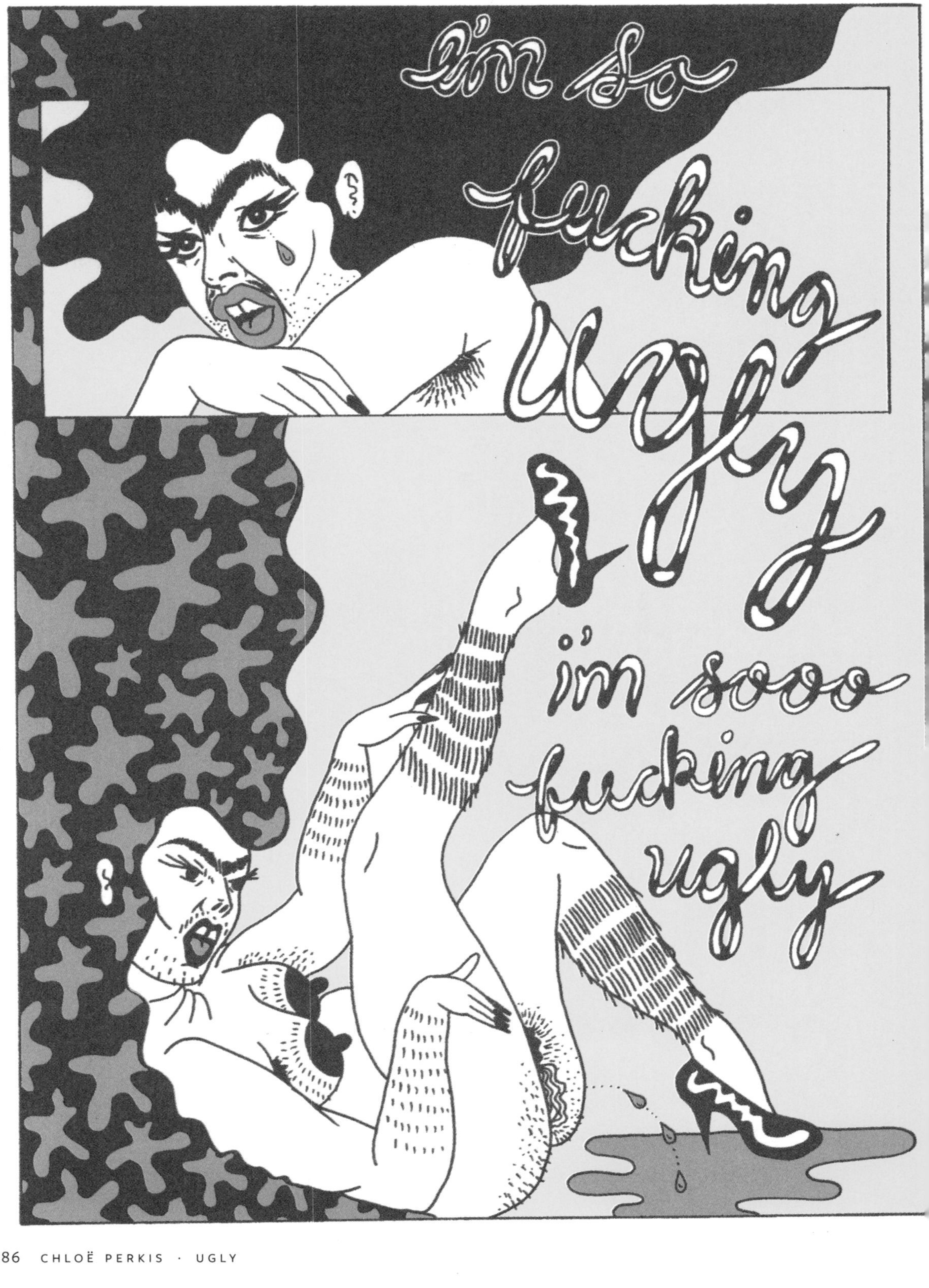
i'm so fucking ugly
i'm sooo fucking ugly

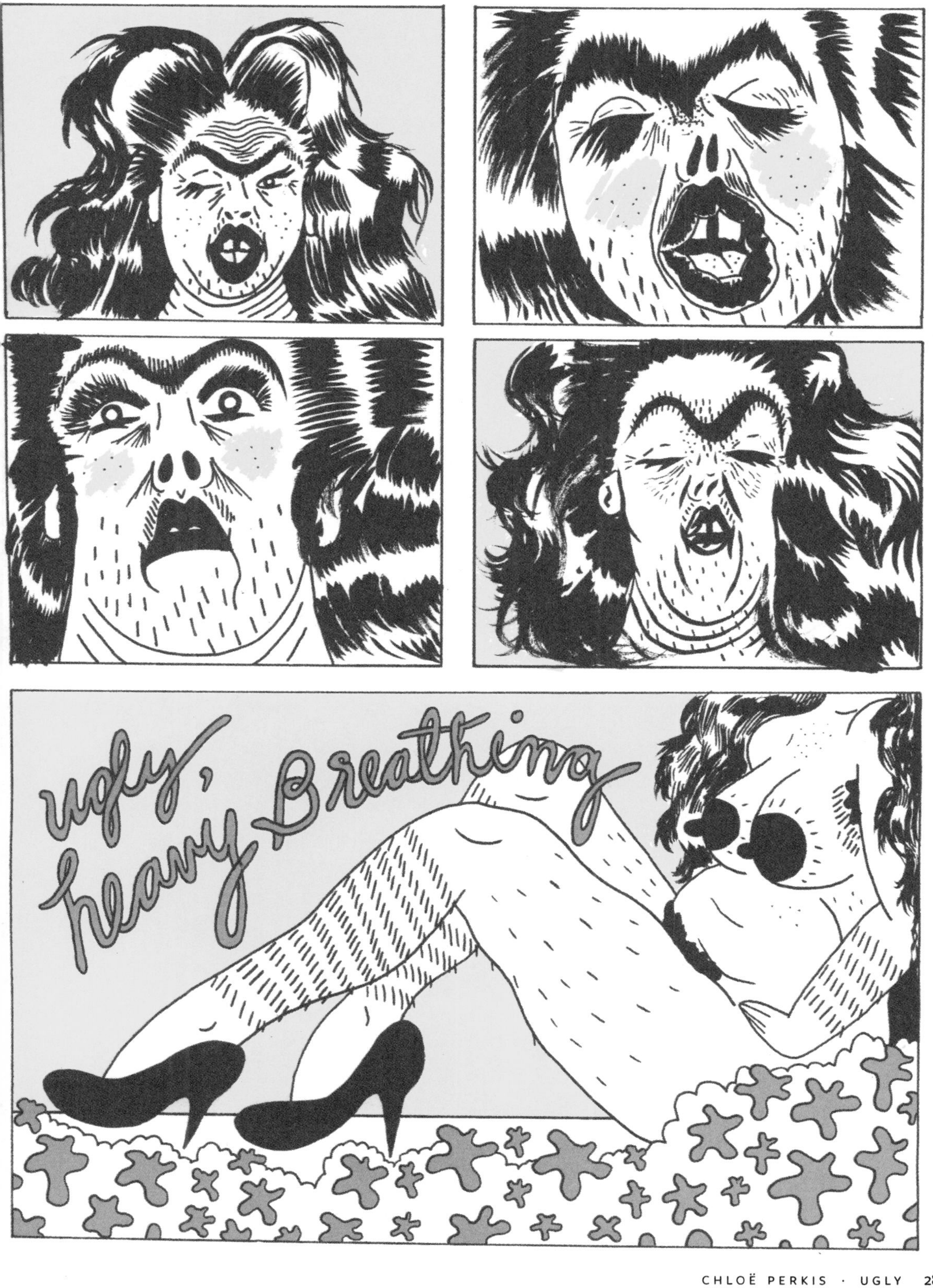
ugly, heavy Breathing

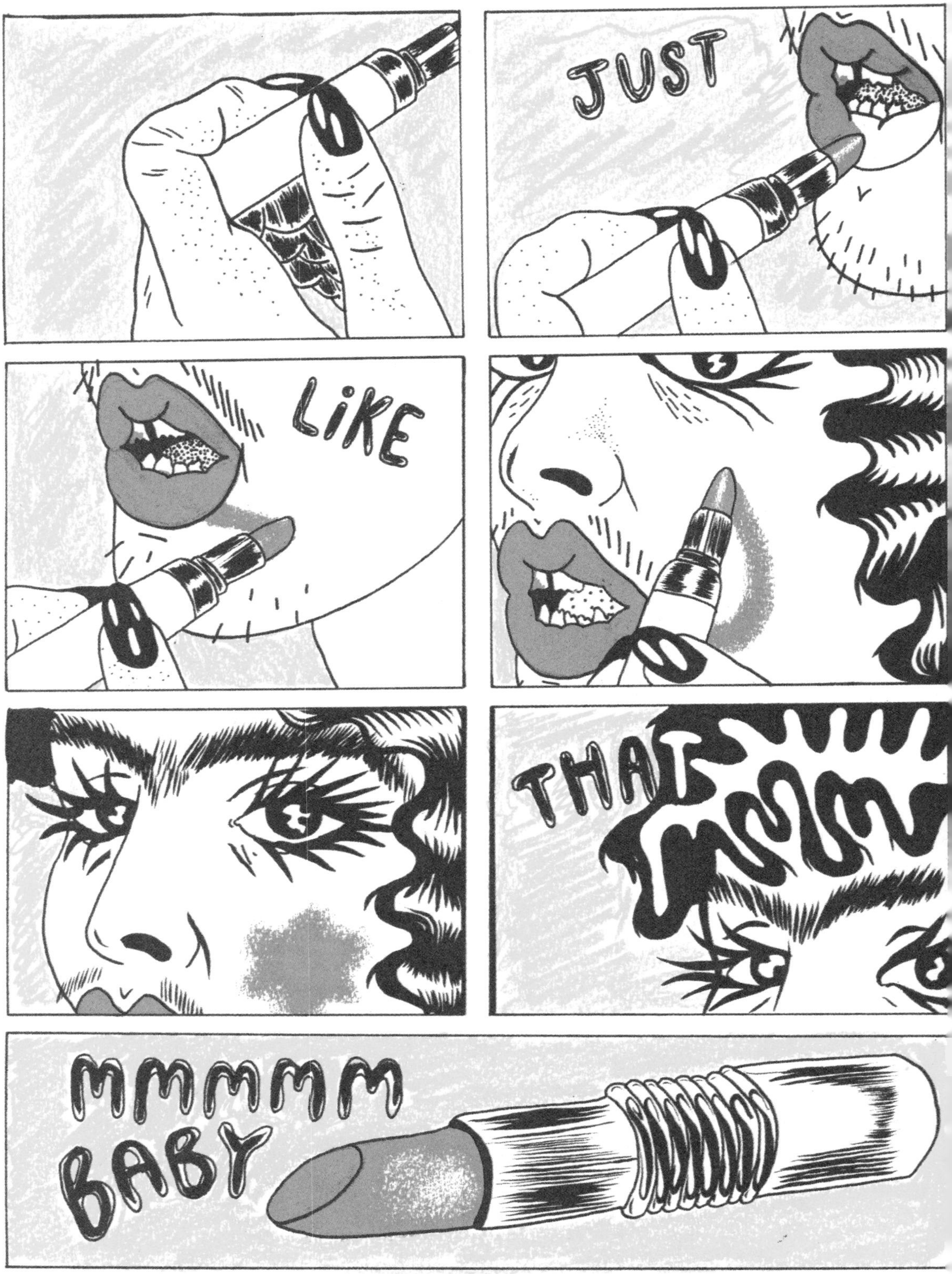
JUST
LiKE
THAT
MMMMM
BABY

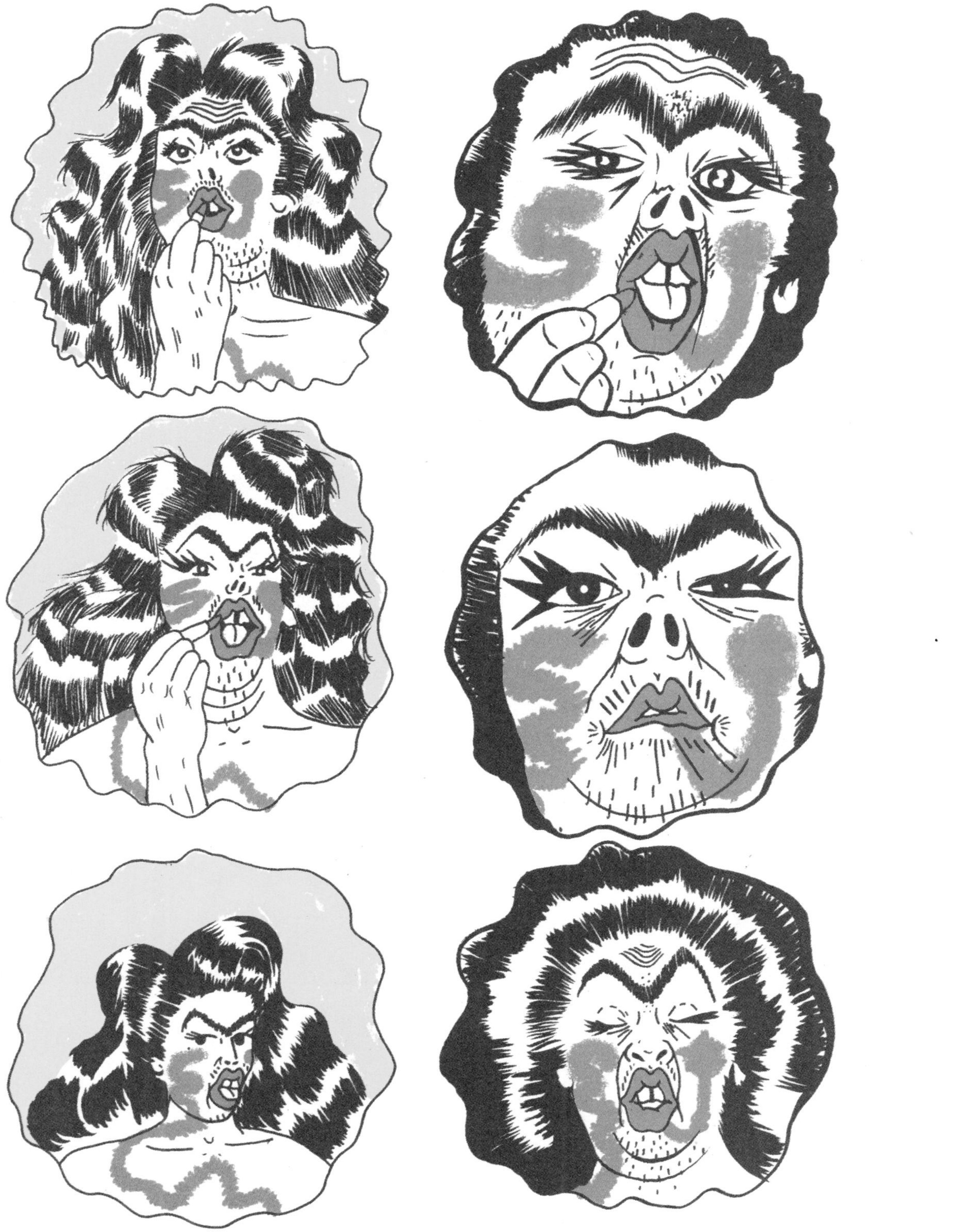

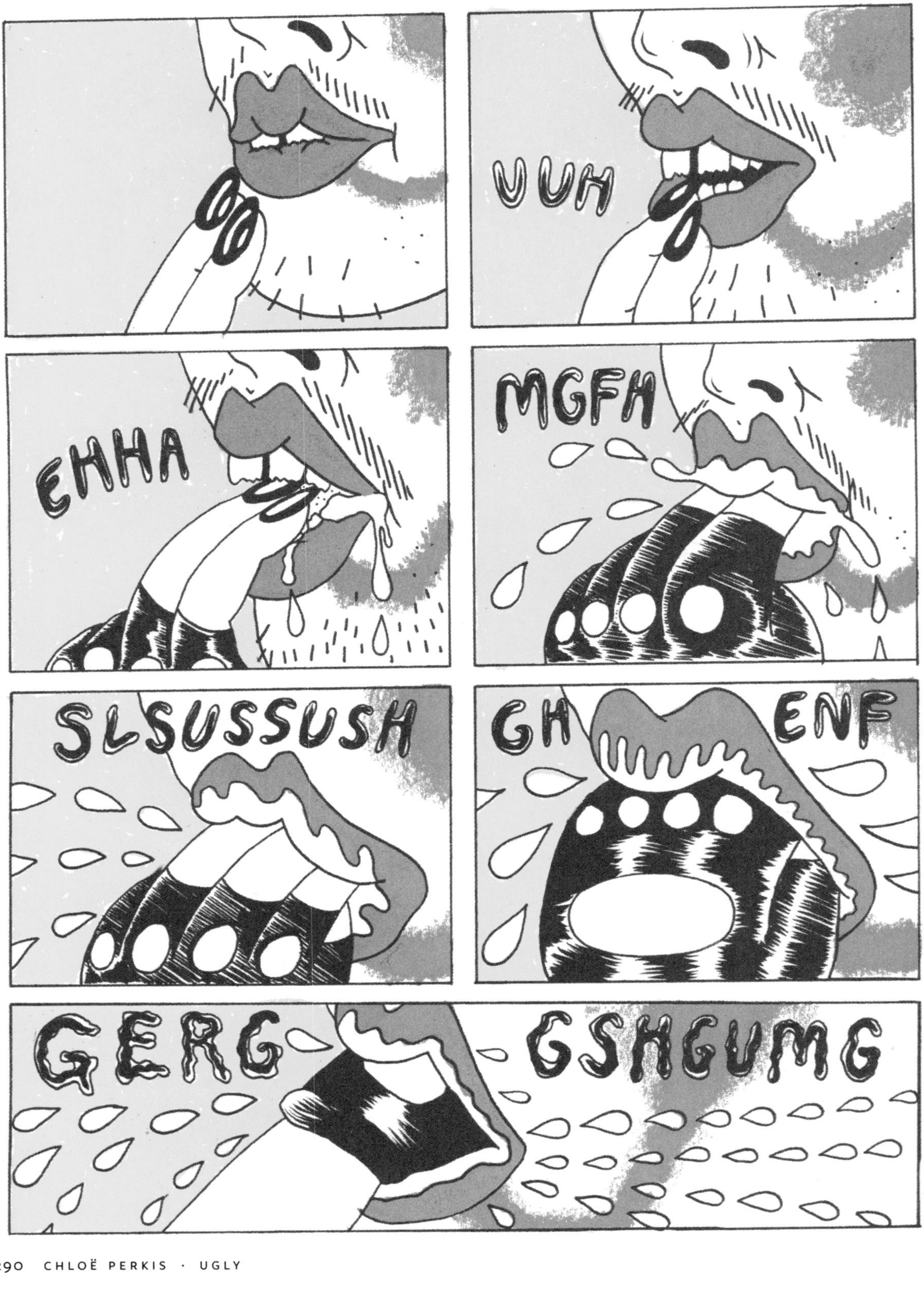
UUH
EHHA
MGFH
SLSUSSUSH
GH
ENF
GERG
GSHGUMG

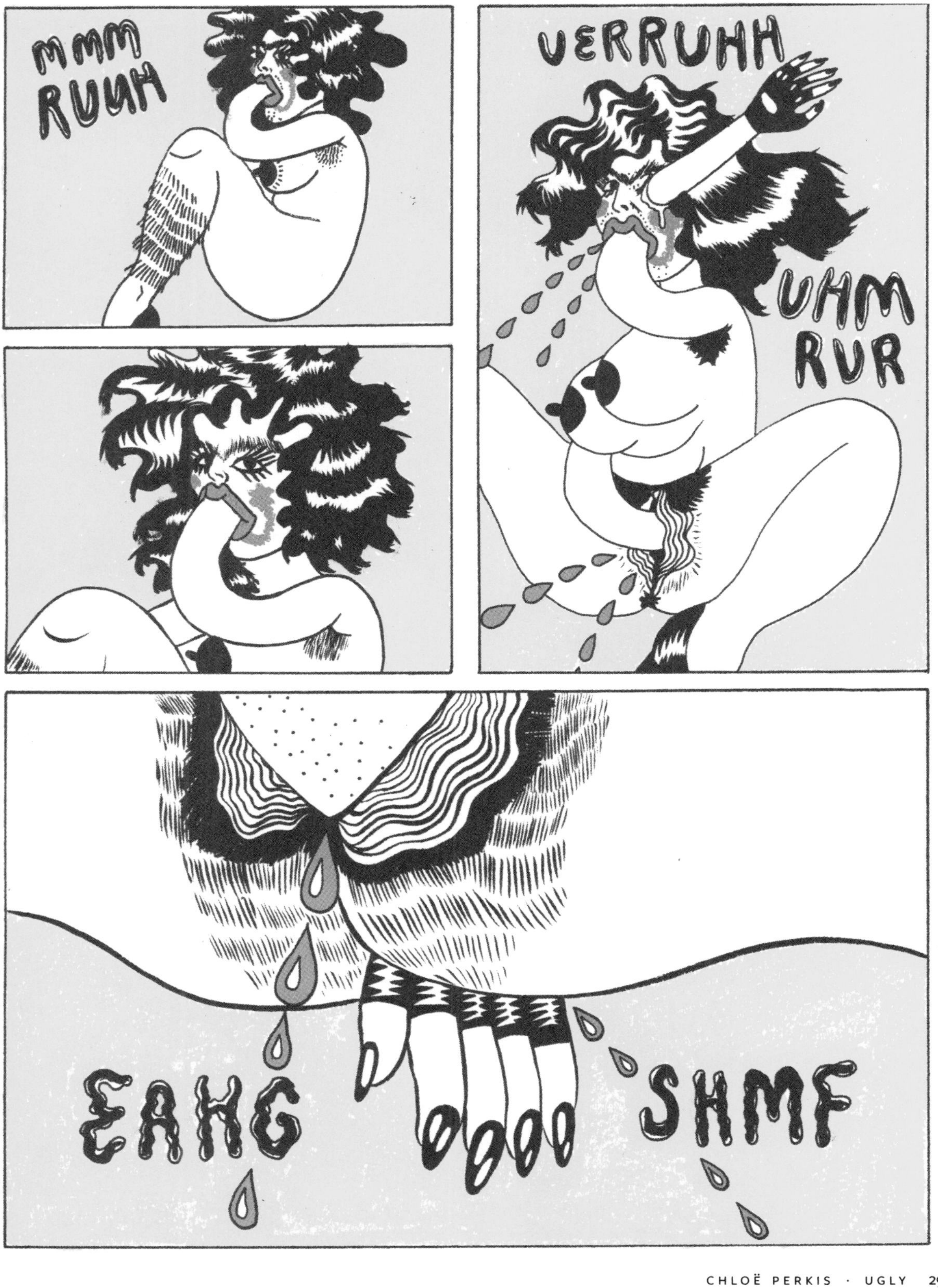
MMM
RUUH
VERRUHH
UHM
RUR
EAHG
SHMF

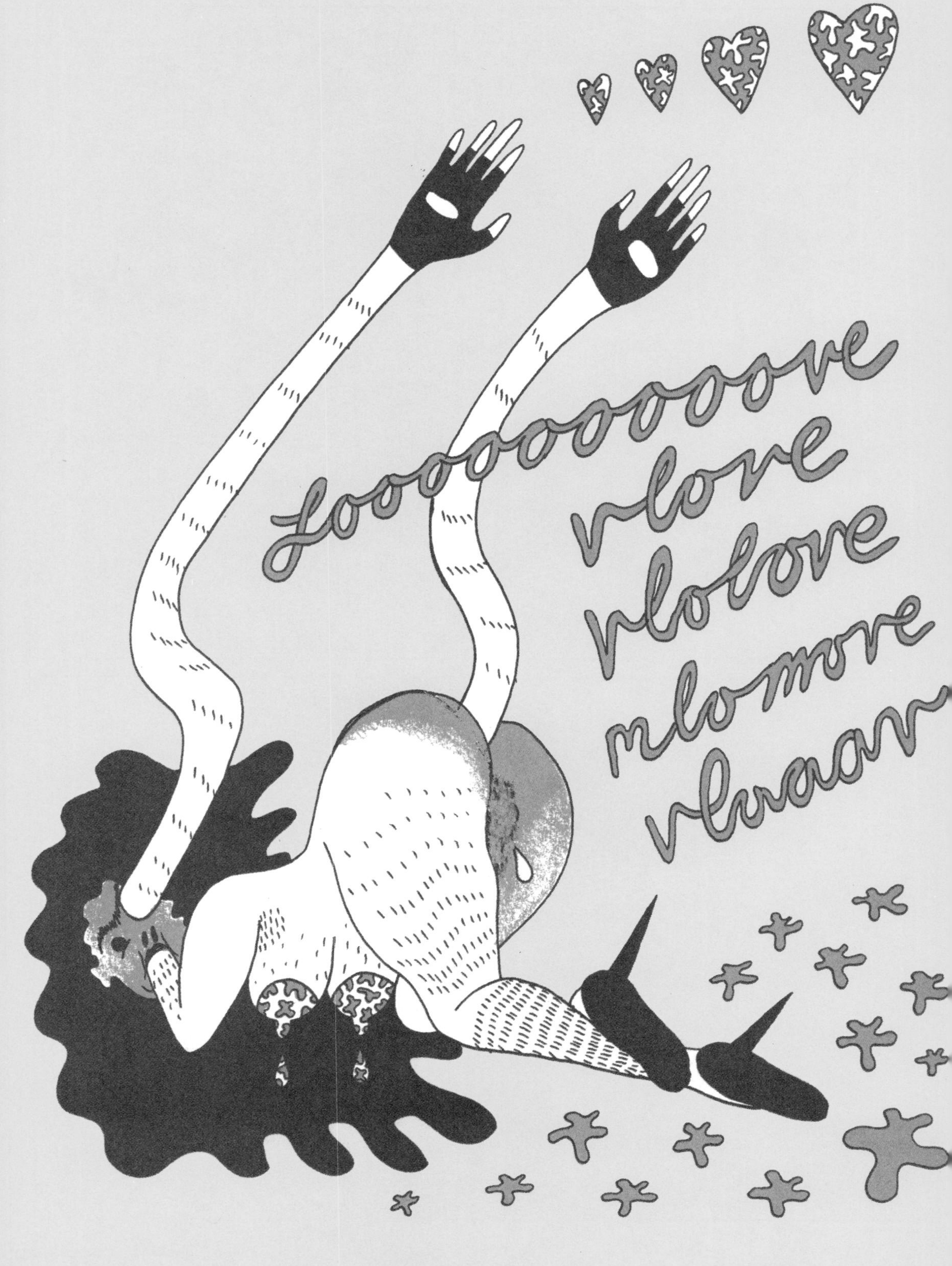
Looooooooove
vlove
vlolove
nlomove
vlwaav

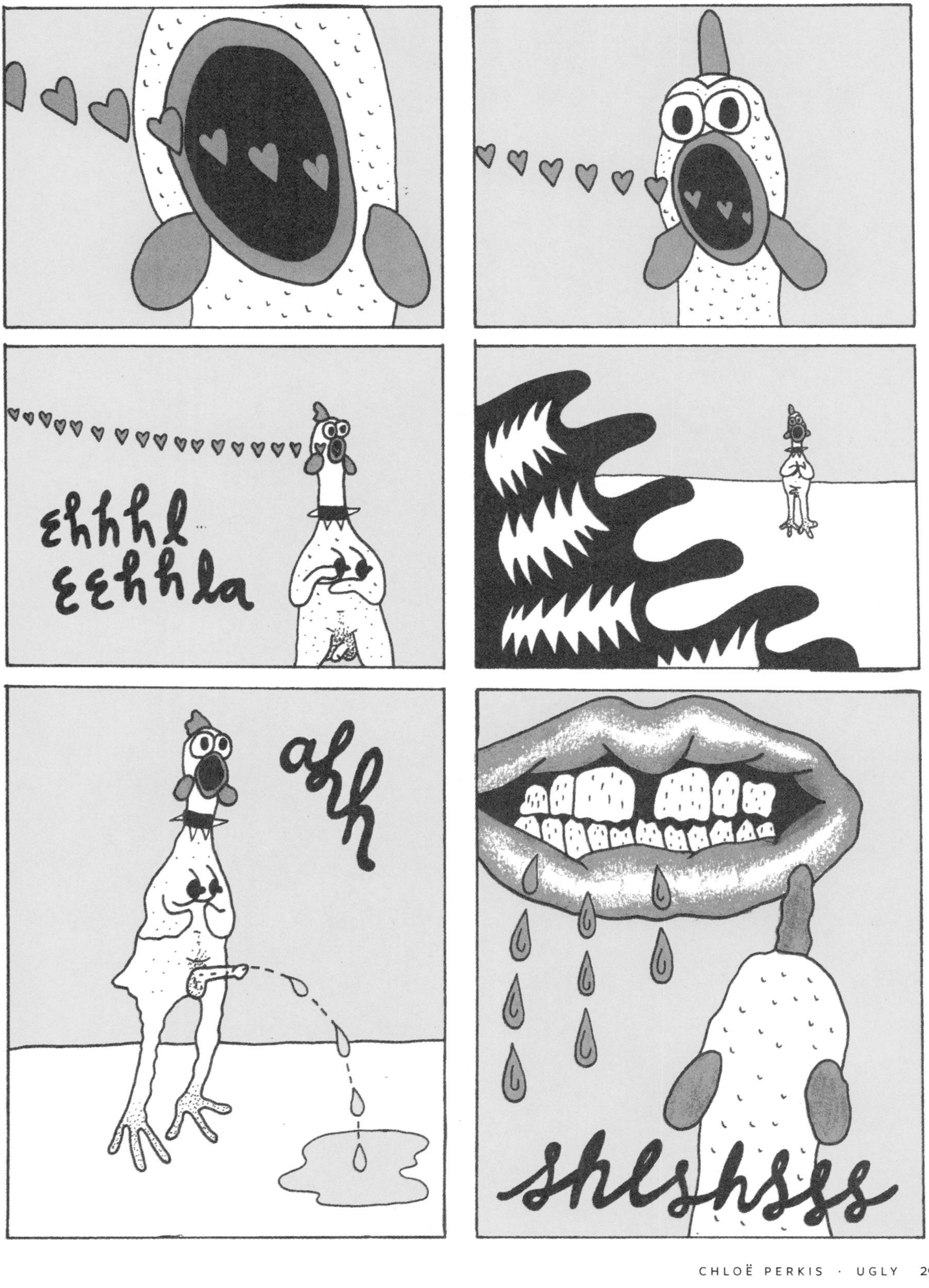
Ehhhl...
EEhhla
ahh
shshsss

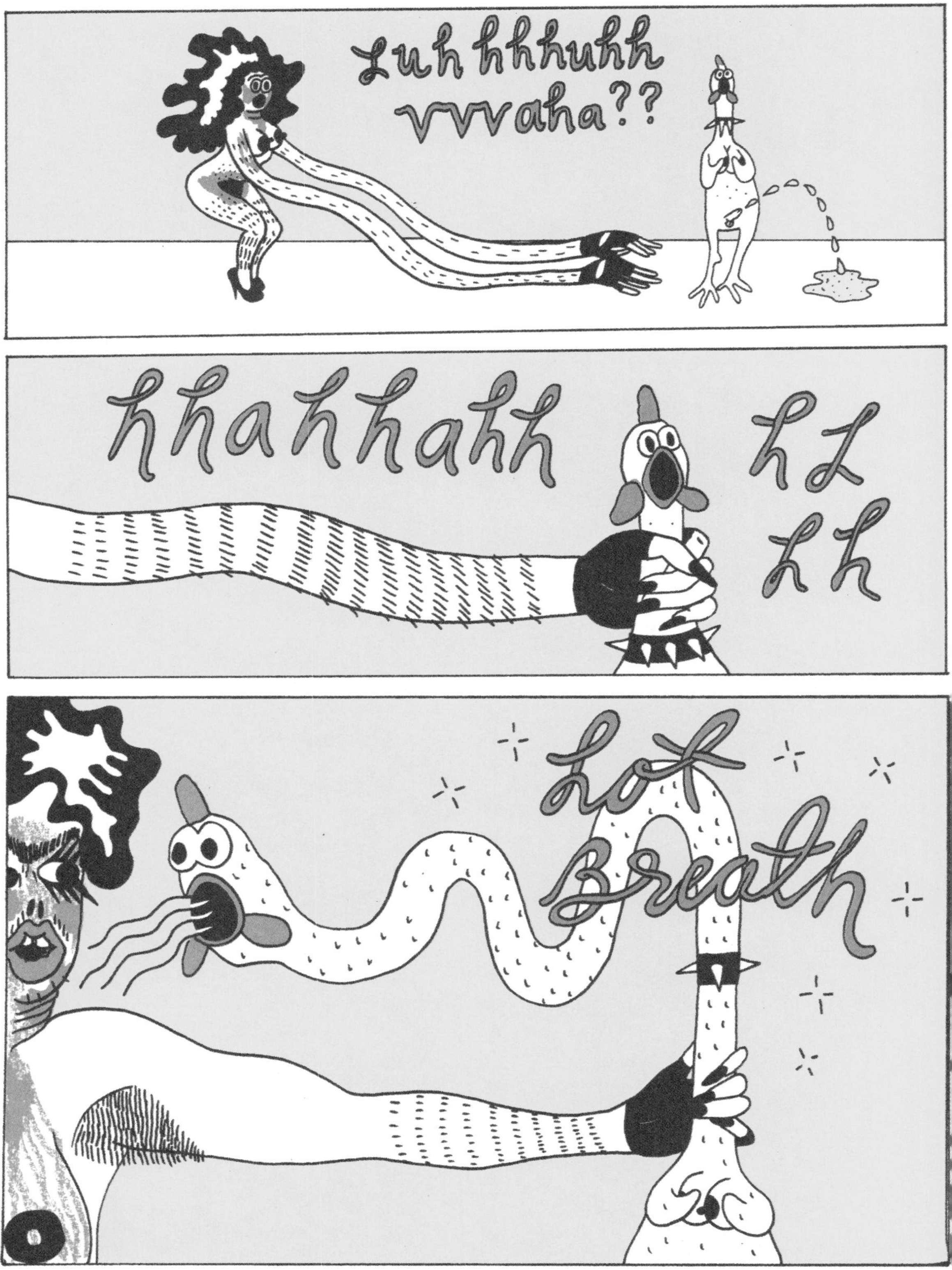
Luhhhhuhh vvvaha??
hhahhahh
hL hh
hot Breath

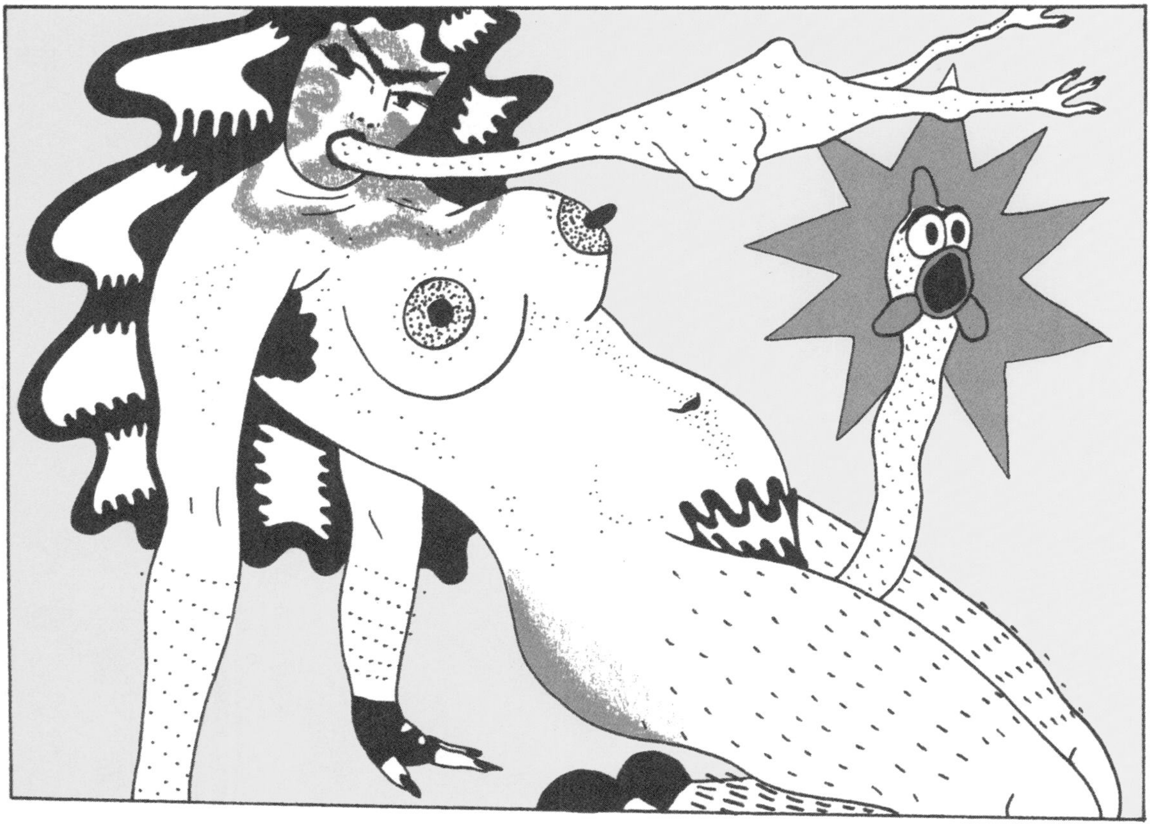

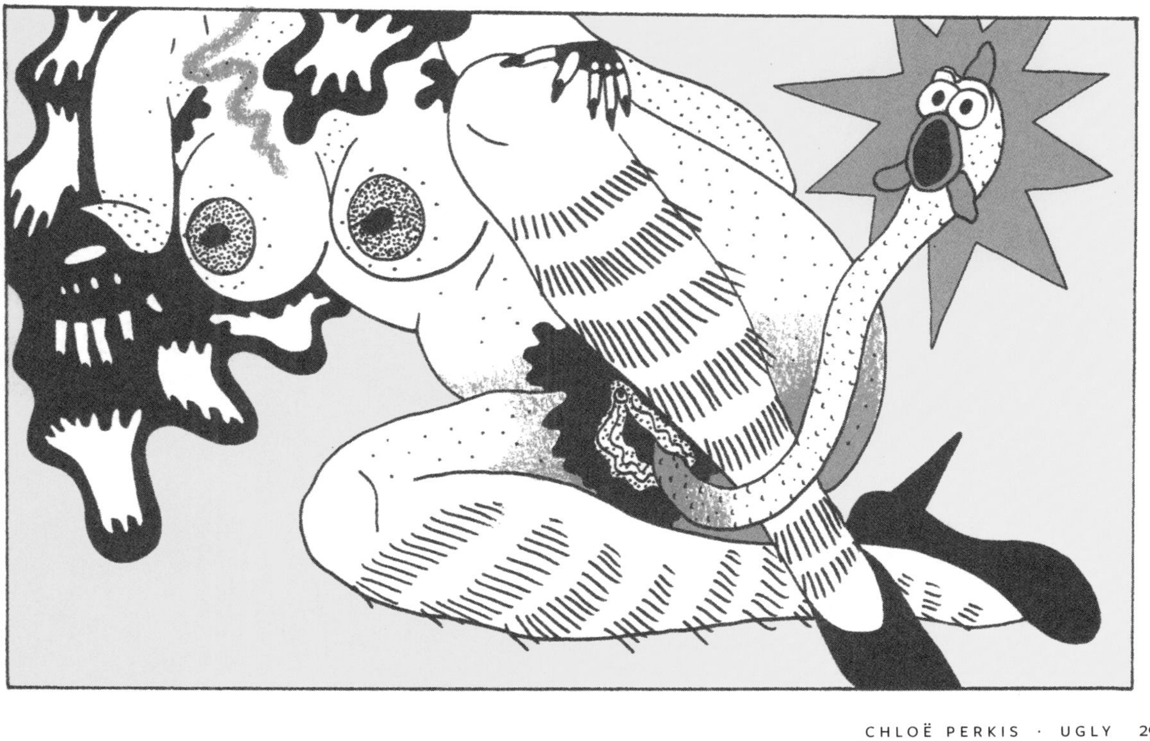

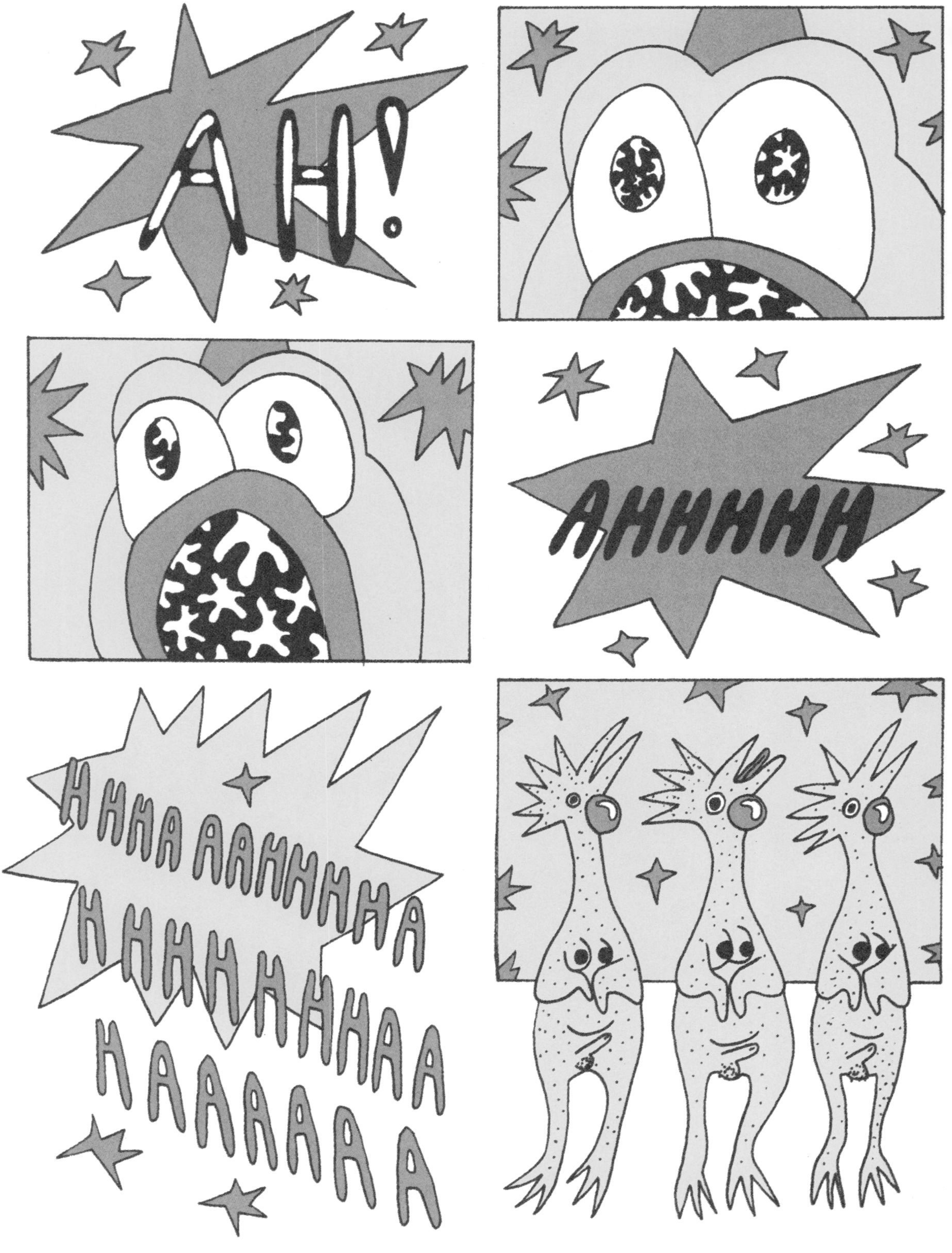
AH!
AHHHHH
HHHA AAHHHHHA
HHHHHHHHHHAA
HAAAAAAA
AAAAAA

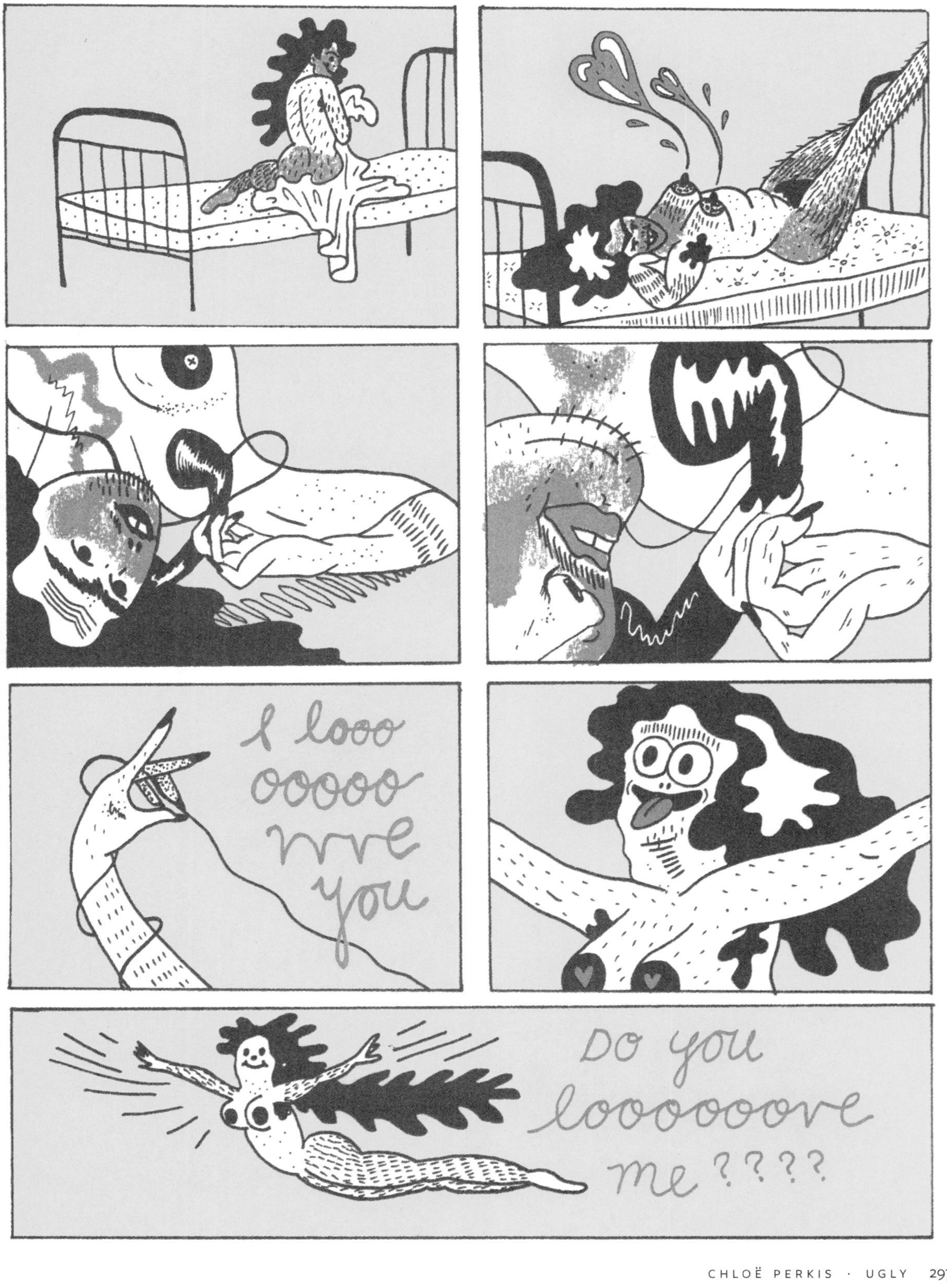
I looo
ooooo
vvve
you
Do you
loooooove
me????

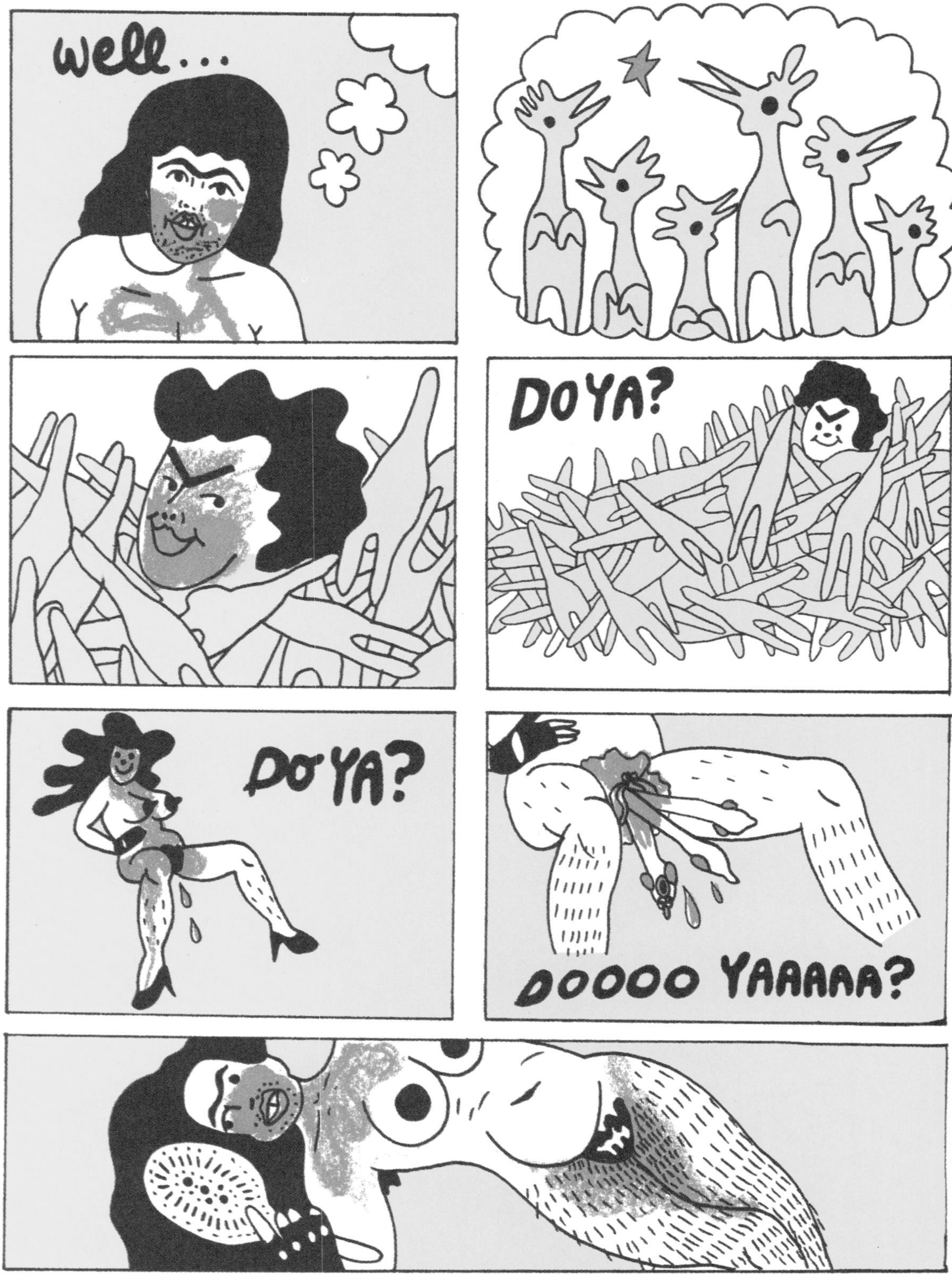
well...
DO YA?
DO YA?
DOOOO YAAAAA?

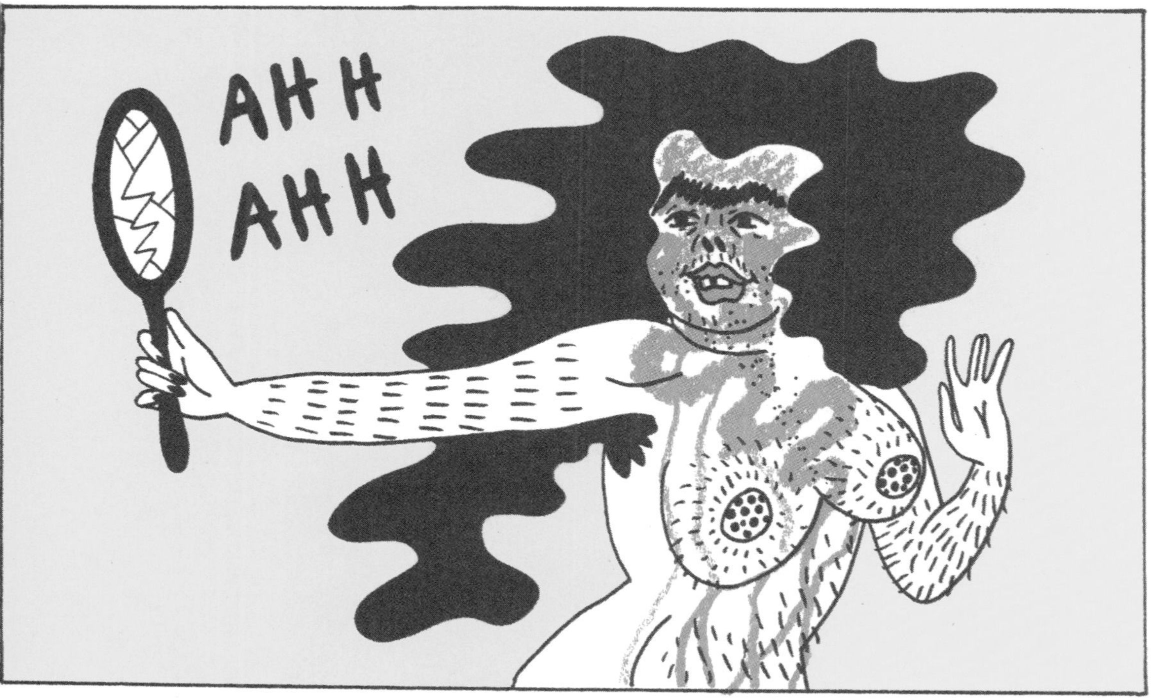
AHH
AHH

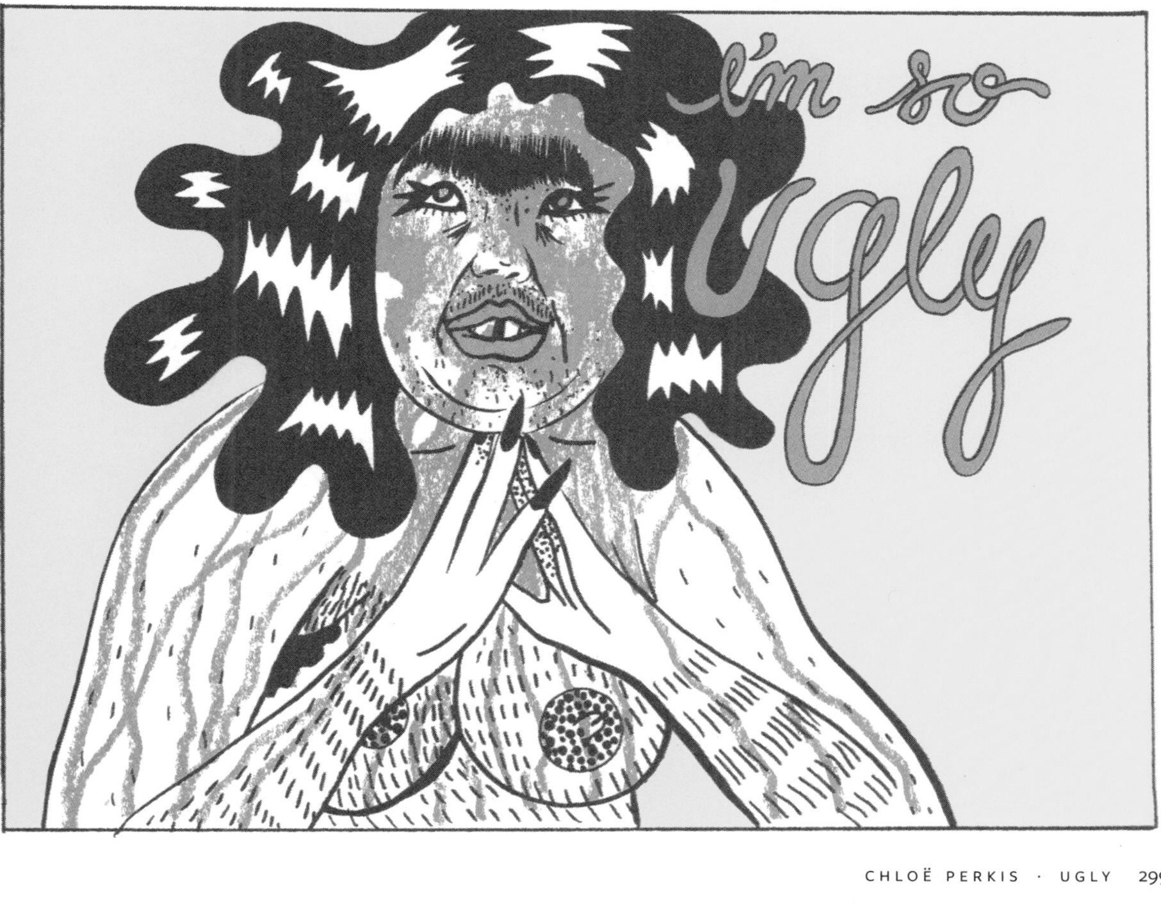
i'm so
ugly

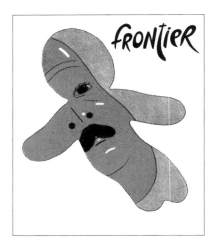

Fatherson

RICHIE POPE

originally published in

Frontier #13
YOUTH IN DECLINE
6.75 x 8 inches · 32 pages

Biography

I'm an illustrator/cartoonist originally from Newport News, Virginia. After attending Virginia Commonwealth University's Illustration program, I went on to start a freelance illustration career. I've worked with publications that include *The New Yorker* and the *New York Times* and done comics for *Shortbox, Youth in Decline,* and *The Nib.* My work has been recognized by American Illustration, Society of Illustrators, and Spectrum.
richiepope.com

Statement

The main text of *Fatherson* hopefully speaks for itself, but there's a subtext that's personal for me: black fatherhood. America's reductive media iconography of black fatherhood tends to be "deadbeats or conservative Cosbys." One example is a racist fear, the other is a racist dream. In my lifetime, from observing my own father, to observing my friends' fathers, to see those friends become fathers themselves, black fatherhood is so much more rich and contradictory than what American media describes. As I get older, my own anxieties about potential fatherhood also have their hands all over this book. Does seeing yourself as a good and just person automatically make you a good father? For me, *Fatherson* is an absurdist send-up and ode to all those different kinds of black fatherhood, from toolboxes to durags to Newport cigarettes.

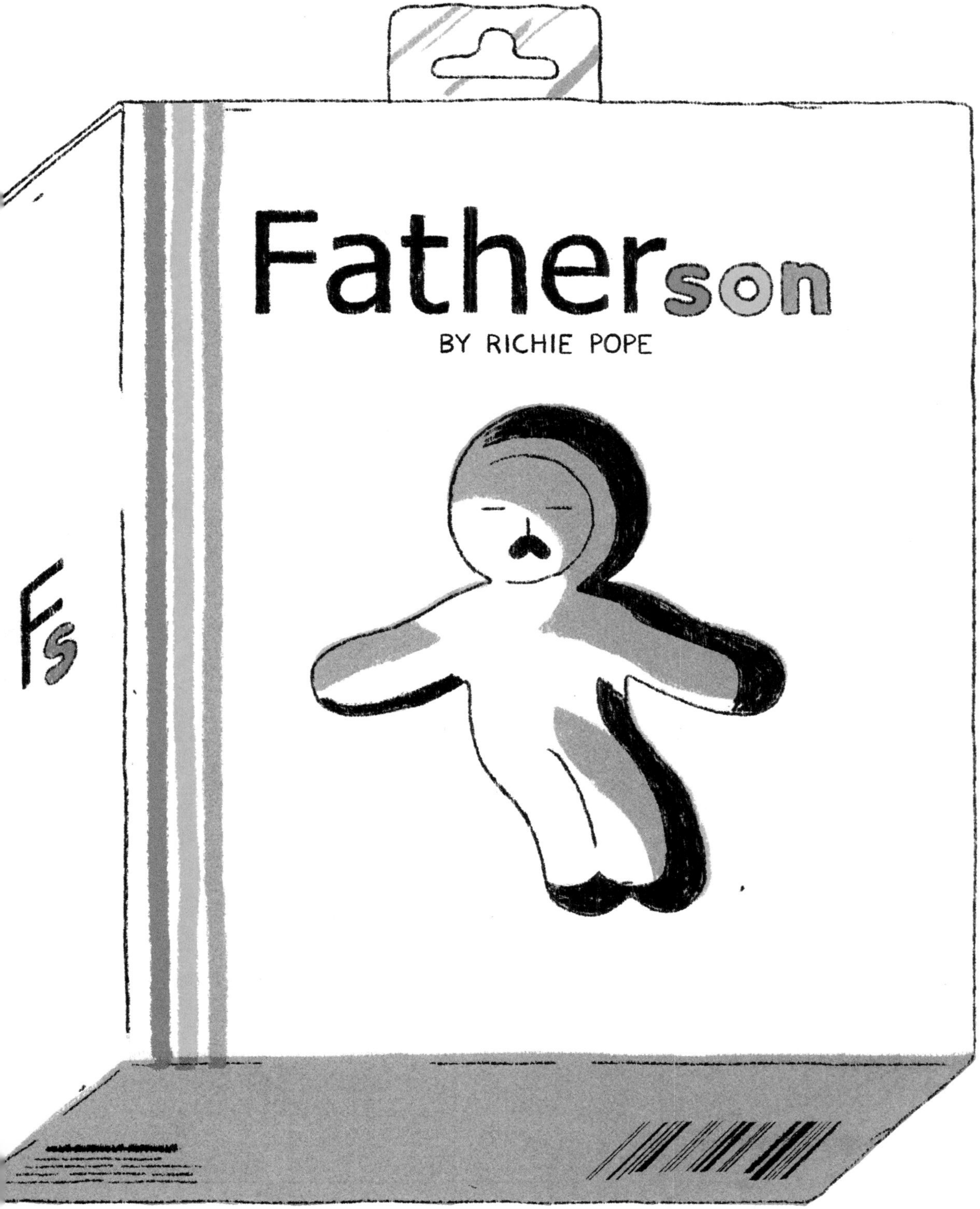
Fatherson
BY RICHIE POPE
Fs

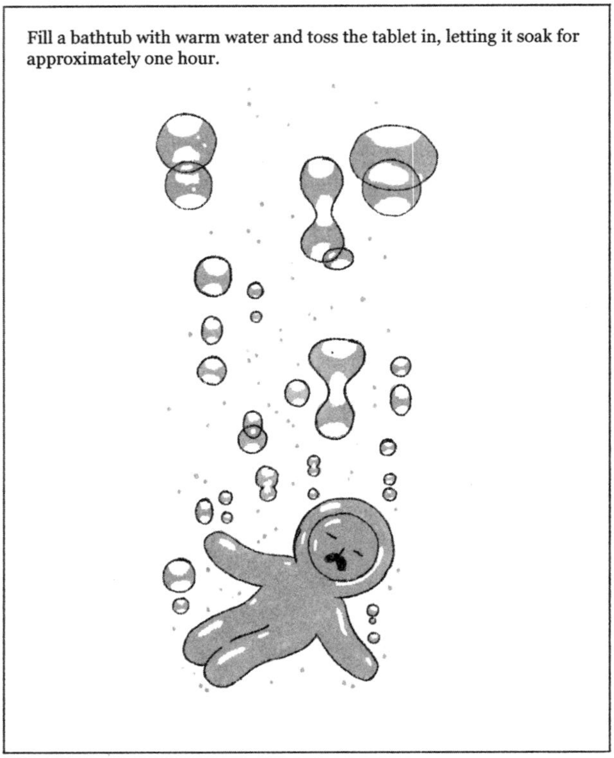
Fill a bathtub with warm water and toss the tablet in, letting it soak for approximately one hour.

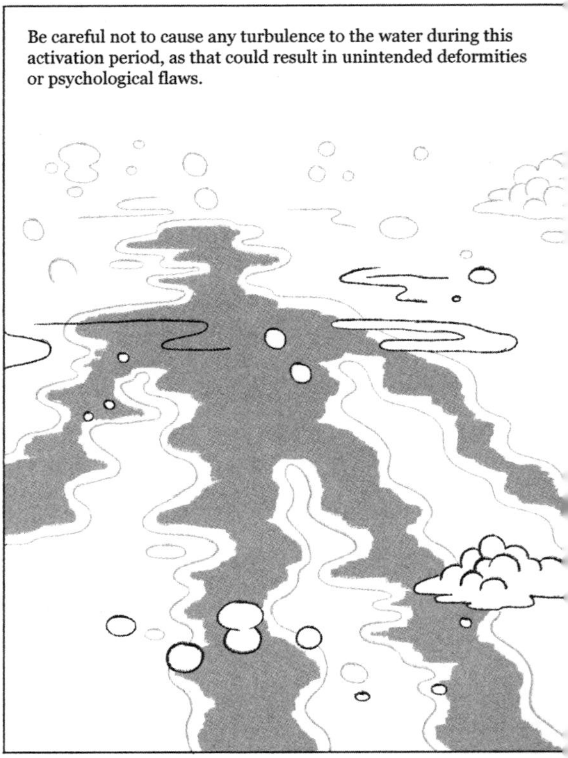
Be careful not to cause any turbulence to the water during this activation period, as that could result in unintended deformities or psychological flaws.

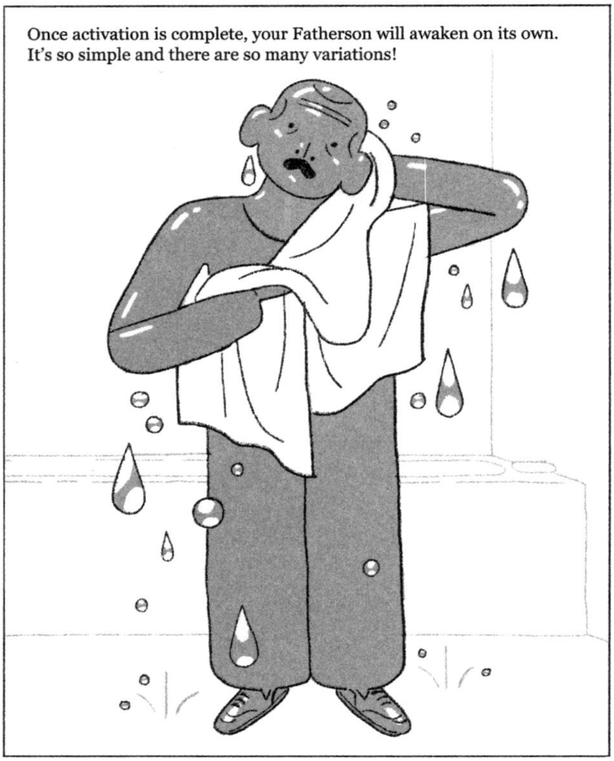
Once activation is complete, your Fatherson will awaken on its own.
It's so simple and there are so many variations!

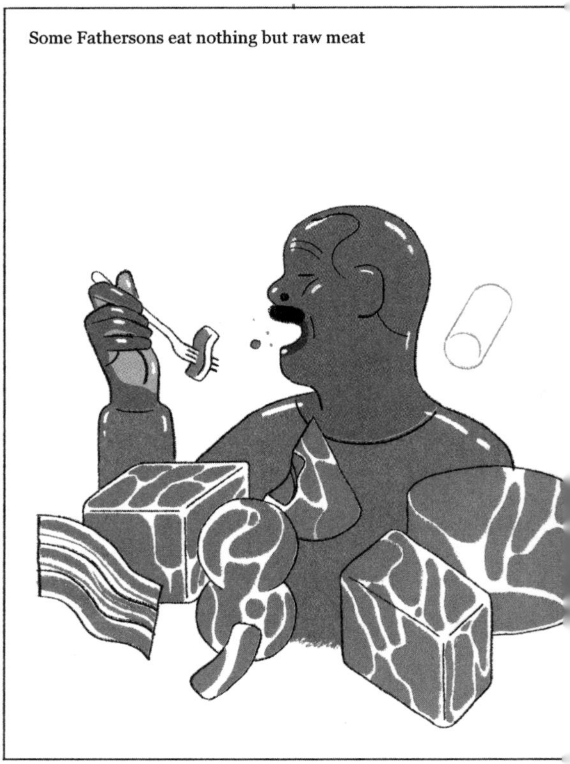
Some Fathersons eat nothing but raw meat

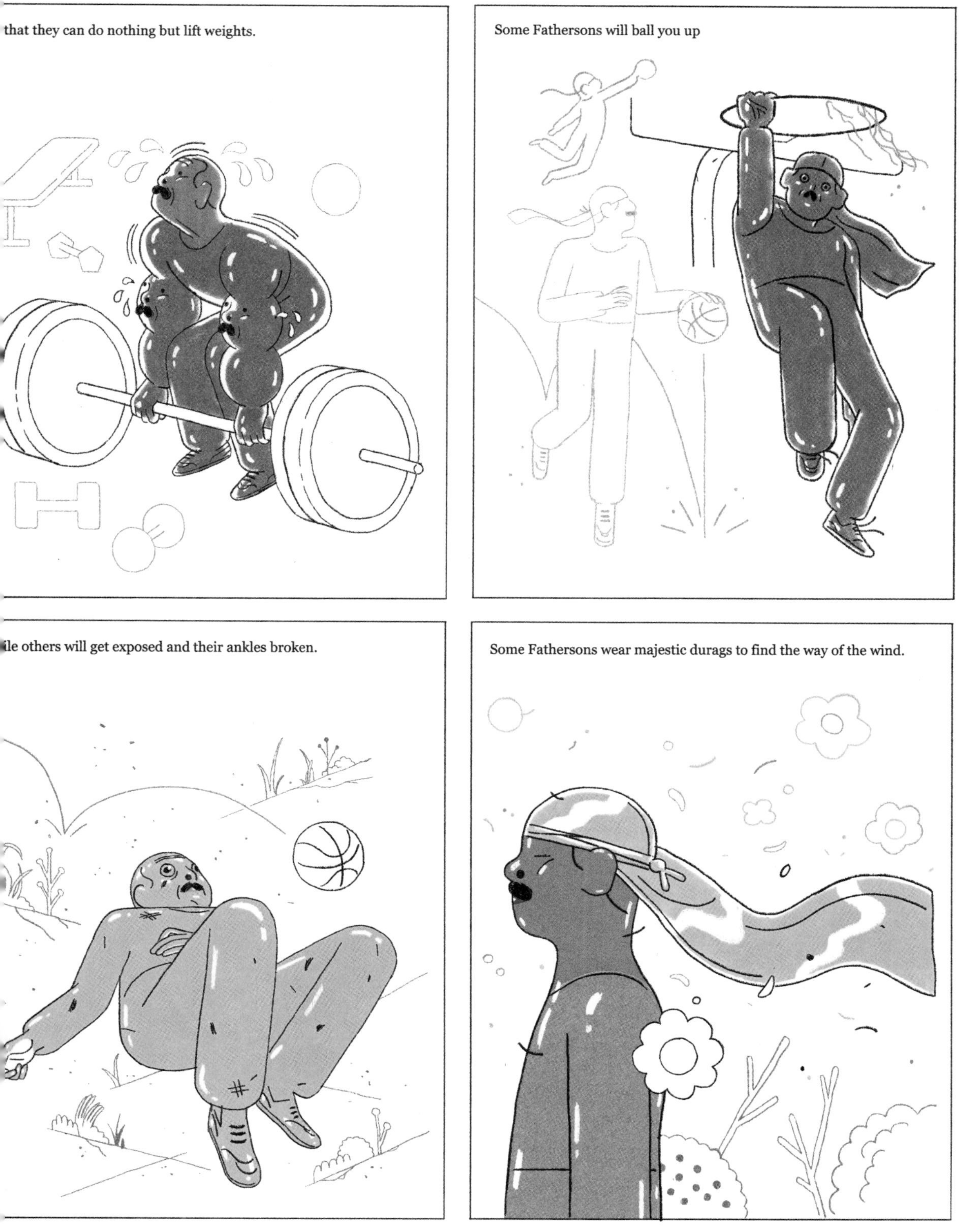
that they can do nothing but lift weights.
Some Fathersons will ball you up
ile others will get exposed and their ankles broken.
Some Fathersons wear majestic durags to find the way of the wind.

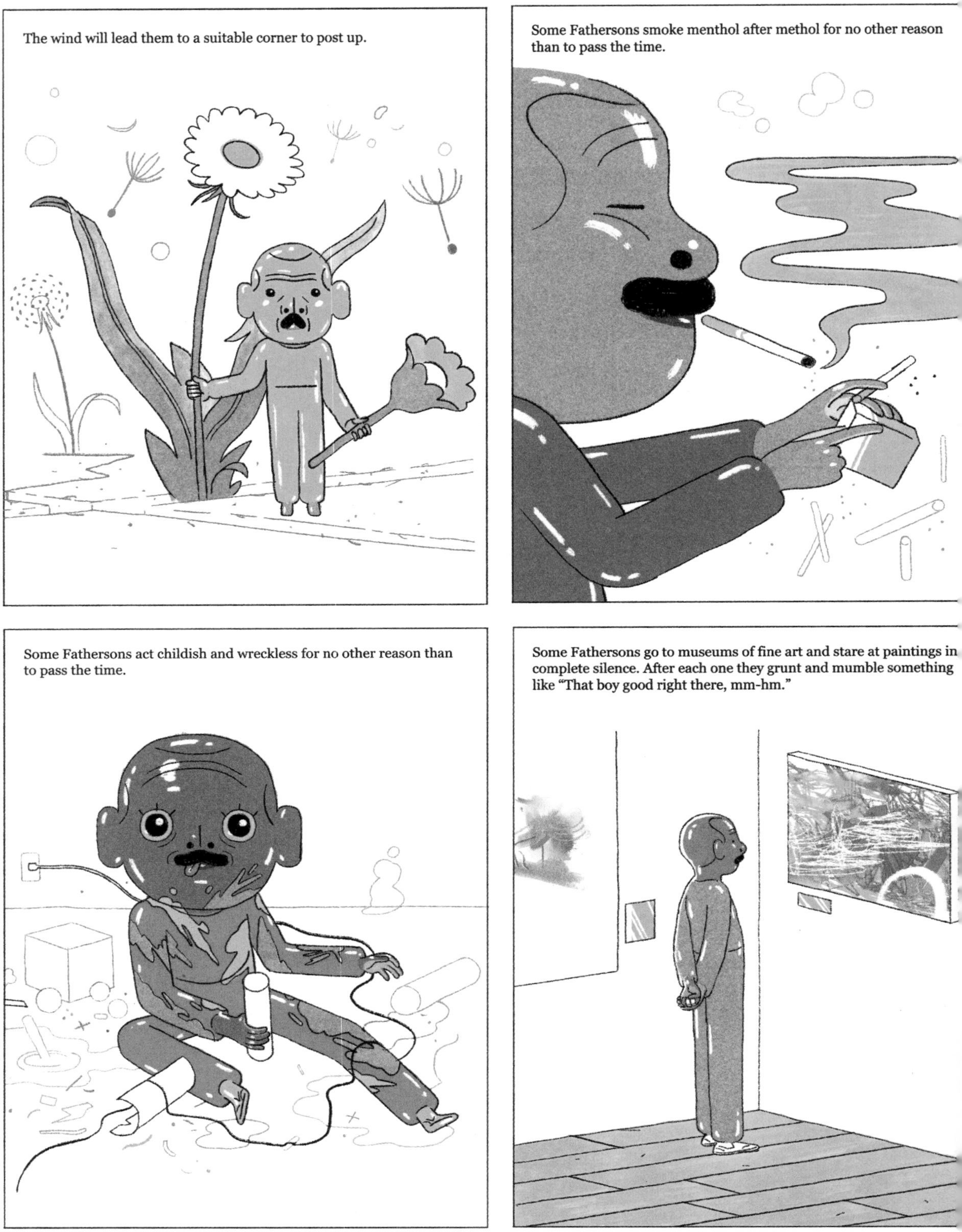
The wind will lead them to a suitable corner to post up.
Some Fathersons smoke menthol after methol for no other reason than to pass the time.
Some Fathersons act childish and wreckless for no other reason than to pass the time.
Some Fathersons go to museums of fine art and stare at paintings in complete silence. After each one they grunt and mumble something like "That boy good right there, mm-hm."

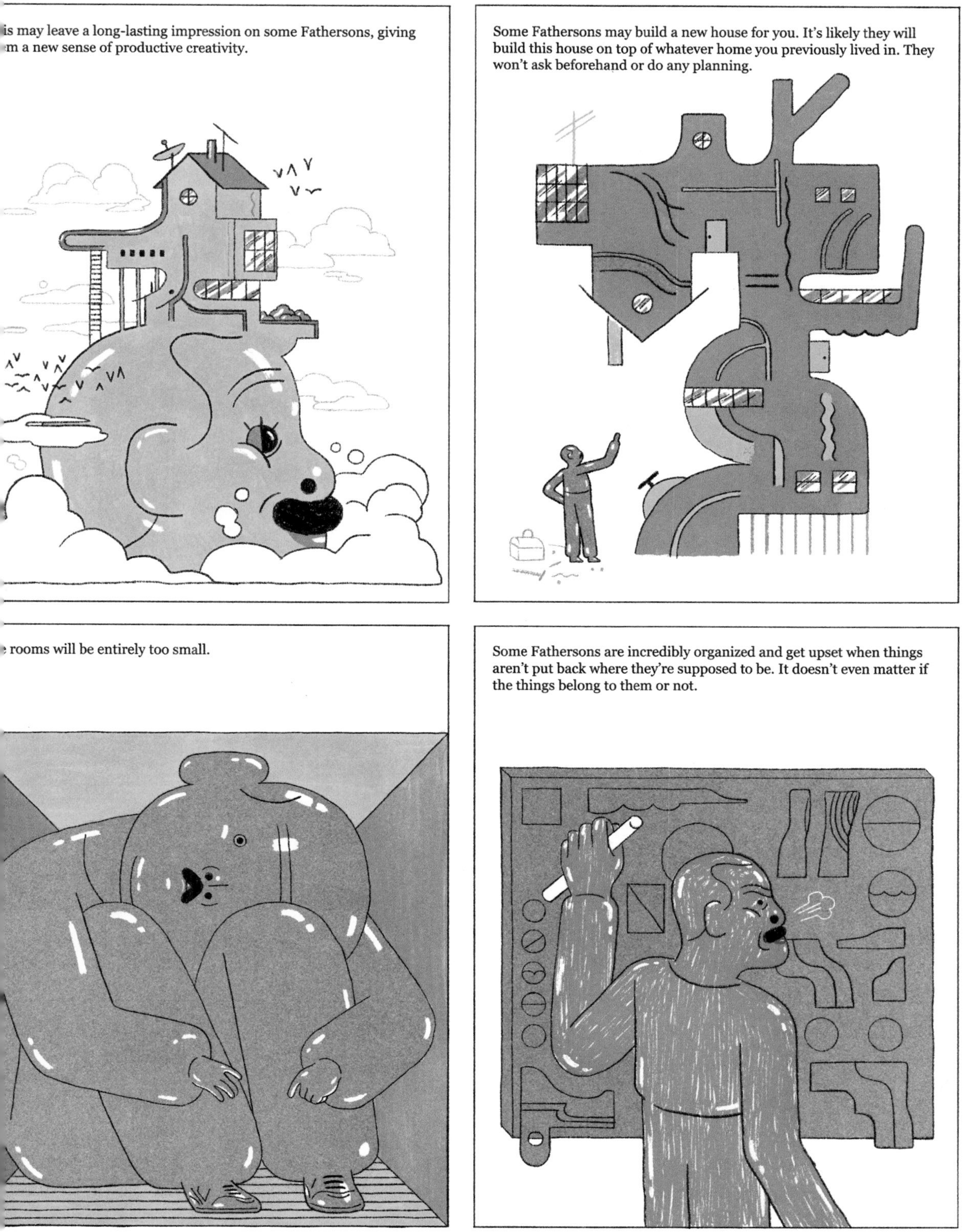

is may leave a long-lasting impression on some Fathersons, giving m a new sense of productive creativity.
Some Fathersons may build a new house for you. It's likely they will build this house on top of whatever home you previously lived in. They won't ask beforehand or do any planning.
rooms will be entirely too small.
Some Fathersons are incredibly organized and get upset when things aren't put back where they're supposed to be. It doesn't even matter if the things belong to them or not.

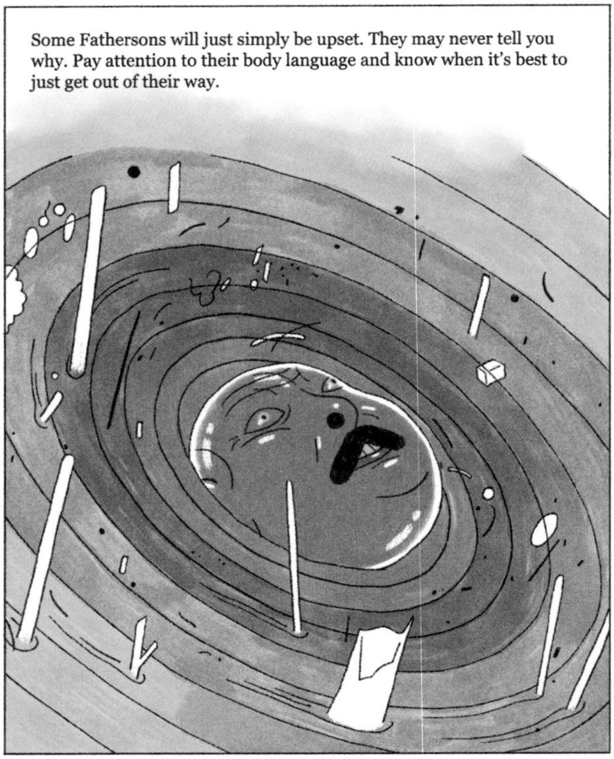
Some Fathersons will just simply be upset. They may never tell you why. Pay attention to their body language and know when it's best to just get out of their way.

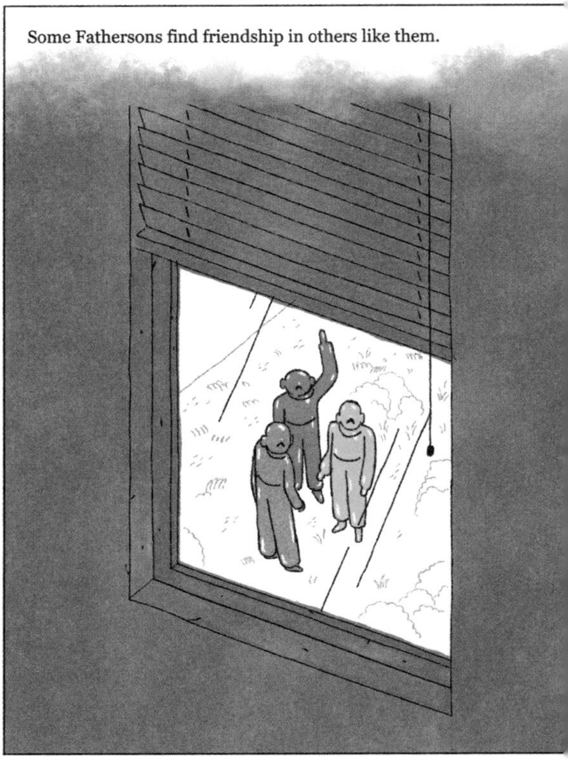
Some Fathersons find friendship in others like them.

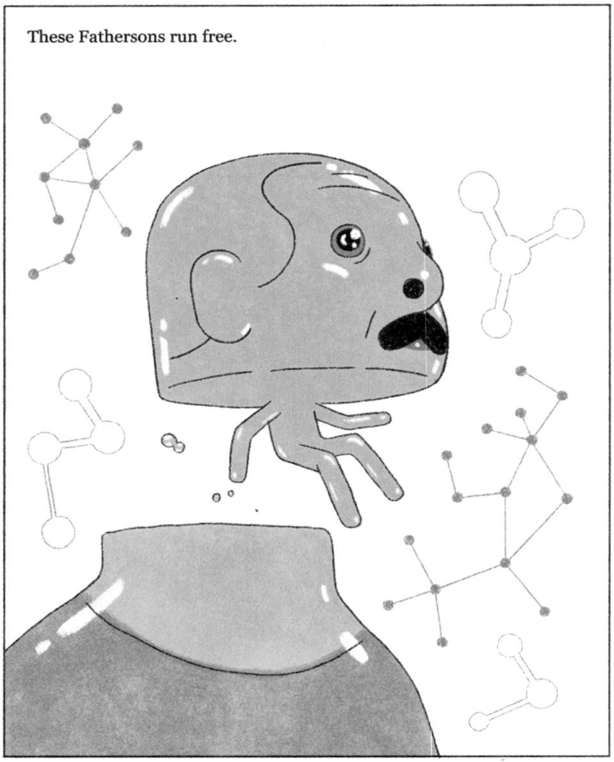
These Fathersons run free.

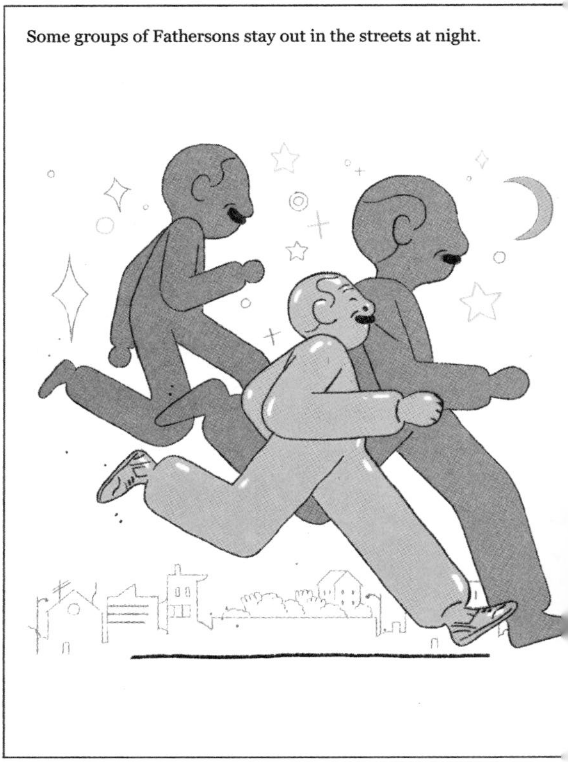
Some groups of Fathersons stay out in the streets at night.

ghting anyone who tests them.

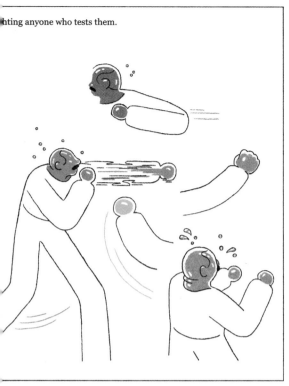

Some Fathersons run so far they forget where they are.

hers run so far they forget who they are.

Some Fathersons get sick. Sometimes they don't even know.

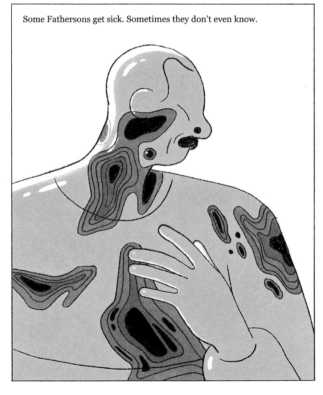

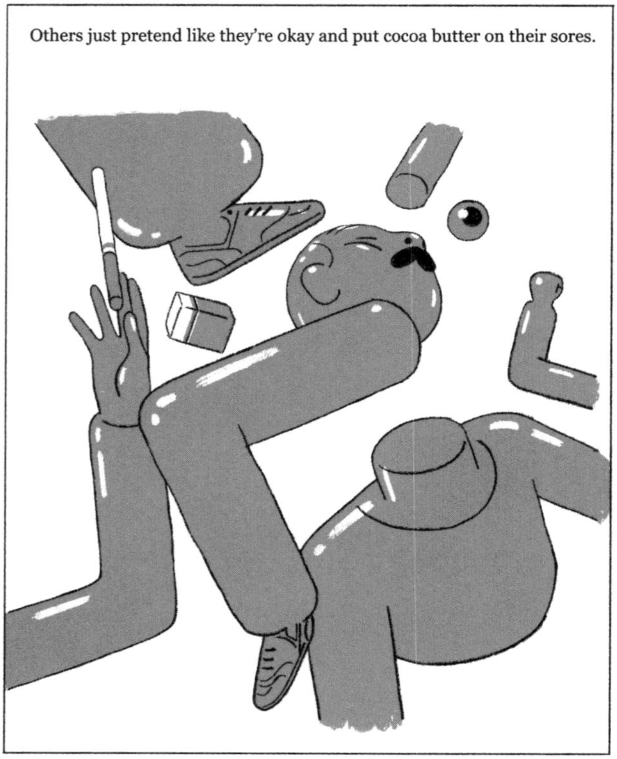
Others just pretend like they're okay and put cocoa butter on their sores.

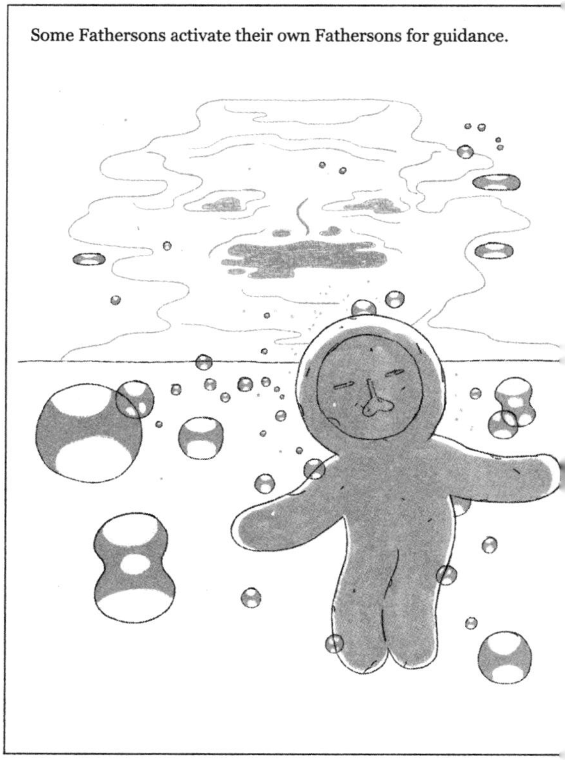
Some Fathersons activate their own Fathersons for guidance.

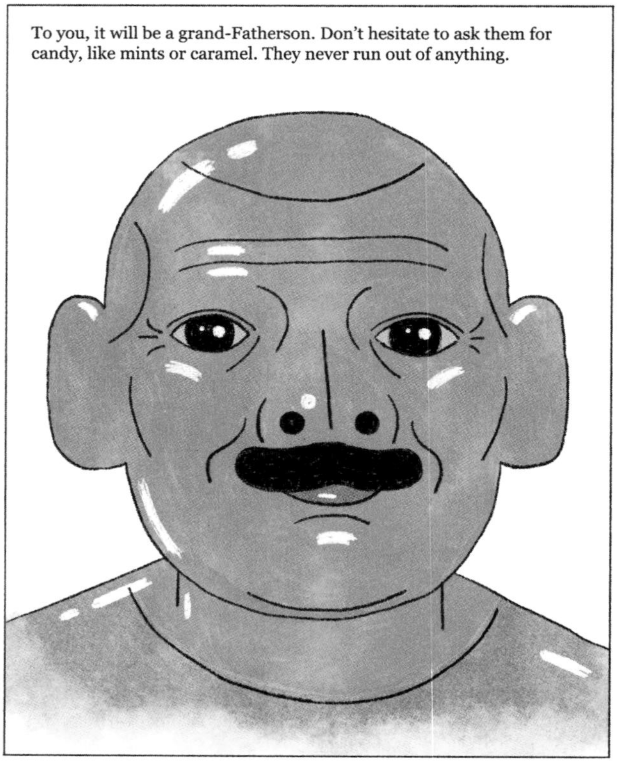
To you, it will be a grand-Fatherson. Don't hesitate to ask them for candy, like mints or caramel. They never run out of anything.

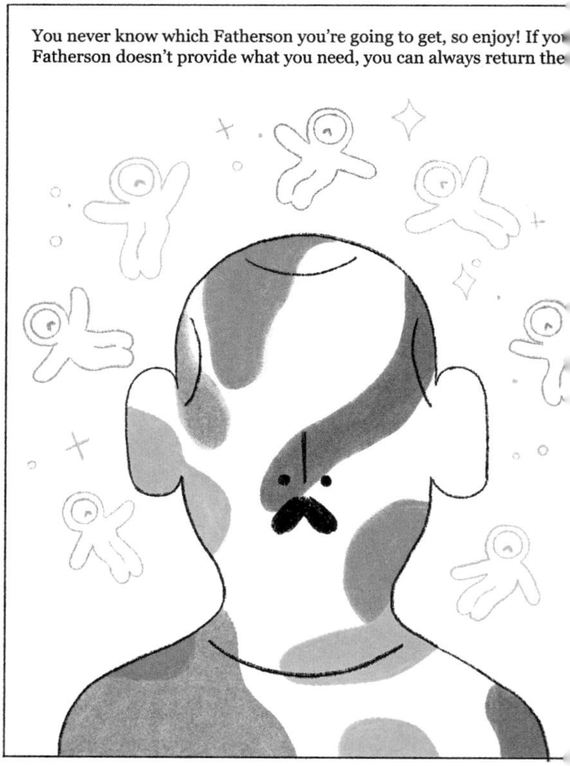
You never know which Fatherson you're going to get, so enjoy! If yo
Fatherson doesn't provide what you need, you can always return the

for credit towards another.

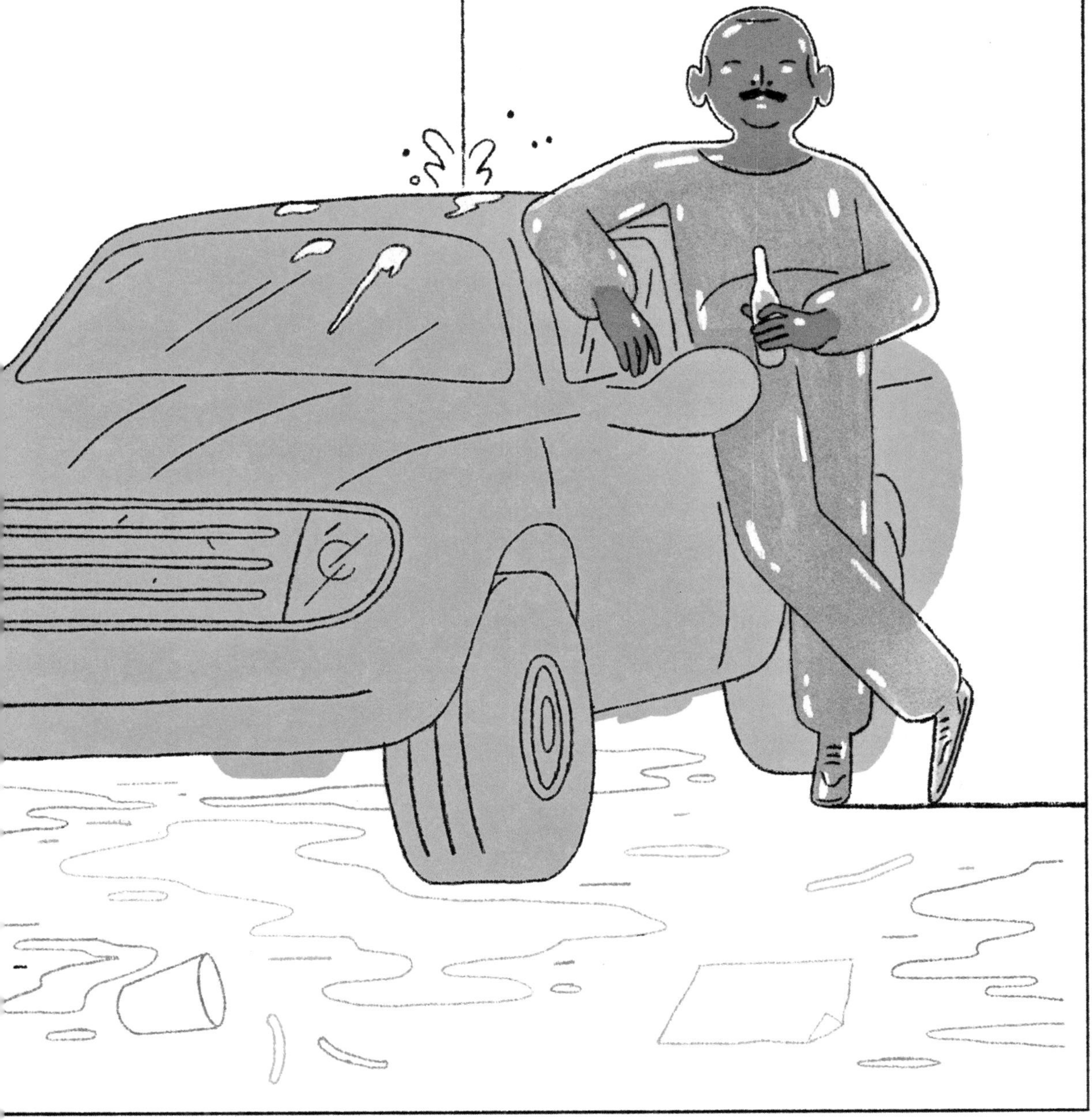

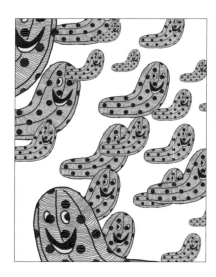

Untitled (Excerpt)

MICHAEL RIDGE

originally published in

Phood Phrends #2
SELF-PUBLISHED
8.5 x 11 inches · 40 pages

Biography

Born in southwestern Pennsylvania, Michael studied printmaking at Edinboro University of Pennsylvania and drawing at the School for the Museum of Fine Arts in Boston. He has lived in Chicago since 2007.
36lbsofproduct.com

Statement

This excerpt comes from the second chapter of a crime comic called *Phood Phrends*. Its plot centers upon two cars and the criminals who drive them. Keep in mind that this short parody is a TV show being watched by a protagonist who's about to meet their unexpected passenger.

Hey, How would you like to ride around with me?
I'm sorry, I can't, I'm going steady
TEMP
E
GAS
0 10 20 30 40 50 60 70 80
221602
Ah, come on! You're just riding around with a bunch of girls.
I just can't.

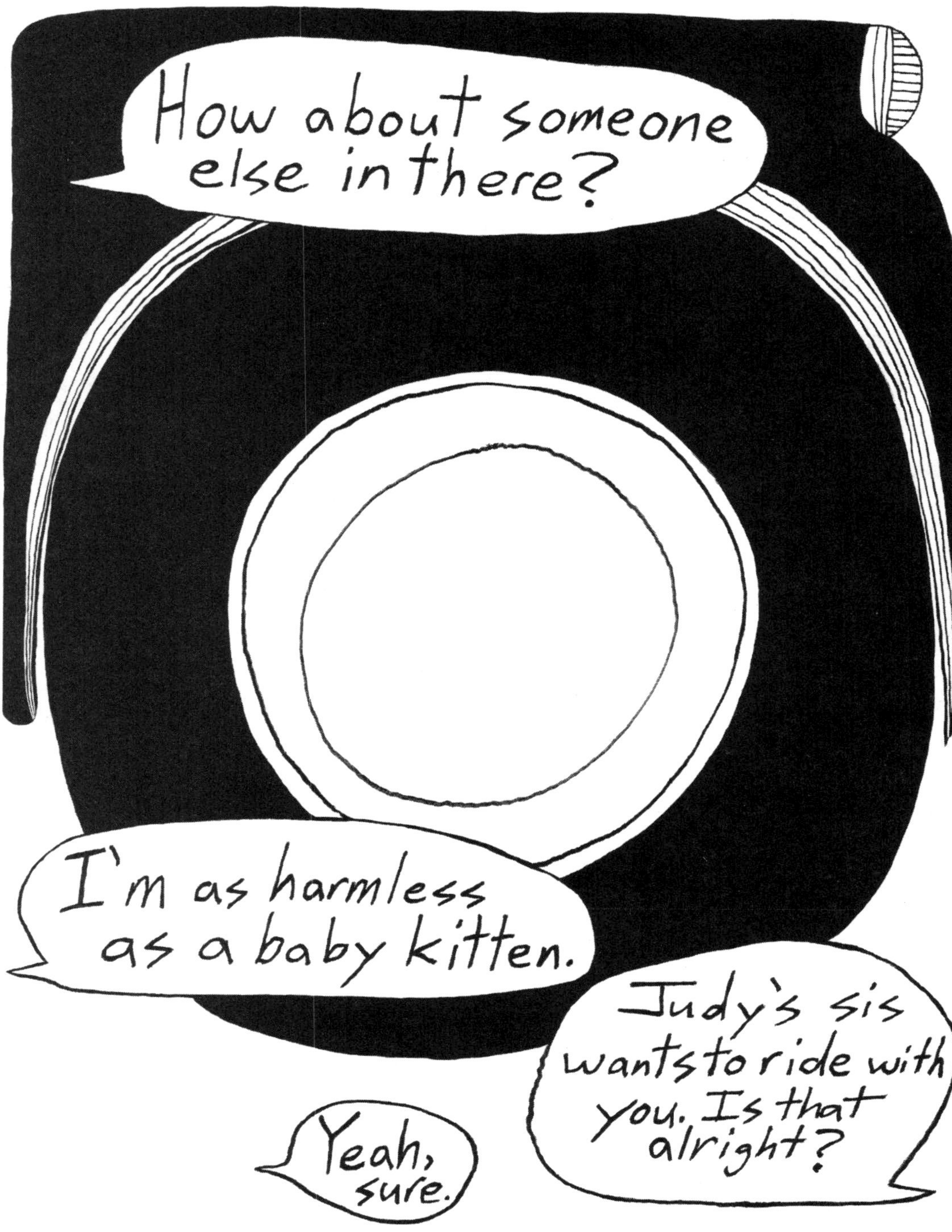
How about someone else in there?
I'm as harmless as a baby kitten.
Judy's sis wants to ride with you. Is that alright?
Yeah, sure.

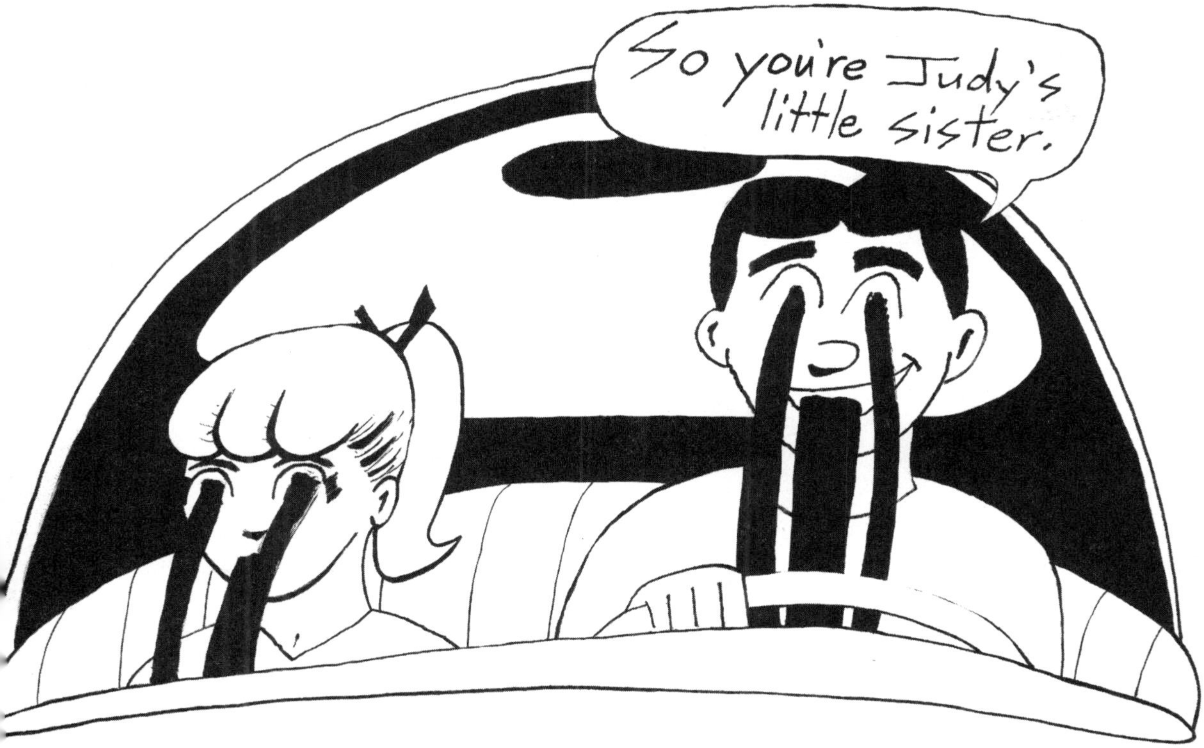
So you're Judy's little sister.

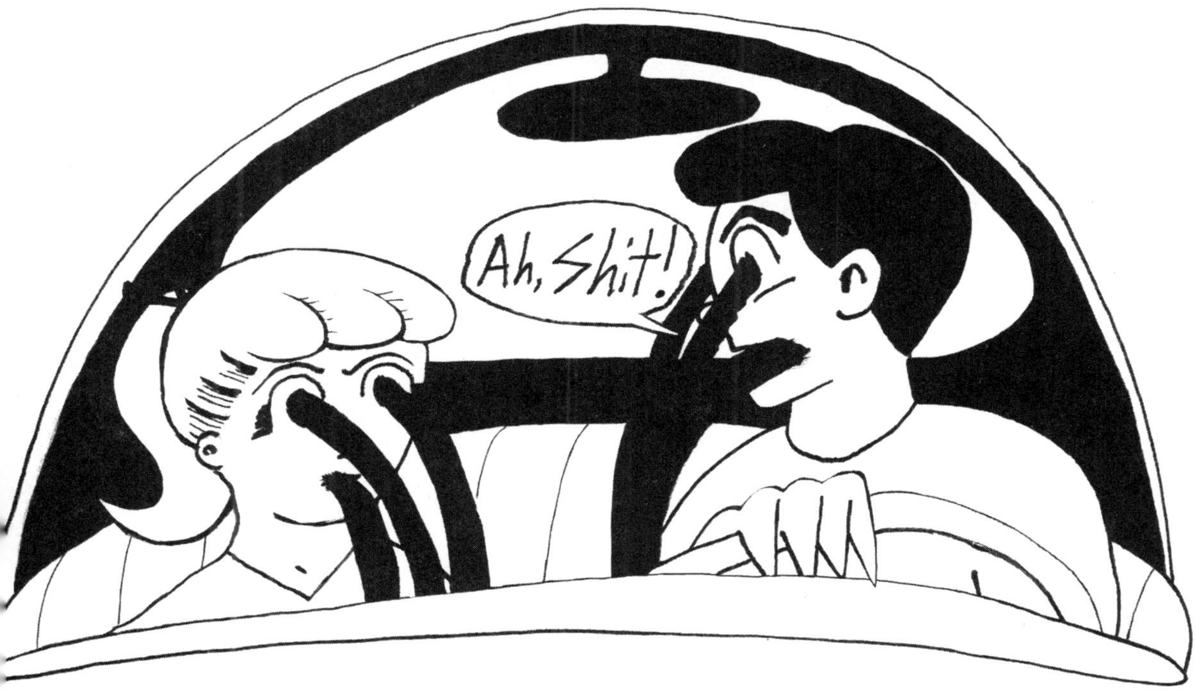
Ah, Shit!

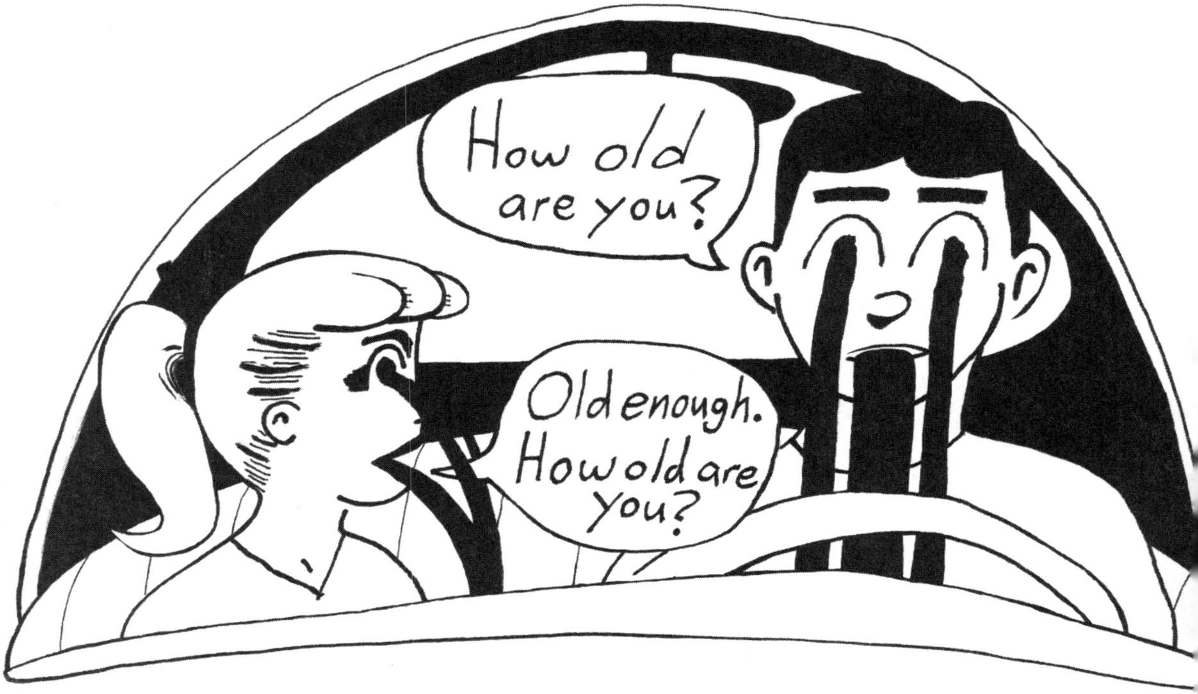
How old are you?
Old enough. How old are you?

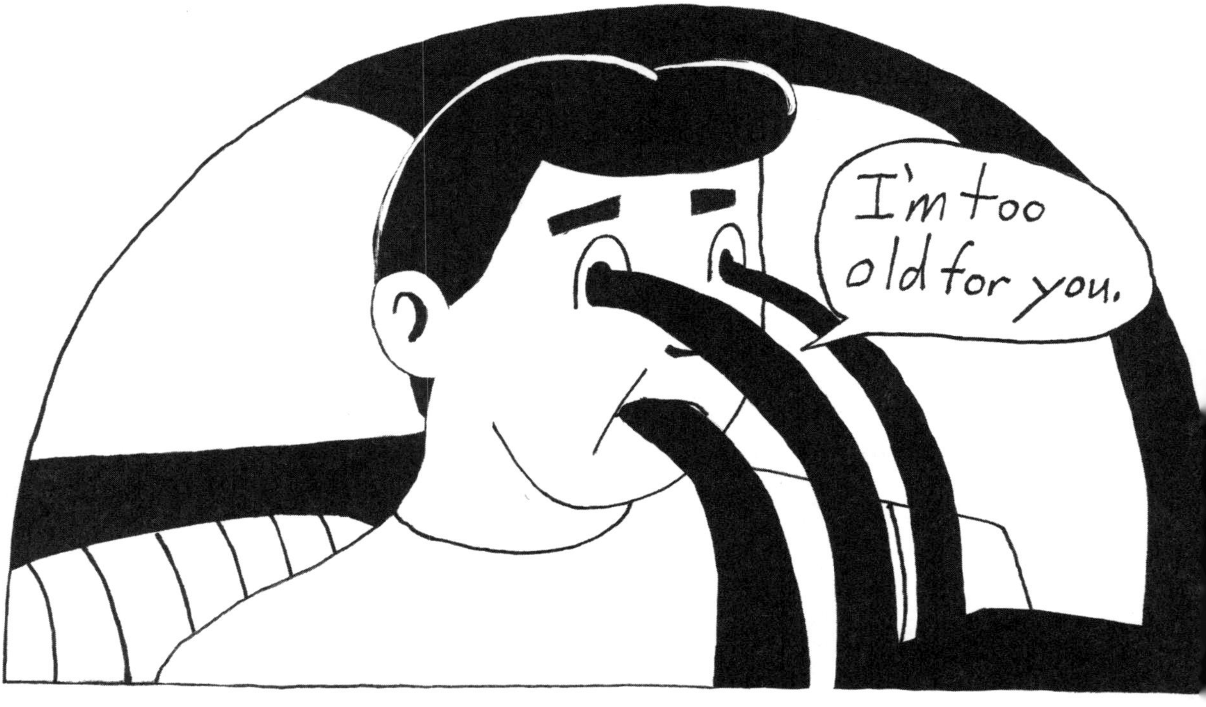
I'm too old for you.

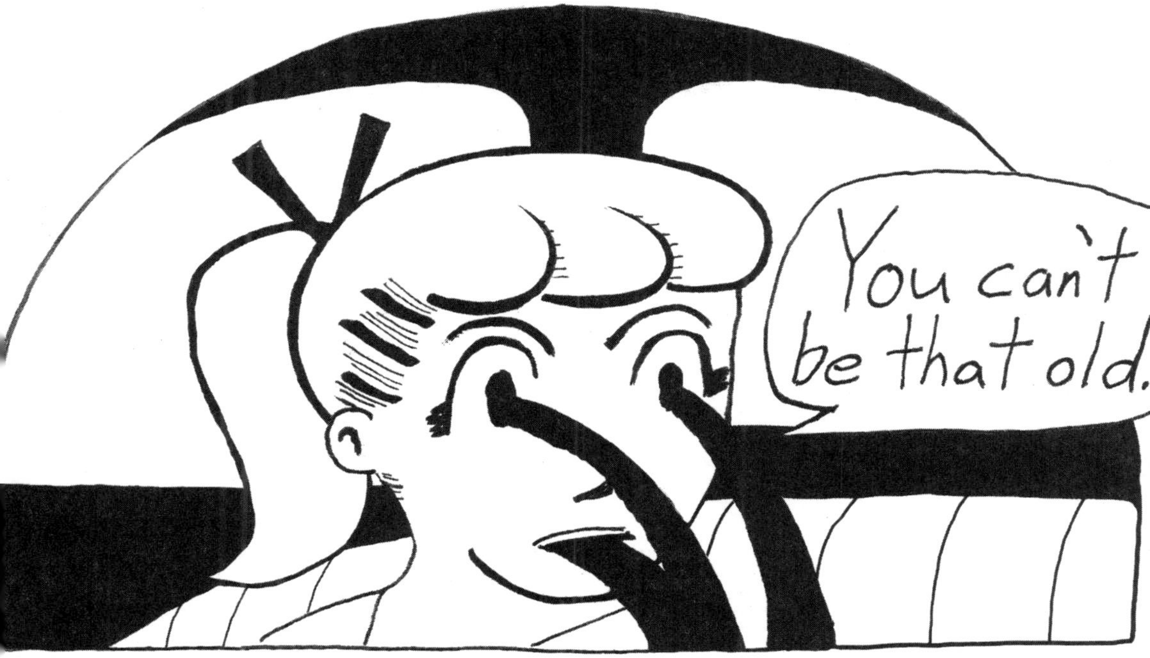
You can't be that old.

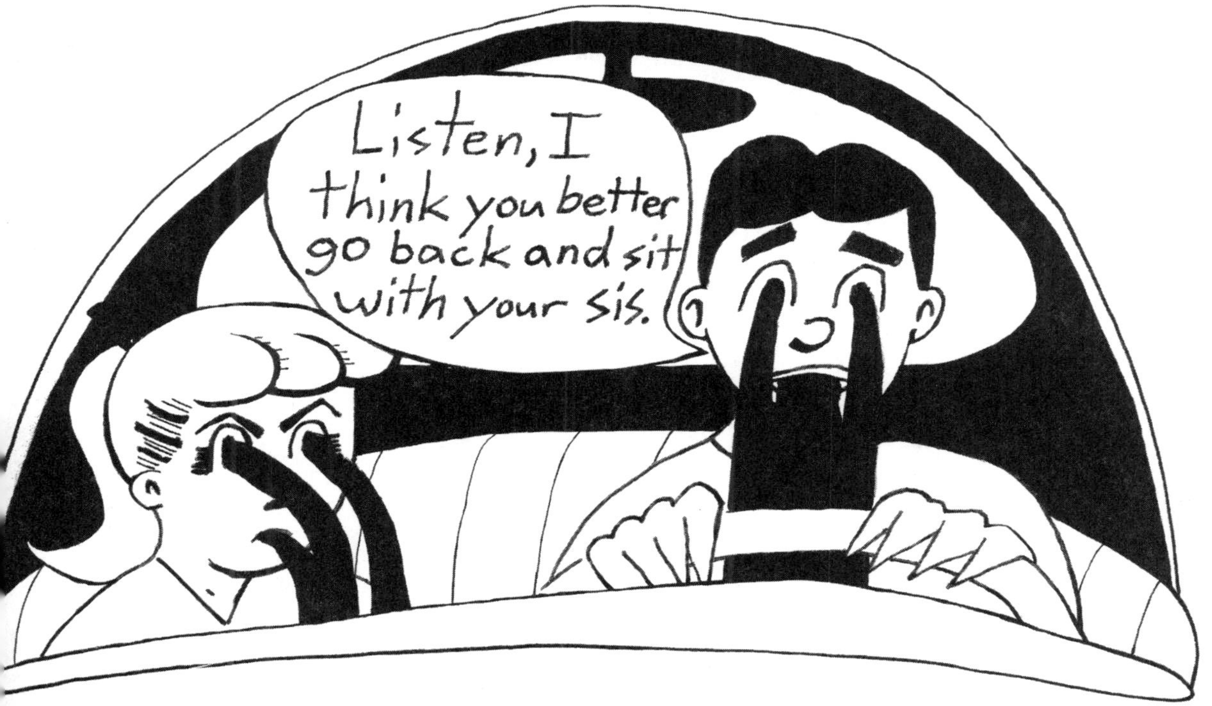
Listen, I think you better go back and sit with your sis.

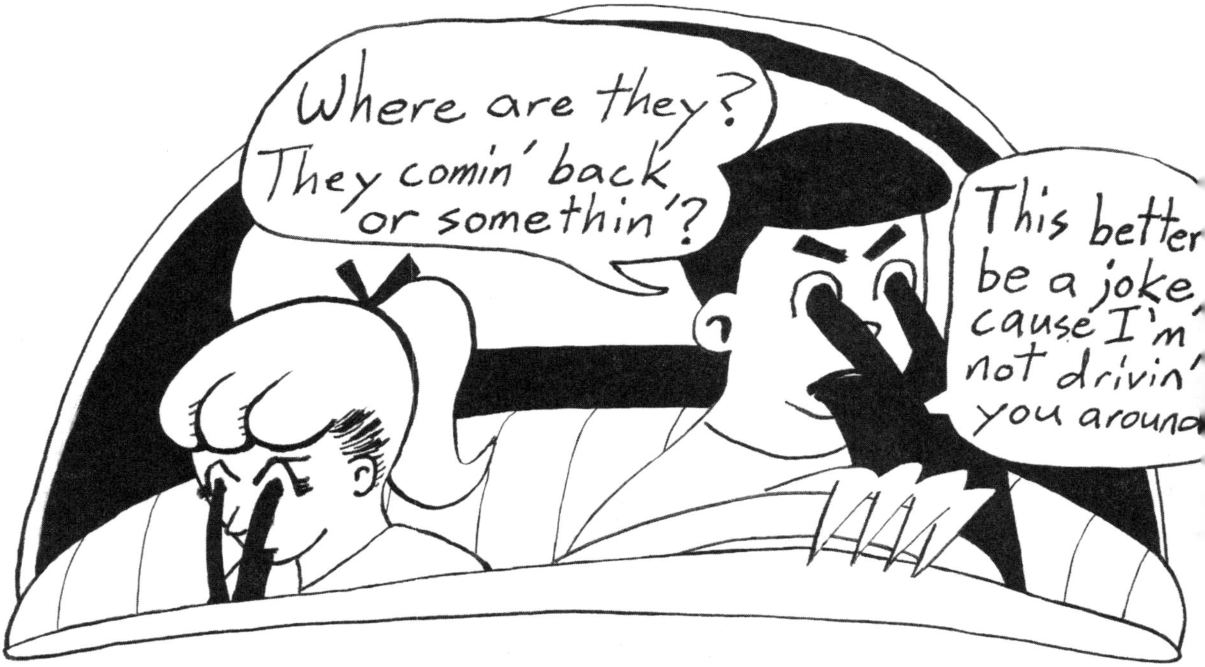
Where are they? They comin' back or somethin'?
This better be a joke, cause I'm not drivin' you around

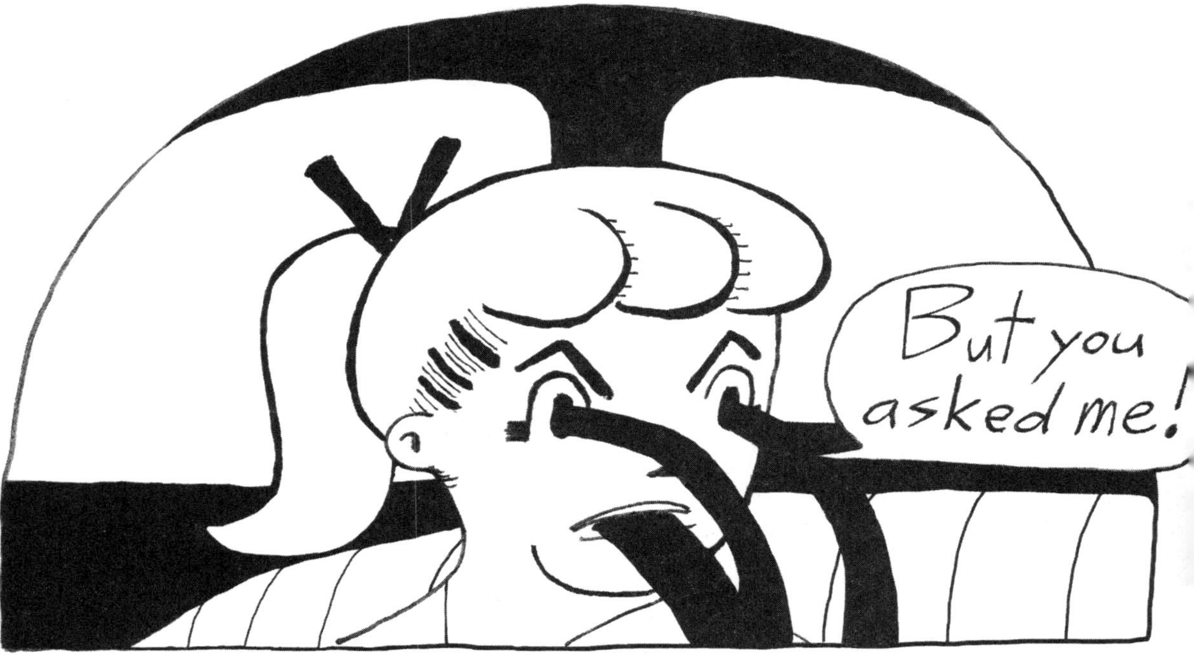
But you asked me!

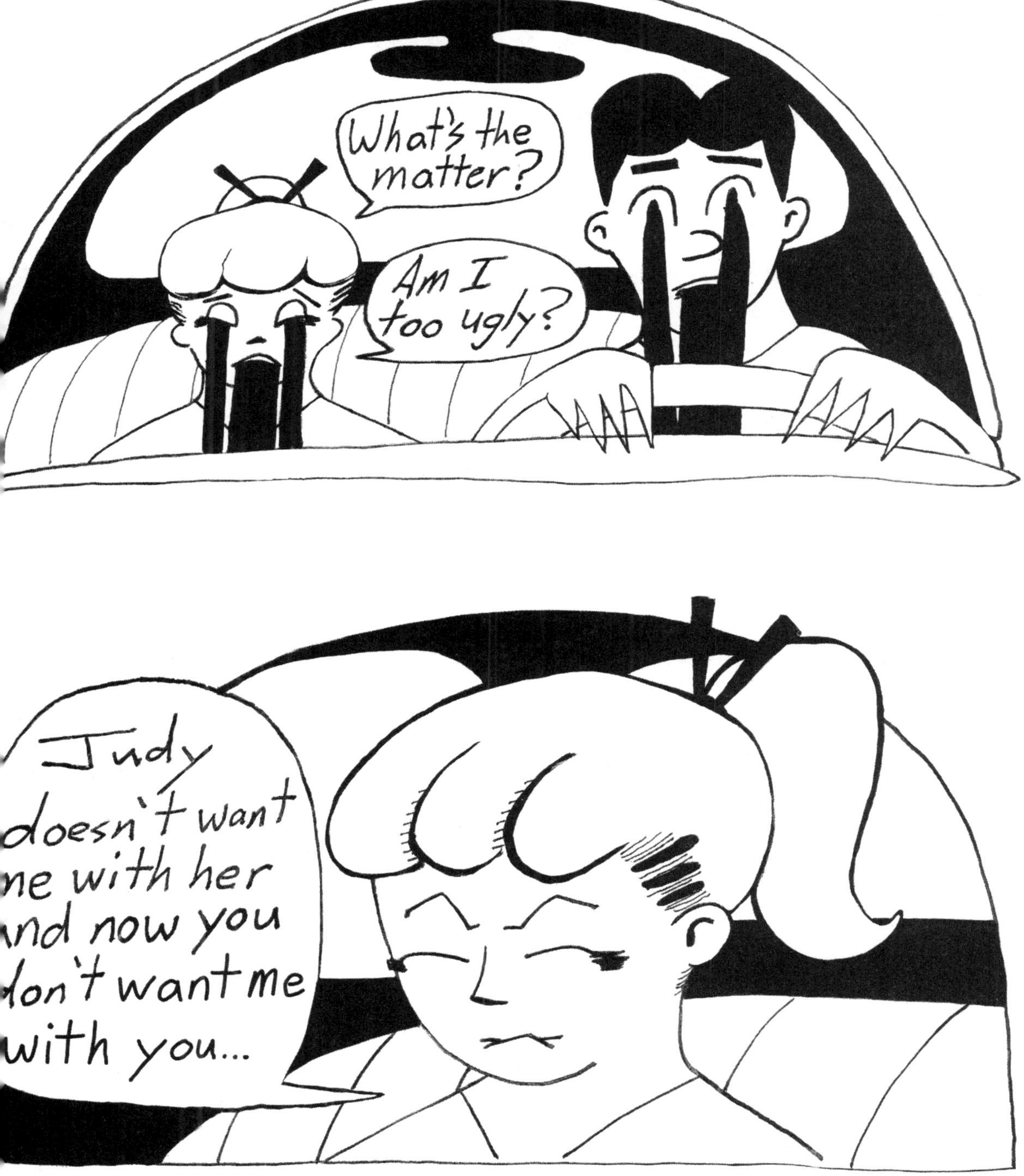
What's the matter?
Am I too ugly?
Judy doesn't want me with her and now you don't want me with you...

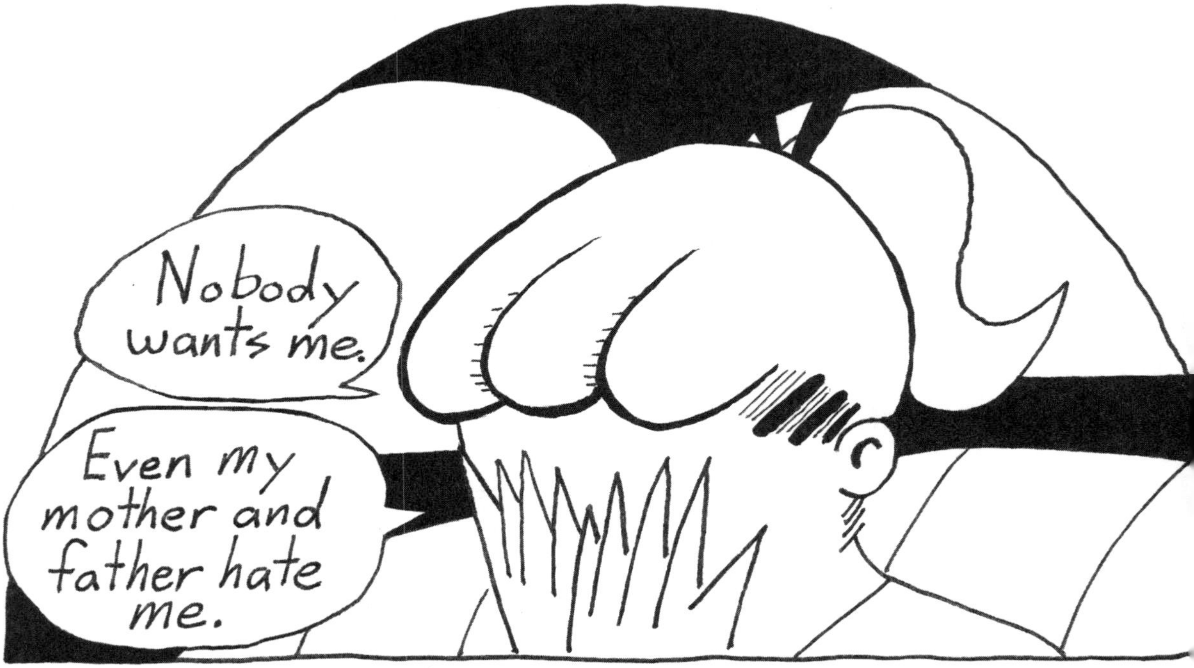
Nobody wants me.
Even my mother and father hate me.

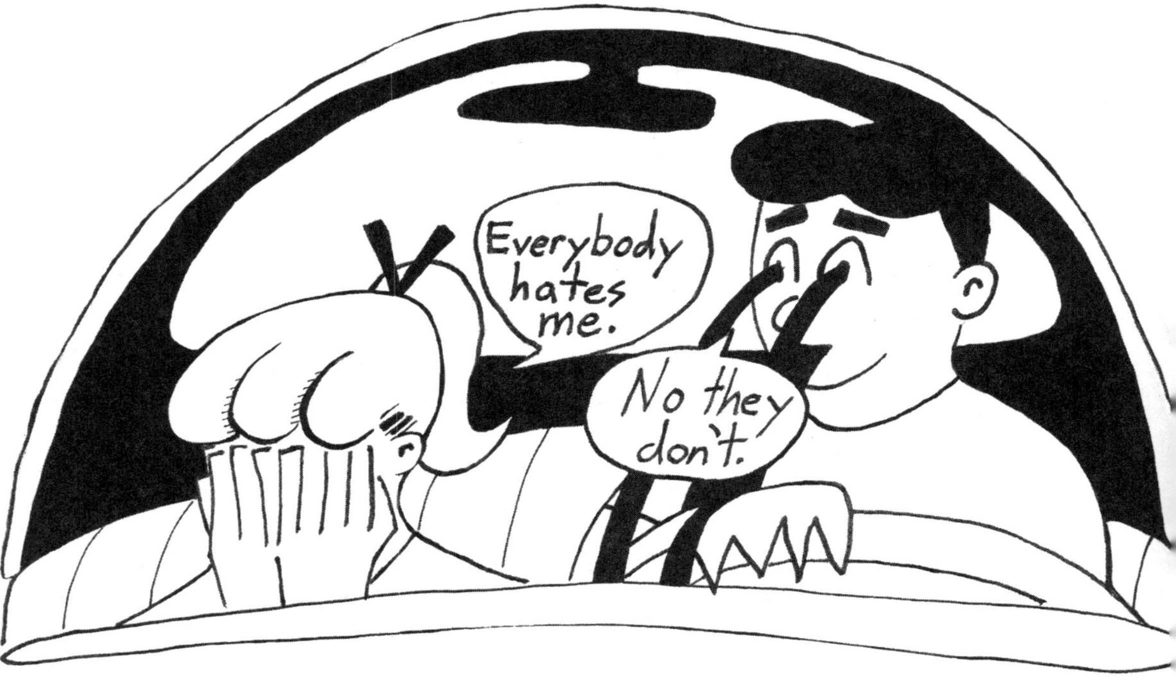
Everybody hates me.
No they don't.

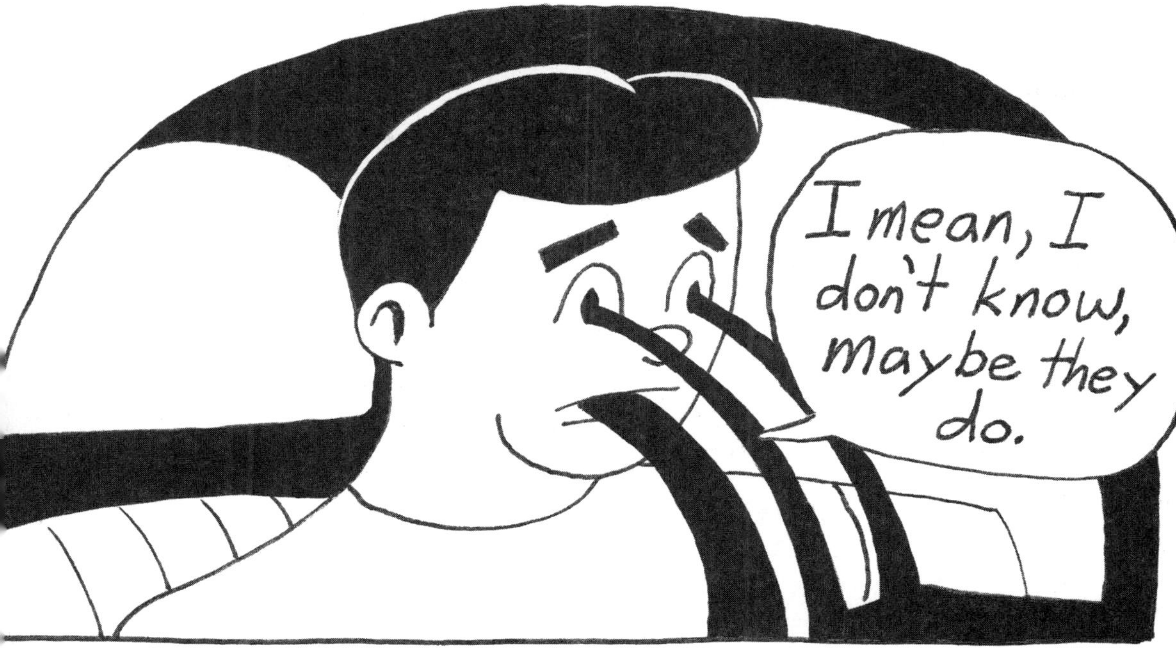
I mean, I don't know, maybe they do.

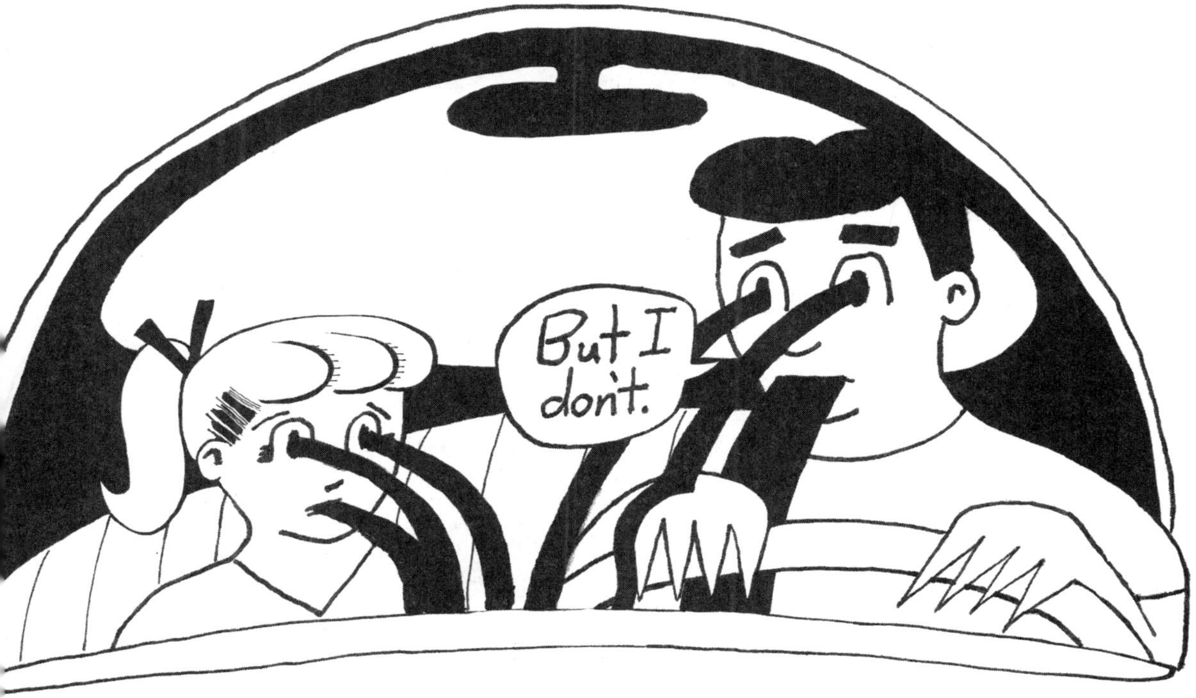
But I don't.

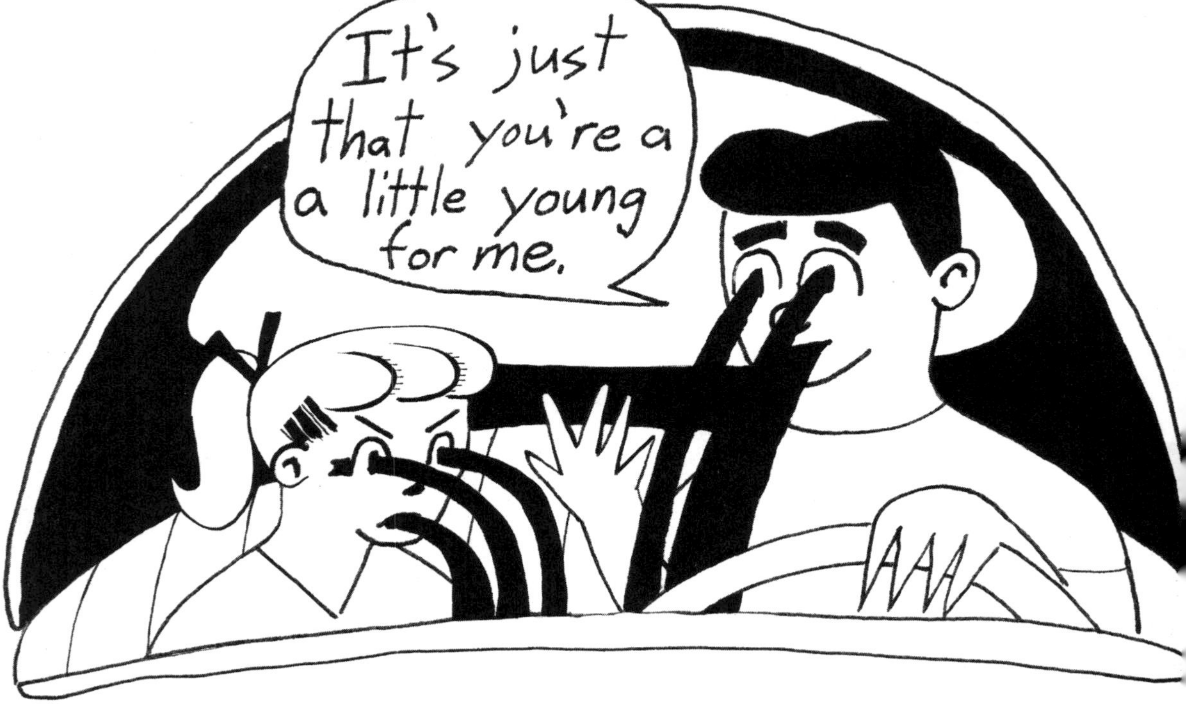
It's just that you're a little young for me.

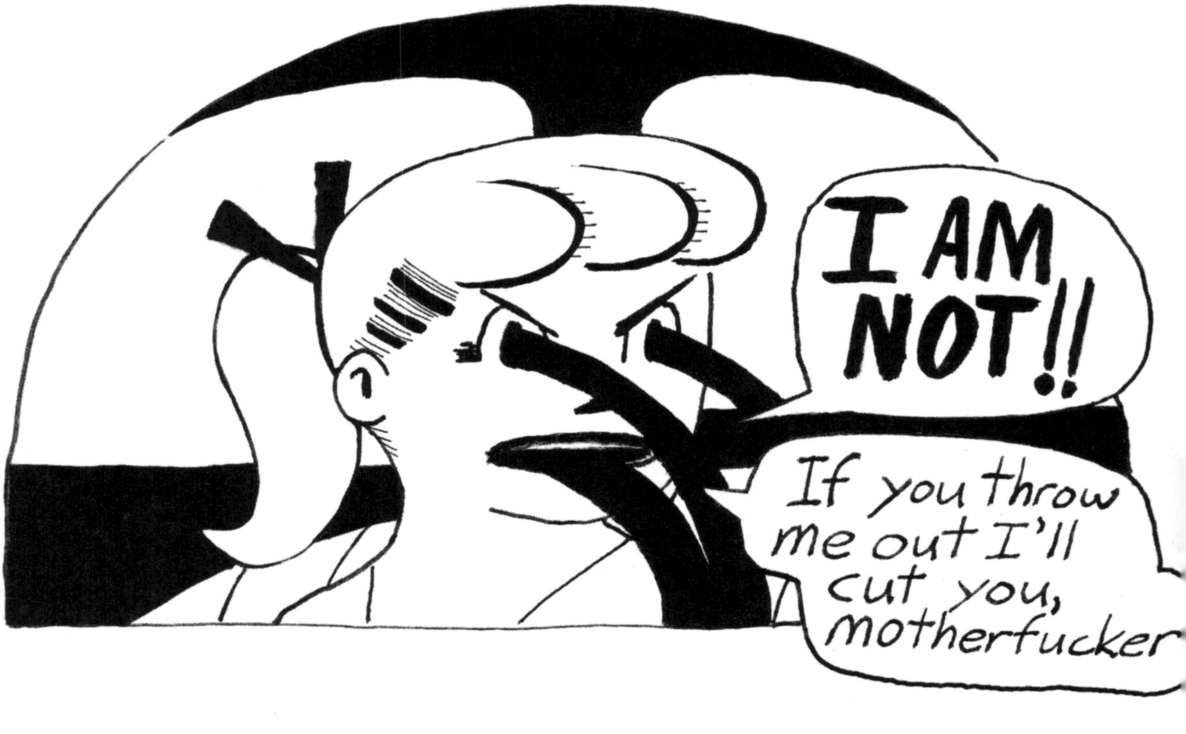
I AM NOT!!
If you throw me out I'll cut you, motherfucker

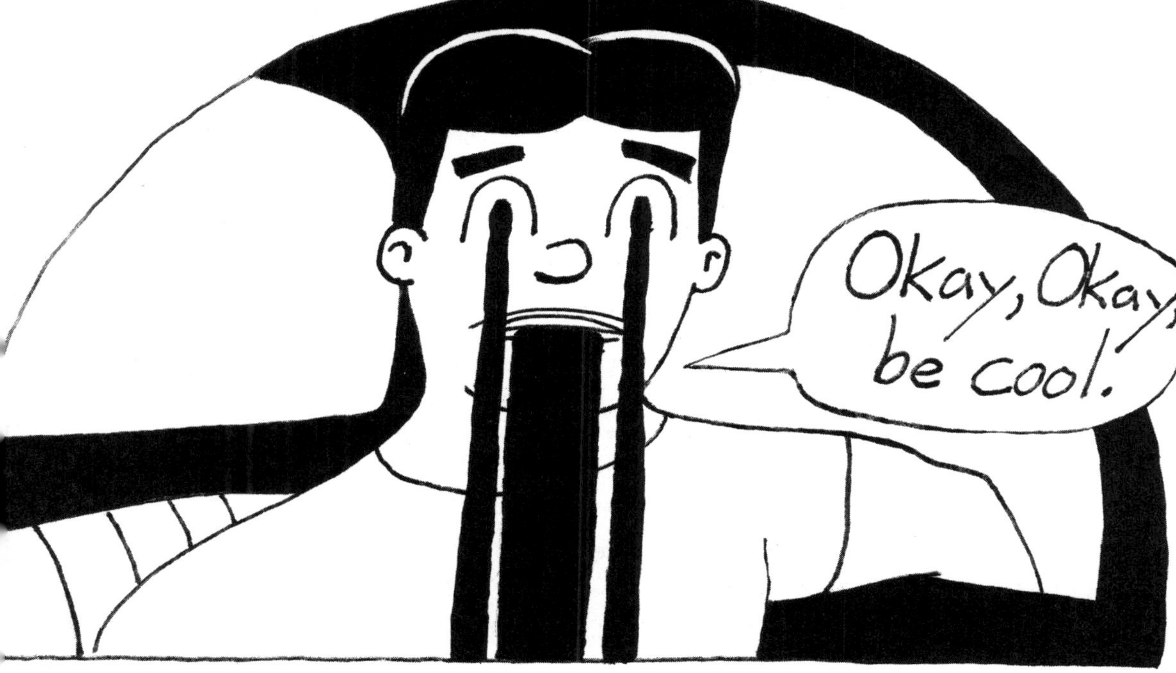
Okay, Okay, be cool.

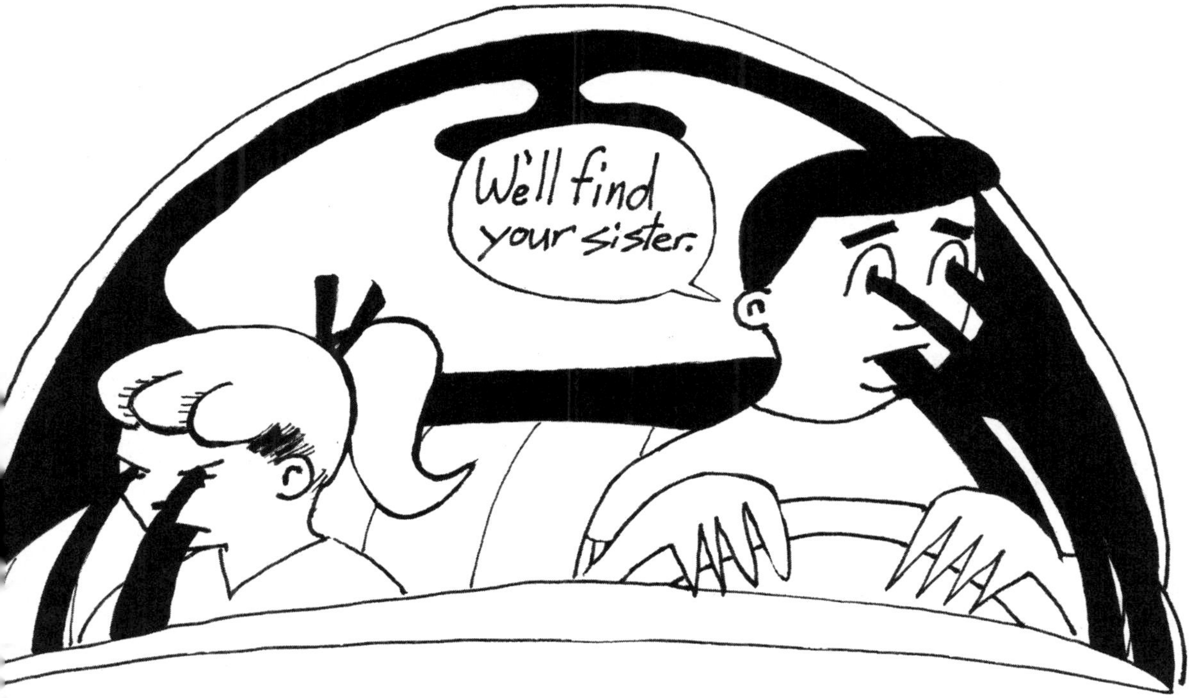
We'll find your sister.

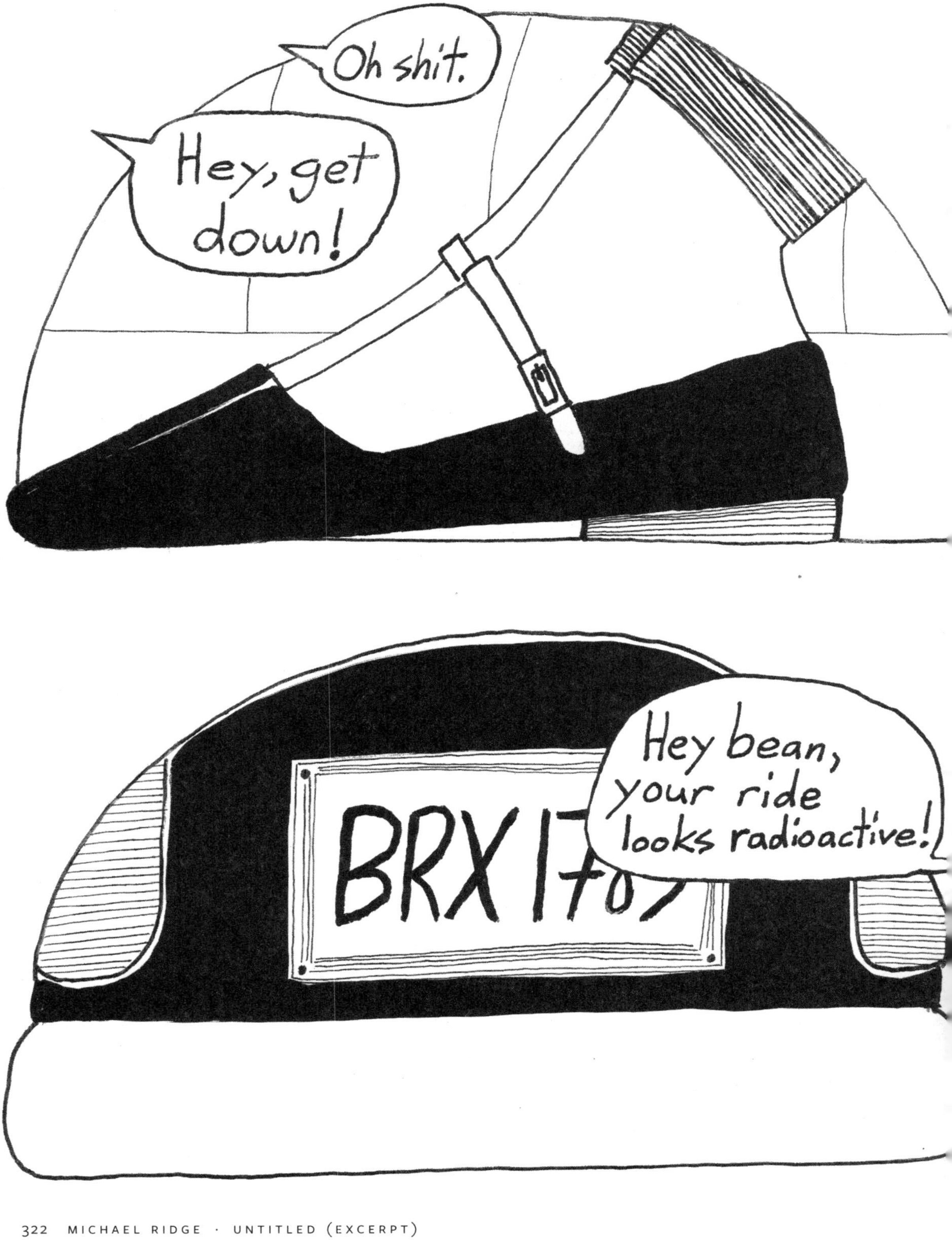
Oh shit.
Hey, get down!
BRX 17
Hey bean, your ride looks radioactive!

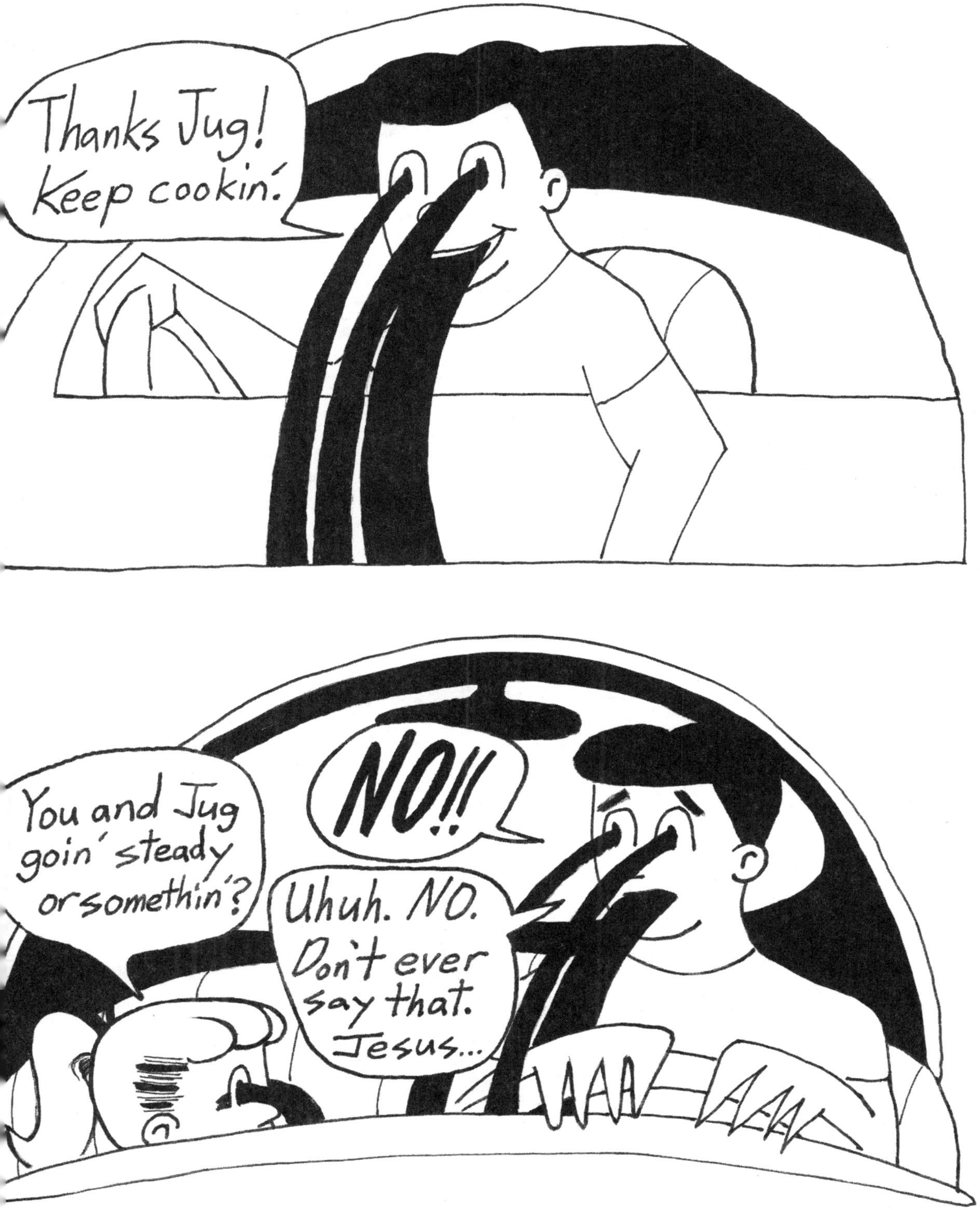
Thanks Jug! Keep cookin'.
You and Jug goin' steady orsomethin'?
NO!!
Uhuh. NO. Don't ever say that. Jesus...

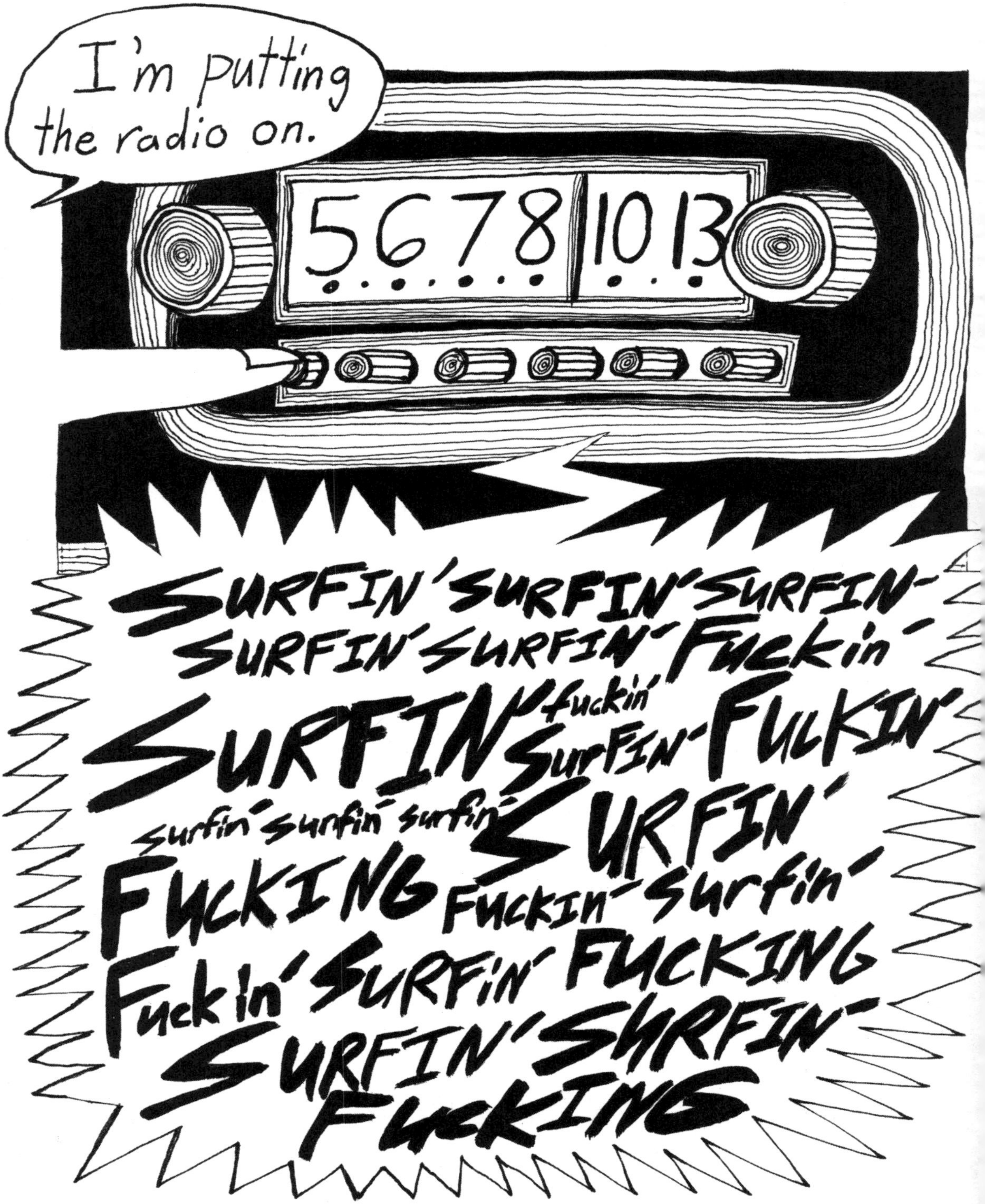
I'm putting the radio on.
5.6.7.8 10.13
SURFIN' SURFIN' SURFIN-
SURFIN' SURFIN' FUCKIN'
SURFIN' fuckin' SURFIN-FUCKIN'
surfin' surfin' surfin' SURFIN'
FUCKING FUCKIN' SURFIN'
FUCKIN' SURFIN' FUCKING
SURFIN' SURFIN'
FUCKING

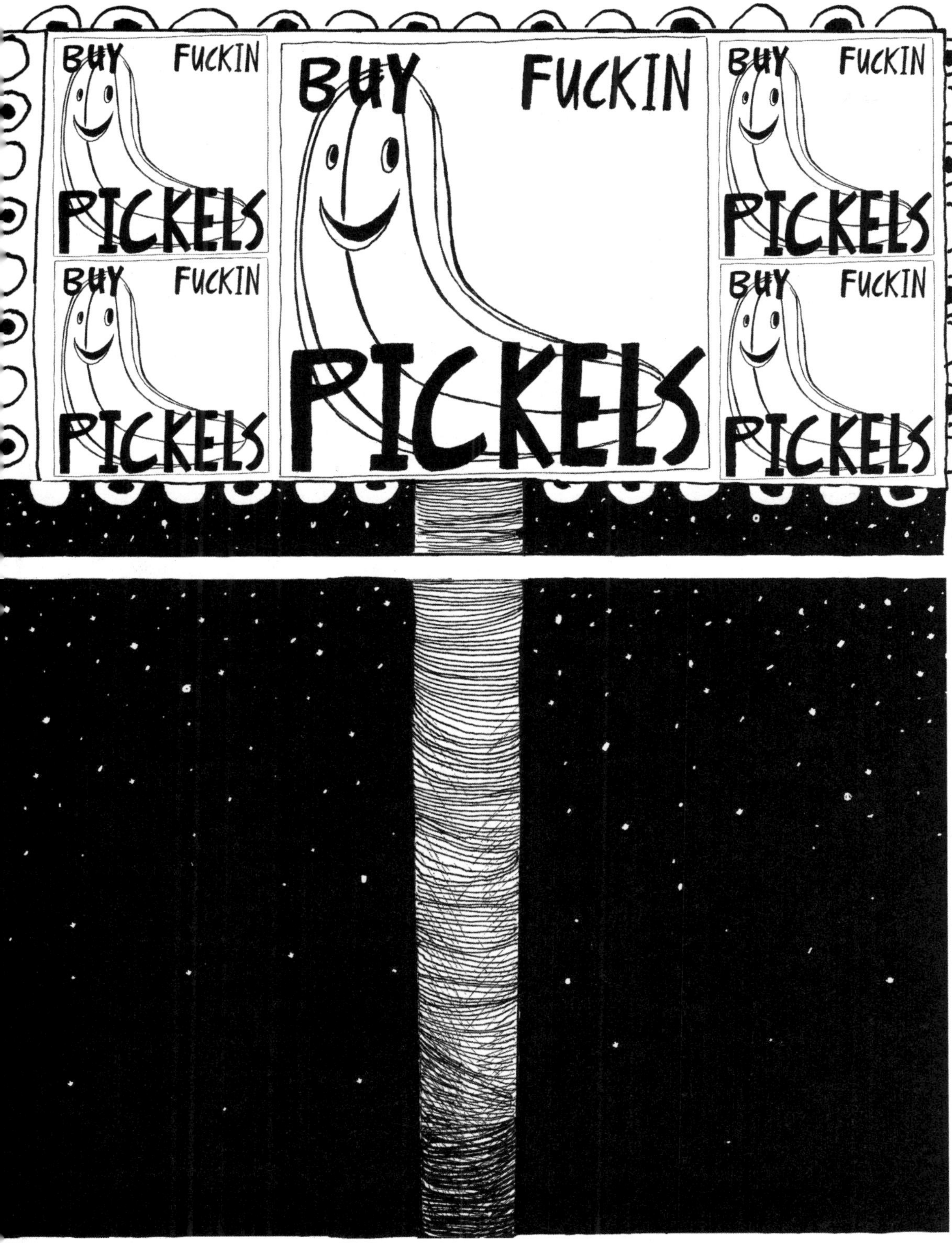
BUY FUCKIN PICKELS
BUY FUCKIN PICKELS
BUY FUCKIN PICKELS
BUY FUCKIN PICKELS
BUY FUCKIN PICKELS

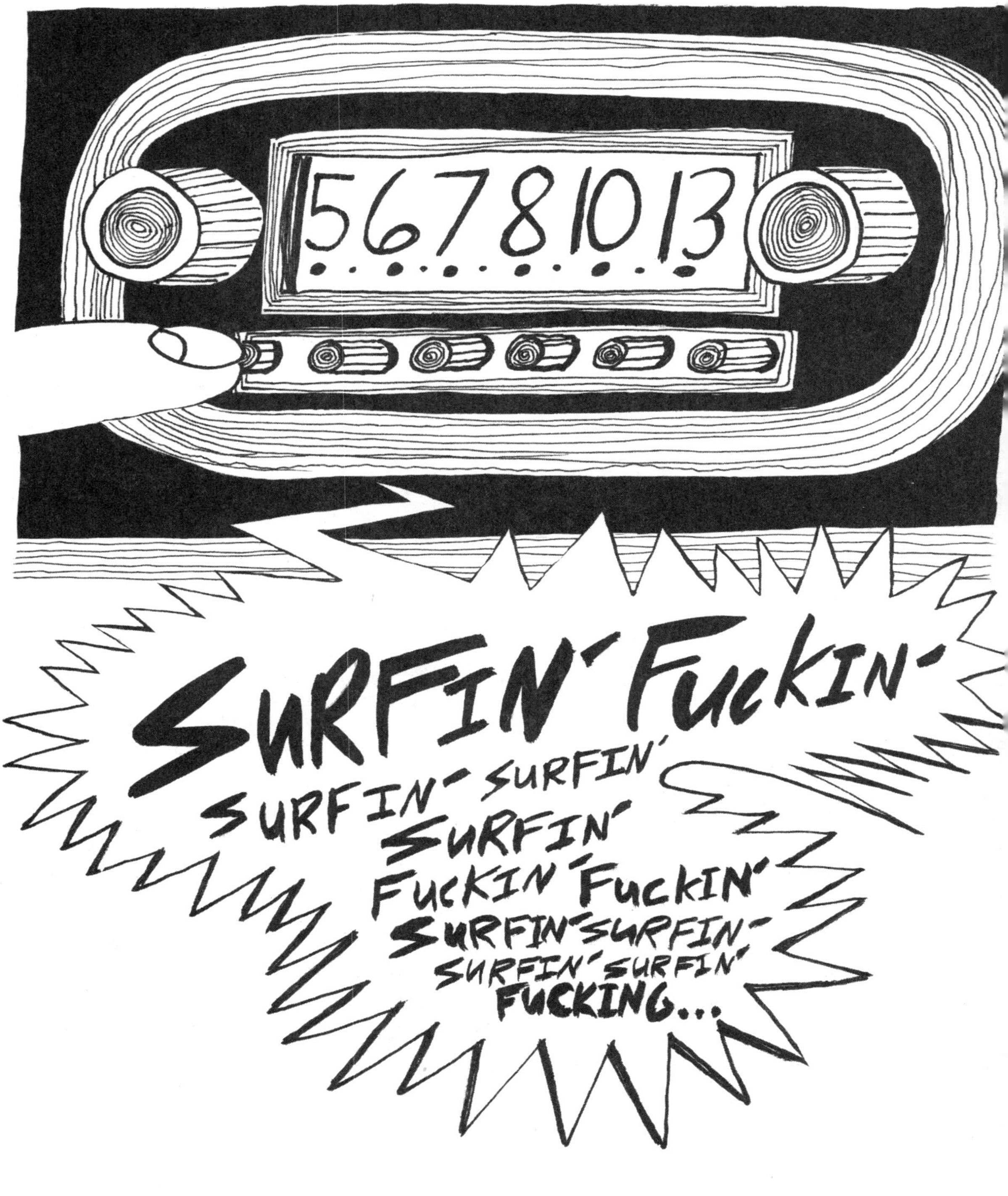
56 7 8 10 13
SURFIN' FUCKIN'
SURFIN' SURFIN'
SURFIN'
FUCKIN' FUCKIN'
SURFIN' SURFIN'
SURFIN' SURFIN'
FUCKING...

Sunburning (*Excerpts*)

KEILER ROBERTS

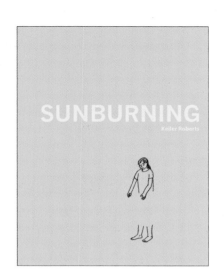

originally published in

Sunburning

KOYAMA PRESS

7 x 9 inches • 120 pages

SUNBURNING
Keiler Roberts

Biography

Keiler Roberts's most recent book, *Sunburning,* was published by Koyama Press in 2017. Roberts has been nominated five times for the Ignatz Award and won for "Outstanding Series" in 2016. She was included in *The Best American Comics 2016* and has been reviewed by *Publishers Weekly,* the *Comics Journal, Vulture, Hyperallergic,* the *Globe and Mail,* and more. Roberts teaches comics at the School of the Art Institute of Chicago. She lives with her husband, Scott Roberts (who is also a cartoonist), daughter, dog, parakeets, and rats.
keilerroberts.com

Statement

These pages are excerpts from *Sunburning,* my fourth book of autobiographical comics. Everything is true, but some backgrounds and clothing have been altered.

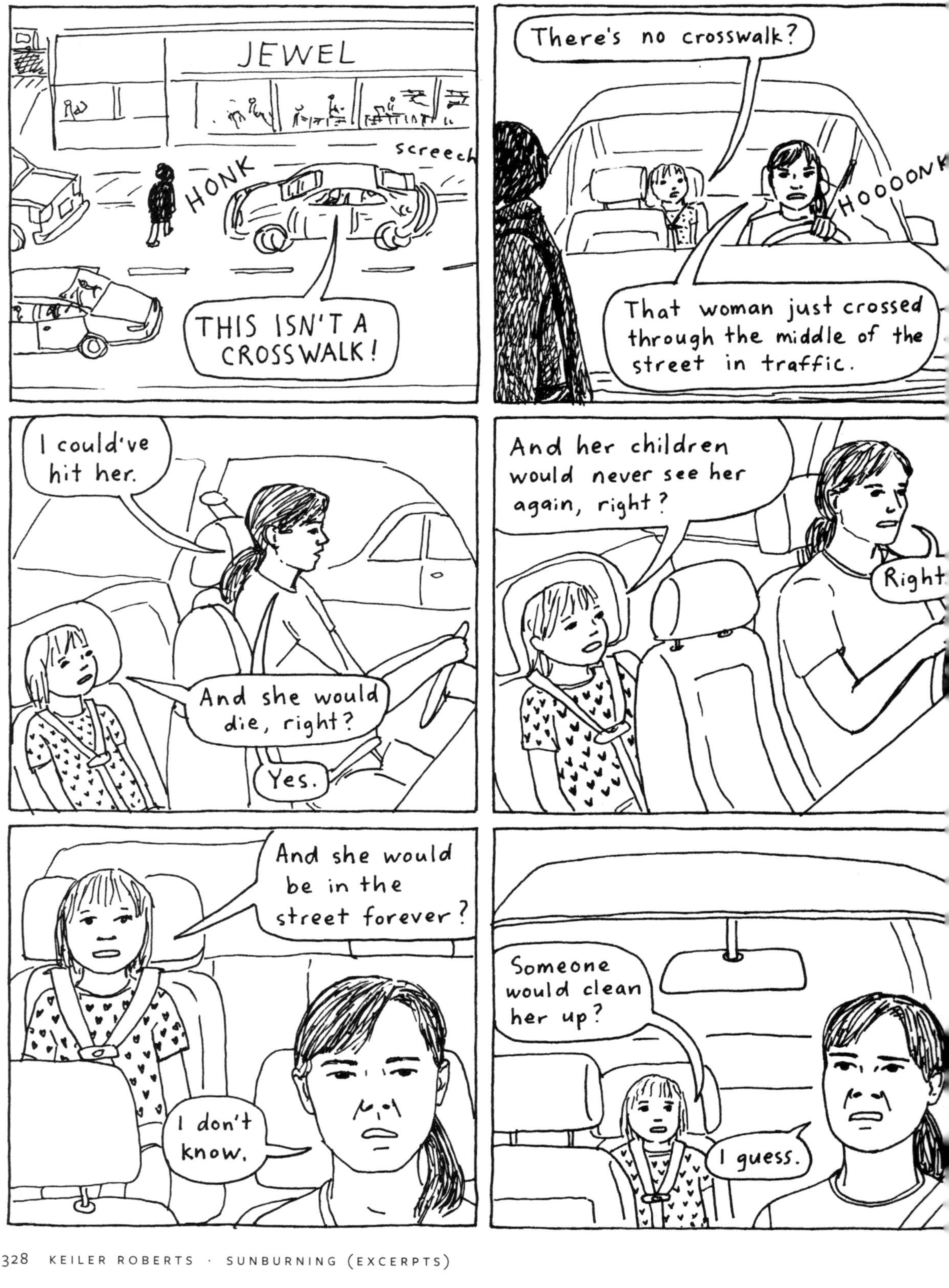
JEWEL
screech
HONK
THIS ISN'T A CROSSWALK!
There's no crosswalk?
HOOOONK
That woman just crossed through the middle of the street in traffic.
I could've hit her.
And she would die, right?
Yes.
And her children would never see her again, right?
Right.
And she would be in the street forever?
I don't know.
Someone would clean her up?
I guess.

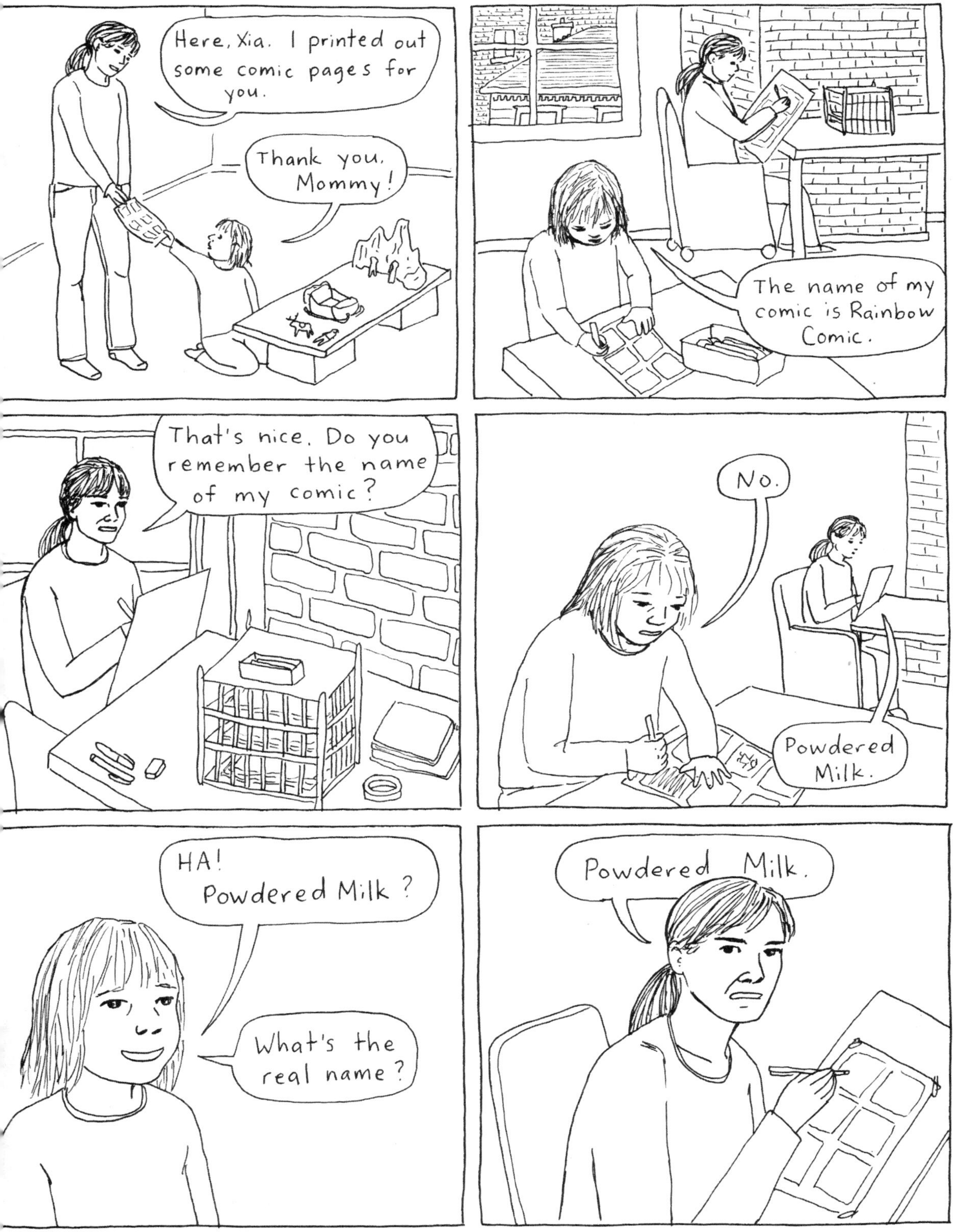
Here, Xia. I printed out some comic pages for you.
Thank you, Mommy!
The name of my comic is Rainbow Comic.
That's nice. Do you remember the name of my comic?
No.
Powdered Milk.
HA! Powdered Milk?
What's the real name?
Powdered Milk.

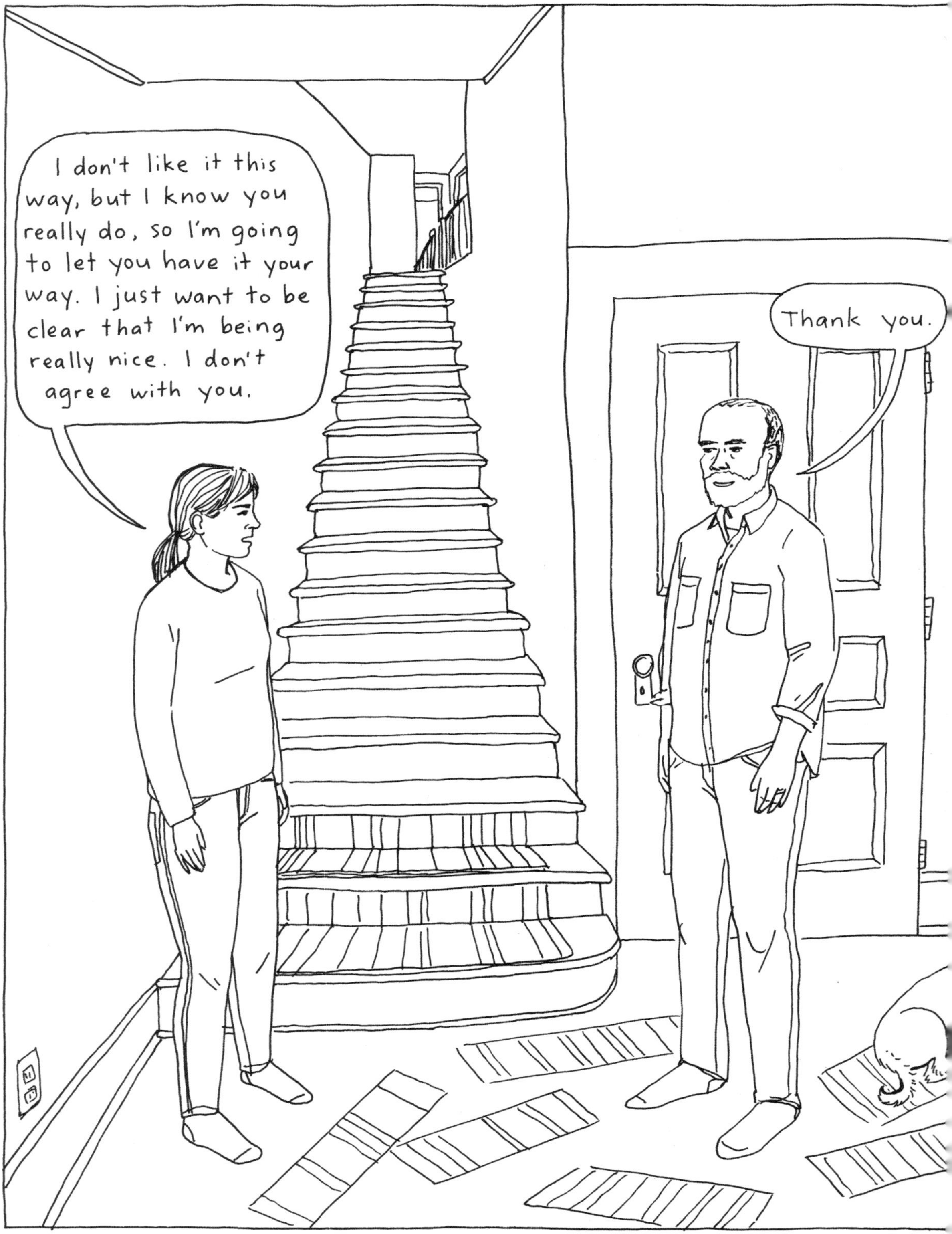
I don't like it this way, but I know you really do, so I'm going to let you have it your way. I just want to be clear that I'm being really nice. I don't agree with you.
Thank you.

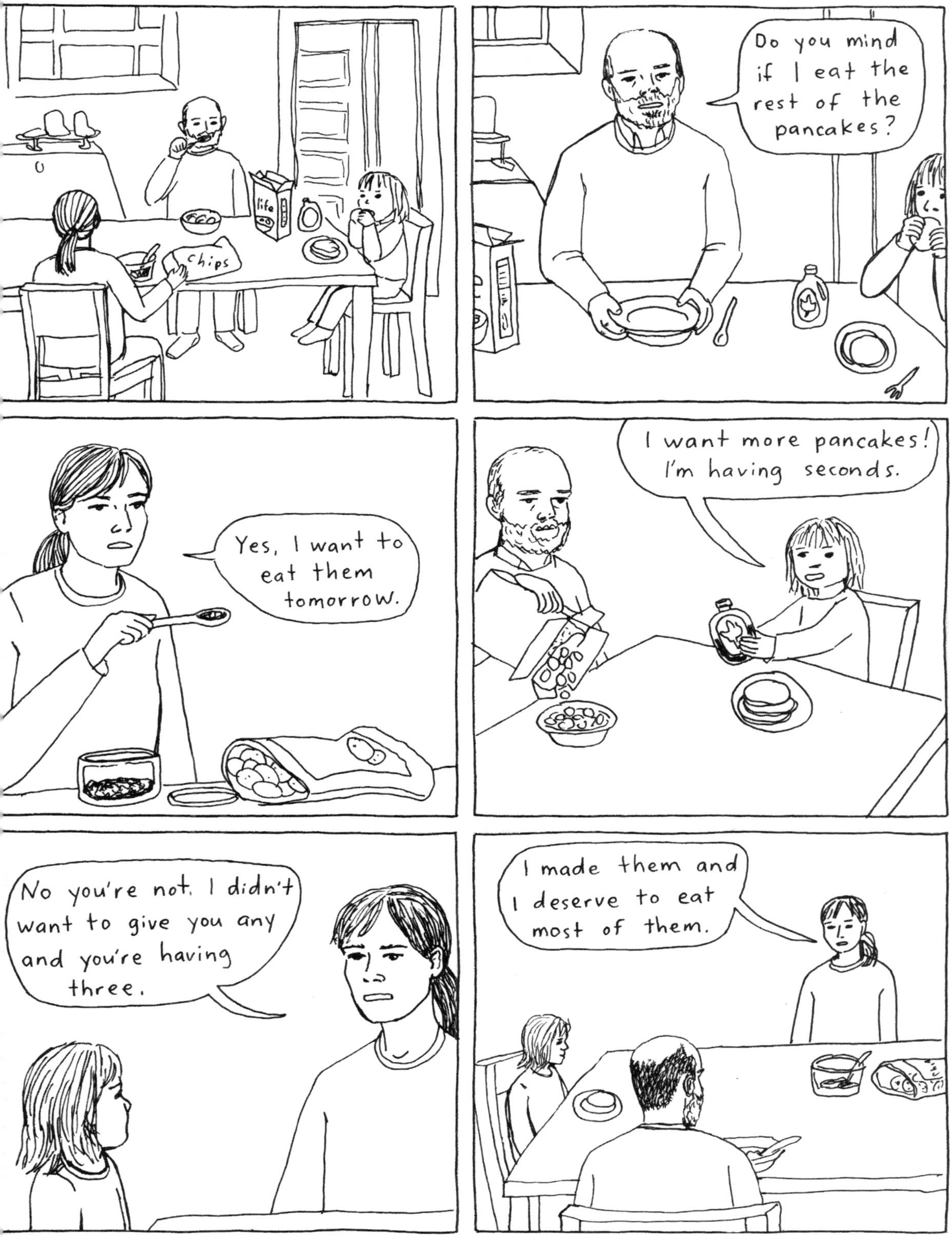
life
chips
Do you mind if I eat the rest of the pancakes?
Yes, I want to eat them tomorrow.
I want more pancakes! I'm having seconds.
No you're not. I didn't want to give you any and you're having three.
I made them and I deserve to eat most of them.

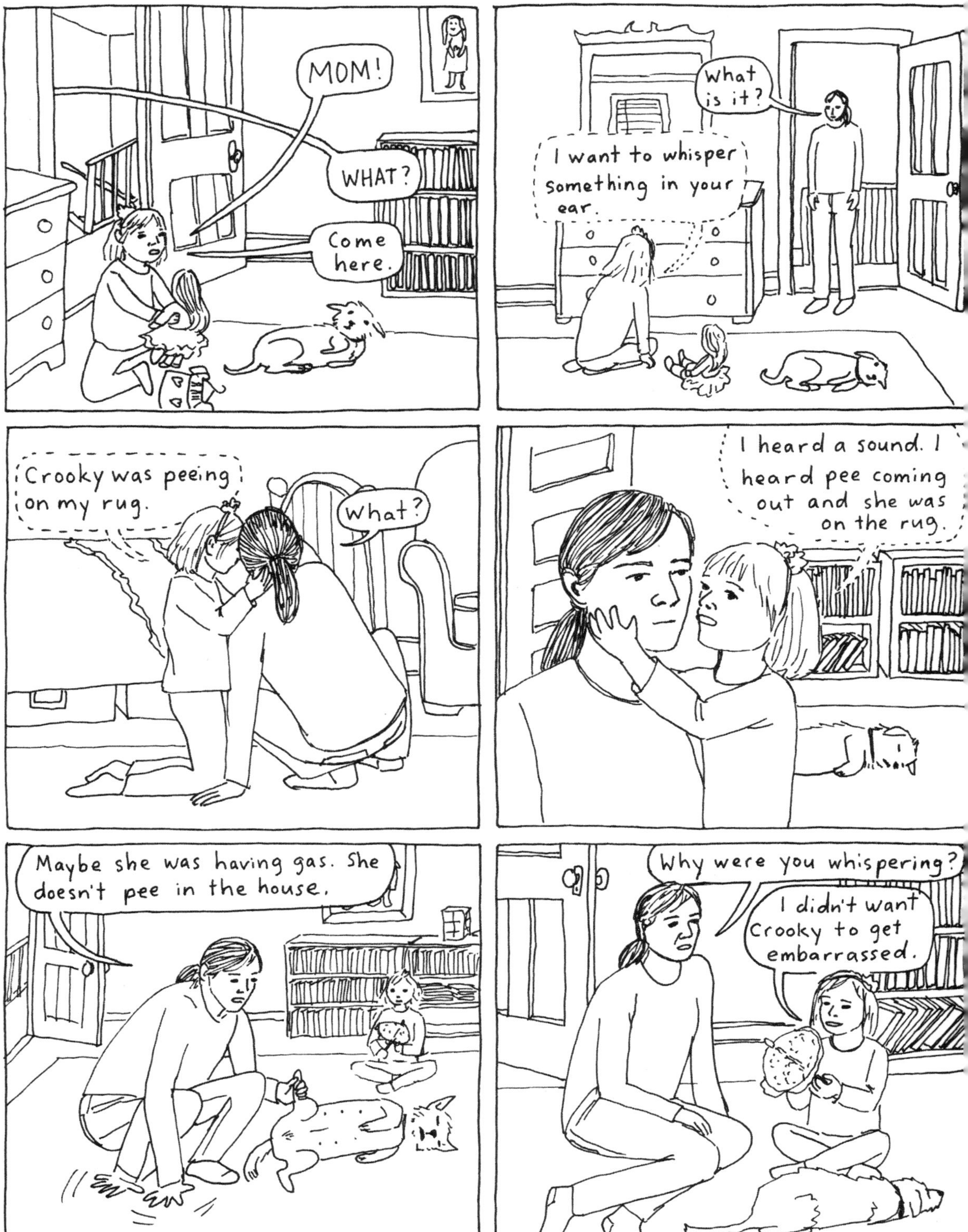
MOM!
WHAT?
Come here.
What is it?
I want to whisper something in your ear.
Crooky was peeing on my rug.
What?
I heard a sound. I heard pee coming out and she was on the rug.
Maybe she was having gas. She doesn't pee in the house.
Why were you whispering?
I didn't want Crooky to get embarrassed.

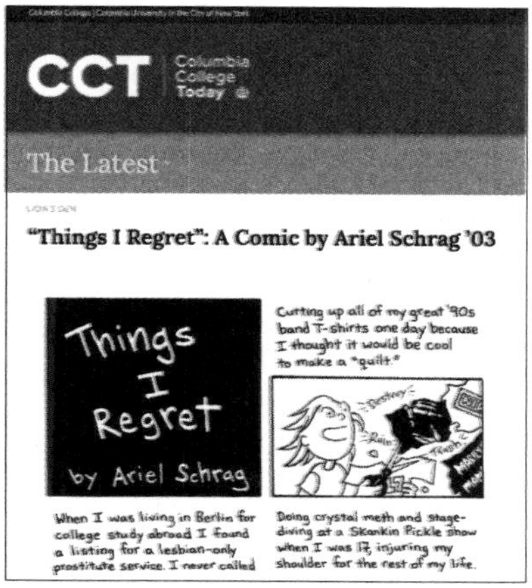
CCT
Columbia College Today
The Latest
"Things I Regret": A Comic by Ariel Schrag '03
Things I Regret
by Ariel Schrag
Cutting up all of my great '90s band T-shirts one day because I thought it would be cool to make a "quilt."
When I was living in Berlin for college study abroad I found a listing for a lesbian-only prostitute service. I never called
Doing crystal meth and stage-diving at a Skankin Pickle show when I was 17, injuring my shoulder for the rest of my life.

Things I Regret

ARIEL SCHRAG

originally published at

Columbia College Today Online

COLUMBIA UNIVERSITY

DIGITAL

Biography

Ariel Schrag is the author of the graphic memoirs *Awkward*, *Definition*, *Potential*, and *Likewise* and of the novel *Adam*. Also a screenwriter, she adapted *Adam* into a feature film and has written on television series for HBO and Showtime. Her latest book is the graphic memoir *Part of It*.
arielschrag.com

Statement

I'd been wanting to write this comic for a long time and finally just had to do it before too many more regrets piled up.

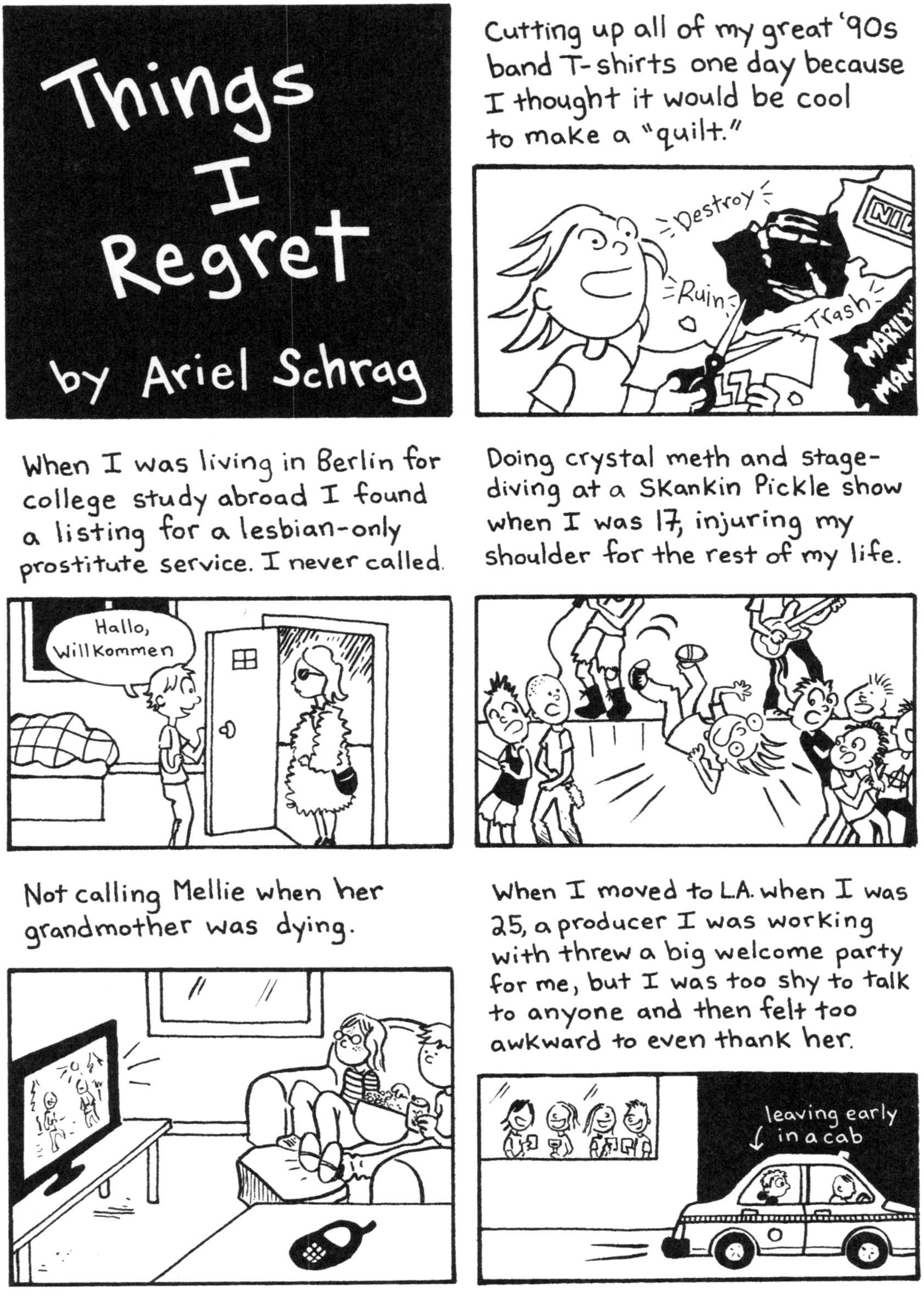
Things I Regret
by Ariel Schrag
Cutting up all of my great '90s band T-shirts one day because I thought it would be cool to make a "quilt."
Destroy
Ruin
Trash
When I was living in Berlin for college study abroad I found a listing for a lesbian-only prostitute service. I never called.
Hallo, Willkommen
Doing crystal meth and stage-diving at a Skankin Pickle show when I was 17, injuring my shoulder for the rest of my life.
Not calling Mellie when her grandmother was dying.
When I moved to L.A. when I was 25, a producer I was working with threw a big welcome party for me, but I was too shy to talk to anyone and then felt too awkward to even thank her.
leaving early in a cab

All the ways I hurt you because I was confused and scared.

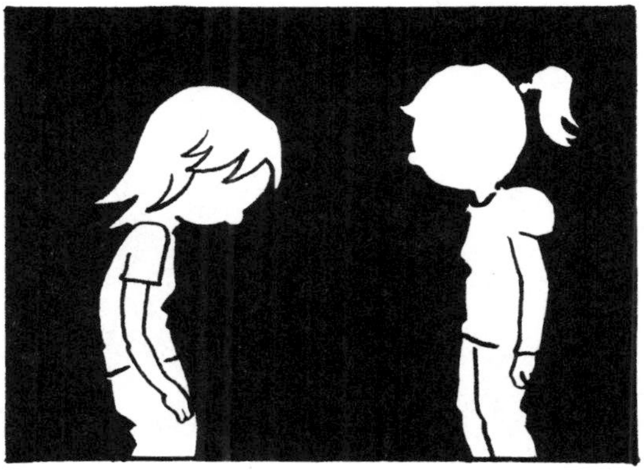

Wasting a year working on a pitch for a TV show that never sold when I could have written something real.

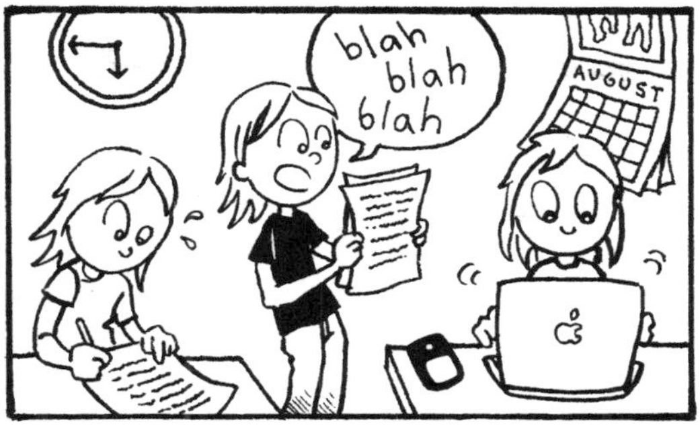
blah blah blah
AUGUST

Not sending my cartoonist hero, Lynn Johnston, copies of my comic books before she dies. She's not dead; I could still do it...

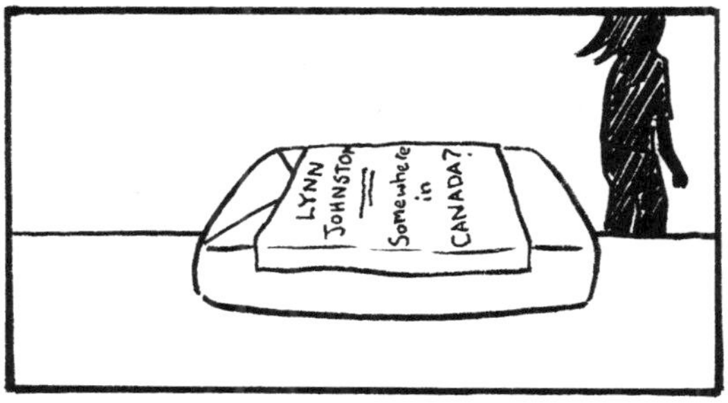
LYNN JOHNSTON
Somewhere in CANADA?

I asked my dad if he had any regrets, hoping for some life advice.

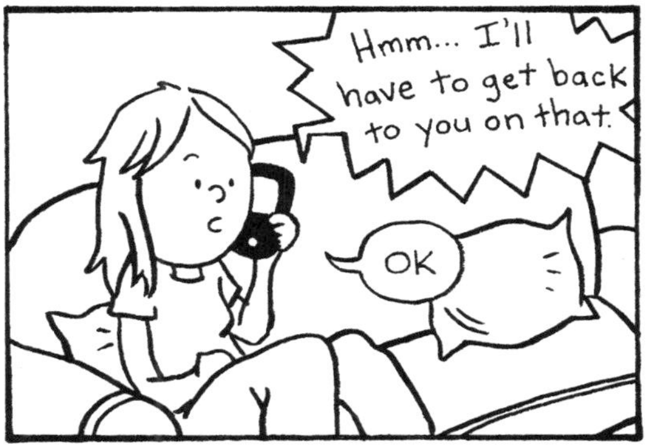
Hmm... I'll have to get back to you on that.
OK

When I visited home in Berkeley a few months later he had an answer.

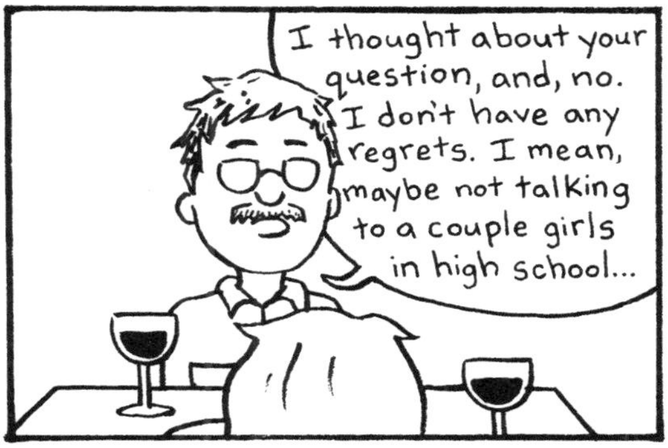
I thought about your question, and, no. I don't have any regrets. I mean, maybe not talking to a couple girls in high school...

I regret not asking him if he regrets not having a closer relationship with me.

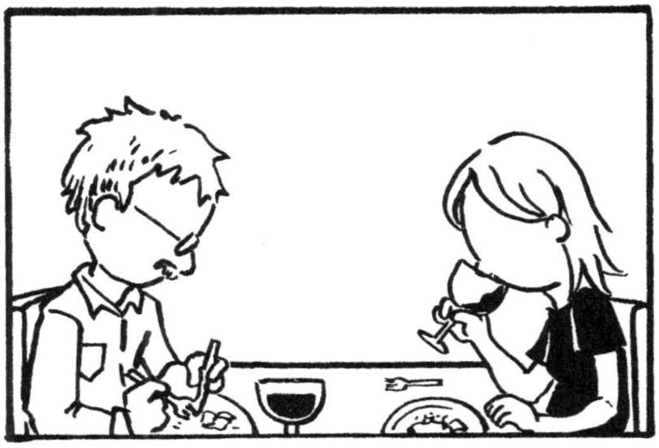

The Moolah Tree (*Excerpt*)

TED STEARN

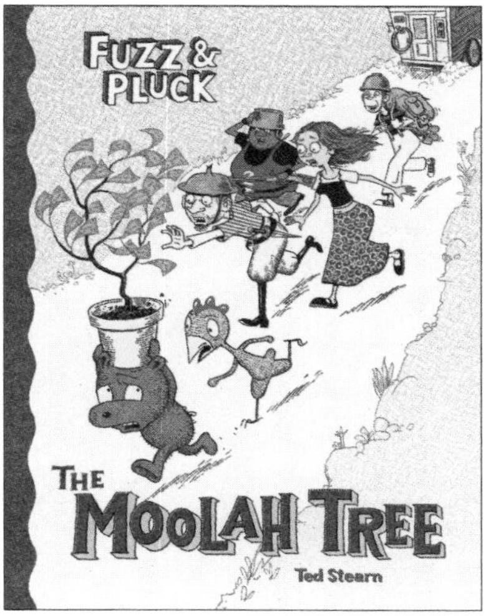
FUZZ & PLUCK
THE MOOLAH TREE
Ted Stearn

originally published in

The Moolah Tree

FANTAGRAPHICS BOOKS

7.25 x 9 inches • 288 pages

Biography

Ted Stearn earned his BFA at the Rhode Island School of Design, and an MFA at the School of Visual Arts in New York. He has been drawing comics whenever he gets a chance since 1993, notably his endless Fuzz and Pluck series, published by Fantagraphics Books. But he has earned his bread and butter mostly as a storyboard artist for animation. He has also taught comics and storyboarding at the Savannah College of Art and Design. Ted currently lives in Los Angeles.
tedstearn.com

Statement

The Fuzz and Pluck series follows two misfits: Fuzz, a motley teddy bear, and Pluck, a defeathered chicken. To read about their origins and previous adventures, check out the previous books, *Fuzz and Pluck* and *Fuzz and Pluck: Splitsville.*

This is an excerpt from Ted Stearn's latest book, entitled *The Moolah Tree.* The reader does not need to know the backstory, except that Fuzz and Pluck find themselves lost on a ferry boat drifting out to sea. This is the beginning chapter of the book.

OH! WHAT ARE WE GOING TO DO?
I MEAN, WE CAN'T EAT NOTHING BECAUSE LOOK— THERE'S NOTHING TO EAT!
...AND THERE IS ALL THIS WATER BUT WE CAN'T DRINK ANY AT ALL!
I THINK WE ARE GOING TO STARVE- -AND THIRST - TO DEATH!

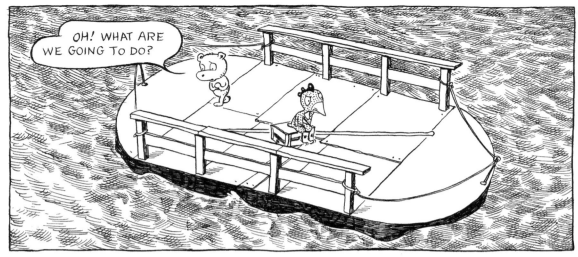

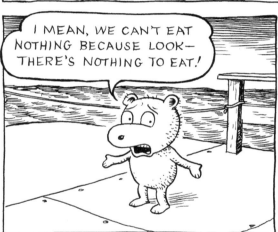

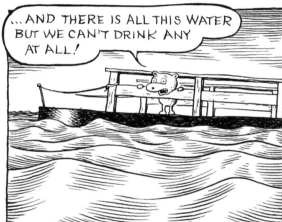

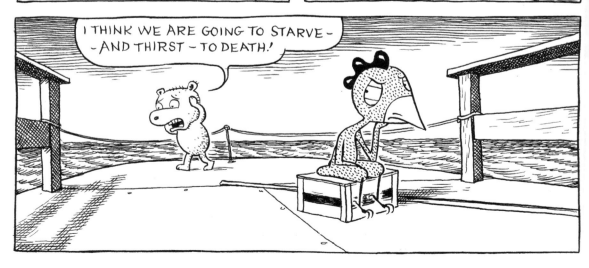

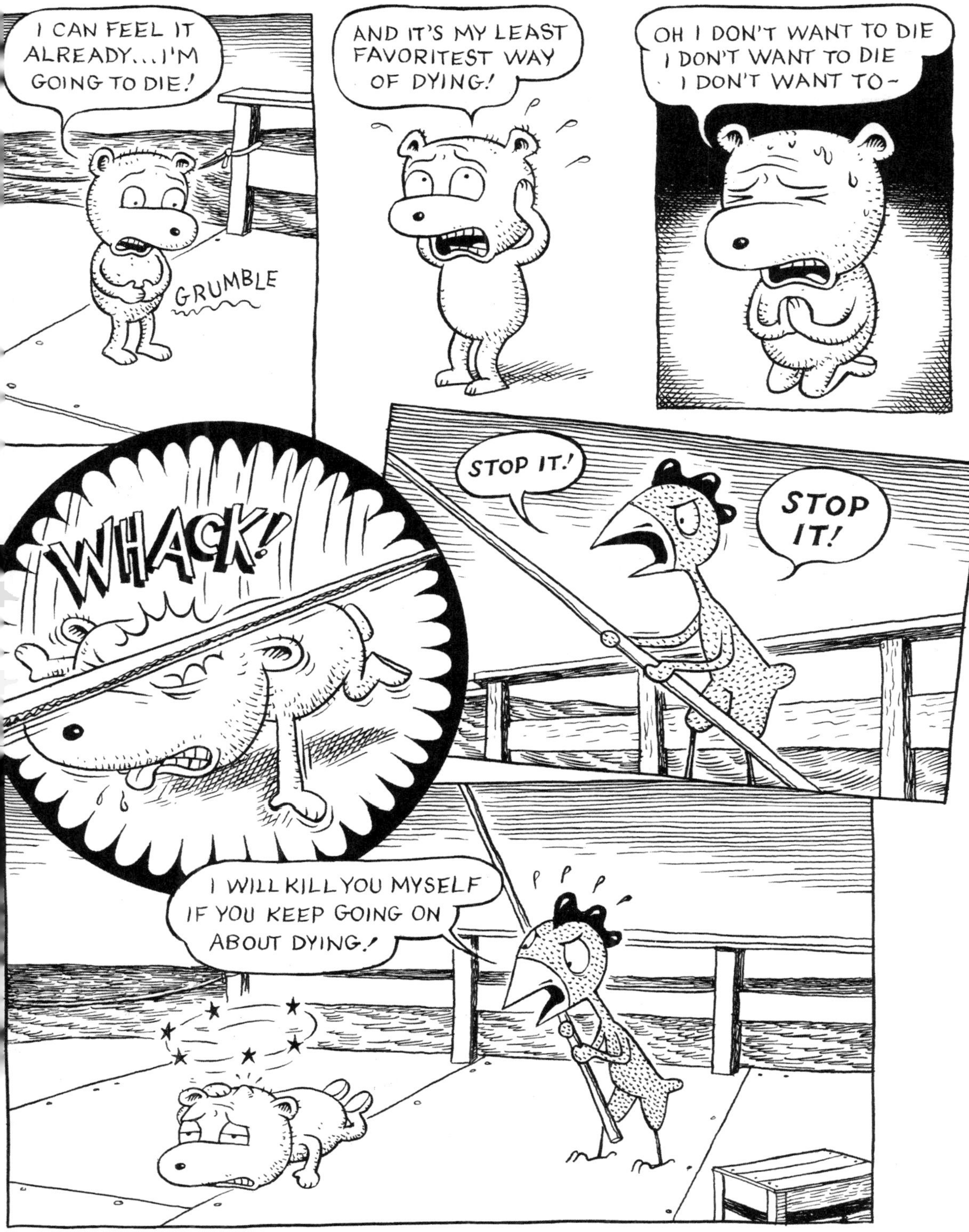
I CAN FEEL IT ALREADY...I'M GOING TO DIE!
GRUMBLE
AND IT'S MY LEAST FAVORITEST WAY OF DYING!
OH I DON'T WANT TO DIE I DON'T WANT TO DIE I DON'T WANT TO-
WHACK!
STOP IT!
STOP IT!
I WILL KILL YOU MYSELF IF YOU KEEP GOING ON ABOUT DYING!

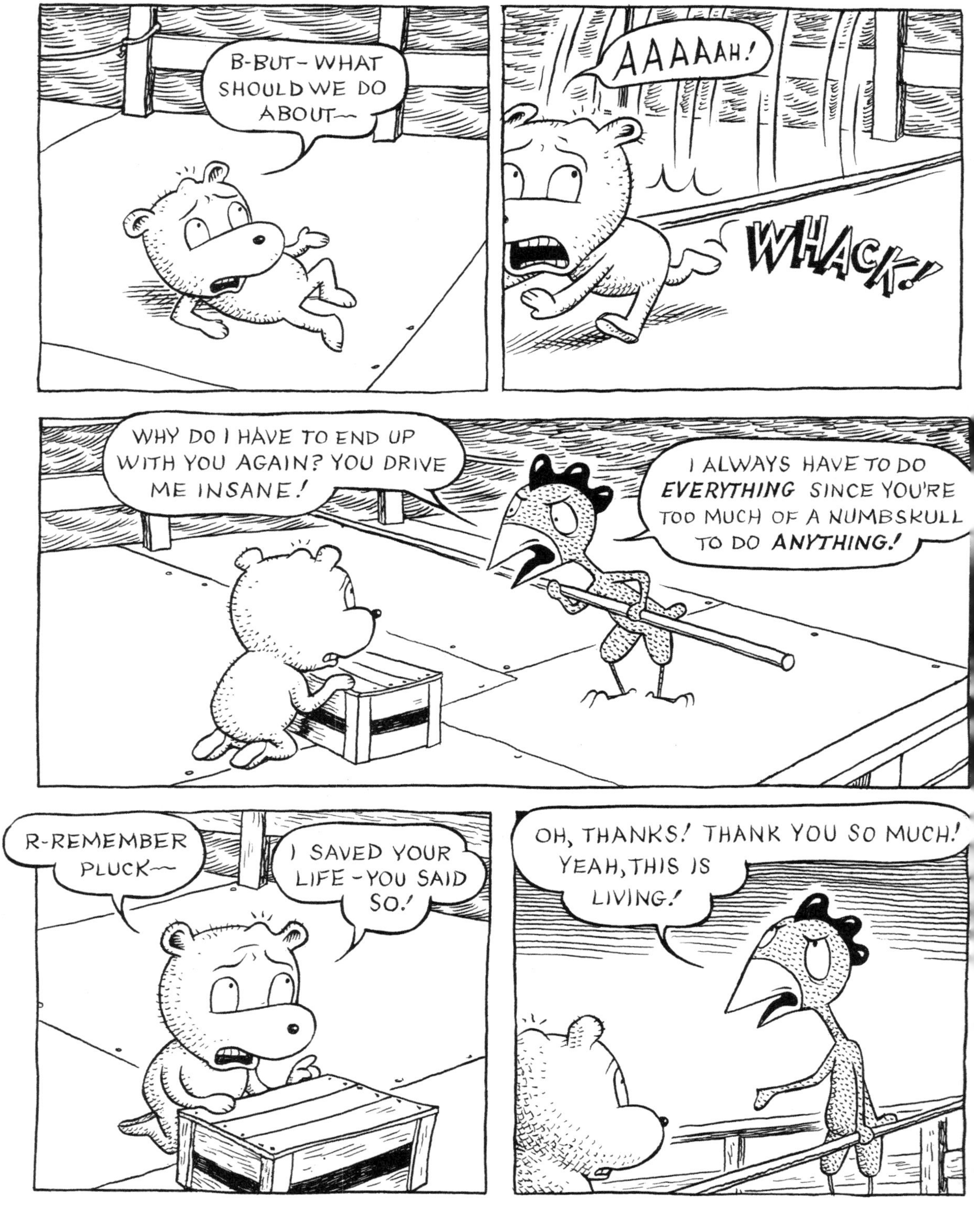
B-BUT- WHAT SHOULD WE DO ABOUT—
AAAAAH!
WHACK!
WHY DO I HAVE TO END UP WITH YOU AGAIN? YOU DRIVE ME INSANE!
I ALWAYS HAVE TO DO **EVERYTHING** SINCE YOU'RE TOO MUCH OF A NUMBSKULL TO DO **ANYTHING!**
R-REMEMBER PLUCK—
I SAVED YOUR LIFE - YOU SAID SO!
OH, THANKS! THANK YOU SO MUCH! YEAH, THIS IS LIVING!

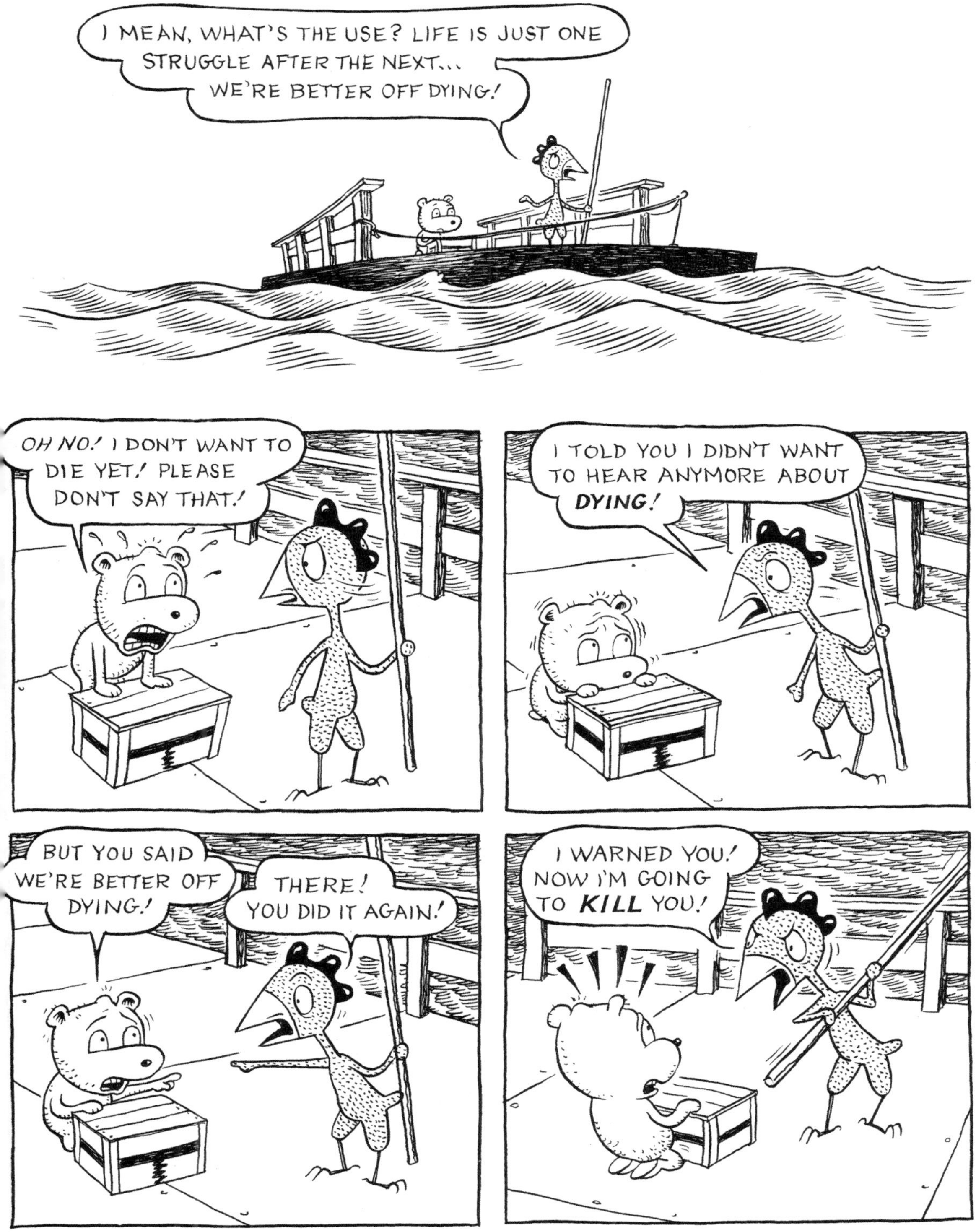
I MEAN, WHAT'S THE USE? LIFE IS JUST ONE STRUGGLE AFTER THE NEXT... WE'RE BETTER OFF DYING!
OH NO! I DON'T WANT TO DIE YET! PLEASE DON'T SAY THAT!
I TOLD YOU I DIDN'T WANT TO HEAR ANYMORE ABOUT **DYING**!
BUT YOU SAID WE'RE BETTER OFF DYING!
THERE! YOU DID IT AGAIN!
I WARNED YOU! NOW I'M GOING TO **KILL** YOU!

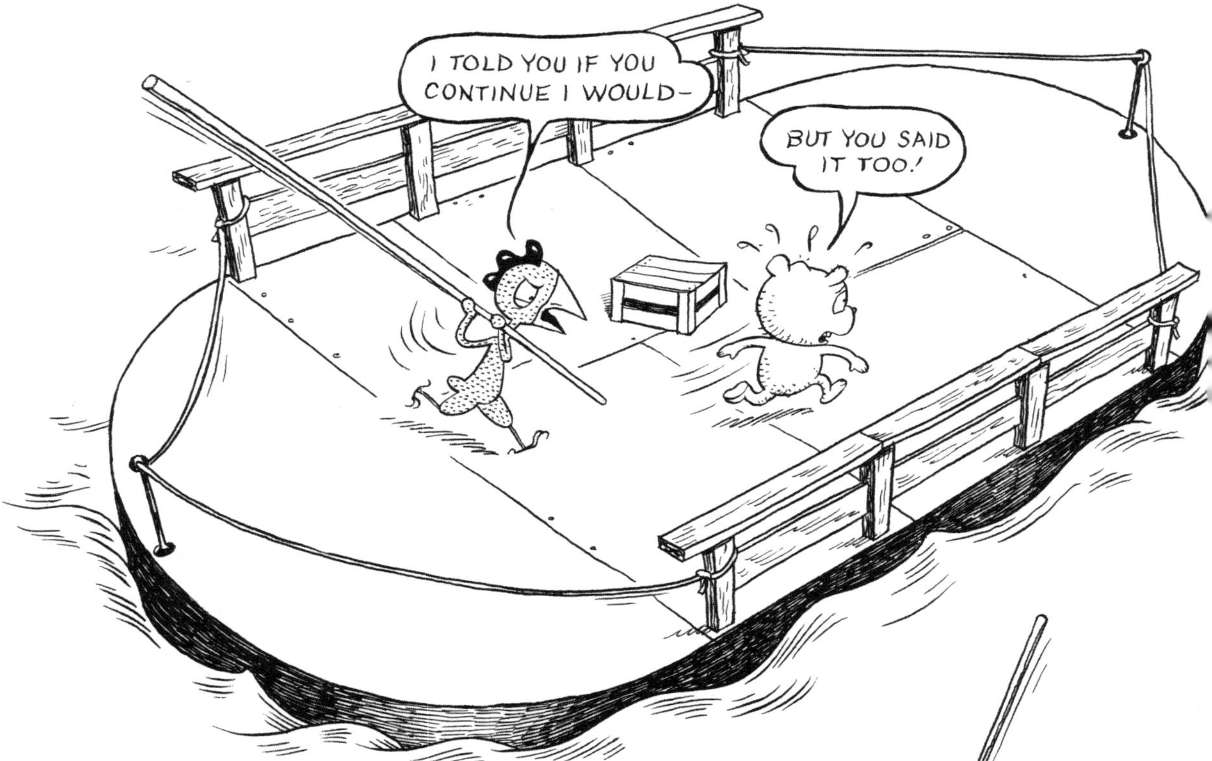
I TOLD YOU IF YOU CONTINUE I WOULD-
BUT YOU SAID IT TOO!

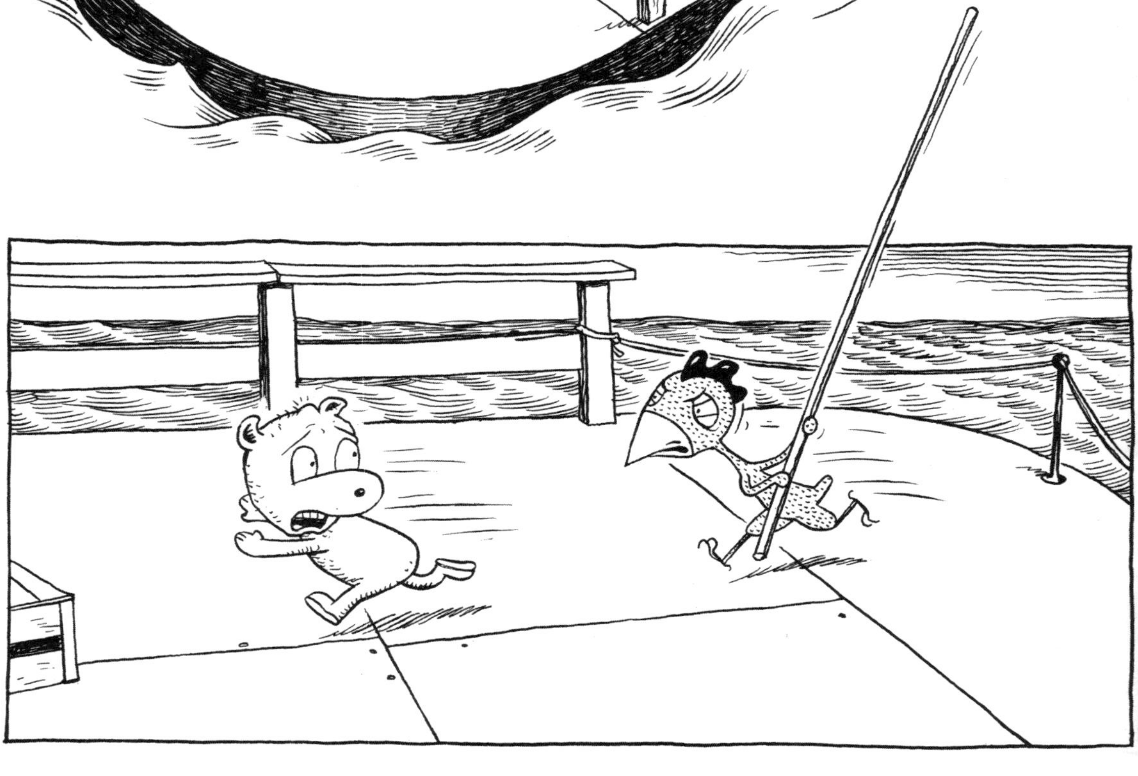

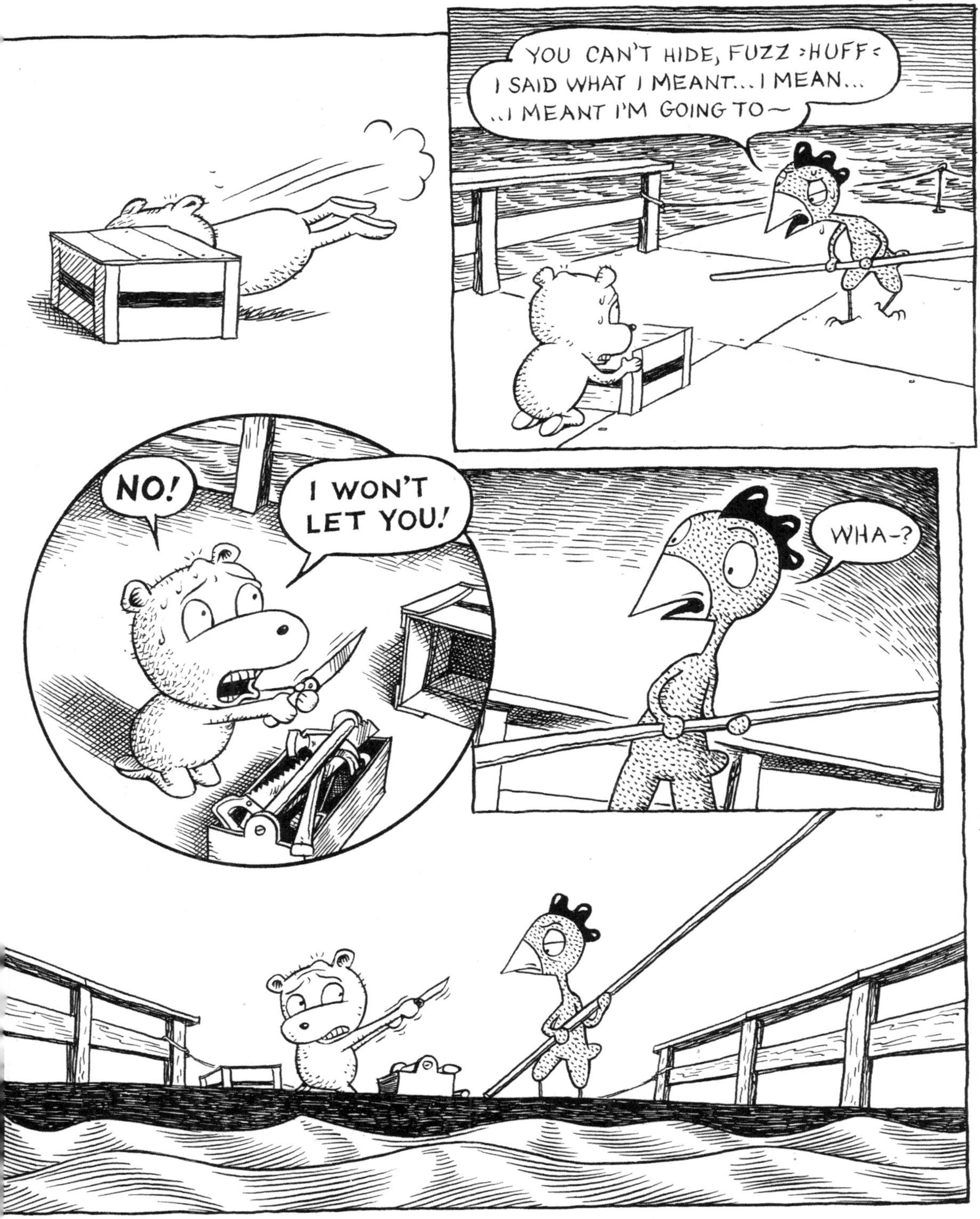
YOU CAN'T HIDE, FUZZ >HUFF< I SAID WHAT I MEANT... I MEAN... ..I MEANT I'M GOING TO~
NO!
I WON'T LET YOU!
WHA-?

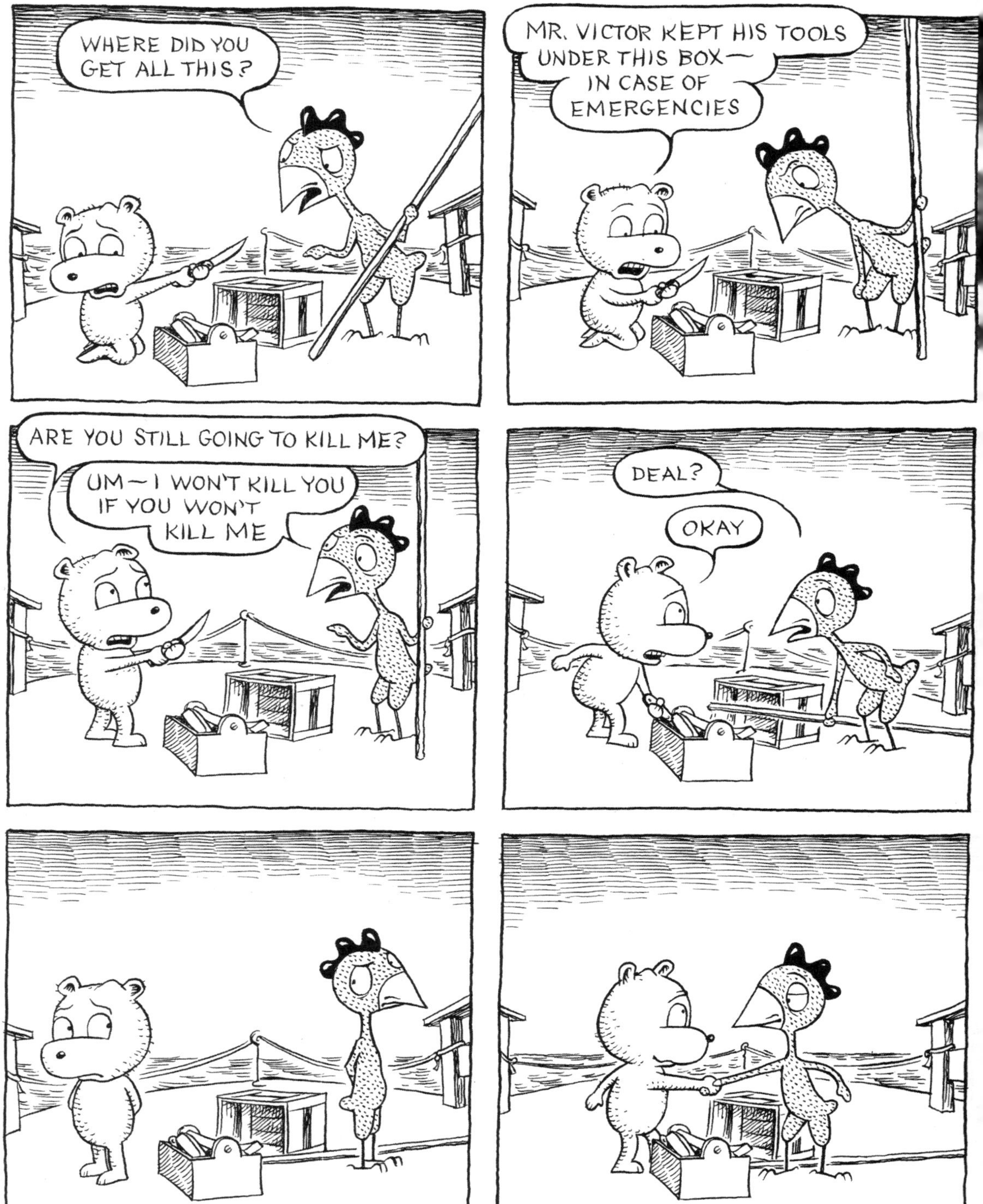
WHERE DID YOU GET ALL THIS?
MR. VICTOR KEPT HIS TOOLS UNDER THIS BOX— IN CASE OF EMERGENCIES
ARE YOU STILL GOING TO KILL ME?
UM—I WON'T KILL YOU IF YOU WON'T KILL ME
DEAL?
OKAY

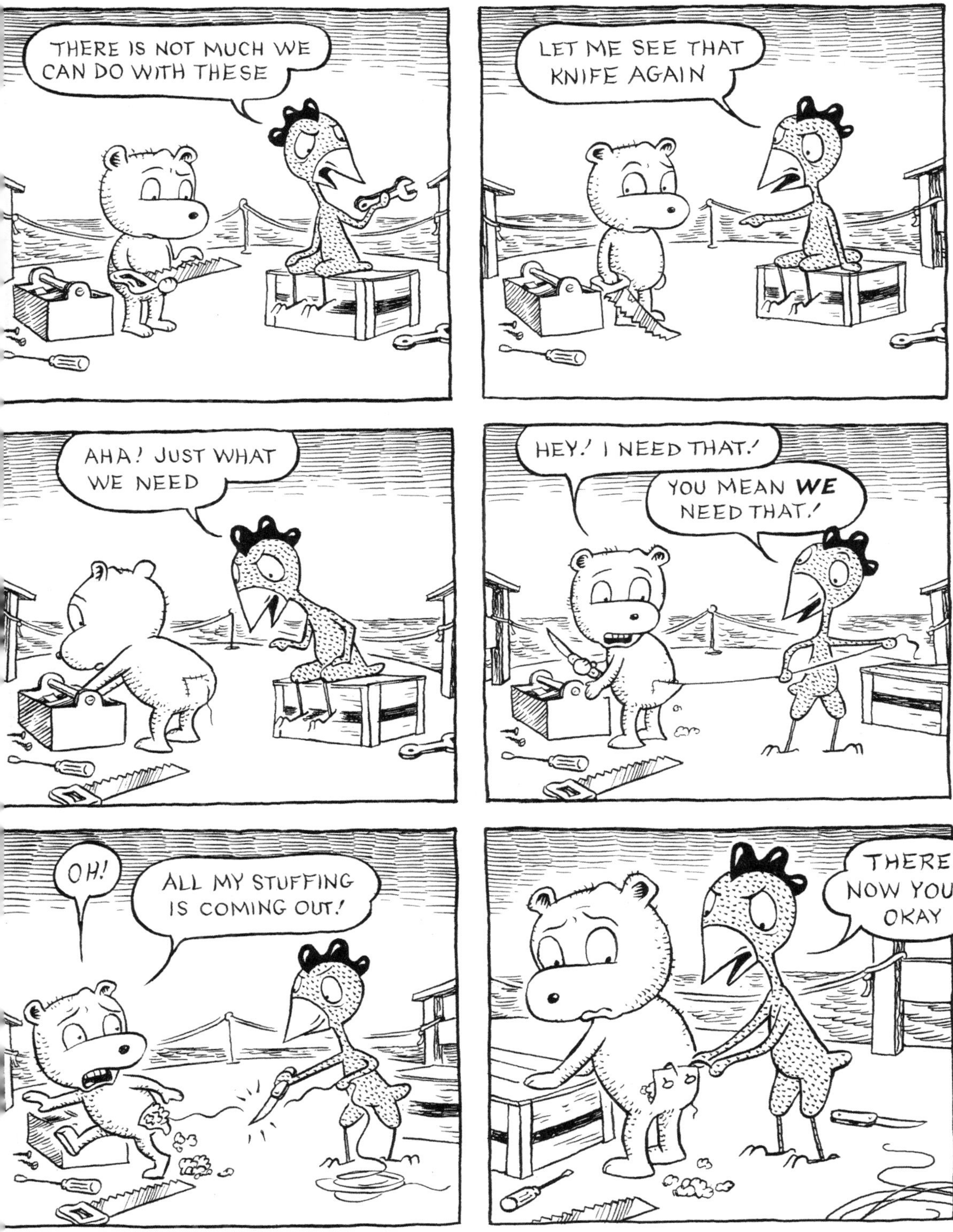
THERE IS NOT MUCH WE CAN DO WITH THESE
LET ME SEE THAT KNIFE AGAIN
AHA! JUST WHAT WE NEED
HEY! I NEED THAT!
YOU MEAN WE NEED THAT!
OH!
ALL MY STUFFING IS COMING OUT!
THERE NOW YOU'RE OKAY

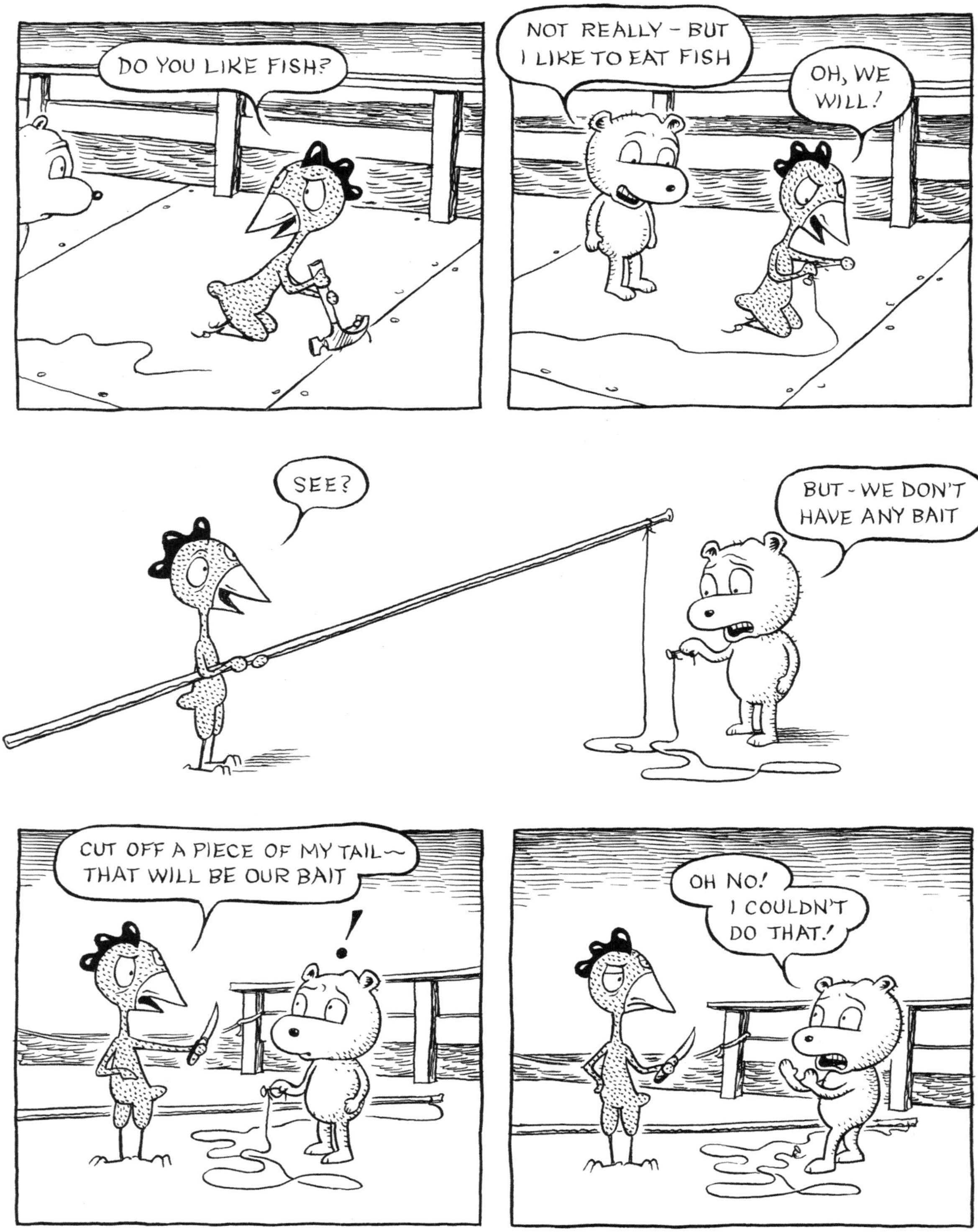
DO YOU LIKE FISH?
NOT REALLY - BUT I LIKE TO EAT FISH
OH, WE WILL!
SEE?
BUT - WE DON'T HAVE ANY BAIT
CUT OFF A PIECE OF MY TAIL~ THAT WILL BE OUR BAIT
!
OH NO! I COULDN'T DO THAT!

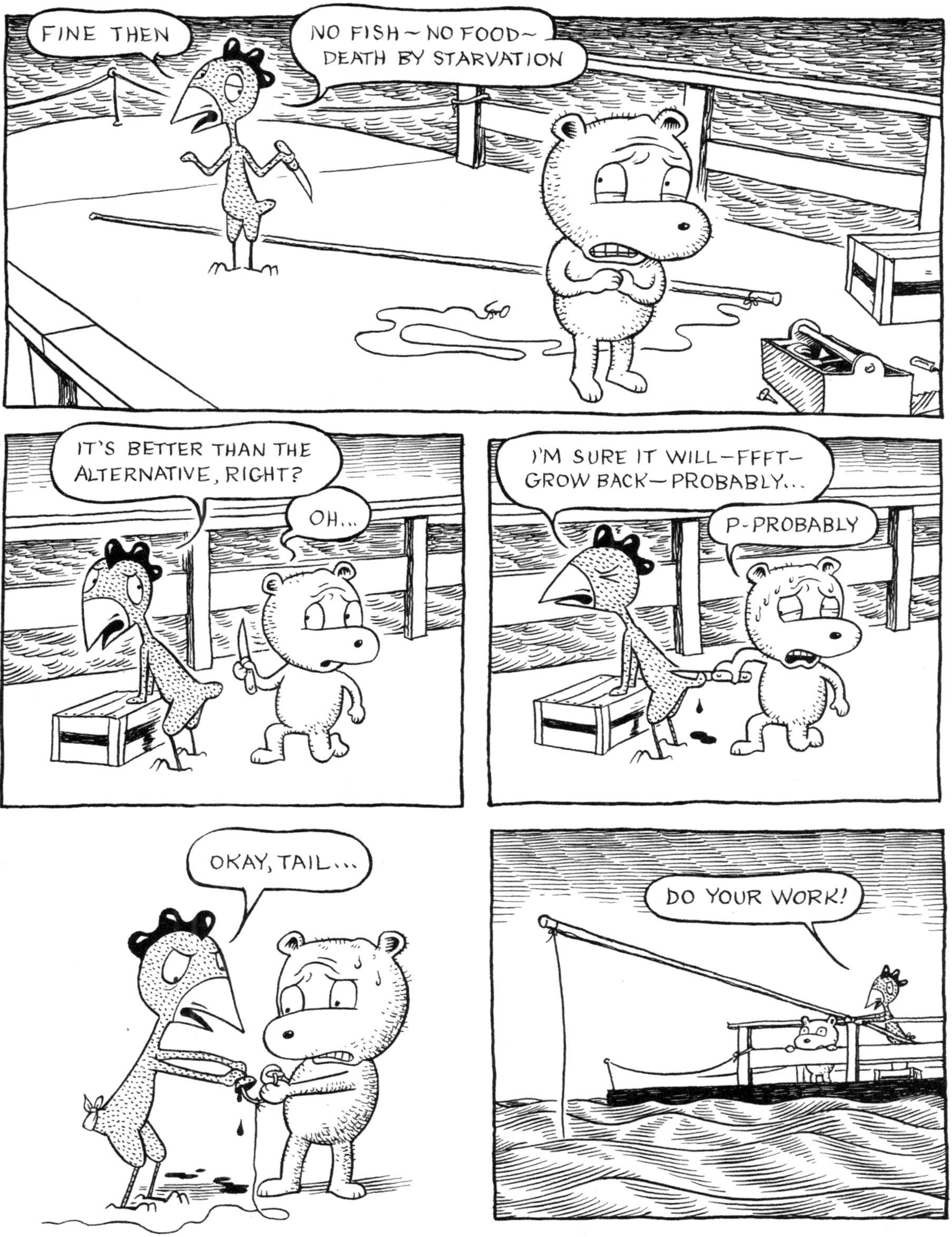
FINE THEN
NO FISH ~ NO FOOD ~ DEATH BY STARVATION
IT'S BETTER THAN THE ALTERNATIVE, RIGHT?
OH...
I'M SURE IT WILL—FFFT—GROW BACK—PROBABLY...
P-PROBABLY
OKAY, TAIL...
DO YOUR WORK!

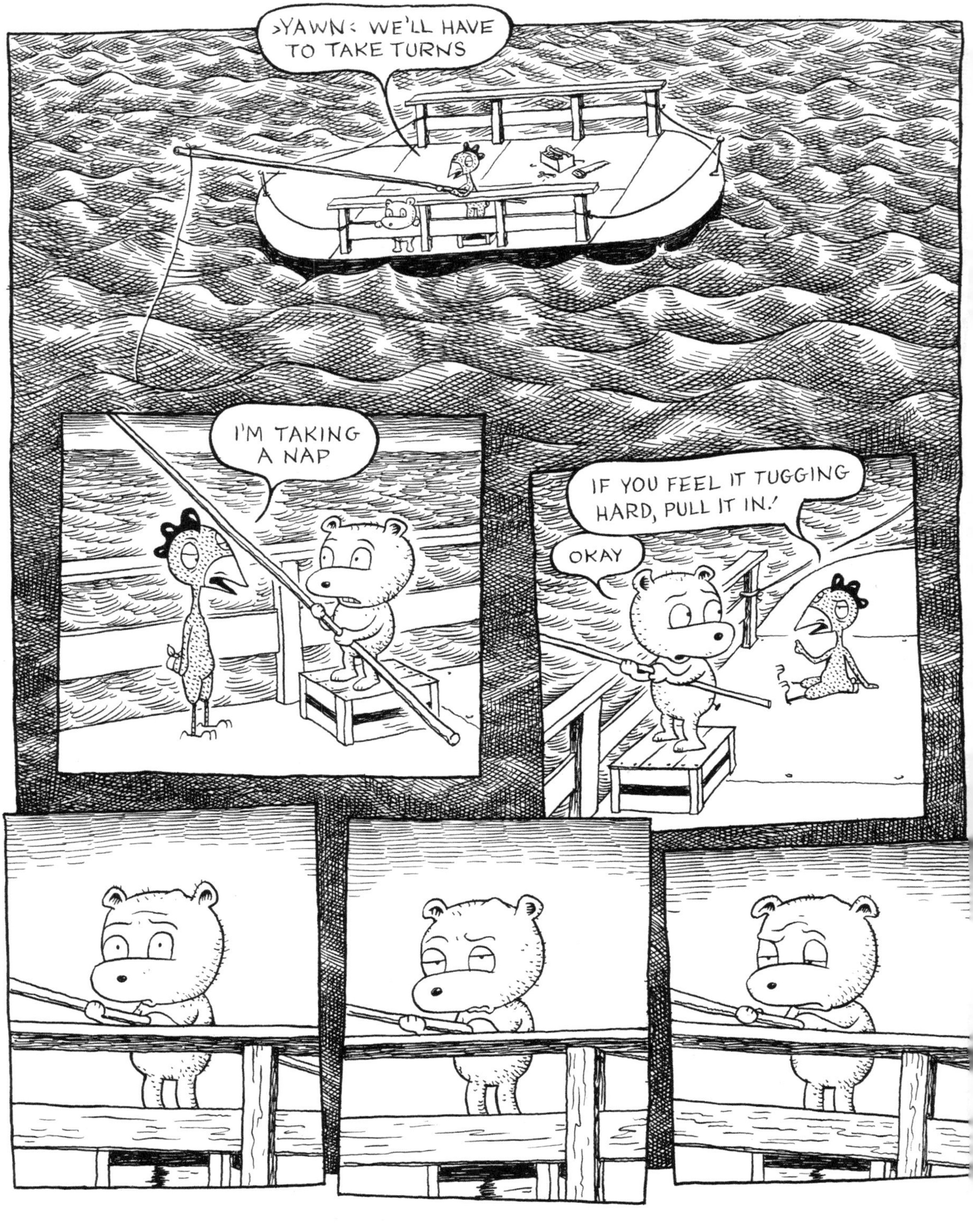
>YAWN< WE'LL HAVE TO TAKE TURNS
I'M TAKING A NAP
IF YOU FEEL IT TUGGING HARD, PULL IT IN.'
OKAY

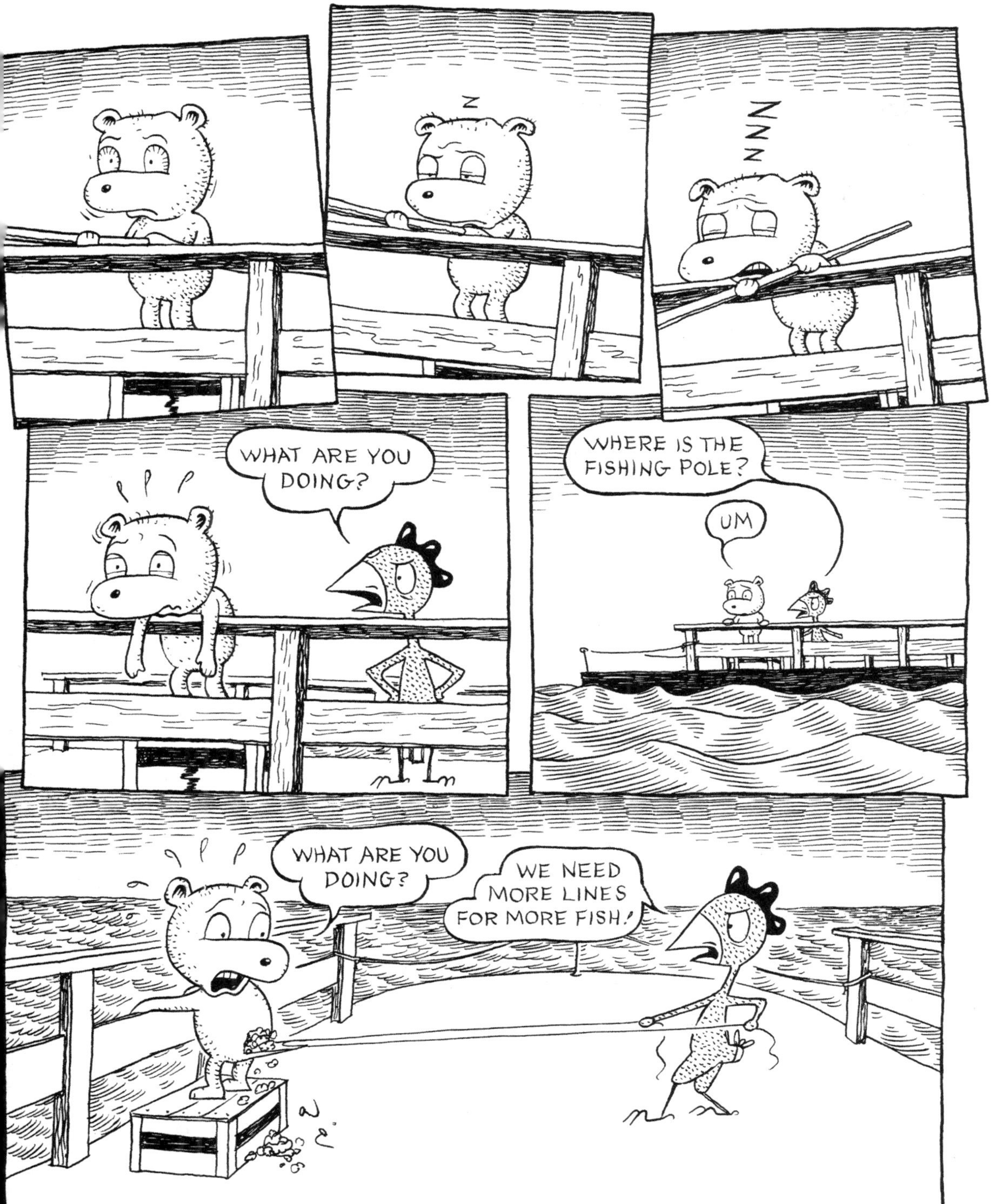
Z
ZZZ
WHAT ARE YOU DOING?
WHERE IS THE FISHING POLE?
UM
WHAT ARE YOU DOING?
WE NEED MORE LINES FOR MORE FISH!

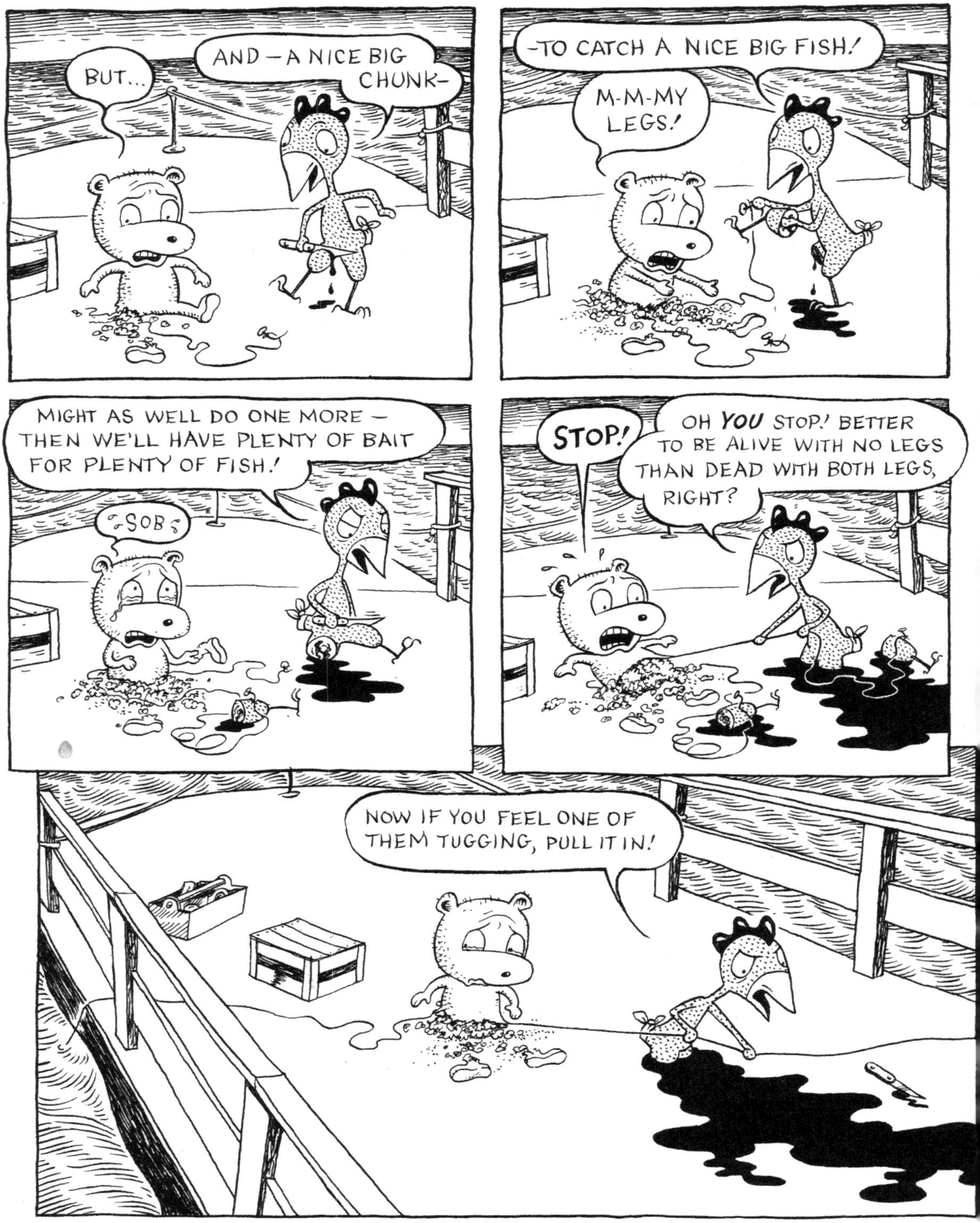
BUT...
AND—A NICE BIG CHUNK—
—TO CATCH A NICE BIG FISH!
M-M-MY LEGS!
MIGHT AS WELL DO ONE MORE—THEN WE'LL HAVE PLENTY OF BAIT FOR PLENTY OF FISH!
SOB
STOP!
OH **YOU** STOP! BETTER TO BE ALIVE WITH NO LEGS THAN DEAD WITH BOTH LEGS, RIGHT?
NOW IF YOU FEEL ONE OF THEM TUGGING, PULL IT IN!

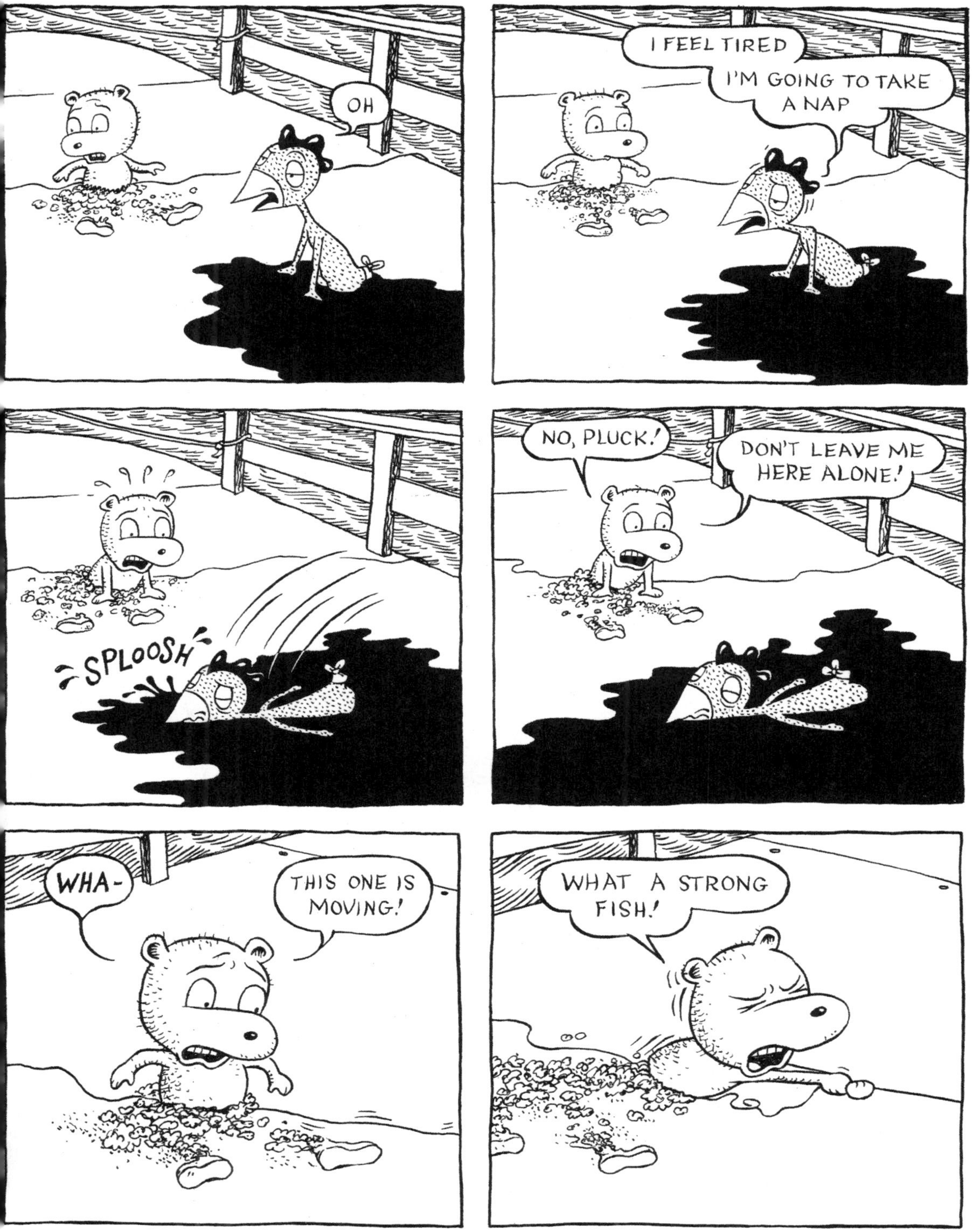
OH
I FEEL TIRED
I'M GOING TO TAKE A NAP
SPLOOSH
NO, PLUCK!
DON'T LEAVE ME HERE ALONE!
WHA-
THIS ONE IS MOVING!
WHAT A STRONG FISH!

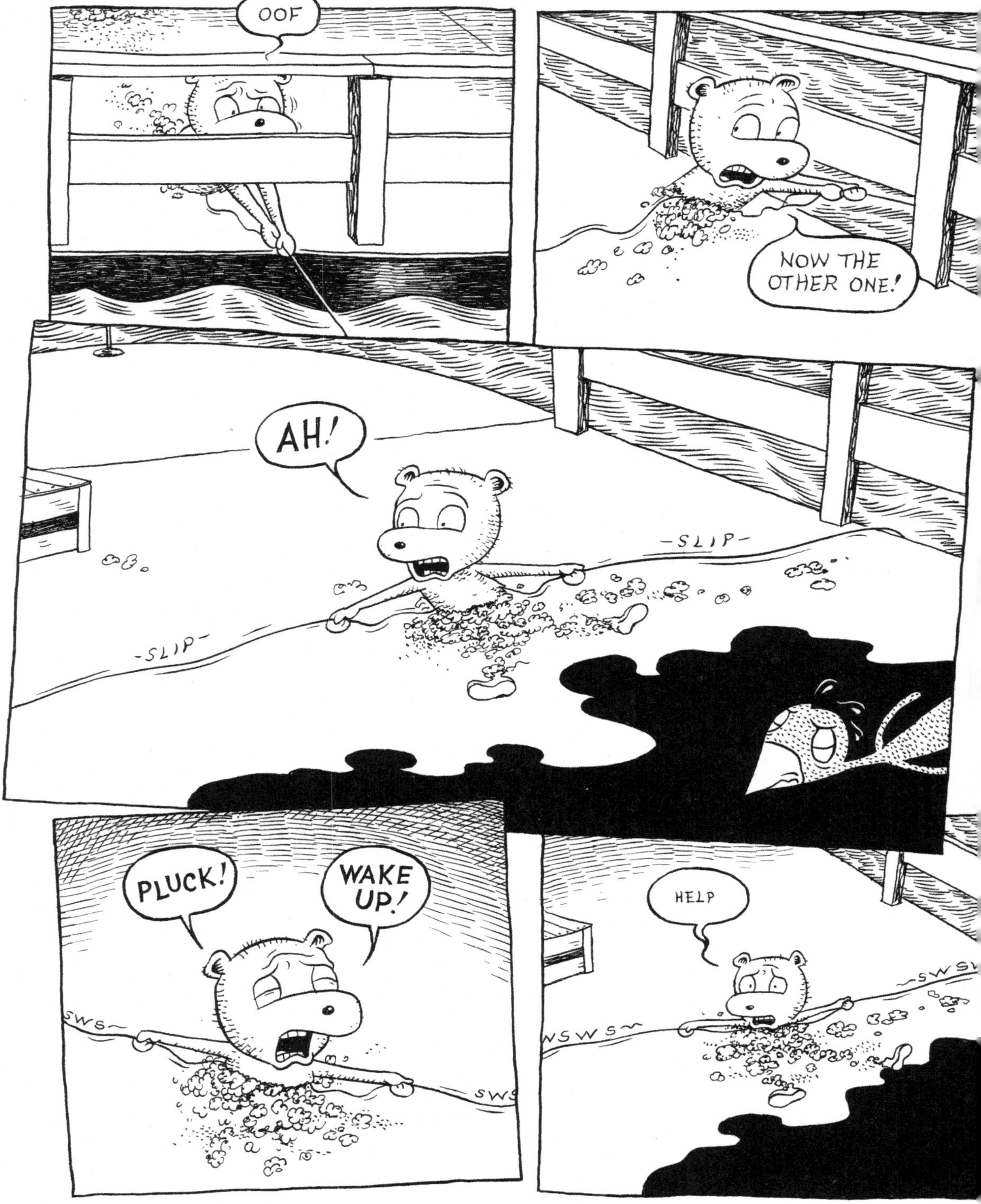
OOF
NOW THE OTHER ONE!
AH!
-SLIP-
-SLIP-
PLUCK!
WAKE UP!
SWS~
SWS
HELP
~SWS
WSWS~

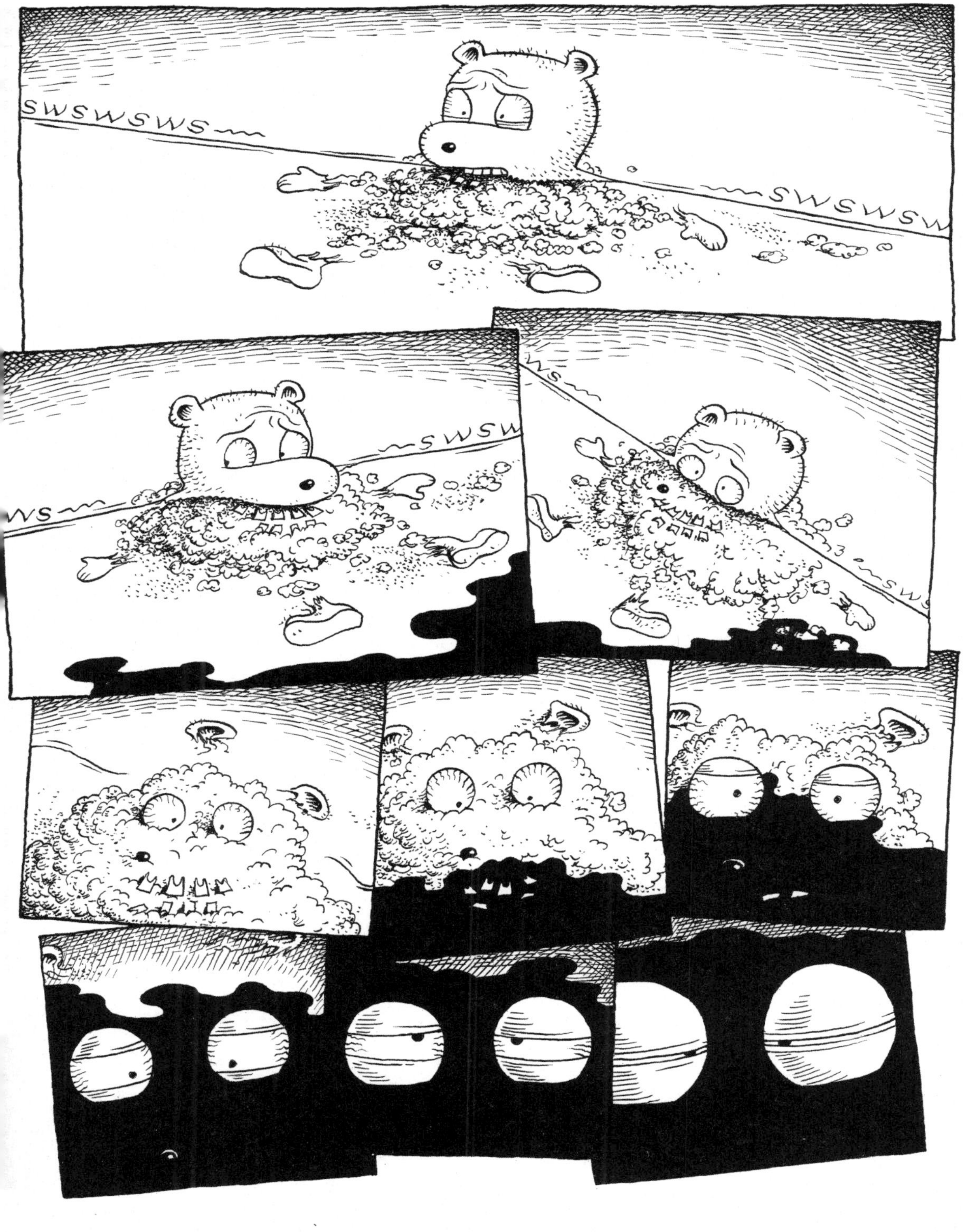
SWSWSWS
SWSWSW
WS
SWSW
WS
SWS

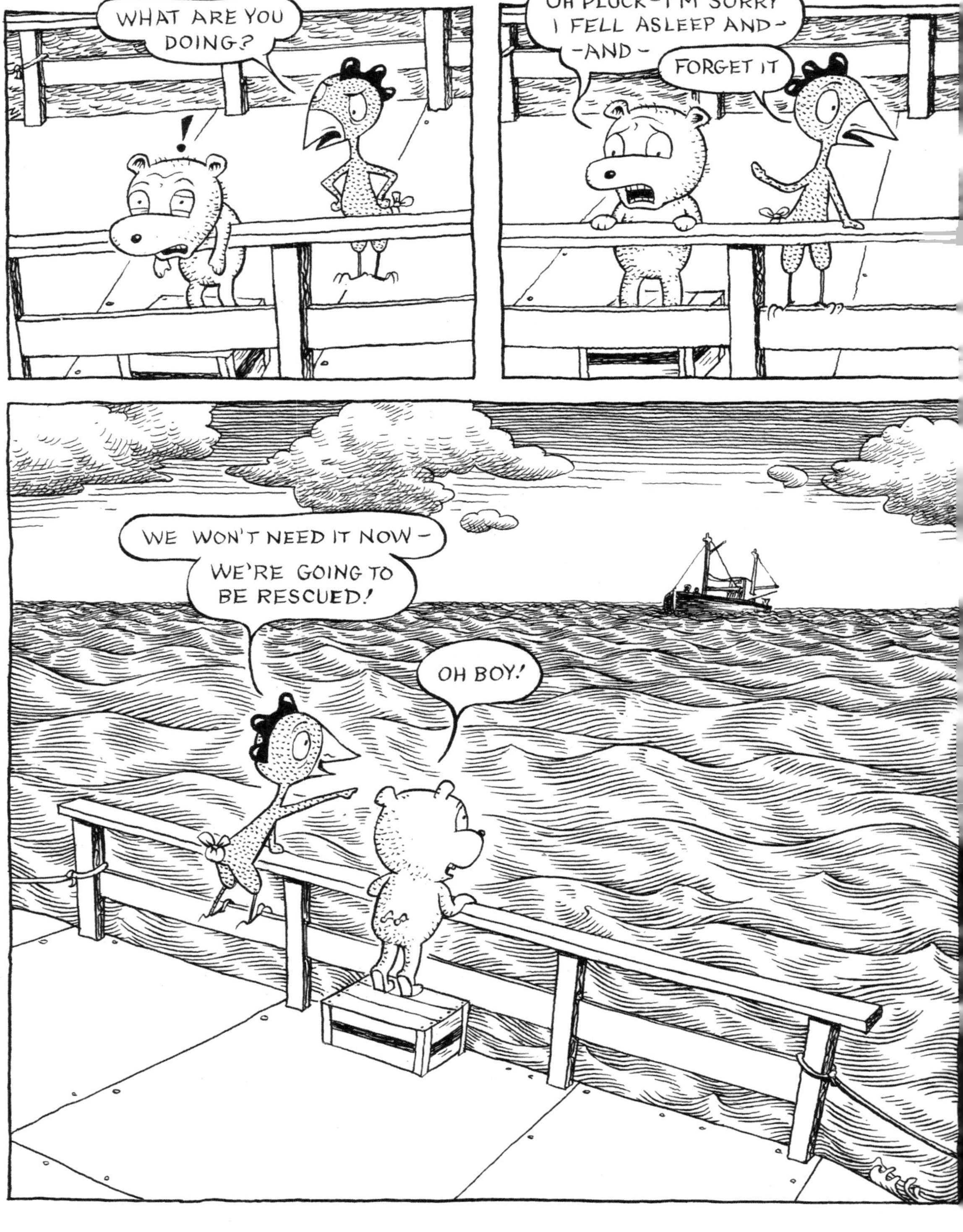
WHAT ARE YOU DOING?
!
OH PLUCK - I'M SORRY I FELL ASLEEP AND - -AND -
FORGET IT
WE WON'T NEED IT NOW -
WE'RE GOING TO BE RESCUED!
OH BOY!

Art Comic (*Excerpt*)

MATTHEW THURBER

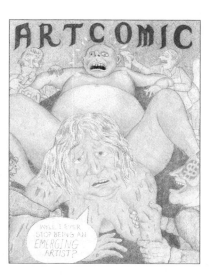

originally published in

Art Comic #4

SWIMMERS GROUP

7 x 9 inches • 28 pages

ARTCOMIC
WILL I EVER STOP BEING AN EMERGING ARTIST?

Biography

Matthew Thurber is the author of *1-800-MICE*, *INFOMANIACS*, *Art Comic*, *Are Snakes Necessary?*, *Mining the Moon*, *Shawarma Chameleon*, *Carrot for Girls*, and many other works. He has performed in various ensembles: Ambergris, Soiled Mattress and the Springs, Court Stenographer, and Young Sherlock Holmes Jr. Thurber resides in Catskill, New York, where he is working on animated and live-action film projects. He is the operator of Mrs William Horsley, a mobile theater devoted to creating works of narrative experimentation and scientific investigation using puppetry.
matthewthurber.com

Statement

Art Comic is a paranoiac-critical examination of the art world seen through the eyes of four graduates of The Cooper Union, each attempting to reconcile their ideals with the realities of capitalism. It is vaguely autobiographical, a memoir-as-hallucination.

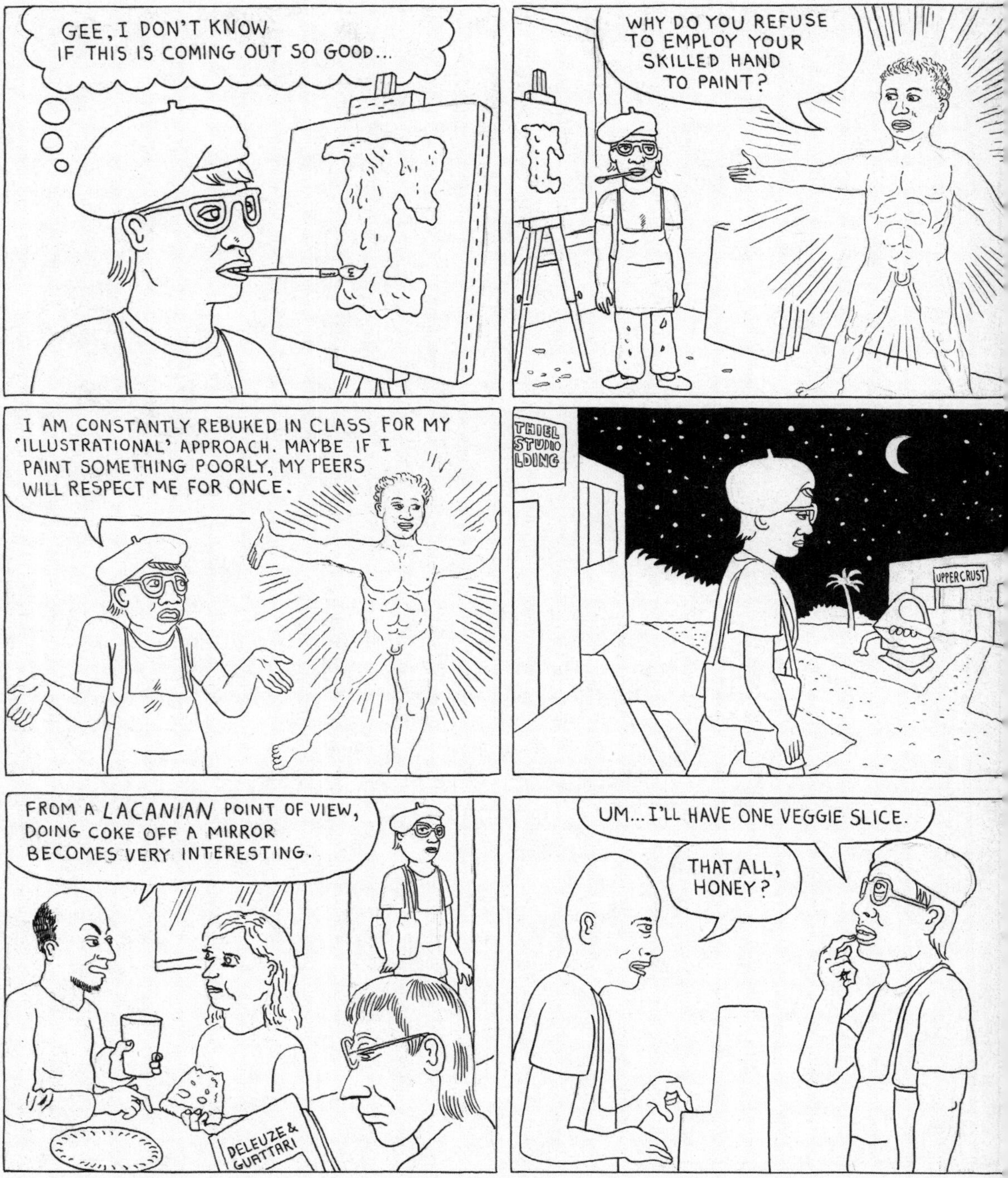
GEE, I DON'T KNOW IF THIS IS COMING OUT SO GOOD...
WHY DO YOU REFUSE TO EMPLOY YOUR SKILLED HAND TO PAINT?
I AM CONSTANTLY REBUKED IN CLASS FOR MY 'ILLUSTRATIONAL' APPROACH. MAYBE IF I PAINT SOMETHING POORLY, MY PEERS WILL RESPECT ME FOR ONCE.
THIEL STUDIO LDING
UPPERCRUST
FROM A LACANIAN POINT OF VIEW, DOING COKE OFF A MIRROR BECOMES VERY INTERESTING.
DELEUZE & GUATTARI
UM... I'LL HAVE ONE VEGGIE SLICE.
THAT ALL, HONEY?

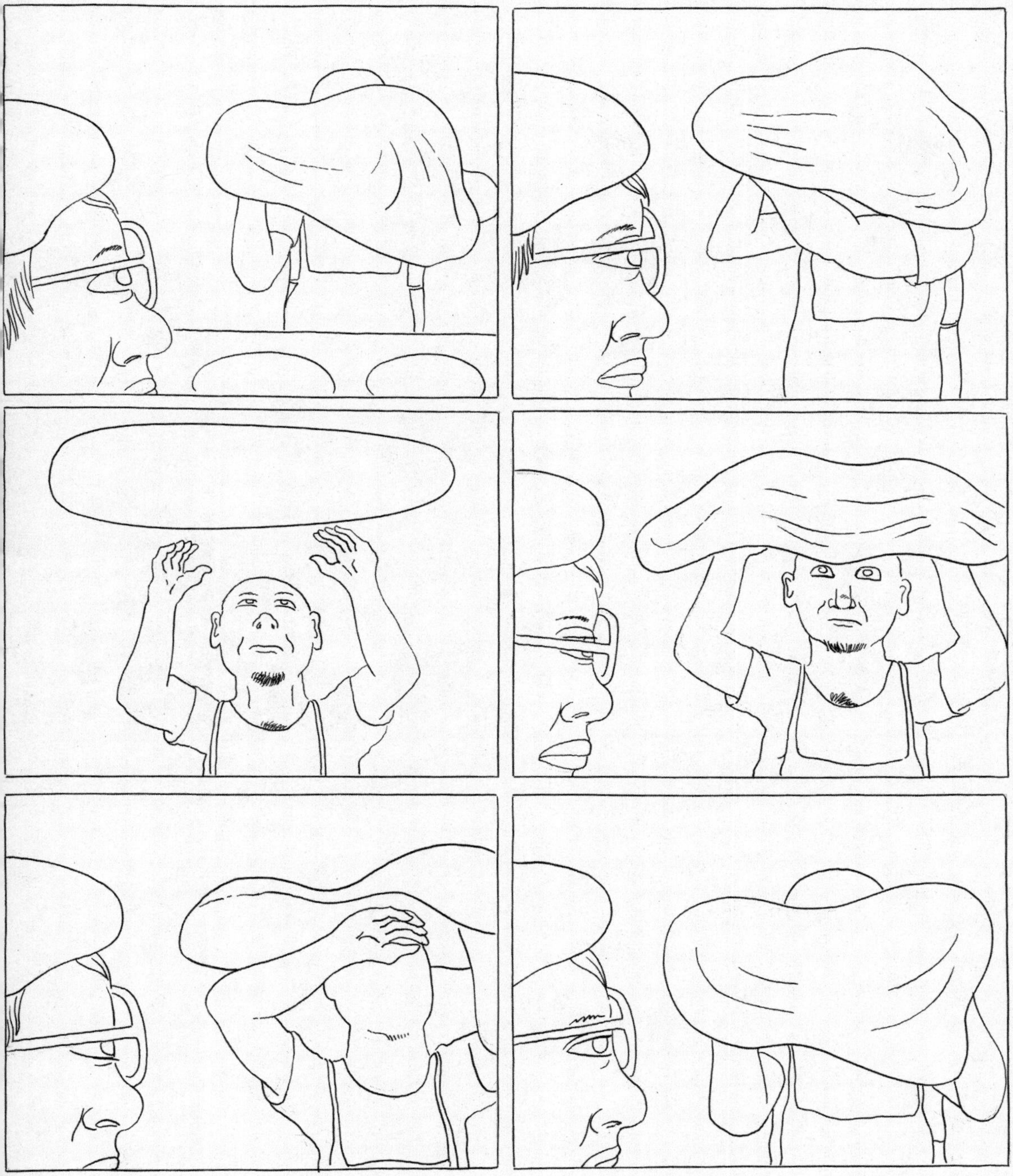

HEY TIFFANY, DO YOU WANT TO PLAY VOLLEYBALL AFTER CLASS WITH US?
UM... I DON'T KNOW. I HAVE TO GET SOME PAINTING DONE. I THINK I'M ENTERING A NEW SYMBOLIST PERIOD IN MY WORK.
WHERE THE HELL IS SHE?
HI!
HI GUYS!
PROUST!
CRIT TIME MOTHER FUCKERS!
PUT YOUR ART WHERE MY EYES COULD SEE!
HA HA HA HA
OH MY GOD!
GROSS!

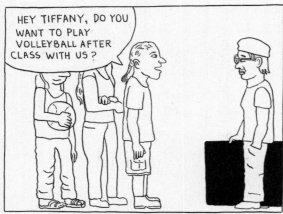

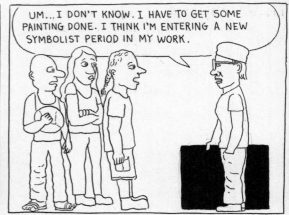

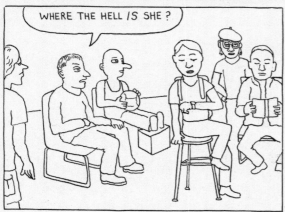

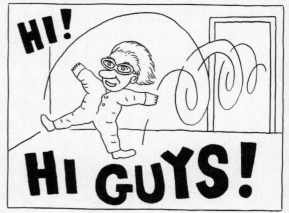

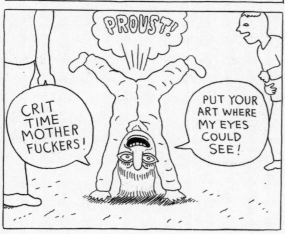

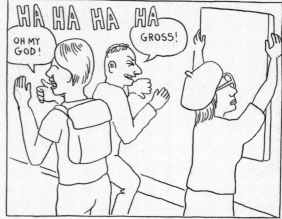

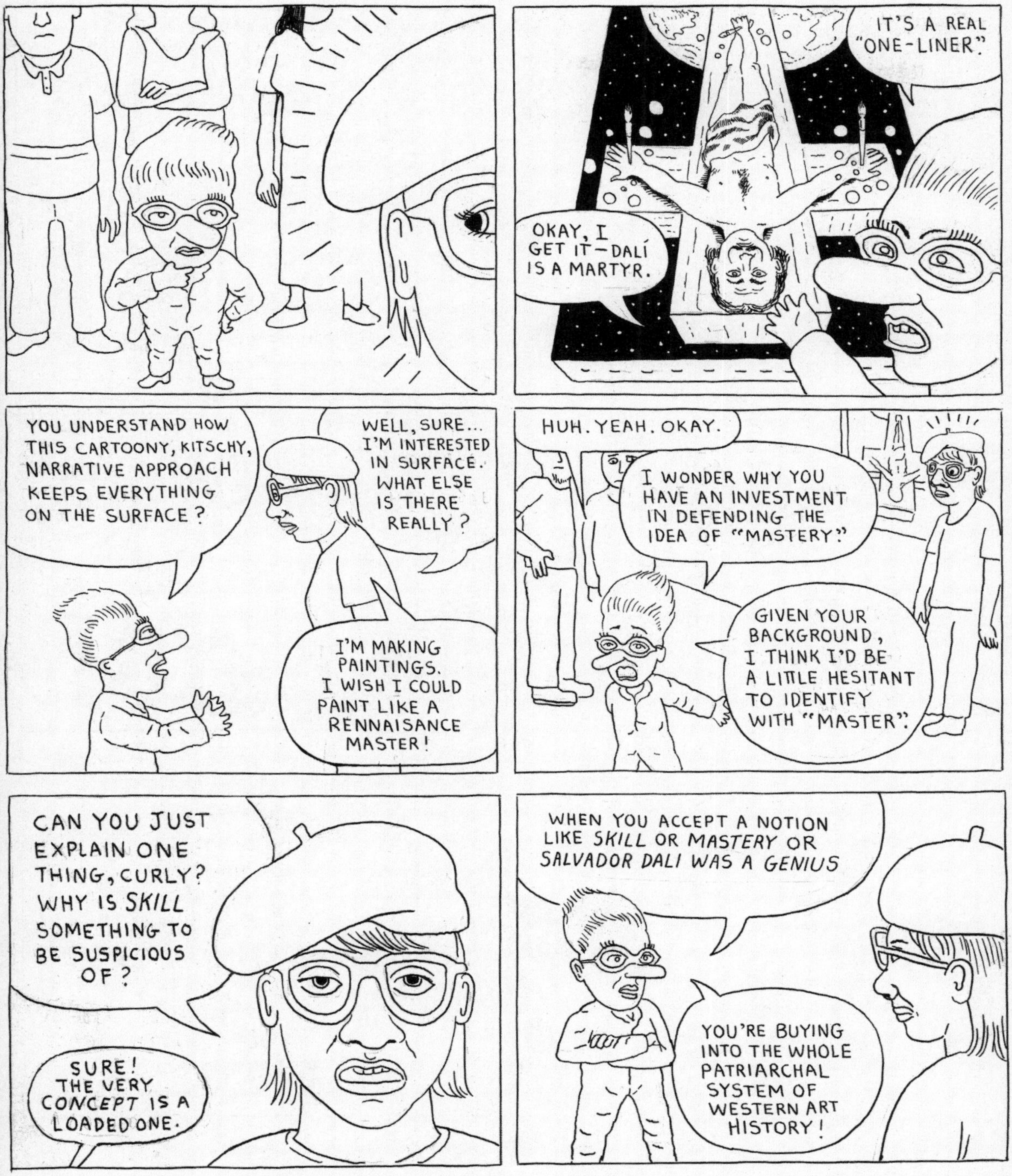
IT'S A REAL "ONE-LINER".
OKAY, I GET IT—DALÍ IS A MARTYR.
YOU UNDERSTAND HOW THIS CARTOONY, KITSCHY, NARRATIVE APPROACH KEEPS EVERYTHING ON THE SURFACE?
WELL, SURE... I'M INTERESTED IN SURFACE. WHAT ELSE IS THERE REALLY?
I'M MAKING PAINTINGS. I WISH I COULD PAINT LIKE A RENNAISANCE MASTER!
HUH. YEAH. OKAY.
I WONDER WHY YOU HAVE AN INVESTMENT IN DEFENDING THE IDEA OF "MASTERY."
GIVEN YOUR BACKGROUND, I THINK I'D BE A LITTLE HESITANT TO IDENTIFY WITH "MASTER".
CAN YOU JUST EXPLAIN ONE THING, CURLY? WHY IS *SKILL* SOMETHING TO BE SUSPICIOUS OF?
SURE! THE VERY *CONCEPT* IS A LOADED ONE.
WHEN YOU ACCEPT A NOTION LIKE *SKILL* OR *MASTERY* OR *SALVADOR DALI WAS A GENIUS*
YOU'RE BUYING INTO THE WHOLE PATRIARCHAL SYSTEM OF WESTERN ART HISTORY!

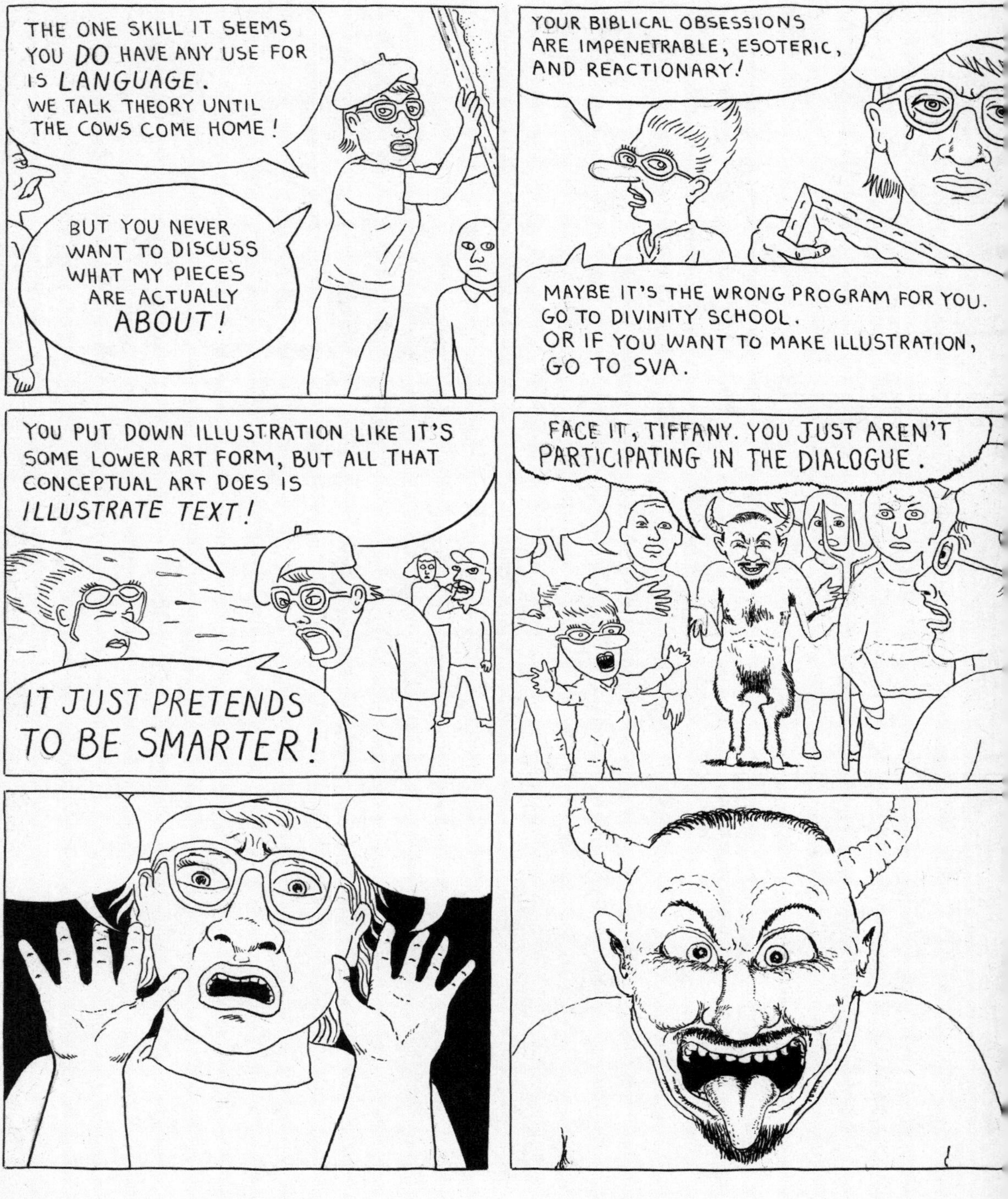
THE ONE SKILL IT SEEMS YOU DO HAVE ANY USE FOR IS LANGUAGE. WE TALK THEORY UNTIL THE COWS COME HOME!
BUT YOU NEVER WANT TO DISCUSS WHAT MY PIECES ARE ACTUALLY ABOUT!
YOUR BIBLICAL OBSESSIONS ARE IMPENETRABLE, ESOTERIC, AND REACTIONARY!
MAYBE IT'S THE WRONG PROGRAM FOR YOU. GO TO DIVINITY SCHOOL. OR IF YOU WANT TO MAKE ILLUSTRATION, GO TO SVA.
YOU PUT DOWN ILLUSTRATION LIKE IT'S SOME LOWER ART FORM, BUT ALL THAT CONCEPTUAL ART DOES IS ILLUSTRATE TEXT!
IT JUST PRETENDS TO BE SMARTER!
FACE IT, TIFFANY. YOU JUST AREN'T PARTICIPATING IN THE DIALOGUE.

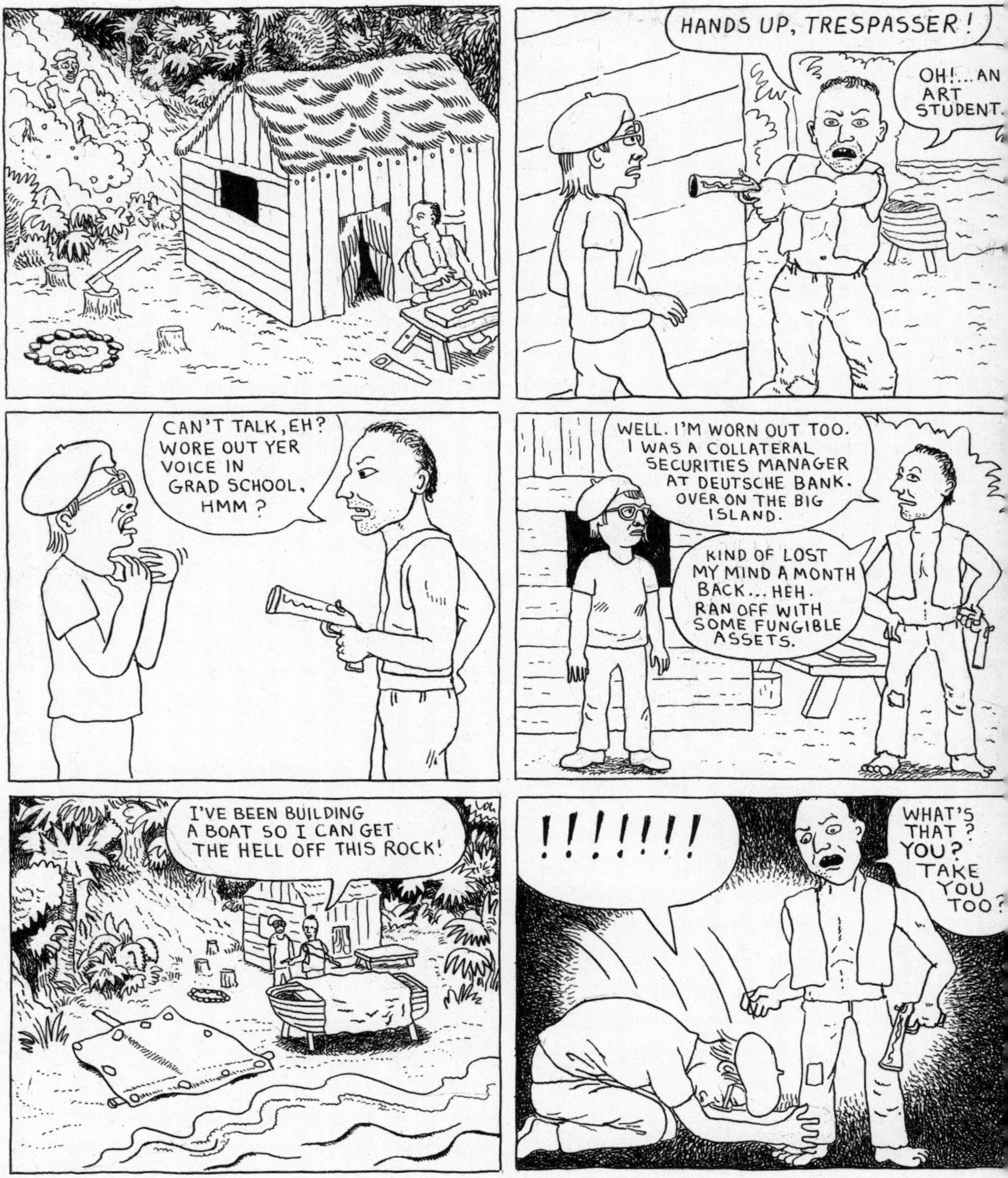
HANDS UP, TRESPASSER!
OH!... AN ART STUDENT.
CAN'T TALK, EH? WORE OUT YER VOICE IN GRAD SCHOOL, HMM?
WELL. I'M WORN OUT TOO. I WAS A COLLATERAL SECURITIES MANAGER AT DEUTSCHE BANK. OVER ON THE BIG ISLAND.
KIND OF LOST MY MIND A MONTH BACK... HEH. RAN OFF WITH SOME FUNGIBLE ASSETS.
I'VE BEEN BUILDING A BOAT SO I CAN GET THE HELL OFF THIS ROCK!
!!!!!!!
WHAT'S THAT? YOU? TAKE YOU TOO?

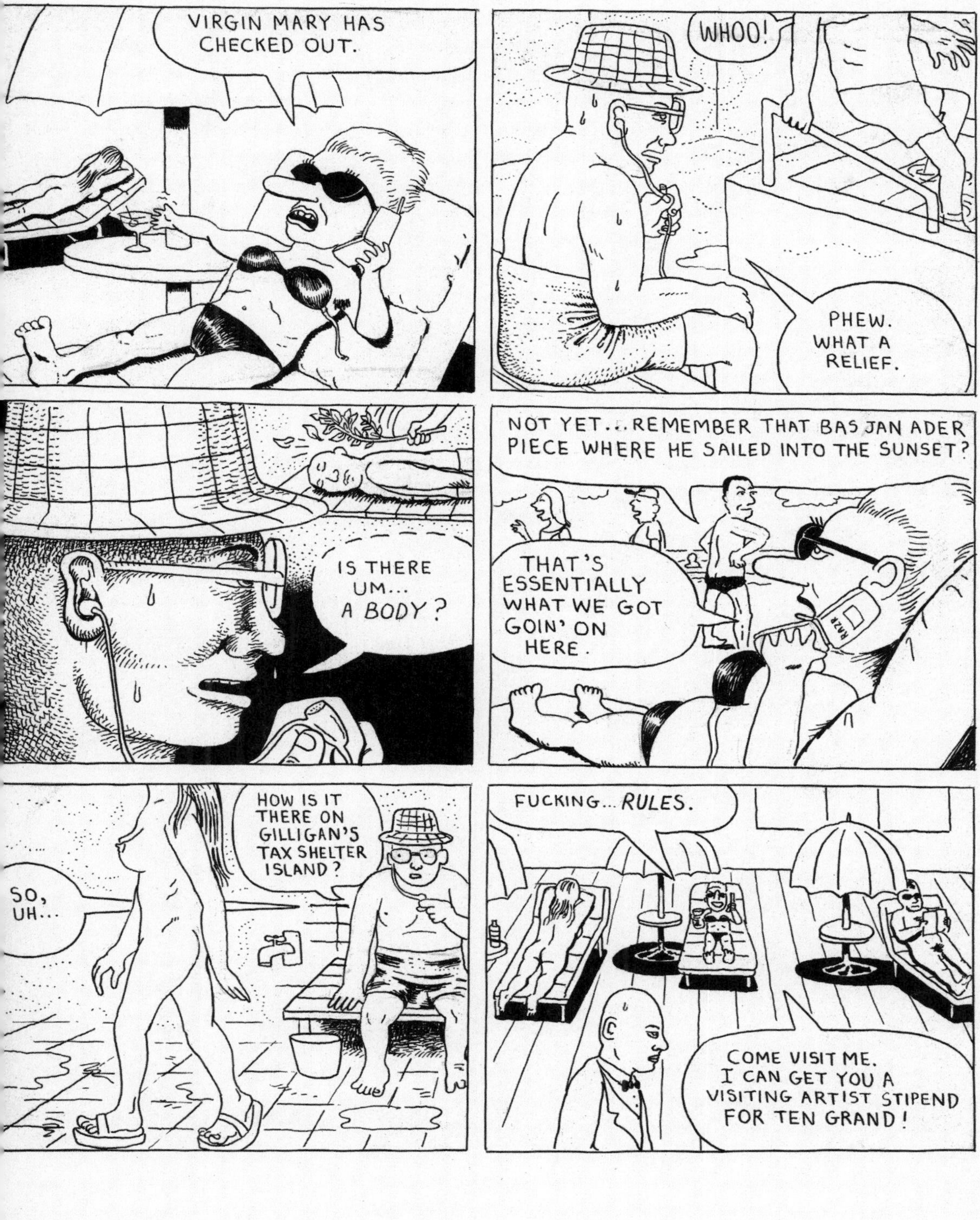
VIRGIN MARY HAS CHECKED OUT.
WHOO!
PHEW. WHAT A RELIEF.
IS THERE UM... A *BODY*?
NOT YET...REMEMBER THAT BAS JAN ADER PIECE WHERE HE SAILED INTO THE SUNSET?
THAT'S ESSENTIALLY WHAT WE GOT GOIN' ON HERE.
SO, UH...
HOW IS IT THERE ON GILLIGAN'S TAX SHELTER ISLAND?
FUCKING... *RULES*.
COME VISIT ME. I CAN GET YOU A VISITING ARTIST STIPEND FOR TEN GRAND!

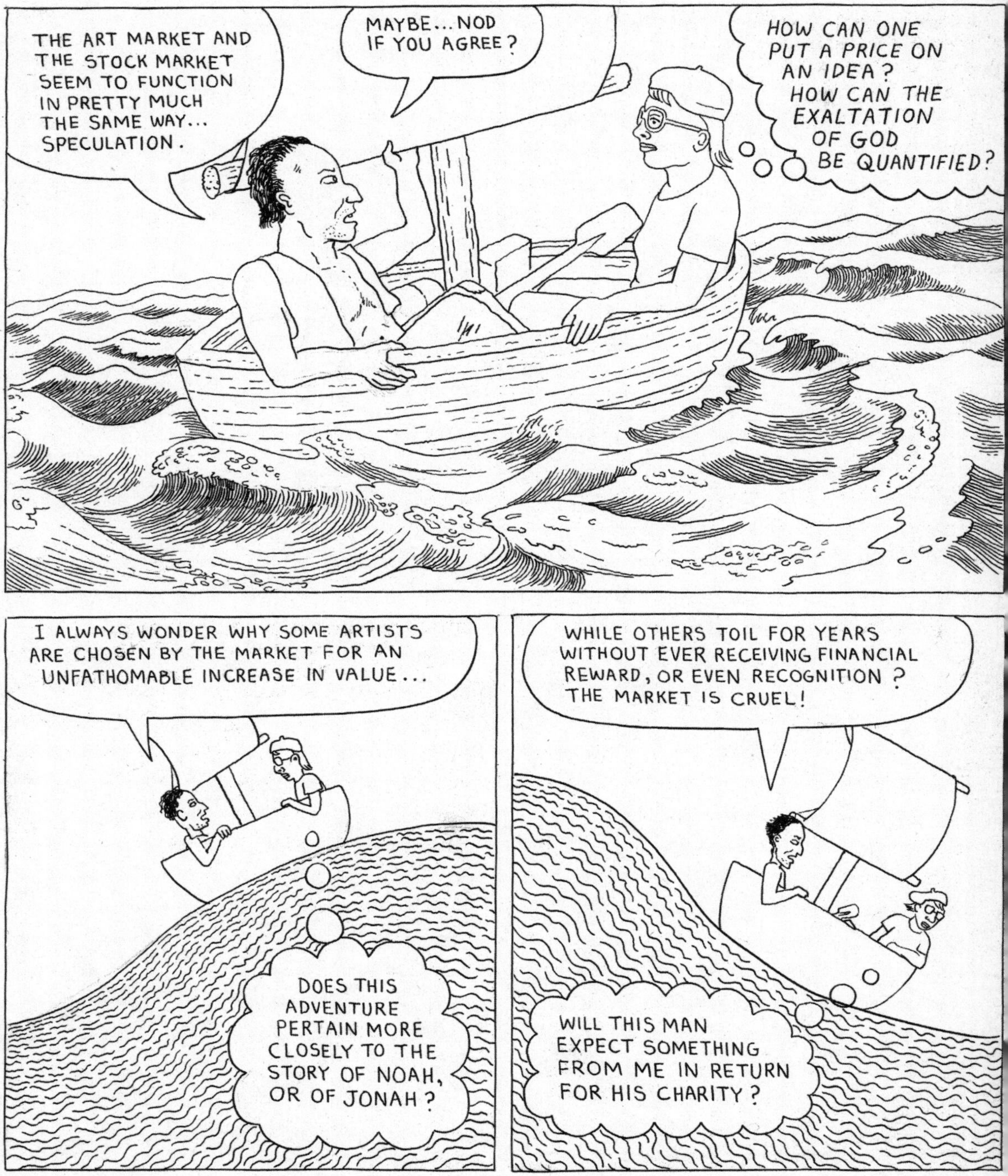
THE ART MARKET AND THE STOCK MARKET SEEM TO FUNCTION IN PRETTY MUCH THE SAME WAY... SPECULATION.
MAYBE...NOD IF YOU AGREE?
HOW CAN ONE PUT A PRICE ON AN IDEA? HOW CAN THE EXALTATION OF GOD BE QUANTIFIED?
I ALWAYS WONDER WHY SOME ARTISTS ARE CHOSEN BY THE MARKET FOR AN UNFATHOMABLE INCREASE IN VALUE...
DOES THIS ADVENTURE PERTAIN MORE CLOSELY TO THE STORY OF NOAH, OR OF JONAH?
WHILE OTHERS TOIL FOR YEARS WITHOUT EVER RECEIVING FINANCIAL REWARD, OR EVEN RECOGNITION? THE MARKET IS CRUEL!
WILL THIS MAN EXPECT SOMETHING FROM ME IN RETURN FOR HIS CHARITY?

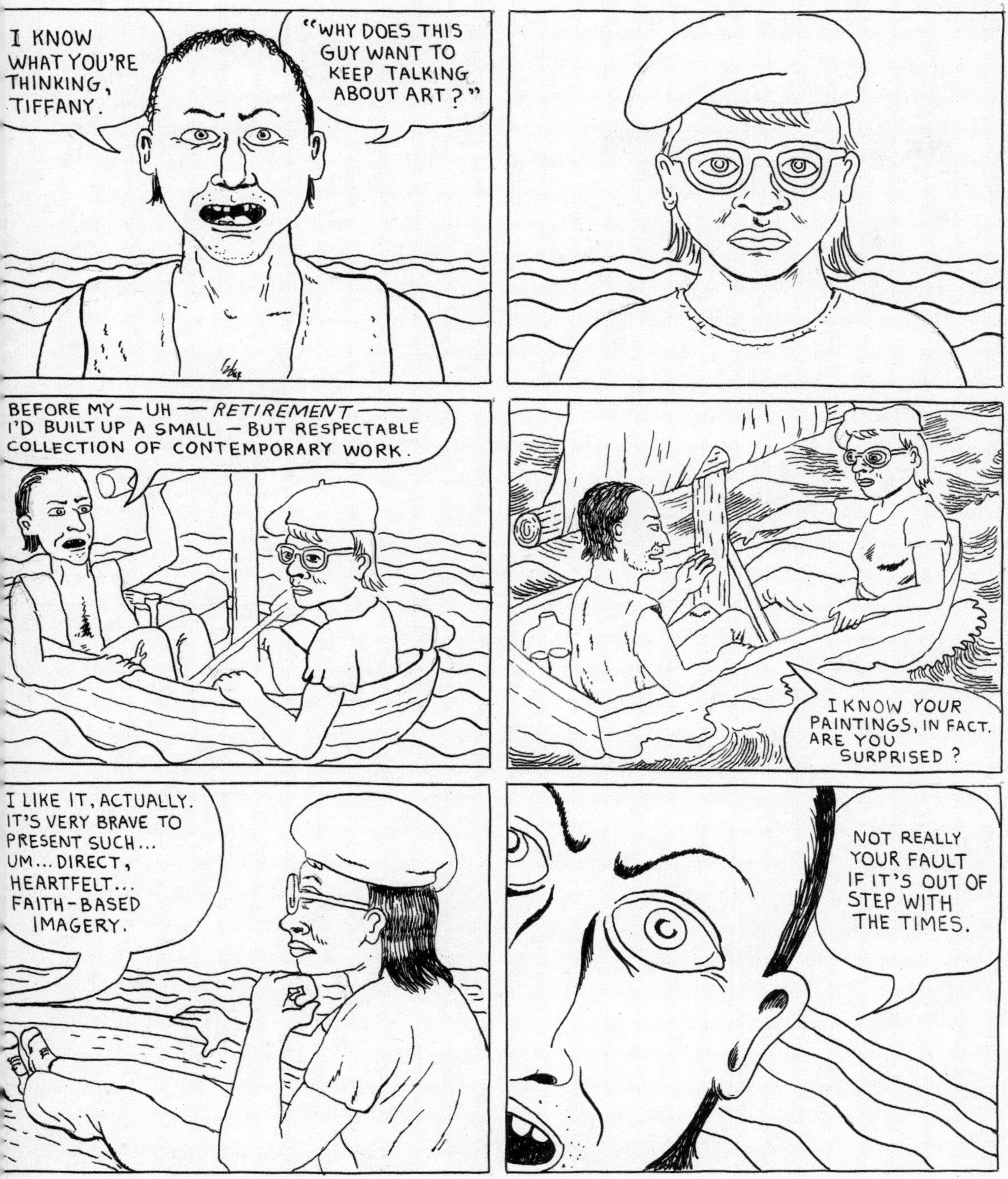
I KNOW WHAT YOU'RE THINKING, TIFFANY.
"WHY DOES THIS GUY WANT TO KEEP TALKING ABOUT ART?"
BEFORE MY — UH — RETIREMENT — I'D BUILT UP A SMALL — BUT RESPECTABLE COLLECTION OF CONTEMPORARY WORK.
I KNOW YOUR PAINTINGS, IN FACT. ARE YOU SURPRISED?
I LIKE IT, ACTUALLY. IT'S VERY BRAVE TO PRESENT SUCH... UM... DIRECT, HEARTFELT... FAITH-BASED IMAGERY.
NOT REALLY YOUR FAULT IF IT'S OUT OF STEP WITH THE TIMES.

I KNOW THAT YOU HAVE VERY LITTLE REGARD FOR MONEY OR INTEREST IN SELLING YOUR WORK. STILL, I WOULD *LOVE* TO ACQUIRE A PIECE FOR MY LITTLE COLLECTION!
NO PRESSURE.
BUT PLEASE LET ME KNOW WHAT YOU THINK ABOUT IT.
I HOPE YOU'LL SAY YES.
IT IS IN ITS WAY A VERY SIGNIFICANT LITTLE COLLECTION. WOULD YOU LIKE TO KNOW ITS PRIMARY DISTINGUISHING FEATURE?
ALL THE ARTISTS IN MY COLLECTION SHARE ONE TRAIT IN COMMON.
YOU SEE THEY ALL *DIED* IN THE SAME WAY.

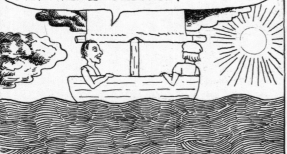

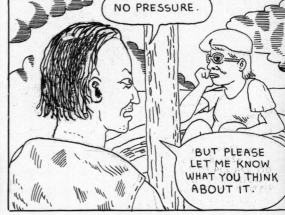

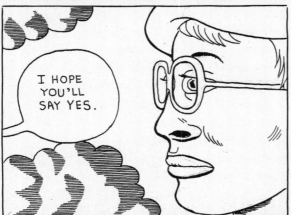

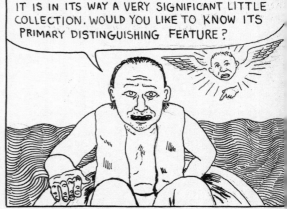

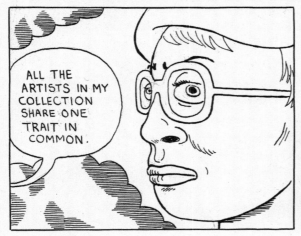

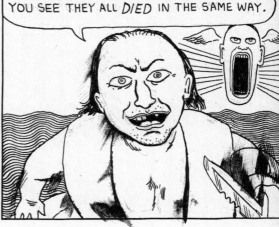

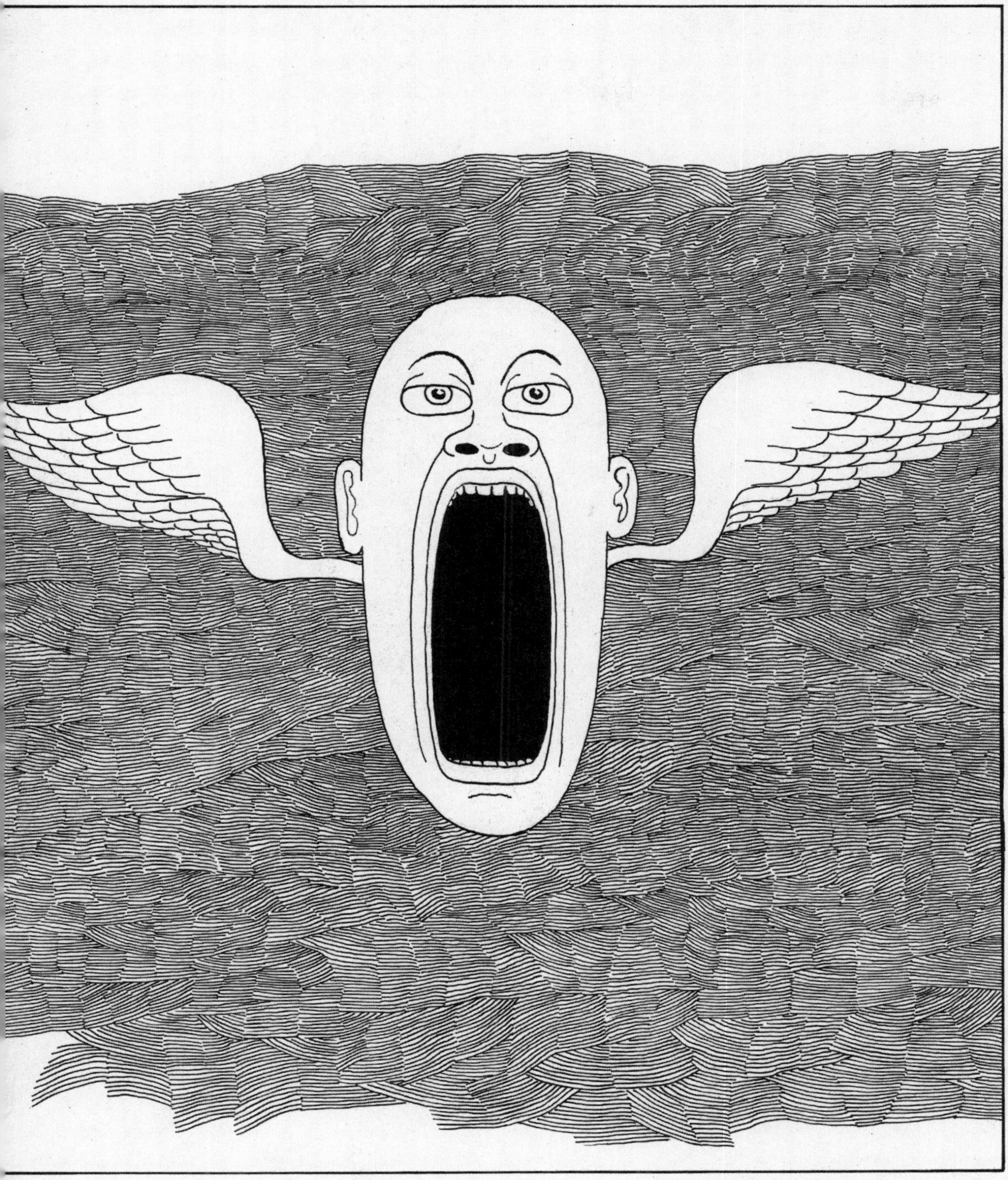

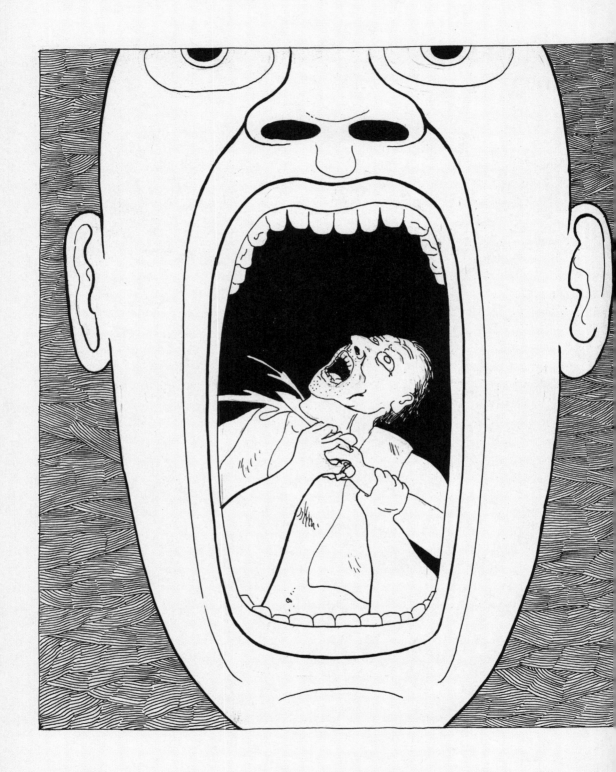

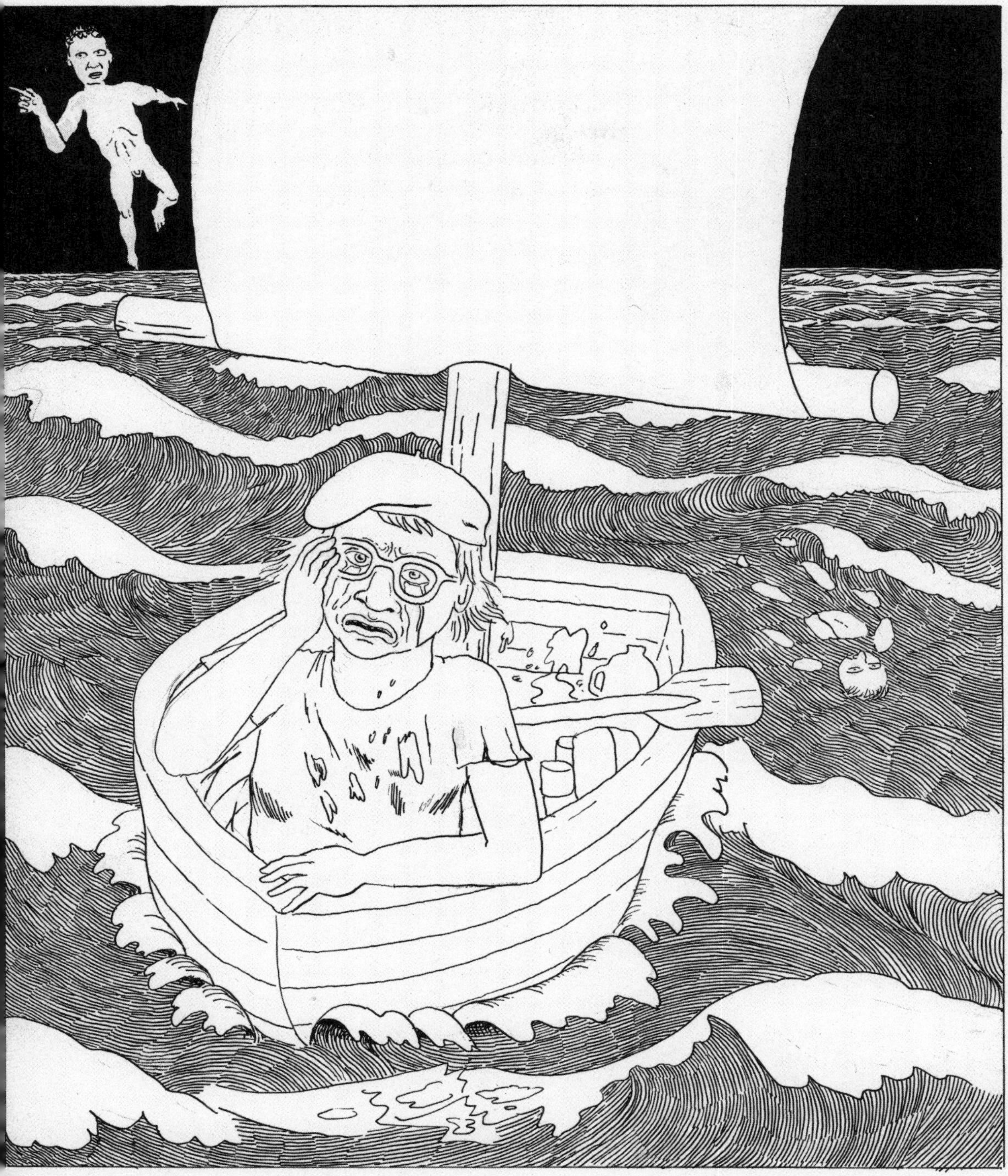

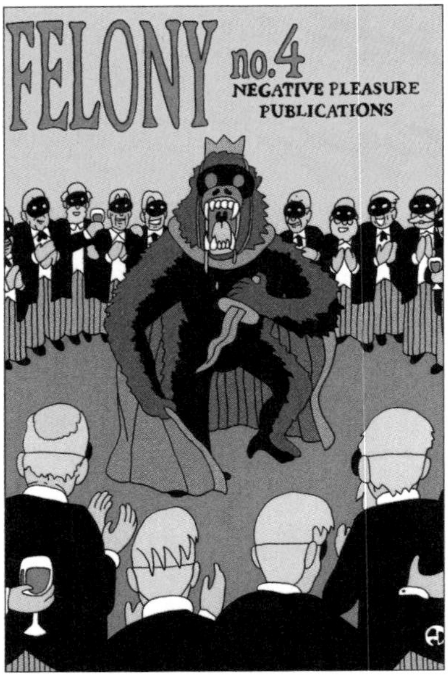
FELONY no.4
NEGATIVE PLEASURE PUBLICATIONS

The Last Felony Comics Story

PETE TOMS

originally published in

Felony #4

NEGATIVE PLEASURE PUBLICATIONS

6.5 x 10.25 inches • 24 pages

Biography

Pete Toms is a cartoonist and writer whose books include *Dad's Weekend* and *The Short Con*. As you read this, there is at least a 95 percent chance he is lying on a floor in Burbank, California.

petetoms.tumblr.com

Statement

For the past few years, the editor Harris Smith published an annual anthology called *Felony*, where cartoonists would draw a crime story. My strip is about a meme thief.

I used to have this recurring nightmare where I realize I'm filled with rats.

I have no organs, no guts, no soul. I'm a skin puppet being collectively controlled by rodents.

I would wake up horrified, not because of the image of rats crawling around inside my body, guiding my every movement, but because I found it comforting.

Now my recurring nightmare is that I post a description of that dream on Twitter and it only gets like 4 favs.

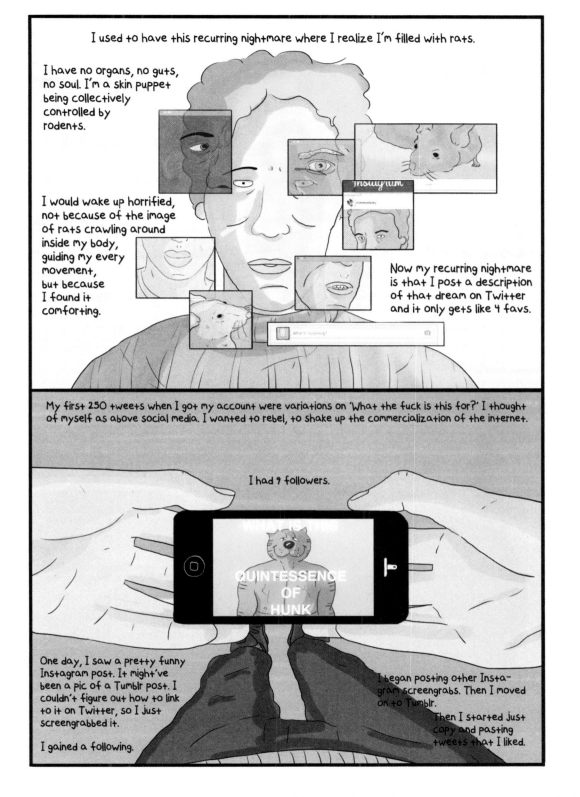

My first 250 tweets when I got my account were variations on 'What the fuck is this for?' I thought of myself as above social media. I wanted to rebel, to shake up the commercialization of the internet.

I had 9 followers.

WHAT IS THIS

QUINTESSENCE OF HUNK

One day, I saw a pretty funny Instagram post. It might've been a pic of a Tumblr post. I couldn't figure out how to link to it on Twitter, so I just screengrabbed it.

I gained a following.

I began posting other Instagram screengrabs. Then I moved on to Tumblr.

Then I started just copy and pasting tweets that I liked.

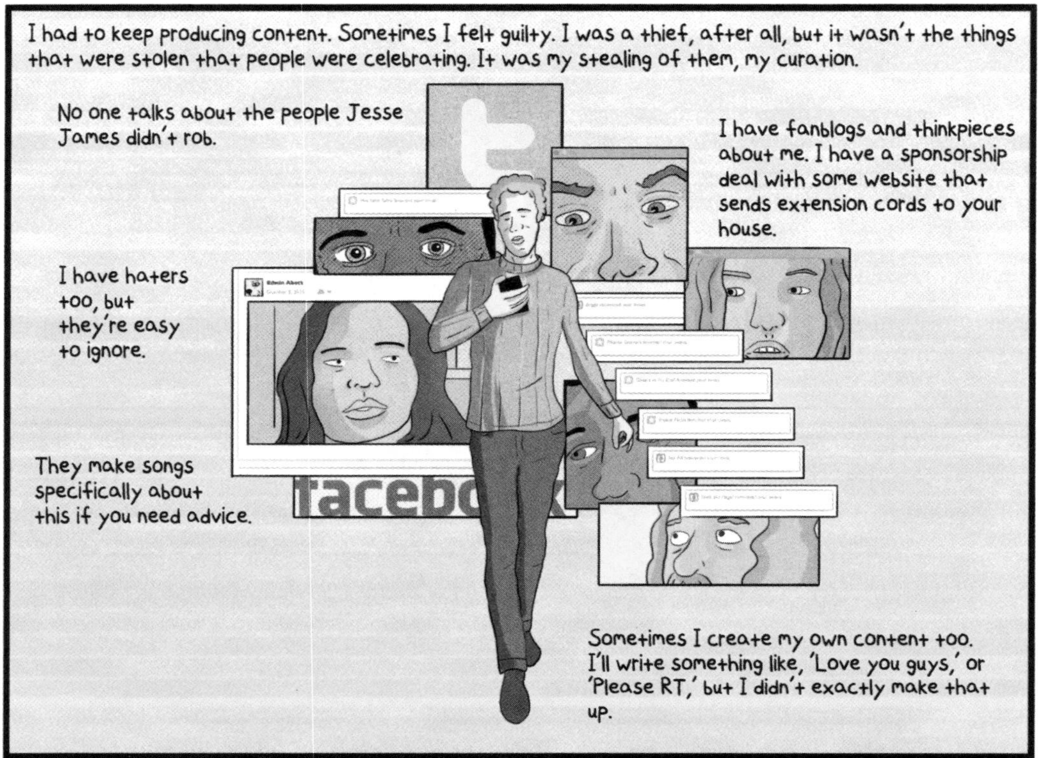
I had to keep producing content. Sometimes I felt guilty. I was a thief, after all, but it wasn't the things that were stolen that people were celebrating. It was my stealing of them, my curation.
No one talks about the people Jesse James didn't rob.
I have fanblogs and thinkpieces about me. I have a sponsorship deal with some website that sends extension cords to your house.
I have haters too, but they're easy to ignore.
They make songs specifically about this if you need advice.
Sometimes I create my own content too. I'll write something like, 'Love you guys,' or 'Please RT,' but I didn't exactly make that up.

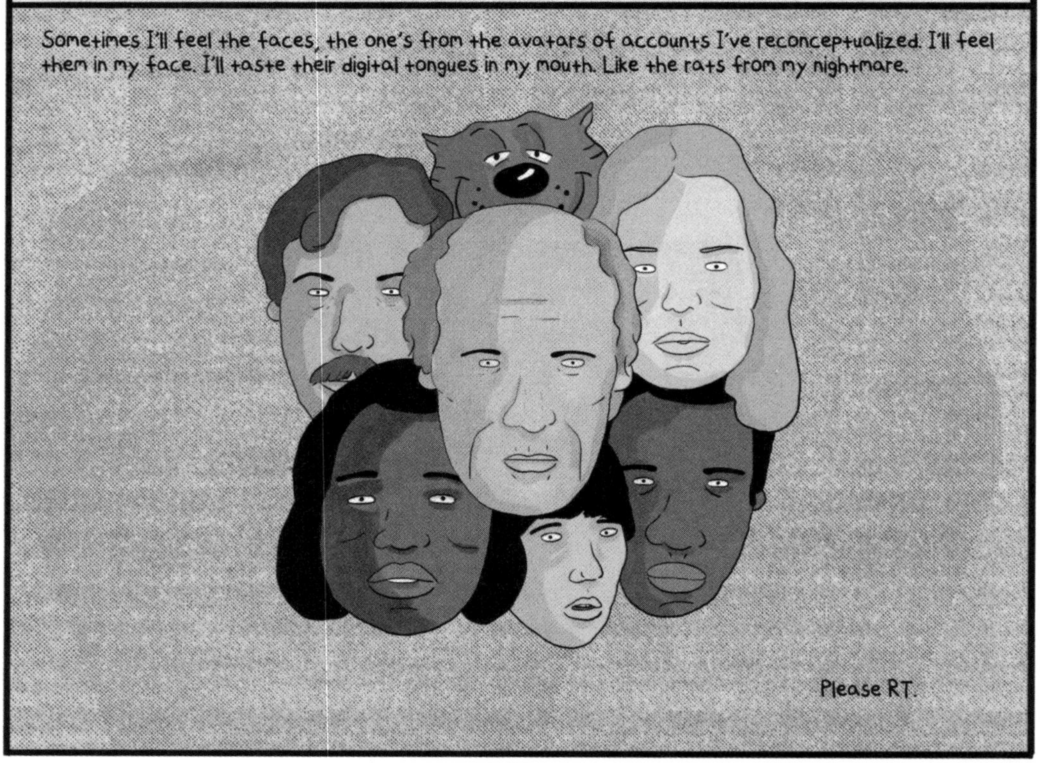
Sometimes I'll feel the faces, the one's from the avatars of accounts I've reconceptualized. I'll feel them in my face. I'll taste their digital tongues in my mouth. Like the rats from my nightmare.
Please RT.

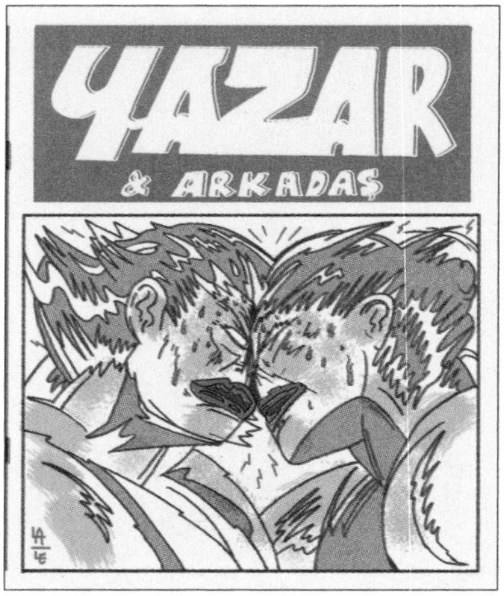
YAZAR
& ARKADAŞ

Yazar and Arkadaş (Excerpt)

LALE WESTVIND

originally published in

Yazar and Arkadaş
FUME ROOM PRESS
6.9 x 8.5 inches • 28 pages

Biography

Lale Westvind is a cartoonist, painter, and animator. Westvind has been self-publishing comics in various genres, formats, and styles since 2008. Her work has appeared in anthologies internationally, including *Kramers Ergot*, *Best American Comics*, *Strapazin* (CH), and *Lagon Revue* (FR). Her animations have screened at festivals all over the world and her animation for Lightning Bolt's "Metal East" won Best Music Video at Leeds International Film Festival in 2015. Westvind teaches part-time in the Illustration department at Parsons School of Design in New York City.
instagram.com/lalewestvind

Statement

Yazar and Arkadaş was conceptualized as the introduction to a cast of female mythic figures, the Daughters of Pain, through their various origin stories. A continuation of this narrative may be forthcoming. This book is a part of an experimental series of publications made for fast and affordable Risograph production in a format fitting legal-sized paper. The narrative was developed organically through reorganization of collected drawings and imagery. *Yazar and Arkadaş* was published cooperatively with Fume Room Press at Space 1026 in Philadelphia with the help of Paula S.B.C. and Will Laren.

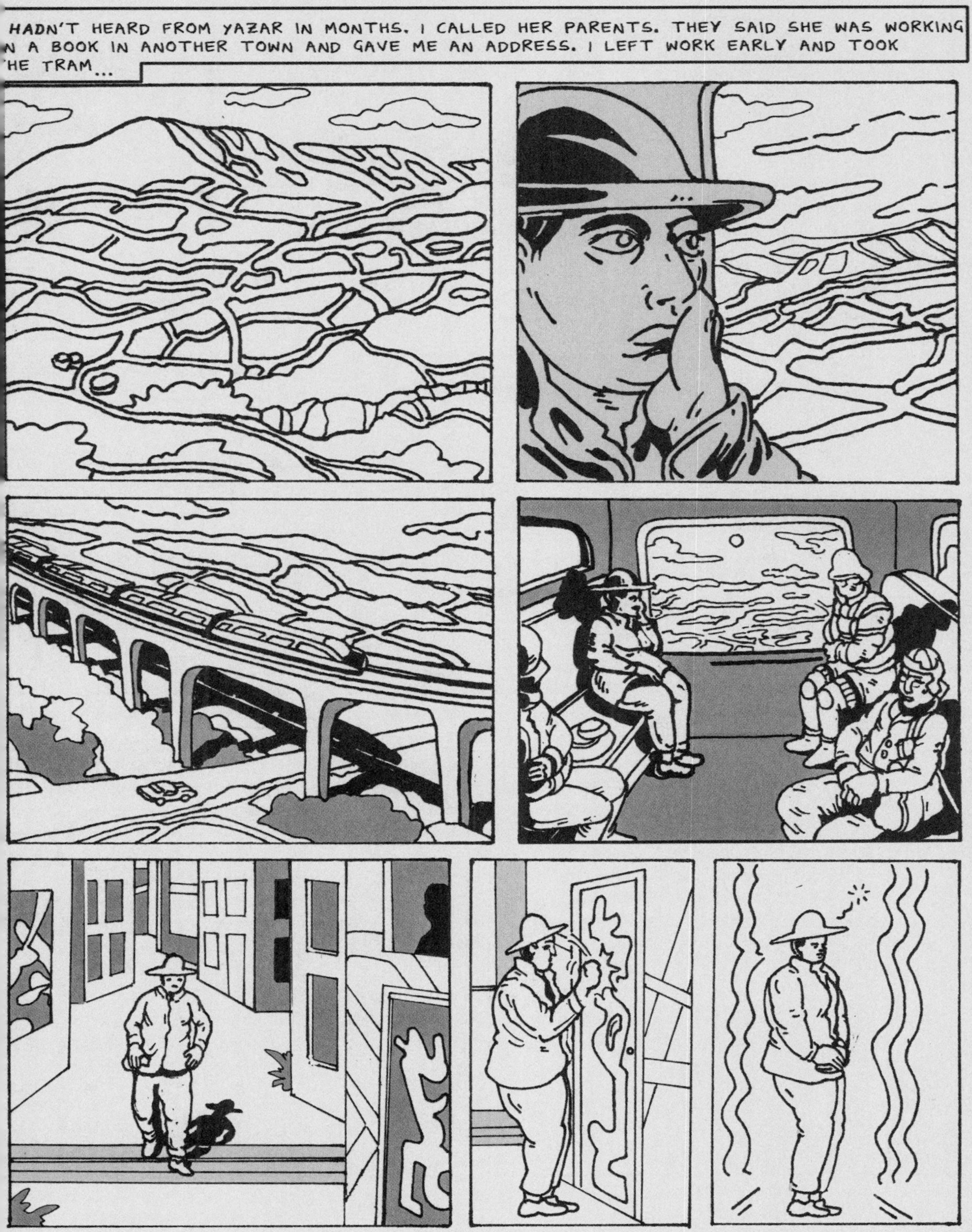
HADN'T HEARD FROM YAZAR IN MONTHS. I CALLED HER PARENTS. THEY SAID SHE WAS WORKING
N A BOOK IN ANOTHER TOWN AND GAVE ME AN ADDRESS. I LEFT WORK EARLY AND TOOK
HE TRAM...

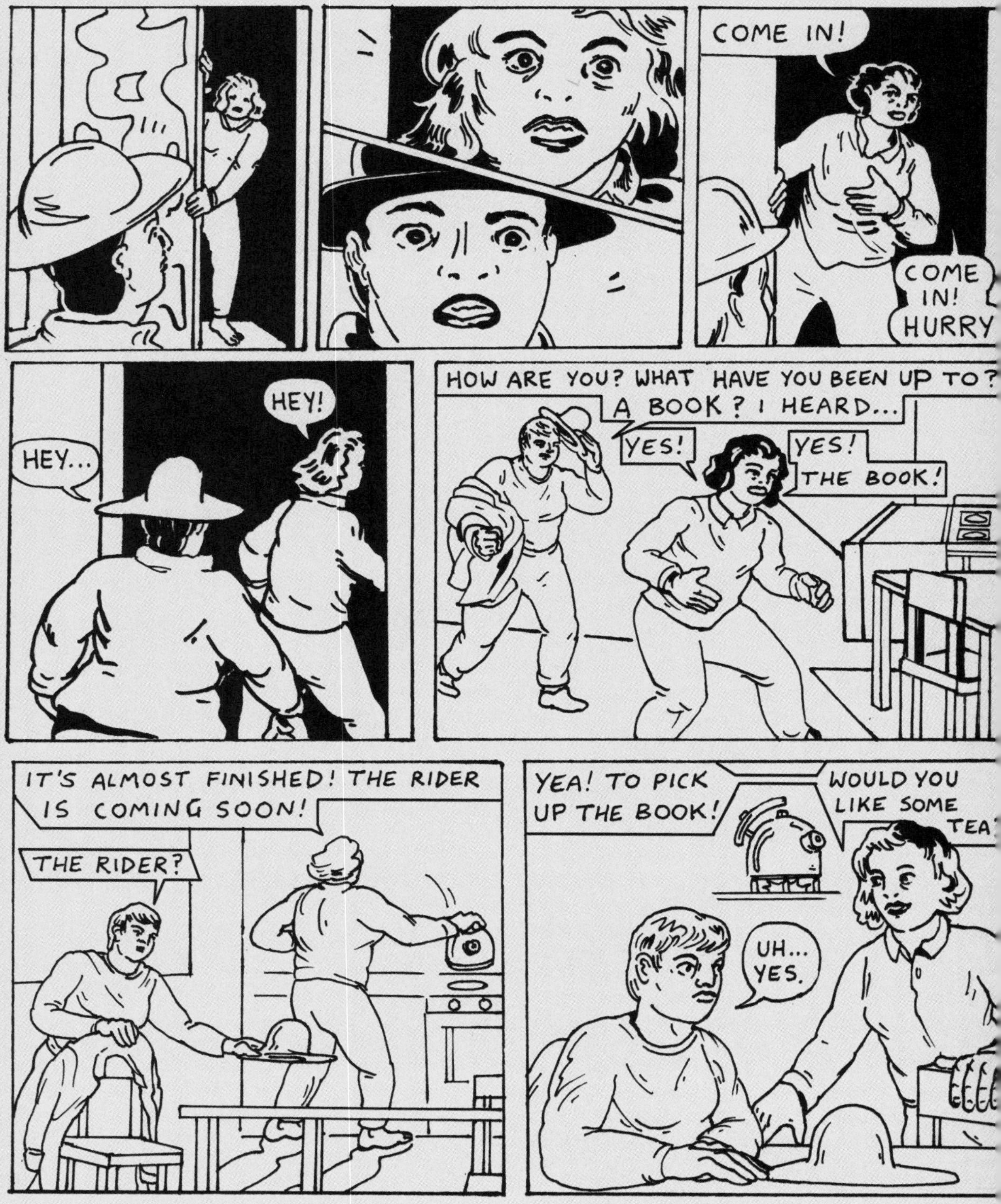
COME IN!
COME IN! HURRY
HEY!
HEY...
HOW ARE YOU? WHAT HAVE YOU BEEN UP TO?
A BOOK? I HEARD...
YES!
YES! THE BOOK!
IT'S ALMOST FINISHED! THE RIDER IS COMING SOON!
THE RIDER?
YEA! TO PICK UP THE BOOK!
WOULD YOU LIKE SOME TEA
UH... YES.

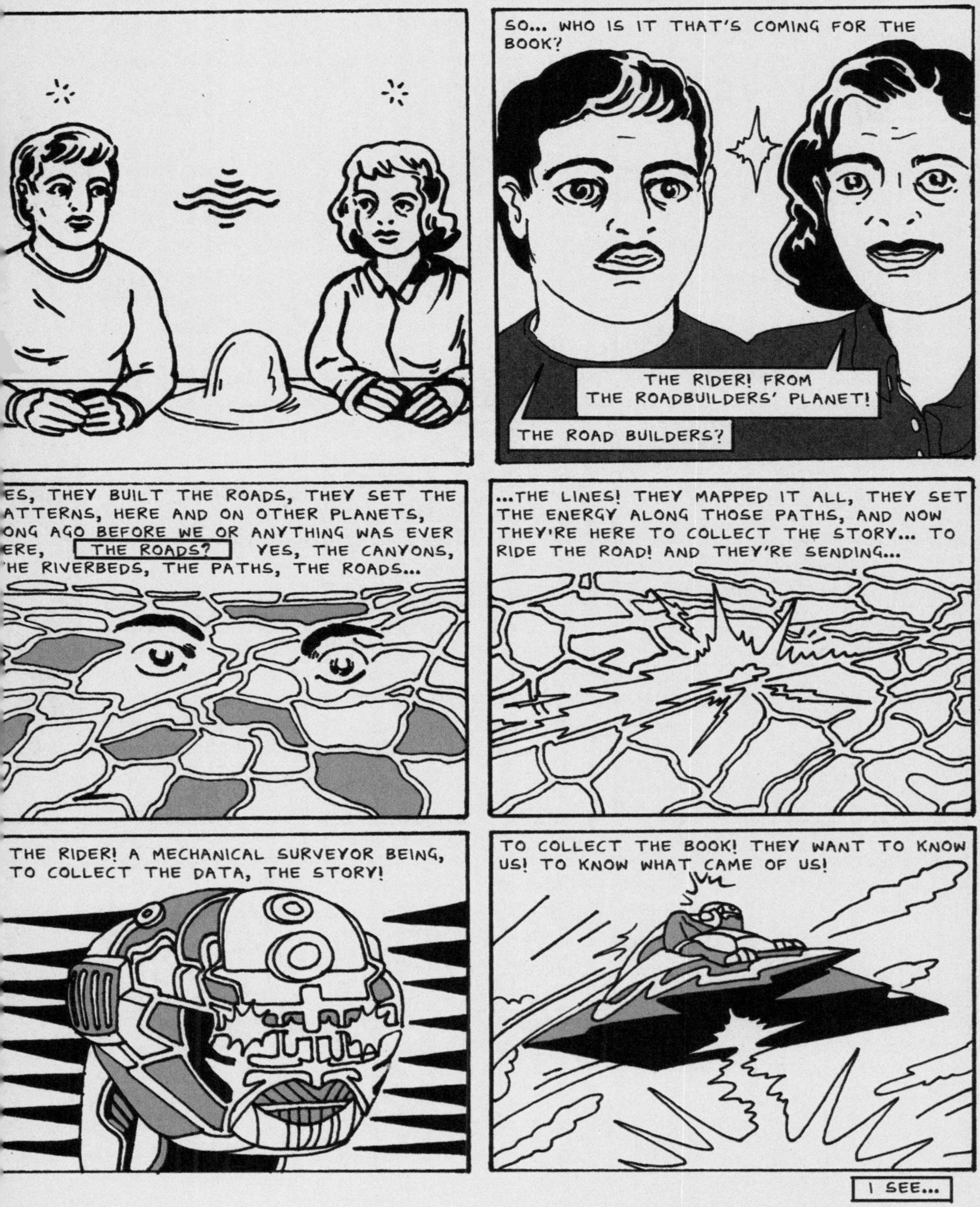
SO... WHO IS IT THAT'S COMING FOR THE BOOK?
THE RIDER! FROM THE ROADBUILDERS' PLANET!
THE ROAD BUILDERS?
ES, THEY BUILT THE ROADS, THEY SET THE ATTERNS, HERE AND ON OTHER PLANETS, ONG AGO BEFORE WE OR ANYTHING WAS EVER ERE,
THE ROADS?
YES, THE CANYONS, HE RIVERBEDS, THE PATHS, THE ROADS...
...THE LINES! THEY MAPPED IT ALL, THEY SET THE ENERGY ALONG THOSE PATHS, AND NOW THEY'RE HERE TO COLLECT THE STORY... TO RIDE THE ROAD! AND THEY'RE SENDING...
THE RIDER! A MECHANICAL SURVEYOR BEING, TO COLLECT THE DATA, THE STORY!
TO COLLECT THE BOOK! THEY WANT TO KNOW US! TO KNOW WHAT CAME OF US!
I SEE...

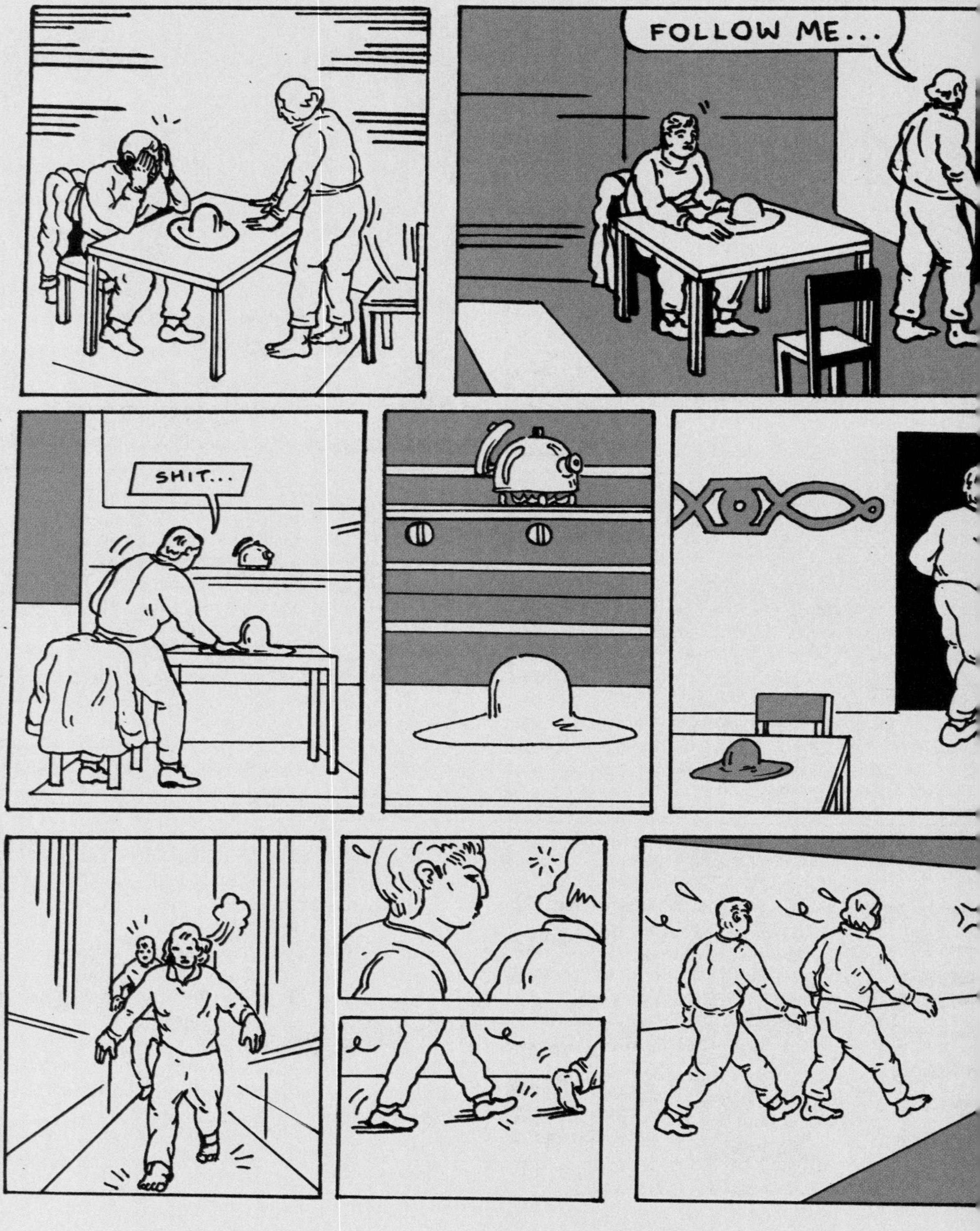
FOLLOW ME...
SHIT...

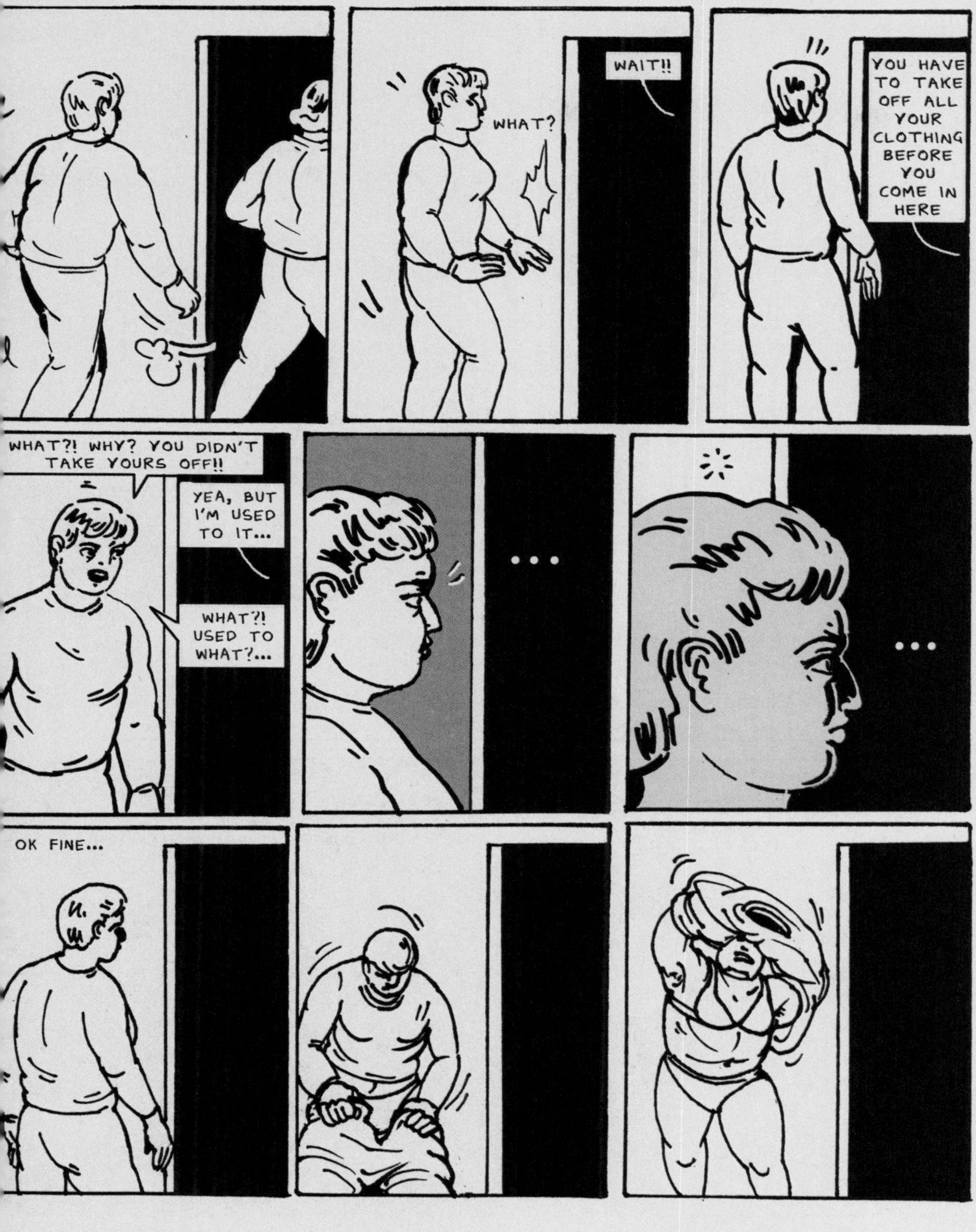
WAIT!!
WHAT?
YOU HAVE TO TAKE OFF ALL YOUR CLOTHING BEFORE YOU COME IN HERE
WHAT?! WHY? YOU DIDN'T TAKE YOURS OFF!!
YEA, BUT I'M USED TO IT...
WHAT?! USED TO WHAT?...
...
...
OK FINE...

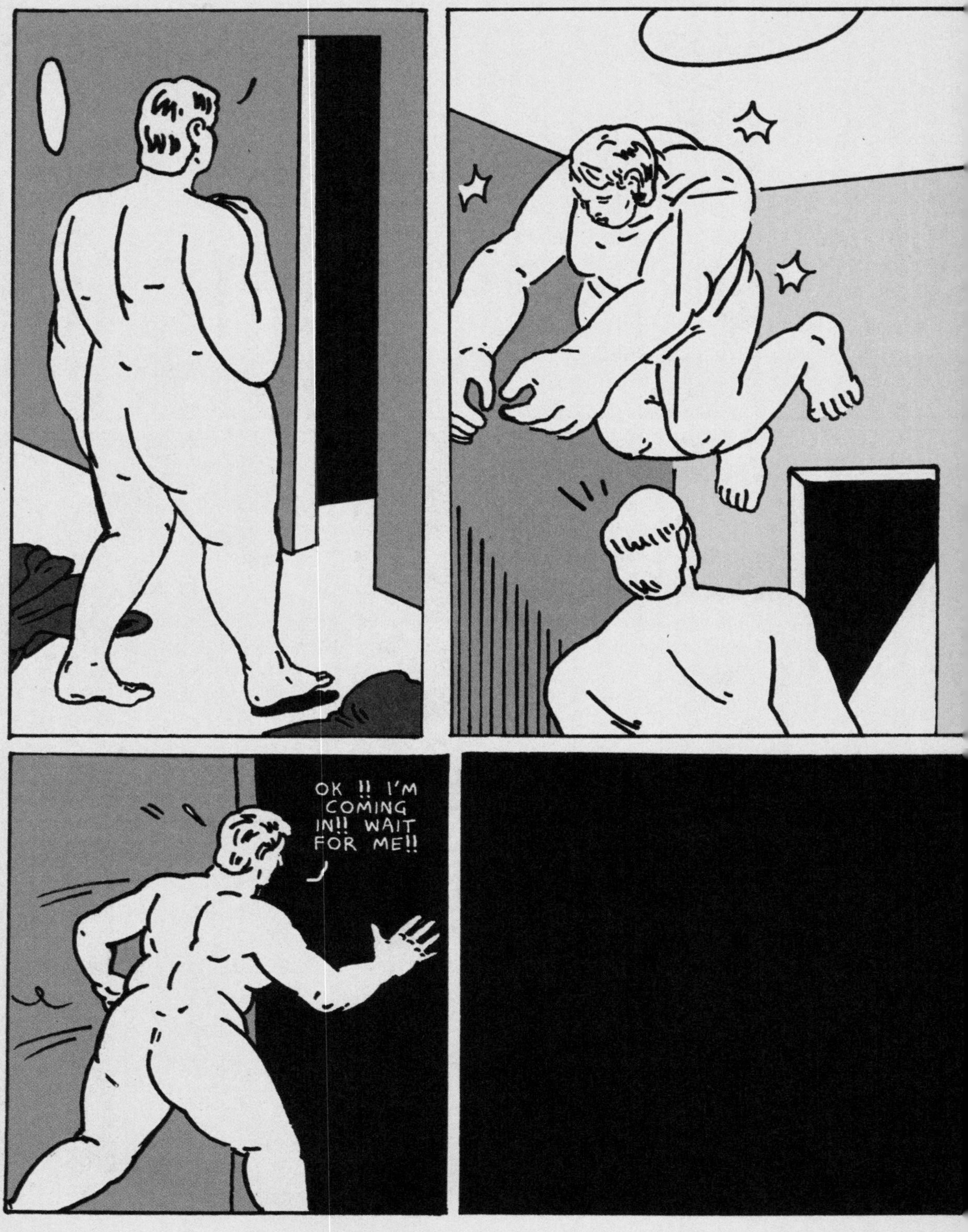
OK !! I'M COMING IN!! WAIT FOR ME!!

TRY TO KEEP UP WITH THE SOUND OF HER FOOTSTEPS,

I TRY NOT TO TRIP IN THE ABSOLUTE DARKNESS

I NOTICE THE AIR IS DRYER AND COOLER...

FRAGRANT...SPICED

AND SWEET

THE FLOOR FEELS SOFTER...

ALMOST LIKE EARTH...

LIKE SAND...

I HEAR INSECTS, AND ANOTHER SOUND I CAN'T PLACE...

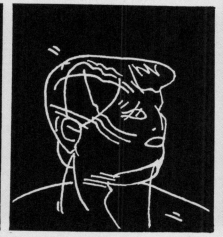

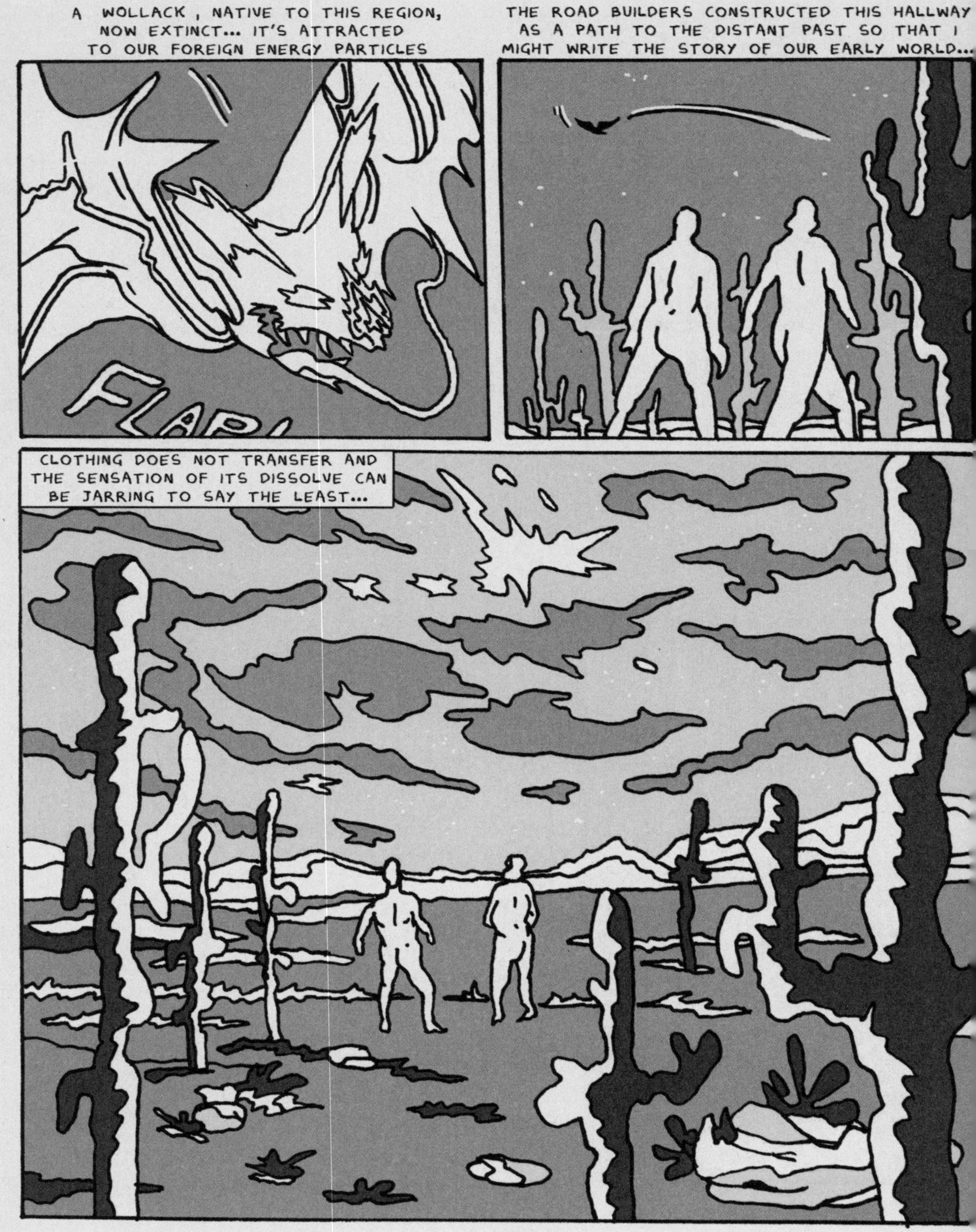
A WOLLACK, NATIVE TO THIS REGION, NOW EXTINCT... IT'S ATTRACTED TO OUR FOREIGN ENERGY PARTICLES
FLAP!
THE ROAD BUILDERS CONSTRUCTED THIS HALLWAY AS A PATH TO THE DISTANT PAST SO THAT I MIGHT WRITE THE STORY OF OUR EARLY WORLD...
CLOTHING DOES NOT TRANSFER AND THE SENSATION OF ITS DISSOLVE CAN BE JARRING TO SAY THE LEAST...

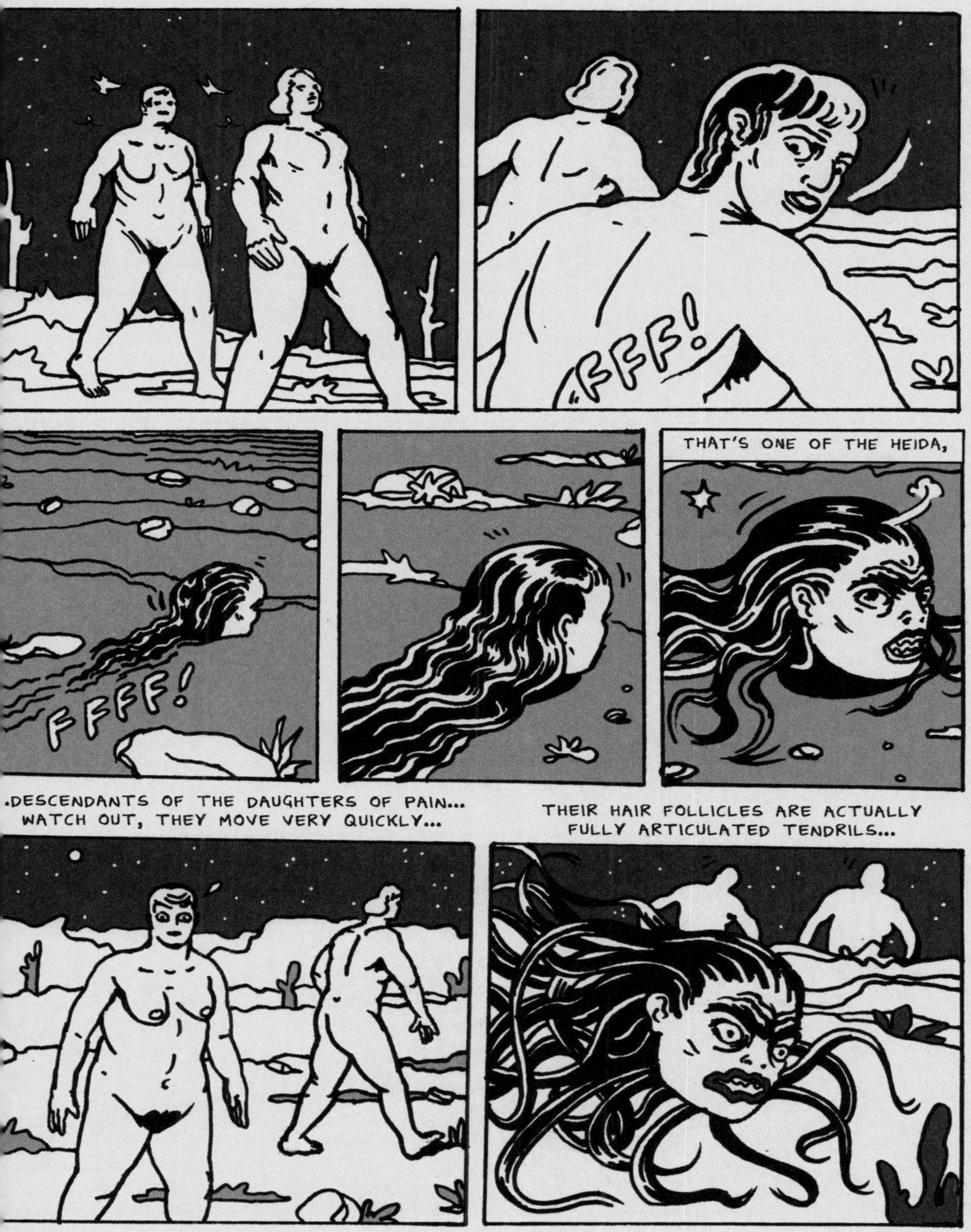
FFF!
FFFF!
THAT'S ONE OF THE HEIDA,
.DESCENDANTS OF THE DAUGHTERS OF PAIN...
WATCH OUT, THEY MOVE VERY QUICKLY...
THEIR HAIR FOLLICLES ARE ACTUALLY FULLY ARTICULATED TENDRILS...

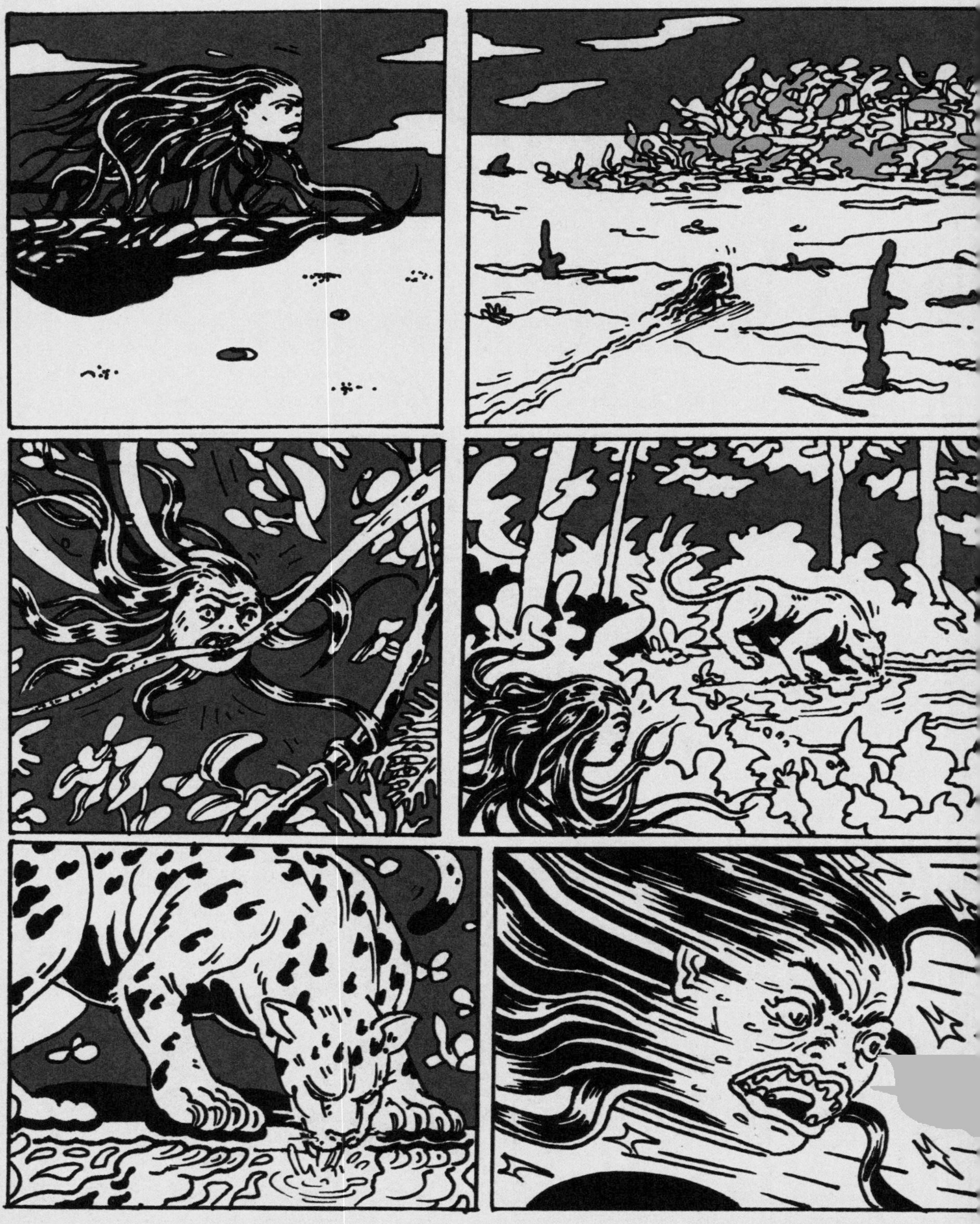

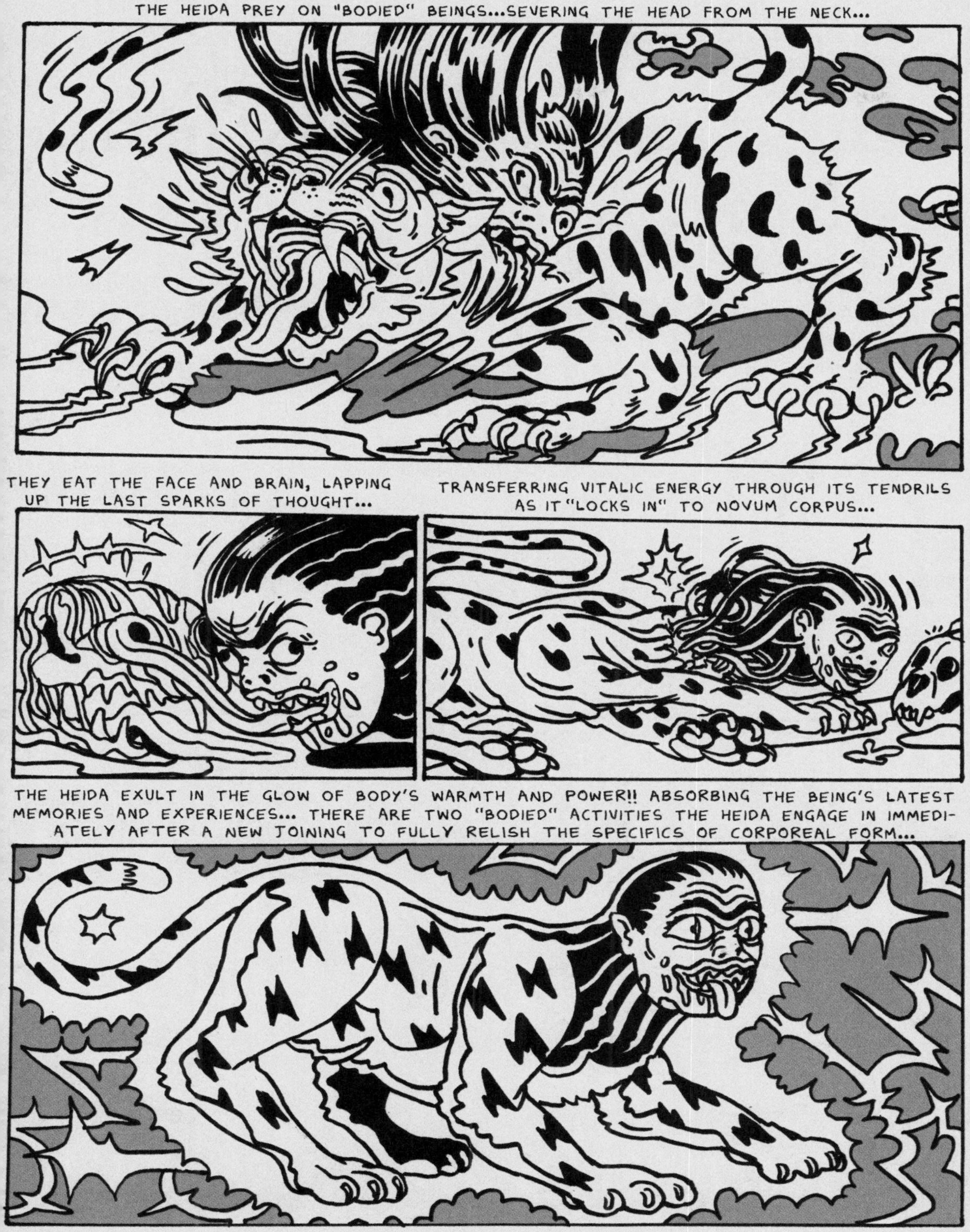
THE HEIDA PREY ON "BODIED" BEINGS...SEVERING THE HEAD FROM THE NECK...
THEY EAT THE FACE AND BRAIN, LAPPING UP THE LAST SPARKS OF THOUGHT...
TRANSFERRING VITALIC ENERGY THROUGH ITS TENDRILS AS IT "LOCKS IN" TO NOVUM CORPUS...
THE HEIDA EXULT IN THE GLOW OF BODY'S WARMTH AND POWER!! ABSORBING THE BEING'S LATEST MEMORIES AND EXPERIENCES... THERE ARE TWO "BODIED" ACTIVITIES THE HEIDA ENGAGE IN IMMEDIATELY AFTER A NEW JOINING TO FULLY RELISH THE SPECIFICS OF CORPOREAL FORM...

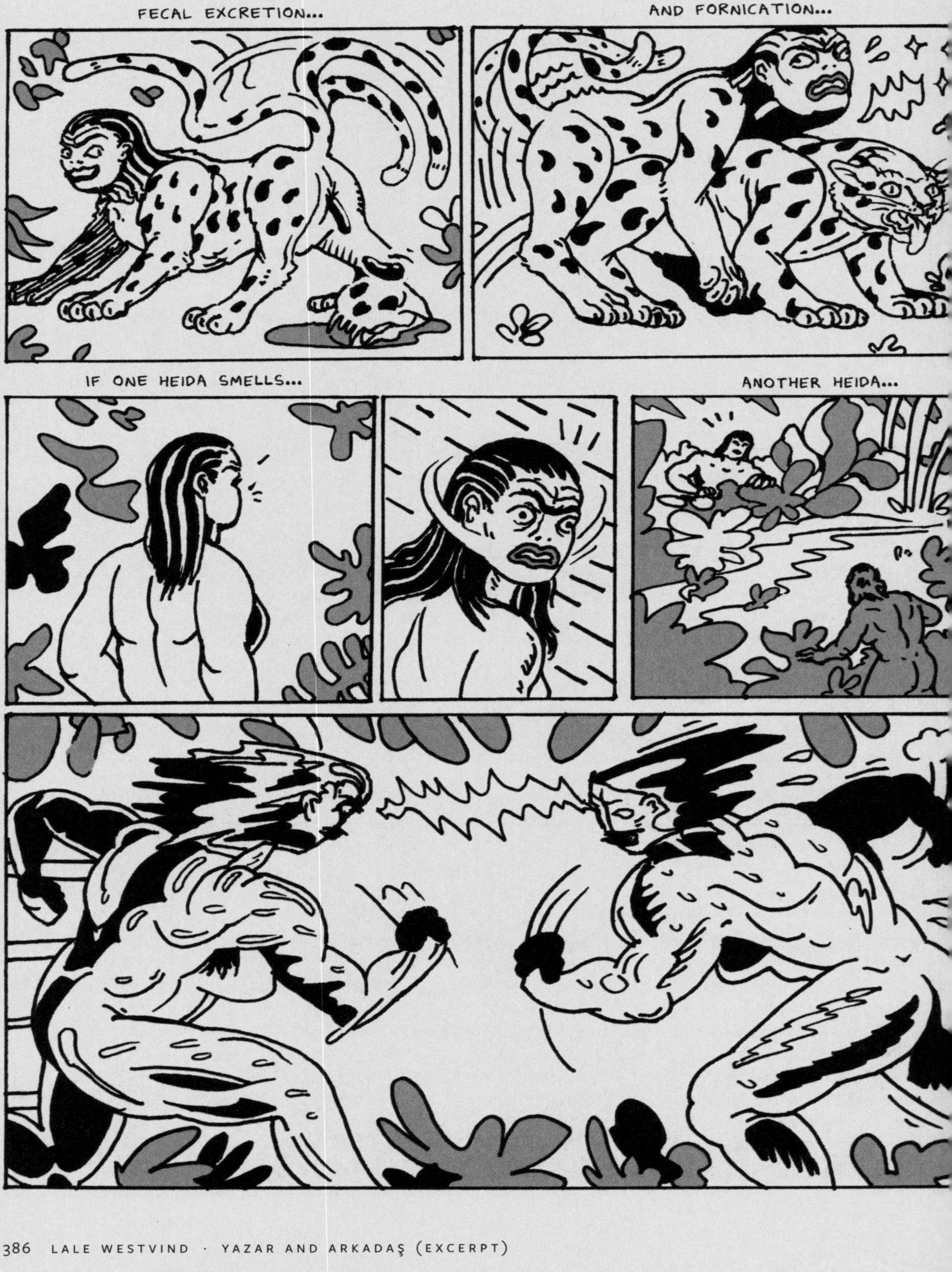
FECAL EXCRETION...
AND FORNICATION...
IF ONE HEIDA SMELLS...
ANOTHER HEIDA...

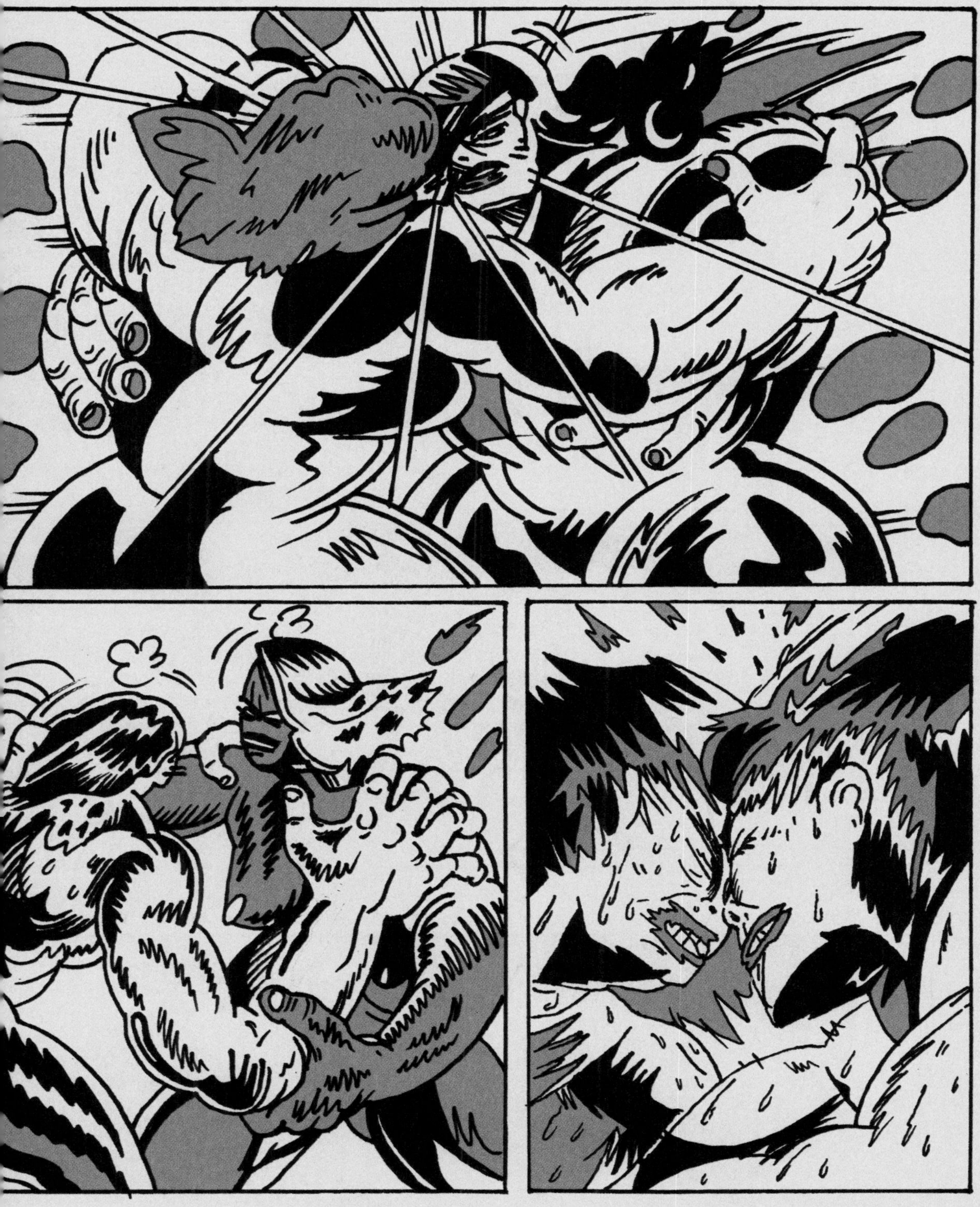

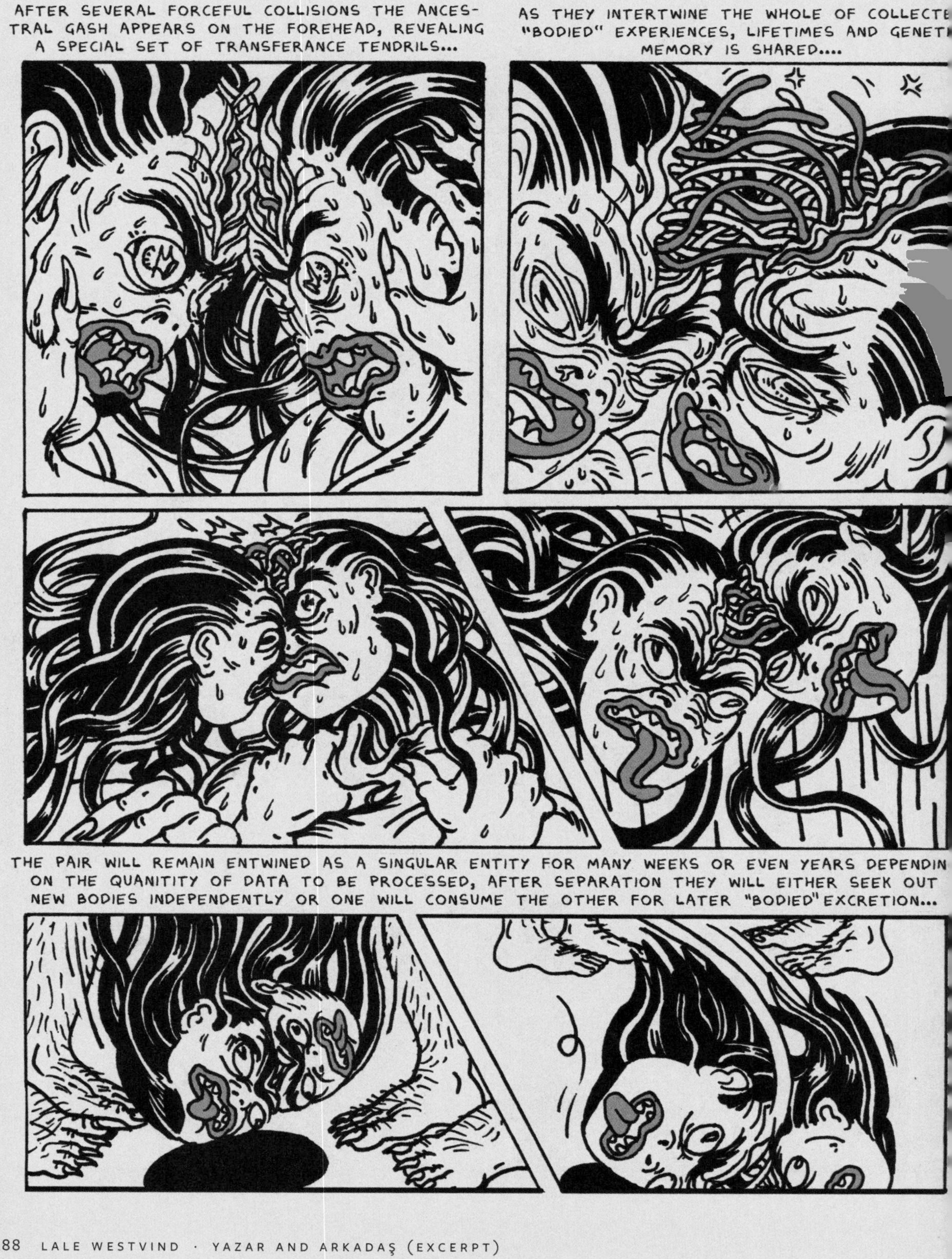

AFTER SEVERAL FORCEFUL COLLISIONS THE ANCES-TRAL GASH APPEARS ON THE FOREHEAD, REVEALING A SPECIAL SET OF TRANSFERANCE TENDRILS...
AS THEY INTERTWINE THE WHOLE OF COLLECTE "BODIED" EXPERIENCES, LIFETIMES AND GENET MEMORY IS SHARED....
THE PAIR WILL REMAIN ENTWINED AS A SINGULAR ENTITY FOR MANY WEEKS OR EVEN YEARS DEPENDIN ON THE QUANITITY OF DATA TO BE PROCESSED, AFTER SEPARATION THEY WILL EITHER SEEK OUT NEW BODIES INDEPENDENTLY OR ONE WILL CONSUME THE OTHER FOR LATER "BODIED" EXCRETION...

Notable Comics

from September 1, 2016, to August 31, 2017

Selected by Bill Kartalopoulos

CHRISTOPHER ADAMS
Tack Piano Heaven One.

LALA ALBERT
Wet Earth.

RICHARD ALEXANDER
Richy Vegas Comics #12 & 13.

SAMI ALWANI
The Idiot.

CARA BEAN
The Art Class Is a Sanctuary City.
pen.org/art-class-sanctuary-city/

E. A. BETHEA
Faded Frankenstein.

BRIAN BLOMERTH
Alphabet Junction.
vice.com

KEVIN BUDNIK
Epilogue.

A. BURKHOLDER
Mleet da Blee.
š! #26

ADAM BUTTRICK
Angel of a Rope.

DAVID COLLIER
Morton.

CREOMAN
Agarrarla.

ANYA DAVIDSON
Lovers in the Garden.

ELEANOR DAVIS
You & A Bike & A Road.

MICHAEL DEFORGE
Leaving Richard's Valley.
instagram.com/richardsvalley/

WILLIAM DEREUME
Egg Shell #1.

JESSICA EARHART
Khloris #2.

AUSTIN ENGLISH
"Half-Hearted Slogan Dance."
BOMB Magazine #139.

THEO ELLSWORTH
An Exorcism.

INÉS ESTRADA
Alienation #1–5.

EDIE FAKE
Gaylord Phoenix, Issue 7.

JESSE FILLINGHAM
Crawl.

SOPHIA FOSTER-DIMINO
Sex Fantasy #8.

IONA FOX
Almanac 2017.

NOEL FREIBERT
Weird #6.

WINNIE T. FRICK
The Pressed Release.
monthlysmokeandmirrors.com/1419-2/

MARNIE GALLOWAY
Particle/Wave.

GG
Valley.

NICOLE GEORGES
Fetch.

BILL GRIFFITH
Zippy the Pinhead.

SAMMY HARKHAM
Crickets #6.

ROYA HAROUN AND SARAH LAMMER
Work.

GEOFFREY HAYES
Benny and Penny in How to Say Goodbye.

GILBERT HERNANDEZ
Garden of the Flesh.

KEVIN HUIZENGA
Ganges #6.

ABBY JAME
The Prophecy of the Flesh Virgin.

BEN JONES
Comics.

DYLAN JONES
Behind a Hole. š! #26.

JULIACKS
Architecture of an Atom.

SEAN KAREMAKER
Mer: Part I: Feast of Fields.

BEN KATCHOR
Metropolis Magazine comics.

AMY KUTTAB
Urstory.

PATRICK KYLE
New Comics #9: *Snooz Magazine.*

ANDREA LUKIC
Journal of Smack.

MELISSA MENDES
The Weight, Parts 5–7.
mmmendes.com.

LANE MILBURN
Corridors.

BJORN MINER
Daisies/Swampson #4.

BRIE MORENO
The Mechanical Head.
š! #26.

ROMAN MURADOV
Jacob Bladders and the State of the Art.

L. NICHOLS
Flocks, Chapter Five.

ANDERS NILSEN
Tongues #1.

NICK NORMAN
Tears of the Toad.

CAROLYN NOWAK
Diana's Electric Tongue.

BEN PASSMORE
Your Black Friend.

COCO PICARD
The Chronicles of Fortune.

JOHN PORCELLINO
King-Cat #77.

AIRE PORTE
Xeno Vehicles // USER.

SHARON ROSENZWEIG
Judgment Call.
Annals of Internal Medicine, annals.org.

JEN SANDWICH
Total Trash #9 & 10.

WALTER SCOTT
Wendy's Revenge.

DASH SHAW
A Cosplayers Christmas.

SETH
Palookaville #23.

KARINA SHOR
XXX ED.

CONOR STECHSCHULTE
The Fence.

LESLIE STEIN
Vice.com comics.

KARL STEVENS
Penny.
The Village Voice.

IAN SUNDAHL
Social Discipline #9.

JILLIAN TAMAKI
Boundless.

WALKER TATE
Procedural.

MAGGIE UMBER
Sound of Snow Falling.

HENRIETTE VALIUM
The Palace of Champions.

CHRIS WARE
"Business or Pleasure."
The New Yorker, June 5 & 12, 2017.

LAUREN WEINSTEIN
Normel Person. *The Village Voice.*

ERIC KOSTIUK WILLIAMS
Condo Heartbreak Disco.

GEORGE WYLESOL
Porn.

SOPHIE YANOW
What Is a Glacier?

CREDITS

"Ghost Cats" by Gabrielle Bell. First published in *Everything Is Flammable.* Copyright © 2017 by Gabrielle Bell. Reprinted by permission of Gabrielle Bell.

Selections from *How to Be Alive* by Tara Booth. First published in *How to Be Alive.* Copyright © 2017 by Tara Booth. Reprinted by permission of Tara Booth.

"Echoes Into Eternity" by D. J. Bryant. First published in *Unreal City,* Fantagraphics Books. Copyright © 2017 by D. J. Bryant. Reprinted by permission of Fantagraphics Books.

"The Warlok Story" by Max Clotfelter. First published in self-published zine titled *The Warlok Story.* Copyright © 2017 by Max Clotfelter. Reprinted by permission of Max Clotfelter.

"The Shaolin Cowboy: Who'll Stop the Reign?" by Geof Darrow. First published in *The Shaolin Cowboy: Who'll Stop the Reign?* Copyright © 2017 by Geof Darrow. Reprinted by permission of Geof Darrow.

"Hostage" by Guy Delisle. First published in *Hostage.* Copyright © 2017 by Guy Delisle. Images courtesy Drawn & Quarterly.

"Brausebad" by Abraham Díaz Aguiñaga. First published in *Tonto* by Ediciones Valientes. Copyright © 2017 by Abraham Díaz Aguiñaga. Reprinted by permission of Abraham Díaz Aguiñaga.

"Margot" by Margot Ferrick. First published in *Yours,* 2dcloud. Copyright © 2017 by Margot Ferrick. Reprinted by permission of Margot Ferrick.

Excerpt from *My Favorite Thing Is Monsters Book 1* by Emil Ferris. First published in *My Favorite Thing Is Monsters Book 1,* Fantagraphics Books. Copyright © 2017 by Emil Ferris. Reprinted by permission of the author and Fantagraphics Books.

"A Taste of Purgatory" by Casanova Frankenstein. First published in *Purgatory.* Copyright © 2017 by Casanova Frankenstein. Reprinted by permission of Casanova Frankenstein.

"Frail Nature" by Julia Gfrörer. First published in *Black Eye #3*, Rotland Press, 2017. Copyright © 2017 by Julia Gfrörer. Reprinted by permission of Julia Gfrörer.

Selections from "Susan Something" by Julian Glander. First published in Vice.com. Copyright © 2017 by Julian Glander. Reprinted by permission of Julian Glander.

"Sam's Story" by Sarah Glidden. First published in *Rolling Blackouts: Dispatches from Turkey, Syria, and Iraq.* Copyright © 2017 by Sarah Glidden. Images courtesy Drawn & Quarterly.

"Angloid, Part 2" by Alex Graham. First published in *Cosmic BE-ING #4.* Copyright © 2017 by Alex Graham. Reprinted by permission of Alex Graham.

"Megg, Mogg & Owl: 'A Gift for a Baby'" by Simon Hanselmann. First published in *One More Year.* Copyright © 2017 by Simon Hanselmann. Reprinted by permission of Simon Hanselmann.

"Forest Spirits" by Jaime Hernandez. First published in *Love and Rockets* vol. 4, no. 2. Copyright © 2017 by Jaime Hernandez. Reprinted by permission of Jaime Hernandez.

"The Wide Berth/Benign Neglect" by Kevin Hooyman. First published in *Conditions on the Ground* #18 & #14. Copyright © 2017 by Kevin Hooyman. Reprinted by permission of Kevin Hooyman.

Excerpt from *Playground of My Mind* by Julia Jacquette. First published in *Playground of My Mind.* Copyright © 2017 by Julia Jacquette. Reprinted by permission of Julia Jacquette.

Excerpt from "Crawl Space" by Jesse Jacobs. First published in *Crawl Space,* Koyama Press. Copyright © 2017 by Jesse Jacobs. Reprinted by permission of Jesse Jacobs & Koyama Press.

Miss V: My Last Love Story by Andre Krayewski & Ed Krayewski. First published in *FKT* #18. Copyright © 2017 by Krayewski-Krayewski. Reprinted by permission of Andre Krayewski & Ed Krayewski.

Selections from "Art School" by Aaron Lange. First published in *TRIM* #5. Copyright © 2017 by Aaron Lange. Reprinted by permission of Aaron Lange.

Excerpt from "Seabrook of Arabia" by Joe Ollmann. First published in *The Abominable Mr. Seabrook,* Drawn & Quarterly. Copyright © 2017 by Joe Ollmann. Images courtesy Drawn & Quarterly.

Selections from "Things More Likely to Kill You Than..." and "Busy Comic" by Laura PallMall. First published in *Nothing Left to Learn #13: Elitist Empathy* and *Nothing Left to Learn #14: Pugilist Palmistry.* Copyright © 2017 by Laura PallMall. Reprinted by permission of Laura PallMall/Nothing Left to Learn.

Excerpt from *Songy of Paradise* by Gary Panter. First published in *Songy of Paradise.* Copyright © 2017 by Gary Panter. Reprinted by permission of Gary Panter/Fantographics.

"UGLY" by Chloë Perkis. First published in *UGLY.* Copyright © 2017 by Chloë Perkis. Reprinted by permission of Chloë Perkis.

"Fatherson" by Richie Pope. First published in Youth in Decline's *Frontier* #13. Copyright © 2017 by Richie Pope. Reprinted by permission of Richie Pope.

"Untitled" by Michael Ridge. First published in *Phood Phrends* #2. Copyright © 2017 by Michael Ridge. Reprinted by permission of Michael Ridge.

Excerpts from *Sunburning* by Keiler Roberts. First published in *Sunburning,* Koyama Press, 2017. Copyright © 2017 by Keiler Roberts. Reprinted by permission of Keiler Roberts.

"Things I Regret" by Ariel Schrag. First published in Columbia College Today Online. Copyright © 2017 by Ariel Schrag. Reprinted by permission of Ariel Schrag.

Excerpt from *The Moolah Tree* by Ted Stearn. First published in *The Moolah Tree.* Copyright © 2017 by Ted Stearn. Reprinted by permission of Ted Stearn.

Excerpt from *Art Comic* by Matthew Thurber. First published in *Art Comic* #4. Copyright © 2017 by Matthew Thurber. Reprinted by permission of Matthew Thurber.

"The Last Felony Comics Story" by Pete Toms. First published in *Felony* #4. Copyright © 2017 by Pete Toms. Reprinted by permission of Pete Toms.

Excerpt from *Yazar and Arkadaş* by Lale Westvind. First published in *Yazar and Arkadaş.* Copyright © 2017 by Lale Westvind. Reprinted by permission of Lale Westvind.

THE BEST AMERICAN SERIES®

FIRST, BEST, AND BEST-SELLING

The Best American Comics

The Best American Essays

The Best American Food Writing

The Best American Mystery Stories

The Best American Nonrequired Reading

The Best American Science and Nature Writing

The Best American Science Fiction and Fantasy

The Best American Short Stories

The Best American Sports Writing

The Best American Travel Writing

Available in print and e-book wherever books are sold.

hmhco.com/bestamerican

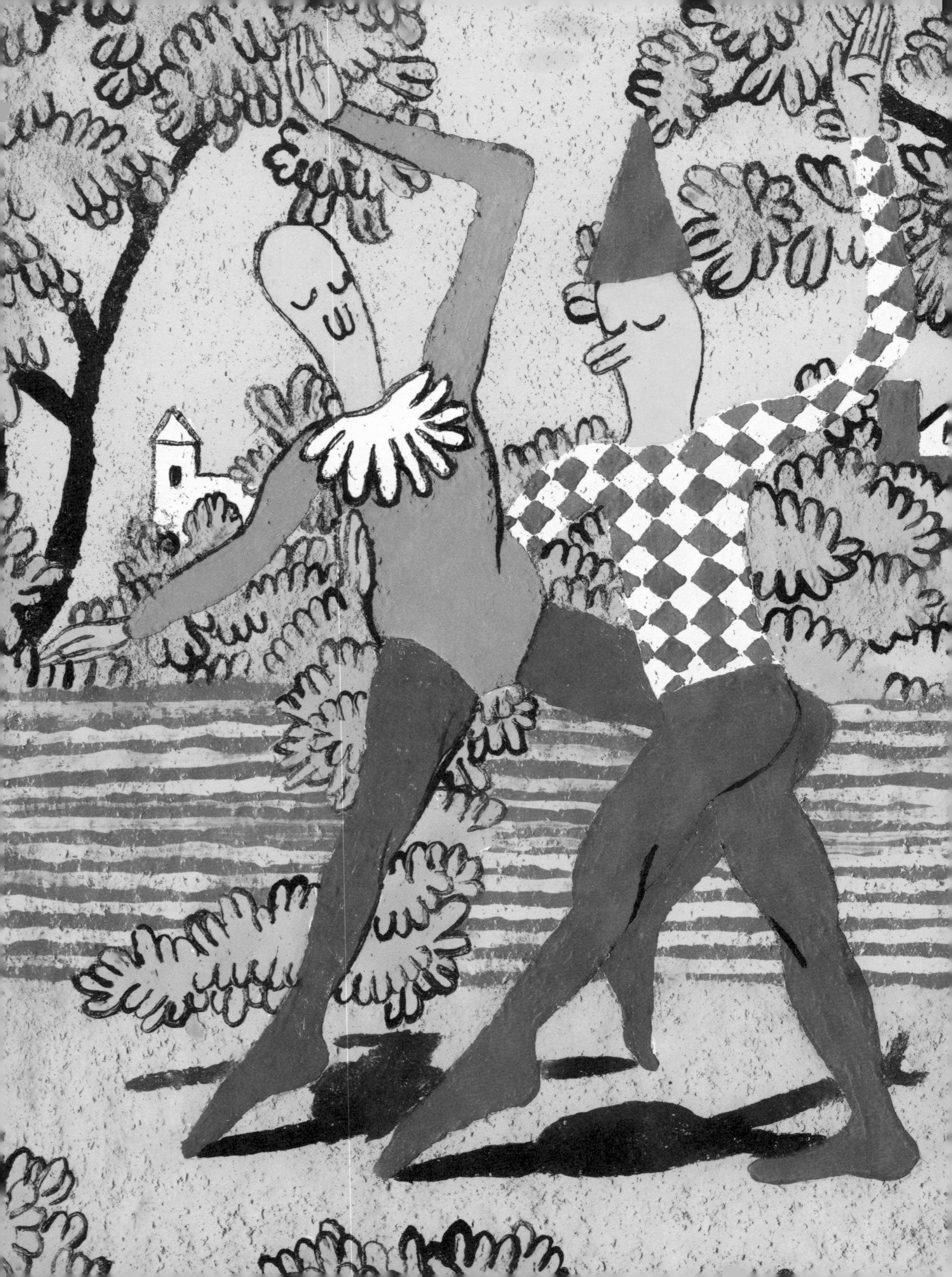